EXTREMELY ENTERTAINING SHORT STORIES

Classic Works of a Master

EXTREMELY ENTERTAINING SHORT STORIES

Stacy Aumonier.

Extremely Entertaining Short Stories

from World War I and the 1920s

—Classic Works of a Master—

by

Stacy Aumonier

PHÆTON
PUBLISHING LTD.

Extremely Entertaining Short Stories

(FIRST PUBLISHED BETWEEN 1914 AND 1928)
THIS COMPILATION PUBLISHED 2008
by Phaeton Publishing Limited, Dublin.

Printed and bound in the United Kingdom
by T J International Limited, Padstow.

British Library Cataloguing In Publication Data: a catalogue record for this book is available from the British Library.

ISBN: 978-0-9553756-3-7 PAPERBACK
ISBN: 978-0-9553756-5-1 HARDBACK

Introduction

FOR MANY DECADES, this most entertaining and insightful of writers has been forgotten, and his wonderful stories out of print.

'A real master of the short story,' John Galsworthy wrote of Stacy Aumonier, '...never heavy, never boring, never really trivial. His humour is sly and dry and frequent...And can't he write.'

Aumonier's comic stories are among the funniest ever written. His serious works observe the human condition with wit and elegance. All are page-turners, full of perception and humanity.

Alfred Hitchcock was an admirer, and had some of his stories adapted for television in the 1950s, including the classic 'Miss Bracegirdle Does Her Duty'.

So what happened? How could a writer so smart, so perceptive and with such a show-stopping turn of phrase have just vanished from memory? In writing a foreword (quoted from above) to a collection of short stories published just after Aumonier's early death at age 51, John Galsworthy finished with what has to be one of the most poignant and, unfortunately, least prophetic sentences in twentieth-century writing: 'But his shade may rest in peace, for in this volume, at least, he will outlive nearly all the writers of his day.'

Inexplicably, that did not happen—and why it did not is one of the sad mysteries of twentieth-century fiction, because his writing was singular: always compelling, sometimes dazzling, and combining great heart with an unprecedented gift for the killer line:

> He was like a man utterly bored with every human experience—except perhaps drink. [THE ROOM]
>
> Was life a rag—a game played by lawyers, politicians, and people? [WHERE WAS WYCH STREET?]
>
> Thus you may see what a domineering personality, backed up by evening dress, may accomplish. [JUXTAPOSITIONS]

Ironically, two of his great strengths—his lightness of touch and his versatility—probably worked against his reputation. He never appeared to take himself seriously and he could not be pigeonholed, writing with ease and skill in a multiplicity of styles. Most of his best stories are comedies. At the same time, the poignant 'The Funny Man's Day' is about as perfect a short story as exists, and 'Burney's Laugh' is an insightful lament for life's inevitable trade-offs. He also wrote detective stories, adventure stories, and a memorably subversive Gothic story ('Old Fags').

About a third of the stories in this volume qualify as classics, and will never be forgotten by anyone who reads them. The rest are first-class, gripping entertainments. All have enough depth and detail to be read repeatedly. It is unusual for purely comic stories to be even funnier on a second reading, but 'The Landlord of The Love-a-Duck', for instance, has so much lurking beneath the surface that it demands to be read more than once. Taken together, these stories add up to to a master-class in short-story writing.

Stacy Aumonier wrote during, and in the decade after, World War I, and that war's battlegrounds and trenches feature in many of his stories. His views on war in general, and what he perceived as the hypocrisy of its rules and values, are summed up movingly in the musings of the naïve protagonist in 'Face':

> He had never conceived that a war could be like this. Sometimes he would lie awake at night and ruminate vaguely on the queer perversity of fate which suddenly made murder popular. He had been turned out of England because he had quite inadvertently killed his father for kicking his mother across the shins, and now he was praised for killing five men within a few minutes. He didn't know, of course, but perhaps some of those men—particularly that elderly plump man who coughed absurdly as he ran on to Caleb's bayonet—perhaps they were better men than his father, although foreigners, although enemy. It was very perplexing...

Impressively, out of the infamous trenches of that war, Stacy Aumonier was able to produce one of the funniest short stories of all time, 'A Source of Irritation'.

He took his characters from every rung of society (sometimes in the one story, as in 'The Octave of Jealousy') and from every walk, and every age, of life: sons who've wasted their inheritance; criminals; farm labourers; a clergyman's sister; gold-diggers; an effective little tyrant (aged 4 or 5?) in 'The Song of Praise'; a divinely-depicted music-hall comedian in the exquisite 'The Funny Man's Day'; the hapless fish-and-chips trader in the hilarious 'A Good Action'.

His talent for putting flesh on those characters in a few words was remarkable, such as in his portrait of the daunting club habitué in 'Juxtapositions':

> In spite of his missing limb, St Clair Chasseloup was the kind of man who always looked as though he had just had a cold bath, done Swedish drill, and then passed through the hairdresser's on his way to your presence.

or of the house-party guests being assessed as the possible perpetrators of a crime in 'Freddie Finds Himself':

> They all looked well off, well fed, and slightly vacant, entirely innocent of anything except the knowledge of what is done or what is not done.

Stacy Aumonier was born near Regent's Park, London in 1877 (not 1887, as often recorded). His French name came from his Huguenot ancestry. His father, William Aumonier, was an architectural sculptor (founder of the Aumonier Studios off Tottenham Court Road) and his uncle was the painter, James Aumonier R.I. Stacy's brother, William (also an architectural sculptor) was responsible for recreating the interiors of Tutankhamun's tomb at the British Empire Exhibition in Wembley in 1924. The landmark sculpture *The Archer* at East Finchley Station in London was the work of his nephew, Eric.

Stacy seemed destined to follow a similar career. He studied decorative design after leaving Cranleigh School in Surrey, and was talented enough as a painter to exhibit both at the Royal Academy and the Royal Institute. In 1908, the catalogue of the Royal Academy described him as an architect (he exhibited a design for the entrance hall of a house).

In that same year, however, he took up an unlikely new line of work—as a stage performer and 'society entertainer', writing and performing his own sketches. He was, according to contemporary reports, very good at this, and enjoyed great popular success.

He was called up for service in World War I in 1917 at age 40, serving first as a private in the Army Pay Corps, and then working as a draughtsman in the Ministry of National Service. The Army medical board in 1916 had put down his occupation as 'actor and writer'. By the end of the following year, he had four books published—two novels and two books of short stories—and his occupation is recorded just as 'author'.

In the 1920s, he enjoyed an unrivalled reputation as a short-story writer. He loved idiosyncracy, and was an outspoken opponent of any push to conform. In an article in the *New York Times* in 1925, he lamented a growing loss of individuality on both sides of the Atlantic, largely blaming industrialisation for this, but also singling out for criticism the English public school system of the time for seeking to enforce conformity through a capricious code of manners and behaviour. Under this unwritten code, he wrote, there were 'unspeakable crimes' such as carrying 'a brown paper parcel or an umbrella', or turning trousers up or not turning them up (depending on which was against the code), or pronouncing French correctly, or showing emotion (or enthusiastism about anything other than sport), and these 'crimes' resulted in instant retribution. The whole purpose of the system, he believed, was to stamp out 'originality, temperament or personal idiosyncrasies'.

He went on to describe a personal experience of being caught wearing 'brown boots in Bond Street in the forenoon' and concluding that he would never be regarded in quite the same way again.

It is hard to read Aumonier's stories without falling in love with the writer. 'It takes years, much training, discipline, and reflection to learn how to become a human being,' he is quoted as saying, and he himself certainly achieved this. Humanity and decency fairly explode out of his stories, and by all contemporary accounts, he was a much-loved man.

'He gets values right,' said Galsworthy of him, 'and that is nearly everything,' adding: 'And how he puts his finger on weak spots!'

He married—in satisfactorily dramatic and romantic circumstances—the international concert pianist, Gertrude Peppercorn, whose father was Arthur Douglas Peppercorn, the landscape painter. The marriage of the then unknown Stacy Aumonier to the already famous musician was reported by the *New York Times* as follows on 8th February 1907:

WILL SING ON HONEYMOON

MISS PEPPERCORN TO SPEND HER FIRST MARRIED WEEKS ON A CONCERT TOUR.

The mystery of Gertrude Peppercorn, the English pianist, who was announced to appear in America during January,

> and who forfeited her contracts at that time, has been solved. The young woman will arrive here today on the steamer *Amerika*. With her she brings her new husband, who was responsible for the cablegram she sent to her managers in January: 'Impossible to come.'
>
> Miss Peppercorn had been booked for an extensive tour beginning on Jan. 15 in Washington. As the day drew near for her first concert, her American managers began to question her by cable. The answers at first were vague. Then, when it was evident that the pianist could not arrive in time for the first concert, she sent the quoted cablegram, implying that she was ill.
>
> Her managers kept the cables hot with hints of what happened to artists who broke contracts and did not have a doctor's certificate. The result is that Miss Peppercorn finally decided to spend her honeymoon in America.
>
> She will make her first appearance in Boston on Feb. 12, and will give a recital here, in Mendelssohn Hall, on Feb. 15. She will be in America at least twelve weeks.

The couple's only child, Timothy, was born in 1921.

In the stories in this volume, Stacy Aumonier has created a real and living history of two extraordinary decades, something he saw as part of the purpose of the artist. He believed that history as recorded by the story-teller was more to be relied on than history as recorded by the scholar, a view he shared with a writer he admired, O. Henry, who had said: 'about the only chance for truth to be told is in fiction.'

In a similar vein, Aumonier wrote in 1923 (in an introduction to *Odd Fish*, a book of character sketches):

> The whole of history is a record of dead dates, dead kings, dead dynasties, dead battles. It is only when the poet and the artist have stepped in that the dreary record has shown signs of vitality…
>
> History, indeed, as recorded in the history books, has never been any good to anyone. It has fanned international

> hatreds, given every small boy in the country a distorted sense of his own country's virtues and achievements, and taught him to worship power and glory…
>
> Before the Great War came you would not have found a hundred people who would have said, 'I hope there'll be a great war,' and yet hundreds of millions of people were involved in it, and conducted it with religious fervour. Let us scrap the old history books, and start with our homely records of living people, so that we may see that human passions and frailties are a common heritage.

In the mid-1920s, Stacy Aumonier was diagnosed with tuberculosis. His graceful, funny essay on falling victim to a terrible disease, 'The Thrill of Being Ill', is included at the end of this volume. He describes how the perception of him changed with the diagnosis:

> …you become subtly aware of a change in attitude in the manner of certain people…You have become dramatically a centre of interest. No miserable cold in the head for you, but something with a name that has the power to frighten and disturb… Indolently you think of various friends who will say, 'Poor old chap! He's got it!'

He was treated for the tuberculosis at a sanatorium in Norfolk in 1927, and wrote the following startling account of the conditions he experienced there in a letter to the writer, Rebecca West, in August 1928, a few months before his death:

> …I was there from August to December last year. Up till the end of September they are all right, but when these white mists begin to roll in from the North Sea it is time to clear. It is the kind of dampness that if you leave a newspaper on the table by the side of your bed at night it is all sodden to the touch in the morning. The huts have no foundations and the wet seems to come right through you from below and above. Last winter, not only the patients but the staff seemed to have

> colds the whole time. When I spoke to Dr — about it, he acknowledged the dampness but said it didn't do the patients any harm. Then he talked about 'the men in the trenches'. I could never quite see the force of this comparison... If well enough, I expect to go to Switzerland in October for the winter.

He and his wife did travel to Montana in Switzerland for the winter of 1928. On 21st December 1928, however, he died of the 'fell and vindictive' disease in the beautiful setting of Clinique La Prairie, Clarens, by Lake Geneva.

The 29 stories included in this volume have been arranged—deliberately—without grouping in relation to style or topic. War stories, thoughtful stories, purely comedic stories are intermixed—and the criterion for their selection was the title on the cover.

For these really are *Extremely Entertaining Short Stories*, and they come with a guarantee. They will compel and amuse you. For a long tedious journey, a sojourn laid up in bed, or just hard times, this book is a sure thing.

S.J.

From a Foreword by John Galsworthy (winner of the Nobel prize for literature in 1932) to a collection of some of Stacy Aumonier's short stories. He wrote it in 1929, the year after Aumonier's death.

I WRITE this Foreword with enthusiasm, for these are... tales of a real master of the short story. The word 'great' has been so overdone, and the word 'genius' is so fly-blown, that I shall use neither. Suffice it to say that Stacy Aumonier is one of the best short-story writers of all time, and that there is certainly no one more readable...

The first essential in a short-story writer is the power of interesting sentence by sentence. Aumonier had this power in prime degree. You do not have to 'get into' his stories. He is especially notable for investing his figures with the breath of life within a few sentences. Take a short story like 'The Funny Man's Day'—how wonderfully well we know that funny man not as a type only but as a human being! How remarkably Miss Bracegirdle, in twenty minutes of our time, becomes a permanent acquaintance!...

There was ... something Gallic in Aumonier's temperament, or at least in his talent—not in his style, which is very English, but in his way of envisaging his subjects. This is not remarkable, considering his name and his face; but in spite of his French look and his Huguenot origin, he was truly English in his humour and attitude to life. French in mind, he was English in heart; for no Frenchman—not even Monsieur André Maurois—could have conceived Alfred Codling—'the man of letters,' or 'the Great Unimpressionable,' or 'The Grayles'...

A short-story writer is always beset by the temptation to be inventive rather than creative or even recreative. This is a temptation to which Aumonier rarely if ever succumbed. He was profoundly in love with life, and impregnated through and through by curiosity about life and its manifestations, whether simple or queer. All types were fish to his net; and he has given us the fruits of his passion for, and his curiosity about, existence with a deft and always interesting fidelity. And with what sympathy he can hit off character! ... His humour is sly and dry and frequent and wholly delightful. And how he puts his finger on weak spots! Yet with what restraint he satirizes!

Stacy Aumonier is never heavy, never boring, never really trivial; interested himself, he keeps us interested. At the back of his tales there is belief in life and a philosophy of life, and of how many short-story writers can that be said? He understands the art of movement in a tale, he has the power of suggestion, he has a sense of line that most of us should envy; he is wholly uninfluenced by the dreary self-consciousness of novelty for novelty's sake. He is not tricky. He follows no fashion and no school. He is always himself. And can't he write? Ah! far better than far more pretentious writers. Nothing escapes his eye, but he describes without affectation or redundancy, and you sense in him a feeling for beauty that is never obtruded. He gets values right, and that is to say nearly everything. The easeful fidelity of his style has militated against his reputation in these somewhat posturing times. But his shade may rest in peace, for in this volume, at least, he will outlive nearly all the writers of his day.

John Galsworthy

Contents

—1—

Miss Bracegirdle Does Her Duty

'THIS IS THE ROOM, madame.'

'Ah, thank you ... thank you.'

'Does it appear satisfactory to madame?'

'Oh, yes, thank you ... quite.'

'Does madame require anything further?'

'Er—if not too late, may I have a hot bath?'

'*Parfaitement*, madame. The bathroom is at the end of the passage on the left. I will go and prepare it for madame.'

'There is one thing more ... I have had a very long journey. I am very tired. Will you please see that I am not disturbed in the morning until I ring.'

'Certainly, madame.'

Millicent Bracegirdle was speaking the truth—she *was* tired. In the sleepy cathedral town of Easingstoke, from which she came, it was customary for everyone to speak the truth. It was customary, moreover, for everyone to lead simple, self-denying lives—to give up their time to good works and elevating thoughts. One had only to glance at little Miss Bracegirdle to see that in her was epitomized all the virtues and ideals of Easingstoke. Indeed, it was the pursuit of duty which had brought her to the Hôtel de l'Ouest at Bordeaux on this summer's night. She had travelled from Easingstoke to London, then without a break to Dover, crossed that horrid stretch of sea to Calais, entrained for Paris, where she of necessity had to spend four hours—a terrifying experience—and then had come on to Bordeaux, arriving at midnight. The reason of this journey being that someone had to come to Bordeaux to meet her young sister-in-law, who was arriving the next day from South America. The sister-in-law was married to a missionary in Paraguay, but the climate not agreeing with her, she was returning to England. Her dear brother, the dean, would have come himself, but the claims on his time were so extensive, the parishioners would miss him so…it was clearly Millicent's duty to go.

She had never been out of England before, and she had a horror of travel, and an ingrained distrust of foreigners. She spoke a little French—sufficient for the purposes of travel and for obtaining any modest necessities, but not sufficient for carrying on any kind of conversation. She did not deplore this latter fact, for she was of opinion that French people were not the kind of people that one would naturally want to have conversation with; broadly speaking, they were not quite 'nice', in spite of their ingratiating manners.

The dear dean had given her endless advice, warning her earnestly not to enter into conversation with strangers, to obtain all information from the police, railway officials—in fact, anyone in an official uniform. He deeply regretted to say that he was afraid that France was not a country for a woman to travel about in *alone*. There were loose, bad people about, always on the lookout…He really thought perhaps he ought not to let her go. It was only by the utmost persuasion, in which she rather exaggerated her knowledge of the French language and character, her courage, and indifference to discomfort, that she managed to carry the day.

She unpacked her valise, placed her things about the room, tried to thrust back the little stabs of homesickness as she visualized her darling room at the deanery. How strange and hard and unfriendly seemed these foreign hotel bedrooms—heavy and depressing, no chintz and lavender and photographs of…all the dear family, the dean, the nephews and nieces, the interior of the cathedral during harvest festival, no samplers and needlework or coloured reproductions of the paintings by Marcus Stone. Oh dear, how foolish she was! What did she expect?

She disrobed and donned a dressing gown; then, armed with a sponge-bag and towel, she crept timidly down the passage to the bathroom, after closing her bedroom door and turning out the light. The gay bathroom cheered her. She wallowed luxuriously in the hot water, regarding her slim legs with quiet satisfaction. And for the first time since leaving home there came to her a pleasant moment—a sense of enjoyment in her adventure. After all, it was rather an adventure, and her life had been peculiarly devoid of it. What queer lives some people must live, travelling about, having experiences! How old was she? Not really old—not by any means. Forty-two? Forty-three? She had shut herself up so. She hardly ever regarded the potentialities of age. As the world went, she was a well-preserved woman for her age. A life of self-abnegation, simple living, healthy walking and fresh air had kept her younger than these hurrying, pampered city people.

Love? yes, once when she was a young girl…he was a schoolmaster, a most estimable kind gentleman. They were never engaged—not actually, but it was a kind of understood thing. For three years it went on, this pleasant understanding and friendship. He was so gentle, so distinguished and considerate. She would have been happy to have continued in this strain forever. But there was something lacking. Stephen had curious restless lapses. From the physical aspect of marriage she shrunk—yes, even with Stephen, who was gentleness and kindness itself. And then one day…one day he went away—vanished, and never returned. They told her he had married one of the country girls—a girl who used to work in Mrs Forbes' dairy—not a very nice girl, she feared, one of these fast, pretty, foolish women. Heigho! well, she had lived that down, destructive as the blow appeared at the time. One lives everything down in time. There is always work, living for others, faith, duty...At the same time she could sympathize with people who found satisfaction in unusual experiences.

There would be lots to tell the dear dean when she wrote to him on the morrow—nearly losing her spectacles on the restaurant car; the amusing remarks of an American child on the train to Paris; the curious food everywhere, nothing simple and plain; the two English ladies at the hotel in Paris who told her about the death of their uncle—the poor man being taken ill on Friday and dying on Sunday afternoon, just before tea-time; the kindness of the hotel proprietor who had sat up for her; the prettiness of the chambermaid. Oh, yes, everyone was really very kind. The French people, after all, were very nice. She had seen nothing—nothing but was quite nice and decorous. There would be lots to tell the dean tomorrow.

Her body glowed with the friction of the towel. She again donned her night attire and her thick, woollen dressing gown. She tidied up the bathroom carefully in exactly the same way she was accustomed to do at home; then once more gripping her sponge-bag and towel, and turning out the light, she crept down the passage to her room. Entering the room, she switched on the light and shut the door quickly. Then one of those ridiculous things happened—just the kind of thing you would expect to happen in a foreign hotel. The handle of the door came off in her hand.

She ejaculated a quiet 'Bother!' and sought to replace it with one hand, the other being occupied with the towel and sponge-bag. In doing this she behaved foolishly, for thrusting the knob carelessly against the steel pin—without properly securing it—she only succeeded in pushing the pin farther into the door and the knob was not adjusted. She uttered another little 'Bother!' and put her sponge-bag and towel down on the floor. She then tried to recover the pin with her left hand, but it had gone in too far.

'How very foolish!' she thought, 'I shall have to ring

for the chambermaid—and perhaps the poor girl has gone to bed.'

She turned and faced the room, and suddenly the awful horror was upon her. *There was a man asleep in her bed!*

The sight of that swarthy face on the pillow, with its black tousled hair and heavy moustache, produced in her the most terrible moment of her life. Her heart nearly stopped. For some seconds she could neither think nor scream, and her first thought was: 'I mustn't scream!'

She stood there like one paralysed, staring at the man's head and the great curved hunch of his body under the clothes. When she began to think she thought very quickly, and all her thoughts worked together. The first vivid realization was that it wasn't the man's fault; it was *her* fault. *She was in the wrong room.* It was the man's room. The rooms were identical, but there were all his things about, his clothes thrown carelessly over chairs, his collar and tie on the wardrobe, his great heavy boots and the strange yellow trunk. She must get out somehow, anyhow.

She clutched once more at the door, feverishly driving her fingernails into the hole where the elusive pin had vanished. She tried to force her fingers in the crack and open the door that way, but it was of no avail. She was to all intents and purposes locked in—locked in a bedroom in a strange hotel alone with a man...a foreigner... *a Frenchman!* She must think. She must think...She switched off the light. If the light was off he might not wake up. It might give her time to think how to act. It was surprising that he had not awakened. If he *did* wake up, what would he do? How could she explain herself? He wouldn't believe her. No one would believe her. In an English hotel it would be difficult enough, but here where she wasn't known, where they were all foreigners and consequently antagonistic...merciful heavens!

She *must* get out. Should she wake the man? No, she couldn't do that. He might murder her. He might...Oh, it was too awful to contemplate! Should she scream? ring for the chambermaid? But no, it would be the same thing. People would come rushing. They would find her there in the strange man's bedroom after midnight—she, Millicent Bracegirdle, sister of the Dean of Easingstoke! Easingstoke!

Visions of Easingstoke flashed through her alarmed mind. Visions of the news arriving, women whispering around tea tables: 'Have you heard, my dear? ... Really no one would have imagined! Her poor brother! He will of course have to resign, you know, my dear. Have a little more cream, my love.'

Would they put her in prison? She might be in the room for the purpose of stealing or ... She might be in the room for the purpose of breaking every one of the ten commandments. There was no explaining it away. She was a ruined woman, suddenly and irretrievably, unless she could open the door. The chimney? Should she climb up the chimney? But where would that lead to? And then she visualized the man pulling her down by her legs when she was already smothered in soot. Any moment he might wake up ...

She thought she heard the chambermaid going along the passage. If she had wanted to scream, she ought to have screamed before. The maid would know she had left the bathroom some minutes ago. Was she going to her room? Suddenly she remembered that she had told the chambermaid that she was not to be disturbed until she rang the next morning. That was something. Nobody would be going to her room to find out that she was not there.

An abrupt and desperate plan formed in her mind. It was already getting on for one o'clock. The man was probably a quite harmless commercial traveller or businessman. He would probably get up about seven or eight o'clock, dress quickly, and go out. She would hide under his bed until he went. Only a matter of a few hours. Men don't look under their beds, although she made a religious practice of doing so herself. When he went he would be sure to open the door all right. The handle would be lying on the floor as though it had dropped off in the night. He would probably ring for the chambermaid or open it with a penknife. Men were so clever at those things. When he had gone she would creep out and steal back to her room, and then there would be no necessity to give any explanation to any one. But heavens! What an experience! Once under the white frill of that bed she would be safe till the morning. In daylight nothing seemed so terrifying.

With feline precaution she went down on her hands and knees and crept toward the bed. What a lucky thing there was that broad white frill! She lifted it at the foot of the bed and crept under. There was just sufficient depth to take her slim body. The floor was fortunately carpeted all over, but it seemed very close and dusty. Suppose she coughed or sneezed! Anything might happen. Of course...it would be much more difficult to explain her presence under the bed than to explain her presence just inside the door. She held her breath in suspense. No sound came from above, but under this frill it was difficult to hear anything. It was almost more nerve-racking than hearing everything ...listening for signs and portents. This temporary escape in any case would give her time to regard the predicament detachedly. Up to the present she had not been able to visualize the full significance of her action. She had in truth lost her head. She had been like a wild animal, consumed with the sole idea of escape...a mouse or a cat would do this kind of thing—take cover and lie low. If only it hadn't all happened *abroad!* She tried to frame sentences of explanation in French, but French escaped her. And then—they talked so rapidly, these people. They didn't listen. The situation was intolerable. Would she be able to endure a night of it?

At present she was not altogether uncomfortable, only

stuffy and...very, very frightened. But she had to face six or seven or eight hours of it—perhaps even then discovery in the end! The minutes flashed by as she turned the matter over and over in her head. There was no solution. She began to wish she had screamed or awakened the man. She saw now that that would have been the wisest and most politic thing to do; but she had allowed ten minutes or a quarter of an hour to elapse from the moment when the chambermaid would know that she had left the bathroom. They would want an explanation of what she had been doing in the man's bedroom all that time. Why hadn't she screamed before?

She lifted the frill an inch or two and listened. She thought she heard the man breathing but she couldn't be sure. In any case it gave her more air. She became a little bolder, and thrust her face partly through the frill so that she could breathe freely. She tried to steady her nerves by concentrating on the fact that—well, there it was. She had done it. She must make the best of it. Perhaps it would be all right after all.

'Of course I shan't sleep,' she kept on thinking, 'I shan't be able to. In any case it will be safer not to sleep. I must be on the watch.'

She set her teeth and waited grimly. Now that she had made up her mind to see the thing through in this manner she felt a little calmer. She almost smiled as she reflected that there would certainly be something to tell the dear Dean when she wrote to him tomorrow. How would he take it? Of course he would believe it—he had never doubted a single word that she had uttered in her life, but the story would sound so...preposterous. In Easingstoke it would be almost impossible to envisage such an experience. She, Millicent Bracegirdle, spending a night under a strange man's bed in a foreign hotel! What would those women think? Fanny Shields and that garrulous old Mrs Rusbridger? Perhaps...yes, perhaps it would be advisable to tell the dear Dean to let the story go no further. One could hardly expect Mrs Rushbridger to ... not make implications ... exaggerate.

Oh, dear! What were they all doing now? They would be all asleep, everyone in Easingstoke. Her dear brother always retired at ten-fifteen. He would be sleeping calmly and placidly, the sleep of the just ... breathing the clear sweet air of Sussex, not this—oh, it was stuffy! She felt a great desire to cough. She mustn't do that. Yes, at nine-thirty all the servants summoned to the library—a short service—never more than fifteen minutes, her brother didn't believe in a great deal of ritual—then at ten o'clock cocoa for every one. At ten-fifteen bed for everyone. The dear sweet bedroom with the narrow white bed, by the side of which she had knelt every night as long as she could remember—even in her dear mother's day—and said her prayers.

Prayers! Yes, that was a curious thing. This was the first night in her life's experience that she had not said her prayers on retiring. The situation was certainly very peculiar ... exceptional, one might call it. God would understand and forgive such a lapse. And yet after all, why ... what was to prevent her saying her prayers? Of course she couldn't kneel in the proper devotional attitude, that would be a physical impossibility; nevertheless, perhaps her prayers might be just as efficacious ... if they came from the heart. So little Miss Bracegirdle curved her body and placed her hands in a devout attitude in front of her face and quite inaudibly murmured her prayers under the strange man's bed.

'Our Father which art in heaven, Hallowed be Thy name. Thy kingdom come. Thy will be done on earth as it is done in heaven; Give us this day our daily bread and forgive us our trespasses ...'

Trespasses! Yes, surely she was trespassing on this occasion, but God would understand. She had not wanted to trespass. She was an unwitting sinner. Without uttering a sound she went through her usual prayers in her heart. At the end she added fervently:

'Please God protect me from the dangers and perils of this night.'

Then she lay silent and inert, strangely soothed by the effort of praying. 'After all,' she thought, 'it isn't the attitude which matters—it is that which occurs deep down in us.'

For the first time she began to meditate—almost to question—church forms and dogma. If an attitude was not indispensable, why—a building, a ritual, a church at all? Of course her dear brother couldn't be wrong, the church was so old, so very old, its root deep buried in the story of human life, it was only that...well, outward forms could be misleading. Her own present position for instance. In the eyes of the world she had, by one silly careless little action, convicted herself of being the breaker of every single one of the ten commandments.

She tried to think of one of which she could not be accused. But no—even to dishonouring her father and mother, bearing false witness, stealing, coveting her neighbour's...husband! That was the worst thing of all. Poor man! He might be a very pleasant honourable married gentleman with children and she—she was in a position to compromise him! Why hadn't she screamed? Too late! Too late!

It began to get very uncomfortable, stuffy, but at the same time draughty, and the floor was getting harder every minute. She changed her position stealthily and controlled her desire to cough. Her heart was beating rapidly. Over and over again recurred the vivid impression of every little incident and argument that had occurred to her from the moment she left the bathroom. This must, of course, be the room next to her own. So confusing, with perhaps twenty bedrooms all exactly alike on one side of a passage—how was one to remember whether one's number was 115 or 116?

Her mind began to wander idly off into her schooldays. She was always very bad at figures. She disliked Euclid and all those subjects about angles and equations—so unimportant, not leading anywhere. History she liked, and botany, and reading about strange foreign lands, although she had always been too timid to visit them. And the lives of great people, most fascinating—Oliver Cromwell, Lord Beaconsfield, Lincoln, Grace Darling—*there* was a heroine for you—General Booth, a great, good man, even if a little vulgar. She remembered dear old Miss Trimming talking about him one afternoon at the vicar of St Bride's garden party. She was so amusing. She ... *Good heavens!*

Almost unwittingly, Millicent Bracegirdle had emitted a violent sneeze!

It was finished! For the second time that night she was conscious of her heart nearly stopping. For the second time that night she was so paralysed with fear that her mentality went to pieces. Now she would hear the man get out of bed. He would walk across to the door, switch on the light, and then lift up the frill. She could almost see that fierce moustached face glaring at her and growling something in French. Then he would thrust out an arm and drag her out. And then? O God in heaven! What then? ...

'I shall scream before he does it. Perhaps I had better scream now. If he drags me out he will clap his hand over my mouth. Perhaps chloroform ...'

But somehow she could not scream. She was too frightened even for that. She lifted the frill and listened. Was he moving stealthily across the carpet? She thought—no, she couldn't be sure. Anything might be happening. He might strike her from above—with one of those heavy boots perhaps. Nothing seemed to be happening, but the suspense was intolerable. She realized now that she hadn't the power to endure a night of it. Anything would be better than this—disgrace, imprisonment, even death. She would crawl out, wake the man, and try and explain as best she could.

She would switch on the light, cough, and say: *'Monsieur!'*

Then he would start up and stare at her.

Then she would say—what should she say?

'Pardon, monsieur, mais je—' What on earth was the French for 'I have made a mistake'?

'J'ai tort. C'est la chambre—er—incorrect. *Voulez-vous*—er—'

What was the French for 'door-knob', 'let me go'?

It didn't matter. She would turn on the light, cough and trust to luck. If he got out of bed, and came toward her, she would scream the hotel down...

The resolution formed, she crawled deliberately out at the foot of the bed. She scrambled hastily toward the door—a perilous journey. In a few seconds the room was flooded with light. She turned toward the bed, coughed, and cried out boldly:

'Monsieur!'

Then, for the third time that night, little Miss Bracegirdle's heart all but stopped. In this case the climax of the horror took longer to develop, but when it was reached, it clouded the other two experiences into insignificance.

The man on the bed was dead!

She had never beheld death before, but one does not mistake death.

She stared at him bewildered, and repeated almost in a whisper:

'Monsieur!... Monsieur!'

Then she tiptoed toward the bed. The hair and moustache looked extraordinarily black in that grey, wax-like setting. The mouth was slightly open, and the face, which in life might have been vicious and sensual, looked incredibly peaceful and far away.

It was as though she were regarding the features of a man across some vast passage of time, a being who had always been completely remote from mundane preoccupations.

When the full truth came home to her, little Miss Bracegirdle buried her face in her hands and murmured:

'Poor fellow... poor fellow!'

For the moment her own position seemed an affair of small consequence. She was in the presence of something greater and more all-pervading. Almost instinctively she knelt by the bed and prayed.

For a few moments she seemed to be possessed by an extraordinary calmness and detachment. The burden of her hotel predicament was a gossamer trouble—a silly, trivial, almost comic episode, something that could be explained away.

But this man—he had lived his life, whatever it was like, and now he was in the presence of his Maker. What kind of man had he been?

Her meditations were broken by an abrupt sound. It was that of a pair of heavy boots being thrown down by the door outside. She started, thinking at first it was someone knocking or trying to get in. She heard the 'boots', however, stamping away down the corridor, and the realization stabbed her with the truth of her own position. She mustn't stop there. The necessity to get out was even more urgent.

To be found in a strange man's bedroom in the night is bad enough, but to be found in a dead man's bedroom was even worse. They could accuse her of murder, perhaps. Yes, that would be it—how could she possibly explain to these foreigners? Good God! they would hang her. No, guillotine her, that's what they do in France. They would chop her head off with a great steel knife. Merciful heavens! She envisaged herself standing, blindfold, by a priest and an executioner in a red cap, like that man in the Dickens story—what was his name?... Sydney Carton, that was it, and before he went on the scaffold he said:

'It is a far, far better thing that I do than I have ever done.'

But no, she couldn't say that. It would be a far, far worse thing that she did. What about the dear Dean? Her sister-in-law arriving alone from Paraguay to-morrow? All her dear people and friends in Easingstoke? Her darling Tony, the large grey tabby cat? It was her duty not to have her head chopped off if it could possibly be avoided. She could do no good in the room. She could not recall the dead to life. Her only mission was to escape. Any minute people might arrive. The chambermaid, the boots, the manager, the gendarmes... Visions of gendarmes arriving armed with swords and notebooks vitalized her almost exhausted energies. She was a desperate woman. Fortunately now she had not to worry about the light. She sprang once more at the door and tried to force it open with her fingers. The result hurt her and gave her pause. If she was to escape she must *think*, and think intensely. She mustn't do anything rash and silly, she must just think and plan calmly.

She examined the lock carefully. There was no keyhole, but there was a slip-bolt, so that the hotel guest could lock the door on the inside, but it couldn't be locked on the outside. Oh, why didn't this poor dear dead man lock his door last night? Then this trouble could not have happened. She could see the end of the steel pin. It was about half an inch down the hole. If any one was passing they must surely notice the handle sticking out too far the other side! She drew a hairpin out of her hair and tried to coax the pin back, but she only succeeded in pushing it a little farther in. She felt the colour leaving her face, and a strange feeling of faintness come over her.

She was fighting for her life, she mustn't give way. She

darted round the room like an animal in a trap, her mind alert for the slightest crevice of escape. The window had no balcony and there was a drop of five stories to the street below. Dawn was breaking. Soon the activities of the hotel and the city would begin. The thing must be accomplished before then.

She went back once more and stared at the lock. She stared at the dead man's property, his razors, and brushes, and writing materials, pens and pencils and rubber and sealing wax... Sealing wax!

Necessity is truly the mother of invention. It is in any case quite certain that Millicent Bracegirdle, who had never invented a thing in her life, would never have evolved the ingenious little device she did, had she not believed that her position was utterly desperate. For in the end this is what she did. She got together a box of matches, a candle, a bar of sealing wax, and a hairpin. She made a little pool of hot sealing wax, into which she dipped the end of the hairpin. Collecting a small blob on the end of it she thrust it into the hole, and let it adhere to the end of the steel pin. At the seventh attempt she got the thing to move. It took her just an hour and ten minutes to get that steel pin back into the room, and when at length it came far enough through for her to grip it with her fingernails, she burst into tears through the sheer physical tension of the strain. Very, very carefully she pulled it through, and holding it firmly with her left hand she fixed the knob with her right, then slowly turned it. The door opened!

The temptation to dash out into the corridor and scream with relief was almost irresistible, but she forbore. She listened; she peeped out. No one was about. With beating heart, she went out, closing the door inaudibly. She crept like a little mouse to the room next door, stole in and flung herself on her bed. Immediately she did so it flashed through her mind that *she had left her sponge-bag and towel in the dead man's room!*

In looking back upon her experience she always considered that that second expedition was the worst of all. She might have left the sponge-bag and towel there, only that the towel—she never used hotel towels—had neatly inscribed in the corner 'M.B.'

With furtive caution she managed to retrace her steps. She re-entered the dead man's room, reclaimed her property, and returned to her own. When this mission was accomplished she was indeed well-nigh spent. She lay on her bed and groaned feebly. At last she fell into a fevered sleep...

It was eleven o'clock when she awoke and no one had been to disturb her. The sun was shining, and the experiences of the night appeared a dubious nightmare. Surely she had dreamt it all?

With dread still burning in her heart she rang the bell. After a short interval of time the chambermaid appeared. The girl's eyes were bright with some uncontrollable excitement. No, she had not been dreaming. This girl had heard something.

'Will you bring me some tea, please?'

'Certainly, madame.'

The maid drew back the curtains and fussed about the room. She was under a pledge of secrecy but she could contain herself no longer. Suddenly she approached the bed and whispered excitedly:

'Oh, madame, I have promised not to tell...but a terrible thing has happened. A man, a dead man, has been found in room 117—a guest. Please not to say I tell you. But they have all been there, the gendarmes, the doctors, the inspectors. Oh, it is terrible...terrible.'

The little lady in the bed said nothing. There was indeed nothing to say. But Marie Louise Lancret was too full of emotional excitement to spare her.

'But the terrible thing is...Do you know who he was, madame? They say it is Boldhu, the man wanted for the murder of Jeanne Carreton in the barn at Vincennes. They say he strangled her, and then cut her up in pieces and hid her in two barrels which he threw into the river ... Oh, but he was a bad man, madame, a terrible bad man ... and he died in the room next door ... suicide they think or was it an attack of the heart? ... Remorse, some shock perhaps ... Did you say a *café complet*, madame?'

'No, thank you, my dear ... just a cup of tea ... strong tea ...'

'*Parfaitement*, madame.'

The girl retired, and a little later a waiter entered the room with a tray of tea. She could never get over her surprise at this. It seemed so—well, indecorous for a man—although only a waiter—to enter a lady's bedroom. There was no doubt a great deal in what the dear Dean said. They were certainly very peculiar, these French people—they had most peculiar notions. It was not the way they behaved at Easingstoke. She got farther under the sheets, but the waiter appeared quite indifferent to the situation. He put the tray down and retired.

When he had gone she sat up and sipped her tea, which gradually warmed her. She was glad the sun was shining. She would have to get up soon. They said that her sister-in-law's boat was due to berth at one o'clock. That would give her time to dress comfortably, write to her brother, and then go down to the docks. Poor man! So he had been a murderer, a man who cut up the bodies of his victims ... and she had spent the night in his bedroom! They were certainly a most—how could she describe it?—people. Nevertheless she felt a little glad that at the end she had been there to kneel and pray by his bedside. Probably nobody else had ever done that. It was very difficult to judge people ... Something at some time might have gone wrong. He might not have murdered the woman after all. People were often wrongly convicted. She herself ... If the police had found her in that room at three o'clock that morning...It is that which takes place in the heart which counts. One learns and learns. Had she not learnt that one can pray just as effectively lying under a bed as kneeling beside it?...Poor man!

She washed and dressed herself and walked calmly down to the writing-room. There was no evidence of excitement among the other hotel guests. Probably none of them knew about the tragedy except herself. She went to a writing-table, and after profound meditation wrote as follows:

My dear brother,

I arrived late last night after a very pleasant journey. Everyone was very kind and attentive, the manager was sitting up for me. I nearly lost my spectacle case in the restaurant car! But a kind old gentleman found it and returned it to me. There was a most amusing American child on the train. I will tell you about her on my return. The people are very pleasant, but the food is peculiar, nothing *plain and wholesome*. I am going down to meet Annie at one o'clock. How have you been keeping, my dear? I hope you have not had any further return of the bronchial attacks.

Please tell Lizzie that I remembered in the train on the way here that that large stone jar of marmalade that Mrs Hunt made is behind those empty tins in the top shelf of the cupboard next to the coach-house. I wonder whether Mrs Butler was able to come to evensong after all? This is a nice hotel, but I think Annie and I will stay at the 'Grand' tonight, as the bedrooms here are rather noisy. Well, my dear, nothing more till I return. Do take care of yourself.

Your loving sister,

Millicent.

Yes, she couldn't tell Peter about it, neither in the letter nor when she went back to him. It was her duty not to tell him. It would only distress him; she felt convinced of it. In this curious foreign atmosphere the thing appeared possible, but in Easingstoke the mere recounting of the fantastic situations would be positively…indelicate. There was no escaping that broad general fact—she had spent a night in a strange man's bedroom. Whether he was a gentleman or a criminal, even whether he was dead or alive, did not seem to mitigate the jar upon her sensibilities, or rather it would not mitigate the jar upon the peculiarly sensitive relationship between her brother and herself. To say that she had been to the bathroom, the knob of the door-handle came off in her hand, she was too frightened to awaken the sleeper or scream, she got under the bed—well, it was all perfectly true. Peter would believe her, but—one simply could not conceive such a situation in Easingstoke deanery. It would create a curious little barrier between them, as though she had been dipped in some mysterious solution which alienated her. It was her duty not to tell.

She put on her hat, and went out to post the letter. She distrusted an hotel letter-box. One never knew who handled these letters. It was not a proper official way of treating them. She walked to the head post office in Bordeaux.

The sun was shining. It was very pleasant walking about amongst these queer excitable people, so foreign and different-looking—and the cafés already crowded with chattering men and women, and the flower stalls, and the strange odour of—what was it? Salt? Brine? Charcoal?… A military band was playing in the square…very gay and moving. It was all life, and movement, and bustle… thrilling rather.

'I spent a night in a strange man's bedroom.'

Little Miss Bracegirdle hunched her shoulders, murmured to herself, and walked faster. She reached the post office and found the large metal plate with the slot for letters and 'R.F.' stamped above it. Something official at last! Her face was a little flushed—was it the warmth of the day or the contact of movement and life?—as she put her letter into the slot. After posting it she put her hand into the slot and flicked it round to see that there were no foreign contraptions to impede its safe delivery. No, the letter had dropped safely in. She sighed contentedly and walked off in the direction of the docks to meet her sister-in-law from Paraguay.

—*II*—

A Source of Irritation

To look at old Sam Gates you would never suspect him of having nerves. His sixty-nine years of close application to the needs of the soil had given him a certain earthy stolidity. To observe him hoeing, or thinning out a broad field of swede turnips, hardly attracted one's attention, he seemed so much part and parcel of the whole scheme. He blended into the soil like a glorified swede. Nevertheless, the half-dozen people who claimed his acquaintance knew him to be a man who suffered from little moods of irritability.

And on this glorious morning a little incident annoyed him unreasonably. It concerned his niece Aggie. She was a plump girl with clear blue eyes and a face as round and inexpressive as the dumplings for which the county was famous. She came slowly across the long sweep of the downland and, putting down the bundle wrapped up in a red handkerchief which contained his breakfast and dinner, she said:

'Well, Uncle, is there any noos?'

Now this may not appear to the casual reader to be a remark likely to cause irritation, but it affected old Sam Gates as a very silly and unnecessary question. It was moreover the constant repetition of it which was beginning to anger him. He met his niece twice a day. In the morning she brought his bundle of food at seven, and when he passed his sister's cottage on the way home to tea at five she was invariably hanging about the gate. And on each occasion she always said, in exactly the same voice:

'Well, Uncle, is there any noos?'

'Noos!' What 'noos' should there be? For sixty-nine years he had never lived farther than five miles from Halvesham. For nearly sixty of those years he had bent his back above the soil. There were indeed historic occasions: once, for instance, when he had married Annie Hachet. And there was the birth of his daughter. There was also a famous occasion when he had visited London. Once he had been to a flower show at Market Roughborough. He either went or didn't go to church on Sundays. He had had many interesting chats with Mr James at 'The Cowman', and three years ago had sold a pig to Mrs Waig. But he couldn't always have interesting 'noos' of this sort up his sleeve. Didn't the silly gaffir know that for the last three weeks he had been thinning out turnips for Mr Dodge on this very same field? What 'noos' could there be?

He blinked at his niece, and didn't answer. She undid the parcel, and said:

'Mrs Goping's fowl got out again last night.'

He replied, 'Ah!' in a non-committal manner, and began to munch his bread and bacon. His niece picked up the handkerchief, and humming to herself, walked back across the field.

It was a glorious morning, and a white sea mist added to the promise of a hot day. He sat there munching, thinking of nothing in particular, but gradually subsiding into a mood of placid content. He noticed the back of Aggie disappear in the distance. It was a mile to the cottage, and a mile and a half to Halvesham. Silly things, girls! They were all alike. One had to make allowances. He dismissed her from his thoughts, and took a long swig of tea out of a bottle. Insects buzzed lazily. He tapped his pocket to assure himself that his pouch of shag was there, and then he continued munching. When he had finished, he lighted his pipe and stretched himself comfortably. He looked along the line of turnips he had thinned, and then across the adjoining field of swedes. Silver streaks appeared on the sea below the mist. In some dim way he felt happy in his solitude amidst this sweeping immensity of earth and sea and sky.

And then something else came to irritate him. It was one of 'these dratted airyplanes'. 'Airyplanes' were his pet aversion. He could find nothing to be said in their favour. Nasty, noisy, vile-smelling things that seared the heavens, and made the earth dangerous. And every day there seemed to be more and more of them. Of course 'this old war' was responsible for a lot of them, he knew. The war was a 'plaguey noosance'. They were short-handed on the farm. Beer and tobacco were dear, and Mrs Stevens' nephew had been and got wounded in the foot.

He turned his attention once more to the turnips. But an 'airyplane' has an annoying genius for gripping one's attention. When it appears on the scene, however much we dislike it, it has a way of taking stage-centre; we cannot help constantly looking at it. And so it was with old Sam Gates. He spat on his hands, and blinked up at the sky. And suddenly the aeroplane behaved in a very extraordinary manner. It was well over the sea when it seemed to lurch in a drunken manner, and skimmed the water. Then it shot up at a dangerous angle and zigzagged. It started to go farther out, and then turned and made for the land. The engines were making a curious grating noise. It rose once more, and then suddenly dived downward, and came plump down right in the middle of Mr Dodge's field of swedes!

Finally, as if not content with this desecration, it ran along the ground, ripping and tearing up twenty-five yards of good swedes, and then came to a stop. Old Sam Gates was in a terrible state. The aeroplane was more than a hundred yards away, but he waved his arms, and called out:

'Hi! you there, you musn't land in they swedes! They're Mister Dodge's.'

The instant the aeroplane stopped, a man leaped out and gazed quickly round. He glanced at Sam Gates, and seemed uncertain whether to address him or whether to concentrate his attention on the flying machine. The latter arrangement appeared to be his ultimate decision. He dived under the engine, and became frantically busy. Sam had never seen anyone work with such furious energy. But all the same, it was not to be tolerated. It was disgraceful. Sam started out across the field, almost hurrying in his indignation. When he appeared within earshot of the aviator, he cried out again:

'Hi! you mustn't rest your old airyplane here. You've kicked up all Mr Dodge's swedes. A nice thing you've done!'

He was within five yards when suddenly the aviator turned and covered him with a revolver! And, speaking in a sharp, staccato voice, he said:

'Old grandfather, you must sit down. I am very much occupied. If you interfere or attempt to go away, I shoot you. So!'

Sam gazed at the horrid glittering little barrel, and gasped. Well, he never! To be threatened with murder when you're doing your duty in your employer's private property! But, still, perhaps the man was mad. A man must be more or less mad to go up in one of those crazy things. And life was very sweet on that summer morning, in spite of sixty-nine years. He sat down among the swedes.

The aviator was so busy with his cranks and machinery that he hardly deigned to pay him any attention except to keep the revolver handy. He worked feverishly, and Sam sat watching him. At the end of ten minutes he appeared to have solved his troubles with the machine, but he still seemed very scared. He kept on glancing round and out to sea. When his repairs were completed, he straightened his back and wiped the perspiration from his brow. He was apparently on the point of springing back into the machine and going off, when a sudden mood of facetiousness, caused by relief from the strain he had endured, came to him. He turned to old Sam and smiled, at the same time remarking:

'Well, old grandfather, and now we shall be all right, isn't it?'

He came close up to Sam, and suddenly started back.

'Gott!' he cried, 'Paul Jouperts!'

Sam gazed at him, bewildered, and the madman started talking to him in some foreign tongue. Sam shook his head.

'You no right,' he remarked, 'to come bargin' through they swedes of Mr Dodge's.'

And then the aviator behaved in a most peculiar manner. He came up and examined his face very closely, and gave a gentle tug at his beard and hair, as if to see whether it was real or false.

'What is your name, old man?' he said.

'Sam Gates.'

The aviator muttered some words that sounded something like 'mare vudish!' and then turned to his machine. He appeared to be dazed and in a great state of doubt. He fumbled with some cranks, but kept glancing at old Sam. At last he got into the car and started the engine. Then he stopped, and sat there deep in thought. At last he suddenly sprang out again, and, approaching Sam, he said very deliberately:

'Old Grandfather, I shall require you to accompany me.'

Sam gasped.

'Eh?' he said. 'What be talkin' about? 'company? I got these here lines o' tarnips—I be already behoind—'

The disgusting little revolver once more flashed before his eyes.

'There must be no discussion,' came the voice. 'It is necessary that you mount the seat of the car without delay. Otherwise I shoot you like the dog you are. So!'

Old Sam was hale and hearty. He had no desire to die so ignominiously. The pleasant smell of the downland was in his nostrils. His foot was on his native heath. He mounted the seat of the car, contenting himself with a mutter:

'Well, that be a noice thing, I must say! Flyin' about the country with all they tarnips on'y half thinned—'

He found himself strapped in. The aviator was in a fever of anxiety to get away. The engines made a ghastly splutter and noise. The thing started running along the ground. Suddenly it shot upward, giving the swedes a last contemptuous kick. At twenty minutes to eight that morning old Sam found himself being borne right up above his fields and out to sea! His breath came quickly. He was a little frightened.

'God forgive me!' he murmured.

The thing was so fantastic and sudden, his mind could not grasp it. He only felt in some vague way that he was going to die, and he struggled to attune his mind to the change. He offered up a mild prayer to God, Who, he felt, must be very near, somewhere up in these clouds. Automatically he thought of the vicar at Halvesham, and a certain sense of comfort came to him at the reflection that on the previous day he had taken a 'cooking of runner beans' to God's representative in that village. He felt calmer after that, but the horrid machine seemed to go higher and higher. He could not turn in his seat and he could see nothing but sea and sky. Of course the man was mad, mad as a March hare. Of what earthly use could he be to any one? Besides, he had talked pure gibberish, and called him Paul Something, when he had already told him that his name was Sam. The thing would fall down into the sea soon, and they would both be drowned. Well, well! He had reached three-score years and ten.

He was protected by a screen, but it seemed very cold. What on earth would Mr Dodge say? There was no one left to work the land but a fool of a boy named Billy Whitehead at Deric's Cross. On, on, on they went at a furious pace. His thoughts danced disconnectedly from incidents of his youth, conversations with the vicar, hearty meals in the open, a frock his sister wore on the day of the postman's wedding, the drone of a psalm, the illness of some ewes belonging to Mr Dodge. Everything seemed to be moving very rapidly, upsetting his sense of time. He felt outraged and yet at moments there was something entrancing in the wild experience. He seemed to be living at an incredible pace. Perhaps he was really dead, and on his way to the Kingdom of God? Perhaps this was the way they took people?

After some indefinite period he suddenly caught sight of a long strip of land. Was this a foreign country? or were they returning? He had by this time lost all feeling of fear. He became interested and almost disappointed. The 'airyplane' was not such a fool as it looked. It was very wonderful to be right up in the sky like this. His dreams were suddenly disturbed by a fearful noise. He thought the machine was blown to pieces. It dived and ducked through the air, and things were bursting all round it and making an awful din; and then it went up higher and higher. After a while these noises ceased, and he felt the machine gliding downwards. They were really right above solid land, trees, and fields, and streams, and white villages. Down, down, down they glided. This was a foreign country. There were straight avenues of poplars and canals. This was not Halvesham. He felt the thing glide gently and bump into a field. Some men ran forward and approached them, and the mad aviator called out to them. They were mostly fat men in grey uniforms, and they all spoke this foreign gibberish. Someone came and unstrapped him. He was very stiff and could hardly move. An exceptionally gross-looking man punched him in the ribs, and roared with laughter. They all stood round and laughed at him, while the mad aviator talked to them and kept pointing at him. Then he said:

'Old grandfather, you must come with me.'

He was led to a zinc-roofed building, and shut in a little room. There were guards outside with fixed bayonets.

After a while the mad aviator appeared again, accompanied by two soldiers. He beckoned him to follow. They marched through a quadrangle and entered another building. They went straight into an office where a very important-looking man, covered with medals, sat in an easy chair. There was a lot of saluting and clicking of heels.

The aviator pointed at Sam and said something, and the man with the medals started at sight of him, and then came up and spoke to him in English.

'What is your name? Where do you come from? Your age? The name and birthplace of your parents?'

He seemed intensely interested, and also pulled his hair and beard to see if they came off. So well and naturally did he and the aviator speak English that after a voluble cross-examination they drew apart, and continued the conversation in that language. And the extraordinary conversation was of this nature:

'It is a most remarkable resemblance,' said the man with medals. '*Unglaublich!* But what do you want me to do with him, Hausemann?'

'The idea came to me suddenly, excellency,' replied the aviator, 'and you may consider it worthless. It is just this. The resemblance is so amazing. Paul Jouperts has given us more valuable information than any one at present in our service. And the English know that. There is an award of twenty-five thousand francs on his head. Twice they have captured him, and each time he escaped. All the company commanders and their staff have his photograph. He is a serious thorn in their flesh.'

'Well?' replied the man with the medals.

The aviator whispered confidentially:

'Suppose, your excellency, that they found the dead body of Paul Jouperts?'

'Well?' replied the big man.

'My suggestion is this. Tomorrow, as you know, the English are attacking Hill 701, which we have for tactical reasons decided to evacuate. If after the attack they find the dead body of Paul Jouperts in, say, the second lines, they will take no further trouble in the matter. You know their lack of thoroughness. Pardon me, I was two years at Oxford University. And consequently Paul Jouperts will be able to—prosecute his labours undisturbed.'

The man with the medals twirled his moustache and looked thoughtfully at his colleague.

'Where is Paul at the moment?' he asked.

'He is acting as a gardener at the Convent of St Eloise, at Mailleton-en-haut, which, as you know, is one hundred metres from the headquarters of the British central army staff.'

The man with the medals took two or three rapid turns up and down the room. Then he said:

'Your plan is excellent, Hausemann. The only point of difficulty is that the attack started this morning.'

'This morning?' exclaimed the other.

'Yes. The English attacked unexpectedly at dawn. We have already evacuated the first line. We shall evacuate the second line at eleven-fifty. It is now ten-fifteen. There may be just time.'

He looked suddenly at old Sam in the way that a butcher might look at a prize heifer at an agricultural show and remarked casually:

'Yes, it is a remarkable resemblance. It seems a pity not to ... do something with it.'

Then, speaking in German, he added:

'It is worth trying, and if it succeeds, the higher authorities shall hear of your lucky accident and inspiration, Herr Hausemann. Instruct Oberleutnant Schutz to send the old fool by two orderlies to the east extremity of trench 38. Keep him there till the order of evacuation is given. Then shoot him, but don't disfigure him, and lay him out face upwards.'

The aviator saluted and withdrew, accompanied by his victim. Old Sam had not understood the latter part of the conversation, and he did not catch quite all that was said in English, but he felt that somehow things were not becoming too promising, and it was time to assert himself. So he remarked when they got outside:

'Now, look'ee here, mister, when be I goin' back to my tarnips?'

And the aviator replied with a pleasant smile:

'Do not be disturbed, old grandfather; you shall...get back to the soil quite soon.'

In a few moments he found himself in a large grey car, accompanied by four soldiers. The aviator left him. The country was barren and horrible, full of great pits and rents, and he could hear the roar of artillery and the shriek of shells. Overhead, aeroplanes were buzzing angrily. He seemed to be suddenly transported from the Kingdom of God to the Pit of Darkness. He wondered whether the vicar had enjoyed the runner beans. He could not imagine runner beans growing here, runner beans, ay! or anything else. If this was a foreign country, give him dear old England.

Gr-r-r-r—Bang! Something exploded just at the rear of the car. The soldiers ducked, and one of them pushed him in the stomach and swore.

'An ugly-looking lout,' he thought. 'If I was twenty years younger I'd give him a punch in the eye that 'ud make him sit up.'

The car came to a halt by a broken wall. The party hurried out and dived behind a mound. He was pulled down a kind of shaft and found himself in a room buried right underground, where three officers were drinking and smoking. The soldiers saluted and handed a typewritten dispatch. The officers looked at him drunkenly, and one came up and pulled his beard and spat in his face, and called him 'an old English swine'. He then shouted out some instructions to the soldiers, and they led him out into the narrow trench. One walked behind him, and occasionally prodded him with the butt-end of a gun. The trenches were half-full of water, and reeked of gases, powder, and decaying matter. Shells were constantly bursting overhead, and in places the trenches had crumbled and were nearly blocked up. They stumbled on, sometimes falling, sometimes dodging moving masses, and occasionally crawling over the dead bodies of men. At last they reached a deserted-looking trench, and one of the soldiers pushed him into the corner of it and growled something, and then disappeared round the angle. Old Sam was exhausted. He lay panting against the mud wall, expecting every minute to be blown to pieces by one of those infernal things that seemed to be getting more and more insistent. The din went on for nearly twenty minutes, and he was alone in the trench. He fancied he heard a whistle amidst the din. Suddenly one of the soldiers who had accompanied him came stealthily round the corner. And there was a look in his eye old Sam did not like. When he was within five yards the soldier raised his rifle and pointed it at Sam's body. Some instinct impelled the old man at that instant to throw himself forward on his face. As he did so, he was conscious of a terrible explosion, and he had just time to observe the soldier falling in a heap near him, when he lost consciousness.

His consciousness appeared to return to him with a snap. He was lying on a plank in a building, and he heard someone say:

'I believe the old boy's English.'

He looked round. There were a lot of men lying there, and others in khaki and white overalls were busy amongst them. He sat up, rubbed his head, and said:

'Hi, mister, where be I now?'

Someone laughed, and a young man came up and said:

'Well, old thing, you were very nearly in hell. Who the devil are you?'

Someone else came up, and two of them were discussing him. One of them said:

'He's quite all right. He was only knocked out. Better

take him to the colonel. He may be a spy.'

The other came up, and touched his shoulder, and remarked:

'Can you walk, uncle?'

He replied:

'Ay, I can walk all right.'

'That's an old sport!'

The young man took his arm and helped him out of the room, into a courtyard. They entered another room, where an elderly, kind-faced officer was seated at a desk. The officer looked up and exclaimed:

'Good God! Bradshaw, do you know who you've got there?'

The younger one said:

'No. Who, sir?'

'By God! it's Paul Jouperts!' exclaimed the colonel.

'Paul Jouperts! Great Scott!'

The older officer addressed himself to Sam. He said:

'Well, we've got you once more, Paul. We shall have to be a little more careful this time.'

The young officer said:

'Shall I detail a squad, sir?'

'We can't shoot him without a court-martial,' replied the kind-faced senior.

Then Sam interpolated:

'Lookee, here, sir. I'm fair sick of all this. My name bean't Paul. My name's Sam. I was a-thinnin' a line of tarnips—'

Both officers burst out laughing, and the younger one said:

'Good! damn good! Isn't it amazing, sir, the way they not only learn the language, but even take the trouble to learn a dialect?'

The older man busied himself with some papers.

'Well, Sam,' he remarked, 'you shall be given a chance to prove your identity. Our methods are less drastic than those of your Boche masters. What part of England are you supposed to come from? Let's see how much you can bluff us with your topographical knowledge.'

'Oi was a-thinnin' a loine o' tarnips this morning at 'alf-past seven on Mr Dodge's farm at Halvesham, when one o' these 'ere airyplanes come roight down among the swedes. I tells 'e to get clear o' that, when the feller what gets owt o' the car, 'e drahs a revowlver and 'e says, "You must 'company —I—" '

'Yes, yes,' interrupted the senior officer; 'that's all very good. Now tell me—where is Halvesham? What is the name of the local vicar? I'm sure you'd know that.'

Old Sam rubbed his chin.

'I sits under the Reverend David Pryce, mister, and a good, God-fearin' man he be. I took him a cookin' o' runner beans on'y yesterday. I works for Mr Dodge what owns Greenway Manor and 'as a stud-farm at Newmarket they say.'

'Charles Dodge?' asked the young officer.

'Ay, Charlie Dodge. You write and ask 'un if he knows old Sam Gates.'

The two officers looked at each other, and the older one looked at Sam more closely.

'It's very extraordinary,' he remarked.

'Everybody knows Charlie Dodge,' added the younger officer.

It was at that moment that a wave of genius swept over old Sam. He put his hand to his head, and suddenly jerked out:

'What's more, I can tell 'ee where this yere Paul is. He's acting a gardener in a convent at—' He puckered up his brow and fumbled with his hat, and then got out:

'Mighteno.'

The older officer gasped.

'Mailleton-en-haut! Good God! What makes you say that, old man?'

Sam tried to give an account of his experience, and the things he had heard said by the German officers. But he was getting tired, and he broke off in the middle to say:

'Ye haven't a bite o' somethin' to eat, I suppose, mister, and a glass o' beer? I usually 'as my dinner at twelve o'clock.'

Both the officers laughed, and the older said:

'Get him some food, Bradshaw, and a bottle of beer from the mess. We'll keep this old man here. He interests me.'

While the younger man was doing this, the chief pressed a button and summoned another junior officer.

'Gateshead,' he remarked, 'ring up G.H.Q. and instruct them to arrest the gardener in that convent at the top of the hill, and then to report.'

The officer saluted and went out, and in a few minutes a tray of hot food and a large bottle of beer were brought to the old man, and he was left alone in the corner of the room to negotiate this welcome compensation. And in the execution he did himself and his county credit. In the meanwhile the officers were very busy. People were coming and going and examining maps, and telephone-bells were ringing furiously. They did not disturb old Sam's gastronomic operations. He cleaned up the mess tins and finished the last drop of beer. The senior officer found time to offer him a cigarette, but he replied:

'Thank'ee kindly, but I'd rather smoke my pipe.'

The colonel smiled, and said:

'Oh, all right. Smoke away.'

He lighted up, and the fumes of the shag permeated the room. Someone opened another window, and the young officer who had addressed him at first suddenly looked at him and exclaimed:

'Innocent, by God! You couldn't get shag like that anywhere but in Norfolk.'

It must have been over an hour later when another officer entered and saluted.

'Message from G.H.Q., sir,' he said.

'Well?'

'They have arrested the gardener at the convent of St Eloise, and they have every reason to believe that he is the notorious Paul Jouperts.'

The colonel stood up, and his eyes beamed. He came over to old Sam and shook his hand.

'Mr Gates,' he said, 'you are an old brick. You will probably hear more of this. You have probably been the means of delivering something very useful into our hands. Your own honour is vindicated. A loving government will probably award you five shillings or a Victoria Cross, or something of that sort. In the meantime, what can I do for you?'

Old Sam scratched his chin.

'Oi want to get back 'ome,' he said.

'Well, even that might be arranged.'

'Oi want to get back 'ome in toime for tea.'

'What time do you have tea?'

'Foive o'clock or thereabouts.'

'I see.'

A kindly smile came into the eyes of the colonel. He turned to another officer standing by the table and said:

'Raikes, is any one going across this afternoon with dispatches?'

'Yes, sir,' replied the other officer. 'Commander Jennings is leaving at three o'clock.'

'You might ask him to come and see me.'

Within ten minutes a young man in a flight-commander's uniform entered.

'Ah, Jennings,' said the colonel, 'here is a little affair which concerns the honour of the British army. My friend here, Sam Gates, has come over from Halvesham in Norfolk in order to give us valuable information. I have promised him that he shall get home to tea at five o'clock. Can you take a passenger?'

The young man threw back his head and laughed.

'Lord!' he exclaimed. 'What an old sport! Yes, I expect I could just manage it. Where is the God-forsaken place?'

A large ordnance-map of Norfolk (which had been captured from a German officer) was produced, and the young man studied it closely.

At three o'clock precisely, old Sam, finding himself something of a hero and quite glad to escape from the embarrassment which this position entailed, once more sped skywards in an 'airyplane'.

At twenty minutes to five he landed once more amongst Mr Dodge's swedes. The breezy young airman shook hands with him and departed inland. Old Sam sat down and surveyed the field.

'A noice thing, I must say,' he muttered to himself as he looked along the lines of unthinned turnips. He still had twenty minutes, and so he went slowly along and completed a line which he had commenced in the morning. He then deliberately packed up his dinner-things and his tools, and started out for home.

As he came round the corner of Stillway's Meadow, and the cottage came in view, his niece stepped out of the copse with a basket on her arm.

'Well, Uncle,' she said, 'is there any noos?'

It was then that old Sam became really irritated.

'Noos!' he said. 'Noos! drat the girl! What noos should there be? Sixty-nine year I live in these here parts, hoein' and weedin' and thinnin' and mindin' Charlie Dodge's sheep. Am I one o' these here story-book folk havin' noos 'appen to me all the time? Ain't it enough, ye silly, dab-faced zany, to earn enough to buy a bite o' some'at to eat, and a glass o' beer, and a place to rest a's head o'night, without always wantin' noos, noos, noos! I tell 'ee, it's this that leads 'ee to 'alf the troubles in the world. Devil take the noos!'

And turning his back on her, he went fuming up the hill.

—*III*—

Juxtapositions

'WHERE WE ARE ALL MIXED UP,' said my friend, Samuel Squidge, vigorously scraping down the *Portrait of the Artist, by Himself* with a palette knife, 'is in our juxtapositions. It's all nonsense, I tell you. People talk about a bad colour. There's no such thing as a bad colour. Every colour is beautiful in its right juxtaposition. When you hear a woman say "I hate puce" or "I love green", she might as well say "I hate sky" or "I love grass". If she had seen puce used in a colour-print as Hiroshige the Second used it—green—fancy *loving* green! The idiot! Do you remember what Corot said? He said Nature was too green and too badly lighted. Now the old man was quite right—'

When Squidge starts talking in this strain he is rather apt to go off the deep end. I yawned and murmured sweetly:

'We were talking about Colin St Clair Chasseloup.'

'Exactly! And I'm trying to point out to you how, with Colin St Clair Chasseloup, it's all a question of juxtapositions. You say that Colin is a frozen drunkard, a surly bore, a high-pressure nonentity. Listen to me. We're all nice people, every one of us. Give a man the right air he should breathe, the right food he should eat, the right work he should do, the right people he should associate with, and he's a perfect dear, every one of him. There isn't a real irreconcilable on the earth. But the juxtaposition—'

'What has Chasseloup to complain of? He has money, a charming wife, children, a place in the country, a flat in town. He does exactly what he likes.'

Squidge surveyed me with amazement.

'You ass! You prize ass! I thought you wrote about people. I thought you were supposed to understand people! And there you go and make a smug, asinine remark like that.'

I blushed, fully conscious that Squidge was being justifiably merciless. It was an asinine statement but then I was merely putting out a feeler, and I could not explain this to the portrait painter. After all, I did not really know St Clair Chasseloup. He was only a club acquaintance, and a very unclubbable acquaintance he was. He appeared to dislike club life. To a stranger he seemed to reek of patrician intolerance. He was an aristocrat of aristocrats. His well-set-up, beautifully groomed figure, clean-cut features, well-poised head, were all in the classic tradition of a ruling caste. It was only about the rather heavy eyelids and the restless mouth that one detected the cynic, the disappointed man, the disillusioned boor. Why?...It was no affair of mine, the secret troubles of this man's heart. But it was his business to behave himself to me decently. To hell with Colin St Clair Chasseloup! I disliked the man. But then we all dislike people who we feel nurture an innate sense of superiority to us. Added to this trying exterior of complete self-absorption and superiority, one had also to allow for the vanity of the cripple.

St Clair Chasseloup had lost his right leg just below the knee. It happened before the war. Indeed, at the time when he was a naval cadet at Osborne, skylarking with other young cadets, he had slipped from a pinnace on a rough day and his right foot had been crushed against the stone wall of a jetty. The leg had to be amputated. That was the end of his naval career. And his father had been a commodore before him, and his father's father was in the Battle of Trafalgar, and so on right away back to the spacious days of Elizabeth—all naval men. Devilish bad luck, you may say! Of course, one had to allow for the bitterness that this misfortune must have produced.

At the same time it doesn't excuse a man not answering when he's spoken to by a fellow-member at the club, or for looking at one—like Chasseloup did!

Squidge's championship of the thwarted seaman amused me. You could not conceive a more remarkable contrast. I was not even aware that they knew each other. In spite of his missing limb, St Clair Chasseloup was the kind of man who always looked as though he had just had a cold bath, done Swedish drill, and then passed through the hairdresser's on his way to your presence. He was aggressively fit. Squidge looked as though a walk to the end of the street would have brought on valvular disease of the heart. From the centre of a dank beard, limp ends of cigarettes eternally clung. Physically, he was just comic. It was his vivid eyes and his queer excitable voice that told you that he was a person of no mean vitality. He was just as sociable and optimistic as Chasseloup was taciturn and moribund. And yet they met on some odd plane, it appeared. Well, well, I could understand Squidge finding merit in Chasseloup, indeed in anyone, but what would Chasseloup's opinion of Squidge be? It made me shudder to contemplate. On the occasion I am recounting it was almost impossible to extract any further intimate details out of Squidge, for he had flown off on one of his pet theoretical tangents.

'It's a queer rum thing,' he was saying, 'why people ever get married at all. You simply can't get level with it—the most unlikely, most outrageous combinations! The more outrageous the more likely they are to be a success. You see some scraggy goat of a woman and you think to yourself, "Poor wretch! whatever sort of chance has she got of getting married?" and the next thing you hear is that she's married to some god who adores her, and they have a large family of boys at Harrow and girls at Girton. Queer! Another woman breathes sunlight and the men pursue her, and nothing happens. She's unhappy. I know a woman who is married to a man she is apparently in love with, and he with her. They have two jolly kids, a boy and a girl. They are a most delightful, happy family. They have money and are bursting with health and good spirits, and yet nearly every year the mother gets fits of melancholia, and has to go away to a nursing home and lie up for months. Some genius has said that when contemplating marriage, what you want to seek in common is not intellectual ambitions and tastes, it's recreations. It's quite right. Generally speaking, a man's at work all day, so is a woman. When they meet in the evening they want to get away from it. It's the time when they spread their feathers. If they can play and fool around they can be happy. Life for the most part is a drab monologue. It's when you come to the accents you want each other...If you can share the same toothbrush with a woman for twenty-five years and she can still surprise you, then you're all right, both of you—'

'My dear Squidge, what has your disgusting notion with regard to the toothbrush to do with St Clair Chasseloup?'

'Nothing. I'm talking.'

'I noticed that. Tell me frankly. Would you say that he and his wife—Aimée, isn't it?—have recreations in common?'

'Yes.'

'What are they?'

'Bach.'

'Bach! what are you talking about? Colin St Clair Chasseloup! Bach!'

'It seems funny to you, doesn't it? You know him and you've seen her. You know him, all beef and phlegm, the immovable mass. A man who thinks of nothing but dumbbells and double Scotches. And you've seen her, the daughter of a hundred earls, highly strung, æsthetic, a little queer, passionately devoted to ultra-modern music, Coué, Montessori, anything and everything that crops up. They've nothing in common, you might say. He's out all day, playing a surly game of golf, or loafing in a club. She's playing the piano, Ravel, Debussy, or some of those queer Russian Johnnies. Or else she's inventing cute devices for the upbringing of the precious children. He lets them rip. She spoils them. When you see them together you would say that they were two people who had just missed their last bus and had to walk home, each thinking it was the other's fault. And yet I tell you they are the only two people suitable to each other. They have a mutual appreciation of accents—the same accents. They meet in the solemn tonal climaxes of Bach—'

'I can't believe that Colin likes Bach.'

'I didn't once. I found out through my pal, Paul Furtwangler, the cellist. He goes there several nights a week—she pays him well, too—and he just plays Bach. It soothes the savage beast. It keeps him at home, quietens him, stays his hand from the whisky bottle. It's marvellous. He can't abide Chopin, or all the jolly tuneful stuff barbarians like you and I enjoy. There's something about it, I suppose, the orderliness, the precision, the organic building up of solemn structures that just fills the kink in his life made by his tragic defection. She hoiks him to St Anne's, Soho, to hear the oratorios. They chase the Bach choir hither and thither. She plays it herself, although she's not much of a performer. That's why she gets Furtwangler and sometimes the Stinzel quartette. When they are listening to Bach together, they meet on a plane of complete satisfaction. Of course, the war didn't do him any good. He used to hobble backwards and forwards to Whitehall doing some ridiculous anti-aircraft intelligence stuff, and he used to look bitterly at his pals when he saw them prancing backwards and forwards, with the salt of the North Sea bitten into their faces. He was a good boy in those days, though. He left the bottle alone, and only groused and grumbled. Weren't we all doing that?... That's what I mean about people—married people especially—you can never tell whether they are happy or not. We all have to live our own lives in our own way. The breezy couple who go about singing "La, too, te rum, tum, tumple, rum, turn, tootle, tootle, lay," and who kiss in public, and say "darling this" and "darling that", you generally find that one or both parties are carrying on a secret liaison with a cook or a chauffeur. Colin has just got to be like that, and the woman understands him. She doesn't want him different. While he is like that she has a more complete grip over him, because she knows that no other woman will understand or tolerate him. And they don't. Of course, they quarrel sometimes, and he goes off and makes no end of a beast of himself. But she knows she is secure. He will come whining back to her like a whipped puppy. And he will grope for her in the darkness, and she will hold his hand, and they will listen to the solemn chords of a Bach fugue, and will feel horribly melancholy, and tremendously moved, and somehow completely satisfied. That's just people, they're like that. It's no good arguing about it. I must be going. I'm going to have a Turkish bath with Smithers.'

The contemplation of Squidge in a Turkish bath talking to Smithers, who is enormously fat, held me for the moment, and then my mind reverted to Chasseloup.

Dash it! you couldn't help being interested in the beast. I had to acknowledge that, in spite of his rudeness and indifference to me, the man had somehow always attracted me. I suppose because I wanted to know him, his rudeness and indifference piqued me all the more. And his wife—well, there it was, I had only seen her in concert-halls and theatres, and riding about in taxis with him, but that peculiarly wistful face would have enslaved anyone. She was slight and fragile, with pale face and very red lips, and that curious gleaming blue-black hair that so often accompanies a pallid complexion. Her eyes were wonderful, large, reflective, dark, with terrific things going on in them all the time. At the same time I shouldn't describe them as altogether unhappy eyes. They reflected too much vital movement for that. The woman was living, and of how many of these hard-bitten society women can you say the same?

It happened that a few nights after my talk with Squidge, I met Chasseloup at the club. He was sitting in a corner of the smoking room, drinking whisky and being talked to by one of the pet club bores. He occasionally growled a monosyllabic reply. After a time the club bore retired and I was left alone with him. I sat back and smoked, but did not speak. We must have sat like that for nearly twenty minutes. There must have been something about this conspiracy of silence which appealed to Chasseloup. I was aware of him occasionally glancing at me, and at length he actually ventured to address a remark. He said:

'This club whisky gets worse every day.'

I believe I must have blushed with pleasure as I hastened to acquiesce.

'Yes, it's awful stuff.'

(Did you ever know a club where the members didn't all agree that the food and drink supplied was the worst in town?)

After a few snappy sentences about the club whisky, Chasseloup even went so far as to generalize. He said:

'Fancy reaching the stage of Colonel Robbins, a man who led a brigade in South Africa, and now there's nothing left for him in life but to serve on wine committees.'

I was startled by this sociable reflection, and before I could reply, he had capped it with:

'Even over that he's come to the end of his tether. His palate is worn out.'

He rose abruptly and rang the bell and ordered some more of the inferior stuff. This insignificant conversation seemed to form a bond between Chasseloup and myself. From that evening onwards his attitude towards me underwent a change. It was not that he talked much, but I was aware that I was one of the few members who didn't get on his nerves. It was extremely flattering.

'All right, my friend,' I thought, 'I'll find out all about you yet.'

Nevertheless, there was a long interval of time between that conversation and the eventful Sunday evening, when I met him and his wife at the Minerva Musical Society's function at the Grafton Galleries.

Now it is not of the slightest importance, except as it affects the chronicle of the events I am about to describe, but I have to say that my own tastes with regard to music are catholic, cosmopolitan, and undistinguished. I like Chopin and Schumann, and most of the Old Masters. I like Bach when I'm in the mood. I even like jazz music sometimes, and foxtrots, and barrel-organs, and Old Bill playing his mouth-organ. But I must confess that what is known as the modern British composer leaves me cold. Perhaps I'm not educated up to him. And the activities of the Minerva Musical Society are almost entirely concerned with the modern British composer. Crowds of very precious overfed and underfed people meet together, and they sit on little gilt chairs and burble with delight about the productions of Mr Cyrus P. Q. H. Robinson, or the tone poem of Ananathius K. Smith. I know nothing about it. They may be right. The only thing I have to record is that it bores me. The only reason I went to this particular evening was—and it is a weakness common to many weak-minded creatures like myself—that my wife took me. She is more eclectic about these matters than I am. She knows more, and so probably she is quite right in believing that Cyrus and Ananathius are geniuses. That isn't the point. The point is, I was frankly bored. And early in the evening, looking round the room, and confessing to myself that I was frankly bored, I suddenly happened to notice that the two people who had just come in and were sitting just behind us were Mr and Mrs Colin St Clair Chasseloup.

Immediately my boredom vanished. Here was a human problem of more interest than the scherzo movement of

Mr Cyrus P. Q. H. Robinson's F minor sonata. I looked round and fidgeted, and my wife said: 'Hush!'

And then without any question I heard Chasseloup say in a rather rude, abrupt voice:

'I'm not going to listen to any more of this drivel.'

And he got up and walked to the back of the room.

With two percent of his aplomb I got up and whispered:

'I don't care for this very much, dear. I'll just go and smoke a cigarette.'

I strolled out and found Chasseloup in the corridor. He was looking thoroughly irritable. I went straight up to him and said:

'What about a drink, Chasseloup?'

His face cleared perceptibly. He gave me quite a friendly nod, and muttered:

'Yes.'

I must now pay a tribute to that most sound of all social conventions—namely, that of evening dress. It will carry one through almost any difficulty. Chasseloup and I were both in evening dress.

We wandered out into Grafton Street just as we were, without hats or coats. We had gone barely twenty yards when I had to exclaim:

'Good God! It's Sunday night! Everything is shut. We are just five minutes too late. I'm awfully sorry, old boy.'

It was interesting to watch the play of expression on Chasseloup's face. The jolt of irritation, the attempt to control a recognition of the jolt, and then the sudden ugly thrust of the chin. He merely said:

'Let's see what we can do.'

But there was in that thrust all the perverse tendency of a man who meant to get a drink, not because he particularly wanted it, but because he was annoyed at being thwarted.

We took two sharp turns to the left—or the right—and we came to a street, the name of which I mustn't tell you, otherwise the whole story becomes almost libellous. In any case, we were not five minutes' walk from the Grafton Galleries, and we were going down a world-renowned street, consecrated chiefly to very swell private clubs. Suddenly Chasseloup jerked out:

'That looks a good place. Let's try it.'

From the exterior it was quite obvious what it was. It was a very select private club, probably an exclusive ornithologists' club, or a club consecrated to men who had won honours for discovering the secrets of subaqueous plant-life. I don't know. Chasseloup didn't know; but without the slightest hesitation we strolled casually into the smoke-room. The commissionaire glanced at us questioningly, but one look at Chasseloup convinced him that he was wrong in his doubts. With a proprietary air, Chasseloup flung himself into an easy chair on the right of the fire, and I occupied the left. There were only two old gentlemen in the room, and they were so absorbed in a conversation about goitres they didn't notice us. An ancient waiter appeared—a man who must have been there at least thirty years—and he came timidly forward. He was about to take orders in a mechanical way, and then he looked at us, and a curious sense of misgiving seemed to creep over him, not as though he were suspecting us, but as though he were suspecting his own memory. Chasseloup, with his white waistcoat and gilt buttons, his braided trousers and commanding atmosphere, couldn't be anything but a most distinguished member.

The waiter fumbled clumsily with a tray, and murmured defensively:

'You gentlemen are stopping the night, I presume?'

An expression of unctuous indignation settled on Chasseloup's features.

'Of course,' he said.

The old waiter almost crawled on the carpet and took our order for two double whiskies. Thus, you may see what a domineering personality, backed up by evening dress, may accomplish. I could not possibly have done this by myself, but in the presence of Chasseloup I felt quite like an old member of this club of which I did not even know the name.

Chasseloup was not by any means a drunkard. But I discovered—at least, I have discovered later—that he considers three double whiskies his right and lawful due for an evening. They do not appear to have the slightest effect on him. We had two in this club—we were in there less than ten minutes—and then he said:

'We'll have one more somewhere else and then toddle back.'

It appeared to me to have been a sufficient triumph to have broken the laws of the land so successfully and speedily without challenging Fate further. Indeed if we wanted one more drink we could easily have obtained it where we were. But it was quite patent that it was the very facility which was the obstacle in Chasseloup's case. It was all too dead easy. There was no fun in having a drink unless you had to fight for it. We had risen and walked to the door. Just as we reached the entrance hall, a man who looked like a butler came stealthily in from the street. He glanced anxiously at us, and then going up to Chasseloup, he whispered:

'Limpo?'

Now Chasseloup naturally had got a limp, and I expected to see this piece of impertinence drastically handled. Whatever was the fool getting at? But Chasseloup gave no sign. He just stared hard at the other, who quickly added:

'Her ladyship says will you come across immediately? I'll show you the way.'

Chasseloup hesitated for a fraction of a second, then, squaring his shoulders, he said:

'Come on, then.'

It was quite apparent that he had not the faintest idea what adventure he was committed to. Crossing the street, I whispered:

'What's it all about?'

And he whispered back:

'I don't know, but I guess we'll get our third drink.'

We went into a palatial block of flats and entered a lift. We were whisked up five floors and ushered into a heavily carpeted hall. The butler left us and did not return for three or four minutes. When he did, he seemed all on edge. He said nervously to Chasseloup: 'Er—would you mind your friend waiting outside, sir?'

Chasseloup spoke emphatically:

'No, tell her ladyship that where Limpo goes Blotto follows.'

There was another interval, and then the butler returned and asked us both to follow him.

We went into a large smoking room, sparsely furnished. The room was occupied by three men. They were all big men, and they were all standing. On the hearth rug stood one of the most sinister-looking individuals I have ever seen. He was very tall, with heavy shoulders and a fierce black moustache and wicked eyes. There was something about the way the men were standing I didn't like. It appeared to be all carefully planned. The big man, whose voice seemed surprisingly thin for his bulk said banteringly:

'Oh, come in, Mr—er—Limpo. Julius Lindt, perhaps I should say. It pains me to tell you that her ladyship is not present, unavoidably detained—see?'

Chasseloup bowed formally, and said in an ice-cold voice:

'I regret to hear it.'

'Um—um—yes. Yes, quite so. I can quite believe it. I presume you are a great reader of the *Times*, Mr—er—Limpo, Lindt I should say.'

'I always read the *Times*,' answered Chasseloup politely.

'Yes, and write for them, advertise, too, Mr—er—Lindt. Nice, friendly, loving little paragraphs, eh?'

He held out a copy of the *Times*, the outside sheet showing. Round one paragraph someone had put a blue pencil line. The big man thrust it in Chasseloup's face and said:

'Just read that out, Mr—er—'

There was a nasty dangerous tone in his voice. I didn't like it at all. I began to think lovingly of the Minerva Society, the little gilt chairs, and Cyrus P. Q. H. Robinson's F minor sonata. Chasseloup was perfectly calm. He never took his eyes off the other man's face. He said coldly:

'My friend, Blotto, will read it.'

The paper was handed to me, and I read out from the agony column:

'Molly. Am yearning for you. Shall be at the Club Sunday night. If the Dragon is away send over for me. All my love. Limpo.'

I was too nervous to see the humour of the situation. Here was the outraged husband, and by great guile he had captured the wrong *tertium quid!* How could one explain? Chasseloup's regrettable limp appeared damning evidence. He had gone there, and deliberately put his head through the noose. The situation was appalling. The worst of it was that, under such circumstances, men do not stop to think and reason. Passion and mob-law are old confederates. This fact was brought home during the ensuing seconds. Everything seemed to happen in a flash. I was conscious of the Dragon stretching out his hand towards a short, stocky riding-whip, which had been concealed by the fireplace; of the other two men stealthily closing in on Chasseloup. And then a fourth man—was it the butler?—gripped me by the throat from behind, and I was jerked towards the door. The idea was to get me out of the way whilst the other three men horsewhipped Chasseloup. I fell backwards into the hall and the door slammed to. At least, it nearly did. It was slammed with terrific violence, but just in the nick of time a leg was thrust through. Now the force with which it was pushed would have broken any ordinary leg, but as it happened the leg that was thrust through was made of wood and steel framing.

The arms above were apparently engaged elsewhere. The sight of that upturned boot spurred me to action. I drove my elbows violently into the ribs of my attacker. I heard him groan, and I leapt forward to the door again. I think he must have been the butler. I never saw him again. When I forced my way back into the room, I think the moral effect of my presence was more valuable to our side than any physical exploit I was likely to offer. Three men against two are not overwhelming odds. The man just in front of the door, who was gripping Chasseloup by the waist, hesitated, and paid the penalty by getting a blow over his left eye. The other two men were closing in, when Chasseloup ducked and got free. It was then that I saw the man as he really was. His eyes were gleaming with exultation. He was thoroughly enjoying himself. With a sudden unexpected swerve he seized a vase and smashed the electric light globes. The room was in darkness.

Now for a mixed body of men to fight in the dark is a dangerous and difficult game. You do not know who is with you or against you. Oaths were exchanged rather than blows. And the Dragon called out:

'Where's Dawson? Where's that — butler?'

Then he gave a curse which showed that he was foolish to reveal his whereabouts. One fool struck a match, which served no better purpose than to reveal the point of his jaw, a fact that was promptly taken advantage of. He went down and out. We were now two against two, and one of them had a black eye that would last many a week. The Dragon was blind with rage. He roared:

'Come out into the hall!'

And he stumbled out there and waved his arms challengingly. We all followed him. The man with the black eye had had enough, and I sat on the opposite side of the hall also a spectator. For it seemed to be suddenly mutually agreed that this was an affair between the Dragon and Chasseloup. They both wanted to fight. I could have yelled out that the whole thing was a mistake, a misunderstanding, that Chasseloup was not the man who had liaisons with the other man's wife; but if I had done so I felt that Chasseloup would never forgive me. He had already taken his coat off, and so had the Dragon. And they fought. An affair of this nature between two heavyweights seldom lasts long. It depends so much on who gets in the first good blow. And in this case the fight certainly didn't last three minutes. It was horrible. I don't know whether the Dragon was much of a boxer. He certainly seemed to have some knowledge of the game, but he never landed a blow. After a few exchanges he received a punch on the nose, and the blood ran down all over his dress shirt. Then he hit wildly, and suddenly received three terrible blows in rapid succession; one on the chin, one on the jaw, and then a fearful thump over the heart, which laid him out. We were now in complete possession of the field, the man with the black eye being the only conscious enemy in the flat, and he had done with fighting for the day.

'Now, where's that butler?' said Chasseloup.

'Oh, come on, for God's sake!' I exclaimed, foreseeing more blood-letting. 'Leave the butler alone. Let's get away.'

'I'm not going till I get what I came for.'

'What's that?'

'That drink.'

The man with the black eye, who appeared to be some sort of hired ruffian, grinned in a sickly manner.

'All right, guv'nor,' he said, 'I can fix that for you.'

He went into the dining room and returned with a tantalus and some glasses.

Chasseloup poured himself out his double whisky, just the exact amount, and no more. Then he put on his coat and readjusted his hair in the mirror. His face was unscratched.

'There's something perfectly disgusting about you,' I thought.

When we left the flat the Dragon was partly conscious, and he was mumbling something about the police and firearms and vengeance. We went down in the lift. Just as we were going out through the entrance hall a typical young-man-about-town came up the steps. He was limping. Chasseloup made to raise his hat.

'Mr Lindt, I presume?'

The young man started. Chasseloup smiled quite graciously.

'Her ladyship is expecting you in the smoke-room,' he said.

'Oh! thank you, thank you, sir.'

The dude blushed and hurried on.

'But, good Lord!' I exclaimed, when we were in the street. 'It's a bit unfair. They'll half murder him.'

'That's his affair,' said Chasseloup. 'Besides, it serves him right—to go fooling about with another man's wife.'

To look back on it, it seems almost unbelievable, but from the moment when we left the Minerva Musical Society to the moment we returned marks the lapse of rather less than an hour. And when we returned nothing might have happened at all. There they all were, the same people, the same little gilt chairs. Everybody looked quite unconcerned, but nobody looked more unconcerned than Colin St Clair Chasseloup, lolling indolently on a stuffed settee at the end of the room.

As it happened, they were just finishing some modern work, and then there was an interval. Both our wives joined us and were introduced. Mrs Chasseloup was charming. She said:

'You bad men! where have you been?'

Without waiting for a reply, she added excitedly:

'Colin, you'll be pleased. Paul Tingleton's ill, and he can't lead his quintette. And I've persuaded Mr Oesler to end up with the Bach fugue you love so much.'

Queer fish, people are. A few minutes later we were drinking lemonade and coffee and talking of such precious intimacies as the colour of a musical phrase, and only a quarter of an hour ago— Then we were back in the concert hall, Chasseloup and his wife and my wife and I, and the great Mr Oesler began to play Bach.

And then the queerest thing of all—Chasseloup! Chasseloup, whose face I had seen but a few minutes before ablaze with anger and cruelty, suddenly mellowing, becoming gentle and wistful. And he leaned forward with his lips parted, and his wife sat beside him with an identical expression on her face. And then I saw his hand steal towards her lap and she took it in both of hers and gripped it greedily. And they sat there, side-by-side, perfectly oblivious to their surroundings, perfectly happy, like two children listening to a fairy-tale.

—*IV*—

The Room

THE ROOM was in Praxton Street, which is not very far from the Euston Road. It was fifteen feet by ten feet six inches. It had a door and a window. The window was covered by stiff lace curtains with several tears in them, framed by red plush curtains, which, if pulled together, failed to meet by nearly a yard. The furniture consisted of a circular mahogany table, a Victorian sideboard with mirrors inset in the panels above, a narrow-seated horsehair chair which had a tendency to shoot the occupant into the fireplace, two other mahogany chairs with green velvet seats, a white enamelled flower-stand supporting a puce-coloured earthenware pot in which a dismal aspidistra struggled for existence. In the angle between the door and the window was an iron frame supporting what proved to be a bed by night and a dumping ground for odds and ends by day. The wall was papered with a strange pattern of violet and pink flowers leaping in irregular waves ceiling-wards. On the walls were many framed oleographs, one of the Crucifixion, one of a small boy holding a piece of sultana cake on a plate and a large collie dog regarding the cake with melancholy greed. There was a photograph of somebody's husband with a square beard and a white stock, two watercolours of some foreign country characterized by blue mountains reflected in a lake, and a large print of the coronation of King George. On the floor was a yellow and red carpet of indeterminate pattern worn right through in all the most frequented spots of the room. Around the gas chandelier a dozen or so flies played their eternal game of touch.

Now this is a brief description of inanimate objects

—except for the flies. But we all know that even inanimate objects—particularly a collection of inanimate objects—have a soul. That is to say that they subtly affect everyone on the spiritual plane. Perhaps it would be safer to say that they have a message.

To James Wilbraham Waite, seated on the horsehair chair on a bright July afternoon, they brought an abrupt message. He looked around the room and he said to himself out aloud:

'This is simply hell!'

He had occupied this room in the lodging-house for seven years, and it had taken all this time to breed in him the special kind of intense loathing and hate which he felt at that moment. It was not the quick hate of sudden anger. It was the slow combustible passion of years of disappointment and dissatisfaction. The room seemed to embody in itself all that he detested and yearned to avoid.

His father had been a small Essex farmer, and James Wilbraham had spent his boyhood on the farm. Owing, however, to Mr Waite senior's lack of concentration on the commercial side of the farm, and his too great concentration on the good stuff served over the bar of the Dog and Destiny, he went bankrupt, and died soon after. His wife had died many years before, and James Wilbraham, being an only son, found himself at the age of eighteen alone in the world without even a mangel-wurzel to his name. He was a dreamy boy, loving an open-air life. He had done fairly well at the Grammar School. He had no head for mathematics, but excelled at theoretical subjects, which brought him no credits or marks. When his father died there was apparently nothing for him to do but become a farm hand. One of the masters at the school, who had taken an interest in him, did his best to dissuade him from this course. His name was Mr Flint, and he pointed out the hopeless future of manual labour without capital. He emphasized the fact that James had

had quite a good education and that he was intelligent, and that he had only to use his brains to make his way in the world. For two years James fought against the good advice of his friend. He worked for a local farmer, and he might be working for the same farmer now but for the fact that he fell in love with a girl he had seen walking about the streets of Pondersham. He never spoke to her, but she stirred some profound note in his nature. It was less the girl herself, perhaps, than the idea of love in the abstract. She was what was known as a lady, inaccessible, remote, fragile as a china vase. He began to regard his rough hands and coarse clothes with misgiving. And then one day he went to the pictures with an acquaintance and found himself suddenly projected into a world of magnificent Life, spelt with a very large L, where gorgeous women flashed in and out of priceless automobiles, and powdered flunkeys ushered them into marvellous palaces. The contrast was too violent. If ever he wanted to possess one of these splendid creatures—well, he could never do so as a farm hand.

His ideas of farming had never been academic, to put it mildly. He had inherited a great deal of his father's vagueness. During his father's lifetime he had regarded the soil as a mysterious substitute for a mother. It succoured him with the good things he liked, and made few calls on his industry. He liked to ride over it, and see the little green shoots budding. Then he would dream by a pond, or idle the hours away with a dog and a ferret.

Consequently when he informed his employer one day, with a sigh, that he had decided to give up farming, that gentleman accepted his resignation with unblushing satisfaction. Through the influence of Mr Flint he got a situation as a clerk in a corn chandler's at Pondersham. He earned seventeen and sixpence a week, and managed to keep himself—in a state of chronic hunger.

He endured this life for over a year, when again through the influence of Mr Flint he considerably improved his position. For he obtained a situation at a scholastic employment agency in London at a salary of thirty shillings a week. It was then that he made his first introduction to the Room. He paid twelve shillings and sixpence a week for it, and that included a breakfast, consisting of tea and a boiled egg. To record his career during the seven years that led up to this particular July afternoon would be tedious in the extreme. It seemed to centre entirely around the Room. By half-crowns and five shillings his salary had now risen to three pounds five shillings. During the next seven years by similar processes it might conceivably rise to five pounds. He would then be thirty-five. But it was not these material considerations and prospects alone which disturbed him. It was that eternal sense of ingrained discontent.

He detested his work. At his desk he was always dreaming. He dreamt of far-off countries, and beauty, and love, and romance. He joined a local library and spent most of his evenings alone reading. And when he had been completely transported into another world he would look up and find himself in the Room. He would catch his own reflection in the crazy mirrors, the boy and sultana cake and the collie dog would appear to be grinning at him insipidly from the wall, the vision of King George in his coronation robes only produced in him a sense of acrid disloyalty. The wallpaper leaping towards the ceiling made him want to scream. Even when he turned out the gas and went to bed he was intensely conscious of enveloping ugliness.

On this particular afternoon his venom focussed on the flies around the chandelier. He had come home early—it was a slack time at the office—and he was reading a novel with a setting in the desert. He became absorbed with visions. He saw the sleepy pile of grey and white buildings against the vivid green of date-palms in an oasis. He could hear the distant sounds of strange music, and breathe the rich perfumes of the African night. Then suddenly he looked up and saw those London flies playing their ridiculous game beneath the chandelier. He felt maddened. He put down the book and made a swipe at them with his handkerchief. They dispersed only to reform a few seconds later. He hit at them again and again without any tangible result. Then he sat down and thought.

'I want a holiday,' he said to himself. 'My nerves are in a rotten state.' Owing to the exigencies of office work he had had his fortnight's holiday in April. He would not get another until—some time next year. And then he would probably go to Hastings, or Bognor, or worse. It was awful, unendurable.

'I won't have you here,' he suddenly said to the flies. There was a look of grim determination on his face. He picked up a towel and slightly damped it, and began a fresh campaign. He soon realized that to hit them in the air was a chance in a hundred. You have to wait till they settle. He tracked them about the room. He killed several on the table, quite a lot on the wall and the window, but nothing seemed to make any difference to the party under the chandelier. He made wild swipes at them and actually hit several on the wing, but back they came. This persistence was either astonishing pluck or astonishing stupidity. It was almost uncanny. He struck wildly at one on the chandelier itself, and then—crash! down came the globe and smashed on the floor. A few minutes later he heard the ponderous steps of his rheumaticky landlady coming up the stairs. He gripped the towel hard. He felt uncertain of himself. 'If the old fool makes a fuss about that globe I'll give her a swipe,' his mind registered. There was the familiar tap on the door and it opened.

To his surprise she held out a letter. She had not apparently heard the globe smash, neither did she notice it.

'Mrs Bean's just left this,' she said. 'It came this morning, but it was addressed to seventy-five.'

He took the letter, and said 'Thanks'; then, feeling that his passions were somewhat vented, he pointed to the globe and said casually:

'I'm afraid I broke the globe, hitting at a fly.'

She said: 'Oh, dear! Hm! I'll go and get a dustpan and brush. My legs are that bad.'

'I'll get it for you if you like,' he answered, feeling suddenly quite amiable.

'I wish you would, Mr Waite; it's under the kitchen dresser.'

The business of getting the dustpan and brush, clearing up the broken glass, and listening to a story about the shocking pain Mr Bean was suffering with his kidney trouble occupied ten minutes. She went at last and he opened the letter. It was from a firm of lawyers in Liverpool informing him that an uncle of his had recently died in Canada, and under the terms of the will he was the inheritor of approximately six hundred pounds.

Six hundred pounds! For the first time he stared at the Room with unseeing eyes. It had no horrors for him. He saw right through the mahogany sideboard and the leaping wallpaper out into the great broad spaces of the world. Gulls screamed above the heaving decks of a mighty ship. He saw white cities with minarets and mosques glittering in the sun. There were valleys aglow with myriad flowers. A woman was coming towards him—

The desire to talk to someone about his amazing news was irresistible. He knew no one in the house except the landlady. He went downstairs and found her ironing some flannel underclothing in the kitchen. He said:

'I say, Mrs Beldam, I've come in for some money.'

The landlady looked up at him with an expression of greedy interest. She said:

'Oh, that's nice, I must say. How much is it?'

'About six hundred pounds.'

She looked down at her flannel petticoat. She was cautiously balancing the potentialities of the situation.

She couldn't exactly see how she was to come in over this. All it would amount to would be that she would probably lose a lodger. She repeated:

'That's nice.' Then, after blowing on her iron, she added:

'You take my advice, young man, and put it all in War Savings Certificates.'

'War Savings Certificates!'

He looked at her with horror. Ah! he could see through it all. This social conspiracy to keep him in the Room. Here was the golden key to freedom, and this woman, this state, social life itself, talked to him about War Savings Certificates. Not likely! He barked at her:

'We shall see,' and almost ran out of the room.

It was nearly a month before he got his cheque. In the meantime he had been carefully maturing his plans. He bought maps, and guides, and works of reference. He gave the scholastic agency a week's notice, and when he was free he devoted his time to reading and polishing up his French, at which he had been fairly proficient at school.

The Room, if anything, seemed more hideous than before. He felt himself already superior to it; nevertheless he was still a little frightened. It had for so long dominated him, with its drab menace, he could not believe that he would ever really escape from its clutches. He dreamed of some feral vengeance. Perhaps on the last night he would get busy with an axe or a poker. But no, this would be very foolish. He would be made to pay, and so the Room would score off him.

And so one day in early September he gave up the key of the Room to the landlady and left it forever.

He had about fifty pounds in cash on him. With the rest of the money he had bought a Worldwide Letter of Credit. What destiny had in store for him when the money was spent he neither knew nor cared. He was achieving his supreme ambition—to escape.

Four days later he arrived at Algiers, tired, bewildered,

but very excited. He regarded Algiers as a good kicking-off place for his adventures. He wanted to get to the desert, but, knowing nothing of the country, he didn't know how to proceed. He stayed there for a week in a quiet hotel, wandering about, and getting lost in the maze of the Arab quarter. The city repelled him a little with its large hotels and terraces of French villas. Even the Arab quarter had a sense of unreality. He felt every moment that he might step out and find himself in the Earl's Court Road. One day at lunch he got into conversation with a Frenchman, who told him about a journey he was about to take to Laghouat in the south. James Wilbraham pricked up his ears. The Frenchman, it appeared, was a traveller in rugs and bric-à-brac. He was making the journey with a companion, and they were going by car. Yes, there were only the three of them, including the chauffeur, and if James cared to join them and pay his share—the contract was concluded then and there.

Three days later the party left. They motored the whole of the first day through the richly fertile country of Northern Algeria, and spent the night at Boghari up in the hills. The two Frenchmen talked the whole time, and James gathered about one-third of their conversation, which was mostly about women, the rate of exchange, French politics, and trade. At Boghari it was very cold and overcast.

The seeker after romance began to feel depressed that night. It was all very beautiful, of course, but somehow things were not for the moment shaping in the way he had hoped. A motor-car was an unromantic way of travelling, and French commercial travellers can be very boring. He felt a tripper, an alien. He wondered whether he would ever fit into any *milieu* in which he found himself. In the early morning he dreamt he was back in the Room, and the chairs, and tables, and lace curtains were laughing at him.

The next day, however, the car wound its way down into

the plain below, and they began to approach the desert. By midday it was very hot. They lunched at Djerfa on fish soup, bustard stewed in oil, and Algerian wine. The food nauseated James, but the Frenchmen became more and more garrulous. He wanted to get on to where romance would begin. At last they started, and all the afternoon the car raced on down a straight road through endless tracks of sand dotted with scrub, clumps of coarse grass, and occasionally pistacia trees. It was nearly sundown before they reached the oasis of Laghouat. They drove up to the little hotel just outside the wall of the town.

Having washed and changed his clothes, James felt a great desire to escape from the two Frenchmen. He put on his hat and hurried out. Immediately outside the hotel he was surrounded by swarms of Arab boys jabbering in French. He tried to shoo them off, but four of them followed him everywhere he went. He learnt afterwards to become accustomed to this attention, but at the moment it annoyed him. He wanted to be alone. He crossed the road and climbed up a rocky eminence, followed by his retinue. Clambering over the last boulder he gave a gasp of astonishment. Laghouat is two thousand feet above sea level, and from it the desert slopes gradually down. At first glance it gave him the impression of the sea, an endless quivering ocean glistening in the sun. In the foreground were thousands of stately date-palms, while on his right the little town, dominated by its minaret, was a pleasant jumble of salmon-pink, grey, white and brown. For the first time since he left the Room he thrilled with a sense of satiety. He sat there for a long while dreaming. The boys chattered to him and among themselves, but he was hardly conscious of them. The sun tipped the horizon, and suddenly he heard a gun fired, a flag fluttered from the top of the minaret, and a diminutive figure in black appeared. Against the clear blue sky, graduated to pale orange on the horizon, the minaret stood out like a pillar of gold. A rich bell-like voice rang out and seemed to reach the furthermost places in the desert. It was the muezzin calling the faithful to prayer.

James Wilbraham gave a sigh of content.

'I have found it,' he thought to himself.

That night he slept badly. He was troubled by the problem of how to keep what he had found. How could he fit into this atmosphere? How could he live? He was at present a foreign guest staying at the only hotel. The town was entirely Arab, its activities almost entirely devoted to the breeding of sheep and cattle. For days he wandered about, listening for signs and portents. The French travellers returned to Algiers. A few other trippers came and went. A week went by. And then one day he met his fate in the person of Giles Duxberry. He was seated on the verandah of the hotel one evening when a tall, angular figure, in a white burnous, came slouching up the path. He seemed to know his way about the hotel, for he made straight for the bell, rang it, and ordered an anisette. Then he retired, washed himself, came back and sat at a table next to James. He poured water into the colourless liquid, drank it in two gulps, and ordered another. When he had consumed four of these insiduous drinks, he suddenly said:

'English, aren't you?'

'Yes,' said James, with surprise.

'Have a drink?'

It would have been inhuman to refuse, and James also had an anisette. He had never drunk it before, and his single one had a much more potent effect on him than the four did on his chance acquaintance. He tried to be conversational, but it was very difficult. Mr Duxberry's skin was almost the colour of an Arab's but his eyes were tired, his manners lethargic. He was like a man utterly bored with every human experience—except perhaps drink. He barked in monosyllables, and explained things in little disconnected sentences.

He was, it appeared, employed by a Lancashire firm

in the halfa business. It seemed that some genius had discovered that the long, coarse halfa-grass, which grew in the desert, was excellent material for making paper. It was garnered by the natives and deposited in bundles in various depots about the country. Giles Duxberry was in charge of a depot in a tiny oasis fifteen miles away. He lived there by himself, and the only thing he could find in the job's favour was that once a week he could come into Laghouat and get drunk. He proceeded to get drunk on this occasion, and before the evening was far advanced he was quite incoherent.

Before he had reached this stage, however, he had asked James to come out and see him, and explained where it was. The only way of getting there was on horseback. James felt grateful for his early years spent on a farm. He could ride. The expedition, moreover, carried with it an element of adventure. Perhaps he, too, could get a similar situation.

It took him three days to obtain the loan of a horse, which he eventually did through the intermediary of four people. He felt singularly like a paladin setting out on some holy quest as he left the town behind and cantered across the desert. He had no difficulty in finding his destination. It was a small oasis with the inevitable date-palms, barley, and castor-oil plants, a low, rambling, lime-washed building made of mud and cement, and some half-dozen nomad tents pitched in the sand. He found Duxberry just sitting down to lunch. Without any particular show of warmth the latter said:

'Hullo, you've come then!'

He shouted something in Arabic into the room beyond. The room was plainly but comfortably furnished, and very clean. They had lunch, and were waited on by an incredibly ugly old Ouled Naïl woman, with the tattoo mark on her forehead and henna stains on her finger-tips. The food was excellently cooked. James talked and asked questions, and received monosyllabic grunts in reply. Afterwards they sat outside in the sun and smoked. During the afternoon Arabs kept on arriving with donkeys laden with bundles of halfa-grass. Duxberry checked their operations with idle indifference. There was an amazing sense of peace and space. In an idle moment James thought of the awful Room. What a contrast! He felt envious of this hard-bitten, sunburnt manager. Before he left he put out a feeler. He asked his host whether he knew if there were any more jobs like that going.

Duxberry stared at him.

'What for?' he asked.

'Me.'

'You!'

He seemed unable to understand.

'But you've got your fare back to England, haven't you?'

'Yes, but I'd rather live here.'

'Rather live out in this God-forsaken place than in England!'

'Much.'

'What is there to it?'

'I don't know. It's just the sense of—oh, freedom and space, and sun and air.'

The older man regarded him gravely.

'Listen, son,' he said; 'when you've had as much of it as I have you'll cut all that stuff out. I ran away from home when I was a boy and worked my passage to South Africa. For thirty years I've beach-combed all over the earth. I've only one ambition.'

'What's that?'

'To get back home.'

'Good God!'

They looked at each other uncomprehendingly, like men who have reached a mental impasse.

James Wilbraham left soon after and returned to Laghouat. For days he wandered around the desert or sat in the hotel, pondering over the problem of his own life. Certain realizations became clear to him. He was unhappy. He wanted to stay out there. Giles Duxberry was unhappy. He wanted to go back to England. Well, surely the situation could be adjusted. Let Giles go back to the Room, and see how he liked it. Let James take his place.

A few days later Giles arrived for his weekly 'drunk'. James waited until he had had his fifth anisette, then he said:

'I say, Duxberry, I'd like to make a proposition to you.'

'Carry on, son.'

'Could you manage to wangle it so that I could take on your job? If you could I would be pleased to give you a hundred pounds to pay your fare back to England.'

The beach-comber's eyes distended. He took a deep draught of the milk-coloured liquid.

'A hundred pounds!' he exclaimed. His eyes said: 'Well, of all the blanketty, blanketty—idiots!'

They discussed ways and means. Two days later James again rode out to see his friend. Yes, it was decided that it might be wangled. Correspondence passed, resulting in James having to make a trip to Algiers to interview a gentleman who was born in Blackburn. The arrangement was satisfactorily made. He returned to Laghouat full of the joy of life. He spent a week with Giles Duxberry, learning the small technicalities of his undertaking. He began to pick up Arabic words and expressions. And then one day he handed over a hundred good English pounds, and Duxberry counted the notes carefully, pouched them, and held out his hand.

'Good luck to you!' he said.

James felt strangely moved. He could hardly speak. It was not that he had developed any particular affection for his new friend, but that he felt him to be a poignant figure in his destiny. He said:

'Good luck to *you!*'

Nothing more was said. Duxberry mounted his horse,

waved a perfunctory farewell, and rode away. James stood there bareheaded, breathing in the warm air, and absorbing the marvellous sense of repose of the desert.

* * *

And so one day Giles Duxberry found himself seated in a horsehair chair that had a tendency to shoot the occupant into the fireplace. He had removed his boots, and was gazing into the fire. Then he looked round and regarded the Room. There was a lovely curly sideboard with mirrors, which reflected the vision of his sunburnt face, a white stand with a pot and a plant, a circular table, two other chairs, a bed. On the wall a pretty pattern and some enchanting pictures—a sacred subject, a boy and a collie dog and a piece of cake, some clever water-colour paintings, King George in his magnificent coronation robes. Civilization!

It was a dream come true—a dream of thirty years. He sighed with happy contentment. He had eighty pounds in cash on him. He had only to stroll out and there were a dozen saloons within a mile, where he could order any drink he liked. There were cinemas and music-halls. There was life passing all the time, strange and amazing things that might happen any moment. He might get a good job, make money, marry some beautiful woman. He gazed fascinated by the Room and murmured:

'Gosh! this is heaven!'

As a man accustomed to live in lonely places he had acquired a habit of talking to himself. He addressed the fire:

'Jeminy! What a fool! what a lunatic! That guy will soon get fed up with it. He'll come bundling back. Anyway, he's not going to take my Room from me. It was a square deal.'

—V—

A Man of Letters

ALFRED CODLING TO ANNIE PHELPS

My Dear Annie,

I got into an awful funny mood lately. You'l think I'm barmy. It comes over me like late in the evenin when its gettin dusky. It started I think when I was in Egypt. Nearly all us chaps who was out there felt it a bit I think. When you was on sentry go in the dessert at night it was so quite and missterius. You felt you wanted to *know* things if you know what I mean. Since I've come back and settled in the saddlery again I still feel it most always. A kind of discontented funny feelin if you know what I mean. Well old girl what I mean is when we're spliced up and settled over in Tibbelsford I want to be good for you and I want to know all about things and that. Well I'm goin to write to Mr Weekes whose a gentleman and who lives in a private house near the church. They say he is a littery society and if it be so I'm on for joinin it. You'l think I'm barmy won't you. It isn't that old dear. Me that has always been content to do my job and draw my screw on Saturday and that. You'l think me funny. When you've lived in the dessert you feel how old it all is. You want something and you don't know what it is praps its just to improve yourself and that. Anyway there it is and I'll shall write to him. See you Sunday. So long, dear.

Alf.

ALFRED CODLING TO JAMES WEEKES, ESQ

Dear Sir,

Someone tells me you are a littery society in Tibbelsford. In which case may I offer my services

as a member and believe me.
Your obedient servant,
ALFRED CODLING.

PENDRED CASTAWAY (SECRETARY TO JAMES WEEKES, ESQ.) TO ALFRED CODLING

DEAR SIR,

In reply to your letter of the 27th inst. I beg to inform you that Mr James Weekes is abroad. I will communicate the contents of your letter to him.

Yours faithfully,
PENDRED CASTAWAY.

ANNIE PHELPS TO ALFRED CODLING

MY DEAR ALF,

You are a dear old funny old bean. What *is* up with you. I expeck you are just fed up. You haven't had another tutch of the fever have you. I will come and look after you Sunday. You are a silly to talk about improvin considerin the money you are gettin and another rise next spring you say. I expeck you got fed up in the dessert and that didn't you. I expeck you wanted me sometimes, eh? I shouldn't think the littery society much cop myself. I can lend you some books. Cook is a great reader. She has nearly all Ethel M. Dell's and most of Charles Garvice. She says she will lend you some if you promiss to cover in brown paper and not tare the edges. They had a big party here over the weekend a curnel a bishop two gentleman and some smart women one very nice she gave me ten bob. We could go to the pictures come Wednesday if agreeable. Milly is walking out with a feller over at Spindlehurst in the grossery a bit flashy I don't like him much. Mrs Vaughan had one of her attacks on Monday. Lord she does get on my nerves when she's like that. Well be good and cheerio must now close.

Love and kisses till Sunday.
ANNIE.

JAMES WEEKES, ESQ. (MALAGA, SPAIN)
TO ALFRED CODLING.

DEAR SIR,

My secretary informs me that you wish to join our literary society in Tibbelsford. It is customary to be proposed and seconded by two members.

Will you kindly send me your qualifications?

Yours faithfully,
JAMES WEEKES.

ALFRED CODLING TO ANNIE PHELPS

MY DEAR ANNIE,

Please thank Cook for the two books which I am keepin rapt up and will not stain. I read the Eagles mate and think it is a pretty story. As you know dear I am no fist at explaining myself. At the pictures the other night you were on to me again about gettin on and that. It isn't that. Its difficul to explane what I mean. I expeck I will always be able to make good money enough. If you havent been throw it you cant know what its like. Its somethin else I want if you know what I mean. To be honest I did not like the picturs the other night. I thought they were silly but I like to have you sittin by me and holding your hand. If I could tell you what I mean you would know. I have heard from Mr Weekes about the littery and am writin off at once. Steve our foreman has got sacked for pinchin lether been goin on for yeres so must close with love till Sunday.

ALF.

ALFRED CODLING TO JAMES WEEKES, ESQ.

DEAR SIR,

As regards your communication you ask what are my quallifications. I say I have no quallifications sir nevertheless I am wishful to join the littery. I will be candid with you sir. I am not what you might call a littery or eddicated man at all. I am in the saddlery. I was all throw Gallipoli and Egypt. L corporal in the 2/15th Mounted Blumshires. It used to come over me like when I was out there alone in the dessert. Prehaps sir you will understand me when I say it for I find folks do not understand me about it not even the girl I walk out with Annie Phelps, who is as nice a girl a feller could wish. Perhaps sir you have to have been throw it if you know what I mean. When you are alone at night in the dessert its all so big and quite you want to get to know things and all about things if you know what I mean sir so prehaps you will pass me in the littery.

Your obedient servant

ALFRED CODLING.

ANNIE PHELPS TO ALFRED CODLING

DEAR ALF,

You was funny Sunday. I dont know whats up with you. You never used to be like that glum I call it. Is it thinking about this littery soc turnin your head or what. Millie says you come into the kitchen like a boiled oul you was. Cheer up ole dear till Sunday week.

ANNIE.

JAMES WEEKES, ESQ., TO ALFRED CODLING

DEAR SIR,

Allow me to thank you for your charming letter. I feel that I understand your latent desires perfectly. I shall be returning to Tibbelsford in a week's time when I hope to make your acquaintance. I feel sure that you will make a desirable member of our literary society.

Yours cordially,

JAMES WEEKES.

JAMES WEEKES TO SAMUEL CHILDERS

MY DEAR SAM,

I received the enclosed letter yesterday and I hasten to send it on to you. Did you ever read anything more delightful? We must certainly get Alfred Codling into our society. He sounds the kind of person who would make a splendid foil to old Baldwin with his tortuous metaphysics—that is, if we can only get him to talk.

Yours ever,

J.W.

SAMUEL CHILDERS TO JAMES WEEKES

My dear chap,

You are surely not serious about the ex-corporal! I showed his letter to Fanny. She simply screamed with laughter. But of course you mean it as a joke proposing him for the 'littery'. Hope to see you on Friday.

Ever yours,

S.C.

ALFRED CODLING TO ANNIE PHELPS

My dear Annie,

I was afraid you would begin to think I was barmy dear I always said so but you musnt take it like that. It is difficult to tell you about but you know my feelins to you is as always. Now I have to tell you dear that I have seen Mr Weekes he is a very nice old gentlemen indeed he is very kind he says I can go to his hous anytime and read his books he has hundreds and hundreds. I have nevver seen so many books you have to have a ladder to clime up to some of them he is very kind he says he shall propose me for the littery soc and I can go when I like he ast me all about mysel and that was very kind and pleesant he told me all about what books I was to read and that so I think dear I wont be goin to the picturs Wednesday but will meet you by the Fire statesion Sunday as usual

Your lovin

Alf.

EPHRAIM BALDWIN TO JAMES WEEKES

MY DEAR WEEKES,

I'm afraid I cannot understand your attitude in proposing and getting Childers to second this hobbledehoy called Alfred Codling. I have spoken to him and I am quite willing to acknowledge that he may be a very good young man in his place. But why join a literary society? Surely we want to raise the intellectual standard of the society, not lower it? He is absolutely ignorant. He knows nothing at all. Our papers and discussions will be Greek to him. If you wanted an extra hand in your stables or a jobbing gardener well and good, but I must sincerely protest against this abuse of the fundamental purposes of our society.

Yours sincerely,

EPHRAIM BALDWIN.

FANNY CHILDERS TO ELSPETH PRITCHARD

DEAR OLD THING,

I must tell you about a perfect scream that is happening here. You know the Tibbelsford literary society that Pa belongs to, and also Jimmy Weekes? Well, it's like this. Dear Old Jimmy is always doing something eccentric. The latest thing is he has discovered a mechanic in the leather trade with a soul! (I'm not sure I ought not to spell it the other way). He is also an ex-soldier and was out in the East. He seems to have become imbued with what they called 'Eastern romanticism'. Anyway, he wanted to join the Society, and old Weekes rushed Pa into seconding him, and they got him through. And now a lot of the others are up in arms about it—especially old Baldwin—you know, we call him 'Permanganate of Potash'. If you saw him you'd know why, but I can't tell you. I have been to two of the meetings specially to observe the mechanic with the soul. He is really quite a dear. A thick-set, square-chinned little man with enormous hands with a heavy silver ring on the third finger of his left, and tattoo marks on his right wrist. He sits there with his hands spread out on his knees and stares round at the members as though he thinks they are a lot of lunatics. The first evening he came the paper was on 'The influence of Erasmus on modern theology', and the second evening 'The drama of the Restoration'. No wonder the poor soul looks bewildered. He never says a word. How is Tiny? I was in town on Thursday and got a duck of a hat. Do come over soon.

Crowds of love,

FAN.

JAMES WEEKES TO ALFRED CODLING

MY DEAR CODLING,

I quite appreciate your difficulty. I would suggest that you read the following books in the order named. You will find them in my library:

Jevons' *Primer of Logic*,
Welton's *Manual of Logic*,
Brackenbury's *Primer of Psychology*, and
Professor James' *Text book of Psychology*.

Do not be discouraged!

Sincerely yours,

JAMES WEEKES.

ANNIE PHELPS TO ALFRED CODLING

DEAR ALF,

I dont think you treat me quite fare You says you are sweet on me and that and then you go on in this funny way It isnt my falt that you got the wind up in Egypt I dont know what you mean by all this I wish the ole littery soc was dead and finish. Cook say you probibly want a blue pill you was so glum Sunday. Dont you see all these gents and girls and edicated coves are pullin youre leg if you dont know what they talkin about and that Your just makin a fule of yourself and then what about me you dont think of me its makin me a fule too. Milly says *she* wouldent have no truck with a book lowse so there it is.

ANNIE.

ALFRED CODLING TO JAMES WEEKES, ESQ.

Dear Sir,

I am much oblidged to you for puttin me on them books. It beats me how they work up these things. I'm afeard I'm not scollard enough to keep the pace with these sayins and that. Its the same with the littery I lissen to the talk and sometimes I think Ive got it and then no. Sometimes I feels angry with the things said I know the speakers wrong but I cant say I feel they wrong but I dont know what to say to say it. Theres some things to big to say isnt that sir. Im much oblidged to you sir for what you done. Beleive me I enjoy the littery altho I most always dont know the talk I know who are the rite ones and who are the rong ones If you have been throw what I have been throw you would know the same sir Beleive me your obedient servant

Alfred Codling.

EPHRAIM BALDWIN TO EDWIN JOPE, SECRETARY TO THE TIBBLESFORD LITERARY SOCIETY

Dear Jope,

For my paper on the 19th prox. I propose to discuss 'The influence of Hegelism on modern psychology'.

Yours ever,

Ephraim Baldwin.

EDWIN JOPE TO EPHRAIM BALDWIN

Dear Mr Baldwin,

I have issued the notices of your forthcoming paper. The subject, I am sure, will make a great appeal to our members, and I feel convinced that we are in for an illuminating and informative evening. With regard to our little conversation on Wednesday last, I am entirely in agreement with you with regard to the quite inexplicable action of Weekes in introducing the 'leather mechanic' into the society. It appears to me a quite superfluous effrontery to put upon our members. We do not want to lose Weekes but I feel that he ought to be asked to give some explanation of his conduct. As you remark, it lowers the whole standard of the society. We might as well admit agricultural labourers, burglars, grooms and barmaids, and the derelicts of the town. I shall sound the opinion privately of other members.

With kind regards,

Yours sincerely,

EDWIN JOPE.

ANNIE PHELPS TO ALFRED CODLING

All right then you stick to your old littery. I am sendin you back your weddin ring you go in and out of that place nevver thinkin of me Aunt said how it would be you goin off and cetterer and gettin ideas into your head what do you care I doant think you care at all I expeck you meet a lot of these swell heads there men *and women* and you get talkin and thinkin you someone All these years you away I wated for you faithfull I never had a thowt for other fellers and then you go on like this and treat me in this way Aunt says she wouldnt put up and Milly says a book lowse is worse than no good and so I say goodby and thats how it is now forever You have broken my hart

ANNE.

ANNIE PHELPS TO ALFRED CODLING

I cried all nite I dindt mean quite all I says you know how I mene dear Alf if you was only reesonible I doant mind you goin the littery if you eggsplain yourself For Gawds sake meet me tonight by the fire stachon and eggsplain everything.

Your broke hearted

ANNE.

JAMES WEEKES TO SAMUEL CHILDERS

MY DEAR SAM,

I hope Harrogate is having the desired effect upon you.

I was about to say that you have missed few events of any value or interest during your absence, but I feel I must qualify that statement. You have missed a golden moment. The great Baldwin evening has come and gone and I deplore the fact that you were not there. My sense of gratification, however, is not due to Ephraim himself but to my unpopular protégé and white elephant—Alfred Codling. I tell you it was glorious! Ephraim spoke for an hour and a half, the usual thing, a dull *réchauffé* of Schopenhauer and Hegel, droning forth platitudes and half-baked sophistries. When it was finished the chairman asked if anyone else wished to speak. To my amazement my ex-lance-corporal rose heavily to his feet. His face was brick red and his eyes glowed with anger. He pointed his big fingers at Ephraim and exclaimed: 'Yes, talk, talk, talk—that's all it is. There's nothing in it at all!' and he hobbled out of the room (you know he was wounded in the right foot). The position, as you may imagine, was a little trying. I did not feel in the mood to stay and make apologies. I hurried after Codling. I caught him up at the end of the lane. I said, 'Codling, why did you do that?' He could not speak for a long time, then he said: 'I'm sorry, sir. It came over me like, all of a sudden.' We walked on. At the corner by Harvey's mill we met a girl. Her face was wet—there was a fine rain pouring at the time. They looked at each other these two, then she suddenly threw out her arms and buried her face on his chest. I realized that this was no place for me and I hurried on. The following morning I received the enclosed letter. Please return it to me.

Yours ever,

JAMES.

ALFRED CODLING TO JAMES WEEKES

DEAR SIR,

Please to irrase my name from the littery soc. I feel I have treated you bad about it but there it is. I apologize to you for treatin you bad like this that is all I regret You have always been kind and pleesant to me lendin me the books and that. I shall always be grateful to you for what you have done. It all came over me sudden like last night while that chap was spoutin out about what you call *physology*. I had never heard tell on the word till you put me on to it and now they all talk about it. I looked it up in the dicktion and it says somethin about the science of mind and that chap went on spoutin about it. I had quarrel with my girl we had nevver quarrel before and I was very down abowt it. She is the best girl a feller could wish and I have always said so. Somehow last night while he was spoutin on it came over me sudden I thowt of the nights I had spent alone in the dessert when it was all quite and missterous and big. I had been throw it all sir. I had seen my pals what was alive one minnit blown to peices the next. I had tramped hunderds of miles and gone without food and watter. I had seen hell itsel sir And when you are always with death like that sir you are always so much alive You are alive and then the next minnit you may be dead and it makes you want to feel in touch like with everythin You cant hate noone when your like that You think of the other feller over there whose thinkin like you are prehaps and he all alone to lookin up the blinkin stars and it comes over you that its only love that holds us all together love and nothin else at all My hart was breakin thinkin of Annie what I had treated so bad and what I had been throw and he went on spoutin and spoutin What does he know about *physology* You have to had been very near death to find the big things thats what I found out and I couldnt tell these littery blokes that thats why I lost my temper and so please to irrase me from the soc They cant teach me nothen that matters I've seen it all and I cant teach them nothin because they havent been throw it What I have larnt is sir that theres somethin big in our lives apart from gettin on and comfits and good times and so sir I am much oblidged for all you done for me and except my appology for the way I treat you

Your obedient servant,

ALFRED CODLING.

JAMES WEEKES TO EDWIN JOPE

DEAR JOPE,

In reply to your letter, I cannot see my way to apologize or even dissociate myself with the views expressed by Mr Alfred Codling at our last meeting, consequently I must ask you to accept my resignation.

Yours very truly,

JAMES WEEKES.

SAMUEL CHILDERS TO EDWIN JOPE

DEAR JOPE,

Taking into consideration all the circumstances of the case, I must ask you to accept my resignation from the Tibbelsford Literary Society.

Yours faithfully,

S. CHILDERS.

ANNIE PHELPS TO ALFRED CODLING

MY DEAR ALF,

Of course its all right. I am all right now dear Alf I will try and be a good wife to you I amnt clever like you with all your big thowts and that but I will and be a good wife to you Aunt Em is goin to give us that horses-hair and mother says therell be twanty five pounds comin to me when Uncle Steve pegs out and he has the dropsie all right already What do you say to Aperil if we can git that cottidge of Mrs Plummers mothers See you Sunday

love from

ANNIE.

xxxxxxxxxx

EPHRAIM BALDWIN TO EDWIN JOPE

Dear Mr Jope,

As no apology has been forthcoming to me *from any quarter* for the outrageous insult I was subjected to on the occasion of my last paper, I must ask you to accept my resignation.

Yours faithfully,

Ephraim Baldwin, O.B.E.

ALFRED CODLING TO ANNIE PHELPS

My dear Anne,

You will be pleased to hear they made me foreman this will mean an increas and so on I think April will be alright Mr Weekes sent me check for fifty pounds to start farnishin but I took it back I said no I could not accep it havin done nothin to earn it and treatin him so bad over that littery soc but he said yes and he put it in such a way that I accep after all so we shall be alright for farnishin at the present He was very kind and he says we was to go to him at any time and I was to go on readin the books he says I shall find good things in them but not the littery soc he says he has left it hisself I feel I treated him very bad but I could not stand that feller spoutin and him nevver havin been throw it like what I have That dog of Charly's killed one of Mrs Reeves chickens Monday so must now close till Sunday with love from

Your soon husband (dont it sound funny?)

Alf.

EDWIN JOPE TO WALTER BUNNING

Dear Sir,

In reply to your letter I beg to say that the Tibbelsford Literary Society is dissolved.

Yours faithfully,

E. Jope.

—*V*—

The Funny Man's Day

HIS ROUND FAT LITTLE FACE appeared seraphic in sleep. If only the hair were not greying at the temples and getting very very thin on top, and the lines about the eyes and mouth becoming rather too accentuated, it might have been the head of one of Donatello's *bambini*. It was not until Mrs Lamb, his ancient housekeeper, bustled into the room with a can and said: 'Your water, Mr Basingstoke'—the intrusion causing him to open his eyes—that it became apparent that he was a man past middle age. His eyes were very large—'goose-gog eyes' the children called them. As elderly people will, it took him some few moments to focus his mentality. A child will wake up, and carry on from the exact instant it went to sleep; but it takes a middle-aged man or woman a moment or so to realize where they are, what day in the week it is, what happened yesterday, what is going to happen today, whether they are happy or not. Certainly with regard to the latter query there is always a subconscious pressure which warns them. Almost before they have decided which day in the week it is, a voice is whispering: 'Something occurred yesterday to make you unhappy,' or 'Things are going well. You are happy just now,' and then the true realization of their affairs, and loves, and passions unfolds itself. They continue yesterday's story.

As to James Jasper Basingstoke, it was not his business to indulge in the slightest apprehension with regard to his condition of happiness or unhappiness. He was a funny man. It was his profession, his mission, his natural gift. From early morning, when his housekeeper awakened him, till, playing with the children—all the children adored him—practising, interviewing managers and costumiers, dropping into the club and exchanging stories with some of the other 'dear old boys', right on until he had finished his second show at night, it was his mission to leave behind him a long trail of smiles and laughter. Consequently, he merely sat up in bed, blinked and called out:

'I am deeply indebted to your Lambship.'

'Nibby's got hiccups,' replied that lady, who was not unused to this term of address. Nibby was Mrs Lamb's grandson. His real name was Percy Alexander. The granddaughter's name was Violetta Gladys, and she was known as Tibby. They lived next door. These names, of course, had been invented by the Funny Man, who lived in a world of make-believe, where no one at all was known by their real name. He himself was known in the theatrical profession as 'Willy Nilly'.

'I am distressed to hear that,' exclaimed Willy Nilly. 'Hiccoughs at nine o'clock in the morning! You don't say so! I always looked upon it as a nocturnal disease. The result of too many hic, haec, hock cups.'

'You must have your fun, Mr Basingstoke, but the pore little feller has been very bad ever since he woke up.'

Willy Nilly leapt out of bed and rolled across to the chest of drawers. He there produced a bottle containing little white capsules, two of which he handed to Mrs Lamb.

'Crunch these up and swallow with a little milk, then lie on his back and think of emerald green parrots flying above a dark forest, where monkeys are hanging by their tails. In our profession the distress of hiccoughs is quite prevalent and we always cure it in this way. A man who can't conquer hiccoughs can never expect to top the bill. Now tell Master Nibby that, dear lady.'

Mrs Lamb looked at the white capsules interestedly.

'Do you really mean that, Mr Basingstoke?'

The little fat man struck a dramatic situation.

'Did you ever find me not a man of my word, Lady Lamb?'

'You are a ONE,' replied the housekeeper, and retired, holding the capsules carefully balanced in the centre of her right palm, as though they contained some secret charm which she was fearful of dispelling by her contact.

The little fat man thrust out his arms in the similitude of some long-forgotten clumsy exercise. Then he regarded himself in the mirror.

'Not too thumbs up, old boy, not too thumbs up. It's going, you know. All the Apollo beauty—oh, you little depraved ruffian, go and hold your head under the tap.'

No, no, it was not the business of Willy Nilly to be depressed by these reflections either in the mirror or upon the mind. He seized the strop suspended from a hook on the architrave of the window and began to flash his razor backwards and forwards while he sang:

'Oh, what care I for a new feather bed,
And a sheet turned down so bravely—O.'

The raggle-taggle gypsies accompanied him intermittently throughout the whole operation of shaving, including the slight cut just beneath the lobe of his left ear. The business of washing and dressing was no perfunctory performance with the Funny Man. He had a personality to sustain. Moreover, among the programme of activities for the day included attendance at a wedding. There is nothing at which a funny man can be so really funny as at a wedding. One funny man at least is almost essential for the success of this time-honoured ritual. And this was a very, very special wedding; the wedding of his two dearest and greatest friends, Katie Easebrook, the pretty comedienne, and Charlie Derrick, that most brilliant writer of ballads. A swell affair it was to be in Clapham Parish Church, with afterwards a reception at the Hautboy Hotel—everything to be done 'in the best slap-up style, old boy'.

No wonder Willy Nilly took an unconscionable time

folding his voluminous black stock, adorned with the heavy gold pin, removing the bold check trousers from under the mattress, tugging at the crisp white waistcoat till it adopted itself indulgently to the curves of his figure, and hesitating for fully five minutes between the claims of seven different kinds of kid gloves. A man who tops the bill at even a suburban music hall cannot afford to neglect these things. It was fully three-quarters of an hour before he presented himself in the dining room below. Mrs Lamb appeared automatically with the teapot and his one boiled egg.

'You'd hardly believe it,' she said, 'but Nibby took them white pills and his hiccups is abated.'

'Ah! What did you expect, my good woman? Was Willy Nilly likely to deceive an innocent child? Did he think of emerald green parrots and a dark forest?'

'I told him what you said, Mr Basingstoke. Here's the letters and the newspaper.'

The Funny Man's correspondence was always rather extensive, consisting for the most part of letters from unknown people commencing: 'Dear Sir,—I wrote the enclosed words for a comic song last Sunday afternoon. I should think set to music you would make them very funny—' or 'Dear Sir,—I had a good idea for a funny stunt for you. Why not sing a song dressed up as a curate called: "The higher I aspire I espy her", and every time you come to the word higher, you trip up over a piece of orange peel. I leave it to you about payment for this idea, but I may say I am in straitened circumstances, and my wife is expecting another next March.'

There was a certain surprising orderliness about the Funny Man's methods. Receipts were filed, accounts kept together and paid fairly regularly, suggestions and ideas were carefully considered, begging letters placed together, with a sigh, 'in case anything could be done a little later on, old boy'. Occasionally would come a chatty letter from some old friend 'on the road', or from his married sister in Yorkshire. But for the most part his correspondence was not of an intimate nature.

His newspaper this morning remained unopened. The contemplation of his own programme for the day was too absorbing to fritter away nervous energy on public affairs. Whilst cracking the egg, he visualized his time-table. At ten o'clock, Chris Read was coming to try over new songs and stunts. At eleven-fifteen, he had an appointment with Albus, the costumier in Long Acre, to set the stamp of his approval upon the wig and nose for his new song: 'I'm one of the Goo-goo boys'. Katie and Charlie's wedding was at twelve-thirty and the wedding breakfast at 'the Hautboy' at one forty-five. In the meantime, he must write two letters and manage to call on old Mrs Labbory, his former landlady, who was very, very ill. Poor old soul! She'd been a brick to him in the old days, when he was sometimes 'out' for seven months in the year, out and penniless. It was only fair now that he should help her a bit with the rent, and see that she had everything she needed.

Willy Nilly's life had been passed through an avenue of landladies, but the position of Mrs Labbory was unique. He had been with her fifteen years and she was intimate with all his intimates.

At three forty-five was a rehearsal with the Railham Empire orchestra. He must get that gag right where he bluffs the trombone player in his song: 'Oh, my in-laws, my in-laws, why don't you leave me be?' Perhaps a cup of tea somewhere, and then an appointment at five-fifteen with Welsh, to arrange terms about the renewal of contract. Knotty and difficult problems—contracts. Everyone trying to do you down—must have a clear head at five-fifteen. If there's time, perhaps pop into the club for half an hour, exchange stories with Jimmy Landish, or old Blakeney. A chop at six-thirty—giving him an hour before making-up for the first house. On at eight-twenty. Three songs and an encore—mustn't forget to speak to

Hignet about that spotlight, the operator must have been drunk last night. Between shows, interview a local pressman and a young man who 'wants to go on the stage, but has had no experience'. Dash round for a sandwich and a refresher. On again at ten twenty-five. Same three songs, same encore, same bluff on the trombone player. Ten-fifty, all clear. Clean up and escape from the theatre if possible.

A last nightcap at the club, perhaps? Oh, but Bird Craft wanted him to toddle along to his rooms and hear a new song he had just acquired, 'a real winner' Bird had said it was, about 'The Girl and the Empty Pram'. Must stand by an old pal. Sometime during the day he must send two suits to be cleaned, and order some new underlinen. A beastly boring business, ordering vests and pants. He knew nothing about the qualities of materials—hosiers surely did him over that. Really a woman's business, women knew about these things. Mrs Lamb! No, not exactly Mrs Lamb. He couldn't ask Mrs Lamb to go and buy him vests and pants. A woman's business, a woman—

Heigho! Nearly ten o'clock already. Chris Read might arrive any minute. The Funny Man dashed downstairs and ran into the house next door. Tibby had already gone off to school, but Nibby had escaped, because at the moment of departure his attack of hiccoughs had reached its apotheosis. Now he was in trouble because it had left off, and his mother now declared he had been pretending. It took the Funny Man fifteen minutes to calm this family trouble. Nibby, putting it on! Nibby, playing the wag! Oh, come! Fie and for shame! Besides did Nibby's mother think that he, Dr Willy Nilly, the eminent specialist of Harley Street, was a quack? Were his remedies spurious remedies?

'Did you think of emerald green parrots in a dark wood, Nibby?'

'Yes.'

'And monkeys hanging by their tails?'

'Yes.'

'There, you see, Mrs Munro! It was a genuine case, and a genuine cure.'

'If he really had it, Mr Basingstoke, I don't believe it was thinking about monkeys what cured him; it was them little white tabloids, and we thank you kindly.'

'Mrs Munro, here are two tickets for the Railham Empire for the first house to-morrow night. Come, and bring your husband, and then you will see that there are more people cured by thinking of monkeys hanging by their tails than there are by swallowing tabloids. That is my business. I am a monkey hanging by its tail, and now I must be off. Goodbye, Nibby old boy. Why, if this isn't a sixpence under the mat. Well, well, this is an age of miracles. No, you keep it, old boy. Good-bye, Mrs Munro. Come round and see me after the show tomorrow. Toot-a-loo, my dear.'

Chris was waiting on the doorstep, a fresh-complexioned young man inclined to corpulence. His face glowed with a kind of vacant geniality.

' Well, old boy, how goes it?'

'I've got a peach this morning, Willy old boy; I think you'll like it.'

'Good boy, come on in.'

The Funny Man's drawing room was comfortably furnished with imitation Carolian furniture, a draped ottoman, and an upright Collard piano. The walls were covered with enlarged photographs of actors and actresses in gold and walnut frames, the majority of them were autographed and contained such inscriptions as: 'To my dear old Willy, from yours devotedly, Cora', 'To Uncle Nilly, one of the best, Jimmy Cotswold (The Blue Girl Company, Aug., 1899)', 'To Willy Nilly, "my heart's afire", Queenie', and so on.

'Now, let's see what you've got, old boy.' Chris sat at the piano, and unwrapped a manuscript score.

'I think this ought to win out, old boy,' he said. 'It's

by Bert Shore. It's called 'The Desert Island'. You see the point is this. You're a bit squiffy, old boy. You see, red nose and battered top hat and your trousers turned up to the knees. You know how when it's been raining on a tarred road it looks like water. Well, we have a set like that. It's really a street island—in Piccadilly, or somewhere. You're on it, and seeing all this shining water, you think you're on a desert island and the lamp-post's a palm tree. You take off your shoes and stockings and there's some good business touching the wet road with your bare toes. See, old boy? There's a thunderin' good tune. Listen to this—tum-te-too-te tum-te-tum, rum-te-too-te-tum-te works up, you see, to a kind of nautical air—then gets back to the plaintive desert stuff—rum-tum-tum-rum-te-tum. Then here's the chorus. Listen to this, old boy:

'Lost in the jungle,
Oh, what a bungle,
Eaten by spiders and ants.
Where is my happy home?
Why did they let me roam?
Where are my Sunday pants?'

Good, eh? What do you think? Make something of it, old boy? Eh?'

The little man's eyes glowed with excitement. Oh, yes, this might assuredly be a winner. It was the kind of song that had made his reputation. The tune of the chorus was distinctly catchy, and his mind was already conceiving various business.

'Let's have a go at it, old boy,' he said.

He leant over the other's shoulder and began to sing. He threw back his head and thrust out his fat little stomach, his eyes rolled, and perspiration streamed down his face. He was really enjoying himself. He had just got to

'Lost in a jungle,
Oh, what a bungle,
Eaten by spiders and ants.'

when there was a knock on the door, and Mrs Lamb thrust her head in and said: 'A telegram for you, Mr Basingstoke.'

'Eh? Oh! Well—er, never mind. Yes, thank you, my dear, give it to me.'

He opened the telegram absently, his mind still occupied with the song. When he had read it, he exclaimed:

'Good God! Poor old Joe! Yes, no, there's no answer, my dear. I must go out.'

Mrs Lamb retired.

'Poor old Joe! Stranded, eh?'

'What is it, old boy?' said Chris.

'Telegram from Joe Bloom. He says: "Can you wire me tenner, very urgent, stranded at Dundee?" Poor old Joe! He has no luck. He was out with "The Queen of the Sea" company. They must have failed. Excuse me Chris, old boy.'

The Funny Man hurried out of the room and ran downstairs. He snatched up his hat and went out. When he got round the corner, he ran. He ran as fast as he could to the High Street till he came to the London, City and Midland Bank. He filled up a cheque for fifteen pounds and cashed it. Then he ran out of the bank and trotted puffily across the road to the post office.

'I want to telegraph fifteen pounds, old girl,' he said to the fair-haired lady behind the wires. Filling up the forms took an unconscionable time, and there all the while was poor old Joe stranded in Dundee, perhaps without food! Dundee! Dundee of all places, a bleak unsympathetic town, hundreds of miles from civilization. Well, that would help him out, anyway. True, he had had to do this twice before for Joe, and Joe had not, so far, paid him back, but Joe was a notoriously unlucky devil, and he, Willy Nilly, topping the bill at the Railham Empire, couldn't let a pal in.

When he got back to his own drawing-room, Chris was stretched at full length on the sofa, smoking a cigarette and drinking whisky and soda.

'Sorry to have kept you Chris, old boy.'

'It's all right, Willy. I've just helped myself to a tot from the sideboard.'

'That's right. That's right. Now let's see, it's a quarter to eleven. I'll have to wash out this trial, old boy. I shall be late for Albus. I like that song. I'd like to have another go at it. Have another tot, Chris, old boy. I'll join you, then I must be off.'

But he didn't get to Albus that morning, because on leaving the house he remembered that he hadn't called on old Mrs Labbory. He *must* just pop in for a few moments. It was only ten minutes' walk away. He purchased a fowl and a bottle of Madeira and hurried to 27, Radnor Street. He found his old landlady propped up on the pillows, looking gaunt and distant, as though she were already regarding the manifestations of social life from a long way off and would never participate in them again.

'Well, Martha, old girl, how goes it? Merry and bright, eh? Oh, you're looking fine. More colour than last week, eh?...eating better, old girl?'

A voice came across the years.

'I'm not so well, Jim. God bless you for coming.'

'Of course I come. I come because I'm a selfish old rascal. I come because I want to, I know where I'm appreciated, eh? Ha, ha, ha, now don't you think you're getting worse. You're getting on fine. We'll soon have you about again, turning out cupboards, hanging wallpapers. Jemimy! Do you remember hanging that convolvulus wallpaper in my bedroom in the Gosport Road, eh?' The Funny Man slapped his leg, and the tears rolled down his cheeks with laughter at the recollection of the episode.

'Do you remember how I helped you? And all I did was to step into a pail of size, nearly broke my leg, and spoilt the only pair of trousers I had! Ha, ha, ha! He, he, he! I had to go to bed for four hours while you washed them out and aired 'em. O dear!'

Old Mrs Labbory began to laugh, too, in a feeble

distant manner. Then she stopped and looked at him wistfully.

'You going to Katie Easebrook's wedding, Jim?'

'Eh? Oh, yes, I'm going, old girl. I'm going straight on now.'

He hadn't meant to mention this. There's something a little crude in talking about a wedding to a dying woman. He paused and looked uncomfortably at his feet. The voice from the past reached him again.

'You ought to have married Katie Easebrook.'

'Eh? What's that? Me? Oh, no, old girl, what are you talking about? Me marry Katie Easebrook? Why, I wouldn't have had the face to ask her. Not when there's a good fellow like Charlie about.'

Like some discerning oracle came the reply.

'Charlie's a good feller, a good-looking feller, too—but you would have made her a better husband, Jim.'

With some curious twist of chivalry and affection the little man gripped the old woman's hand and kissed it.

'You've always thought too much of me, Martha, old girl.'

'I've had good cause to, Jim... Goodbye.'

He walked a little unsteadily down Radnor Street. A pale October sun filtered through a light mist, and gave to the meagre front gardens a certain glamour. Fat spiders hung in glistening webs between the shrubs and Japanese anemones. Children were playing absorbing games with chalk and stones upon the pavement. Cats looked down sleepily from the security of narrow walls. He had to pat a little girl's head and arbitrate in a dispute between two girls and a boy regarding the laws of a game called 'Snowball'.

'Life is a lovely thing,' he thought as he hurried on. 'Poor old Martha!... She's going out.'

He was, of course, late for the service in the church.

In some way he did not regret this. He slipped quietly into a seat at the back, unobserved. A hymn was being sung, or was it a psalm? He didn't know. There was something about a church service he didn't like. It disturbed him at some uncomfortable level. Charlie was standing by the altar, looking self-conscious and impatient. Katie was a ghostly unrecognisable figure, like a fly bound up in a spool in a spider's web. Thirty or forty people were scattered on either side of the central aisle. He could only see their backs. The parson began to drone the service, slowly enunciating the prescribed purposes of the married state. Willy Nilly felt a flush of discomfort. It somehow didn't seem right that Katie should have to stand there before all these people and have things put to her quite so straight.

'Rather detailed, old boy,' he thought. 'Perhaps that's why a bride wears a veil.'

When it was over, he walked boldly up the aisle and followed a few intimates into the vestry. He was conscious of people indicating him with nudges and whispering: 'Look! That's Willy Nilly!'

'In the vestry, Katie's mother was weeping, and Katie appeared to be weeping with one eye and laughing with the other. A few relatives were shaking hands, kissing and talking excitedly. Someone said: 'Here's Willy Nilly.'

Charlie gripped his hand and whispered:

'Come on Willie, old boy, kiss the bride.' The bride looked up at him with her glorious eyes, and held out her arms.

'Dear old Willie…so glad you came, old boy.'

He kissed the bride all right, and held her from him.

'God bless you, dear old girl. God bless you. May you…may all your dreams come true, old girl.'

In most weddings there is a streak of pathos, but in theatrical weddings the note is predominant. It is as though the lookers-on realize that these people whose life is passed in make-believe are bound to burn their fingers when they begin to touch reality. Perhaps their reactions are too violent to be bound within the four walls of a contract.

Katie's wedding certainly contained a large element of sadness.

'She looks so sweet and fragile. I hope he'll be good to her,' women whispered.

The lunch at the Hautboy Hotel was hilarious to an almost artificial degree. A great deal of champagne was drunk, and toasts were prolific. It was here that Willy Nilly came in. The Funny Man excelled himself. He was among the people who knew him and loved him. He made goo-goo eyes at the bridesmaids, he told stories, he imitated all the denizens of a farmyard, he gave a mock conjuring display, and his speech in proposing the health of the bride's father and mother was the hit of the afternoon. (He was not allowed the principal toast as that had been allocated to Charlie's father, who was a stockbroker.) To the waiter who hovered behind chairs with napkined magnums of champagne, he kept on saying:

'Not too much, old boy. I've a rehearsal at three-forty.'

Nevertheless, he drained his glass every time it was filled. The craving to be funny exceeded every other craving. Willy Nilly had knocked about the world in every kind of company. It took a lot to go to his head. It was almost impossible to make him drunk. When at three o'clock it was time for the bride and bridegroom to depart he was not by any means drunk, certainly not so drunk as Charlie, but he was in a slightly detached comatose state of mind. He kissed the bride once more, and to Charlie he said:

'God bless you, old boy. Be good to her. You've got the dearest woman in the world.'

And Charlie replied:

'I know, old boy. You've been a brick to us. You oughtn't to have sent the cheque as well as all that silver. Good luck, old boy.'

'O my in-laws, my in-laws, why don't you leave me be?'
It seemed but a flash from one experience to another, from pressing the girl's dainty shoulders in a parting embrace to stamping about on the draughty stage and calling into the void:

'Now, Mr Prescott, I want a little more slowing down of this passage. Do you see what I mean, old boy? It gives me more time for the business.'

The gag with the trombone player was considerably improved. Must keep going, doing things—a contract to sign at five-fifteen. He was feeling tired when the rehearsal was over—mustn't get tired before the two shows tonight. Perhaps he could get half an hour's nap after seeing the agent before it was time to feed. Someone gave him a cup of tea in the theatre, and a dresser told him a long story about a disease which his wife's father got through sitting on a churchyard wall waiting for the village pub to open at six.

There appeared no interval of time between this and sitting in front of the suave, furtive-looking gentleman named Welsh who 'handled' him on behalf of the United Varieties Agency. He was conscious of not being at his best with Welsh. He believed that he could have got much better terms in his new contract, but somehow the matter did not appear to him to be of great importance. He changed the subject and told Welsh the story about the sea captain and the Irish stewardess. Welsh laughed immoderately. After all, quite a good fellow—Welsh. He was anxious to get away and see some boys at the club. Jimmy would certainly have a new story ready. He hadn't seen Jimmy for four days.

Jimmy was certainly there, and not only Jimmy, but old Barrow, and Sam Lenning, and a host of others. He had a double Scotch whisky and proceeded to take a hand in the game of swapping improper stories. At one time something seemed to jog at his consciousness and say: 'Do you really think much of this kind of thing, old boy?' And another voice replied: 'What does it matter?...They've just arrived at Brighton railway station. In another ten minutes they'll be at "The Ship".'

'I thought you were going to have a chop at six-thirty, Willy,' someone remarked to him suddenly.

'So I am, old boy.'

'It's seven-fifteen now.'

Good gracious! So it was! Well, he didn't particularly want a chop. He would have a couple of sandwiches and another double Scotch. He was quite himself again in his dressing room at the theatre. He loved the smell of grease paint and spirit gum, the contact of fantastic whiskers and clothes, the rather shabby mirror under a strong light. His first song was going to be 'Old Fags', the feckless ruffian who picks up cigarette ends. The dresser, whose name was Flood and who always called him Mr Nilly, was ready with his three changes.

'Number five's on,' came the message down the corridors. Good! There was only 'Charlemayne', the equilibrist, between him and 'his people'.

Willy Nilly had got to love 'his people' as he mentally designated them. He knew them, and they knew him—the reward of many years' hard work. He loved stumbling down the corridors, through the iron doors, and groping his way amidst the dim medley of the wings, where gorgeous unreal women and men in bowler hats patted him as he passed and whispered:

'Hullo, Willy, old boy! Good luck!'

He loved to wait there and hear his number go up; the roar of welcome which greeted it was music to his soul.

'Number seven!'

The orchestra played the opening bars and then with a queer shuffle he was before them, a preposterous figure with a bright red nose, a miniature bowler hat, and a fearful old suit with ferns growing out of the seams, and a heavy sack slung across his back.

'Old Fags! Old Fags!
See my collection of fine old fags.
If you want to be happy,
If you want to be gay,
Empty your sack
At the fag-end of the day.'

Oh, yes, you ought to see Willy Nilly in 'Old Fags'.

The habitués at the Railham Empire will tell you all about him. The doleful wheezy voice, the quaint antics, and then the screamingly funny business when he empties the sack of cigarette ends all over the stage and, of course, at the bottom is a bottle of gin and a complete set of ladies' undies (apparently new and trimmed in pink). Then the business of finding innumerable cigarette ends in his unmanageable beard.

On that night, Willy Nilly was at his best. A lightning change and he came on as 'The Carpet Salesman' in which he brought on a roll of carpet, the opportunities concerning which are obvious. Then followed 'The Lady who Works for the Lady Next Door'. The inevitable encore—prepared for and expected—followed. A terrible Russian—more whiskers, red this time—singing:

'O Mary-vitch,
O Ada-vitch,
I don't know which
Ich lieber ditch;
I told your pa
I'd got the itch;
He promptly hit me
On the snitch.'

It was difficult for Willy to escape after this valiant satirical digression.

He fled perspiring to his dressing-room.

'Give me a drink, old boy,' he gasped to the lugubrious Flood.

He had smothered his face in cocoa butter, when there was a knock on the door.

'Mr Peter Wilberforce, representing the *Railham Mercury*.'

'Ah, yes, come in, old boy.'

Mr Wilberforce was in no hurry to depart. He had a spot—'just a couple of fingers, old boy' of whisky.

He wanted a column of bright stuff for the next issue of the weekly. 'Is Railham behind the other suburbs in humour? Interview with the famous Willy Nilly—our local product.'

'You just give me a lead,' said Mr Wilberforce, 'I'll fill in the padding.'

Willy Nilly found turning out the bright stuff immediately after his performance the most exhausting experience of the day. He was quite relieved when, at the end of forty minutes, there was a knock at the door and a woman with a lanky son was shown in. This was the young man who wanted to go on the stage. The pressman departed and the mother started forth on a long harangue about what people said about her son's remarkable genius for acting. Before Willy Nilly knew where he was, he was listening to the boy giving imitations of Beerbohm Tree and Henry Ainley. It was quite easy to tell which was meant to be which, and so Willie grasped the young man's hand and said:

'Very good, old boy! Very good.'

He promised to do what he could, but by the time the mother had gone all over the same ground three times he found it was too late to pop round to the club again. It was nearly time to make up for the second show. He dozed in the chair for a few moments. Suddenly he thought:

'They've had dinner. They're probably taking a stroll on the front before turning in.'

He poured himself out another tot of whisky and picked up his red nose.

'O God! How tired I feel! ... Not quite the man you were, old boy.'

He found it a terrible effort to go on that second time.

'Old Fags' seemed flat. He began to be subtly aware that the audience knew that he knew that the song wasn't really funny at all. At the end the applause was mild. 'The Carpet Salesman' went even worse.

'Pull yourself together, old boy,' he muttered as he staggered off. It wouldn't do. A man who tops the bill can't afford not to bring the house down with every song. He made a superhuman effort with 'The Lady who Works for the Lady Next Door'. It certainly went better than the others, just well enough to take an encore rather quickly. On this occasion he altered his encore. Instead of 'Mary-vitch', he sang a hilarious song with the refrain:

'O my! Hold me down!
My wife's gone away till Monday!'

At the end of the first verse he felt that he had got them. Success excited him. He went for it for all he was worth. Willy Nilly was himself again. The house roared at him. He had the greatest difficulty in escaping without giving a further encore. As he stumbled up the stone staircase to his dressing-room, he suddenly thought:

'They've gone to bed now.'

The imperturbable Flood followed him in, laden with properties.

'I'll just have one more spot, Flood, old boy.'

How tired he was! He cleaned up languidly and got into his normal clothes.

'Well, that's that, old boy,' he said to Flood. 'Now I think we'll toddle off to our bye-byes.'

'Excuse me, Mr Nilly, wasn't you going round to Mr Bird Crafts?'

Eh? Oh, yes, for sure; he'd forgotten about poor old Bird. Couldn't exactly let an old pal in. Well, he would have a cab and hang the expense—just stay a few minutes—dear old Bird would understand. But he stayed an hour at Bird Craft's. He listened to three new comic songs and a lot of patter.

'Yes, you've got a winner there, old boy,' he remarked at the end of each song.

It was nearly one o'clock when he groped his way up the dim staircase of his own house. The bedroom looked bleak and uninteresting. It had never struck him before in quite that way. He had always liked his bedroom with its heavy mahogany furniture and red plush curtains, but somehow tonight the place seemed forlorn...as though something was terribly lacking.

'You're tired, old boy.'

He undressed and threw his clothes carelessly on chairs and tables. He got into bed and regarded the room, trying with his tired brain to think what was wrong. His clothes ought not to have been thrown about like that, of course. He felt that they and he were out of place in the large room. A strange feeling of melancholy crept over him.

'It's badly ordered...it's all badly ordered, old boy.'

He had a great desire to cry, so weak he felt. But no, a man mustn't do that; a funny man certainly mustn't. His mind wandered back to his old mother. He remembered the days when she had taught him to pray. He would give anything for the relief of prayer. But he couldn't do that either. It didn't seem exactly playing the game. He had put all that kind of thing by so long ago. He despised those people who lead unvirtuous lives and then in the end turned religious. He wasn't going to pretend. He turned out the light, and closed his eyes. He would neither weep nor pray, but he must express himself somehow. Perhaps he compromised between these two human frailties. Certainly his voice was very near a sob, and his accents vividly alive with prayer as he cried to the darkness:

'Charlie, old boy, be good to her...For God's sake be good to her.'

—VI—

Where Was Wych Street?

IN THE PUBLIC BAR of the 'Wagtail', in Wapping, four men and a woman were drinking beer and discussing diseases. It was not a pretty subject, and the company was certainly not a handsome one. It was a dark November evening, and the dingy lighting of the bar seemed but to emphasize the bleak exterior. Drifts of fog and damp from without mingled with the smoke of shag. The sanded floor was kicked into a muddy morass not unlike the surface of the pavement. An old lady down the street had died from pneumonia the previous evening, and the event supplied a fruitful topic of conversation. The things that one could get! Everywhere were germs eager to destroy one. At any minute the symptoms might break out. And so—one foregathered in a cheerful spot amidst friends, and drank forgetfulness.

Prominent in this little group was Baldwin Meadows, a sallow-faced villain with battered features and prominent cheekbones, his face cut and scarred by a hundred fights. Ex-seaman, ex-boxer, ex-fish-porter—indeed, to everyone's knowledge, ex-everything. No one knew how he lived. By his side lurched an enormous coloured man who went by the name of Harry Jones. Grinning above a tankard sat a pimply-faced young man who was known as 'The Agent'. Silver rings adorned his fingers. He had no other name, and most emphatically no address, but he 'arranged things' for people, and appeared to thrive upon it in a scrambling, fugitive manner. The other two people were Mr and Mrs Dawes. Mr Dawes was an entirely negative person, but Mrs Dawes shone by virtue of a high, whining, insistent voice, keyed to within half a note of hysteria.

Then, at one point, the conversation suddenly took a peculiar turn. It came about through Mrs Dawes mentioning that her aunt, who died from eating tinned lobster, used to work in a corset shop in Wych Street. When she said that, 'The Agent', whose right eye appeared to survey the ceiling, whilst his left eye looked over the other side of his tankard, remarked:

'Where was Wych Street, ma?'

'Lord!' exclaimed Mrs Dawes. 'Don't you know, dearie? You must be a young 'un, you must. Why, when I was a gal everyone knew Wych Street. It was just down there where they built the Kingsway, like.'

Baldwin Meadows cleared his throat and said:

'Wych Street used to be a turnin' runnin' from Long Acre into Wellington Street.'

'Oh, no, old boy,' chipped in Mr Dawes, who always treated the ex-man with great deference. 'If you'll excuse me, Wych Street was a narrow lane at the back of the old Globe Theatre, that used to pass by the church.'

'I know what I'm talkin' about,' growled Meadows.

Mrs Dawes's high nasal whine broke in:

'Hi, Mr Booth, you used ter know yer wye abaht. Where was Wych Street?'

Mr Booth, the proprietor, was polishing a tap. He looked up. 'Wych Street? Yus, of course I knoo Wych Street. Used to go there with some of the boys when I was Covent Garden way. It was at right angles to the Strand, just east of Wellington Street.'

'No, it warn't. It were alongside the Strand, before yer come to Wellington Street.'

The coloured man took no part in the discussion, one street and one city being alike to him, provided he could obtain the material comforts dear to his heart; but the others carried it on with a certain amount of acerbity.

Before any agreement had been arrived at three other men entered the bar. The quick eye of Meadows recognized them at once as three of what was known at that time as 'The Gallows Ring'. Every member of 'The Gallows Ring' had done time, but they still carried on a lucrative industry devoted to blackmail, intimidation, shop-lifting, and some of the clumsier recreations. Their leader, Ben Orming, had served seven years for bashing a Chinaman down at Rotherhithe.

'The Gallows Ring' was not popular in Wapping, for the reason that many of their depredations had been inflicted upon their own class. When Meadows and Harry Jones took it into their heads to do a little wild prancing they took the trouble to go up into the West End. They considered 'The Gallows Ring' an ungentlemanly set; nevertheless, they always treated them with a certain external deference—an unpleasant crowd to quarrel with.

Ben Orming ordered beer for the three of them, and they leant against the bar and whispered in sullen accents. Something had evidently miscarried with the Ring. Mrs Dawes continued to whine above the general drone of the bar. Suddenly she said:

'Ben, you're a hot old devil, you are. We was just 'aving a discussion like. Where was Wych Street?'

Ben scowled at her, and she continued:

'Some sez it was one place, some sez it was another. I *know* where it was, 'cors my aunt what died from blood p'ison, after eatin' tinned lobster, used to work at a corset shop...'

'Yus,' barked Ben, emphatically. 'I know where Wych Street was—it was just sarth of the river, afore yer come to Waterloo Station.'

It was then that the coloured man, who up to that point had taken no part in the discussion, thought fit to intervene.

'Nope. You's all wrong, cap'n. Wych Street were alongside de church, way over where the Strand takes a side line up west.'

Ben turned on him fiercely.

'What the blazes does a blanketty nigger know abaht it? I've told yer where Wych Street was.'

'Yus, and I know where it was,' interposed Meadows. 'Yer both wrong. Wych Street was a turning running from Long Acre into Wellington Street.'

'I didn't ask yer what *you* thought,' growled Ben.

'Well, I suppose I've a right to an opinion?'

'You always think you know everything, you do.'

'You can just keep yer mouth shut.'

'It 'ud take more'n you to shut it.'

Mr Booth thought it advisable at this juncture to bawl across the bar:

'Now, gentlemen, no quarrelling—please.'

The affair might have been subsided at that point, but for Mrs Dawes. Her emotions over the death of the old lady in the street had been so stirred that she had been, almost unconsciously, drinking too much gin. She suddenly screamed out:

'Don't you take no lip from 'im, Mr Medders. The dirty, thieving devil, 'e always thinks 'e's goin' to come it over every one.'

She stood up threateningly, and one of Ben's supporters gave her a gentle push backwards. In three minutes the bar was in a complete state of pandemonium. The three members of 'The Gallows Ring' fought two men and a woman, for Mr Dawes merely stood in a corner and screamed out:

'Don't! Don't!'

Mrs Dawes stabbed the man, who had pushed her, through the wrist with a hatpin. Meadows and Ben Orming closed on each other and fought savagely with the naked fists. A lucky blow early in the encounter sent Meadows reeling against the wall, with blood streaming down his temple. Then the coloured man hurled a pewter tankard straight at Ben and it hit him on the knuckles. The pain maddened him to a frenzy. His other supporter had immediately got to grips with Harry Jones, and picked up one of the high stools and, seizing an opportunity, brought it down crash on to the coloured man's skull.

The whole affair was a matter of minutes. Mr Booth was bawling out in the street. A whistle sounded. People were running in all directions.

'Beat it! Beat it, for God's sake!' called the man who had been stabbed through the wrist. His face was very white, and he was obviously about to faint.

Ben and the other man, whose name was Toller, dashed to the door. On the pavement there was a confused scramble. Blows were struck indiscriminately. Two policemen appeared. One was laid *hors de combat* by a kick on the knee-cap from Toller. The two men fled into the darkness, followed by a hue-and-cry. Born and bred in the locality, they took every advantage of their knowledge. They tacked through alleys and raced down dark mews, and clambered over walls. Fortunately for them, the people they passed, who might have tripped them up or aided in the pursuit, merely fled indoors. The people in Wapping are not always on the side of the pursuer. But the police held on. At last Ben and Toller slipped through the door of an empty house in Aztec Street barely ten yards ahead of their nearest pursuer. Blows rained on the door, but they slipped the bolts, and then fell panting to the floor. When Ben could speak, he said:

'If they cop us, it means swinging.'

'Was the nigger done in?'

'I think so. But even if 'e wasn't, there was that other affair the night before last. The game's up.'

The ground-floor rooms were shuttered and bolted, but they knew that the police would probably force the front door. At the back there was no escape, only a narrow stable yard, where lanterns were already flashing. The roof only extended thirty yards either way, and the police would probably take possession of it. They made a round of the house, which was sketchily furnished.

There was a loaf, a small piece of mutton, and a bottle of pickles, and—the most precious possession—three bottles of whisky. Each man drank half a glass of neat whisky, then Ben said: 'We'll be able to keep 'em quiet for a bit, anyway,' and he went and fetched an old twelve-bore gun and a case of cartridges. Toller was opposed to this last desperate resort, but Ben continued to murmur, 'It means swinging, anyway.'

* * *

And thus began the notorious siege of Aztec Street. It lasted three days and four nights. You may remember that, on forcing a panel of the front door, Sub-Inspector Wraithe, of the V Division, was shot through the chest. The police then tried other methods. A hose was brought into play without effect. Two policemen were killed and four wounded. The military was requisitioned. The street was picketed. Snipers occupied windows of the houses opposite. A distinguished member of the Cabinet drove down in a motor-car, and directed operations in a top hat. It was the introduction of poison gas which was the ultimate cause of the downfall of the citadel. The body of Ben Orming was never found, but that of Toller was discovered near the front door with a bullet through his heart.

The medical officer to the Court pronounced that the man had been dead three days, but whether killed by a chance bullet from a sniper or whether killed deliberately by his fellow-criminal was never revealed. For when the end came Orming had apparently planned a final act of venom. It was known that in the basement a considerable quantity of petrol had been stored. The contents had probably been carefully distributed over the most inflammable materials in the top rooms. The fire broke out, as one witness described it, 'almost like an explosion'. Orming must have perished in this. The roof blazed up, and the sparks carried across the yard and started a stack of light timber in the annexe of Messrs Morrel's piano-factory. The factory and two blocks of tenement buildings were burnt to the ground. The estimated cost of the destruction was one hundred and eighty thousand pounds. The casualties amounted to seven killed and fifteen wounded.

* * *

At the inquiry held under Justice Pengammon various odd interesting facts were revealed. Mr Lowes-Parlby, the brilliant young K.C., distinguished himself by his searching cross-examination of many witnesses. At one point a certain Mrs Dawes was put in the box.

'Now,' said Mr Lowes-Parlby, 'I understand that on the evening in question, Mrs Dawes, you, and the victims, and these other people who have been mentioned, were all seated in the public bar of the "Wagtail", enjoying its no doubt excellent hospitality and indulging in a friendly discussion. Is that so?'

'Yes, sir.'

'Now, will you tell his lordship what you were discussing?'

'Diseases, sir.'

'Diseases! And did the argument become acrimonious?'

'Pardon?'

'Was there a serious dispute about diseases?'

'No, sir.'

'Well, what was the subject of the dispute?'

'We was arguin' as to where Wych Street was, sir.'

'What's that?' said his lordship.

'The witness states, my lord, that they were arguing as to where Wych Street was.'

'Wych Street? Do you mean W-Y-C-H?'

'Yes, sir.'

'You mean the narrow old street that used to run across the site of what is now the Gaiety Theatre?'

Mr Lowes-Parlby smiled in his most charming manner.

'Yes, my lord, I believe the witness refers to the same street you mention, though, if I may be allowed to qualify your lordship's description of the locality, may I suggest that it was a little further east—at the side of the old Globe Theatre, which was adjacent to St Martin's in the Strand? That is the street you were all arguing about, isn't it, Mrs Dawes?'

'Well, sir, my aunt who died from eating tinned lobster used to work at a corset-shop. I ought to know.'

His lordship ignored the witness. He turned to the counsel rather peevishly.

'Mr Lowes-Parlby, when I was your age I used to pass through Wych Street every day of my life. I did so for nearly twelve years. I think it hardly necessary for you to contradict me.'

The counsel bowed. It was not his place to dispute with a justice, although that justice be a hopeless old fool; but another eminent K.C., an elderly man with a tawny beard, rose in the body of the court, and said:

'If I may be allowed to interpose, your lordship, I also spent a great deal of my youth passing through Wych Street. I have gone into the matter, comparing past and present ordnance survey maps. If I am not mistaken, the street the witness was referring to began near the hoarding at the entrance to Kingsway and ended at the back of what is now the Aldwych Theatre.'

'Oh, no, Mr Backer!' exclaimed Lowes-Parlby.

His lordship removed his glasses and snapped out:

'The matter is entirely irrelevant to the case.'

It certainly was, but the brief passage-of-arms left an unpleasant tang of bitterness behind. It was observed that Mr Lowes-Parlby never again quite got the prehensile grip upon his cross-examination that he had shown in his treatment of the earlier witnesses. The coloured man, Harry Jones, had died in hospital, but Mr Booth, the proprietor of the 'Wagtail', Baldwin Meadows, Mr Dawes, and the man who was stabbed in the wrist, all gave evidence of a rather nugatory character. Lowes-Parlby could do nothing with it. The findings of this special inquiry do not concern us. It is sufficient to say that the witnesses already mentioned all returned to Wapping. The man who had received the thrust of a hatpin through his wrist did not think it advisable to take any action against Mrs Dawes. He was pleasantly relieved to find that he was only required as a witness of an abortive discussion.

* * *

In a few weeks' time the great Aztec Street siege remained only a romantic memory to the majority of Londoners. To Lowes-Parlby the little dispute with Justice Pengammon rankled unreasonably. It is annoying to be publicly snubbed for making a statement which you know to be absolutely true, and which you have even taken pains to verify. And Lowes-Parlby was a young man accustomed to score. He made a point of looking everything up, of being prepared for an adversary thoroughly. He liked to give the appearance of knowing everything. The brilliant career just ahead of him at times dazzled him. He was one of the darlings of the gods. Everything came to Lowes-Parlby. His father had distinguished himself at the Bar before him, and had amassed a modest fortune. He was an only son. At Oxford he had carried off every possible degree. He was already being spoken of for very high political honours.

But the most sparkling jewel in the crown of his successes was Lady Adela Charters, the daughter of Lord Vermeer, the Minister for Foreign Affairs. She was his *fiancée*, and it was considered the most brilliant match of the season. She was young and almost pretty, and Lord Vermeer was immensely wealthy and one of the most influential men in Great Britain. Such a combination was irresistible. There seemed to be nothing missing in the life of Francis Lowes-Parlby, K.C.

* * *

One of the most regular and absorbed spectators at the Aztec Street Inquiry was old Stephen Garrit. Stephen Garrit held a unique but quite inconspicuous position in the legal world at that time. He was a friend of judges, a specialist at various abstruse legal rulings, a man of remarkable memory, and yet—an amateur. He had never taken silk, never eaten the requisite dinners, never passed an examination in his life; but the law of evidence was meat and drink to him. He passed his life in the Temple, where he had chambers. Some of the most eminent counsel in the world would take his opinion, or come to him for advice. He was very old, very silent, and very absorbed. He attended every meeting of the Aztec Street Inquiry, but from beginning to end he never volunteered an opinion.

After the inquiry was over, he went and visited an old friend at the London Survey Office. He spent two mornings examining maps. After that he spent two mornings pottering about the Strand, Kingsway, and Aldwych; then he worked out some careful calculations on a ruled chart. He entered the particulars in a little book which he kept for purposes of that kind, and then retired to his chambers to study other matters. But before doing so, he entered a little apophthegm in another book. It was apparently a book in which he intended to compile a summary of his legal experiences. The sentence ran:

'The basic trouble is that people make statements without sufficient data.'

Old Stephen need not have appeared in this story

at all, except for the fact that he was present at the dinner at Lord Vermeer's, where a rather deplorable incident occurred. And you must acknowledge that in the circumstances it is useful to have such a valuable and efficient witness.

Lord Vermeer was a competent, forceful man, a little quick-tempered and autocratic. He came from Lancashire, and before entering politics had made an enormous fortune out of borax, artificial manure, and starch.

It was a small dinner party, with a motive behind it. His principal guest was Mr Sandeman, the London agent of the Ameer of Bakkan. Lord Vermeer was very anxious to impress Mr Sandeman and to be very friendly with him: the reasons will appear later. Mr Sandeman was a self-confessed cosmopolitan. He spoke seven languages and professed to be equally at home in any capital in Europe. London had been his headquarters for over twenty years. Lord Vermeer also invited Mr Arthur Toombs, a colleague in the Cabinet, his prospective son-in-law, Lowes-Parlby K.C., James Trolley, a very tame Socialist M.P., and Sir Henry and Lady Breyd, the two latter being invited, not because Sir Henry was of any use, but because Lady Breyd was a pretty and brilliant woman who might amuse his principal guest. The sixth guest was Stephen Garrit.

The dinner was a great success. When the succession of courses eventually came to a stop, and the ladies had retired, Lord Vermeer conducted his male guests into another room for a ten minutes' smoke before rejoining them. It was then that the unfortunate incident occurred. There was no love lost between Lowes-Parlby and Mr Sandeman. It is difficult to ascribe the real reason of their mutual animosity, but on the several occasions when they had met there had invariably passed a certain sardonic by-play. They were both clever, both comparatively young, each a little suspect and jealous of the other; moreover, it was said in some quarters that Mr Sandeman had had intentions himself with regard to Lord Vermeer's daughter, that he had been on the point of a proposal when Lowes-Parlby had butted in and forestalled him.

Mr Sandeman had dined well, and he was in the mood to dazzle with a display of his varied knowledge and experiences. The conversation drifted from a discussion of the rival claims of great cities to the slow, inevitable removal of old landmarks. There had been a slightly acrimonious disagreement between Lowes-Parlby and Mr Sandeman as to the claims of Budapest and Lisbon, and Mr Sandeman had scored because he extracted from his rival a confession that, though he had spent two months in Budapest, he had only spent two days in Lisbon. Mr Sandeman had lived for four years in either city. Lowes-Parlby changed the subject abruptly.

'Talking of landmarks,' he said, 'we had a queer point arise in that Aztec Street Inquiry. The original dispute arose owing to a discussion between a crowd of people in a pub as to where Wych Street was.'

'I remember,' said Lord Vermeer. 'A perfectly absurd discussion. Why, I should have thought that any man over forty would remember exactly where it was.'

'Where would you say it was, sir?' asked Lowes-Parlby.

'Why to be sure, it ran from the corner of Chancery Lane and ended at the second turning after the Law Courts, going west.'

Lowes-Parlby was about to reply, when Mr Sandeman cleared his throat and said, in his supercilious, oily voice:

'Excuse me, my lord. I know my Paris, and Vienna, and Lisbon, every brick and stone, but I look upon London as my home. I know my London even better. I have a perfectly clear recollection of Wych Street. When I was a student I used to visit there to buy books. It ran parallel to New Oxford Street on the south side, just between it and Lincoln's Inn Fields.'

There was something about this assertion that infuriated Lowes-Parlby. In the first place, it was so hopelessly wrong and so insufferably asserted. In the second place, he was already smarting under the indignity of being shown up about Lisbon. And then there suddenly flashed through his mind the wretched incident when he had been publicly snubbed by Justice Pengammon about the very same point; and he knew that he was right each time. Damn Wych Street! He turned on Mr Sandeman.

'Oh, nonsense! You may know something about these—eastern cities; you certainly know nothing about London if you make a statement like that. Wych Street was a little further east of what is now the Gaiety Theatre. It used to run by the side of the old Globe Theatre, parallel to the Strand.'

The dark moustache of Mr Sandeman shot upwards, revealing a narrow line of yellow teeth. He uttered a sound that was a mingling of contempt and derision; then he drawled out:

'Really? How wonderful—to have such comprehensive knowledge!'

He laughed, and his small eyes fixed his rival. Lowes-Parlby flushed a deep red. He gulped down half a glass of port and muttered just above a whisper: 'Damned impudence!' Then, in the rudest manner he could display, he turned his back deliberately on Sandeman and walked out of the room.

* * *

In the company of Adela he tried to forget the little contretemps. The whole thing was so absurd—so utterly undignified. As though *he* didn't know! It was the little accumulation of pinpricks all arising out of that one argument. The result had suddenly goaded him to—well, being rude, to say the least of it. It wasn't that Sandeman mattered. To the devil with Sandeman! But what would his future father-in-law think? He had never before given way to any show of ill-temper before him. He forced himself into a mood of rather fatuous jocularity. Adela was at her best in those moods. They would have lots of fun together in the days to come. Her almost pretty, not too clever face was dimpled with kittenish glee. Life was a tremendous rag to her. They were expecting Toccata, the famous opera-singer. She had been engaged at a very high fee to come on from Covent Garden. Mr Sandeman was very fond of music.

Adela was laughing and discussing which was the most honourable position for the great Sandeman to occupy. There came to Lowes-Parlby a sudden abrupt misgiving. What sort of wife would this be to him when they were not just fooling? He immediately dismissed the curious, furtive little stab of doubt. The splendid proportions of the room calmed his senses. A huge bowl of dark red roses quickened his perceptions. His career… The door opened. But it was not La Toccata. It was one of the household flunkies. Lowes-Parlby turned again to his inamorata.

'Excuse me, sir. His lordship says will you kindly go and see him in the library?'

Lowes-Parlby regarded the messenger, and his heart beat quickly. An uncontrollable presage of evil racked his nerve-centres. Something had gone wrong; and yet the whole thing was so absurd, trivial. In a crisis—well, he could always apologize. He smiled confidently at Adela, and said:

'Why, of course; with pleasure. Please excuse me, dear.'

He followed the impressive servant out of the room. His foot had barely touched the carpet of the library when he realized that his worst apprehensions were to be plumbed to the depths. For a moment he thought Lord Vermeer was alone, then he observed old Stephen Garrit, lying in an easy chair in the corner like a piece of crumpled parchment. Lord Vermeer did not beat about the bush. When the door was closed, he bawled out, savagely:

'What the devil have you done?'

'Excuse me, sir. I'm afraid I don't understand. Is it Sandeman...?'

'Sandeman has gone.'

'Oh, I'm sorry.'

'Sorry! By God, I should think you might be sorry! You insulted him. My prospective son-in-law insulted him in my own house!'

'I'm awfully sorry. I didn't realize...'

'Realize! Sit down, and don't assume for one moment that you continue to be my prospective son-in-law. Your insult was a most intolerable piece of effrontery, not only to him, but to me.'

'But I...'

'Listen to me. Do you know that the Government were on the verge of concluding a most far-reaching treaty with that man? Do you know that the position was just touch-and-go? The concessions we were prepared to make would have cost the State thirty million pounds, and it would have been cheap. Do you hear that? It would have been cheap! Bakkan is one of the most vulnerable outposts of the Empire. It is a terrible danger zone. If certain powers can usurp our authority—and, mark you, the whole blamed place is already riddled with this new pernicious doctrine—you know what I mean—before we know where we are the whole East will be in a blaze. India! My God! This contract we were negotiating would have countered this outward thrust. And you, you blockhead, you come here and insult the man upon whose word the whole thing depends.'

'I really can't see, sir, how I should know all this.'

'You can't see it! But, you fool, you seemed to go out of your way. You insulted him about the merest quibble—in my house!'

'He said he knew where Wych Street was. He was quite wrong. I corrected him.'

'Wych Street! Wych Street be damned! If he said Wych Street was in the moon, you should have agreed with him. There was no call to act in the way you did. And you—you think of going into politics!'

The somewhat cynical inference of this remark went unnoticed. Lowes-Parlby was too unnerved. He mumbled:

'I'm very sorry.'

'I don't want your sorrow. I want something more practical.'

'What's that, sir?'

'You will drive straight to Mr Sandeman's, find him, and apologize. Tell him you find that he was right about Wych Street after all. If you can't find him tonight, you must find him tomorrow morning. I give you till midday tomorrow. If by that time you have not offered a handsome apology to Mr Sandeman, you do not enter this house again, you do not see my daughter again. Moreover, all the power I possess will be devoted to hounding you out of that profession you have dishonoured. Now you can go.'

Dazed and shaken, Lowes-Parlby drove back to his flat at Knightsbridge. Before acting he must have time to think. Lord Vermeer had given him till tomorrow midday. Any apologizing that was done should be done after a night's reflection. The fundamental purposes of his being were to be tested. He knew that. He was at a great crossing. Some deep instinct within him was grossly outraged. Is it that a point comes when success demands that a man shall sell his soul? It was all so absurdly trivial—a mere argument about the position of a street that had ceased to exist. As Lord Vermeer said, what did it matter about Wych Street?

Of course he should apologize. It would hurt horribly to do so, but would a man sacrifice everything on account of some footling argument about a street?

In his own rooms, Lowes-Parlby put on a dressing-gown, and, lighting a pipe, he sat before the fire. He would have given anything for companionship at such a moment—the right companionship. How lovely it would be to have—a woman, just the right woman, to talk this all over with; someone who understood and sympathized. A sudden vision came to him of Adela's face grinning about the prospective visit of La Toccata, and again the low voice of misgiving whispered in his ears. Would Adela be—just the right woman? In very truth, did he really love Adela? Or was it all—a rag? Was life a rag—a game played by lawyers, politicians, and people?

The fire burned low, but still he continued to sit thinking, his mind principally occupied with the dazzling visions of the future. It was past midnight when he suddenly muttered a low 'Damn!' and walked to the bureau. He took up a pen and wrote:

> Dear Mr Sandeman,
>
> I must apologize for acting so rudely to you last night. It was quite unpardonable of me, especially as I since find, on going into the matter, that you were quite right about the position of Wych Street. I can't think how I made the mistake. Please forgive me.
>
> Yours cordially,
>
> Francis Lowes-Parlby.

Having written this, he sighed and went to bed. One might have imagined at that point that the matter was finished. But there are certain little greedy demons of conscience that require a lot of stilling, and they kept Lowes-Parlby awake more than half the night. He kept on repeating to himself, 'It's all positively absurd!' But the little greedy demons pranced around the bed, and they began to group things into two definite issues. On the one side, the great appearances; on the other, something at the back of it all, something deep, fundamental, something that could only be expressed by one word—truth. If he had *really* loved Adela—if he weren't so absolutely certain that Sandeman was wrong and he was right—why should he have to say that Wych Street was where it wasn't?

'Isn't there, after all,' said one of the little demons, 'something which makes for greater happiness than success? Confess this, and we'll let you sleep.'

Perhaps that is one of the most potent weapons the little demons possess. However full our lives may be, we ever long for moments of tranquillity. And conscience holds before our eyes the mirror of an ultimate tranquillity. Lowes-Parlby was certainly not himself. The gay, debonair, and brilliant egoist was tortured, and tortured almost beyond control; and it had all apparently risen through the ridiculous discussion about a street. At a quarter past three in the morning he arose from his bed with a groan, and, going into the other room, he tore the letter to Mr Sandeman to pieces.

* * *

Three weeks later old Stephen Garrit was lunching with the Lord Chief Justice. They were old friends, and they never found it incumbent to be very conversational. The lunch was an excellent, but frugal, meal. They both ate slowly and thoughtfully, and their drink was water. It was not till they reached the dessert stage that his lordship indulged in any very informative comment, and then he recounted to Stephen the details of a recent case in which he considered that the presiding judge had, by an unprecedented paralogy, misinterpreted the Law of Evidence. Stephen listened with absorbed attention. He took two cob-nuts from the silver dish, and turned them over meditatively, without cracking them. When his lordship had completely stated his opinion and peeled a pear, Stephen mumbled:

'I have been impressed, very impressed indeed. Even in my own field of—limited observation—the opinion of an outsider, you may say—so often it happens—the trouble caused by an affirmation without sufficiently established data. I have seen lives lost, ruin brought about, endless suffering. Only last week, a young man—a brilliant career—almost shattered. People make statements without—'

He put the nuts back on the dish, and then, in an apparently irrelevant manner, he said abruptly:

'Do you remember Wych Street, my lord?'

The Lord Chief Justice grunted.

'Wych Street! Of course I do.'

'Where would you say it was, my lord?'

'Why, here, of course.'

His lordship took a pencil from his pocket and sketched a plan on the tablecloth.

'It used to run from there to here.'

Stephen adjusted his glasses and carefully examined the plan. He took a long time to do this, and when he had finished his hand instinctively went towards a breast pocket where he kept a notebook with little squared pages. Then he stopped and sighed. After all, why argue with the law? The law was like that—an excellent thing, not infallible, of course (even the plan of the Lord Chief justice was a quarter of a mile out), but still an excellent, a wonderful thing. He examined the bony knuckles of his hands and yawned slightly.

'Do you remember it?' said the Lord Chief Justice.

Stephen nodded sagely, and his voice seemed to come from a long way off:

'Yes, I remember it, my lord. It was a melancholy little street.'

—VIII—

The Spoil-Sport

I CAN'T REMEMBER HOW WE GOT ON TO the question of 'spoil-sports', but I know that the Colonel suddenly became very indignant about them. He, Jimmy Tamaren, and I were seated in a large flat-bottomed punt, tied up to stakes, in the middle of a backwater on the grounds of old Sir John Gostard, whose guests we were. We were lolling there, smoking and talking, and waiting for the sun to get lower in the heavens, at which time we proposed to do a little of what is known as rough fishing. I think the subject of spoil-sports must have arisen from the obvious beauty and attractiveness of our setting: a perfect place and time of day for lovers. It seemed absurd somehow that three men should monopolise it all. And there was something pleasantly ironical in the situation that the eldest of us, to whom erotic experiences could have been little more than a fragrant memory, was the one to wax indignant about this tampering with the prerogatives of lovers.

'These blackmailers that you hear of in the parks and on heaths,' he said. 'I'd like to wring their necks.' He wasted three matches getting a light for his pipe, and then continued in a more subdued tone:

'I often think how damned hard it is on the lower middle classes, the artisan, and working classes generally, in the big cities. A fellow meets a girl and gets keen on her, and he never gets a chance to get her all alone to himself. Where can they go? Probably both his people and her people are living in more or less congested conditions. If he calls on her or she calls on him, they never get a room to themselves. There's nothing to do but to walk about the streets, or sit on a seat in the park. They are being watched all the time. How can you make love to a girl when you know that if you give her more than a brotherly peck on the cheek when you meet and when you part, you will be accused of some sort of criminal intentions?'

'They can always go to the pictures,' suggested Jimmy.

The Colonel's eyes and moustache twitched in unison.

'That's a nice, stuffy, dirty solution,' he spluttered. 'The very worst atmosphere for young lovers. There's nothing to do there but grasp at each other in the dark. How can they talk, and say all the things that lovers want to say with a frowsy band playing ragtime, and the people round them demanding silence? How can you make love to a woman if you can't look into her eyes? How can you concentrate when you are being constantly distracted by close-ups of murders?'

'I leave it to you, partner,' said Jimmy, nonchalantly.

A motorboat went 'touf-toufing' down the main stream, and our punt rocked pleasantly under the effect of its backwash.

The Colonel for the moment seemed to have spent his indignation, and Jimmy took up the thread:

'I'm not sure it's not a salutary restriction for this particular class. You see, I'm frankly a snob. When I was very young I used to be a red-hot socialist like the Colonel.'

'A socialist!' barked that gentleman, from his layers of cushions. 'What the devil—'

'Some genius once said that if a man is not a socialist up to the age of twenty-five it shows he has no heart. If he is a socialist after twenty-five it shows he has no brains. This fits in with my own case precisely. The Colonel's age I wouldn't like to guess at.'

'Who said anything about being a socialist?'

'The word was not used, but you implied that the

lower classes in this respect were being abused at the expense of the upper classes. I'm rather inclined to think it's the other way about. The passing of the chaperon has been a serious disaster to what is known as the upper classes. I'm not a prig—at least I hope I'm not—but I believe all our young people are being spoilt by too much freedom. It is not so much that they go morally wrong as that they go romantically wrong. Or rather that they lose romance altogether. What happens to that exquisite thrill you get in touching a girl's hand in a crowded room, the mysterious and entrancing propinquity of her, when you know quite well you have only got to ask her to come up the river with you, and she will turn up, with her bobbed hair, her cigarettes, and her bare legs, and be quite content to spend the afternoon with you in an obscure backwater, and talk unblushingly about—well, the awful and intimate things that girls do talk about these days. In my opinion it would be to everyone's advantage, instead of agitating for more freedom, to agitate for more chaperons, spoil-sports, and Nosey Parkers.'

'There is an element of bitterness in your comments, Jimmy,' I remarked.

Swallows were flying low, apparently supping on the swarms of midges, upon whom unfortunately they seemed to make no impression. An orange-coloured dragonfly darted hither and thither among the reeds. The Colonel was heard banging out his pipe.

'I met a spoil-sport once,' said Jimmy, reminiscently.

'It sounds like the beginning of a story,' I said. 'Once upon a time there was a spoil-sport—'

'It does almost make a story,' he replied.

'Well, I hope you threw him into the river,' suddenly bawled the Colonel. 'If you didn't throw him into the river I shall go to sleep.'

'It happened in a country singularly free from rivers, although there were many dried-up river courses. It was indeed in Northern Africa quite near the desert.'

'Nothing will be rising for half-an-hour, Jimmy, so let's have the yarn,' I said.

Jimmy re-lighted his pipe with slow deliberation.

'It happened a good twenty years ago,' he began. 'I remember there had been a little dust-up at the time because I wanted to marry a girl, whom some people averred to be the first woman chemist. In any case, she used to make up prescriptions for her father, who had a chemist's shop at Staines, where we were then living. I have entirely forgotten the girl's face, although I believe she was dark, and used to wear bangles.

'I know that the upshot was that my father very generously sent me abroad for three months by myself to study and reflect. He was a great believer in travel and had already taken me with him to Holland once, and to France twice. But this was to be an entirely novel experience. I was, as it were, thrown into the deep end.

'I want to begin appropriately enough at Charing Cross Station. Since those days I have been on the Continent some fifteen or twenty times, and one thing always impresses me. You see the French satirical journals with caricatures of English tourists, and you are apt to say: "Absurd!" but go to Charing Cross or Victoria Station and see the Continental Express go off and lo and behold! There they all are. Where do they come from, these people? You never see them in England, except at these stations. And then an hour before the train starts they come pouring in—elderly ugly women, with mackintoshes, and protruding teeth; fat, red-faced men, with walrus moustaches, wearing cloth caps and plus-fours. They swarm all over the train, and they swarm all over the Continent. Wherever they go they clamour for eggs and bacon, and marmalade, and whisky, and steak, and bass, and the *Daily Mail*, and cold baths at inconvenient moments.

'On the morning I left England there was this usual galaxy. My father, who came to see me off, had booked me a corner seat, which was fortunate, as the train was very full. When I took my seat I was relieved to find that the rest of the party in my carriage were not all of the "Englishman abroad" type. There was an elderly gentleman with his wife, obviously cultured people, and their two good-looking daughters, who were probably college girls. In spite of my political creed the snob in me warmed to these pleasant people, and I felt correspondingly shy in their presence. The journey promised to be entertaining. About a quarter of an hour before the train started, however, there was a certain amount of commotion in the corridor, and in bundled one of my pet aversions—a living model of a French caricature. He was wearing loud tweeds and knickerbockers—we didn't call them plus-fours in those days—and he was thick-set, red-cheeked, and he had a fair drooping moustache. He had a seat right opposite me.

'I had of course no tangible reason to be aggrieved with this individual, except that he made himself immediately so very much at home, and in certain readjustments of the luggage rack he called me "ma lad", which made me feel young and ridiculous in the presence of those other people; and when my father made some suggestion about one of my bags, he said: "That's all right, pa. I'll manage it." Which made my father seem old and somehow absurd. I went hot and cold with the thought that these other highly respectable people might think he was a friend or connection of mine. Such is extreme youth!

'When the train started he immediately began talking to me in a broad Lancashire accent. He said he came from Blundellsands and was in the jute trade. I did not object to this so much; what exasperated me was the fact that he began to pump me in a loud voice about who I was, what I was doing, and what my business was. I simply detested the man, and quite deliberately snubbed him by muttering monosyllables over the top of a magazine cover. I had no chance of conversation with the charming family.

'On the boat I lost them, and never saw them again. That is one of the curses of travel, one is always meeting people who you feel might be your bosom friends for life, and then Nemesis in the form of a guard or a ticket collector comes along and snatches them away from you.

'Of course I saw plenty of the man from Blundellsands. He was promenading the deck, smoking a bulldog pipe, and talking in a loud voice to all and sundry. Once or twice he came up and spoke to me—he seemed to have quite overlooked my attempts at snubbing. He apparently regarded me as a small boy.

'He repeated: "Well, lad, are ye all reet?" (I can't imitate Lancashire accent, so don't ask me!) On the Paris train, to my delight, I quite lost track of him, I hoped for ever.

'My plans were rather indefinite. I intended in any case to visit Northern Italy, and possibly afterwards go south to Sicily. But I had booked nothing beyond Paris. I may say that I had not been many days in that intriguing city before my passion for the girl who made up prescriptions began to wane. Paris smelt good. There was that curious peaty, coffeeish smell about it that seemed to betoken adventure. I stayed there a week, and then I booked a ticket through to Milan.

'The night before I left I wandered around alone, and late in the evening strolled into the Olympia. The entertainment was singularly boring, consisting mostly of freak dancing or equilibrists. After a time I went to the long bar at the back, and had a demi-bock. I had only been sitting there five minutes when a hand slapped me on the back and a voice said: "Hallo, ma lad, how art thee gettin' on?"

'I felt a curious sinking feeling at the pit of my stomach. What a nuisance the man was! A moment's reflection told me that of course this was just the kind of place I should meet him. It was my own fault. I was as polite as I could be. He said: "Ay, lad, when thou'rt in a foreign country it's soomtimes nice to meet one of th' own people."

'One of my own people! In this cosmopolitan place chiefly patronised by English and Americans it seemed rather an extravagant form of solicitude. There being no one else to talk to, however, and the evening being young for Paris, I stayed with him, and afterwards we took a taxi out to Montparnasse, and my youthful vanity was a little flattered by being able to show off my inner knowledge of night life to this ponderous Lancastrian, who must have been a good twenty years my senior.

'We parted in a friendly enough spirit, and he wanted to make an appointment for the morrow, but I gave some evasive answer. I felt I had done my duty by "one of my own people".

'I left the next day for Milan, and forgot all about him, which was not surprising, for it was there that I met Desirée Freyre. I ran plump into her in the lounge of the Hotel Bristol, after dinner. I will not bore you with a description of her. It is sufficient to say that within five minutes of our meeting, the girl who made up prescriptions, and indeed all the other girls who had made my youthful heart to flutter, promptly became back numbers.

'I don't even remember how I got into conversation with her. She was travelling with a companion, a very plain, genial soul much older than herself. Desirée was of the limpid, helpless sort, with large appealing eyes, a manner that suggested hidden fires beneath an easy-going companionable exterior. She was the kind of woman who called you "my dear" on first acquaintanceship, and persuaded you that your troubles were her troubles.

'We spent the next two days doing the sights of Milan together, though what they were I couldn't tell you, for my eyes were entirely occupied with my companion.

'I found that she and her friend had just done Northern Italy and were on their way to Genoa, and then by easy stages along the Côte d'Azur to Marseilles, where they had booked berths to Algiers. They proposed spending three months in Algeria.

'I had taken a ticket through to Florence, but when I suggested cancelling it, and accompanying these two ladies to Algeria, I found that the suggestion was accepted with encouraging readiness. I wrote rather a light-headed letter to my father, telling him of my change of plans, but of course not giving the reason.

'We left a few days later. I cannot describe that journey to Marseilles. We stayed days and nights at Genoa, Bordighera, Mentone, Monaco, and Nice. As my father wanted to eradicate the memory of the chemist's assistant I'm sure he could not have chosen a more effective way himself, though I am a little dubious whether he would have chosen precisely these means. I was madly in love, and this love had for its setting, instead of the familiar byways of Staines, a novel and romantic atmosphere of tamarisks, deep blue sea, orange groves, picturesque people, and the eternal accompaniment of bands of nomad musicians. I believe we were a fortnight getting to Marseilles, but it went like a flash.

'We spent the first few days there lazing in the sun, inhaling the perfume of early summer flowers, playing with the tame monkeys that used to come down and gambol in the wood beyond the garden, and occasionally going for a short drive in the vicinity. I got more intimate with Desirée here than I had done before. There were times when she became serious, and told me about her mother, who had been an opera singer, and her father, who had been an engineer, and had invented some contraption for making thin steel plates, and had made a lot of money and lost it, and made it again, and lost it again. Both her parents were now dead.

'And one night, under a clump of pistoia trees, with the moon making patterns on the ground at our feet, and on the white shawl of my companion, she told me something which aroused my interests even more, about her—husband, a major in the Artillery, who had been killed in the South African war. And when she told me,

I could not see her face, for it was pressed against my own, but I could feel her warm tears on my own cheek. She had a way, when I think she felt she was becoming too intimate, of giving me an almost savage pat on the cheek and saying: "Oh, you boy, you!" She did so on this occasion, and I felt my love for her ennobled by a great wave of compassion.

'I must confess that there were moments when I was free from the embraces of my beloved that I had moments of apprehension. She was so entirely alien to the world I came from. I could not conceive her as fitting into the social environment of Staines! My father for instance—I dared not imagine a meeting between him and Desirée.

'In the hotel at Algiers were many interesting people. I was not unmindful—and indeed a little proud of—the glances of envy that followed me about when I strolled on the terrace or into the dining room, accompanied by the beautiful Desirée Freyre. Of course, the eyes were focussed on her, but I knew that they also looked at me to see who the lucky fellow was who had captured so dazzling a prize. On only one occasion was I made to feel a little disconcerted. One evening I was talking to the companion in the lounge, waiting for Desirée. She had some little business to discuss with the hall-porter, and was talking to him at the door. A party of French people—newcomers—came down the stairs. There was an elderly man with a black moustache. He glanced in the direction of Desirée, and then turned, and I heard him say to an old lady in French: "Gracious, mamma! Do you see who's here?"

'The old lady looked in the same direction, and another woman came up. I could not hear what was said, but there was a good deal of whispering and laughing, and shrugging of shoulders.

'The table of these people was within sight of ours, and I saw Desirée glance once in their direction. I thought I observed a little frown pucker her brow as she turned away. She did not look at them again.

'The next day she was anxious to put into effect a project we had been discussing for some time. That was a visit to Constantine, a wonderful old town, built on a limestone plateau.

'It was nearly two hundred miles from Algiers, but we could take a train to El-Guerrah, and from there, it was just a comfortable five hours' ride in a diligence.

'I was hoping that I might have Desirée's company alone on this trip—or in any case with only one companion—but as she could not resist discussing it rather animatedly with the other hotel habitués, several of them expressed a desire to accompany us, and it would have been churlish to refuse. It was not till late in the evening that I managed to get Desirée to myself, and then we escaped to a small summerhouse in the grounds. That was an eventful night for me, for she promised to marry me.

'The night air was intoxicating with its rich aroma of flowers and unfamiliar herbs. My mind was in a whirl of ecstasy and anticipation. I little suspected the unpleasant little shock being prepared for me in the morning. Our diligence was to leave at eleven o'clock, and we were to have lunch at a caravanserai on the way.

'The diligence turned up rather before its time, and our party began to assemble, I was talking to a Russian princess, and feeling very much of the great world, when a thick-set figure in tweeds came out of the hotel with the Commissionaire and made straight for the diligence. I felt a wave of positive horror. It was the man from Blundellsands!

'He did not see me for a moment. He was busy giving instructions about luggage. Indeed, the whole party had collected and were ready to get aboard when he saw me. His face lighted up:

'"Ay, laddie!" he exclaimed. "Fancy seeing thee! Well, now, that's fine. Art going Constantine by cooch?"

'I felt myself going hot and cold all over. I could tell

by the faces of the others that they were thinking: Who on earth is this awful bourgeois person?

'But what could I do? There was no escaping from him. And he was quite as justified in taking the trip as I was. The worst of it was he insisted on sitting next to me, and bawling out about the places he had been to, and asking me questions. And of course he reiterated: "Ay, when thee gets right away in a foreign country, lad, it's fine to meet a fellow-countryman!"

'Fellow-countryman! I didn't want to talk to him, or have anything to do with him. I wished he'd die. I felt, in truth, that he had turned up as a kind of fate, an unpremeditated spoil-sport between myself and Desirée.

'We stopped at several Arab villages on the way and probed about in the markets which struck us as being curiously deserted. Desirée was angry with me. "Can't you get rid of this awful person?" she whispered. I could only shrug my shoulders and feel helpless. He was wearing in his buttonhole a ridiculously large bunch of purple heather. Seeing me look at it, he said: "Lad, see yon heather. Cooms all tha way from Bloondellsands. Ma sister sent it wrapped oop in ma socks." "Rather like coals to Newcastle," I tried to sneer. "Ay," he answered. "But when it cooms from th' own people—There's a bit of common just outside oor toon—"

'I managed to get to the other end of the diligence on the way to the caravanserai. There we partook of a strange and wonderful lunch, in which stewed bustard was a feature, I remember.

'Now in the strange occurrence that happened to me that day I was convinced that the stewed bustard played the leading rôle. I was to learn a long while later that it had nothing to do with it. But at the time I was dominated by this illusion. Hanging up in the caravanserai had been a stuffed bustard. I had never seen one before. In the middle of the afternoon, as we drove over the sandy waste thickly studded with scrub and halfagrass, the bustard I had eaten and the bustard that was hanging up became one and the same bird. It seemed to flutter against the roof of the diligence and make it darker and darker. I had the greatest difficulty in seeing, hearing, or breathing. I remember at one time a crowd of faces staring at me, and I was not certain who they were, and not particularly interested. I knew I was ill, and that all my powers of resistance were vanishing. My head seemed to be in iron clamps, and my body was throbbing as though stirred by a hundred fevers. I had no sense of time, only a sense of impenetrable darkness, that increased, that increased—'

Jimmy shook himself and gave a little shiver. The Colonel was silent and invisible behind my back. The sun had already tipped the horizon. There was no need for me to interrupt the flow of his story, and he continued:

'I don't know whether you have ever been unconscious for a long time under the pressure of raging fever. It is horrible. Apart from racking pains one is desperately unhappy in an inexplicable way. The fever seems to get right through to one's soul. I had glimpses of semi-consciousness, in which all the people I had ever known became inconsequentially involved. After some interminable passage of time I had a glimpse of reality. I awakened in some dim light, and was aware of a woman in white gliding about the room. "I have been very ill" was the first intelligible thought I had had for a long time, and then a name came involuntarily to my lips, "Desirée!"

'I know not how long passed between this brief return to consciousness and another more placid one. It was a twilight hour, and I felt cool, and master of myself. I waited patiently, and the woman in white came back. It was not Desirée. A wave of disappointment flooded me, and I tried to speak, to protest against this outrage. The nurse said in English: "There, there! that's better! Don't talk. I will give you something." She poured a white liquid between my lips. I gradually felt stronger, but she would not talk or answer my questions. A French doctor came and examined me. He came every day. At the end of nearly a week the nurse talked a little. She told me I was in a ward of the Isolation Hospital of the White Sisters at Algiers. "But what has been the matter with me? I feel as though I have had something awful—like typhoid." "You have had something worse than that," she said.

'"What was it?" I asked.

'"Typhus," she said quietly.

'"Typhus!"

'"There was a little epidemic of it in some of the villages along the coast, brought they say by a coaster from the Levant."

'"But you are English," I said, fencing for time, my mind occupied with other aspects of the case.

'"I am an Irish nun," she answered. "They put me to nurse you because I speak English."

'I waited, not quite knowing how to frame the questions I was burning to ask. At last I said: "I was with a party, going to Constantine. Tell me, what happened to them?"

'"When they heard what was the matter with you they fled. They hired a car and drove to El-Guerrah, and took the next train back to Algiers."

'"All of them?" I faltered.

'"No, one remained behind and nursed you, and somehow got you back here."

'I sighed contentedly. My spirits rose. I knew that *she* in any case would not have deserted me under those conditions. After a pause I whispered hoarsely: "Where is she now?"

'"It was a he," said the nurse in a low voice. "An Englishman. He said he came from Lancashire. Had it not been for him you would have died."

'I turned my face away, for I did not want the Irish nurse to see it. I tried to speak as casually as I could.

'"Oh," I said, "what was his name? Did he leave his address?"

'"No," she answered, "he went away quietly one morning. He left neither name nor address. But look! he left his bunch of heather. He said it was for luck—'look' he called it. He waited till you were out of danger. On the morning he left he came and saw you and said: 'Poor laddie! I had a boy like you.' He told me his boy was killed in the South African war. And then as though to apologise for his emotion, he said something about one must do what one can for a fellow countryman."

'"And then he went away?"

'"Yes, we none of us knew his name. He was very generous. By the way," she added, "your father is here in Algiers. We telegraphed to him. As soon as you are free from contagion we shall send you to him."'

'You never saw the man from Blundellsands again?' I ventured. 'And what about the—your fiancée?'

'You must remember,' said Jimmy, 'all this happened about twenty years ago. Honestly I have no clearer recollection of her face than I have of the girl who made up prescriptions. No, I never saw—any of the party again. But from what I since heard one other man came out of the affair with credit.'

'Who was that?'

'The Frenchman who laughed in that hotel at Mustapha. Come, let's get busy. The fish are rising.'

'And the Colonel has gone to sleep,' I answered. 'That's because you didn't throw your spoil-sport into the river!'

'Poor old chap! don't let's wake him up,' said Jimmy.

'I'm afraid we shall have to,' I said. 'He's gone to sleep on the gentles.'

—*XI*—

The Deserter

HE WAS CONSCIOUS THAT some of the men in cloth caps were sniggering at him. They sat there in rows in the bare room, swinging their legs, smoking cigarettes, laughing, muttering coarse jests. They had all been thrown together that morning for the first time, but they appeared drawn to each other by some instinctive comradeship. Wainwright alone felt himself shut out, a being apart. He had already spent three hours with them awaiting his turn to go before the Medical Board, but his tentative approaches towards companionship had been still-born. He was acutely self-conscious, and his furtive offers of cigarettes to the men next to him were received with chilling unresponsiveness. If he addressed one, the answer would be:

'Eh?' or 'What d'yer sye?'

They did not seem to be able to understand what he said, any more than he could understand what they said. He made a bold attempt on two occasions to be friendly, to make some laughing comment, and the failure froze him. More and more he felt himself thrust apart, until he was aware of small groups whispering together and laughing at him. Doubtless his olive skin with the mop of dark hair, and the patent fact that he was better dressed, better educated, might act as a barrier, but the knowledge distressed him. He did not feel himself superior to his fellow men, whatever his character or position, but how to cross this terrible mental chasm? A sergeant and two privates were walking in and out of the room, with lists of names and innumerable army forms. The men in driblets of dozens, passed through to another room, stripped and went before the Board. When Wainwright's turn came he felt a curious choking feeling, as though he could not get his breath. He felt a desire to make a sudden dash from the building, and then there dawned upon him for the first time the realization of a sudden and terrible experience. He had lost his liberty. He was twenty-four, and all his life to that minute he had been an absolutely free man. He had occasionally been checked by small fetters, but none which could not be instantly broken if he desired it very much. He had been to school, and after school he had been articled to an architect in London, an old friend of his father. The indenture implied certain mutual obligations, but it was one that could have been terminated at any time. There was no hint of bondage. All his life he had been generously treated, perhaps spoilt. His father, who was a vicar in the East Riding of Yorkshire, had died when he was at school. His mother had worshipped him, and she had died only three years before. His only living relative was his sister, who was married to a wealthy flax-merchant at Huddersfield. In London he had few friends but he was comfortable and happy in his quiet introspective way. His parents had left him a small private income, and he was absorbed in his work. He occupied a commodious suite of rooms on Adelphi Terrace, well stocked with old furniture and books. He had never been interested in politics and had not given the subject of war half-an-hour's consideration in his life. Nevertheless he was not entirely a book-worm. At school he had been keen on cricket and hockey, and the latter game he still kept up and he played tennis in the summer. He was perhaps highly strung, but apart from that he was not aware of any physical disability. When the war had come it had seemed so preposterous he tried to thrust it aside as much as possible. He wildly hoped that it would suddenly end in the same cyclonic way it had begun. He would not argue about it. He dismissed it again and again with the simple expression 'Ridiculous!' He could not feel a thing that was so much outside himself, and he harboured the eternal suspicion which the artist always had for the politician. And then suddenly had come that little buff slip of paper *ordering* him to appear before a certain Medical Board on a certain day at a certain time. Even then he had not grasped the full significance of this onslaught on his liberty. He still thought it was 'ridiculous'. Something would happen. He would get out of it. It was not till that moment when he stood naked among a crowd of naked men that he realized that his liberty was really at stake; that the war was something which tremendously concerned himself. He followed them into another room, where an old man was sitting at a desk talking to a lieutenant, and a plump doctor in civilian clothes appeared to be chasing naked men about the room and calling out remarks in a mechanical voice to a clerk. They were weighed, measured, examined in every detail, made to hop, skip, jump and bend. Nothing seemed to be overlooked. Man was reduced to a physical automaton, and nothing else appeared of the slightest consequence. Wainwright hopped, skipped and jumped with the rest. The doctor asked one or two questions, and he found himself replying huskily: 'Yes, sir,' or 'No, sir,' as the case might be. Eventually he found himself standing before the old major and the doctor, feeling more naked than ever, and the major was saying:

'You've never suffered from any organic disease then?'

'No, sir.'

They drew apart and talked, and he suddenly felt a desire to go up and say:

'I say, you know, I shan't be any good at this sort of thing.'

But that choking sense prevented him from doing this, and also the realization that from their point of view this would also be 'ridiculous'.

In a few moments the doctor turned round and said:

'All right. Dress up.'

He dressed and waited interminably in another room, among his friends in the cloth caps. At length they were despatched to a corridor, where they waited for their names to be called out. He received another buff slip of paper. He had been passed A1. He was liable to be called in fourteen days' time as a first-class fighting man in the Great War!

He walked out of the building, greedy for his momentary liberty, but dazed by the astounding position he faced. He walked all the way to Adelphi Terrace and let himself in. The quiet dignity and beauty of his sitting room calmed him. The soothing proportions of his William and Mary walnut furniture, the Adams' bay-window overlooking the river, on the table an open book on *Old English Mansions*, and a pile of *Architectural Reviews* and *Builders*. A fire glowing in the grate and inviting him to warm his toes as he reclined on the tall easy chair, by the side of which was a book-rest and his favourite pipe. This was reality, and the menacing disturbance outside was a dream. In any case here he was himself, and here he could think this thing out to its bitter conclusion.

And so from that time Wainwright began to try and think earnestly and intensely about the war and his own position. And if the conclusions he came to were not ours, we must in any case give him the credit for having tried very hard to get his thoughts into a true focus, and we must allow considerably for his upbringing and environment. For the mind of Wainwright was a very complex affair, and the effect of the war was like that of a bear disturbing a beehive. If you conceive a swarm of bees intent on the delicate construction of a hive, and suddenly having their well-laid plans obliterated by the nozzle of the fierce monster, you may imagine how for some time his thoughts buzzed round in a complete state of panic. There was no cohesion, no unity, no concentration. He felt personally outraged. He had no feeling of animosity to any living thing. He had read very little history and no political economy. He abhorred politics, and lived for beauty. He had been brought up to see the good in everything, to believe the best in everyone, and in the unswerving faith that war was a thing of pre-civilized ages. Incidentally he distrusted newspapers and was always inclined to see the other fellow's point of view more insistently than his own. He became convinced that the war was a politico-economic affair waged by two groups of uninspired and quite uninteresting people.

The outcome of Wainwright's reflections was a determination to become a deserter.

Now Wainwright was a Yorkshireman, that is to say, he had the power of combining his idealism with its full quota of hard-headed sense. When he had once made up his mind to desert, he decided to do the thing thoroughly and with the greatest degree of circumspection. He spent a week thinking it all out in detail and then acted deliberately. He was in a peculiarly good position to desert, for he had money and very few friends. There were barely half a dozen people who would be likely to cause trouble: his employer Mr Haynes, who was getting on in years and spent his whole life at the office, except to go backwards and forwards to his house at Northwood; two assistants who led a very similar life; the woman who came to work for him; his landlord; his lawyer and two or three others whose habitation and movements were familiar to him. The whole scheme was daringly simple. He did not go away and hide in a cave in the Welsh hills, or disguise himself as a blind pedlar, but he simply moved from Adelphi Terrace to South Kensington on the very day that the calling-up notice was served upon him.

Now for anyone who wishes to desert or to escape from the eyes of the world we cannot imagine a safer or more appropriate retreat than South Kensington. Nobody in South Kensington takes the slightest notice of anybody else. The tall supercilious houses look right over your head. The broad streets and pavements hold your neighbours at a distance. Provided you are decently dressed, no one takes any interest in you at all. A respectable person might wander there unobserved for ever, like a conventional ghost in a city of make-believe. Inquisitiveness soon exhausts itself in the atmosphere of the Cromwell Road. The vast museum and institutions have the faculty of making the individual appear trivial and inconsequential. This is of course all assuming—as we have said—that the individual is *respectable*. If a gentleman in a cloth cap and a scarf instead of a tie—such as Wainwright encountered when he went before his Medical Board—were to make it a practice to lounge about the Exhibition Road, we do not presume to know what secret machinery might be set in motion to make enquiries as to his *raison d'être*, but a clean collar and a well-cut suit will always act as a soporific in this select neighbourhood. Moreover, there are innumerable buildings which were at that time occupied by gentlemen, dressed very like Wainwright, who were employed in multifarious and mysterious ways in 'getting on with the war'. All of this is nobody else's business. Certainly not yours or mine. There is not the slightest doubt but that Wainwright might have been wandering about there comfortably to this day, had it not been for certain circumstances which we shall disclose presently.

He took a suite of furnished rooms in a quiet square at the back of South Kensington Station, in the name of

George Plinth. He liked the name of George Plinth. He took a long time inventing it. It gave a pleasant suggestion of his profession, and seemed peculiarly appropriate to the neighbourhood. He estimated that the 'ridiculous' war would be over within six months or in any case a year, and then he would be able to return and everything would go on as usual. He took two hundred pounds out of the bank and told his lawyer he was going up to Yorkshire on business and would send his address later. He told Mr Haynes he regretted to leave his employ, but he had been called up to do war work and he hoped to come back to him after. He gave the woman who worked for him a handsome tip and told her he was going to France. When she had gone he took three taxi-loads of books, drawing materials and household goods to his new address. He wrote to the landlord and sent a year's rent and told him he was going to Scotland. He wrote to two other people and told one he was going to Bristol and the other that he was leaving to take up Red Cross work in Serbia. Having completed this campaign of mellow mendacity, he locked up the flat on Adelphi Terrace and left no address.

'They can take their choice,' he said to himself that night in his new rooms as he lighted his pipe after supper. Satisfied that his plans had been executed with complete skill and foresight, he sedulously dismissed the Army authorities from his mind and buried himself in the study of architecture. His landlady was a lantern-jawed, forlorn-looking widow with three young children. She kept the place adequately clean, cooked well, and took no further interest in him beyond that of securing her rent in advance and stealing some of his butter and sugar, altogether an ideal landlady for his purpose. He spent his days studying, partly in his rooms and partly in the Victoria and Albert Museum. It was for the time very satisfactory. When the whole of Europe was in a death-grip, he commenced to compile a book on *Doorways in the Reign of Charles II.*

Occasionally he went for strolls in Kensington Gardens, and he did not hesitate to venture further afield if he felt in the mood; though he timed his visits to the West End when he would not be likely to meet Mr Haynes or any other people who knew him. As time went on he became bolder in these enterprises. He went to Hampstead and occasionally into the country for a day. The summer exhausted itself and still the 'ridiculous' war went on. He settled down to 'stick it' through the winter. His work absorbed him, but he began to experience transient moods of unrest. When he withdrew from his books or his drawing-board, he was acutely conscious of an alien world in the making. Everything socially appeared to be changing kaleidoscopically. New uniforms both for men and women appeared upon the streets every day. Everyone seemed intent and occupied, women especially. He would notice them hurrying along the streets with their little despatch cases, and a new light of independence and enthusiasm in their eyes. And he felt shut out from all this. He would occasionally talk to people, but he avoided controversy. He made no friends and encountered no enemies. He passed thousands of officers, and groups of military police, but no one took any notice of him. He refused to take any interest in the war except to glance at the papers to see if there were any probability of it coming to an end.

One night he was awakened by the sound of guns. He jumped up and went to the window. Flashlights were whipping the sky with jerky movements. He could hear the drone of engines, and below in the street he heard a woman scream. He dressed quickly and went out. The streets were deserted. The night was very dark, and the guns were booming thunderously. He could not see the Zeppelin, but he walked quickly on. Occasionally someone would rush past him, or a motorcar dash drunkenly into the darkness. He felt an odd sense of exhilaration in this experience. He thought to himself:

'Up there somewhere are ten or fifteen men—men of flesh and blood like myself—seated in a cage, and their idea is to kill me or anyone else they can.'

The thing seemed to present itself at an unusual angle. It appeared very real, but if anything more ridiculous than ever. Why on earth should ten or fifteen good gentlemen whom he had never met want to kill him or anyone else? He had never felt any desire to kill anyone, not even in a passion. At the corner of a square he ran into an oldish man with a grey beard gazing upwards. He looked eccentric. Perhaps he too shared Wainwright's views. Wainwright spoke to him. He spoke impulsively with that freedom common to men who share a danger. The old man mumbled his replies. Wainwright brought his harangue to the point of the 'ridiculousness' of the war. Suddenly the old man turned on him and said:

'Boy, anything that's worth having is worth fighting for. I've got three lads out there. Why aren't you?'

Wainwright stole furtively away into the night, tingling with a dull sense of disappointment. He hardly knew how he got through the winter. Periods of depression became more and more acute, and more and more frequent. The book on *Charles II Doorways* was half-finished and then discarded. He lost interest in it. He took up the study of Gothic tracery, but he found his mind wandering. There dawned upon him at times the realization that he hadn't perhaps faced the thing quite squarely, but that it was now too late. You cannot destroy a thing by calling it ridiculous. Perhaps it would have been better to become a conscientious objector and to have gone to prison. It would certainly have been more courageous, only... he knew he was not a conscientious objector. He would assuredly fight for anything he believed in. It was only that he objected to be made to fight for some affair he knew nothing about, somebody else's affair. But it must soon be over now.

The winter passed, but not the war. It appeared indeed to be extending, to be developing, to have 'only just begun', some people said. He saw the snowdrops and the violets come and go in Kensington Gardens, and then the daffodils raise their heads and nod at him indifferently. And then one day he met Emma.

It was a warm day at the end of April. It was essentially a day when the heart should be singing, but Wainwright was disconsolate. The sunlight seemed to mock him. He sat on a bench gazing idly at the flowers and listening to the drone of the traffic. Nursemaids passed pushing go-carts and perambulators, children laughed, and their high-spirited voices epitomized the gaiety of the day. He became aware that one perambulator had passed him twice and was returning. He looked up and into the eyes of—Emma.

She was a little thing, round and soft like a bird, with grey mothering eyes ever watchful. She was undeniably pretty, with pallid cheeks, glowing with a kind of warmth more emotional than physical. She had a small nose and a full but not too firm mouth, and a strand of light brown hair waved from under her nurse's cap. As she passed she did not take her eyes from Wainwright's, but she went on.

Twenty paces on she turned and looked timidly back. Then she went on again. Wainwright looked at his hands.

'Somehow, somewhere, somewhere, I have looked into those eyes before,' he thought.

He had been instantly conscious of some sudden vital contact. Something peculiar had happened. He had been raised in a flash from the lowest depths of despair to an emotional plane that was in any case exhilarating. He couldn't understand it and so he looked helplessly and wonderingly and for no reason at all at his hands. Then he shifted his legs and looked after her. She was walking very, very slowly, and there was something peculiarly enticing and feline about her movements. She saw him watching her. After a time she turned and came back. Wainwright felt his heart beating in an unaccountable manner. He wondered whether he should get up and bolt, but his limbs appeared atrophied and he sat there still staring at his hands. Very, very slowly she approached once more, and this time she gave him an almost imperceptible smile. She spoke to the baby, and her voice was soft and purry. The baby made a little noise and it became necessary to rearrange its pillow. After she had done this, still talking to the baby, and as though not conscious of her own action, she sat down at the other end of the bench, and Wainwright became aware of being engulfed in the vortex of a strange and quite inexpressible emotional experience. She appeared to half glance at him occasionally, as though expecting him to speak, but he merely sat there trembling and distracted at his own helplessness.

After a time, the baby not requiring any further attention, she sat back and looked around her, like a little bird perched on a bough. Then she took out a notebook and started to feel in her bag. She was evidently in distress.

Then Wainwright behaved like a man.

'Excuse me,' he said, 'do you happen to want a pencil?'

The grey eyes looked right into his, and the lips parted in a slow smile.

'Yes, thank you. Could you—?'

Wainwright snatched the pencil out of his pocket

and handed it to her. She thanked him, and made some scribbling entry in the book and returned it.

'It's a nice day,' she said.

'Yes—ripping,' replied the young man.

'The daffodils are pretty,' she remarked after a pause.

'Yes, aren't they fine!' he replied eagerly.

There was a most disconcerting pause, and then Wainwright in desperation stood up and peered into the perambulator. He could just see the tip of a pink nose. He said:

'I say, what a jolly baby!'

'Yes, it is pretty, isn't it?' she replied.

'Is it yours?'

She laughed a low gurgly laugh.

'Not much. What do *you* think?'

'Oh, I'm sorry. I didn't know,' exclaimed Wainwright, who felt he'd made a very tactless remark.

'Oh, I don't mind. I wish it was.'

'Do you like babies?'

'Rather. I wish I had one of my own.'

This seemed a desperate plunge into the most sacred intimacies and in order to gain time to focus this tremendous confession, Wainwright remarked:

'You're not married then?' To his surprise she appeared suddenly very solemn.

She nodded and said:

'Yes, I'm married.'

'Oh!'

There was another uncomfortable pause, and then she became jerkily confidential.

'I only do this of a morning—to oblige Mrs Merryfeather of Knightsbridge. I'm married myself. We live at Hammersmith. I used to do type-writing at one time.'

It seemed difficult to reply to these disconnected

comments, but Wainwright felt that their acquaintanceship was sufficiently developed to venture:

'Have you been married long?'

'Three years.'

'Is your husband—in business?'

'He's foreman in a stonemason's yard. He's a very strong man.'

'I see.'

The principal thing that Wainwright could see was that it was extremely regrettable that so lovable and attractive a little person should not have babies if she desired them. But he felt that he had pursued the matter as far as it was decently appropriate, and he added quickly:

'Do you come here often?'

'Every morning now. I only started last week.'

'I seem to know you or to have met you before.'

For reply she looked out at him from under her lowered lids and smiled. He added:

'I must be going. Perhaps I'll see you again, then.'

She leant forward as though making a mysterious and solemn acquiescence and rose from the bench. Their ways parted and she did not look back.

It may be difficult to gather what gleams of spiritual comfort Wainwright managed to deduce from the foregoing banal conversation, but it is an undoubted fact that it raised him to an unexpected pinnacle of bliss. Possibly it was the things not said rather than the things said, or it may have been the sudden contact with an all-too-human creature after a long period of emotional starvation. In any case it is certain that the experience turned his head. For the rest of the day he walked on air. Those grey eyes were between him and his drawing-board. He could not work and he could not think. Through the dull mists of his austere life, and the desperate negation of these latter days, there suddenly fluttered the pennant of a cavalier, a reckless dare-devil fellow, with boots and spurs, and a quick desire for action. He flung his books aside and went for a long walk. In the evening he swaggered unblushingly into a music-hall. It is quite on the cards that if he had met his former colleagues at Mr Haynes' or any others likely to be informers, he would not have hesitated to speak to them. Fortunately for him no such contretemps materialized. But the music only maddened him the more, and he returned to his rooms late at night to dream of grey eyes and the morrow.

Wainwright was young, somehow impulsive, and generally illogical, but he was not a fool. Even in those first days when the full glamour of that experience was on him, he entertained no illusions on the score of Emma. He believed himself to be desperately in love with her, but he knew that it was a love without the hope of fruition. Apart from the fact of her being a married woman he realized that she was a being quite apart from himself. She was primitive, uneducated, amazingly ignorant, but the very thought of her stimulated him, and her presence intoxicated him. He had been brought up on strictly puritanical lines, and a reverence for woman was ingrained in his nature. He had never been in love before and literature which reflected variations of the erotic passion did not interest him greatly. But this to him was something altogether unique. No human being had ever been brought face to face with so engaging an experience.

Every morning he went to meet her in the gardens, and sometimes in the afternoon, when she was free of the baby, they would meet again by appointment. They went to Richmond, and Kew, and Hampton Court; but she always insisted on being back at her home at Hammersmith at seven o'clock, because 'he' came home at half-past, and she had to prepare 'his' supper.

Once Wainwright took her up into Richmond Park. They sat on a low bench among the young ferns, far from the gaze of all living things. She was in one of her unbreakable silent moods, leaning forward on her knees and occasionally glancing at him furtively with her cat-like eyes.

'What are your thoughts, little witch?' he said.

She smiled vaguely and shook her head. Wainwright took her hand in his and kissed it.

'Tell me all about everything,' he said.

'What do you mean by "everything"?' she answered faintly.

'You, your life, your home. Are you happy?'

She seemed to catch her breath. Then she nodded and replied unconvincingly,

'Yes.'

He put his arm round her waist and pulled her to him.

'Let me help you. Let me make you happy, Emma.'

She half-closed her eyes as though she were slipping away from him. He kissed her on the cheek and she neither responded nor checked him. She sat there brooding and unanswering. Wainwright was tortured by the unbridgeable chasm that always seemed to lie between them. She appeared to be drawn to him, to like him and want him, but then there came a point beyond which everything seemed empty and unresponsive. And he was choking for want of sympathy and understanding. A lark swung upwards and started its song above the chestnut trees. The river away beneath them trembled in a warm mist. Suddenly Wainwright slipped on to his knees, and buried his head in her lap. And then he held her hands over his eyes and he told her everything. He told her about his parents and his upbringing, and his work, and his experience at the Medical Board. He told her he was a deserter, and he explained his views and reasons. He held his cheek against hers, and whispered hoarsely:

'Do you blame me?'

He felt her bosom heaving as she replied simply:

'No. Everybody for himself, I say.'

She would not kiss him, but she stroked his hair and after a time she said:

'We must be going back, I think.'

He lifted her up, and for a moment she clung limply to him. Then they sauntered across the grass back to the station.

After that they seemed more to each other. Although Emma would not speak to him of her home life, he found her more companionable. He chatted to her indiscriminately about anything that came into his head. Sometimes he made her laugh. He was happier, even when he was not with her. He launched into his work once more. He took a fresh interest in the *Charles II Doorways*. The war became more and more a matter of minor importance. He found in Emma the thing he had been looking for. She became his mother-confessor. He idealized her. He basked in the self-martyrdom of believing that he loved her and of controlling his passion. His attitude towards her should always be knightly and chivalrous. He gloried in the agony of wanting to kiss her lips, and then forbearing. He had strange dreams concerning her, in which he always played the part of Sir Launcelot.

One morning he noticed that her nurse's cap was pulled down further across her brow than usual. He would not have commented upon it only that once as she was stooping over the baby he observed something else. He said:

'Emma, pull back your cap.'

She frowned and shook her head.

'Emma, dear, you've got a bruise on your temple. How did you do it?'

For a moment she was silent, and then her eyes were filled with tears.

'I didn't do it.'

'Who did it?'

'*He* did.'

Wainwright started.

'What do you mean? He did it?'

She was shaking and she would not answer. He pressed her arm and whispered:

'Tell me.'

But she only shook herself free and answered:

'Oh, it's all right.'

From that day Wainwright passed through periods of maddening disquiet. There dawned upon him the complete solution of her moods of sullen unresponsiveness, weighed down as she must be by her secret tragedy. Whenever he hinted that he should come to see her in her home, she shivered and implored him not to. Neither would she speak of it unless forced to. For the most part her attitude remained watchful, supplicating, mildly playful. That she was fond of him and liked to have him dancing attendance was patent. That he stirred any deeper chords in her nature remained problematical.

In any case, they still continued meeting nearly every day, and the fine-drawn skeins of chivalry were tested to their utmost strength. Sometimes she would come to him playful, gay, almost yielding. At other times with dark rims and pink lids to her eyes, distracted and unresponsive. Once she did not appear for nearly a week, and then no cunning arrangement of hat or coiffure could conceal the fact that she was barely recovered from the effects of a black eye. It was the evidence of this phenomenon which stirred the cavalier to drastic action. For on that evening he followed her home to that block of tenements down by the river at Hammersmith, grandiloquently named 'Northallerton Buildings'. Stealthily he tracked her to Number 473B. But he did not on that occasion catch sight of her husband, Jim Stroud.

He wandered the neighbourhood of wharfs, narrow gullies, deserted plots of land, meagre dwellings, and vast factories, and a feeling of despair and pity possessed him. For almost the first time he felt dragged from the lure of books and precious study by the call of the grim and terrible social realities. And as the days and nights went by he found himself more and more frequently, without any idea of meeting Emma, haunting this unattractive neighbourhood. It fascinated him. It was nearly three weeks later that he first beheld Jim Stroud. He had been wandering down by the river one evening and, turning the corner of a passage-way, he crossed a mean street of buff-coloured houses when he beheld a man and woman walking thirty paces ahead. He recognized Emma at once. The man was a big heavy chunk of humanity, clumsily built. He was slouching along several yards ahead of the woman, and appeared to be drunk. He was in any case rolling peculiarly and growling at her. Sometimes he would lurch sideways and appear to be going to strike her, and she seemed to shrink back and to be on the alert for some such contingency. Wainwright increased his pace. As he approached he could hear the man's remarks and curses, but he continued stumbling forward. In a few minutes the gaunt frame of Northallerton Buildings loomed against the sky, and swallowed them up as though fully aware that its expansive body had been nourished for generations upon a diet of similar morsels. Wainwright returned home consumed with a melancholy resolution.

On the morrow he found Emma more morose than usual. She said she was tired and did not want to go far. They went and sat on a seat on the Chiswick side of the river. They were both unusually silent. At length Wainwright said:

'Look here, Emma, this can't go on. I saw you last night with your husband. He was cursing you. He looked as though he were going to strike you any minute. Emma, dear, this can't go on. You must leave him. You can't love him. Listen, you shall leave him and go where you like. I will look after you. I promise you I'll never do anything you don't wish me to. I will just be your servant. We will leave London. Go right into the country—anywhere you like. Say you will, Emma.'

She was crying. She dabbed her eyes with her handkerchief and shook all over. He kept trying to soothe her, touching her hands and muttering 'Emma dear'.

At last she said:

'I lied to you. He is not my husband.'

Wainwright started.

'What do you mean?'

'He is not my husband. He is my—man!'

'My God!'

The calm assertion of this amazing news left Wainwright stupefied. He stared at the girl, at the river and at the sky. Then gripping her forearm, he exclaimed:

'Then, by God, that settles it. But why haven't you left him before?'

'He's my man,' she answered simply.

'But, my dear—' Wainwright stood up. He found himself groping amidst incomprehensible things. He stretched out his arms.

'You'll come with me now though, won't you, Emma? You'll put up with no more of this. Come, we'll start all over again, both of us.' He pulled her up to him, and she swayed passively. Her bosom was still heaving, and she could not control her voice to speak all the way along to the bridge. As they approached the turning that led to the Buildings, Wainwright lowered his voice.

'Emma,' he whispered imploringly, 'you will come, won't you? You will come to me, or if you won't, you'll promise me to leave him? I will pay for a room for you. You shall go unmolested. You shall be free. Promise me you'll leave him.'

For a moment she appeared as she had when they first met, a small, fluffy bird hovering on a branch, liable to dart away in any direction. He squeezed her hands supplicatingly. Suddenly her eyes lighted up with an incomprehensible burst of anger. She forced herself free and cried out:

'He is my man.'

And he beheld her small cat-like body gliding away into the fading light. A little way down the street, she turned and threw him a kiss, and then ran on. Wainwright began to realize that there are things which you cannot get to learn in books. And in the days that followed he felt odd forces working within him. Something was hardening. Some inner impulse clamouring for concrete expression. He remembered the old man's saying on the night of the Zeppelin raid:

'Anything that's worth having is worth fighting for!'

He began to see himself in a different light, to be conscious of a social entity. There were other people in the world besides himself, inextricably interdependent. There must be reasons for everything. And if one asserts oneself, struggles for what one believes in, there must be inevitably—conflict.

'He shan't knock her about! He shan't knock her about in any case,' he kept on repeating to himself.

He met her again. She was still incomprehensible, bewildering and more attractive than ever. She seemed at pains to atone for her repulsion of his chivalry. She allowed him to see her home, and she showed him the stone-mason's yard where her man worked. It stood at the angle of the river and a tiny canal. A narrow passage with a low stone wall connected it with the Causeway and a little frequented road. On the left one passed a deserted wharf. It is necessary to briefly describe this wharf, because it was in this that the affairs of Wainwright reached a crisis on a certain Monday evening in June. A black door always ajar in the midst of a long stretch of black hoarding led into an L-shaped piece of ground, partly mud and weeds, but flanked on one side by a strip of broken stone pavement. The land was protected from the river by a stone building with its windows boarded up and its solitary crane out of repair, whilst on the other side was a high wooden fencing, and three tarred huts stood at right angles to the lane.

On the Monday evening we have mentioned it had been raining and the air was still moist and the sky overcast. As Jim Stroud came up the lane from the yard, a young man with a pale face and a mop of dark hair appeared at the doorway of this deserted wharf. He put his head out and said:

'Mr Stroud.'

Jim stared at this peculiar apparition without much interest or apprehension, merely acknowledging his name by not denying it. And then the young man suddenly delivered himself of the following incredible speech. He said:

'Look here, Jim Stroud. This has got to stop. No one can prevent you living with Emma if she wishes it. But if she does you've got to treat her decently. If you strike her or knock her about again, you'll have to answer for it.'

Jim Stroud was a man of remarkably few words when sober. He would frequently go through a day's work without speaking to anyone. On this occasion he did not belie his reputation in this respect. He simply pushed through the doorway and pushed the young man back. He then forced the door to behind him. They were then alone in the deserted wharf. Even then he did not seem to show any inclination to speak. He came grimly onwards till he had the young man's face silhouetted against the black hoarding and then he struck at it with his right fist.

In the fight which followed one of the most disconcerting things for Wainwright was this utter silence of his opponent. He never said a word. Whether he knew all about Wainwright and his relationship to Emma, or whether he looked upon this as merely an ordinary wharfside social amenity, Wainwright was never able to determine.

Wainwright had done a little boxing at school, but he had never fought with bare knuckles in his life. He knew that his chances against the stone-mason were about one in a hundred, but it required some fantastic demand on fate such as these odds suggested to attune him to his new mood. His mind was working very rapidly. He felt exhilarated and utterly indifferent to his danger. He knew that there were one or two things in his favour. He was quicker than his opponent, and he had plenty of elbow room. There was, moreover, no friendly referee to give a breather. His tactics must be to exhaust and wind his man. He met the first onrush of Stroud's terrific blows on his arms. They hurt, and so did his own knuckles when he got them to Stroud's ribs. The man was horribly strong. Wainwright darted round him, and sometimes simply ran away. If he could have got the other to run after him the tactics might have paid, but Stroud was in no hurry. He just turned and followed him grimly and slowly, certain of his prey. Wainwright tried to remember some of the instructions of his old gym instructor up in Yorkshire. He remembered one point, though rather vaguely. It concerned what he called 'in-fighting'. He knew that if he could get his opponent to lunge heavily at his face, and then step quickly to the left he could crash with his right to the other's jaw. He knew that the jaw was the place to go for.

'You could knock a giant out if you tap him on the side of the jaw,' he seemed to hear his old instructor say. Stroud's jaw was a massive affair, and it seemed terribly inaccessible, with two steel bands swinging in front of it. Nevertheless, Wainwright made a sudden determination to try desperately for the other's jaw. He went straight at him, giving blow for blow. In two minutes he was lying on his back in the mud, a blow over the heart like a kick from a horse having laid him there. He leapt to his feet, and rushed in again. Four times he tried these rushing tactics, and four times he measured his length on the ground. Something else would have to be done. A fine rain was falling, some gulls were whining overhead. Blood was flowing from his mouth, the result of some blow of which he had no recollection. He knew he was badly cut, bruised, and damaged, but it didn't seem to matter. He became like a primitive thing, indifferent to pain, obsessed with the one idea—to get one blow in on the point of that jaw. He was fighting, being beaten and was enjoying the analysis of his sensations under the trial. He had no idea the mind could think so quickly; he was intensely alert for any strategic advantage; at the same time all sorts of other things kept racing through his brain, odd and ridiculous trifles, snatches of music, nothing whatever to do with the bitter case in hand. He fought mechanically, darting in and breaking away, receiving punishment and inflicting none. Little pools of water lay about the yard. The men would sometimes splash into them, and Stroud's iron-bound boots would slip upon a stone.

'If I can get him on to that wet pavement, he might

trip up in those boots,' suddenly occurred to Wainwright. He worked his way round so that his back was to the pavement. He was getting weaker. Stroud came on doggedly, driving him back. Foot by foot he gave way. At last he felt his heel touch the stone. Now was the time to be wary. He appeared to be making a great effort, and then suddenly threw up his arms helplessly and fell back. Stroud with a growl rushed in to finish him off. Wainwright heard his iron-clamped boots strike the stone pavement. He saw his malevolent face as he struck with his left. Wainwright side-stepped, and knew that the other had missed and lost his balance. He felt the blow graze his temple, and then with every ounce of strength that was left in him, he swung his right to the point of the stonemason's jaw.

It was not till he beheld his opponent lying insensible on the pavement that Wainwright realized that three spectators had been watching the fight. They were three other men from the mason's yard, and they might have been there all the time for all he knew. They ran up, and one said:

'Bravo, lad, you're a bonny fighter. My God! You've knocked out old Jim Stroud!'

They seemed immensely impressed by the fact, and quite indifferent to the cause of the quarrel. On Wharfside men often fight for the sake of fighting.

Two of them propped Jim up and bathed his face.

'You put him to sleep a treat,' said one. 'He'll be all right in half an hour. What's your name, lad?'

'Plinth.'

'Plinth! That's a funny name. You ought to be a stonemason.'

'Plinth' bathed his face and staggered home. He was feeling very groggy. He managed to stagger to bed. He stayed there for three days, telling his forlorn landlady that he had been in a cab accident. She said: 'Reely! How awful!' but took no further interest in the matter. All night he was in a mild fever, going over every incident of the fight. He was obsessed by one fantastic whim. He wished Emma had been there to see it!

He had done it for her, fought for her, proved that in the end he was more of a man than her man. It was only right she should have beheld his triumph. Besides, it might have made all the difference. This man had no more legal claim on her than he had. She was only frightened of him. She was attracted by certain virile qualities in him, and somehow Wainwright had not so far impressed her in that way. And yet, God in Heaven! what did she think? Were all women enigmas?

Come what may, nothing would ever be quite the same after this. When he got about again he avoided Kensington Gardens and their other favourite haunts.

'She must send for me,' he thought autocratically.

Ten days went by, and he was becoming anxious.

And then one morning there arrived by post a scrawled note.

> Meet me to-morrow night at the lane by Potter's Wharf at nine o'clock. E.

A quiet sense of triumph stole over him. She had had to write after all. He had asserted his position as the dynamic male. Probably she had heard of his victory and his courage. Now everything would become gradually different. He spent the day calmly at his work, the *Charles II Doorways* being nearly complete.

At half-past eight he left home. He knew Potter's Wharf well. The little winding lane at the back was a popular rendezvous of theirs. There were some quiet seats near there underneath a clump of willows by the riverside. It was a favourite resort of Hammersmith lovers. It was getting dark as he crossed the bridge, but the sky was clear and the air warm with the breath of early summer. A glorious evening for lovers. He hummed to himself as he took the first turning in Potter's Lane.

And then the thing happened with dramatic suddenness. There was a sharp bend by the wall and an open piece of land stretching to the water-side. As he swung round the corner, four figures closed on him. They were in khaki. A red-faced sergeant said:

'This is the young man we want. You're under arrest, Mr Plinth or Wainwright or whatever you call yourself. Fall in, son.'

For a fraction of a second the world seemed to rock, his heart beat with sickening fear, the colour left his lips. Then he looked up. Some gulls went screaming into the evening sky, the great river still glided to the wastes. All was movement, and betokened a world of invisible activities. Low against a wall a girl was crouching, a girl with grey watchful eyes, the only person who knew, the only one he had ever told that he was a deserter. The evening star glimmered above the bridge in a sky that appeared too light and fragile to hold so precious a diadem. He looked round at the men, then pulling himself up, he faced about and said quietly:

'All right, Sergeant. I'm ready.'

—x—

The Landlord of 'The Love-a-Duck'

I FORGET THE NAME of the wag in our town who first called him Mr Seldom Right, but the name caught on. His proper name was James Selden Wright, and the inference of this obvious misnomer was too good to drop. James was invariably wrong, but so lavishly, outrageously, magnificently wrong that he invariably carried the thing through with flying colours. He was a kind of Tartarin of Tibbelsford, which was the name of the town.

Everything about Mr Seldom Right was big, impressive, expansive. He himself was an enormous person, with fat, puffy cheeks with no determinate line between them and his innumerable chins. His large grey eyes with their tiny pupils seemed to embrace the whole universe in a glance. Upon his pendulous front there dangled thick gold chains with signets and seals like miniature flat-irons. His fingers were ribbed with gold bands like curtain-rings. His wife was big; his daughter was big; the great shire horses which worked on his adjoining farm seemed quite normal creatures in this Gargantuan scheme of things.

Above all, 'The Love-a-Duck' was big. It appeared to dominate the town. It was built at the top of the hill, with great rambling corridors, bars, coffee-rooms, dilapidated ballrooms, staircases of creaking deal, bedrooms where a four-post bed was difficult to find, a cobbled courtyard with a covered entrance drive where two brewer's drays could have driven through abreast. There was no social function, no town council, no committee of importance that was not driven to meet at 'The Love-a-Duck'. But the biggest thing in Tibbelsford was the voice of the landlord. At night amidst the glittering taps and tankards he would 'preside'. By this you must understand that the word be taken liberally. He was no ordinary potman to hand mugs of ale across the bar to thirsty carters, or nips of gin to thin-lipped clerks. He would not appear till the evening was well advanced, and then he would stroll in and lean against the bar, his sleepy eyes adjusting the various phenomena of this perspective to a comfortable focus.

And then the old cronies and characters of Tibbelsford would touch their hats and say:

''Evening, Mr Wright!' And he would nod gravely, like an Emperor receiving the fealty of his serfs. And a stranger might whisper:

'Who is this fat old guy?'

And the answer would be 'H'sh!' for the eyes of Mr Seldom Right missed nothing. Bumptious strangers were treated with complete indifference. If they addressed him, he looked right through them, and breathed heavily. But for the cronies and characters there was a finely-adjusted scale of treatment, a subtle under-current of masonry. To get into favour with Mr Seldom Right one had to work one's way up and any bad mistake would land one back among the strangers. In which case one would be served fairly and squarely, but there the matter would end. For it should be stated at this point that everything about 'The Love-a-Duck' was good in quality, and lavish in quantity, and the rooms, in spite of their great size, were always spotlessly clean.

Having carefully considered the relative values of this human panorama, the landlord would single out some individual fortunate enough to catch his momentary favour, and in a voice which seemed to make the glasses tremble and the little Chelsea figures on the high mantel-shelf gasp with surprise, he would exclaim:

'Well, Mr Topsmith, and how are we? Right on the top o' life? Full of beans, bone, blood and benevolence, eh? Ha, ha, ha!'

And the laugh would clatter among the tankards, twist the gas-bracket, go rolling down the corridor, and make the dogs bark in the kennels beyond the stables. And Mr Topsmith would naturally blush, and spill his beer, and say:

'Oh, thank you, sir, nothin' to grumble about; pretty good goin' altogether.'

'That's right! that's RIGHT!'

There were plenty of waitresses and attendants at 'The Love-a-Duck', but however busy the bars might be, the landlord himself always dined with his wife and daughter, at seven-thirty precisely, in the oblong parlour at the back of the saloon bar. And they dined simply and prodigiously. A large steaming leg of mutton would be carried in, and in twenty minutes' time would return a forlorn white fragment of bone. Great dishes of fried potatoes, cabbages, and marrow, would all vanish. A stilton cheese would come back like an over-explored ruin of some ancient Assyrian town. And Mine Host would mellow these simple delicacies with three or four tankards of old ale. Occasionally some of the cronies and characters were invited to join the repast, but whoever was there, the shouts and laughter of the landlord rang out above everything, only seconded by the breezy giggles of Mrs Wright, whose voice would be constantly heard exclaiming:

'Oh, Jim, you are a fule!'

It was when the dinner was finished that the landlord emerged into the president. He produced a long churchwarden and ambled hither and thither with a pompous, benevolent, consciously proprietary air. The somewhat stilted formality of his first appearance expanded into a genial but autocratic courtliness. He was an Edwardian of Edwardians. He could be surprisingly gracious, tactful and charming, and he also had that Hanoverian faculty of seeing right through one—a perfectly crushing mannerism.

By slow degrees he would gently shepherd his favourite flock around the fire in the large bar parlour, decorated with stags' heads, pewter and old Chelsea. Then he would settle himself in the corner of the inglenook by the right side of the fire. Perhaps at this time I may be allowed to enumerate a few of the unbreakable rules which the novice had to learn by degrees. They were as follows:

You must always address the landlord as 'sir'.

You must never interrupt him in the course of a story.

You must never appear to disbelieve him.

You must never tell a bigger lie than he has just told.

If he offers you a drink you must accept it.

You must never, under any circumstances, offer to stand him a drink in return.

You may ask his opinion about anything, but never any question about his personal affairs.

You may disagree with him, but you must not let him think that you're not taking him seriously.

You must not get drunk.

These were the broad, abstract rules. There were other bye-laws and covenants allowing for variable degrees of interpretation. That, for instance, which governed the improper story. A story could be suggestive but must never be flagrantly vulgar or profane. Also one might have had enough to drink to make one garrulous, but not enough to be boisterous, or maudlin, or even over-familiar.

I have stated that the quality of fare supplied at 'The Love-a-Duck' was excellent; and so it was. Beyond that, however, our landlord had his own special reserves. There was a little closet just off the central bar where on occasions he would suddenly disappear, and when in the humour produce some special bottle of old port or liqueur. He would come toddling with it back to his seat and exclaim:

'Gentlemen, this is the birthday of Her Imperial Highness the Princess Eulalie of Spain. I must ask you to drink her good health and prosperity!'

And the bar, who had never heard of the Princess Eulalie of Spain, would naturally do so with acclamation.

Over the little glasses he would tell most impressive and incredible stories. He had hunted lions with the King of Abyssinia. He had dined with the Czar of Russia. He had been a drummer-boy during the North and South war in America. He had travelled all over Africa, Spain, India, China and Japan. There was no crowned head in either of the hemispheres with whom he was not familiar. He knew everything there was to know about diamonds, oil, finance, horses, politics, Eastern religions, ratting, dogs, geology, women, political economy, tobacco, corn, or rubber. He was a prolific talker, but he did not object to listening, and he enjoyed an argument. In every way he was a difficult man to place. Perhaps in thinking of him one was apt not to make due allowance for the rather drab background against which his personality stood out so vividly. One must first visualise the company of 'The Love-a-Duck'.

There was old Hargreaves, the local estate agent: a snuffy, gingery, pinched old ruffian, with a pretty bar-side manner, an infinite capacity for listening politely: one whose nature had been completely bowdlerised by years of showing unlikely tenants over empty houses, and keeping cheerful in draughty passages. There was Mr Bean, the corn-merchant, with a polished red-blue face and no voice. He would sit leaning forward on a thin gold-knobbed cane, and as the evening advanced he seemed to melt into one vast ingratiating smile. One dreaded every moment that the stick would give way and that he would fall forward on his face. There was an argumentative chemist, whose name I have forgotten; he was a keen-faced man, and he wore gold-rimmed spectacles which made him look much cleverer than he really was. There was old Phene Sparfitt. Nobody knew how he lived. He was very old, much too old to be allowed out at night, but quite the most regular and persistent customer. He drank quantities of gin-and-water, his lower lip was always moist, and he professed an intimate knowledge of the life of birds. Dick Toom, the owner of the local livery stables, was a spasmodic visitor. He generally came accompanied by several horsey-looking gentlemen. He always talked breezily about some distressing illness he was suffering from, and would want to make a bet with anyone present about some quite ridiculous proposition: for instance that the distance from the cross-roads to the stone wall by Jenkins' black-pig farm was greater than the distance from the fountain in the middle of Piccadilly Circus to the tube station in Dover Street. A great number of these bets took place in the bar, and the fact that the landlord always lost was one of the reasons of his nickname.

It cannot be said that the general standard of intelligence reached a very high level, and against it, it was difficult to tell quite how intelligent the landlord was. If he were not a well-educated man he certainly had more than a veneer of education. In an argument he was seldom extended. Sometimes he talked brilliantly for a moment, and then seemed to talk out of his hat. He had an extravagant, theatrical way of suddenly declaiming a statement, and then sinking his voice and repeating it. Sometimes he would be moodish and not talk at all. But at his best he was very good company.

It would be idle to pretend that the frequenters of the bar believed the landlord's stories. On the contrary, I'm afraid we were a very sceptical lot. Most of us had never been farther than London or the seaside, and our imagination shied at episodes in Rajahs' palaces and receptions in Spanish courts. It became a byword in the town: 'Have you heard old Seldom Right's latest?' Nevertheless he was extremely popular. At the time of which I write the landlord must have been well over sixty years of age, and his wife was possibly forty-five. They appeared to be an extremely happy and united family.

And then Septimus Stourway appeared on the scene.

He was an acid, angular, middle-aged man, with sharp features, a heavy black moustache, and eyes too close together. He was a chartered accountant, and he came to the town to audit the books of a large brewery nearby, and one or two other concerns. He brought his wife and his son, who was eleven years old. He was a man whom everybody disliked from the very beginning. He was probably clever at his job, quick thinking, self-opinionated, precise, argumentative, aggressively assertive and altogether objectionable.

The very first occasion on which he visited 'The Love-a-Duck' he broke every rule of the masonic ring except the one which concerned getting drunk. The company was in session under its president, and he bounced into the circle and joined in the conversation. He interrupted the landlord in the middle of a story, and plainly hinted that he didn't believe him. He called him 'old chap', and offered to stand him a drink. He then told a long, boring story about some obscure episode in his own life. The effect of this intrusion was that the landlord, who never replied to him at all, rose heavily from his seat and disappeared. The rest of the company tried to show by their chilling unresponsiveness that they disapproved of him. But Mr Stourway was not the kind of person to be sensitive to this. He rattled on, occasionally taking tiny sips of his brandy-and-water. He even had the audacity to ask old Hargreaves who the fat disagreeable old buffer was! And poor old Hargreaves was so upset that he nearly cried. He could only murmur feebly:

'He's the landlord.'

'H'm! a nice sort of landlord! Now I know a landlord at—'

The company gradually melted away and left the stranger to sip his brandy-and-water alone.

Everybody hoped, of course, that this first visit would also be the last. But oh, no! The next evening, at the same time, in bounced Mr Septimus Stourway, quite uncrushed.

Again the landlord disappeared, and the company melted away. The third night some of them tried snubbing him and being rude, but it had no effect at all. At every attempt of this sort he merely laughed in his empty way, and exclaimed:

'My dear fellow, just listen to me—'

Before a week was out Mr Septimus Stourway began to get on the nerves of the town. He swaggered about the streets as though he was doing us a great honour by being there at all. His wife and son were also seen. His wife was a tall, vinegary looking woman in a semi-fashionable, semi-sporting get-up. She wore a monocle and a short skirt, and carried a cane. The boy was a spectacled, round-shouldered, unattractive-looking youth, more like the mother than the father in appearance. He never seemed to leave his mother's side for an instant.

It appeared that his name was Nick, and that he was the most remarkable boy for his age who had ever lived. He knew Latin, and Greek, and French, and history, and mathematics, and philosophy, and science. Also he had a beautiful nature. Mr Stourway spent hours boring anyone he could get to listen with the narration of his son's marvellous attributes. If the *habitués* of 'The Love-a-Duck' tired of Mr Stourway, they became thoroughly fed up with his son.

It was on the following Wednesday evening that the dramatic incident happened in the bar-parlour of the famous inn. The landlord had continued his attitude of utter indifference to the interloper. He had been just as cheerful and entertaining, only when Mr Stourway entered the bar he simply dried up. But during the last two days he appeared to be thinking abstractedly about something. He was annoyed.

On this Wednesday evening the usual company had again assembled, and the landlord appeared anxious to resume his former position of genial host, when in came Mr Septimus Stourway again. He had not been in the previous evening, and everyone was hoping that at last he had realised that he was not wanted. Up rose the landlord at once, and went away. There was an almost uncontrolled groan from the rest. Mr Stourway took his seat, and began to talk affably.

It was then observed that the landlord, instead of going right away, was hovering about behind the bar. I don't know how the conversation got round to poetry, but after a time Mr Stourway started talking about his son's marvellous memory for poetry.

'That boy of mine, you know,' he said, 'he would simply astound you. He remembers everything. The poetry he's learnt off by heart! Miles and miles of it! I don't suppose there's another boy of his age in the country who could quote half as much.'

It was then that the bombshell fell. The landlord was leaning across the bar, and suddenly his enormous voice rang out:

'I'll bet you five pounds to one that I know a little boy of five who could quote twice as much poetry as your son!'

There was a dead silence, and everybody looked from the landlord to Mr Stourway. That gentleman grinned superciliously, then he rubbed his hands together and said:

'Well, well, that's interesting. I can't believe it. My son's eleven. A boy of five? Ha, ha! I'd like to get a wager like that!'

The landlord's voice, louder than ever, exclaimed:

'I'll bet you a hundred pounds to five!'

Mr Stourway looked slightly alarmed, but his eyes glittered.

'A hundred pounds to five! I'm not a betting man, but, by God! I'll take that.'

'Is your son shy?'

'Oh, no, he enjoys reciting poetry.'

'Would he come here and have an open competition?'

'H'm. Well, well, I don't know. He might. I should have to ask his mother. Who is this wonderful boy you speak of?'

'My nephew over at Chagham. They could drive him over in the dogcart.'

It need hardly be said that the members of 'The Love-a-Duck' fraternity were worked up to a great state of excitement over this sudden challenge. What did it all mean? No one knew that old Seldom Right had any relatives in the country. But then he was always such a secretive old boy about his own affairs. Could a little boy of five possibly remember and repeat more poetry—twice as much!—than this phenomenal Nick Stourway? How was it all to be arranged?

It became evident, however, that the landlord was very much in earnest. He had apparently thought out all the details. It should be an open competition. It could take place in the ballroom of the hotel. The two boys should stand on the platform with their parents, and should recite poems or blank verse in turn. A small committee of judges should count the lines. When one had exhausted his complete répertoire the other, of course, would have won; but it would be necessary for Stephen—that was the name of old Wright's nephew—to go on for double the number of lines that Nick had spoken to win the wager for his uncle.

When it was first put to him Mr Stourway looked startled, but on going into the details he soon became eager. It was the easiest way of making a hundred pounds he had ever encountered. Of course the little boy might be clever and have a good memory, but that he could possibly recite *twice* as much as the wonderful Nick was unthinkable. Moreover his back was up, and he hated the landlord. He knew that he snubbed him on every occasion, and this would be an opportunity to score. There was just the mild risk of losing a fiver, and his wife to be talked over, but—he thought he could persuade her. The rumour of the competition spread like wildfire all over the town.

It was not only the chief topic of conversation at 'The Love-a-Duck' but at all places where men met and talked. It cannot be denied that a considerable number of bets were made. Mr Seldom Right's tremendous optimism found him many supporters, but the great odds and the fact that he invariably lost in wagers of this sort drove many into the opposing camp of backers.

A committee of ways and means was appointed the following night after Mrs Septimus Stourway had given her consent and Nick had signified his willingness to display his histrionic abilities to a crowd of admirers.

Old Hargreaves, Mr Bean, and a schoolmaster named McFarlane were appointed the judges. The ballroom was to be open to anyone, and there was to be no charge for admission. The date of the competition was fixed for the following Saturday afternoon, at five o'clock.

I must now apologise for intruding my own personality into this narrative. I would rather not do so, but it is inevitable. It is true my part in the proceedings was only that of a spectator, but from your point of view—and from mine—it was an exceedingly important part. I must begin with the obvious confession that I had visited 'The Love-a-Duck' on occasions, and that is the kind of adventure that one naturally doesn't make too much of. Nevertheless I can say with a clear conscience that I was not one of the inner ring. I had so far only made the most tentative efforts to get into the good graces of the landlord. But everyone in Tibbelsford was talking of the forthcoming remarkable competition, and I naturally made a point of turning up in good time.

I managed to get a seat in the fourth row, and I was very fortunate, for the ballroom was packed, and a more remarkable competition I have never attended. The three judges sat in the front row, facing the platform. The Stourway party occupied the right side of the platform and the Wrights the left. The landlord sat with his party, but in the centre, so that he could act as a kind of chairman. He appeared to be in high good-humour, and he came on first and made a few facetious remarks before the performance began. In the first place, he apologised for the lighting. It was certainly very bad. There originally had been footlights, but it was so long since they had been used that they were out of repair. The large room was only lighted by a gas chandelier in the centre, so that the stage was somewhat dim, but, as he explained, this would only help to obscure the blushes of the performers when they received the plaudits of such a distinguished gathering.

The Stourway party entered first. They came in from a door at the back of the platform, Mr Stourway noisily nonchalant, talking to everyone at random, in a tail-coat, with grey spats; his wife in a sports skirt and a small hat, looking rather bored and disgusted; and the boy in an Eton jacket and collar with a bunchy tie, and his hair neatly brushed. He looked very much at home and confident. It was obvious that he was out to enjoy himself. Numerous prize-distributions at which he had played a conspicuous part had evidently inured him to such an ordeal.

And then the other party entered, and the proceedings seemed likely to end before they had begun. Mrs Wright came on first, followed by a lady dressed in black, leading a most diminutive boy. They only reached the door when apparently the sight of the large audience frightened the small person, and he began to cry. The landlord and his wife rushed up and with the mother tried to encourage him, and after a few minutes they succeeded in doing so. The lady in black, however—who was presumably the widowed mother—picked him up and carried him in and sat him on her knee.

The audience became keenly excited, and everyone was laughing and discussing whether the affair would materialize or not. At length they seemed to be arranged, and the landlord came forward and said:

'Ladies and gentlemen, allow me to introduce you to

the competitors—Master Nick Stourway, Master Stephen Wright. Good gracious! It sounds as though I were announcing the competitors in a prize-ring. But this is to be a very peaceful competition—at least, I hope so! I think you all know the particulars. We're simply going to enjoy ourselves aren't we, Nick? Aren't we, Stephen?'

Nick smiled indulgently, and said, 'Yes, sir.'

Stephen glanced up at him for a second, and then buried his face in his mother's lap.

'Well, well,' said the landlord, 'I will now call on Master Nick to open the ball.'

Master Nick was nothing loth. He stood up and bowed, and holding his right arm stiff, and twiddling a button of his waistcoat with his left, he declaimed in ringing tones:

> 'It was the schooner *Hesperus*
> That sailed the wintry sea;
> And the skipper had taken his little daughter
> To bear him company.'

There were twenty-two verses of this, of four lines each, and the audience were somewhat impatient, because they had not come there to hear Master Nick recite. They had come for the competition, and it was still an open question whether there would be any competition. They were anxiously watching Master Stephen. He spent most of the period of his rival's recitation of this long poem with his face buried in his mother's lap, in the dark corner of the platform. His mother stroked his hair and kept on whispering a word to him, and occasionally he would peer round at Nick and watch him for a few seconds; then he glanced at the audience, and immediately ducked out of sight again.

When Nick had finished, he bowed and sat down, and there was a mild round of applause. The judges consulted, and agreed that he had scored 88 lines.

Now, what was going to happen?

The small boy seemed to be shaking his head and stamping his feet, and his mother was talking to him. The landlord coughed. He was obviously a little nervous. He went over to the group and said in a cheerful voice:

'Now, Stephen, tell us a poem!'

A little piping voice said, 'No!' and there were all the wriggles and shakes of the recalcitrant youngster. Murmurs ran round the room, and a lot of people were laughing. The Stourway party was extremely amused. At length the landlord took a chair near him, and produced a long stick of barley-sugar.

'Now, Stephen,' he said, 'if you won't talk to these naughty people, tell me a poem. Tell me that beautiful "Hymn to Apollo" that you told me last winter.'

'The little boy looked up at him and grinned; then he looked at his mother. Her widow's veil covered the upper part of her face. She kissed him, and said:

'Go on, dear; tell Uncle Jim.'

There was a pause; the small boy looked up and down, and then, fixing his eyes solemnly on the landlord's face, he suddenly began in a queer little lisping voice:

'God of the golden bow,
  And of the golden lyre,
And of the golden hair,
  And of the golden fire;
    Charioteer
    Round the patient year,
  Where—where slept thine ire?'

It was a short poem, but its rendering was received with vociferous applause. There was going to be a competition, after all! People who had money at stake were laughing and slapping their legs, and people who hadn't were doing the same. Everyone was on the best of terms with each other. There was a certain amount of trouble with the judges, as they didn't know the poem, and they didn't grasp the length of the lines. Fortunately the schoolmaster had come armed with books, and after some discussion the poem was found to have been written by Keats, and Master Stephen was awarded thirty-six lines. He was cheered, clapped, and kissed by the landlord, and his aunt, and his mother.

Master Nick's reply to this was to recite 'The Pied Piper of Hamelin', a performance which bored everyone to tears, especially as he would persist in gesticulating and doing it in a manner as though he thought that the people had simply come to hear his performance. 'The Pied Piper of Hamelin' is 195 lines. This made his score 283.

The small boy was still very shy, and seemed disinclined to continue, but the landlord said:

'Now, come on, Stephen; I'm sure you remember some more beautiful poetry.' At last, to everyone's surprise, he began to lisp:

> 'Once more unto the breach, dear friends, once more—'

It was screamingly funny. He went right through the speech, and when he got to:

> 'Cry "God for Harry, England, and Saint George!"'

the applause was deafening. People were calling out, and some of the barrackers had to be rebuked by the landlord. King Henry's speech was only 35 lines, so Master Stephen's total was 71. Nick then retaliated with an appalling poem, which commenced:

> 'She stood at the bar of Justice,
> A creature wan and wild,
> In form too small for a woman,
> In feature too old for a child.'

Fortunately, it was not quite as long as the other two,

and only brought him 60 lines, making a total of 343.

Stephen, who seemed to be gaining a little more confidence and entering into the spirit of the thing, replied with Robert Herrick's 'Ode to a Daffodil', a charming little effort, although it only brought in 20 lines.

Master Nick now broke into Shakespeare, and let himself go on:

> 'Friends, Romans, countrymen, lend me your ears.'

He only did twenty-three lines, however, before he broke down and forgot. The committee had arranged for this. It was agreed that in the event of either competitor breaking down, he should still score the lines up to where he broke down, and at the end he should be allowed to quote odd lines, provided there were more than one.

At this point there was a very amusing incident. Master Stephen hesitated for some time, and then he began 'Friends, Romans, countrymen,' etc., and he went right through the same speech without a slip! It was the first distinct score for the landlord's party, and Master Stephen was credited with 128 lines. The scores, however, were still 366 to 219 in Nick's favour, and he proceeded to pile on the agony by reciting 'Beth Gelert'. However, at the end of the twelfth verse he again forgot, and only amassed 48 lines.

Balanced against his mother's knee, and looking unutterably solemn—as far as one could see in the dim light—and only occasionally glancing at the audience, Stephen then recited a charming poem by William Blake called 'Night', which also contained 48 lines.

Nick then collected 40 lines with 'Somebody's Darling', and as a contrast to this sentimental twaddle Stephen attempted Wordsworth's 'Ode on Intimations of Immortality'. Unfortunately it was his turn to break down, but not till he had notched 92 lines. It was quite a feature of the afternoon that whereas Nick's contributions for the most part were the utmost trash, Stephen only did good things.

It would perhaps be tedious to chronicle the full details of the poems attempted and the exact number of lines scored, although, as a matter of fact, at the time I did keep a careful record. But on that afternoon it did not appear tedious, except when Nick let himself go rather freely over some quite commonplace verse. Even then there was always the excitement as to whether he would break down. The audience indeed found it thrilling, and it became more and more exciting as it went on, for it became apparent that both boys were getting to the end of their tether. They both began to forget, and the judges were kept very busy, and the parents were as occupied as seconds in a prize-ring. It must have been nearly half-past six when Master Nick eventually gave out. He started odds and ends, and forgot, and his parents were pulled up for prompting. He collected a few odd lines, and amassed a total of 822, a very considerable amount for a boy of his age.

At this point he was leading by 106 lines. So for Stephen to win the wager for the landlord he would not only have to score that odd 106, but he would have to remember an additional 822 lines! And he already gave evidence of forgetting! There was a fresh burst of betting in odd parts of the hall, and Dick Toom was offering 10 to 1 against the landlord's *protégé* and not getting many takers. The great thing in his favour was that he seemed to have quite lost his nervousness. He was keen on the job, and he seemed to realise that it *was* a competition, and that he had got to do his utmost. The landlord's party were allowed to talk to him and to make suggestions, but not to prompt if he forgot. There was a short interval, in which milk and other drinks were handed round. The landlord had one of the other drinks, and then he said:

'Ladies and gentlemen, I'm going to ask your indulgence to be as quiet as possible. My small nephew has to recall

928 lines, to win the competition, and he is going to try to do it.'

The announcement was received with cheers. And then Stephen started again. He began excellently with Keats' 'Ode to a Nightingale', and scored 80 lines, and without any pause went on to Milton's 'L'Allegro', of which he delivered 126 lines before breaking down. He paused a little, and then did odds and ends of verses, some complete, and some not. Thomas Hood's 'Departure of Summer' (14 lines), Shelley's 'To Night' (35) and a song by Shelley commencing:

> 'Rarely, rarely comest thou
> Spirit of Delight!' (48 lines)

I will not enumerate all these poems, but he amassed altogether 378 lines in this way. Then he had another brief rest, and reverted once more to Shakespeare. In his little sing-song voice, without any attempt at dramatic expression, he reeled off 160 lines of the Balcony Scene from *Romeo and Juliet*; 96 lines of the scene between Hamlet and the Queen; 44 lines of the Brutus and Cassius quarrel; 31 of Jaques' speech on 'All the world's a stage'. It need hardly be said that by this time the good burghers of Tibbelsford were in a state of the wildest excitement.

The schoolmaster announced that Master Stephen had now scored 689 of the requite 928, so that he only wanted 240 more to win. Mr Stourway was biting his nails and looking green. Mrs Stourway looked as though she was disgusted with her husband for having brought her among these common people. Nick sneered superciliously.

But in the meantime, there was no question but that Master Stephen himself was getting distressed. His small voice was getting huskier and huskier, and tears seemed not far off. I heard Mrs Rusbridger, sitting behind me, remark:

'Poor little mite! I calls it a shime!'

It was also evident that he was getting seriously to the end of his quoting répertoire. He had no other long speeches. The landlord's party gathered round him and whispered. He tried again, short stanzas and odd verses, sometimes unfinished. He kept the schoolmaster very busy; but he blundered on. By these uncertain stages he managed to add another 127 lines; and then he suddenly brought off a veritable *tour de force*. It was quite uncanny. He quoted 109 lines of Spenser's *Faerie Queene*! The matter was quite unintelligible to the audience, and they were whispering to each other and asking what it was. When he broke down, the schoolmaster announced that it was quite in order, and that Master Stephen's total lines quoted now amounted to 1640, and therefore he only required four lines to win!

Even then the battle was apparently not over. Everyone was cheering and making such a noise that the small boy could not understand it, and he began crying. A lot of people in the audience were calling out 'Shame!' and there was all the appearance of a disturbance. The landlord's party were very occupied. It was several minutes before order was restored and then the landlord rapped on the table and called out 'Order! Order!'

He drank a glass of water, and there was dead silence. Stephen's mother held the little boy very tight, and smiled at him. At last, raising his voice for this last despairing effort, he declaimed quite loudly:

'Why all the Saints and Sages who discuss'd
   Of the two Worlds so wisely—they are thrust
Like foolish Prophets forth; their Words to Scorn
   Are scatter'd, and their Mouths are stopt with Dust.'

The cheers which greeted this triumphant climax were split by various disturbances, the most distressing coming from Stephen himself, for almost as he uttered the last word he gave a yell, and burst into sobs. And he sobbed, and sobbed, and sobbed. And his mother picked him up and rocked him, and the landlord and his wife did what they could. But it was quite hopeless. Stephen was finished. His mother picked him up and hurried out of the door at the back with him. The Stourway party melted away. There were no more speeches, but people crowded on to the platform, and a lot of the women wanted to just kiss Stephen before he went away; but Mrs Wright came back and said the poor child was very upset. She was afraid they ought not to have let him do it. His mother was putting him to bed in one of the rooms, and they were giving him some sal volatile. He would be all right soon. Of course it was a tremendous effort—such a tiny person, too!

Someone offered to go for the doctor, but Mrs Wright said they would see how he was, and if he wasn't better in half-an-hour's time they'd send over to Dr Winch.

Everyone was congratulating the landlord, and he was clasping hands and saying:

'A marvellous boy! a marvellous boy! I knew he would do it!'

The party gradually broke up.

I must now again revert to myself. I was enormously impressed by what I had seen and heard, and for the rest of the evening I could think of nothing else. After dinner I went out for a stroll. It was early March, and unseasonably cold. When I got down to the bridge, over which the high-road runs across the open country to Tisehurst, large snow-flakes were falling. I stood there for some time, looking at our dim little river, and thinking of the landlord and Stephen. And as I gazed around me I began to wonder what it was about the snow-flakes which seemed to dovetail with certain sub-conscious movements going on within me.

And suddenly a phrase leapt into my mind. It was:

'Rotten cotton gloves!'

Rotten cotton gloves! What was the connection? The snow, the mood, something about Stephen's voice quoting the *Faerie Queene*. Very slowly the thing began to unfold itself. And when I began to realise it all, I said to myself, 'Yes, my friend, it was the *Faerie Queene* which gave the show away. The rest might have been possible. You were getting rather hard put to it!' The snow was falling heavily. It was Christmas-time—good Lord! I did not like to think how long ago. Thirty years? Forty years? My sister and I at Drury Lane pantomime. 'Rotten cotton gloves!' Yes, that was it! I could remember nothing at all of the performance. But who was that great man they spoke of? The star attraction?—Some name like 'The Great Borodin', the world's most famous humorist and ventriloquist. We were very excited, Phyllis and I, very small people then, not, surely, much older than Stephen himself. I could not remember the great Borodin, but I remembered that one phrase. There was a small lay figure which said most amusing things. It was called—No, I have forgotten. It was dressed in an Eton suit and it wore rather dilapidated-looking white cotton gloves. And every now and then, in the middle of a dialogue or discourse it broke off, looked at its hands, and muttered:

'Rotten cotton gloves!'

It became a sort of catch-phrase in London in those days. On buses and trains people would murmur 'Rotten cotton gloves!' A certain vague something about the way that Stephen recited Spenser's *Faerie Queene*...Was it possible?

And then certain very definite aspects of the competition presented themselves to my mind's eye. It had all been very cleverly stage-managed. It must be observed that Stephen neither walked on nor walked off. He did not even stand. He hardly looked at the audience. And then the lighting was inexcusably bad. Even some of the lights in the central chandelier had unaccountably failed. And the landlord's party had chosen the darkest side of the stage. No one had spoken to the boy. No one had seen him arrive, and immediately after the competition he had gone straight to bed.

I tried to probe my memory for knowledge of 'The Great Borodin', but at eight or nine one does not take great interest in these details. I know there was something...I remember hearing my parents talking about it—some great scandal soon after I had seen him. He was disgraced, I am sure. I have a vague idea he was in some way well-connected. He was to marry a great lady, and then perhaps he eloped with a young barmaid? I cannot be certain. It was something like that. I know he disappeared from public life, for in after years, when people had been to similar performances, I had heard our parents say:

'Ah, but you should have seen "The Great Borodin".'

These memories, the peculiar thrill of the competition, the cold air, the lazy snow-flakes drifting hither and thither, all excited me. I walked on further and further into the country trying to piece it all together. I liked the landlord, and I shared the popular dislike of Mr Stourway.

After a time I returned, and making my way towards the north of the town, I started to walk quickly in the direction of 'The Love-a-Duck'. If I hurried I should be there ten minutes or so before closing time.

When I entered the large bar-parlour the place was very crowded. I met old Hargreaves by the door. I'm afraid a good many of the rules of the society had been broken that evening. Old Hargreaves was not the only one who had had quite enough liquid refreshment. Everybody was in high spirits, and they were still all talking about the competition. I met Mr Bean near the fireplace, and I said:

'Well, Mr Bean, and have you heard how the boy is?'

'Oh, ay,' he replied. 'He soon got all right. Mrs Wright says he were just a bit upset. He went off home not an hour since.'

'Did you see him?'

'Eh? Oh, no, I didn't see'm. Mrs Wright says he looked quite hisself.'

The landlord was moving ponderously up and down behind the bar. I thought he looked tired, and there were dark rims round his eyes. I moved up towards the bar, and he did not notice me. The noise of talking was so loud that one could speak in a normal voice without being heard. Everything had apparently gone off quite successfully. Mr Stourway had sent along his cheque for five pounds and it was not reckoned that he would ever show his face in 'The Love-a-Duck' again. I waited.

At last I noticed that the landlord was quite alone. He was leaning against the serving-hatch, flicking some crumbs from his waistcoat, as though waiting for the moment of release. I took my glass and sidled up to him. I leant forward as though to speak. He glanced at me, and inclined his head with a bored movement. When his ear was within a reasonable distance, I said quietly:

'Rotten cotton gloves!'

I shall never forget the expression on the face of the landlord as he slowly raised his head. I was conscious of being a pinpoint in a vast perspective. His large, rather colourless eyes appeared to sweep the whole room. They were moreover charged with a perfectly controlled expression of surprise, and a kind of uncontrolled lustre of ironic humour. I had a feeling that if he laughed it would be the end of all things. He did not laugh; he looked lugubriously right through my face, and breathed heavily. Then he swayed slightly from side to side, and looking at my hat, said:

'I've got some cherry-brandy here you'd like. You must have a glass, Mr—'

Now, I do not wish to appear to you either as a prig, a traitor, or a profiteer. I am indeed a very ordinary, perhaps over-human member of Tibbelsford society. If I have taken certain advantages of the landlord, you must at any rate give me the credit of being the only member of a large audience who had the right intuitions at the right moment. In all other respects you must acknowledge that I have treated him rather well.

In any case, I became prominent in the inner circle without undergoing the tortuous novitiateship of the casual stranger.

The landlord and I are the best of friends today, although we exchange no confidences. I can break all the rules of the masonic understanding without getting into trouble. Some of the others are amazed at the liberties I take.

And in these days, when licensing restrictions are so severe, when certain things are not to be got (officially), and when I see my friends stealing home to a bone-dry supper, I only have to creep into the bar of 'The Love-a-Duck' and whisper 'Rotten cotton gloves!' and lo! all these forbidden luxuries are placed at my disposal! Can you blame me?

I have said that we exchange no confidences, and indeed I feel that that would be going too far, taking too great an advantage of my position. There is only one small point I would love to clear up, and I dare not ask. Presuming my theory to be right about 'The Great Borodin'—which was he?

The landlord? Or the widow?

—*XI*—

The Grayles

HENRY COTTESBY GRAYLE was a publisher of architectural and archaeological books. He was a widower and lived with his son and two daughters in a small house to which was attached a studio and a large garden in the neighbourhood of Regent's Park.

At the time of which I write the Grayles had become the centre of a set of people of varying degrees of celebrity in the artistic and dramatic world and it is perhaps a little difficult to account for this. They were certainly a very devoted and likeable family, and the children called their father 'Harry'. One felt at once their innate kindness, and their loyal affection for each other, but the mentality of none of them was of a very high order, and I do not remember hearing any one of them express any particularly original or individual point of view. They were physically unattractive, having badly proportioned figures and they were all short sighted, both the girls, Wanda and Olivia (or 'Pan' as we called her) as well as the father wearing thick glasses. The son, Arthur, was less short-sighted, he only wore pince-nez for reading, but he was an awkward-looking chap with a head that seemed too heavy for his shoulders. To say that they were unselfish would be putting too mild a term to their dominant characteristic. I should imagine that they were one of the most elaborately unselfish families that ever existed. They carried this system of unselfishness to such a degree that it was always defeating its own end. For instance, Mr Grayle, who hated the East Coast, would get an idea into his head that the East Coast was good for the girls, so he would let fall a hint that he would like to go to the East Coast for his holidays. Now Wanda and Pan also hated the East Coast, and a doctor had told Pan that it was bad for her, but they would pretend that they loved the East Coast, and would not like to go anywhere else, because they secretly thought that their father wanted to go there. And Arthur would give up an invitation to go and stay with friends in Devonshire—a county that he adored—in order to enjoy the dubious benefits of the east wind, for the same reason. And so any member of the family hardly ever got what he or she really wanted, except the satisfaction of feeling that they had done the right thing. Perhaps one of the most attractive features of the Grayle establishment was the tennis court and garden. It was really an excellent court backed by a dark hedge on three sides, and the garden was remarkable for London, with a very alluring terrace just above the tennis court, where tea went on at sporadic intervals from four o'clock till half past six. The house was easy of access from any part of London, and it was very pleasant to pop in there in the afternoon and to be certain of finding people who were pleased to see one, and to play tennis and to talk. Besides there was always an element of surprise at the Grayles', one never knew whom one would meet. And then there were two extremely pretty girls, and great friends of Wanda and Pan. Their names were Toni and Mildred Sholt. They were actresses by profession, although they never by any chance seemed to have an engagement, except to play at special matinées for some society for the advancement of the Drama, but they were fluffy companionable girls. They seemed to know every member of the dramatic profession by some intimate nickname, and they were always bringing new people to the tennis court. They even brought two of the Russian dancers from Drury Lane one day, and Guy Haveling, the famous Comedian, who set everyone in roars of laughter by his antics when serving.

There seemed an endless procession of girls who were

Wanda and Pan's 'dearest friends', there were people who were just beginning to be talked about, architects, writers, musicians and Pagans of every description. In the winter, or when the weather was unpleasant in the summer, we used to go into the studio, and Wanda and Pan roasted chestnuts and we played most preposterous paper games, and talked. If the conversation at times became a little 'precious', it had the compensating advantage of being extremely naïve, and often engagingly personal. We were always talking about each others' characters, and fiercely criticizing each other behind our backs. This was not done in a spirit of tittle-tattle or malice. It was pure interest, and a love of analysis.

People began to refer to the 'Grayle set', but I am not sure that the Grayles themselves were the pivots of this set, though their garden and studio were undoubtedly its headquarters. I'm afraid many of us used to laugh about the Grayles even on their own court and in their own studio. In spite of the open house they kept, and the erratic company that enjoyed their hospitality, they had peculiar fussy little mannerisms. And they encouraged each other in these. There were certain things that had always been and consequently *had* to be. Arthur had to have porridge with his breakfast—although the others never touched it—and he had to have a tray of biscuits and anchovy paste and a glass of lime juice to take up to his bedroom at night. 'Harry' must not under any circumstances be disturbed between the hours of six thirty and seven thirty in the evening, which he spent alone in the room upstairs. Pan had to have a glass of hot milk at eleven fifteen every morning, and always scrambled eggs on toast for breakfast. Wanda would not touch tea if the milk had been put in first, and no one would dream of interfering with the tradition that gave her the right to take the rest of the family to three lectures at the Royal Society of Arts every year. She had at some remote period joined this Society, and although the lectures bored the whole family to death, they would come out chatting gaily, and persuade each other that the lecture was even more interesting than the last.

In fine, the family was intensely sentimental. They would not have acknowledged that, in fact they laughed at and scorned sentimentality as expressed in sentimental plays and stories. They simply did not realise that the only difference lay in the fact that they did not express it. Of course they all kissed each other, but they never gave expression to any extremely endearing or emotional terms. But they watched each other with a sort of furtively erotic zest, they pampered each others' whims, and silently studied and prophesied each others' desires. The girls would scheme together to forestall their father's and brother's wishes, and the father or brother would lie awake at night thinking how best to please the girls. One shuddered to think of the effect of the emotionalism of these good people if they had given it rein.

In addition to the people who came to tennis and tea and supper, there were invariably people staying in the house, cousins, and various deserving people working in obscure causes. I remember also that there was an American woman who was nearly always there. She rejoiced in the name of Florence Cheesewright Cannifer. She was not so formidable a person as her name might suggest, in fact she was delightful. She was broad—in every sense—she had broad shoulders and hips, and a broad low brow and deep set kind grey eyes. I could never quite locate her, she may have been some sort of relation. All the family kissed her (including Mr Grayle) and they called her 'Bee'. She was the sort of person that one kissed automatically. It always surprised me how badly all the Grayles played tennis, considering they played nearly every day in the summer and had done so for so long as anyone could remember. This may have been due largely to their defective eyesight. They were extremely good at indoor games, being very quick, and all having a mathematical sense. They had a most bewildering repertoire of games of all sorts, and they would sit in the studio with all the windows shut, and the air blue with tobacco smoke, and play games with frenzied excitement very often till two or three in the morning.

I need hardly tell you that all of us in the Grayle set were Socialists, at least when I say Socialists, I mean that we were people supremely discontented with existing social conditions, although this discontent manifested itself in different ways. Mr Grayle who was a little more inured to these social conditions, voted Liberal as a sort of compromise, but both the girls and Arthur belonged to some Socialist organisation in Gray's Inn, and pursued an active propaganda; the majority of us limited our activities to the point of sneering at Constitutions and monarchies, and politicians, and of adopting an attitude of extreme superiority to these mundane things.

When the War broke out, the news dropped like a bombshell into the security of our comfortable ideals. I knew that the Grayles, with their intense humanitarian instincts, and their hatred of cruelty in any form, would be upset; but I hardly expected them to be as affected as they were. On the evening when it was announced that England had declared war, I found the whole family in the studio with Florence Cheesewright Cannifer, and the Sholt girls and a sculptor named Rohan Lees who was supposed to be more or less engaged to Mildred Sholt. They were sitting round in a circle immersed in newspapers looking scared and tragic and what surprised me most—definitely angry.

'It's detestable!' Wanda was muttering.

'Disgusting patriotism!' Pan ejaculated.

Toni Sholt tried to be facetious but was hushed up, while Rohan Lees' occasional attempts to sing 'Land of Hope and Glory' in falsetto were received in chilling silence. It is true that later in the evening we tried to play a game called 'Ware Wilkins'. It was a poor game at its best, but on this evening it fell particularly flat. I forget the rules, but I remember that it was played with cards and just before you suspected someone of playing a certain card—I think it was the Queen of Diamonds—you had to call out 'Ware Wilkins' and then there were forfeits and so on. It was a game that Mr Grayle usually shone at, but on this occasion he was always at fault, which was deplorable, in as much as Wanda and Pan had obviously suggested the game to distract his mind. His mind was not distracted, and he only played because he imagined that the girls wanted to. The only member of the family who seemed at all reasonable about it all was Arthur, who confessed to me on the quiet that he was reserving his judgement, but at present he had to say that he could hardly see how Sir Edward Grey could have acted otherwise.

After that it became a sort of understood thing that the War was a subject not to be discussed in the Grayle family. It was avoided—like an unclean thing. Occasionally people would be brought who did not understand this and they would launch into discussions about the War, but they found themselves isolated, talking in detached groups and the conversation never became general.

Certain events which followed were precipitated by the oratory of a certain Mr Robson, who appeared at that time. I don't know where he came from or what his relationship was. He seemed to be a friend of Mr Grayle. He was an elderly man, with a sour lugubrious countenance and a stoop. He had lived on the East Coast of Africa for seven years, and had contracted some chronic internal trouble that doctors agreed was incurable, but he might live for a long time. He spoke with a deep booming voice like a park-keeper at closing time. He seemed quite out of his element at the Grayles, but indifferent to the fact. One got the idea that he would boom on in that voice, enunciating his unpalatable sophistries, in any climate or in any society. It made no difference to him if he were addressing a gang of coloured plate-layers on an African

Railway or a young ladies' school on the South Coast. The mere fact of us calling him *Mr* Robson showed that he was not one of us. He seemed like some vague impersonal force, against which all our most cherished ideas dashed in vain. One knew of course that the Grayle family thought about the War. In fact they thought about it too much, and they each secretly devoured the newspapers. With their quick intuitions and sympathies they suffered many of the horrors of the whole thing, only the ambition of each was that the others should not suffer these horrors. But Mr Robson had no such scruples. He boomed on about the War from morning to night. He might have been Hansard himself doomed to an eternal punishment of declaiming the redundant products of his volumes. Nothing could stop him, but occasionally some member of the family or their friends would flash bitingly across his path, and interject some facile argument. He would look at them with an expression of unutterable sadness like one who has lost the faculty of listening but who deplores any diversion to a prescribed idea, and would then continue from the point at which he was interrupted.

I remember Arthur telling me one day that any doubts he held that the War was in any way justifiable were entirely dispelled by listening to Mr Robson.

'I don't mean to say,' he said, 'that the English Government is any more culpable than the German, probably it's not. But there's not much to choose between them. Civilisation is rotten to the core. The whole thing has been worked by contractors, politicians, and wire pullers all over the World. This Robson represents the official mind. You can do nothing with it. It has no fluidity, no sympathy, no intelligence. It's just an atrophied organ.'

It was surprising therefore to hear Arthur that same evening break a lance with Mr Robson and even get angry with him, and he was vigorously seconded by Wanda and Pan, and in a more cold-blooded manner by Rohan Lees. No one could ever quite understand how Mildred

Sholt got engaged to Rohan Lees. He was a queer little chap, and looked rather dirty. He smoked about sixty cigarettes during the day, was a sort of Art madman. He did impressionist sculpture that no one could make head or tail of, and always suggested that his work was the sort of thing that Rodin was trying to do. For some reason or other Mr Robson fixed on Rohan, and suddenly asked him if he weren't going to join the Army, and do something for his King and Country. Now we all knew that if Rohan held any political views at all they were entirely anarchical, and we all laughed. But Rohan took the matter up, and said: 'I tell you what, Robson,' (he was the only one of us who didn't call him *Mr* Robson) 'I'm an outsider. I never *have* done anything conventional or fashionable, why should I? I don't care a damn about Society. They don't appreciate me or want me. Well, I mean to stick like it. When it's been fashionable to go grouse shooting, or go to bridge parties, or play golf, I've stopped at home and gone on with my work. Now it happens to be the thing to go out and do a bit of killing or being killed. Well, let those people who always have to do the right thing, keep on doing it. I'm going to remain unconventional.'

'Do you never consider what you owe to your country? Liberty, freedom—Power?'

'Yes,' interposed Pan, 'or slums, wretchedness, and disgraceful society inequality?'

'The social system,' continued Mr Robson, 'was not invented in a night by some fiend as some of you young people seem to think. It is the result of the steady growth of thousands of years, history, character, environment, the survival of the fittest.'

'Of the physically fittest,' said Wanda. 'It's no good, Mr Robson. Nothing can justify War. It's simply a return to the beast age.'

Florence Cheesewright Cannifer took pity on the poor man and told us we were not to bully him for being a patriot. 'It's natural to love one's country,' she said. We all agreed with her, but protested that one should not love one's country at the expense of other countries. The discussion took its normal course, that is to say, round in a circle without leading anywhere, when 'Harry' Grayle came in. I thought he looked tired, and I knew that as a matter of fact he was a little worried by a newspaper agitation for conscription. Of course he said nothing about this, but I noticed him looking narrowly at Arthur, and I believed he was summing up the physical attributes of his son, and wondering whether he would pass the Army doctor, if conscription were brought in. There was a little chap called Skinner who used to come and play tennis sometimes. I don't know what he was by profession. We used to call him 'Scaly Skinner'. I think because he used to get very hot, and his nose peeled in the summer. Directly the War broke out Scaly Skinner rushed off and joined something, and was made a Corporal. We were all very much amused about this, and often laughed about Corporal Scaly Skinner! When Mr Grayle came in on this evening, he told us quietly that he had just heard that 'Scaly Skinner' had been killed. I need hardly say that this news caused a profound impression. Pan, with genuine tears in her eyes, emphasized her view that the whole idea of War was more unspeakable and disgusting than ever, and we all felt that if Mr Robson said much more we should jump on him.

As a matter of fact, this gentleman said very little more, but he made one cryptic utterance, that was destined to have a far-reaching effect. He looked lugubriously round the studio and sighed, as though he had gathered the full complement of our idealistic thoughts and then his voice once more boomed forth in level tones.

'Do you ever realise that you are only allowed to have these ideas, and to express them, by virtue of the fact that men like your friend, Mr Scaly Skinner, are out at the Front fighting for you and giving their lives for you?'

There was an imperceptible pause, and then Mr Grayle,

glancing at his son, nodded and said—'That's very true.' I believe he glanced at Arthur apprehensively because he dreaded what effect this unarguable remark might have on his impressionable son.

He muttered, 'That's very true,' almost automatically because he realised that it *was* an abstract truth. It came out before he had had time to consider the effect. I saw Arthur catch his father's eye, and take in his pale, worried glance, and I know that in a flash he thought 'Father thinks I ought to join. He's too decent to say so, but he's a little ashamed of me.' Incidentally, too, he thought of Scaly Skinner. It seemed appalling to think of a chap like Scaly Skinner whom they had all despised, going out and fighting so that he (Arthur) should be safe at home, and free to express any views he liked.

I remember very little more of what was said that evening. I think Florence Cheesewright came to the rescue by talking about 'some dandy ponjee' she'd bought that afternoon at a store on Oxford Street. I know we didn't play any games and we broke up early.

My next intimation of a development in the matter came by way of a visit from Wanda two days later. She said she and Pan were in trouble. It was like this. They—the girls—had come to the conclusion that Arthur was worrying. They believed that he felt a call to join the Army. Of course he was much too unselfish to worry *them* about it, and they believed that he thought too much about their feelings. They didn't think he *would* join, simply because he knew how unhappy it would make them. It was very difficult for them. Of course they simply *loathed* the idea of his going, at the same time it would be selfish to impose their own feelings to such an extent that he acted against his own conscience and inclination.

I asked them what their father thought, but they said that he had not spoken, and they should not worry him about it, especially as there might be nothing in it. I said that if it would be satisfactory to them, I would sound Arthur and find out what he did think.

I tackled him the same evening, but he would only talk about Scaly Skinner. Mr Robson's remark about Scaly Skinner seemed to have bitten deep, but I believe he was really thinking more about his father's glance, and his acquiescence to Mr Robson's view. I could only report to Wanda that it *did* seem as though his conscience troubled him in the matter. After that the girls, I thought, behaved very splendidly. In an almost imperceptible manner they mollified their views. By gentle degrees they allowed that under certain circumstances War might be possibly justifiable, if honourably conducted. They listened more leniently to Mr Robson's diatribe, and took a more technical interest in the operations on hand. This change of view was not lost on Arthur. He thought 'The girls think I ought to go.' And Mr Grayle thought 'The girls think Arthur ought to join. It would be selfish of me to interpose.'

I do not want to dwell on the heartburnings that went on in the Grayle family up to that time when Arthur walked down one morning to a recruiting office in the Strand and offered himself as a private. I can only say that he joined the Army in the way that he went to the East Coast, because he somehow believed his family wished it. Everybody was tremendously surprised that Arthur was accepted, for he was the most unmilitary looking person you can imagine. But when it comes to a fine point, one found that there was nothing really radically wrong with him, and he was fairly wiry, and occasionally had camped out in August. He was sent first of all down to a place near Bedford and occasionally got a few days' leave. The atmosphere of the Grayles house seemed entirely altered. This was in October, so of course the garden was deserted, and the girls and 'Harry' seemed to prefer the drawing room or their bedroom to the studio. Mr Robson had taken his departure, as though his mission were fulfilled, and he were at liberty to scatter the seeds of his moribund philosophy in some other clime. Florence Cheesewright was still there and I must say that she was splendid all through that time, mothering the trembling fabrics of the Grayle family in turn. We never played games and the girls started their interminable knitting.

They always spoke of Arthur in cheerful voices, but they could not control their strained faces when one heard the cold rain driving down on the studio roof on the dark evenings. One instinctively thought of anchovy biscuits and lime juice, and wondered how Arthur was faring. When he came home on leave he looked surprisingly fit, and spoke cheerfully, though he told me on the quiet that 'it was damnable' and that 'he was heartily fed up with it'.

On those occasions we always held high revel, and played 'Ware Wilkins', or some such game in the studio and the Sholt girls came in and anyone else who got wind of it. I got the impression that the Grayle family did not desire tremendously to be alone on these occasions, I think they were a little afraid. It is so much easier to keep bright and gay when there are others about.

Arthur did not go till April, and I had the doubtful privilege of being present at his last leave. I must say candidly that it was awful. It was so horribly strained and unreal. We played games desperately and talked of most trivial things as though they were matters of tremendous moment. When it came time for Arthur to go, the only person who was allowed to cry was Florence Cannifer, and this she did right royally. He might have been going to post a letter for all the effusion there was between his family and himself. They pecked at each other as though they were kissing through a glass screen, and thought it rather amusing but impossible. Arthur said 'So long, Harry' to his father, and the latter said 'Bye-bye! have you packed that stuff for your feet?'

They watched him go furtively, hovering amongst each

other, and afraid to look at each others' faces. We went back to the drawing room after he had gone, and I talked to Mr Grayle about early French renaissance architecture and the girls encouraged me. I felt that it gave them power to look at their father's face. I admired old Grayle very much that evening, he controlled himself amazingly, for I believe he was much more upset than the girls. I wondered whether at night they all lay shivering apart, but they undoubtedly showed the traces of anxious dread upon their faces the next day.

Of course the very thing happened that one would expect to happen to a family nervously constituted like the Grayles, and it happened with dramatic suddenness. Arthur had been out there less than a month, and they had received three letters from him, all couched in cheery terms. He did not seem to have received any of the elaborate packages that had been sent, but he was apparently having the time of his life. And then one day the news came crashing across the horizon of three strained lives. Arthur was 'missing, believed killed'. This is perhaps the most disturbing news any family can receive, and the Grayles no longer pretended to ride serenely. They were terribly distraught, and Pan developed an illness which served the useful purpose of distracting the other two. It seemed she had been taking sleeping draughts, and had taken too much. Wanda and her father did not acknowledge that they also had been in the habit of taking sleeping draughts. But they nursed Pan assiduously, and Pan kept up her illness as long as possible, because she saw that it was doing the others good.

A week later a correction appeared in the official announcements. Previously 'missing, believed killed' should now read 'wounded, not missing':

MIDDLESUSSEX, 7th (T.F.): GRAYLE, 9093 A.G.

When I saw the face of old Mr Grayle reading this

correction I thought that the gods could not have chosen a more unfortunate victim for their unholy jest. He cried in front of the girls. Of course the matter only lasted inside a minute but it was the most terrible minute I ever lived through.

Then they all went to the War Office. They spent ten days there asking questions of most unlikely people, and making each other drink copious draughts of hot milk in an A.B.C. in Westminster Bridge Road. It was a time of great congestion, and they got no information till they heard that Arthur was back and in a hospital at Folkestone. The poor chap had been badly wounded and had lost his right leg below the knee and had a shrapnel wound in his back. I did not see the Grayles when the news of this arrived, they had all gone to Folkestone, and there they remained for three months till Arthur was well enough to be moved. But in the meantime more surprising news had arrived which was nothing less than that Arthur had received a D.S.O. or was it a D.C.M.? It was not in any case a V.C., but it was some high order given in recognition of conspicuous gallantry in face of the enemy!

The official story was that he held a section of a trench single handed, when all the other defenders had been killed or wounded, for seven hours, till reinforcements arrived, and thus saved an important position in the line.

I went down to Folkestone twice and saw Arthur when he was on the move again. He seemed quite cheerful, and they had fitted him up with a very nice artificial leg. He seemed disinclined to talk about his experiences, so I naturally avoided referring to the War. The family were living in rooms down there, and Mr Grayle came up to town twice a week to business. It was not till about two months later—when Arthur had been invalided out of the Army—and the family were once more back at the house in Regent's Park, that he gave me any intimation that he would care to talk. We were sitting in his room upstairs after dinner one evening, and finding him in the mood I asked him if he could tell me how he won his medal. He puffed at his pipe for a long time and then he said:

'Honestly my dear chap, I only have the vaguest notion. I knew I should be frightened, but I never thought it possible to have such a ghastly fear. When I first came under fire I was sick—actually physically sick... I don't remember a bit how long the whole thing lasted. I blazed away from the trench with my rifle whenever there was an excuse, it seemed to comfort me. One felt that one was looking out over the edge of creation and trying to keep back things that wanted to prove one had never lived. I was horribly frightened. Believe me, I wasn't thinking of the guv'nor or the girls, I was in a stark staring terror of death and damnation... For I felt that after this there could be nothing... it was just pre-neolithic, as though man had never been born, as though there was nothing... When night came I didn't believe it had ever been daylight. A shell struck the angle of our trench, four chaps were blown to nothing, a chap named Rettison—he was rather a cad as a matter of fact—he was smashed up near me... I felt his blood running over my boots. The trench was crumbling—honestly I went mad—There was a whole bunch of those damned little things you throw—you know 'grenades.' I picked them up one at a time and threw them about... I threw one at the dead body of Rettison—I felt I couldn't stand it there—if ever I saw anything move I flung a grenade. I denied God and I believe I foamed at the mouth. I may have thrown them at English or French or anyone—I should have thrown one at our Colonel if he had been there—perhaps I did—I had lost all cosmic sense... I was nothing—just a crumbling negation waiting for the earth to close up. And then something vital happened—I believe I dropped one of the damned things on my foot... I swung out into a darkness.'

Arthur coughed and rolled his pipe round in his

mouth. His lips were trembling in a peculiar way, and I said I thought I heard someone downstairs calling. I thought it better for us to go, so I took Arthur's arm, and we found them all in the drawing room. On a table there was the medal that Arthur had lately received from the King. They were looking at it as we came in, and they all looked round at us. There was a curiously strained moment, in which a jumble of emotions seemed to vibrate through the room. I did not know why this should be so, or how much of Arthur's story the others knew, but it was Florence Cheesewright's suave voice as usual, with its soothing upward inflection that seemed to relieve the tension.

'My! what a dandy ribbon!'

—XII—

An Adventure in Bed

THERE WAS SOMETHING ESSENTIALLY CHINESE about the appearance of George as he lay there propped up against the pillows. His large flabby face had an expression of complete detachment. His narrowing eyes regarded me with a fatalistic repose. Observing him, I felt that nothing mattered, nothing ever had mattered, and nothing ever would matter. And I was angry. Pale sunlight filtered through the curtains.

'Good Lord!' I exclaimed. 'Still in bed! Do you know it's nearly twelve o'clock?'

An almost inaudible sigh greeted my explosion.

George occupied the maisonette below me. Some fool of an uncle had left him a small private income, and he lived alone, attended by an old housekeeper. He did nothing, absolutely nothing at all, not even amuse himself, and whenever I went in to see him he was invariably in bed. There was nothing wrong with his health. It was sheer laziness. But not laziness of a negative kind, mark you, but the outcome of a calm and studied policy. I knew this, and it angered me the more.

'What would happen if the whole world went on like you?' I snapped.

He sighed again, and then replied in his thin, mellow voice: 'We should have a series of ideal states. There would be no wars, no crimes, no divorce, no competition, no greed, envy, hatred or malice.'

'Yes, and no food.'

He turned slightly on one side. His accents became mildly expostulating, the philosopher fretted by an ignorant child.

'How unreasonable you are, dear boy. How unthinking! The secret of life is complete immobility. The tortoise lives four hundred years; the fox terrier wears itself out in ten. Wild beasts, fishes, savages, and stockbrokers fight and struggle and eat each other up. The only place for a cultivated man is—bed. In bed he is supreme—the arbiter of his soul. His limbs and the vulgar carcase of his being constructed for purely material functioning are concealed.

His head rules him. He is the autocrat of the bolster, the gallant of fine linen, the master of complete relaxation. Believe me, there are a thousand tender attitudes of repose unknown to people like you. The four corners of a featherbed are an inexhaustible field of luxurious adventure. I have spent more than half my life in bed, and even now I have not explored all the delectable crannies and comforts that it holds for me.'

'No,' I sneered, 'and in the meantime other people have to work to keep you there.'

'That is not my fault. A well-ordered state should be a vast caravanserai of dormitories. Ninety-nine per cent of these activities you laud so extravagantly are gross and unnecessary. People should be made to stay in bed till they have found out something worth doing. Who wants telephones, and cinemas, and safety razors? All that civilisation has invented are vulgar luxuries and time-saving devices. And when they have saved the time, they don't know what to do with it. All that is required is bread, and wine, and fine linen. I—even I would not object to getting up for a few hours every week to help to produce these things.' He stroked the three weeks' growth on his chin, and smiled magnanimously. Then he continued:

'The world has yet to appreciate the real value of passivity. In a crude form the working classes have begun to scratch the edge of the surface. They have discovered the strike. Now, observe that the strike is the most powerful political weapon of the present day. It can accomplish nearly everything it requires, and yet it is a condition of immobility. So you see already that immobility may be more powerful than activity. But this is only the beginning. When the nations start going to bed, and stopping there, then civilisation will take a leap forward. You can do nothing with a man in bed—not even knock him down. My ambition is to form a League of Bedfellows. So that if one day some busybody or group of busybodies says: "We're going to war with France, or Germany, or America," we can reply, "Very well. Then I'm going to bed." Then, after a time, they would have to go to bed too. And they would eventually succumb to the gentle caresses of these sheets and eiderdowns. All their evil intentions would melt away. The world should be ruled not by Governments or Soviets, but by national dosshouses.'

He yawned, and I pulled up the blind.

'What about the good activities?' I replied. For a moment I thought I had stumped him, or that he was not going to deign to reply. Then the thin rumble of his voice reached me from across the sheets.

'What you call the good activities can all be performed in bed. That is to say, they can be substituted by a good immobility. The activities of man are essentially predatory. He has learnt nothing and forgotten nothing. He is a hunter and slayer and nothing else at all. All his activities are diversions of this instinct. Commerce is war, capital is a sword, labour is a stomach. Progress means either filling the stomach, or chopping someone else's head off with the sword. Science is an instrument that speeds up the execution. Politics is a game. Colonisation is straightforward daylight burglary.'

'I'm not going to waste my morning talking to a fool like you,' I said. 'But what about art, and beauty, and charity, and love?'

'In bed,' he mumbled. 'All in bed... They are all spiritual things. Bed is the place for them. Was Keats' "Ode to a Nightingale" any finer because he got up and wrote it down and sent it off to a fool of a publisher? Charity! Give a man a bed, and charity ceases to have any significance. Love! What a fool you are! Is a bed a less suitable place for love than a County Council tramcar?'

His voice died away above the coverlet. I was about to deliver a vitriolic tirade against his ridiculous theories, but I did not know where to begin, and before I had framed a suitable opening, the sound of gentle snoring reached me.

I record this conversation as faithfully as I can recollect because it will help you to share with me the sense of extreme surprise at certain events which followed, two months later. Of course George did occasionally get up. Sometimes he went for a gentle stroll in the afternoon, and he belonged to a club down town where he would go and dine in the evening. After dinner he would watch some of the men play billiards, but he invariably returned to his bed about ten o'clock. He never played any game himself, neither did he apparently write or receive letters. Occasionally he read in bed, but he never looked at a newspaper or a magazine. He once said to me that if you read the newspapers you might as well play golf, and the tremulous shiver of disgust in his voice when he uttered the word 'golf' is a thing I shall never forget.

I ask you, then, to imagine my amazement when, two months later, George shaved himself, got up to breakfast, reached a city office at nine o'clock, worked all day, and returned at seven in the evening. You will no doubt have a shrewd idea of the reason, and you are right. She was the prettiest little thing you can imagine, with chestnut hair and a solemn, babish pucker of the cheeks. She was as vital as he was turgid. Her name was Maisie Brand. I don't know how he met her, but Maisie, in addition to being pretty and in every way attractive, was a practical modern child. George's two hundred a year might be sufficient to keep him in bed, but it wasn't going to be enough to run a household on. Maisie had no use for this bed theory. She was a daughter of sunshine and fresh air, and frocks, and theatres, and social life. If George was to win her he must get up in the morning.

On the Sunday after this dramatic change I visited him in his bedroom. He was like a broken man. He groaned when he recognised me.

'I suppose you'll stop in bed all day today?' I remarked jauntily.

'I've got to get up this afternoon,' he growled. 'I've got to take her to a concert.'

'Well, how do you like work?' I asked.

'It's torture … agony, hell. It's awful. Fortunately, I found a fellow-sufferer. He works next to me. We take it in turn to have twenty-minute naps, while the other keeps watch.'

I laughed, and quoted: 'Custom lies upon us with a weight, heavy as frost and deep almost as night.' Then I added venomously: 'Well, I haven't any sympathy for you. It serves you right for the way you've gone on all these years.'

I thought he was asleep again, but at last his drowsy accents proclaimed:

'What a perfect fool you are! You always follow the line of least resistance.'

I laughed outright at that, and exclaimed: 'Well, if ever there was a case of the pot calling the kettle black!'

There was a long interval, during which I seemed to observe a slow, cumbrous movement in the bed. Doubtless he was exploring. When he spoke again, there was a faint tinge of animation in his voice.

'You are not capable, I suppose, of realising the danger of it all. You fool! Do you think I follow the line of least resistance in bed? Do you think I haven't often wanted to get up and do all those ridiculous things you and your kind indulge in? Can't you see what might happen? Suppose these dormant temptations were thoroughly aroused! Good God! It's awful to contemplate. Habit, you say? Yes, I know. I know quite well the risk I am running. Am I to sacrifice all the epic romance of this life between the sheets for the sordid round of petty actions you call life? I was a fool to get up that day. I had a premonition of danger when I awoke at dawn. I said to myself, "George, restrain yourself. Do not be deceived by the hollow sunlight. Above all things, keep clear of the park." But, like a fool, I betrayed my sacred trust. The premonitions which come to one in bed are always right. I got up. And now... My God! It's too late.'

Smothered sobs seemed to shake the bed.

'Well,' I said, 'if you feel like that about it; if you think more of your bed than of the girl, I should break it off. She won't be missing much.'

He suddenly sat up, and exclaimed:

'Don't you dare—'

Then he sank back on the pillow, and added dispassionately:

'There, you see, already the instinct of activity. A weak attitude. I could crush you more successfully with complete immobility. But these movements are already beginning. They shake me at every turn. Nothing is secure.'

Inwardly chuckling at his discomfiture, I left him.

* * *

During the months that followed I did not have the opportunities of studying George to the extent that I should have liked, as my work carried me to various parts of the country, but what opportunities I did have I found intriguing. He certainly improved in health. A slight colour tinged his cheeks. He seemed less puffy and turgid. His movements were still slow, but they were more deliberate than of old. His clothes were neat and brushed. The girl was delightful. She came up and chatted with me, and we became great friends. She talked to me quite frankly about George. She laughed about his passion for bed, but declared she meant to knock all that sort of thing out of him. She was going to thoroughly wake him up. She said laughingly that she thought it was perfectly disgusting the way he had been living. I used to try and visualise George making love to her, but somehow the picture would never seem convincing. I do not think it could have been a very passionate affair. Passion was the last thing you would associate with George. I used to watch them walking down the street, the girl slim and vivid, swinging along with broad strides, George, rather flustered and disturbed, pottering along by her side, like a performing bear that is being led away from its bun. He did not appear to look at her, and when she addressed him vivaciously, he bent forward his head and held his large ear close to her head. It was as though he was timid of her vitality.

At first this spectacle amused me, but after a time it produced in me another feeling altogether.

'This girl is being thrown away on him. It's horrible. She's much too good for George.'

And when I was away I was constantly thinking of her, and dreading the day of the wedding, praying that something would happen to prevent it. But to my deep concern nothing did happen to prevent it, and they were duly married the following April. They went for a short honeymoon to Brittany, and then returned and occupied George's old maisonette below me. The day after their return I had to face a disturbing realisation. I was falling hopelessly in love with Maisie myself. I could not think of George or take any interest in him. I was always thinking of her. Her face haunted me. Her charm and beauty, and the pathos of her position, gripped me. I made up my mind that the only thing to do was to go away. I went to Scotland, and on my return took a small flat in another part of London. I wrote to George and gave him my address, and wished him all possible luck. I said I hoped 'some day' to pay them a visit, but if at any time I could be of service, would he let me know.

I cannot describe to you the anguish I experienced during the following twelve months. I saw nothing of George or Maisie at all, but the girl was ever present in my thoughts. I could not work. I lived in a state of feverish restlessness. Time and again I was on the point of breaking my resolve, but I managed to keep myself in hand.

It was in the following June that I met Maisie herself walking down Regent Street. She looked pale and worried. Dark rings encircled her eyes. She gave a little gasp when she saw me, and clutched my hand. I tried to be formal, but she was obviously labouring under some tense emotion.

'My flat is in Baker Street,' I said. 'Will you come and visit me?'

She answered huskily, 'Yes, I will come tomorrow afternoon. Thank you.'

She slipped away in the crowd. I spent a sleepless night. What had happened? Of course I could see it all. George had gone back to bed. Having once secured her, his efforts had gradually flagged. He had probably left his business—or been sacked—and spent the day sleeping. The poor girl was probably living a life of loneliness and utter poverty. What was I to do? All day long I paced up and down my flat. I dreaded that she might not come. It was just after four that the bell went. I hastened to answer it myself. It was she. I led her into the sitting room, and tried to be formal and casual. I made some tea and chatted impersonally about the weather and the news of the day. She hardly answered me. Suddenly she buried her face in her hands, and broke into tears. I sprang to her and patted her shoulder.

'There, there,' I said. 'What is it? Tell me all about it, Maisie.'

'I can't live with him! I can't live with him any longer!' she sobbed.

I must acknowledge that my heart gave a violent bump,

not entirely occasioned by contrition. I murmured as sympathetically as I could, but with prophetic assurance:

'He's gone back to bed.'

'Oh, no, no,' she managed to stammer. It's not that. It's just the opposite.'

'Just the opposite?'

'He's so restless, so exhausting. Oh, dear! Yes, please, Mr Wargrave, give me a cup of tea, and I will tell you all about it.'

For a moment I wondered whether the poor girl's mental balance had been upset. I poured her out the tea in silence. George restless! George exhausting! Whatever did she mean? She sipped the tea meditatively; then she dabbed her beautiful eyes, and told me the following remarkable story:

'It was all right at first, Mr Wargrave. We were quite happy. He was still—you know, very lazy, very sleepy. It all came about gradually. Every week, however, he seemed to get a little more active and vital. He began to sleep shorter hours and work longer. He liked to be entertained in the evening or to go to a theatre. On Sunday he would go for quite long walks. It went on like that for months. Then they raised his position in the firm. He seemed to open out. It was as though during all those years he had spent in bed he had been hoarding up remarkable stores of energy. And suddenly some demon of restlessness got possession of him. He began to work frenziedly. At first he was pleasant to me; then he became so busy he completely ignored me. At the end of six months they made him manager of a big engineering works at Walham Green. One of the directors, a Mr Sturge, said to me one day, "That husband of yours is a remarkable man. He is the most efficient and forceful person we have ever employed. What has he been doing all these years? Why haven't we heard of him before?" He would get up at six in the morning, have a cold bath, and study for two hours before he went off to work. He would work all day, like a fury.

They say he was a perfect slave driver in the works. Only last week he sacked a man for taking a nap five minutes over his lunch hour. He would get home about eight o'clock, have a hurried dinner, and then insist on going to the opera or playing bridge. When we got back he would read till two or three in the morning. Oh, Mr Wargrave, he has got worse and worse. He never sleeps at all. He terrifies me. On Sunday it is just the same. He works all the morning. After lunch he motors out to Northwood, and plays eighteen holes before tea, and eighteen after.'

'What!' I exclaimed. 'Golf!'

'Golf, and science, and organisation are his manias. They say he's invented some wonderful labour-saving appliances on the plant, and he's planning all kinds of future activities. The business at the firm is increasing enormously. They pay him well, but he still persists in living in that maisonette. He says he's too busy to move.'

'Is he cruel to you?'

'If complete indifference and neglect is cruelty, he is most certainly cruel. Sometimes he gives me a most curious look, as though he hated me, and yet he can't account for me. He allows me no intimacy of any sort. If I plead with him he doesn't answer. I believe he holds me responsible for all these dormant powers which have got loose and which he cannot now control. I do not think his work gives him any satisfaction. It is as though he were driven on by some blind force. Oh, Mr Wargrave, I can't go on. It is killing me. I must run away and leave him.'

'Maisie!' I murmured, and I took her hand.

The immediate subsequent proceedings are not perhaps entirely necessary to record in relating this story, which is essentially George's story. The story of Maisie and myself could comfortably fill a stout volume, but as it concerns two quite unremarkable people, who were just human and workaday I do not expect that you would be interested to read it. In any case, we have no intention of writing it, so do not be alarmed. I can only tell you that during that year of her surprising married life, Maisie had thought of me not a little, and this dénouement rapidly brought things to a head. After this confession we used to meet every day. We went for rambles, and picnics, and to matinées, and of course that kind of thing cannot go on indefinitely. We both detested the idea of an intrigue. And eventually we decided that we would cut the Gordian knot and make a full confession. Maisie left him and went to live with a married sister. That same morning I called on George. I arrived at the maisonette just before six o'clock as I knew that that was the most likely time to catch him. Without any preliminary ceremony I made my way into the familiar bedroom. George was in bed. I stood by the door and called out:

'George!'

Like a flash he was out of bed, and standing in his pyjamas, facing me. He had changed considerably. His face was lined and old, but his eyes blazed with a fury of activity. He awed me. I stammered out my confession.

'George, I'm awfully sorry, old chap. I have a confession to make to you. It comes in the first place from Maisie. She has decided that she cannot live with you any longer. She thinks you have neglected her, and treated her badly. She refuses to come back to you under any circumstances. Indeed, she—she and I—er—'

I tailed off dismally and looked at him. For a moment I thought he was going to bear down on me. I know that if he had I should have been supine. I should have stood there and let him slaughter me. I felt completely overpowered by the force of his personality. I believe I shivered. He hovered by the edge of the bed, then he turned and looked out of the window. He stood there solemnly for nearly a minute; then he emitted a profound sigh. Without more ado, he got back into bed. There was an immense upheaval of the sheets. He seemed to be burrowing down into some vast and as yet unexplored cave of comfort. He rolled and heaved and at length became inert. I stood there, waiting for my answer. Sparrows twittered outside on the window box. I don't know how long I waited. I felt that I could not go until he had spoken.

At length his voice came. It seemed to reach me across dim centuries of memory, an old, tired, cosy, enormously contented, sleep-encrusted voice.

''S'all right,' said the voice. 'Tell Mrs Chase she needn't bring up my shaving-water this morning.'

—XIII—

Burney's Laugh

AFTER BREAKFAST was a good time. Throughout the day there was no moment when his vitality rose to such heights as it did during the first puffs of that early cigar. He would stroll out then into the conservatory, and the bright colour of the azaleas would produce in him a strange excitement. His senses would seem sharpened, and he would move quickly between the flowers, and would discuss minor details of their culture with Benyon the gardener. Then he would stroll through the great spaces of his reception-rooms with his head bent forward. The huge Ming pot on its ebony stand would seem to him companionable and splendid, the Majolica plaques which he had bought at Padua would glow serenely. He would go up and feast his eyes on the Chinese lacquer cabinet, on its finely wrought gilt base; and his lips would quiver with a tense enjoyment as he lingered by the little carved Japanese ivories in the recess. Above all, he liked to stand near the wall and gaze at the Vandyke above the fireplace. It looked well in the early morning light, dignified and impressive.

All these things were his. He had fought for them in the arena of the commercial world. He had bought them in the teeth of opposition. And they expressed *him*, his sense of taste, his courage, his power, his relentless tenacity, the qualities that had raised him above his fellows to the position he held. The contemplation of them produced in him a curious vibrant exhilaration. Especially was this so in the early morning when he rose from the breakfast-table, and lighted his first cigar.

The great hall, too, satisfied his quivering senses. The walnut panelling shone serenely, and brass and pewter bore evidence that the silent staff whom his housekeeper controlled had done their work efficiently. It was early—barely nine o'clock—but he knew that in the library Crevace and Dilgerson, his private secretaries, would be fidgeting with papers and expecting him. He would keep them waiting another ten minutes while he gratified this clamorous proprietary sense. He would linger in the drawing room, with its long, grey panels and splendid damask hangings, and touch caressingly the little groups of statuary. The unpolished satinwood furniture appealed to some special aesthetic appetite. It was an idea of his own. It seemed at once graceful and distinguished.

He seemed to have so little time during the rest of the day to feel these things. And if he had the time, the satisfaction did not seem the same, for this was the hour when he felt most virile.

In the library the exultation that he had derived from these æsthetic pleasures would gradually diminish. It is true that Dilgerson had prepared the rough draft of his amendment to the new Peasant Allotment Bill, and it was an amendment he was intensely interested in, for if it passed it might lead to the overthrow of Chattisworth, and that would be a very desirable thing, but nevertheless his interests would flag.

He had a fleeting vision of a great triumph in the House, and himself the central figure. He settled down to discuss the details with Dilgerson. Dilgerson was a very remarkable person. He had a genius for putting his finger on the vital spot of a bill, and he had moreover an unfathomable memory. But gradually the discussion of involved financial details with Dilgerson would tire him. He would get restless and say, 'Yes, yes. All right, Dilgerson. Put it your own way.'

He turned aside to the table where Crevace, coughing

nervously, was preparing some sixty-odd letters for him to sign. A charming young man, Crevace, with gentle manners and a great fund of concentration. He was the second son of Emma Countess of Waddes. He had not the great abilities of Dilgerson, but he was conscientious, untiring, and infinitely ornamental.

He discussed the letters and a few social matters with Crevace, while Dilgerson prepared the despatch-case for the Cabinet meeting at twelve o'clock.

At half-past eleven a maid entered and brought him a raw egg beaten up with a little neat brandy, in accordance with custom.

He told her that Hervieu, the chauffeur, need not come for him. He would walk over to Downing Street with Mr Dilgerson. As a matter of fact, there were still one or two points upon which he was not quite clear about the rights of rural committees. Dilgerson had made a special study of these questions. It was a great temptation to rely more and more on Dilgerson.

He enjoyed a Cabinet meeting. He felt more at home there than in the House. He liked the mixture of formality and urbanity with which the most important affairs were discussed. He liked to sit there and watch the faces of his fellow-ministers. They were clever, hard-headed men, men who like himself had climbed, and climbed, and climbed. They shared in common certain broad political principles, but he did not know what was at the back of any one of their minds. It amused him to listen to Brodray elaborating his theories about the Peasant Allotment Bill, and enunciating commendable altruistic principles. He knew Brodray well. He was a good fellow, but he did not really believe what he was saying. He had another axe to grind, and he was using the Peasant Allotment Bill as a medium. The divagations of 'procedure' were absorbing. It was on the broad back of 'procedure' that the interests of all were struggling to find a place. It was the old parliamentary hand who stood the best chance of finding a corner for his wares. The man who knew the ropes. He, too, had certain ambitions...

It seemed strange to look back on. He had been in political affairs longer than he dare contemplate. Two distinct decades. He had seen much happen. He had seen youth and ambition ground to powder in the parliamentary machine. He had seen careers cut short by death or violent social scandal. Some men were very foolish, foolish and lacking in—moral fibre, that must be it. Moral fibre! the strength not to overstep the bounds, to keep passion and prejudice in restraint, like hounds upon a leash, until their veins become dried and atrophied, and they lack the desire to race before the wind...

He had done that. And now he sat there in the sombre room among the rustling papers, and the greatest Minister of them all was speaking to him, asking his opinion, and listening attentively to his answers. He forced himself to a tense concentration on the issue. He spoke quietly but well. He remembered all the points that the excellent Dilgerson had coached him in. He was conscious of the room listening to him attentively. He knew they held the opinion that he was—safe, that he would do the best thing in the interest of the Party.

O'Bayne spoke after that, floridly, with wild dashes of Celtic fun, and they listened to him, and were amused but not impressed. O'Bayne, too, had an axe to grind, but he showed his hand too consciously. He did not know the ropes.

As the meeting broke up, Brodray came up to him and said:

'Oh, by the way, you know I'm dining with you tonight. May I bring my young nephew with me? He's a sub, in town for a few days' leave.'

Of course he smiled and said it would be delightful. What else could he say?

As a matter of fact he would rather not have had the young sub. He had arranged a small bachelors' dinner—just eight of them—and he flattered himself he had arranged it rather skilfully. There was to be Brodray, and Nielson, the director of the biggest agricultural instrument works in the country, Lanyon the K.C., Lord Bowel of the Board of Trade, Tippins, a big landowner from the North, Sir Andrew Griggs, the greatest living authority on the Land Laws (he had also written a book on 'artificial manures'), and Sir Gregory Caste, director of the Museum of Applied Arts.

The latter, he felt, would be perhaps a little out of it with the rest, but he would help to emphasize his own aspect of social life, its irreproachable taste and patronage of the arts. It would be a very eclectic dinner party, and one in which the fusion of the agricultural interests might tend to produce certain opinions and information of use in conducting the Peasant Allotment Bill, and a young red-faced sub dumped into the middle of it would be neither appropriate nor desirable. There was, however, nothing to be done. He and Brodray had always been great friends—that is to say, they had always worked hand in hand.

He rested in the afternoon, for as the years advanced he found this more and more essential. There were the strictest instructions left that under no circumstances was he to be disturbed till half-past four. In the meanwhile the egregious Dilgerson would cope with his affairs.

At half-past four he rose and bathed his face, and after drinking one cup of tea he rejoined his secretaries in the library. In his absence many matters had developed. There was a further accumulation of correspondence, and a neat typewritten list of telephone messages and applications for appointments. But there was no flurry about Dilgerson; everything was in order, and the papers arranged with methodical precision.

He lighted his second cigar of the day and sat down. The graceful head of Crevace was inclined over the papers, and the suave voice of Dilgerson was saying:

'I see, sir, that Chattisworth has been speaking up in Gaysfield. Our agent has written, he thinks it might be advisable for you to go up North and explain our attitude towards the Bill to your constituents. They must not be—er—neglected for long in these restless times.'

Yes, there was something satisfying in this. The sense of power, or rather the sense of being within the power focus, the person who understood, who knew what power meant, and yet was great enough to live outside it. Strange why today he should be so introspective, why things should appear so abstract! He had a curious feeling as though everything was slipping away, or as though he were seeing himself and his setting from a distance.

He gazed at Dilgerson with his square chin, and his neat moustache, deftly stowing papers into a file whilst he spoke. He momentarily envied Dilgerson with his singular grip on life. He was so intense, so sure...

'Yes...yes,' he said after a time, 'we'd better go up there, Dilgerson. As you say, they get restless. You might draft me a rough summary of Chattisworth's points. Let me know what you would suggest—precedents, historical parallels and so on. It is true; they so soon get restless.'

A feeling of apathy came to him after a time, and he left his secretaries and strolled out into the Mall. A fine rain was drifting from the south, and the tops of the winter trees seemed like a band of gauze veiling the buildings of Whitehall. He went into St James's Park and watched the pale lights from the Government Buildings. Some soldiers passed him, and a policeman touched his hat.

Usually these things moved him with a strange delight. They were the instruments of power, the symbols of the world he believed in. But tonight the vision of them only filled him with an unaccountable melancholy.

He suddenly remembered a day when he had strolled here with his wife twenty-five years ago…

He passed his hand across his brow and tried to brush back a certain memory. But it would not be denied. It was a grey day like this. She had made some remark, something sentimental and—entirely meretricious. He remembered vividly that he had chided her at the time. One must not think like that; one must restrain and control these emotional impulses. They are retrograde, destroying. He had succeeded, risen to the position he held, because—he had always been master of himself.

After his wife's death it had been easier to do this. His two daughters had married well, one to the Bishop of St Lubin, and the other to Viscount Chesslebeach, a venerable but well-informed gentleman, who had been loyal to the Party. His son was now in India, holding a position of considerable responsibility. He was free, free to live and struggle for his great ambitions. He was fortunate in that respect; in fact, he had always been fortunate.

He made his way back across the muddy pathway of the Mall, imbued with a sudden uncontrollable desire for light and warmth.

Gales met him in the hall and relieved him of his coat. There was an undeniable sense of comfort and security about Gales. He glanced furtively at the ponderous figure of his head 'man', who had been with him now longer than he could remember. He muttered something about the inclemency of the weather, and it soothed him to note the ingratiating acquiescence of the servant, as though by addressing him he had conferred a great benefit upon him. He heard the heavy breathing of Gales as he bustled away with his hat and coat, and then he warmed his hands by the fire, and strolled upstairs to dress.

As he entered his bedroom an indefinable feeling of dreariness came over him again. It was very silent there, and well-modulated lights above the dressing table revealed his gleaming silver brushes and the solid properties of the mahogany bed. He looked at the fire and lighted a cigarette, a very unusual habit for him. Then he went into his dressing room and noted his clothes all neatly laid out for him, and the brass can of hot water wrapped in the folds of a rough towel. The door half-open revealed the silver rails and taps in the bathroom, and a very low hum of sound suggested a distant power station or the well-oiled machinery of a lift. It was all wonderfully ordered, wonderfully co-ordinated.

He strolled from one room to the other on the thick pile carpet, trying to thrust back the waves of dejection that threatened to envelop him.

At last he threw his cigarette away, and, disrobing himself, he washed and dressed.

He felt better then, a little more alert and interested. He turned down the light and went downstairs. He felt suddenly curiously nervous and apprehensive about the dinner party. He went into the dining room and found Gales instructing a new butler in the subtleties of his profession. The table was laid for nine, and indeed looked worthy of Gales and of himself. There was a certain austerity and distinction about the three bowls of red tulips that were placed at intervals along it, and the old silver and the Nuremberg glasses, and the cunning arrangements of concealed lights emphasized his own sure taste and discrimination. Nevertheless, he felt nervous. He fussed about the table, and took the champagne bottles from their ice beds to satisfy himself that Gales had brought up the right year. He fidgeted with one of the typewritten menu-cards, and told Gales that on a previous occasion Fouchet had overdone the Lucca oil in the Hollandaise. He must speak to him. He was not sure that Fouchet was not going off. His eyesight was failing, or he was becoming careless. The straw potatoes served with the pheasant had been cut too thick, and his savouries were apt to be too dry. Gales listened to these criticisms with a lugubrious sympathy, and, bowing, he left the room to convey them to the chef.

After that he retired to the small Japanese room on the ground floor. When he had a bachelor party he preferred to receive his guests there. There was something about the black walls, and the grotesquely carved fireplace, and the heavily timbered ceiling, also carved and painted dark red, that appealed to his sense of appropriateness in a men's dinner-party. It was essentially a man's room, a little foreboding and bizarre. It symbolized also his appreciation of a race who were above all things clever: clever and patient, industrious, æsthetic, with some quality that excited the mystic tendencies of the cultivated Westerner.

He had not long to wait before two of his guests arrived—Sir Gregory Caste and Lanyon the K.C. They had met in the cloakroom, and, having previously made each other's acquaintance at an hotel at Baden-Baden, were discussing the medical values of rival Bavarian springs. It was a subject on which he himself was no mean authority. The conversation had not progressed far before Lord Bowel was shown in. He was a very big man with a heavy dome of a head, large pathetic eyes and a thick grey beard. He shook hands solemnly without any gleam of welcome, and immediately gave an account of an incurable disease from which his sister was suffering.

Tippins then arrived, a square-headed North-countryman, who did not speak all the evening except in self-defence, and he was followed by Sir Andrew Griggs and Nielson. Sir Andrew was well into the eighties, and Nielson was a thin, keen-faced man with very thick glasses. There was a considerable interval before Brodray arrived with his nephew. They were at least ten minutes late, and Brodray was very profuse with apologies.

It was curious that the young man was almost precisely as he had pictured him. He was just a red-faced boy in khaki. He fancied that Brodray introduced him as

'Lieutenant Burney', but he was not sure. It was in any case some such name, something ordinary and insignificant.

They then all adjourned to the dining room without breaking the general level of their conversation and sat down.

On his right he had Lord Bowel, and on his left Sir Andrew Griggs. Brodray faced him with Sir Gregory Caste on his right and his nephew on the left. Lanyon sat next to the lieutenant, and Nielson and Tuppins occupied the intervening spaces. He had thought this arrangement out with considerable care.

It was not until the sherry and caviare had fulfilled their destiny that Lord Bowel managed to complete the full description of his sister's disease. He spoke very slowly and laboriously, and moved his beard with a curious rotary movement as he masticated his food.

Sir Andrew Griggs then managed to break into the conversation with a dissertation on the horrors of being ill in a foreign hotel. He had once been suddenly seized with a serious internal trouble and had had to undergo an operation in an hotel in Zermatt. It was very trying, and the hotel people were very unreasonable.

Brodray sang the praises of a new American osteopath during the removal of the soup plates, and the salmon found the director of the National Museum of Applied Arts dilating upon the virtues of grapefruit as a breakfast food.

The host was in no hurry. He knew that the course of events would be bound to draw the conversation into channels connected with matters that were of moment to the construction of the Peasant Allotment Bill.

What more natural than that the virtues of grapefruit should lead to the virtues of fresh air and exercise, and then obviously to horseflesh. At the first glass of champagne the company were already in the country. Horses and dogs! Ah! how difficult to eliminate them from the conversation of a party of representative Englishmen!

Lord Bowel was the first to express his views upon the Bill. The conversation led to it quite naturally at the arrival of the pheasant. They were better cooked tonight, and the potatoes were thinner, more refined.

He watched the curious movement of Lord Bowel's beard as he bit the pheasant, and said in his sepulchral voice:

'The Groynes Amendment will in my opinion inflict a grave injustice on the agricultural classes. You may remember that in Gangway's Rural Housings Bill in eighteen ninety-five, Lord Pennefy, who was then on the Treasury Bench, said...'

The ball had started. He had a curious feeling that he wished Dilgerson were there. Dilgerson had such a remarkable memory. He particularly wanted to get Lanyon's views. Lanyon had a great reputation among the people who knew. Unfortunately he was not a good Party man. They said of him that he had a mind like a double-edged sword. He was keen, analytical, and recondite; and he did not mind whom he struck. The lawyer was listening to Lord Bowel intently. His skin was dry and cracked into a thousand little crevices, his cheekbones stood out, and his cold, abstract eyes were gazing through his rimless pince-nez at his empty glass. For he did not drink.

Lord Bowel dwelt at great length on the Bill's unfortunate attitude towards the agricultural labourer, and at even greater length on the probable result of that attitude upon the agricultural labourer at the polls. When he mentioned the Party he sank his voice to a lower key, and spoke almost humanly.

The pheasants had disappeared, and little quails in aspic had quivered tremulously in the centre of large plates surrounded by a vegetable salad, the secret of which he himself had discovered when living in Vienna, before Lanyon entered the arena with a cryptic utterance, quoting from an Act of James II. He spoke harshly and incisively, like a judge arraigning a criminal. It was very interesting, for the host became aware that as Lanyon proceeded he was not speaking from conviction. He had heard that Lanyon had ambitions of a certain legal position. The Bill would not affect it one way or the other, but his reputation as a dialectician must be established beyond question. He had his game to play, too.

Nielson broke in and seemed to the host to agree with Lord Bowel in an almost extravagant manner. He, too, spoke feelingly when the Party was the theme. It was said that Lord Bowel was the power behind the Chief. He certainly exerted a great influence in the selection of office-holders. Men whose political reputation was not made invariably agreed with Lord Bowel, in any case before his face.

The game pursued its normal course, the even tenor of the men's voices sounded one long drone of abstract passionless sound. Under the influence of the good wine, and the solemn procession of cunningly arranged foods, they sank into a detached unity of expression. They looked at each other tolerantly, listening for signs and omens, and measuring the value of each other's remarks. There was no enthusiasm, no passion, nothing to belie the suave and cultivated accents of their voices. They seemed perhaps unreal to each other, merely a segregation of ideas meeting in a mirage, without prejudice, or bias, or any great desire for personal expression.

It was as the savoury was being removed that young Burney laughed. The host did not catch what it was that made him laugh, neither did he ever know. It was probably some wildly humorous remark of Tippins. But it came crashing through the room like the reel of pipes in a desert. It was not a boisterously loud laugh, but it was loud enough to rise above the general din. It was the quality of it that seemed to rend the air like an electric thrill. It was clear, mellow, vibrant, and amazingly free. It rang out with an unrestrained vibrato of enjoyment. It hung in the air and satisfied its purpose; it seemed to lash the walls of the room and hurl its message defiantly at the ceiling. It could not be subdued, and it could never be forgotten. It was an amazing laugh. It was like the wind on the moors, or the crash of great high waves breaking on a rock, something that had been imprisoned and suddenly breaks free and rides serenely to its end...

'And the saintly Cybeline—'

It was curious. Why, immediately he heard the young man's laugh, did this line occur to him? Gales was standing by the sideboard looking flustered and perturbed. People did not laugh in the presence of Gales. He had a faculty of discouraging any flippant digressions from the dignity of politics or dinner. Lanyon was looking in the young man's direction, his keen eyes surveying the wine glasses set there.

Old Sir Andrew looked at him also and smiled dimly; but, surprisingly enough, the others hardly seemed to have noticed the laugh.

Lord Bowel was saying:

'If therefore we are prepared to accept this crisis which the Opposition—with a singular lack of insight in my opinion—seem disposed to precipitate upon the country, we shall be—er—lacking in loyalty not only to the—er—Constitution, but to ourselves, and I said to the Chief on Wednesday...'

'And the saintly Cybeline—'

What on earth did it mean? What was Lord Bowel talking about? Why did the young man's laugh still seem to be ringing round the room? He looked at him, the boy was talking animatedly to Brodray and grinning; he thought he caught something about 'we didn't sleep under cover for a fortnight'. He had not been drinking—certainly not to excess. No one had had sherry except the silent

Tippins. He might have had three glasses of champagne. It certainly didn't account for the laugh; besides, it was not that sort of laugh.

'There was something, something, something,
  And the something will entwine,
And the something, something, something,
  With the saintly Cybeline.'

A shadowy vision glimmered past the finger-bowl in front of him. He remembered now—it was in Frodsee's room at Magdalen. There was a tall chap, with curly dark hair, sitting on Frodsee's table swinging his legs. He was in 'shorts', and his bare knees and stockings were splashed with mud. Frodsee himself was standing by the window, declaiming his ridiculous jingle. And there was a third boy there who was laughing uncontrollably.

'With the saintly Cybeline.'

He wished he could remember the rest of the words. The sun was streaming through the window, and the young willows were whispering above the river. The jingle finished and they all laughed, and one laugh rang out above the rest. Strange that it should all come rushing back to him at that moment—the free ring of his own laughter across the years! He had something then, he couldn't think what it was, something that he had since lost.

'Even if in the end we have to sacrifice some of these minor principles, I am inclined to think, sir, that the broader issues will be better served...The interests of the Party are interdependent...'

Nielson was speaking, nervously twisting the cigar in his mouth.

He made a desperate plunge to find his place in the flow of this desultory discussion. He mumbled some inchoate remark upon the Land Laws. It was not in any way germane to what had just been said, and he knew it, only he wanted them to draw him back among them, to protect him from the flood of perverse memories that strove to increase his melancholy.

But the memory of that laugh unnerved him. He could not concentrate. He longed once more for Dilgerson, or for some power that would give him a grip upon his concrete existence. He rose from the table and led his guests back into the Japanese room. He lighted a cigar, and, contrary to his custom, he indulged in a liqueur. His guests formed themselves into little groups, and he hovered between them, afraid to remain with either long, in case they should discover his horror, that in that hour—all through a boy's laugh—he had lost the power to concentrate.

Perhaps something in his manner conveyed itself to his guests, for they broke up early. First old Griggs, then Nielson, then Brodray, and the boy. He shook the boy's hand, but made no comment.

Lanyon took his departure alone, and Tippins followed. Lord Bowel seemed the only one disposed to remain. He sank back in an easy chair and talked interminably, unconscious of any psychological change in the atmosphere of the room. He found a patient listener in Gregory Caste, to whom the discussions of a Government official were as balm.

The host moved restlessly, blinking at his two remaining guests. Sometimes he would sit furtively on the edge of a chair and listen, and nod his head, and say, 'Yes…yes, I quite agree. Yes, that is so.'

Then he would rise, and walk to the fireplace and move some object an inch or two from the position in which it was placed, and then move it back again. He drank a glass of lemon-water, a row of which was placed on a silver tray by the wall, and smoked another cigarette. Then the instinct of common courtesy prompted him once more to join his two remaining guests. He looked closely at Lord Bowel's heavy cheeks, and a curious feeling of disgust came over him. The voice of the Board of Trade official boomed on luxuriously about the arts of the Eastern people, about ceramics, about the diseases of bees, the iniquity of licensing restrictions, the influence of Chaldean teaching on modern theology, on the best hotel in Paris, on the vacillating character of the principal leaders of the Opposition. There seemed no end to the variety of theme, and no break in the dull monotony of voice.

It must have been well after midnight that Lord Bowel suddenly sighed heavily and rose. He took his host's hand and said gloomily:

'It has been a most delightful evening.'

He watched the two men pass out into the hall, and saw Gales come ponderously forward and help them with their coats. Then he drew back and looked into the fire. He pressed his hand to his brow. He had not a headache, but he felt peculiarly exhausted, as though he had been through some great strain. In the fire he saw again the nodding heads of willows and the young clouds scudding before the wind...He started. He could not understand; he could have sworn that at that moment he again heard some one laugh. He looked round to convince himself that he was alone in the room. He shivered and stood up. He was not well. He was getting old. A time comes to all men—Anyway, he had not been a failure. He had succeeded, in fact, beyond his wildest dreams. His name was known to everyone in England. His features even graced the pages of the satiric journals. He was the 'safe' man of the Party. One paper had nicknamed him 'Trumps', the safest card in the pack. It was something to have achieved this, even if—he had sacrificed things, impulses, convictions, passions, the fierce joy of expressing his primitive self. Perhaps in the process he had lost something.

Ah, God! He wished the young man had not laughed. There was a gentle tap on the door, and Gales came in.

'Oh, I beg your pardon, sir!' he murmured softly.

'It's all right. I'm going to bed.'

He rose weakly from the chair and went upstairs. Once more in the bedroom, the silence tormented him. The furniture seemed no longer his own, no longer an expression of himself, but a cold, frigid statement of dead conformity. He touched the bed, and then walked up and down. What could he do? He had no power to combat the strange terrors of remorse that flooded him. He sat there silently waiting for the mood to pass. He knew that if he struggled it *would* pass. He would be himself again. It was all so foolish, so unworthy of him. He kept saying that to himself, but underneath it all something else seemed stirring, something that went to the roots of his being and shook him violently.

He waited there a long time, till the house seemed given over to the embraces of the night, then he stealthily crept downstairs again. It was all in darkness. He turned on the light in the hall and dining room. He wandered to his accustomed chair at the dining table and huddled into it. He struggled to piece together the memories of days of freedom and splendour, when he had sacrificed nothing, when life was an open book.

He visualized little incidents of his childhood and school-days, but they seemed trivial and without significance or humour.

Ah, God! if he could laugh!

He started suddenly at the sound of someone moving in the hall. He knew instinctively it would be Gales. He jumped up. He did not want his loyal retainer to think him a fool. It would be the most terrible thing of all to appear ridiculous to Gales. He walked round the room nervously peering at the floor.

Gales blinked at him. He was in a dressing gown, and he mumbled:

'I beg your pardon, sir?'

He glanced at Gales but said nothing. He continued searching the floor. Gales advanced into the room and coughed, and looked at him curiously. He had never known Gales look at him before in quite that way. He felt suddenly angry with the servant and wanted to get rid of him, but at the same time he was self-conscious and afraid. He was aware of the level tones of Gales's voice murmuring:

'Excuse me, sir, may I help you? Have you lost anything? Can I—'

The horror came home to him with increased violence as he glanced at the puffy cheeks of the butler. He felt that he could not endure him for another moment. He almost ran to the door, calling out in a harsh voice as he did so:

'Yes … yes. I've lost something.'

He brushed past the butler, his cheeks hot and dry, and his eyes blazing with an unforgiving anger. He did not turn again, but hurried away, like an animal that is ashamed to be seen, and ran whimpering upstairs to his bedroom.

—*XIV*—

The Great Unimpressionable

Ned Picklekin was a stolid chunk of a young man, fair, blue-eyed, with his skin beaten to a uniform tint of warm red by the sun and wind. For he was the postman at the village at Ashalton. Except for two hours in the little sorting-office, he spent the whole day on his bicycle, invariably accompanied by his Irish terrier, Toffee. Toffee was as well known on the countryside as Ned himself. He took the business of delivering letters as seriously as his master. He trotted behind the bicycle with his tongue out, and waited panting outside the gates of gardens while the important government business was transacted. He never barked, and had no time for fighting common, unofficial dogs. When the letters were delivered, his master would return to his bicycle, and say: 'Coom ahn, boy!' and Toffee would immediately jump up, and fall into line. They were great companions.

Ned lived with his mother, and also he walked out with a young lady. Her name was Ettie Skinner, and she was one of the three daughters of old Charlie Skinner, the corn merchant. Charlie Skinner had a little establishment in the station-yard. He was a widower, and he and his three daughters lived in a cottage in Neap's Lane. It was very seldom necessary to deliver letters at the Skinners' cottage, but every morning Ned had to pass up Neap's Lane, and so, when he arrived at the cottage, he dismounted, and rang his bicycle bell. The signal was understood by Ettie, who immediately ran out to the gate, and a conversation somewhat on this pattern usually took place:

'Hulloa!'

'Hulloa!'

'All right?'

'Ay.'

'Busy?'

'Ay. Mendin' some old cla'es.'

'Oo-ay!'

'Looks like mebbe a shower.'

'Mebbe.'

'Comin' along tonight?'

'Ay, if it doan't rain.'

'Well, so long!'

'So long, Ned.'

In the evenings the conversation followed a very similar course. They waddled along the lanes side by side and occasionally gave each other a punch. Ned smoked his pipe all the time, and Toffee was an unembarrassed cicerone. He was a little jealous of this unnecessary female, but he behaved with a resigned acquiescence. His master could do no wrong. His master was a god, a being apart from all others.

It cannot be said that Ned was a romantic lover. He was solemn, direct, imperturbable. He was a Saxon of Saxons, matter-of-fact, incorruptible, unimaginative, strong-willed, conscientious, not very ambitious, and suspicious of the unusual and the unknown. When the war broke out he said:

'Ay, but this is a bad business!'

And then he thought about it for a month. At the end of that time he made up his mind to join. He rode up Neap's Lane one morning and rang his bell. When Ettie appeared the usual conversation underwent a slight variant:

'Hulloa!'

'Hulloa!'

'All right?'

'Ay.'

'Doin' much?'

'Oo—mendin' pa's night-gown.'

'Oh! I be goin' to jine up.'

'Oo-oh! Be 'ee?'

'Ay.'

'When be goin'?'

'Monday with Dick Thursby and Len Cotton. An' I think young Walters, and Binnie Short mebbe.'

'Oh, I say!'

'Ay. Comin' along tonight?'

'Ay, if it doan't rain.'

'Well, see you then.'

'So long, Ned.'

On the following Monday Ned said good-bye to his mother, and sweetheart, and to Toffee, and he and the other four boys walked over to the recruiting-office at Carchester. They were drafted into the same unit, and sent up to Yorkshire to train. (Yorkshire being one hundred and fifty miles away was presumably the most convenient and suitable spot.)

They spent five months there, and then Len Cotton was transferred to the Machine Gun Corps, and the other four were placed in an infantry regiment and sent out to India.

They did not get an opportunity of returning to Ashalton, but the night before they left Ned wrote to his mother:

> DEAR MOTHER, I think we are off to-morrow. They don't tell us where we are going but they seem to think it's India because of the Eastern kit served out and so on. Everything all right, the grub is fine. Young Walters has gone sick with a bile on his neck. Hope you are all right. See Toffee don't get into Mr Mears yard for this is about the time he puts down that poison for the rats. Everything all O.K. love from NED.

He wrote a very similar letter to Ettie, only leaving out the instructions about Toffee, and adding, 'don't get overdoing it now the warm weathers on.'

They touched at Gibraltar, Malta, Alexandria, and Aden. At all these places he merely sent the cryptic postcard. He did not write a letter again until he had been three weeks up in the hills in India. As a matter of fact it had been a terribly rough passage nearly all the way, especially in the Mediterranean, and nearly all the boys had been seasick most of the time. Ned had been specially bad and in the Red Sea had developed a slight fever. In India he had been sent to a rest-camp up in the hills. He wrote:

> DEAR MOTHER, everything all right. The grub is fine. I went a bit sick coming out but nothing. Quite all O.K. now. This is a funny place. The people would make you laugh to look at. We beat the 2nd Royal Scots by two goals to one. I wasn't playing but Binnie played a fine game at half-back. He stopped their centre forward an old league player time and again. Hope you are keeping all right. Does Henry Thatcham take Toffee out regler. Everything serene. love from NED.

In this letter the words '2nd Royal Scots' were deleted by the censor.

India at that time was apparently a kind of training ground for young recruits. There were a few recalcitrant hill-tribes upon whom to practise the latest developments of military science, and Ned was mixed up in one or two of these little scraps. He proved himself a good soldier, doing precisely what he was told and being impervious to danger. They were five months in India, and then the regiment was suddenly drafted back to Egypt. Big things were afoot. No one knew what was going to happen. They spent ten days in a camp near Alexandria. They were then detailed for work in connection with the protection of the banks of the Canal, and Ned was stationed near the famous pyramid of Gizeh. He wrote to his mother:

> DEAR MOTHER, everything all right. Pretty quiet so far. This is a funny place. Young Walters has gone sick

> again. We had the regimental sports Thursday. Me and Bert Carter won the three-legged race. The grub is fine and we get dates and figs for nuts. Hope your cold is all right by now. Thanks for the parcel which I got on the 27th. Everything all right. Glad to hear about Mrs Parsons having the twins and that. Glad to hear Toffee all right and so with love your loving son NED.

They had not been at Gizeh for more than a week before they were sent back to Alexandria and placed on a transport. In fifteen days after touching at Imbros, Ned and his companions found themselves on Gallipoli peninsula. Heavy fighting was in progress. They were rushed up to the front line. For two days and nights they were in action and their numbers were reduced to one-third their original size. For thirty hours they were without water and were being shelled by gas, harried by flame-throwers, blasted by shrapnel and high explosive. At the end of that time they crawled back to the beach at night through prickly brambles which poisoned them and set up septic wounds if they scratched them. They lay there dormant for two days, but still under shellfire, and then were hurriedly re-formed into a new regiment, and sent to another part of the line. This went on continuously for three weeks, and then a terrible storm and flood occurred. Hundreds of men—some alive and some partly alive—were drowned in the ravines. Ned and his company lost all their kit, and slept in water for three nights running. At the end of four weeks he obtained five days' rest at the base. He wrote to Ettie:

> DEAR ETTIE, A long time since I had a letter from you. Hope all right. Everything all right so far. We had a bad storm but the weather now keeps fine. Had a fine bathe this morning. There was a man in our company could make you laugh. He is an Irish Canadian. He plays the penny whistle fine and sings a bit too. Sorry to say young Walters died. He got enteric and phewmonnia

and so on. I expect his people will have heard all right. How is old Mrs Walters? Dick Thursby got a packet too and Mrs Quinby's boy I forget his name. How are them white rabbits of yours. I met a feller as used to take the milk round for Mr Brand up at Bodes farm. Funny wasn't it. Well nothing more now. I hope this finds you as it leaves me your affectionate NED.

Ned was three months on Gallipoli peninsula, but he left before the evacuation. During the whole of that time he was never not under shellfire. He took part in seven attacks. On one occasion he went over the top with twelve hundred others, of whom only one hundred and seven returned. Once he was knocked unconscious by a mine explosion which killed sixty-seven men. At the end of that period he was shot through the back by a sniper. He was put in a dressing-station, and a gentleman in a white overall came and stuck a needle into his chest and left him there in state of nudity for twelve hours. Work at the field hospitals was very congested just then. He became a bit delirious and was eventually put on a hospital ship with a little tag tied to him. After some vague and restless period he found himself again at Imbros and in a very comfortable hospital. He stayed there six weeks and his wound proved to be slight. The bone was only grazed. He wrote to his mother:

DEAR MOTHER, Everything all right. I had a scratch but nothing. I hope you enjoyed the flower show. How funny meeting Mrs Perks. We have a fine time here. The grub is fine. Sorry to say Binnie Short went under. He got gassed one night when he hadn't his mask on. The weather is mild and pleasant. Glad to hear Henry takes Toffee out all right. Have not heard from Ettie for some time. We had a fine concert on Friday. A chap played the flute lovely. Hope you are now all right again.

Your loving son, NED.

In bed in the hospital at Imbros a bright idea occurred to Ned. He made his will. Such an idea would never have occurred to him had it not been forced upon him by the unusual experiences of the past year. He suddenly realised that of all the boys who had left the village with him only Len Cotton, as far as he knew, remained. So one night he took a blunt-pointed pencil, and laboriously wrote on the space for the will at the end of his pay-book:

> I leave everything Ive got to my mother Anne Picklekin including Toffee. I hope Henry Thatcham will continue to look after Toffee except the silver bowl which I won at the rabbit show at Oppleford. This I leave to Ettie Skinner as a memorial of me.

One day Ned enjoyed a great excitement. He was under discharge from the hospital, and a rumour got round that he and some others were to be sent back to England. They hung about the island for three days, and were then packed into an Italian fruit-steamer—which had been converted into a transport. It was very over-crowded and the weather was hot. They sailed one night and reached another island before dawn. They spent three weeks doing this. They only sailed at night, for the seas about there were reported to be infested with submarines. Every morning they put in at some island in the Greek archipelago, or at some port on the mainland. At one place there was a terrible epidemic of illness, owing to some Greek gentleman having sold the men some doped wine. Fifteen of them died. Ned escaped from this, as he had not had any of the wine. He was practically a teetotaller except for an occasional glass of beer. But he was far from happy on that voyage. The seas were rough and the transport ought to have been broken up years ago, and this didn't seem to be the right route for England.

At length they reached a large port called Salonika. They never went into the town, but were sent straight out to a camp in the hills ten miles away. The country was very wild and rugged, and there was great difficulty with water. Everything was polluted and malarial. There was very little fighting apparently, but plenty of sickness. He found himself in a Scottish regiment. At least, it was called Scottish, but the men came from all parts of the world, from Bow Street to Hong Kong.

There was to be no Blighty after all, but still—there it was! He continued to drill, and march and clean his rifle and play the mouth-organ and football. And then one morning he received a letter from his mother, which had followed him from Imbros. It ran as follows:

> My Dear Ned, How are you, dear? I hope you keep all right. My corf is now pretty middlin otherwise nothin to complain of. Now dear I have to tell you something which greives me dear. Im afraid its no good keepin it from you ony longer dear. *Ettie is walkin out with another feller.* A feller from the air station called Alf Mullet. I taxed her with it and she says yes it is so dear. Now dear you mustnt take on about this. I told her off I says it was a disgraceful and you out there fightin for your country and that. And she says nothin excep yes there it was and she couldnt help it and her feelins had been changed you being away and that. Now dear you must put a good face on this and remember theres just as good fish in the sea as ever came out of it as they say dear. One of Mr Beans rabbits died Sunday they think it over-eating you never know with rabbits. Keep your feet warm dear I hope you got them socks I sent. Lizzie was at chapel Sunday she had on her green lawn looked very nice I thought but I wish she wouldnt get them spots on her face perhaps its only the time of year. Toffee is all right he had a fight with a hairdale Thursday Henry says got one of his eres bitten but nothin serous. So now dear I must close as Mrs Minchin wants me to go and take tea with her has Florrie has gone to the school treat at Furley. And so dear with love your lovin Mother.

When he had finished reading this letter he uttered an exclamation, and a cockney friend sitting on the ground by his side remarked:

'What's the matter, mate?'

Ned took a packet of cigarettes out of his pocket and lighted one. Then he said:

'My girl's jilted me.'

The cockney laughed and said:

'Gawd! is that all? I thought it was somethin' serious!' He was cleaning his rifle with an oil rag, and he continued:

'Don't you worry, mate. Women are like those blinkin' little Greek islands, places to call at but not to stay. What was she like?'

'Oo—all right.'

'Pretty?'

'Ay—middlin.'

''As she got another feller?'

'Ay.'

'Oh, well, it's all in the gime. If you will go gallivanting about these foreign parts enjoyin' yerself, what d'yer expect? What time's kick-off this afternoon?'

'Two o'clock.'

'Reckon we're goin' to win?'

'I doan't know. 'Pends upon whether McFarlane turns out.'

'Yus, 'e's a wonderful player. Keeps the team together like.'

'Ay.'

'Are you playin'?'

'Ay. I'm playin' right half.'

'Are yer? Well, you'll 'ave yer 'ands full. You'll 'ave to tackle Curly Snider.'

'Ay.'

Ned's team won the match that afternoon, and he wrote to his mother afterwards:

> DEAR MOTHER, We just had a great game against 15/Royal South Hants. McFarlane played centre half

and he was in great form. We lead 2—0 at half time and they scored one at the beginnin of the second half but Davis got thro towards the end and we beat them by 3—1. I was playin quite a good game I think but McFarlane is a real first class. I got your letter all right, am glad your corf is getting all right. I was sorry about Ettie but of course she knows what she wants I spose. You don't say what Toffee did to the *other dog*. You might tell Henery to let me have a line about this. Fancy Liz being at chapel. I almos forget what shes like. Everything is all right. The grub is fine. This is a funny place all rocks and planes. The Greeks are a stinkin lot for the most part so must now close with love. NED.

Having completed this letter, Ned got out his pay-book and revised his will. Ettie Skinner was now deleted, and the silver bowl won at the rabbit-show at Oppleford was bequeathed to Henry Thatcham in consideration of his services in taking Toffee out for runs.

They spent a long and tedious eight months on the plains of Macedonia, dodging malaria and bullets, cracking vermin in their shirts, playing football, ragging, quarrelling, drilling, manoeuvring, and, most demoralising of all, hanging about. And then a joyous day dawned. This hybrid Scottish regiment was ordered home! They left Salonica in a French liner and ten days later arrived at Malta. But in the meantime the gods had been busy. The wireless operators had been flashing their mysterious signals all over the Mediterranean and the Atlantic. At Malta the order was countermanded. They remained there long enough to coal, but the men were not even given shore leave. The next day they turned eastwards again and made for Alexandria.

The cockney was furious. He had the real genius of the grouser, with the added venom of the man who in the year of grace had lived by his wits and now found his wits enclosed in an iron cylinder. It was a disgusting anti-climax.

'When I left that filthy 'ole,' he exclaimed, 'I swore to God I'd try and never remember it again. And now I'm darned if we ain't goin' back there. As if once ain't enough in a man's lifetime! It's like the blooming cat with the blankety mouse!'

'Eh, well, mon,' interjected a Scotsman, 'there's ane thing. They canna keel ye no but once.'

'It ain't the killing I mind. It's the blooming mucking about. What d'yer say, Pickles?'

'Ah, well...there it is,' said Ned sententiously.

There was considerable 'mucking about' in Egypt, and then they started off on a long trek through the desert, marching on wire mesh that had been laid down by the engineers. There was occasional skirmishing, sniping, fleas, delay, and general discomfort. One day, in Southern Palestine, Ned was out with a patrol party just before sundown. They were trekking across the sand between two oases when shots rang out. Five of the party fell. The rest were exposed in the open to foes firing from concealment on two sides. The position was hopeless. They threw up their hands. Two more shots rang out and the cockney next to Ned fell forward with a bullet through his throat. Then dark figures came across the sands towards them. There were only three left, Ned, a Scotsman, and a boy who had been a clerk in a drapery store at Lewisham before the war. He said:

'Well, are they going to kill us?'

'No,' said the Scotsman. 'Onyway, keep your hands weel up and pray to God.'

A tall man advanced, and to their relief beckoned them to follow. They fell into single file.

'These are no Tur-r-ks at all,' whispered the Scotsman. 'They're some nomadic Arab tribe.'

The Scotsman had attended evening continuation

classes at Peebles, and was rather fond of the word 'nomadic'.

They were led to one of the oases, and instructed to sit down. The Arabs sat round them, armed with rifles. They remained there till late at night, when another party arrived, and a rope was produced. They were handcuffed and braced together, and then by gesticulation told to march. They trailed across the sand for three hours and a half. There was no moon, but the night was tolerably clear. At length they came to another oasis, and were bidden to halt. They sat on the sand for twenty minutes, and one of the Arabs gave them some water. Then a whistle blew, and they were kicked and told to follow. The party wended its way through a grove of cedar-trees. It was pitch-dark. At last they came to a halt by a large hut. There was much coming and going. When they entered the hut, in charge of their guard, they were blinded by a strong light. The hut was comfortably furnished and lighted by electric light. At a table sat a stout, pale-faced man, with a dark moustache—obviously a German. By his side stood a tall German orderly. The German official looked tired and bored. He glanced at the prisoners and drew some papers towards him.

'Come and stand here in front of my desk,' he said in English.

They advanced, and he looked at each one carefully. Then he yawned, dipped his pen in ink, tried it on a sheet of paper, swore, and inserted a fresh nib.

'Now you,' he said, addressing the Scotsman, when he had completed these operations. 'Name, age, profession, regiment. Smartly.'

He obtained all these particulars from each man. Then he got up and came round the table, and looking right into the eyes of the clerk from Lewisham, he said:

'We know, of course, in which direction your brigade is advancing, but from which direction is the brigade commanded by Major-General Forbes Fittleworth advancing?'

The three of them all knew this, for it was common gossip of the march. But the clerk from Lewisham said:

'I don't know.'

The German turned from him to the Scotsman and repeated the question.

'I don't know,' answered the Scotsman.

'From which direction is the brigade commanded by Major-General Forbes Fittleworth advancing?' he said to Ned.

'Naw! I doan't know,' replied Ned.

And then a horrible episode occurred. The German suddenly whipped out a revolver and shot the clerk from Lewisham through the body twice. He gave a faint cry and crumbled forward. Without taking the slightest notice of this horror, the German turned deliberately and held the revolver pointed at Ned's face. In a perfectly unimpassioned, toneless voice he repeated:

'From which direction is the brigade commanded by Major-General Forbes Fittleworth advancing?'

In the silence which followed, the only sound seemed to be the drone of some machine, probably from the electric light plant. The face of Ned was mildly surprised but quite impassive. He answered without a moment's hesitation:

'Naw! I doan't know.'

There was a terrible moment in which the click of the revolver could almost be heard. It seemed to hover in front of his face for an unconscionable time, then suddenly the German lowered it with a curse, and leaning forward he struck Ned on the side of his face with the flat of his hand. He treated the Scotsman in the same way, causing his nose to bleed. Both of the men remained quite impassive. Then he walked back to his seat, and said calmly:

'Unless you can refresh your memories within the next two hours you will both share the fate of—that swine.

You will now go out to the plantation at the back and dig your graves. Dig three graves.'

He spoke sharply in Arabic to the guards, and they were led out. They were handed a spade each, two Arabs held torches for them to work by, and four others hovered in a circle twelve paces away. The soil was light sand, and digging was fairly easy. Each man dug his own grave, making it about four feet deep. When it came to the third grave the Scotsman whispered:

'Dig deep, mon.'

'Deeper than others?'

'Ay, deep enough to make a wee trench.'

'I see.'

They made it very deep, working together and whispering. When it was practically completed, apparently a sudden quarrel arose between the men. They swore at each other and the Scotsman sprang out of the trench and gripped Ned by the throat. A fearful struggle began to take place on the edge of the grave. The guard ran up and tried to separate them. And then, during the brief confusion there was a sudden dramatic development. Simultaneously they snatched their spades. Both the men with the torches were knocked senseless, and one of them fell into the third grave. The torches were stamped out and a rifle went off. It was fired by a guard near the hut, and the bullet struck another Arab who was trying to use his bayonet. Ned brought a fourth man down with his spade and seized his rifle, and the Scotsman snatched the rifle of the man who had been shot, and they both leapt back into their purposely prepared trench.

'We shallna be able to hold this long, but we'll give them a grand run for their money,' said the Scotsman.

The body of one Arab was lying on the brink of their trench and the other in the trench itself. Fortunately they both had bandoliers, which Ned and his companion instantly removed.

'You face east and I'll take west,' said the Scotsman,

his eyes glittering in the dim light. 'I'm going to try and scare that Boche devil.'

He peppered away at the hut, putting bullets through every window and smashing the telephone connection, which was a fine target at the top of a post against the sky. Bullets pinged over their heads from all directions, but there was little chance of them being rushed while their ammunition held out. However, it became necessary to look ahead. It was the Scotsman's idea in digging the graves to plan them in zigzag formation. The end of the furthest one was barely ten paces from a clump of aloes. He now got busy with his spade whilst Ned kept guard in both directions, occasionally firing at the hut and then in the opposite direction into the darkness. In half-an-hour the Scotsman had made a shallow connection between the three graves, leaving just enough room to crawl through. They then in turn donned the turbans of the two fallen Arabs, who were otherwise dressed in a kind of semi-European uniform.

They ended up with a tremendous fusillade against the hut, riddling it with bullets; then they crept to the end of the furthest grave, and leaving their rifles, they made a sudden dash across the open space to the group of aloes, bending low and limping like wounded Arabs. They reached them in safety, but there were many open spaces to cover yet. As they emerged from the trees Ned stumbled on a dark figure. He kicked it and ran. They both ran zigzag fashion, and tore off their turbans as they raced along. They covered nearly a hundred yards, and then bullets began to search them out again. They must have gone nearly a mile before the Scotsman gave a sudden slight groan.

'I'm hit,' he said.

He stumbled on into a clump of bushes, and fell down.

'Is it bad?' asked Ned.

'Eh, laddie, I'm doon,' he said quietly. He put his hand

to his side. He had been shot through the lungs. Ned stayed with him all night, and they were undisturbed. Just before dawn the Scotsman said:

'Eh, mon, but yon was a bonny fight,' and he turned on his back and died.

Ned made a rough grave with his hands, and buried his companion. He took his identification disc and his pocket book and small valuables, with the idea of returning them to his kin if he should get through himself. He also took his water-flask, which still fortunately contained a little water. He lay concealed all day, and at night he boldly donned his turban, issued forth and struck a caravan-trail. He continued this for four days and nights, hiding in the daytime and walking at nights. He lived on figs and dates, and one night he raided a village and caught a fowl, which also nearly cost him his life.

On the fourth night his water gave out, and he was becoming light-headed. He stumbled on into the darkness. He was a desperate man. All the chances were against him, and he felt unmoved and fatalistic. He drew his clasp knife and gripped it tightly in his right hand. He was hardly conscious of what he was doing, and where he was going. The moon was up, and after some hours he suddenly beheld a small oblong hut. He got it into his head that this was the hut where his German persecutor was. He crept stealthily towards it.

'I'll kill that swine,' he muttered.

He was within less than a hundred yards of the hut, when a voice called out:

''Alt! Who goes there?'

'It's me,' he said. 'Doan't thee get in my way. I want to kill him. I'm going to kill him. I'm going to stab him through his black heart.'

'What the hell—!'

The sentry was not called upon to use his rifle, for the turbaned figure fell forward in a swoon.

Three weeks later Ned wrote to his mother from

Bethlehem (where Christ was born), and this is what he said:

> Dear Mother, Everything going on all right. I got three parcels here altogether as I had been away copped by some black devils an unfriendly tribe. I got back all right though. The ointment you sent was fine and so was them rock cakes. What a funny thing about Belle getting lost at the picnick. We got an awful soaking from the Mid-Lancs Fusiliers on Saturday. They had two league cracks playing one a wonderful centreforward. He scored three goals. They beat us by 7—0. The weather is hot but quite plessant at night. We have an old sergeant who was born in America does wonderful tricks with string and knots and so on. He tells some very tall yarns. You have to take them with a pinch of salt. Were getting fine grub here pretty quiet so far. Hope Henry remembers to wash Toffee with that stuff every week or so. Sorry to hear Len Cotton killed. Is his sister still walking out with that feller at Aynham. I never think he was much class for her getting good money though. Hope you have not had any more trouble with the boiler. That was a good price to get for that old buck rabbit. Well there's nothing more just now and so with love your loving son, Ned.

Ned went through the Palestine campaign and was slightly wounded in the thigh. After spending some time in hospital he was sent to the coast and put on duty looking after Turkish prisoners. He remained there six months and was then shipped to Italy. On the way the transport was torpedoed. He was one of a party of fifty-seven picked up by French destroyers. He had been for over an hour in the water in his life belt. He was landed in Corsica and there he developed pneumonia. He only wrote his mother one short note about this:

> Dear Mother, Have been a bit dicky owing to falling in the water and getting wet. But going on all

right. Nurses very nice and one of the doctors rowed for Cambridge against Oxford. I forget the year but Cambridge won by two-and-a-half lengths. We have very nice flowers in the ward. Well not much to write about and so with love your loving son, NED.

Ned was fit again in a few weeks and he was sent up to the Italian front. He took part in several engagements and was transferred to the French front during the last months of the war. He was in the great retreat in March 1918, and in the advance in July. After the armistice he was with the army of occupation on the banks of the Rhine. His mother wrote to him there:

MY DEAR NED, Am glad that the fightin us now all over dear. How relieved you must be. Mr Filter was in Sunday. He thinks there will be no difficulty about you gettin your job back when you come back dear. Miss Siffkins as been deliverin but as Mr Filter says its not likely a girl is going to be able to deliver letters not like a man can and that dear. So now you will be comin home soon dear. That will be nice. We had a pleesant afternoon at the Church needlewomens gild. Miss Barbary Banstock sang very pleesantly abide with me and the vicar told a very amusing story about a little girl and a prince she didn't know he was a prince and talked to him just as though he was a man it was very amusin dear. I hear Ettie is goin to get married next month they wont get me to the weddin was it ever so I call it disgraceful and I have said so. Maud Bean is expectin in April that makes her forth in three years. Mr Bean as lost three more rabbits they say its rats this time. The potaters are a poor lot this time but the runners and cabbidge promiss well. So now dear I will close. Hoppin to have you back dear soon.

YOUR LOVING MOTHER.

It was, however, the autumn before Ned was

demobilised. One day in early October he came swinging up the village street carrying a white kit bag slung across his left shoulder. He looked more bronzed and perhaps a little thinner, but otherwise little altered by his five years of war experiences. The village of Ashalton was quite unaltered, but he observed several strange faces; he only met two acquaintances on the way to his mother's cottage, and they both said:

'Hullo, Ned! Ye're home agen then!'

In each case he replied:

'Ay,' and grinned, and walked on.

He entered his mother's cottage, and she was expecting him. The lamp was lighted and a grand tea was spread. There was fresh boiled beetroot, tinned salmon, salad, cake, and a large treacle tart. She embraced him and said:

'Well, Ned! Ye're back then.'

He replied: 'Ay.'

'Ye're lookin' fine,' she said. 'What a fine suit they've given ye!'

'Ay,' he replied.

'I expect you want yer tea?'

'Ay.'

He had dropped his kit bag, and he moved luxuriously round the little parlour, looking at all the familiar objects. Then he sat down, and his mother brought the large brown teapot from the hob and they had a cosy tea. She told him all the very latest news of the village, and all the gossip of the countryside, and Ned grinned and listened. He said nothing at all. The tea had progressed to the point when Ned's mouth was full of treacle tart, when his mother suddenly stopped, and said:

'Oh, dear, I'm afraid I have somethin' distressin' to tell ye, dear.'

'O-oh? what's that?'

'Poor Toffee was killed.'

'What!'

Ned stopped suddenly in the mastication of the treacle

tart. His eyes bulged and his cheeks became very red. He stared at his mother wildly, and repeated:

'What's that? What's that ye say, Mother?'

'Poor Toffee, my dear. It happened right at the crossroads. Henry was takin' him out. It seems he ran round in front of a steamroller, and a motor came round the corner sudden. Henry called out, but too late. Went right over his back. Poor Henry was quite upset. He brought him home. What's the matter, dear?'

Ned had pushed his chair back, and he stood up. He stared at his mother like a man who has seen horror for the first time.

'Where is— where was—' he stammered.

'We buried 'im, dear, under the little mound beyond the rabbit hutches.'

Ned staggered across the room like a drunken man and repeated dismally:

'The little mound beyond the rabbit hutches!'

He lifted the latch, and groped his way into the garden. His mother followed him. He went along the mud path, past the untenanted hutches covered with tarpaulin. Some tall sunflowers stared at him insolently. A fine rain was beginning to fall. In the dim light he could just see the little mound—signifying the spot where Toffee was buried. He stood there bareheaded, gazing at the spot. His mother did not like to speak. She tiptoed back to the door. But after a time she, called out:

'Ned! ... Ned!'

He did not seem to hear, and she waited patiently. At the end of several minutes she called again:

'Ned! ... Ned dear, come and finish your tea.'

He replied quite quietly:

'All right, Mother.'

But he kept his face averted, for he did not want his mother to see the tears which were streaming down his cheeks.

—XV—

One Sunday Morning

THE IRON FINGERS OF HABIT probed his consciousness into the realization that it was seven-thirty, the hour to rise. He sighed as he pushed his way to the surface through the pleasant obscurity of tangled dreams. And then, oh, joy! his conscious brain registered the abrupt reflection that it was Sunday. Oh, happy thought. Oh, glorious and soporific reflection! He sunk back again, like a deep-sea monster plunging into the dark waters of its natural environment. There passed a long untroubled passage of time, in which his sub-conscious mind dallied with ecstatic emotions. Then slowly and reluctantly he blinked once more into the light of day and knowingness. This re-entry was accompanied by the pleasant sound of running water. His wife was in the bathroom, already getting up. Her activity and the sound of her ablutions added a piquance to the luxury of his own state. Oh, Sunday, glorious and inactive day!

His mind became busy with the anticipations of his own inactivity.

Breakfast in bed! When he won the Calcutta Sweepstake he would always have breakfast in bed. There was something irresistibly luxurious about sitting up snugly in the warmed bed, eating toast and bacon and drinking hot tea that someone else, pottering about in the cold, had had to prepare. And when one had had breakfast one was a man, fortified for anything, even to the extent of getting up.

His wife came back into the bedroom, wearing—oh, those funny things that women wear underneath deceptive frocks. He had been married for sixteen years and the vision of his wife in these habiliments did not produce in him any great manifestation of interest. He realized that he wanted his tea, and his interests were more nearly concerned with the estimate of how long it would take her to finish dressing and go downstairs and make it. And after breakfast—oh, that first cigarette and the indolent stimulus of reading the Sunday newspaper from cover to cover. His wife was chatting away about the cook-general, who was ill, and he boomed out a lethargic yes or no according to the decision which he believed that she expected. Oh, luxurious and delicious indifference!

She bustled away at last, and he listened entranced to the distant sound of rattling plates and tea-cups. A pity that Jenny had to get the breakfast herself, but there! she didn't have to go to the city every day in the week, and besides—it was the woman's sphere. His conscience was serene and satisfied, his senses aroused almost to exultation by the sudden and insidious smell of frying bacon.

When she brought the tray he roused himself valiantly to say the gracious thing, for he realized that the situation was a little dangerous. His wife was not in too good a temper over this affair of the fool of a cook. If he was not careful, she would want him to do something, chop wood or bring up coals, some angular and disturbing abrasion upon the placidity of his natural rights. However, she left the breakfast tray without any such disquieting threats.

He stared at the tray, when she had gone, as a cat may look at a mouse which he has cornered, realizing that the great charm of the situation lies in the fact that there is no hurry. At last he poured himself out a large cup of tea, and drank it in gulps. He then got busy on the bacon and the toast. He ate up all the bacon carefully and thoughtfully, cleaning up the liquid fat with a piece of bread. He began to feel good. He drank more tea, and ate slice after slice of buttered toast, piled up with marmalade. At last he sank back on the pillow replete.

Then he reached out and took his cigarette case out of his coat pocket. He lighted a cigarette and opened the Sunday newspaper. Then indeed did he reach the culmination of all his satisfactions. Strange how much more interesting and readable a Sunday newspaper is than a daily paper. A daily paper is all rush and headlines, designed entirely for the strap-hanger. The Sunday paper was conceived in the interest of breakfasters in bed. It is all slow-going and familiar. You know just where to look for everything, and you almost know what will be printed there. He first of all read carefully the results of all the previous day's football. Queer that he should do so, for he had not played football for twenty-five years, and then very indifferently. But he had sneaking affections for certain clubs and he looked eagerly to see how they were faring. Then he read the General news. Everything seemed interesting; even political speeches were not too dull, but divorce and criminal cases were thrilling. He took no interest in literature, drama or music, but sayings of the week, police-court news, foreign intelligence, even Court chat, absorbed him. He read the advertisements and then the football news again, knocking the ash off his cigarette into the teacup. Sometimes his arms would get cold holding the paper, and he would put it down and tuck them under him. He would stare around the room, and glow with proprietorial delight. Then he would pick up the paper and start all over again. His splendid reveries were eventually disturbed by the voice of his wife calling from below:

'Jim, are you going to get up today or tomorrow?'

Dear, oh dear! Disturbing and alarming creatures, women. No sense of repose, no appreciation of real tranquillity. However, it must be getting late, and the morning constitutional to give one an appetite for lunch must not be disregarded. He devoted another ten minutes to an inert contemplation of the function of rising and dressing, and then rolled out of bed. He went into the bathroom, and lighted the geyser for his weekly bath. When the water was hot enough he drew off some for shaving, and returned to the bedroom for his new packet of safety razors. He caught sight of himself in the long mirror which his wife used. The reflection was so familiar that it produced in him no emotion whatever. He felt no misgiving about the puffy modelling of the face, the dishevelled strands of disappearing hair, the taut line made by the cord of his dressing gown where it met around his middle. He was just himself, getting up. Besides, no man looks his best first thing in the morning.

When he returned to the bathroom he was in gay spirits. During the operation of shaving he made curious volcanic noises meant to represent the sound of singing. Running water always affected him like that. The only disquieting element in this joyous affair was the fact that steam from the bath kept on clouding the mirror. He kept on rubbing it with a towel, shaving a little bit, then rubbing again, to the accompaniment of many damns and confounds. When that was over he pondered for some moments on the question of whether he should clean his teeth first, or have his bath. As the room was beginning to get full of steam, he decided on the latter course. He got in and let himself down slowly, for the water was very hot, and though his legs could stand it, other portions of his anatomy were more sensitive. He let in some cold water and settled down with a plomp. He soaped himself, and rubbed himself, and lay on his back, splashing gently. Glorious and delightful sensation. If he had time he would like to have a hot bath every day, but how could you expect a fellow to when he had to be in the city every day at nine-thirty? He got out of the bath, hot and pink and shiny. He dried himself, and cleaned his teeth. There! all the serious side of getting up was accomplished. During the performance of dressing he smoked another cigarette. He dressed very slowly, and deliberately, putting on a clean shirt, vest, socks and collar.

Golly! he felt good. He puffed out his chest, opened the window, and brushed his hair. He was rather pleased with his general appearance of respectability.

Now came the dangerous moment. He had to go downstairs. Would he be able to escape without being ordered to perform some unpleasant task by his wife? He went down, humming soulfully. In the sitting room the fire was burning brightly, but Jennie was not there. He could hear her bustling about in the kitchen, already preparing the solemn rites affecting the Sunday joint...no insignificant ritual. He wandered about the room, touching things, admiring their arrangement. He picked up two letters, which had come by the last post the previous night, and read them again. One was from his wife's sister at Ramsgate, full of details about the illness of her husband. The other was from a gentleman offering to lend him any sum of money from £5 to £10,000 on note of hand alone, without security. He tried to visualize £10,000, what he could do with it, the places he could visit, the house he could rent on the top of Hampstead Heath, a few dinners at the Savoy perhaps, a month in Paris (he had never been abroad). Then he tore the letter up and went into the kitchen.

'Er—anything I can do, my dear?'

'No, except to get out of the way.'

She was obviously on edge. Women were like that, especially first thing in the morning...curious creatures. He picked his teeth with a broken match, which happened to be conveniently in a waistcoat pocket. Anyway, he had done his duty. He had faced the music.

'Well, I'll just go for a stroll round,' he murmured ingratiatingly. He had escaped! A pallid sun was trying to penetrate a nebulous bank of clouds. The air was fresh and stimulating. A muffin man came along, ringing his bell. He passed two anaemic women carrying prayer books. At the corner of the road was a man with an impromptu kiosk of newspapers. He hesitated as to whether he should buy another newspaper. His wife wouldn't approve. She would say it was extravagant. Well, he could read on a seat on the top of the heath, and leave it there. But still—he resisted the temptation and walked on. The streets had their definitely Sunday look. You could tell it was Sunday in a glance…milk, prayer books, newspapers, muffins, wonderful! Dear England! A crowd of hatless young men on bicycles came racing along the Finchley Road, swarms of them, like gnats, and in the middle a woman riding behind a man on a tandem. They were all laughing and shouting with rather common voices…enjoying themselves though, off to the country for the day.

'The woman looks like the queen gnat,' he reflected. 'They are pursuing her. The race to the swift, the battle to the strong.' He was pleased with the luminance of this reflection. A boy asked him for a cigarette picture. He shook his head and passed on. Then he wondered whether…well, he had several in his pocket, but somehow he felt it would look silly to be giving cigarette pictures to a boy in the street. He didn't like that kind of thing. It made him conspicuous. Passers-by might look at him and say: 'Look at that fat man giving a boy cigarette pictures.' And they might laugh. It was all very curious, foolish perhaps, but there it was.

He knew he was going to walk up to the top of the heath, and along the Spaniards' Road, but he never liked to make up his mind to. He walked there by instalments, sometimes almost deciding to turn back, but he invariably got there in the end. Besides, what else could he do? Dinner was not till half-past one. He couldn't go home, and there was nowhere to sit down. Going up the hill he was conscious of the disturbance of his pulmonary organs…heart not too good, either, you know. The day would come when this would be too much for him. He enjoyed it when he got there. Oh, yes, this was a joyous place…heartening. He liked the noise, and bustle, and sense of space and light. Nearly every Sunday for twenty years he had walked up here. It was where the Cockney came to peep out of London, and regard the great world, the unexplored vista of his possessions. He was a little shy of it. He didn't look at the view much, but he liked to feel it was there. He preferred to watch boys sailing miniature yachts on the round pond, or to listen to a Socialist lecturer being good-humouredly heckled by a crowd. Every Sunday he had pondered an identical problem—why these public lecturers always chose the very noisiest spot on the whole heath, near the pond, amidst the yelping of dogs, the tooting of motor horns, the back-firing of motor bikes, and the din of a Salvation Army band. But there it was! This was England, perhaps the most English thing in all England. There were the young men in plus-fours, without hats, old men with their dogs, red-cheeked women riding astride brown mares...cars, bicycles, horses, dogs, even yachts! There were the fat policemen in couples, talking lazily, their mission being apparently to see that the fiery gentleman by the pond was allowed free speech...There were boys with kites, and boys with scooters, boys with nursemaids. Oh, a man's place this. Many more men than women. Did not the predominance signify something vital, something pertinent to the core of English life—the Sunday joint? It was only the women with cooks who were allowed to adorn this gay company. And even then—could a cook be trusted? Wasn't the wife's or mother's true place basting the sirloin, or regulating the gas-stove so that the roast shoulder should be done to a turn?

These reflections caused him to focus his attention upon the personal equation. What was to be the Sunday joint today? He was already beginning to feel those first delightful pangs of hunger, the just reward of exercise in fresh air. The Sunday joint? Why, yes, of course, he had heard Jenny say that she had ordered a loin of pork. Pork! delicious and seductive word. He licked his lips, and visualized the set board. It was not entirely a misfortune that the cook was ill, for Jenny was a much better cook. The pork would be done to a turn, with its beautiful brown encasement of crackling. There would be applesauce, Brussels sprouts, and probably lovely brown potatoes. He would carve. It was only right of course that the master of the house—the breadwinner—should control this ceremonial. There were little snippy brown bits—and that little bit of kidney underneath—that—well, one didn't give to a servant for instance.

He passed the orator once more, and overheard this remark:

'The day is coming when these blood-suckers will be forced to disgorge. They will be made to stew in their own juice. Look at Russia!'

Nobody appeared to be looking at Russia. With their pipes in the corner of their mouths they were looking stolidly at the speaker, or at the boys and their yachts. Dogs were barking furiously, and motor horns drowned any further declamation till he was out of hearing. The two fat policemen were talking about horse-racing. Oh, wonderful and imperishable country!

He had heard men talk in that strain before—but only in the city or in stuffy tea-shops. They spoke with fear in their hearts. Something was always going to happen. They didn't quite know what, but it was always something awful, and the country was just on the eve of it. But up here, amidst these dogs and bikes and horses you knew that nothing could ever happen to England. Everybody just went on doing things, making the best of things. The air was sweet and good. There was the Sunday joint in the offing, and the Cup Final next Sunday to be discussed.

He looked at his watch and proceeded to walk slowly homewards. It cannot be said that he thought about anything very definite on the way back, but his mind was pleasantly attacked by fragmentary thoughts, half-fledged ambitions to make more money, anticipations of a Masonic dinner the following week, the dim vision of an old romance with a girl in a tobacconist shop at Barnes. But at the back of his mind there loomed the solid assurance of the one thing that mattered—pork! He played with the vision, not openly but secretly. After the pork there would be pudding. He didn't care much about pudding, but there was a very good old gorgonzola to follow, and then a glass of port. After dinner a cigar, and then the Sunday newspaper again until he fell into that delightful doze in front of the fire. Oh, blessed day!

His timing was superb. He arrived at 'The Dog and Dolphin' at exactly one o'clock, in accordance with a time-honoured tradition—the gin-and-bitters to put the edge on one's appetite for dinner. The bar was filled with the usual Sunday morning crowd, some who had risen just in time for the bar to open, other stalwarts like himself, who had earned their appetiser through walking.

He was just ordering a gin-and-bitters when a voice said:

'Hullo, old boy, have this with me.'

He turned and beheld Beeswax, a fellow city man. They had known each other for fifteen years, meeting nearly every day, but neither had ever visited the other's house. He said:

'No, go on, you have it with me.'

They went through the usual formula of arguing who should pay for the first drink, both knowing quite well that the other would inevitably have to stand another drink in return. They stood each other two drinks, making four in all. In the meantime they discussed old so-and-so and old thingummy, trade, dogs, tobacco and females. Then he looked at his watch again. Just five-and-twenty past—perfect!

'Well, old boy, I must be off or I shall get into trouble with the missus.'

He walked quite briskly up the street, feeling good.

Life wasn't such a bad business to a normal man, if he looked after himself, and on the bright side of things. Pork, eh?

He knocked his pipe out against the parapet in the front garden, walked up the steps, and let himself in. He hung up his coat and hat, and was about to enter the sitting room, when he became abruptly sensitive to disaster. It began in the realization that there was no smell of roasting pork, no smell of anything cooking. He felt angry. Fate was going to cheat him in some way or the other. He did not have long to wait. His wife came screaming down the stairs, her face deadly white, her hair awry.

'Jim! Jim!' she shouted, 'rush to the corner quick. Fetch a policeman!'

'What?' he said.

'Fetch a policeman!'

'What for?'

'Moyna. She's dead. I went upstairs an hour ago and found her lying fully dressed on the floor. The gas stove was turned on. She looked awful, but she wasn't quite dead. I dragged her into our room, and fetched a doctor. He did what he could, but she died. She's lying dead on our bed. The doctor's up there now.'

'Yes, but—'

'Don't argue. Fetch a policeman. The doctor says we must.'

He fumbled his way out into the hall, and put on his hat and coat again. He knew it was no good arguing with his wife when she was like that. Damn! How wretched and disturbing and—inconvenient. He walked slowly up the street. What a disgusting and unpleasant job—fetching a policeman—beastly! He found a ripe specimen at the corner, staring at nothing. He explained the situation apologetically to the officer. The latter turned the matter over in his mind and made a noise that sounded like:

'Huh-huh.'

Then the two strolled back to the house at the law's pace, and talked about the weather. He found his wife in the sitting room, sobbing and carrying on, and the doctor was there too, and another woman from next door.

'I believe these women rather enjoy this kind of thing,' he reflected, the fires of hunger and anger burning within him. They all went upstairs and left him to ruminate. What a confounded and disgusting nuisance! Anyway, what did Jenny want to carry on like that for about a servant. Who was she? She hadn't been there long, about two weeks. She was an Irish girl, not bad-looking in that dark way. He seemed to remember that Jenny said she was married or something. Some man had been cruel to her, cruel and callous, she had said. She used to cry. Confound it! Why was it so difficult to get a good servant? But there it was. Jenny would carry on and be hysterical all the afternoon. There would be no dinner. Perhaps a snack of cheese or something on the quiet. Women were absurd, impossible. You couldn't cope with them. They had no reasoning power, no logic, no sense of fatality, no repose. It was enough to make one boil…pork, too!

—XIV—

Two of Those Women

WHEN TRAVELLING ON THE CONTINENT one must always be impressed, I think, by curious types of Englishwomen whom one never sees in their own country. One regards the French caricaturists' impression of the Englishwomen as a piece of absurd extravagance until one joins the Paris express at Charing Cross or Victoria. Very often they are middle-aged or quite elderly, and they go about singly, or in pairs, or sometimes in a party of three or four, like flocks of drab swallows. There is something terribly pathetic in their demeanour, particularly when one begins to realise the fact that they are not tourists, but hotel habituées. For there is a difference. The tourist is there temporarily for pleasure or sight-seeing, but the hotel habituée is a permanent, tragic, and often inexplicable figure. All over the South of France and Italy particularly there are thousands of these women staying at pensions and small hotels, drifting from place to place, rudderless, unwanted, and patently unhappy. They have the atmosphere of exiles, as of people who have committed some crime in their own country, and dare not return. And in many cases the crime that they have committed is, I suspect, the unpardonable crime of poverty. Women who have held some kind of social position in their own country, and become impoverished, develop the not unreasonable idea that they can live more cheaply, and with more dignity, in a foreign hotel. Some are exiled for reasons or illusions of health, or because someone has disappointed them or broken their hearts. These women in any case never give the impression that their mode of life is an entirely voluntary one. Although they may assume a perfunctory interest in the life and activities of the place of their sojourn, I have noticed that their chief concern is invariably—the next mail from England.

The story that I am going to tell is about two such women, and if I appear as a rather unscrupulous eavesdropper, you must please understand that I was a very unwilling one. In fact, I derived no actual enjoyment from it at all.

The accommodation in the little Hôtel Beau-Séjour at Antibes is very limited. I was trying to write something at the only writing table in the lounge, when two of these women—as I will call them—came along and seated themselves opposite me, and began to talk in languid voices.

Now I don't know what your powers of concentration are, but personally whenever I hear people talking I am bound to listen to what they say, however banal and trivial it may be. On this occasion I honestly did try to concentrate for a time, but their conversation soon usurped my entire attention. I realised that it was going to be no good, and so I drifted into the dishonest but popular habit of drawing diagrams on the back of hotel envelopes.

One of these women was about sixty, the other could hardly have been thirty, and they were obviously strangers to each other. But they had one thing in common. It might be called a kind of soul-weariness. Both were tired and bored, existing only in reminiscences. And it became very apparent that neither wanted to listen to the other. The old lady wanted to talk about her son. The younger one wanted to talk about some other man, and having missed the opening sentences I could not gather at first whether it was her brother, her lover, or her husband. But I could not help being impressed by the impatient attitude of either, while the other was speaking. They kept on interjecting: 'Yes, yes. No. Really! Fancy!' and the way they said it showed that neither had taken in a word of what the other had said.

'I shall never forget the pranks he used to play at Bolsover House School,' the elder woman was saying. 'There was a Euclid and gymnastic master there none of the boys liked...what was his name? I have forgotten. And there was a Miss Beaswyck, the matron, a very prim and severe person, who always wore black kid gloves. One day she annoyed Georgie very much. I have forgotten why. And Mr Raynes—yes, that was his name, funny how it comes to you when you're telling a story, and not trying to remember—well, he had punished Georgie for not doing his homework. When Mr Raynes went to bed that night he found Miss Beaswyck's black kid gloves, filled with cold porridge, in his bed. And Miss Beaswyck found Mr Raynes boxing gloves filled with cold porridge in *her* bed. Oh dear! there was a to-do!'

'Really! how amusing!' said the younger woman, without enthusiasm. 'Well, it happened in the very early spring...'

'Of course, where Georgie was so splendid was, he confessed. He confessed simply because the master suspected one of the other boys, and although nothing could be proved, he couldn't bear the idea of the other boy living under this eternal stigma.'

'Quite right,' said the younger woman. 'There are so few people with any sense of altruism. Now when I first met Peter, I was coming off duty at the base hospital at Amiens. We had had a terrible thirty-six hours. I was feeling awful—done up and finished. I must have looked awful. It was just after dawn. In the courtyard I suddenly felt my knees sagging. I was talking to an orderly, when I heard a voice say "Can't you see she's going to faint?" Before I did faint, I just had time to glimpse a pair of deep blue eyes, and the kindest face I have ever seen. He carried me somewhere. He never asked my name. He just did the kind thing and went away—'

'Ah, yes, my dear, there were some wonderful men in the War. Some vile, some sublime. My son, for instance. Ah, yes, we women...We women...It was wicked of me,

I suppose, but oh, how I used to pray that it would be over before my Georgie came of age! Oh, why couldn't they have come to some arrangement!'

'I know. I believe we women who...who had some one in it we loved all felt that. Of course, I did see him again, otherwise, I shouldn't be telling you all this...'

The elder woman uttered a deep sigh.

'We were so helpless though. Georgie never told me. He joined up a year before he was qualified, as a *private*, mind you! a private! and to think that my uncle commanded a brigade in the South African War! Of course he was such a splendid boy. He stood nearly six feet when he was eighteen. He looked every inch an officer even in his Tommy's uniform. A lot of the others used instinctively to call him 'Sir'. He wrote me such lovely letters, so cheerful, so gay, even when he was down with fever in those dreadful swamps in Greece. He used to write home about—oh, about everything except the war. It was just as though he were more interested in our little doings at Battlinghurst than he was in—in himself and the war.'

'Yes, yes,' said the younger woman wearily. 'I met Peter a few days later quite by chance in a narrow street near the railway station. He walked straight up to me and gravely asked me how I was. I was amazed that he remembered me. He looked, in the curious outfit they used to wear in the trenches, like one of those mediaeval knights. He told me he was going up to the front line in two hours' time. We had only a few hurried words and then he went.'

The elder woman clicked her tongue with what was meant to be a display of sympathy and interest, but her aged and short-sighted eyes were elsewhere.

'Games! that was what he was so good at. Cricket, football, all those things. They said there were several colleges at both Oxford and Cambridge anxious to have him because he could run a hundred yards in—ten minutes, was it? and he could knock anybody over at football. And yet the wonderful thing was he was so gentle with it all.

He wouldn't hurt a fly if he could help it. Of course he got his commission, my dear, did I tell you?'

I saw on the face of the younger woman a sudden expression of utter disgust and annoyance. She was, I am sure, thinking: 'Oh, you tedious old fool! What do I care about your ridiculous son! Don't you understand I'm trying to tell you about Peter. Peter! you know, my Peter, the most wonderful person in the world.'

The old lady was continuing:

'It seems strange to me, my dear, that after all these years, that part of it seems unreal. I can remember very little about it. Nothing at all about names and places and regiments and all those things. It was just a terrible nightmare coming between me and Georgie. When I think of him it is always of him when he was a baby or a boy. Everything, everything, I remember everything of those early days.'

The expression of the younger woman suggested: What was the interest of a baby and a schoolboy compared with the interest of a young man in the first flush of virile manhood? She fidgeted in her chair, and there was a silence. The two of them seemed to fall apart and forget each other. After a pause they drifted together again like migratory birds on a long flight. Strangely enough, it was the elder woman who seemed first conscious of their need for some kind of communion. Perhaps her conscience stabbed her that she had occupied too much of the conversation. She said hesitatingly:

'Did you marry this—did you marry the young man, my dear?'

It was evident that the question moved the younger woman profoundly.

She put her hand to her throat, and whispered almost inaudibly:

'No.'

Then controlling herself with an effort she continued:

'No, no, no. But you may guess the reason.'

'He was killed?'

The younger woman shook her head, and her voice shaking with tears, said:

'I do not know. In the war it was so easy to lose touch with people. We only met four times. But he swore that he loved me at our last meeting. God knows I loved him. Soon after he went I developed typhoid fever. I was terribly ill and sent to England. When I recovered I could find no trace of him. Whether he had been killed or sent to another front, perhaps killed there, perhaps married to someone else...I don't know, I tell you, I don't know. I shall never know. It was more than ten years ago this coming April, when the chestnut trees were blossoming along the banks of the Canal...I was only a girl then...oh, my God!'

She was trembling from the effect of this little outbreak, but in the pause she seemed to realise that it was she who had been monopolising the conversation. It was comforting to have *anyone* to tell all this to, you could see. And after all, the poor old lady had lost her son. Could it be as terrible to lose a son as a lover? Controlling herself she said:

'Where was your boy killed?'

The older woman was apparently reacting to this emotional display. Her eyes were fixed on the ground, and her tongue was beating a little tattoo between her lips. She did not answer the question.

'That dreadful uncertainty!' she suddenly exclaimed, 'how it has eaten me up. Men have never quite known what it means. Why do they have these wars? Why can't they come to some arrangement, I say? You are young, my dear. You may yet have a son, and pour out all your substance into making him a man. And when he has arrived at that...'

She shrugged her shoulders helplessly, and the younger woman said:

'No, I shall never have a son. I could never, never,

love anyone but Peter.'

It was quite apparent that during the last few minutes the women had been drawn more closely together. A link was formed by their common grief. Neither of them was any longer entirely preoccupied with her individual trouble. The younger woman repeated her question:

'Where was your boy killed, Mrs—er—?'

In her effort to appear interested she was handicapped by not knowing her companion's name, and she plainly did not like to address her as she herself was addressed as 'my dear'. What did it matter? They had drifted together, as they would drift apart. A name or a term meant nothing. Then the elder woman made a remark which surprised me:

'My son was not killed. He is still alive.'

I think this interested me more than it did the younger woman. Indeed, her brow puckered into a little perplexed frown, as though she thought that the other had not been quite playing the game. Why all this extravagant grief if she had not lost the boy after all? What was the old woman making this fuss about? The latter was continuing:

'He was captured by the Turks, you know. Did I tell you? Was it the Turks or the Arabs? some of those dark people, anyway, over there …'

She made a vague gesture in the direction of the North Pole.

'Georgie was two and a half years in one of their foul prisons. Ah! how vile it is that a man should be sent to prison for merely serving his country! Oh, and the conditions of it, the misery the torture, the anguish! No, I think for part of the time it was a Russian prison. I can't remember all that. I was so distracted. He lost an eye, a leg, and memory to a large extent. He had fever, I know. He hardly told us anything. And when in the end he came back, everything about him seemed to be lost. All his youth, and spirits. He hardly seemed to remember or care for me. Before he went out he was engaged to Millicent Brander, our vicar's daughter, as nice a girl as you could wish to meet. He would have nothing to do with her. And she was quite willing to marry him in spite of his missing eye, and leg, and memory. In delirious moments he swore he loved some other woman he had met on the Continent. I'm not sure it wasn't other women—vague names he mumbled. Absurd, of course, it all was. The doctors tried to persuade me that he would get right. He was chock full of illusions and panics...But eight years have passed, and he is little better. He takes little interest in anything except carpentry, and flowers, and keeping bees.'

'Where does he live?'

'At present he is in Switzerland. Someone persuaded me, I've forgotten who. He's staying with one of these new German doctors they make so much fuss about these days. You know, what do they call it? men who treat the mind. I don't believe in it, but he might as well be there as anywhere. Oh, yes, I believe it was my brother who persuaded me, and he is a doctor himself. A qualified medical man, but he dabbles in this other business. But why should I distress you, my dear, with all this? I'm an old fool, I know. Tell me more about your—Stephen, wasn't it? What is he like?'

'The younger woman heaved a deep sigh. I could see that she considered the story unsatisfactory and inconclusive. Then as though relieved to turn to a more congenial subject, she said:

'Peter? oh, Peter...' A long pause. 'He had deep blue eyes, very wide apart, a square chin, clean shaven. He was tall and strong, and there was a kind of—kind of elasticity about him. Elastic in mind and body. Beneath the gay exterior you were conscious of something profound and strong.'

The elder woman's interest appeared vaguely aroused.

'But,' she said, 'didn't you—didn't you enquire at the War Office? the Records Office, wasn't it? they knew pretty well.'

'That was the absurd part about it. I—we—' a girlish blush came to the younger woman's face. 'You see, well, when we first met it was just a flirtation. I christened him Peter. He made up a name for me. Life was so unreal in those days. Death seemed to be the only reality. What did it matter what we were called, who we were, or, for that matter, what we did? Oh, yes...we did flirt. We had...lovely times together. It was not till that last meeting when we both realised that the thing had gone far—become very serious. Just before he was leaving when it dawned upon us that neither knew the other's real name, and we had of course promised to correspond! There were other officers at the station, and he took out a card, scribbled his address on it, and thrust it into my hand. I didn't look at it, but slipped it into my purse. When I got back to the hospital the purse had disappeared! He had gone and I did not even know his name! So absorbed had we been with all the foolish little things that—people like us talk about—you've no idea how in those days we conspired together, men and women, to ignore the War—I did not even know his regiment. I only knew that he was in the heavy artillery.'

'Heavy artillery,' repeated the elder woman dully.

'Three days later I developed my fever. Oh, I'm not sure—I was so worried—I think the fever started before—I nearly went out of my mind.'

'You are sure it was the *heavy* artillery?' said the elder woman.

The younger one dabbed her nose and nodded. Both seemed to have fallen apart once more. The elder appeared to be ruminating. As though to herself she muttered, 'These German doctors say that there is only one thing that could cure my Georgie...but suppose...'

She took off her spectacles, wiped them, and regarded the other with the impaired vision of her naked sight, as though by this means she could observe something, unobserved herself.

'What was the pet name he called you, my dear?'

The younger woman appeared to hesitate. This was sacred ground. This old woman had no right to trespass. And yet, after all, she had already said so much. Greedy for sympathy and understanding, she said in a quiet clear voice:

'Little Wind-flower.'

The elder woman stood up and faced the window. She was still not wearing her glasses. The girl could not see her face, but I could. And I have never seen a stranger expression on the face of any living creature. Her eyes were wide open, and probably seeing nothing, but to me they seemed to absorb all the phenomena of existence at a glance. They were alight with amazement, and questioning. She was trembling violently, her lips were shaking, and I quite expected her to swoon. I felt most terribly embarrassed, as though I had stepped into a forbidden sanctuary. I did not know how to act. Neither of the women had taken the slightest notice of me. They had spoken in the quiet normal voices which women of their kind usually employ in an hotel, rather indifferent as to whether they are overheard or not by the other hotel guests. They had probably been aware of me at first, when the conversation opened so conventionally, but had forgotten me when they began to exchange their profound confidences.

But the elder woman did not swoon. After considerable effort she repeated in a perfectly controlled voice:

'Little Wind-flower!'

She turned and glanced overtly at the younger, but whether she could see her or not I could not say. Then she sat down, put on and carefully adjusted her spectacles. With a motherly gesture she put her hand on the other's, and said casually:

'What are your plans, my dear?'

The younger woman shrugged her shoulders, in the manner of one to whom plans have no longer interest or significance.

'Listen, then,' said the elder. 'Will you do me a favour?

I am leaving on Thursday for Lausanne to see my son. Will you come as my companion?'

The younger woman hesitated, and the elder seemed to press her hands harder, and she spoke earnestly and vehemently:

'Please do, my dear. I had a companion, and she had to leave because of illness in her family. I don't know what your position is, but I would gladly pay you. I am not badly off. My uncle, the brigadier, left me money last year. Please come. Oh, do please come.'

'You are extremely kind,' said the younger woman. 'I must think. I—have no plans, but this is—oh, please forgive me if I go away and think. It is most generous of you. I have just enough to pig along at these little hotels. But still—please forgive me.'

She gave both her companion's hands a tight squeeze and hurried out of the lounge. The old lady removed her spectacles once more. She wiped them with her handkerchief, and again dabbed her eyes. She was entirely oblivious to my presence. Her whole character seemed to have changed. She was still shaking, but it was with a kind of elation. For several minutes she sat there, mumbling to herself. Twice I heard her mutter:

'Little Wind-flower! Peter, she called him, did she?'

Unaccountable tears clouded her old eyes. Pressing her hand to her temple she whispered hoarsely: 'Oh, if it should be—'

She rose very slowly, and appeared to grope her way out of the room.

I sat there for a long time until it began to get dark.

A waiter came in.

'Shall I turn on the light, monsieur?'

'No, please,' I said, 'leave it all just as it is.'

And I continued to stare at my empty writing pad.

Two of those women? God forgive me!

—*XVII*—

'Old Fags'

THE BOYS CALLED HIM 'Old Fags', and the reason was not far to seek. He occupied a room in a block of tenements off Lisson Grove, bearing the somewhat grandiloquent title of Bolingbroke Buildings, and conspicuous among the many doubtful callings that occupied his time was one in which he issued forth with a deplorable old canvas sack, which, after a day's peregrination along the gutters, he would manage to partly fill with cigar and cigarette ends. The exact means by which he managed to convert this patiently gathered garbage into the wherewithal to support his disreputable body nobody took the trouble to enquire. Neither were their interests any further aroused by the disposal of the contents of the same sack when he returned with the gleanings of dustbins distributed thoughtfully at intervals along certain thoroughfares by a maternal borough council.

No one had ever penetrated to the inside of his room, but the general opinion in Bolingbroke Buildings was that he managed to live in a state of comfortable filth. And Mrs Read who lived in the room opposite, NO. 477, with her four children was of opinion that 'Old Fags 'ad 'oarded up a bit'. He certainly never seemed to be behind with the payment of the weekly three-and-sixpence that entitled him to the sole enjoyment of NO. 475, and when the door was opened, among the curious blend of odours that issued forth, that of onions and other luxuries of this sort was undeniable.

Nevertheless, he was not a popular figure in the Buildings. Many, in fact, looked upon him as a social blot on the Bolingbroke escutcheon. The inhabitants were mostly labourers and their wives, charwomen and lady helps, dressmakers' assistants, and several mechanics. There was a vague tentative effort among a great body of them to be a little respectable, and among some even to be clean.

No such uncomfortable considerations hampered the movements of Old Fags. He was frankly and ostentatiously a social derelict. He had no pride and no shame. He shuffled out in the morning, his blotchy face covered with dirt and black hair, his threadbare green clothes tattered and in rags, the toes all too visible through his forlorn-looking boots. He was rather a large man with a fat flabby person and a shiny face that was over-affable and bleary through a too constant attention to the gin bottle. He had a habit of ceaseless talk. He talked and chuckled to himself all the time, he talked to everyone he met in an undercurrent of jeering affability. Sometimes he would retire to his room with a gin bottle for days together and then (the walls at Bolingbroke Buildings are not very thick) he would be heard to talk and chuckle and snore alternately, until the percolating atmosphere of stewed onions heralded the fact that Old Fags was shortly on the war-path again.

He would meet Mrs Read with her children on the stairs and would mutter, 'Oh, here we are again! All these dear little children been out for a walk, eh? Oh these dear little children!' and he would pat one of them gaily on the head.

And Mrs Read would say: ''Ere, you keep your filthy 'ands off my kids, you dirty old swine, or I'll catch you a swipe over the mouth!'

And Old Fags would shuffle off muttering: 'Oh, dear! Oh, dear! these dear little children! Oh, dear! Oh dear!'

And the boys would call after him and even throw orange peel and other things at him, but nothing seemed to disturb the serenity of Old Fags. Even when young

Charlie Good threw a dead mouse that hit him on the chin he only said: 'Oh, these boys! these *boys!*'

Quarrels, noise and bad odours were the prevailing characteristics of Bolingbroke Buildings, and Old Fags, though contributing in some degree to the latter quality, rode serenely through the other two in spite of multiform aggression. The penetrating intensity of his onion stews had driven two lodgers already from NO. 476, and was again a source of aggravation to the present holders, old Mrs Birdle and her daughter Minnie.

Minnie Birdle was what was known as a 'tweeny' at a house in Hyde Park Square, but she lived at home. Her mistress—to whom she had never spoken, being engaged by the housekeeper—was Mrs Bastien-Melland, a lady who owned a valuable collection of little dogs. These little dogs somehow gave Minnie an unfathomable sense of respectability. She loved to talk about them. She told Mrs Read that her mistress paid ''undreds and 'undreds of pahnds for each of them.' They were taken out every day by a groom on two leads of five—ten highly groomed, bustling, yapping, snapping, vicious little luxuries. Some had won prizes at dog shows, and two men were engaged for the sole purpose of ministering to their creature comforts.

The consciousness of working in a house which furnished such an exhibition of festive cultivation brought into sharp relief the degrading social condition of her next room neighbour.

Minnie hated Old Fags with a bitter hatred. She even wrote to a firm of lawyers who represented some remote landlord and complained of 'the dirty habits of the old drunken wretch next door.' But she never received any answer to her complaint. It was known that Old Fags had lived there for seven years and paid his rent regularly.

Moreover, on one critical occasion, Mrs Read, who had periods of rheumatic gout, and could not work, had got into hopeless financial straits, having reached the very limit of her borrowing capacity, and being three weeks in arrears with her rent, Old Fags had come over and had insisted on lending her fifteen shillings! Mrs Read eventually paid it back, and the knowledge of the transaction further accentuated her animosity toward him.

One day Old Fags was returning from his dubious round and was passing through Hyde Park Square with his canvas bag slung over his back, when he ran into the cortège of little dogs under the control of Meads, the groom.

'Oh, dear! Oh, dear!' muttered Old Fags to himself. 'What dear little dogs! H'm! What dear little dogs!'

A minute later Minnie Birdle ran up the area steps and gave Meads a bright smile.

'Good-night, Mr Meads,' she said.

Mr Meads looked at her and said: ''Ullo! you off?'

'Yes!' she answered.

'Oh, well,' he said, 'Good-night! Be good!'

They both sniggered and Minnie hurried down the street. Before she reached Lisson Grove Old Fags had caught her up.

'I say,' he said, getting into her stride. 'What dear little dogs those are! Oh, dear! what dear little dogs!'

Minnie turned, and when she saw him her face flushed, and she said: 'Oh, you go to hell!' with which unladylike expression she darted across the road and was lost to sight.

'Oh, these women!' said Old Fags to himself, 'these *women!*'

It often happened after that Old Fags's business carried him in the neighbourhood of Hyde Park Square, and he ran into the little dogs. One day he even ventured to address Meads, and to congratulate him on the beauty of his canine protégés, an attention that elicited a very unsympathetic response, a response, in fact, that amounted to being told to 'clear off'.

The incident of Old Fags running into this society was

entirely accidental. It was due in part to the fact that the way lay through there to a tract of land in Paddington that Old Fags seemed to find peculiarly attractive. It was a neglected strip of ground by the railway that butted at one end on to a canal. It would have made quite a good siding but that it seemed somehow to have been overlooked by the railway company and to have become a dumping ground for tins and old refuse from the houses in the neighbourhood of Harrow Road. Old Fags would spend hours there alone with his canvas bag.

When winter came on there was a great wave of what the papers call 'economic unrest'. There were strikes in three great industries, a political upheaval, and a severe 'tightening of the money market'. All these misfortunes reacted on Bolingbroke Buildings. The dwellers became even more impecunious, and consequently more quarrelsome, more noisy and more malodorous. Rents were all in arrear, ejections were the order of the day, and borrowing became a tradition rather than an actuality. Want and hunger brooded over the dejected buildings. But still Old Fags came and went, carrying his shameless gin and permeating the passages with his onion stews.

Old Mrs Birdle became bedridden and the support of room NO. 476 fell on the shoulders of Minnie. The wages of a 'tweeny' are not excessive, and the way in which she managed to support herself and her invalid mother must have excited the wonder of the other dwellers in the building if they had not had more pressing affairs of their own to think about. Minnie was a short, sallow little thing, with a rather full figure, and heavy grey eyes that somehow conveyed a sense of sleeping passion. She had a certain instinct for dress, a knack of putting some trinket in the right place, and of always being neat.

Mrs Bastien-Melland had one day asked who she was. On being informed, her curiosity did not prompt her to push the matter further, and she did not speak to her, but the incident gave Minnie a better standing in the domestic household at Hyde Park Square. It was probably this attention that caused Meads, the head dog groom, to cast an eye in her direction. It is certain that he did so, and, moreover, on a certain Thursday evening had taken her to a cinema performance in the Edgware Road. Such attention naturally gave rise to discussion and alas! to jealousy, for there was an under-housemaid and even a lady's maid who were not impervious to the attentions of the good-looking groom.

When Mrs Bastien-Melland went to Egypt in January she took only three of the small dogs with her, for she could not be bothered with the society of a groom, and three dogs were as many as her two maids could spare time for after devoting their energies to Mrs Bastien-Melland's toilette. Consequently, Meads was left behind, and was held directly responsible for seven—five Chows and two Pekinese, or, as he expressed it, 'over a thousand pounds' worth of dogs'.

It was a position of enormous responsibility. They had to be fed on the very best food, all carefully prepared and cooked and in small quantities. They had to be taken for regular exercise and washed in specially prepared condiments. Moreover, at the slightest symptom of indisposition he was to telephone to Sir Andrew Fossiter, the great veterinary specialist, in Hanover Square. It is not to be wondered at that Meads became a person of considerable standing and envy, and that little Minnie Birdle was intensely flattered when he occasionally condescended to look in her direction. She had been in Mrs Bastien-Melland's service now for seven months and the attentions of the dog groom had not only been a matter of general observation for some time past, but had become a subject of reckless mirth and innuendo among the other servants.

One night she was hurrying home. Her mother had been rather worse than usual of late, and she was carrying a few scraps that the cook had given her. It was a wretched night and she was not feeling well herself, a mood of tired dejection possessed her. She crossed the drab street off Lisson Grove and as she reached the curb her eye lighted on Old Fags. He did not see her. He was walking along the gutter patting the road occasionally with his stick.

She had not spoken to him since the occasion we have mentioned. For once he was not talking: his eyes were fixed in listless apathy on the road. As he passed she caught the angle of his chin silhouetted against the window of a shop. For the rest of her walk the haunting vision of that chin beneath the drawn cheeks, and the brooding hopelessness of those sunken eyes, kept recurring to her. Perhaps in some remote past he had been as good to look upon as Meads, the groom! Perhaps someone had cared for him! She tried to push this thought from her, but some chord in her nature seemed to have been awakened and to vibrate with an unaccountable sympathy towards this undesirable fellow lodger.

She hurried home and in the night was ill. She could not go to Mrs Melland's for three days and she wanted the money badly. When she got about again she was subject to fainting fits and sickness. On one such occasion, as she was going upstairs at the Buildings, she felt faint, and leant against the wall just as Old Fags was going up. He stopped and said: 'Hullo, now, what are we doing? Oh, dear! Oh, dear!' and she said: 'It's all right, old 'un.' These were the kindest words she had ever spoken to Old Fags.

During the next month there were strange symptoms about Minnie Birdle that caused considerable comment, and there were occasions when old Mrs Birdle pulled herself together and became the active partner and waited on Minnie. On one such occasion Old Fags came home late and, after drawing a cork, varied his usual programme of talking and snoring by singing in a maudlin key, and old Mrs Birdle came banging at his door and shrieked out: 'Stop your row, you old— My daughter is ill. Can't you hear?' And Old Fags came to his door and blinked at her and said: 'Ill, is she? Oh, dear! Oh, dear! Would she like some stew, eh?' And old Mrs Birdle said: 'No, she don't want any of your muck,' and bundled back. But they did not hear any more of Old Fags that night or any other night when Minnie came home queer.

Early in March Minnie got the sack from Hyde Park Square. Mrs Melland was still away, having decided to winter in Rome; but the housekeeper assumed the responsibility of this action, and in writing to Mrs Melland justified the course she had taken by saying that 'she could not expect the other maids to work in the same house with an unmarried girl in that condition.' Mrs Melland, whose letter in reply was full of the serious illness of poor little Anisette (one of the Chows) that she had suffered in Egypt on account of a maid giving it too much rice with its boned chicken, and how much better it had been in Rome under the treatment of Dr Lascati, made no special reference to the question of Minnie Birdle, only saying that she was '*so* sorry if Mrs Bellingham was having trouble with these tiresome servants.'

The spring came and the summer, and the two inhabitants of Room 476 eked out their miserable existence. One day Minnie would pull herself together and get a day's charing, and occasionally Mrs Birdle would struggle along to a laundry in Maida Vale where a benevolent proprietress would pay her one shilling and threepence to do a day's ironing, for the old lady was rather neat with her hands. And once when things were very desperate a nephew from Walthamstow turned up. He was a small cabinet maker by trade, and he agreed to allow them three shillings a week 'till things righted themselves a bit'. But nothing was seen of Meads, the groom. One night Minnie was rather worse and the idea occurred to her that she would like to send a message to him. It was right that he should know. He had made no attempt to see her since she had left Mrs Melland's service. She lay awake thinking of him and wondering how she could send a message when she suddenly thought of Old Fags. He had been quiet of late; whether the demand for cigarette ends was abating and he could not afford the luxuries that their disposal seemed to supply, or whether he was keeping quiet for any ulterior reason she was not able to determine.

In the morning she sent her mother across to ask him if he would 'oblige by calling at Hyde Park Square and asking Mr Meads if he would oblige by calling at 476, Bolingbroke Buildings to see Miss Birdle.' There is no record of how Old Fags delivered this message, but it is known that that same afternoon Mr Meads did call. He left about three-thirty in a great state of perturbation and in a very bad temper. He passed Old Fags on the stairs, and the only comment he made was: 'I never have any luck! God help me!' and he did not return, although he had apparently promised to do so.

In a few weeks' time the position of the occupants of Room 476 became desperate. It was, in fact, a desperate time all round. Work was scarce and money scarcer. Waves of ill-temper and depression swept Bolingbroke Buildings. Mrs Read had gone—heaven knows where. Even Old Fags seemed at the end of his tether. True, he still managed to secure his inevitable bottle, but the stews became scarcer and less potent. All Mrs Birdle's time and energy were taken up in nursing Minnie, and the two somehow existed on the money now increased to four shillings a week, which the sympathetic cabinet maker from Walthamstow allowed them. The question of rent was shelved. Four shillings a week for two people means ceaseless gnawing hunger. The widow and her daughter lost pride and hope, and further messages to Mr Meads failed to elicit any response. The widow became so desperate that she even asked Old Fags one night if he could spare a little stew for her daughter who was starving. The pungent odour of the hot food was too much for her. Old Fags came to the door.

'Oh, dear! Oh, dear!' he said, 'What trouble there is! Let's see what we can do!' He messed about for some time and then took it across to them. It was a strange concoction. Meat that it would have been difficult to know what to ask for at the butcher's, and many bones, but the onions seemed to pull it together. To anyone starving it was good. After that it became a sort of established thing—whenever Old Fags *had* a stew he sent some over to the widow and daughter. But apparently things were not doing too well in the cigarette end trade, for the stews became more and more intermittent, and sometimes were desperately 'bony'.

And then one night a terrible climax was reached. Old Fags was awakened in the night by fearful screams. There was a district nurse in the next room, and also a student from a great hospital. No one knows how it all affected Old Fags. He went out at a very unusual hour in the early morning, and seemed more garrulous and meandering in his speech. He stopped the widow in the passage and mumbled incomprehensible solicitude. Minnie was very ill for three days, but she recovered, faced by the insoluble proposition of feeding three mouths instead of two, and two of them requiring enormous quantities of milk.

This terrible crisis brought out many good qualities in various people. The cabinet maker sent ten shillings extra and others came forward as though driven by some race instinct. Old Fags disappeared for ten days after that. It was owing to an unfortunate incident in Hyde Park when he insisted on sleeping on a flower bed with a gin-bottle under his left arm, and on account of the uncompromising attitude that he took up towards a policeman in the matter. When he returned things were assuming their normal course. Mrs Birdle's greeting was:

'Ullo, old 'un, we've missed your stoos.'

But Old Fags had undoubtedly secured a more stable position in the eyes of the Birdles, and one day he was even allowed to see the baby.

He talked to it from the door. 'Oh, dear! Oh, dear!' he said. 'What a beautiful little baby! What a dear little baby! Oh, dear! Oh, dear!'

The baby shrieked with unrestrained terror at sight of him, but that night some more stew was sent in.

Then the autumn came on. People whose romantic instincts had been touched at the arrival of the child gradually lost interest and fell away. The cabinet maker from Walthamstow wrote a long letter saying that after next week the payment of the four shillings would have to stop. He 'hoped he had been of some help in their trouble, but that things were going on all right now. Of course he had to think of his own family first,' and so on. The lawyers of the remote landlord, who was assiduously killing stags in Scotland, 'regretted that their client could not see his way to allow any further delay in the matter of the payment of rent due.' The position of the Birdle family became once more desperate. Old Mrs Birdle had become frailer, and though Minnie could now get about she found work difficult to obtain, owing to people's demand for a character from the last place. Their thoughts once more reverted to Meads, and Minnie lay in wait for him one morning as he was taking the dogs out. There was a very trying scene ending in a very vulgar quarrel, and Minnie came home and cried all the rest of the day and through half the night. Old Fags' stews became scarcer and less palatable. He, too, seemed in dire straits.

We now come to an incident that we are ashamed to say owes its inception to the effect of alcohol. It was a wretched morning in late October, bleak and foggy. The blue-grey corridors of Bolingbroke Buildings seemed to exude damp. The strident voices of the unkempt children quarrelling in the courtyard below permeated the whole Buildings. The strange odour that was its characteristic lay upon it like the foul breath of some evil God. All its inhabitants seemed hungry, wretched and vile. Their lives of constant protest seemed for the moment lulled to a sullen indifference, whilst they huddled behind their gloomy doors and listened to the rancorous railings of their offspring. The widow Birdle and her daughter sat silently in their room. The child was asleep. It had had its milk, and it would have to have its milk whatever happened. The crumbs from the bread the women had had at breakfast lay ungathered on the bare table. They were both hungry and very desperate. There was a knock at the door. Minnie went to it, and there stood Old Fags. He leered at them meekly and under his arm carried a gin-bottle three parts full.

'Oh, dear!' Oh, dear!' he said. 'What a dreadful day! What a dreadful day! Will you have a little drop of gin to comfort you? Now! What do you say?'

Minnie looked at her mother; in other days the door would have been slammed in his face, but Old Fags had certainly been kind in the matter of the stews. They asked him to sit down. Then old Mrs Birdle did accept 'just a tiny drop of gin,' and they both persuaded Minnie to have a little. Now neither of the women had had food of any worth for days, and the gin went straight to their heads. It was already in Old Fags' head firmly established. The three immediately became garrulous. They all talked volubly and intimately. The women railed Old Fags about his dirt, but allowed that he had 'a good 'eart'. They talked longingly and lovingly about his 'stoos', and Old Fags said:

'Well, my dears, you shall have the finest stoo you've ever had in your lives to-night.'

He repeated this nine times, only each time the whole sentence sounded like one word. Then the conversation drifted to the child, and the hard lot of parents, and by a natural sequence to Meads, its father. Meads was discussed with considerable bitterness, and the constant reiteration of the threat by the women that they meant to ''ave the lor on 'im all right', mingled with the jeering sophistries of Old Fags on the 'genalman's behaviour', and the impossibility of expecting 'a dog groom to be sportsman', lasted a considerable time.

Old Fags talked expansively about 'leaving it to him', and somehow as he stood there with his large puffy figure looming up in the dimly lighted room, and waving his long arms, he appeared to the women a figure of portentous significance. He typified powers they had not dreamt of. Under the veneer of his hide-bound depravity Minnie seemed to detect some slow-moving force trying to assert itself. He meandered on in a vague monologue, using terms and expressions they did not know the meaning of. He gave the impression of some fettered animal launching a fierce indictment against the fact of its life. At last he took up the gin-bottle and moved to the door and then leered round the room. 'You shall have the finest stoo you've ever had in your life to-night, my dears!' He repeated this seven times again and then went heavily out.

That afternoon a very amazing fact was observed by several inhabitants of Bolingbroke Buildings. Old Fags washed his face! He went out about three o'clock without his sack. His face had certainly been cleaned up and his clothes seemed in some mysterious fashion to hold together. He went across Lisson Grove and made for Hyde Park Square. He hung about for nearly an hour at the corner, and then he saw a man come up the area steps of a house on the south side and walk rapidly away. Old Fags followed him. He took a turning sharp to the left through a mews and entered a narrow street at the end. There he entered a deserted-looking pub kept by an ex-butler and his wife. He passed right through to a room at the back and called for some beer. Before it was brought Old Fags was seated at the next table ordering gin.

'Dear, oh dear! what a wretched day!' said Old Fags.

The groom grunted assent. But Old Fags was not to be put off by mere indifference. He broke ground on one or two subjects that interested the groom, one subject in particular being dog. He seemed to have a profound knowledge of dog, and before Mr. Meads quite realized what was happening he was trying gin in his beer at Old Fags' expense. The groom was feeling particularly morose that afternoon. His luck seemed out. Bookmakers had appropriated several half-crowns that he sorely begrudged, and he had other expenses. The beer-gin mixture comforted him, and the rambling eloquence of the old fool who seemed disposed to be content paying for drinks and talking, fitted in with his mood.

They drank and talked for a full hour, and at length got to a subject that all men get to sooner or later if they drink and talk long enough—the subject of woman. Mr Meads became confiding and philosophic. He talked of women in general and what triumphs and adventures he had had among them in particular. But what a trial and tribulation they had been to him in spite of all. Old Fags winked knowingly and was splendidly comprehensive and tolerant of Meads' peccadillos.

'It's all a game,' said Meads. 'You've got to manage 'em. There ain't much I don't know, old bird!'

Then suddenly Old Fags leaned forward in the dark room and said:

'No, Mr Meads, but you ought to play the game you know. Oh, dear, yes!'

'What do you mean, *Mister Meads*?' said that gentleman sharply.

'Minnie Birdle, eh? you haven't mentioned Minnie Birdle yet!' said Old Fags.

'What the devil are you talking about?' said Meads drunkenly.

'She's starving,' said Old Fags, 'starving, wretched, alone with her old mother and your child. Oh, dear! yes, it's terrible!'

Meads' eyes flashed with a sullen frenzy but fear was gnawing at his heart, and he felt more disposed to placate this mysterious old man than to quarrel with him.

'I tell you I have no luck,' he said after a pause. Old Fags looked at him gloomily and ordered some more gin. When it was brought he said:

'You ought to play the game, you know, Mr. Meads—after all—luck? Oh, dear! Oh, dear! Would you rather be the woman? Five shillings a week you know would—'

'No, I'm damned if I do!' cried Meads fiercely. 'It's all right for all these women. Gawd! How do I know if it's true? Look here, old bird, do you know I'm already done in for two five bobs a week, eh? One up in Norfolk and the other at Enfield. Ten shillings a week of my — money goes to these blasted women. No fear, no more, I'm through with it!'

'Oh, dear! Oh, dear!' said Old Fags, and he moved a little further into the shadow of the room and watched the groom out of the depths of his sunken eyes. But Meads' courage was now fortified by the fumes of a large quantity of fiery alcohol, and he spoke witheringly of women in general and seemed disposed to quarrel if Old Fags disputed his right to place them in the position that Meads considered their right and natural position. But Old Fags gave no evidence of taking up the challenge: on the contrary he seemed to suddenly shift his ground. He grinned and leered and nodded at Meads' string of coarse sophistry, and suddenly he touched him on the arm and looked round the room and said very confidentially:

'Oh, dear! yes, Mr Meads. Don't take too much to heart what I said.'

And then he sniffed and whispered:

'I could put you on to a very nice thing, Mr Meads. I could introduce you to a lady I know would take a fancy to you, and you to her. Oh, dear, yes!'

Meads pricked up his ears like a fox-terrier and his small eyes glittered.

'Oh!' he said. 'Are you one of those, eh, old bird? Who is she?'

Old Fags took out a piece of paper and fumbled with a pencil. He then wrote down a name and address somewhere at Shepherd's Bush.

'What's a good time to call?' said Meads.

'Between six and seven,' answered Old Fags.

'Oh, hell!' said Meads, 'I can't do it. I've got to get back and take the dogs out at half-past five, old bird. From half-past five to half-past six. The missus is back, she'll kick up a hell of a row.'

'Oh, dear! Oh, dear!' said Old Fags. 'What a pity! The young lady is going away, too!'

He thought for a moment, and then an idea seemed to strike him.

'Look here, would you like me to meet you and take the dogs round the park till you return?'

'What!' said Meads. 'Trust you with a thousand pounds' worth of dogs! Not much!'

'No, no, of course not, I hadn't thought of that!' said Old Fags humbly.

Meads looked at him, and it is very difficult to tell what it was about the old man that gave him a sudden feeling of complete trust. The ingenuity of his speech, the ingratiating confidence that a mixture of beer-gin gives, tempered by the knowledge that famous pedigree Pekinese would be almost impossible to dispose of, perhaps it was a combination of these motives. In any case a riotous impulse drove him to fall in with Old Fags' suggestion and he made the appointment for half-past five.

* * *

Evening had fallen early, and a fine rain was driving in fitful gusts when the two met at the corner of Hyde Park. There were ten little dogs on their lead, and Meads with a cap pulled close over his eyes.

'Oh, dear! Oh, dear!' cried Old Fags as he approached. 'What dear little dogs! What dear little dogs!'

Meads handed the lead over to Old Fags, and asked

more precise instructions of the way to get to the address.

'What are you wearing that canvas sack inside your coat for, old bird, eh?' asked Meads, when these instructions had been given.

'Oh, my dear sir,' said Old Fags. 'If you had the asthma like I get it, and no underclothes on these damp days! Oh, dear! Oh, dear!'

He wheezed drearily and Meads gave him one or two more exhortations about the extreme care and tact he was to observe.

'Be very careful with that little Chow on the left lead. 'E's got his coat on, see? 'E's 'ad a chill and you must keep 'im on the move. Gently, see.'

'Oh, dear! Oh, dear! Poor little chap! What's his name?' said Old Fags.

'Pelleas,' answered Mr Meads.

'Oh, poor little Pelleas! Poor little Pelleas! Come along. You won't be too long, Mr Meads, will you?'

'You bet I won't,' said the groom, and nodding he crossed the road rapidly and mounting a Shepherd's Bush motor-bus he set out on his journey to an address that didn't exist.

Old Fags ambled slowly round the Park, snuffling and talking to the dogs. He gauged the time when Meads would be somewhere about Queen's Road, then he ambled slowly back to the point from which he had started. With extreme care he piloted the small army across the high road and led them in the direction of Paddington. He drifted with leisurely confidence through a maze of small streets. Several people stopped and looked at the dogs, and the boys barked and mimicked them, but nobody took the trouble to look at Old Fags. At length he came to a district where their presence seemed more conspicuous. Rows of squalid houses and advertisement hoardings. He slightly increased his pace, and a very stout policeman standing outside a funeral furnishers' glanced at him with a vague suspicion. However, in strict accordance with an ingrained officialism that hates to act 'without instructions', he let the cortège pass. Old Fags wandered through a wretched street that seemed entirely peopled by children. Several of them came up and followed the dogs.

'Dear little dogs, aren't they? Oh my, yes, dear little dogs!' he said to the children. At last he reached a broad gloomy thoroughfare with low irregular buildings on one side, and an interminable length of hoardings on the other that screened a strip of land by the railway—land that harboured a wilderness of tins and garbage. Old Fags led the dogs along by the hoarding. It was very dark. Three children, who had been following, tired of the pastime, had drifted away. He went along once more. There was a gap in a hoarding on which was notified that 'Pogram's Landaulettes could be hired for the evening at an inclusive fee of two guineas. Telephone 47901 Mayfair.' The meagre light from a street lamp thirty yards away revealed a colossal coloured picture of a very beautiful young man and woman stepping out of a car and entering a gorgeous restaurant, having evidently just enjoyed the advantage of this peerless luxury. Old Fags went on another forty yards and then returned. There was no one in sight.

'Oh, dear little dogs,' he said. 'Oh, dear! Oh, dear! What dear little dogs! Just through here, my pretty pets. Gently, Pelleas! Gently, very gently! There, there, there! Oh, what dear little dogs!'

He stumbled forward through the quagmire of desolation, picking his way as though familiar with every inch of ground, to the further corner where it was even darker, and where the noise of shunting freight trains drowned every other murmur of the night.

* * *

It was eight o'clock when Old Fags reached his room in Bolingbroke Buildings carrying his heavily laden sack across his shoulders. The child in Room 476 had been peevish and fretful all the afternoon and the two women were lying down exhausted. They heard Old Fags come in. He seemed very busy, banging about with bottles and tins and alternately coughing and wheezing. But soon the potent aroma of onions reached their nostrils and they knew he was preparing to keep his word.

At nine o'clock he staggered across with a steaming saucepan of hot stew. In contrast to the morning's conversation, which though devoid of self-consciousness, had taken on at times an air of moribund analysis, making little stabs at fundamental things, the evening passed off on a note of almost joyous levity. The stew was extremely good to the starving women, and Old Fags developed a vein of fantastic pleasantry. He talked unceasingly, sometimes on things they understood, sometimes on matters of which they were entirely ignorant and sometimes he appeared to them obtuse, maudlin and incoherent.

Nevertheless he brought to their room a certain light-hearted raillery that had never visited it before. No mention was made of Meads. The only blemish to the serenity of this bizarre supper party was that Old Fags developed intervals of violent coughing, intervals when he had to walk around the room and beat his chest. These fits had the unfortunate result of waking the baby. When this undesirable result had occurred for the fourth time Old Fags said:

'Oh, dear! Oh, dear! This won't do! Oh, no, this won't do. I must go back to my hotel!' a remark that caused paroxysms of mirth to old Mrs Birdle.

Nevertheless, Old Fags retired and it was then just on eleven o'clock. The women went to bed, and all through the night Minnie heard the old man coughing. And while he is lying in this unfortunate condition let us follow the movements of Mr Meads.

Meads jumped off the bus at Shepherd's Bush and hurried quickly in the direction that Old Fags had instructed him. He asked three people for the Pomeranian

Road before an errand boy told him that he 'believed it was somewhere off Giles Avenue,' but at Giles Avenue no one seemed to know it. He retraced his steps in a very bad temper and enquired again. Five other people had never heard of it. So he went to a post office and a young lady in charge informed him that there was no such road in the neighbourhood.

He tried other roads whose names vaguely resembled it then he came to the conclusion 'that that blamed old fool had made a silly mistake.' He took a bus back with a curious fear gnawing at the pit of his stomach, a fear that he kept thrusting back; he dare not allow himself to contemplate it. It was nearly seven-thirty when he got back to Hyde Park and his eye quickly scanned the length of railing near which Old Fags was to be. Immediately that he saw no sign of him or the little dogs, a horrible feeling of physical sickness assailed him. The whole truth flashed through his mind. He saw the fabric of his life crumble to dust. He was conscious of visions of past acts and misdeeds tumbling over each other in a furious kaleidoscope.

The groom was terribly frightened. Mrs Bastien-Melland would be in at eight o'clock to dinner, and the first thing she would ask for would be the little dogs. They were never supposed to go out after dark, but he had been busy that afternoon and arranged to take them out later. How was he to account for himself and their loss?

He visualized himself in a dock, and all sorts of other horrid things coming up—a forged character, an affair in Norfolk and another at Enfield, and a little trouble with a bookmaker seven years ago. For he felt convinced that the dogs had gone for ever, and Old Fags with them.

He cursed blindly in his soul at his foul luck and the wretched inclination that had lured him to drink 'beer-gin' with the old thief. Forms of terrific vengeance passed through his mind, if he should meet the old devil again. In the meantime what should he do? He had never even thought of making Old Fags give him any sort of address. He dared not go back to Hyde Park Square without the dogs. He ran breathlessly up and down peering in every direction. Eight o'clock came and there was still no sign! Suddenly he remembered Minnie Birdle. He remembered that the old ruffian had mentioned and seemed to know Minnie Birdle. It was a connection that he had hoped to have wiped out of his life, but the case was desperate.

Curiously enough, during his desultory courtship of Minnie he had never been to her home, but on the only occasion when he had visited it, after the birth of the child, he had done so under the influence of three pints of beer, and he hadn't the faintest recollection now of the number or the block. He hurried there, however, in feverish trepidation. Now Bolingbroke Buildings harbour some eight hundred people, and it is a remarkable fact that although the Birdles had lived there about a year, of the eleven people that Meads asked not one happened to know the name. People develop a profound sense of self-concentration in Bolingbroke Buildings. Meads wandered up all the stairs and through the slate-tile passages. Twice he passed their door without knowing it: on the first occasion only five minutes after Old Fags had carried a saucepan of steaming stew from NO. 475 to NO. 476.

At ten o'clock he gave it up. He had four shillings on him and he adjourned to a small pub hard by and ordered a tankard of ale, and as an afterthought, three pennyworth of gin which he mixed in it. Probably he thought that this mixture, which was so directly responsible for the train of tragic circumstances that encompassed him, might continue to act in some manner towards a more desirable conclusion. It did indeed drive him to action of a sort, for he sat there drinking and smoking Navy Cut cigarettes, and by degrees he evolved a most engaging but impossible story of being lured to the river by three men and chloroformed, and when he came to, finding that the dogs and the men had gone. He drank a further quantity of 'beer-gin' and rehearsed his role in detail, and at length brought himself to the point of facing Mrs Melland...

It was the most terrifying ordeal of his life. The servants frightened him for a start. They almost shrieked when they saw him and drew back. Mrs Bastien-Melland had left word that he was to go to a breakfast-room in the basement directly he came in and she would see him. There was a small dinner party on that evening and an agitated game of bridge. Meads had not stood on the hearthrug of the breakfast-room two minutes before he heard the foreboding swish of skirts, the door burst open and Mrs Bastien-Melland stood before him, a thing of penetrating perfumes, high-lights and trepidation.

She just said 'Well!' and fixed her hard bright eyes on him. Meads launched forth into his improbable story, but he dared not look at her. He tried to gather together the pieces of the tale he had so carefully rehearsed in the pub, but he felt like some helpless barque at the mercy of a hostile battle fleet, the searchlights of Mrs Melland's cruel eyes were concentrated on him, while a flotilla of small diamonds on her heaving bosom winked and glittered with a dangerous insolence. He was stumbling over a phrase about the effects of chloroform when he became aware that Mrs Melland was not listening to the matter of his story, she was only concerned with the manner. Her lips were set and her straining eyes insisted on catching his. He looked full at her and caught his breath and stopped.

Mrs Melland still staring at him was moving slowly to the door. A moment of panic seized him. He mumbled something and also moved towards the door. Mrs Melland was first to grip the handle. Meads made a wild dive and seized her wrist. But Mrs Bastien-Melland came of a hard-riding Yorkshire family. She did not lose her head. She struck him across the mouth with her flat hand, and as he reeled back she opened the door and called to the servants. Suddenly Meads remembered that the rooms had a French window on to the garden. He pushed her clumsily against the door and sprang across the room. He clutched wildly at the bolts while Mrs Melland's voice was ringing out:

'Catch that man! Hold him! Catch thief!'

But before the other servants had had time to arrive he managed to get through the door and to pull it to after him. His hand was bleeding with cuts from broken glass but he leapt the wall and got into the shadow of some shrubs three gardens away. He heard whistles blowing and the dominant voice of Mrs Melland directing a hue and cry. He rested some moments, then panic seized him and he laboured over another wall and found the passage of a semi-detached house. A servant opened a door and looked out and screamed. He struck her wildly and unreasonably on the shoulder and rushed up some steps and got into a front garden. There was no one there and he darted into the street and across the road.

In a few minutes he was lost in a labyrinth of back streets and laughing hysterically to himself. He had two shillings and eightpence on him. He spent fourpence of this on whisky, and then another fourpence just before the pubs closed. He struggled vainly to formulate some definite plan of campaign. The only point that seemed terribly clear to him was that he must get away. He knew Mrs Melland only too well. She would spare no trouble in hunting him down. She would exact the uttermost farthing. It meant gaol and ruin. The obvious impediment to getting away was that he had no money and no friends. He had not sufficient strength of character to face a tramp life. He had lived too long in the society of the pampered Pekinese. He loved comfort.

Out of the simmering tumult of his soul grew a very definite passion—the passion of hate. He developed a vast, bitter, scorching hatred for the person who had caused this ghastly climax to his unfortunate career—Old Fags. He went over the whole incidents of the day again rapidly recalling every phase of Old Fags' conversation and manner. What a blind fool he was not to have seen through the filthy old swine's game! But what had he done with the dogs? Sold the lot for a pound, perhaps! The idea made Meads shiver. He slouched through the streets harbouring his pariah-like lust.

* * *

We will not attempt to record the psychologic changes that harassed the soul of Mr Meads during the next two days and nights, the ugly passions that stirred him and beat their wings against the night, the tentative intuitions urging towards some vague new start, the various compromises he made with himself, his weakness and inconsistency that found him bereft of any quality other than the sombre shadow of some ill-conceived revenge. We will only note that on the evening of the day we mention he turned up at Bolingbroke Buildings. His face was haggard and drawn, his eyes blood-shot and his clothes tattered and muddy. His appearance and demeanour were unfortunately not so alien to the general character of Bolingbroke Buildings as to attract any particular attention, and he slunk like a wolf through the dreary passages and watched the people come and go.

It was at about a quarter to ten when he was going along a passage in Block 'F' that he suddenly saw Minnie Birdle come out of one door and go into another.

His small eyes glittered and he went on tip-toe. He waited till Minnie was quite silent in her room and then he went stealthily to Room 475. He tried the handle and it gave. He opened the door and peered in. There was a cheap tin lamp guttering on a box that dimly revealed a room of repulsive wretchedness. The furniture seemed mostly to consist of bottles and rags. But in one corner on a mattress he beheld the grinning face of his enemy—Old Fags. Meads shut the door silently and stood with his back to it.

'Oh!' he said. 'So here we are at last, old bird, eh!'

This move was apparently a supremely successful dramatic coup, for Old Fags lay still, paralyzed with fear, no doubt.

'So this is our little 'ome, eh?' he continued, 'where we bring little dogs and sell 'em. What have you got to say, you old —'

The groom's face blazed into a sudden accumulated fury. He thrust his chin forward and let forth a volley of frightful and blasting oaths. But Old Fags didn't answer; his shiny face seemed to be intensely amused with this outburst.

'We got to settle our little account, old bird, see?' and the suppressed fury of his voice denoted some physical climax. 'Why the hell don't you answer?' he suddenly shrieked, and springing forward he lashed Old Fags across the cheek.

And then a terrible horror came over him. The cheek he had struck was as cold as marble and the head fell a little impotently to one side. Trembling, as though struck with an ague, the groom picked up the guttering lamp and held it close to the face of Old Fags. It was set in an impenetrable repose, the significance of which even the groom could not misunderstand. The features were calm and childlike, lit by a half smile of splendid tolerance that seemed to have overridden the temporary buffets of a queer world. Meads had no idea how long he stood there gazing horror-struck at the face of his enemy. He only knew that he was presently conscious that Minnie Birdle was standing by his side and as he looked at her, her gaze was fixed on Old Fags and a tear was trickling down either cheek.

''E's dead,' she said. 'Old Fags is dead. 'E died this morning of noomonyer.'

She said this quite simply as though it was a statement that explained the wonder of her presence. She did not look at Meads or seem aware of him. He watched the flickering light from the lamp illumining the underside of her chin and nostrils and her quivering brows.

''E's dead,' she said again, and the statement seemed to come as an edict of dismissal as though love and hatred and revenge had no place in these fundamental things. Meads looked from her to the tousled head leaning slightly to one side of the mattress and he felt himself in the presence of forces he could not comprehend. He put the lamp back quietly on the box and tip-toed from the room.

Out once more in the night, his breath came quickly and a certain buoyancy drove him on. He dared not contemplate the terror of that threshold upon which he had almost trodden. He only knew that out of the surging maelstrom of irresolution some fate had gripped him. He walked with a certain elasticity in the direction of Millwall. There would be doss-houses and docks there and many a good ship that glided forth to strange lands, carrying human freight of whom few questions would be asked, for the ship wanted them to ease her way through the regenerating seas...

And in the cold hours of the early dawn Minnie Birdle lay awake listening to the rhythmic breathing of her child. And she thought of that strange old man, less terrible now in his mask of death than when she had first known him. No one tomorrow would follow to his pauper's grave, and yet at one time—who knows? She dared not speculate upon the tangled skein of this difficult life that had brought him to this. She only knew that somehow from it she had drawn a certain vibrant force that made her build a monster resolution. Her child! She would be strong, she would throw her frail body between it and the shafts of an unthinking world. She leant across it, listening intensely, then kissed the delicate down upon its skull, crooning with animal satisfaction at the smell of its warm soft flesh.

—XVIII—

The Octave of Jealousy

I

A TRAMP came through a cutting by old Jerry Shindle's nursery, and crossing the stile, stepped into the glare of the white road. He was a tall swarthy man with stubby red whiskers which appeared to conceal the whole of his face, except a small portion under each eye about the size of a two shilling piece. His skin showed through the rents in a filthy old black-green garment, and was the same colour as his face, a livid bronze. His toes protruded from his boots, which seemed to be home-made contraptions of canvas and string. He carried an ash stick, and the rest of his worldly belongings in a spotted red and white handkerchief. His worldly belongings consisted of some rags, a door-knob, a portion of a foot-rule, a tin mug stolen from a workhouse, half a dozen date stones, a small piece of very old bread, a raw onion, the shutter of a camera and two empty matchboxes.

He looked up and down the road as though uncertain of his direction. To the north it curved under the wooded opulence of Crawshay Park. To the south it stretched like a white ribbon across a bold vista of shadeless downs. He was hungry and he eyed, critically, the potential possibilities of a cottage standing back from the road. It was a shabby little three-roomed affair with fowls running in and out of the front door, some washing on a line, and the sound of a child crying within. While he was hesitating, a farm labourer came through a gate to an adjoining field, and walked toward the cottage. He, too, carried property tied up in a red handkerchief. His other hand balanced a steel fork across his left shoulder. He was a thick-set, rather dour-looking man. As he came up the tramp said:

'Where does this road lead to, mate?'

The labourer replied brusquely:

'Pondhurst.'

'How far?'

'Three and a half miles.'

Without embroidering this information any further he walked stolidly across the road and entered the garden of the cottage. The tramp watched him put the fork down by the lintelled door. He saw him enter the cottage, and he heard a woman's voice. He sighed and muttered into his stubbly red beard: 'Lucky devil!' Then, hunching his shoulders, he set out with long flat-footed strides down the white road which led across the downs.

II

Having kicked some mud off his boots, the labourer, Martin Crosby, said to his wife:

'Dinner ready?'

Emma Crosby was wringing out some clothes. Her face was shiny with the steam and the heat of the day. She answered petulantly:

'No, it isn't. You'll have to wait another ten minutes, the 'taters aren't cooked. I've enough to do this morning I can tell you, what with the washing, and Lizzie screaming with her teeth, and the biler going wrong.'

'Ugh! There's allus somethin'.'

Martin knew there was no appeal against delay. He had been married four years; he knew his wife's temper and mode of life sufficiently well. He went out into the garden and lighted his pipe. The fowls clucked round his feet and he kicked them away. He, too, was hungry. However, there would be food of a sort—in time. Some greasy pudding and potatoes boiled to a liquid mash, a piece of cheese perhaps. Well, there it was. When you work in the open air all day you can eat anything. The sun was pleasant on his face, the shag pungent and comforting. If only old Emma weren't such a muddler! A good enough piece of goods when at her best, but always in a muddle, always behind time, no management, and then resentful because things went wrong. Lizzie: seven months old and two teeth through already and another coming. A lovely child, the spit and image of—what her mother must have been. Next time it would be a boy. Life wasn't so bad—really.

The gate clicked, and the tall figure of Ambrose Baines appeared. He was dressed in a corduroy coat and knickers, stout brown gaiters and square thick boots. Tucked under his arm was a gun with its two barrels pointing at the ground. He was the gamekeeper to Sir Septimus Letter. He stood just inside the gate and called out:

'Mornin', Martin.'

Martin replied: 'Mornin'.'

'I was just passin'. The missus says you can have a cookin' or so of runner beans if you wants 'em. We've got more than enough, and I hear as yours is blighty.'

'Oh! ... ay, thank'ee.'

'Middlin' hot to-day.'

'Ay ... terrible hot.'

'When'll you be comin'?'

'I'll stroll over now. There's nowt to do. I'm waitin' dinner. I 'specks it'll be a half-hour or so. You know what Emma is.'

He went inside and fetched a basket. He said nothing to his wife, but rejoined Baines in the road. They strolled through the cutting and got into the back of the gamekeeper's garden just inside the wood. Martin went along the row and filled his basket. Baines left him and went into his cottage. He could hear Mrs Baines singing and washing up.

Of course *they* had had their dinner. It would be like that. Mrs Baines was a marvel. On one or two occasions

Martin had entered their cottage. Everything was spick and span, and done on time. The two children always seemed to be clean and quiet. There were pretty pink curtains and framed oleographs. Mrs Baines could cook, and she led the hymns at church—so they said. Even the garden was neat, and trim, and fruitful. Of course *their* runner beans would be prolific while his failed. Mrs Baines appeared at the door and called out:

'Mornin', Mr Crosby.'

He replied gruffly: 'Mornin', Mrs Baines.'

'Middlin' hot.'

'Ay... terrible hot.'

She was not what you would call a pretty, attractive woman; but she was natty, competent, irrepressibly cheerful. She would make a shilling go as far as Emma would a pound. The cottage had five rooms, all in a good state of repair. The roof had been newly thatched. All this was done for him, of course, by his employer. He paid no rent; Martin had to pay five shillings a week, and then the roof leaked, and the boiler never worked properly—but perhaps that was Emma's fault. He picked up his basket and strolled toward the outer gate. As he did so, he heard the two children laughing, and Baines's voice joining in.

'Some people do have luck,' Martin murmured, and went back to his wife.

III

'Jack and Jill went up the hill
    To fetch a pail of water;
Jack fell down and broke his crown
    And Jill came tumbling after!'

It was very pretty—the way Winny Baines sang that, balancing the smaller boy on her knee, and jerking him skyward on the last word. Not what the world would call a pretty woman, but pretty enough to Ambrose, with her clear skin, kind motherly eyes, and thin brown hair. Her voice had a quality which somehow always expressed her gentle and unconquerable nature.

'She's too good for me,' Ambrose would think at odd moments. 'She didn't ought to be a gamekeeper's wife. She ought to be a lady—with carriages, and comforts, and well-dressed friends.'

The reflection would stir in him a feeling of sullen resentment, tempered with pride. She was a wonderful woman. She managed so well; she never complained. Of course, so far as the material necessities were concerned, there was enough and to spare. The cottage was comfortable, and reasonably well furnished—so far as he could determine. Of food there was abundance: game, rabbits, vegetables, eggs, fruit. The only thing he had to buy in the way of food was milk from the farm, and a few groceries from Mr Mead's shop. He paid nothing for the cottage and yet—he would have liked to have made things better for Winny. His wages were small, and there were clothes to buy, all kinds of little incidental expenses. There never seemed a chance to save and soon there would be the boy's schooling.

In spite of the small income, Winny always managed to keep herself and the children neat and smart, and even to help others like the more unfortunate Crosbys. She did all the work of the cottage, the care of the children, the mending and washing, and still found time to make jam, to preserve fruit, to grow flowers, and to sing in the church choir. She was the daughter of a piano tuner at Bladestone, and the glamour of this early connection always hung between Ambrose and herself. To him a piano tuner appeared a remote and romantic figure. It suggested a world of concerts, theatres, and Bohemian life. He was never quite clear about the precise functions of a piano tuner, but he regarded his wife as the daughter of a public man, coming from a world far removed from the narrow limits of the life she was forced to lead with him.

In spite of her repeated professions of happiness, Ambrose always felt a shade suspicious, not of her, but of his own ability to satisfy her every demand. Sometimes he would observe her looking round the little rooms, as though she were visualising what they might contain. Perhaps she wanted a grand piano, or some inlaid chairs, or embroidered coverings. He had not the money to buy these things, and he knew that she would never ask for them; but still it was there—that queer gnawing sense of insecurity. At dawn he would wander through the coppices, drenched in dew, the gun under his arm, and the dog close to heel. The sunlight would come rippling over the jewelled leaves, and little clumps of primroses and violets would reveal themselves. Life would be good then, and yet somehow—it was not Winny's life. Only through their children did they seem to know each other.

'Jack and Jill went up the hill
To fetch a pail of water;
Jack fell down and broke his crown
And Jill came tumbling after!'

'Oo—Ambrose,' the other boy was tugging at his beard, when Winny spoke. He pretended to scream with pain before he turned to his wife.

'Yes, my dear?'

'Will you be passing Mr Mead's shop? We have run out of candles.'

'Oh? Roight be, my love. I'll be nigh there afore sundown. I have to order seed from Crumblings.'

He was later than he expected at Mr Mead's shop. He had to wait whilst several women were being served. The portly owner's new cash register went 'tap-tapping!' five times before he got a chance to say:

'Evenin', Mr Meads, give us a pound of candles, will ye?'

Mrs Meads came in through a parlour at the back, in a rustling black dress. She was going to a welfare meeting at the vicar's. She said:

'Good evening, Mr Baines, hope you are all nicely.'

A slightly disturbing sight met the eye of Ambrose. The parlour door was open, and he could see a maid in a cap and apron clearing away tea things in the gaily furnished room. The Meads had got a servant! He knew that Meads was extending his business. He had a cheap clothing department now, and he was building a shed out at the back with the intention of supplying petrol to casual motorists, but—a servant!

He picked up his packet of candles and muttered gruffly:

'Good evenin'.'

Before he had reached the door he heard 'Tap-tapping!' *His* one and twopence had gone into the box. As he swung down the village street, he muttered to himself:

'God! I wish I had his money!'

IV

When Mrs Meads returned from the welfare meeting at half-past eight, she found Mr Meads waiting for her in the parlour, and the supper laid. There was cold veal and beetroot, apple pie, cheese and stout.

'I'm sorry I'm late, dear,' she said.

'That's all right, my love,' replied Mr Meads, not looking up from his newspaper.

'We had a lovely meeting—Mrs Wonnicott was there, and Mrs Beal, and Mrs Edwin Pillcreak, and Mrs James, and Ada, and both the Jamiesons, and the Vicar was perfectly sweet. He made two lovely speeches.'

'Oh, that was nice,' said Mr Meads, trying to listen and read a piquant paragraph about a divorce case at the same time.

'I should think you want your supper.'

'I'm ready when you are, my love.'

Mr Meads put down his newspaper, and drawing his chair up to the table, began to set about the veal. He was distinctly a man for his victuals. He carved rapidly for her, and less rapidly for himself. From this you must not imagine that he treated his wife meanly. On the contrary, he gave her a large helping, but a close observer could not help detecting that when carving for himself he seemed to take more interest in his job. Then he rang a little tinkly hand-bell and the new maid appeared.

'Go into the shop, my dear,' he said, 'and get me a pot of pickled walnuts from the second shelf on the left before you come to them bales of calico.'

The maid went, and Mrs Meads clucked:

'Um—being a bit extravagant to-night, John.'

'The labourer is worthy of his hire,' quoted Mr Meads sententiously. He put up a barrage of veal in the forefront of his mouth—he had no back teeth, but managed to penetrate it with an opaque rumble of sound. 'Besides we had a good day today—done a lot of business. Pass the stout—'

'I'm glad to hear it,' replied Mrs Meads. 'It's about time things began to improve, considerin' what we've been through. Mrs Wonnicott was wearin' her biscuit-coloured taffeta with a new lace yoke. She looked smart, but a bit stiff for the Welfare to my way of thinkin'.'

'Ah!' came rumbling through the veal.

'Oh, and did I tell you Mrs Mounthead was there, too? She was wearing her starched ninon—no end of a swell she looked.'

Mr Meads's eyes lighted with a definite interest at last.

Mrs Mounthead was the wife of James Mounthead, the proprietor of that handsome hostelry, 'The Die is Cast'. When his long day's work was over, Mr Meads would not infrequently pop into 'The Die is Cast' for an hour or so before closing time and have a long chat with Mr James Mounthead. He swallowed half a glass of stout at a gulp, and helped himself liberally to the pickled walnuts which the maid had just brought in. Eyeing the walnuts thoughtfully, he said:

'Oh, so she's got into it, too, has she?'

'Yes, she's really quite a pleasant body. She told me coming down the street that her husband has just bought Bolder's farm over at Pondhurst. He's setting up his son there who's marrying Kate Steyning. Her people have got a bit of money, too, so they'll be all right. By the way, we haven't heard from Charlie for nearly three weeks.'

Mr Meads sighed. Why were women always like that? There was Edie. He was trying to tell her that things were improving, going well in fact. The shed for petrol and motor accessories was nearly finished; the cheap clothing department was in full swing; he had indulged in pickled walnuts for supper (her supper, too); and there she must needs talk about—Charlie! Everybody in the neighbourhood knew that their son Charlie was up in London, and not doing himself or anybody else any good. And almost in the same breath she must needs talk about old Mounthead's son. Everyone knew that young Mounthead was a promising industrious fellow. Oh! and so James had bought him Bolder's farm, had he? That cost a pretty penny, he knew. Just bought a farm, had he? Not put the money into his business; just bought it in the way that he, Sam Meads, might buy a gramophone, or an umbrella. Psaugh!

'I don't want no tart,' he said, on observing Edie begin to carve it.

'No tart!' she exclaimed. 'Why, what's wrong?'

'Oh, I don't know,' he replied. 'Don't feel like it—working too hard—bit flatulent. I'll go out for a stroll after supper.'

An hour later he was leaning against the bar of 'The Die is Cast', drinking gin and water, and listening to Mr Mounthead discourse on dogs. The bar of 'The Die is Cast' was a self-constituted village club. Other cronies drifted in. They were all friends of both Mr Meads and Mr Mounthead. Mrs Mounthead seldom appeared in the bar, but there was a potman and a barmaid named Florrie;

and somewhere in the rear a cook, two housemaids, a scullery maid, a boy for knives and boots, and an ostler. Mr Mounthead had a victoria and a governess car, as well as a van for business purposes, a brown mare and a pony. He also had his own farm well stocked with pigs, cattle, and poultry. While taking his guests' money in a sleepy leisurely way, he regaled them with the rich fruits of his opinions and experiences. Later on he dropped casually that he was engaging an overseer at four hundred a year to take his son's place. And Mr Meads glanced round the bar and noted the shining glass and pewter, the polished mahogany, the little pink and green glasses winking at him insolently.

'He doesn't know what work is either,' suddenly occurred to him. Mr Mounthead's work consisted mostly in a little bookkeeping, and in ordering people about. He only served in the shop as a kind of social relaxation. If he, Sam Meads, didn't serve in his shop himself all day from early morning till late evening, goodness knows what would happen to the business. Besides—the pettiness of it all! Little bits of cheese, penny tins of mustard, string, weighing out sugar and biscuits, cutting bacon, measuring off ribbons and calico, and flannelette. People gossiping all day, and running up little accounts it was always hard to collect. But here—oh, the snappy quick profit. Everybody paying on the nail, served in a second, and what a profit! Enough to buy a farm for a son as though it was—an umbrella. Walking home, a little dejectedly, later on, he struck the road with his stick, and muttered:

'Damn that man!'

V

Mrs James Mounthead was rather pleased with her starched ninon. She leant back luxuriously in the easy chair, yawned, and pressed her hands along the sides of her well-fitting skirt. Gilt bangles round her wrists rattled pleasantly during this performance. A paste star glittered on her ample bosom. She heard James moving ponderously on the landing below; the bar had closed. He came puffily up the stairs and opened the door.

'A nightcap, Queenie?' he wheezed through the creaking machinery of his respiratory organs.

Mrs Mounthead smiled brightly. 'I think I will tonight, Jim.' He went to a cabinet and poured out two mixed drinks. He handed his wife one, and raising the other to his lips said:

'Well, here's to the boy!'

'Here's to James the Second!' she replied, and drank deeply. Her eyes sparkled. Mrs Mounthead was excited. The bangles clattered against the glass as she set it down.

'Come and give me a kiss, old dear,' she said, leaning back.

Without making any great show of enthusiasm, James did as he was bidden. He, too, was a little excited, but his excitement was less amorous than commercial. He had paid nearly twelve hundred pounds less for Bolder's farm than he had expected. The news of his purchase was all over the neighbourhood. It had impressed everyone. People looked at him differently. He was becoming a big man, *the* big man in those parts. He could buy another farm tomorrow, and it wouldn't break him. And the boy—the boy was a good boy; he would do well, too.

A little drink easily affected Mrs Mounthead. She became garrulous.

'I had a good time at the Welfare, though some of the old cats didn't like me, I know. Ha, ha, ha, what do I care? We could buy the whole lot up if we wanted to, except perhaps the Wonnicotts. Mine was the only frock worth a tinker's cuss. Lord! You should have seen old Mrs Meads! Looked like a washerwoman on a Sunday. The vicar was ever so nice. He called me madam, and said he 'oped I often come. I gave a fiver to the fund. Ha, ha, ha, I didn't tell 'em that I made it backing "Ringcross" for the

Nunhead Stakes yesterday! They'd have died.'

During this verbal explosion, James Mounthead thoughtfully regarded his glass. And he thought to himself: 'Um. It's a pity Queenie gives herself away sometimes.' He didn't particularly want to hear about the Welfare. He wanted to talk about 'James the Second' and the plans for the future. He wanted to indulge in the luxury of talking about their success, but he didn't want to boast about wealth in quite that way. He had queer ambitions not unconnected with the land he lived on. He had not always been in the licensing trade. His father had been a small landed proprietor and a stock breeder; a man of stern, unrelenting principles. From his father he, James Mounthead, had inherited a kind of reverence for the ordered development of land and cattle, an innate respect for the sanctity of tradition, caste, property and fair dealing. His wife had always been in the licensing trade. She was the daughter of a publican at Pondhurst. As a girl she had served in the bar. All her relations were licensing people. When she had a little to drink—she was apt to display her worst side, to give herself away. James sighed.

'Did Mrs Wonnicott say anything about her husband?' he asked to change the subject.

'You bet she did. Tried to put it across us—when I told her about us buying Bolder's farm—said her old man had thought of bidding for it, but he knew it was poor in root crops and the soil was no good for corn, and that Sturge had neglected the place too long. The old cat! I said: "Yes, and p'raps it wouldn't be convenient to pay for it just now, after 'aving bought a lawn mower!" Ha, ha, ha. He, he, he. Oh my!'

'I shouldn't have said that,' mumbled Mr Mounthead, who knew, however, that anything was better than one of Queenie's violent reactions to quarrelsomeness. 'Come on let's go and turn in, old girl.'

An hour later, James Mounthead was tossing restlessly

between the sheets. Queenie's reference to the Wonnicotts had upset him. He could read between what she had said sufficiently to envisage a scene, which he himself deplored. Queenie, of course, had given herself away again to Mrs Wonnicott. He knew that both the Wonnicotts despised her, and through her, him. He had probably as much money as Lewis Wonnicott, if not more. He certainly had a more fluid and accumulative way of making it, but there the matter stopped. Wonnicott was a gentleman; his wife a lady. He, James, might have been as much a gentleman as Wonnicott if—circumstances had been different. Queenie could never be a lady in the sense that Mrs Wonnicott was a lady. Wonnicott led the kind of life *he* would like to live—a gentleman farmer, with hunters, a little house property, and some sound vested interests; a man with a great knowledge of land, horses, finance, and politics.

He loved Queenie in a queer enduring kind of way. She had been loyal to him, and she satisfied most of his needs. She loved him, but he knew that he could never attain the goal of his vague ambitions, with her clinging to his heels. He thought of Lewis Wonnicott sleeping in his white panelled bedroom with chintz curtains and old furniture, and his wife in the adjoining room, where the bay window looked out on to the downs; and the heart of James became bitter with envy.

VI

'I don't think I shall attend those Welfare meetings any more,' remarked Mrs Lewis Wonnicott with a slight drawl. She gathered up her letters from the breakfast table and walked to the window.

In the garden below, Leach, the gardener, was experimenting with a new mower on the well-clipped lawns. The ramblers on the pergola were at their best. Her husband in a broad check suit and a white stock, looked up from the *Times* and said:

'Oh, how is that, my dear?'

'They are getting such awful people in. That dreadful woman, the wife of Mounthead, the publican, has joined.'

'Old Mounthead's all right—not a bad sort. He knows a gelding from a blood mare.'

'That may be, but his wife is the limit. I happened to say something about the new mower, and she was simply rude. An awful vulgar person, wears spangles, and boasts about the money her husband makes out of selling whisky.'

'By gad! I bet he does, too. I wouldn't mind having a bit in his pub. Do you see Canadian Pacifics are still stagnant?'

'Lewis, I sometimes wish you wouldn't be so material. You think about nothing but money.'

'Oh, come, my dear, I'm interested in a crowd of other things—things which I don't make money out of, too.'

'For instance?'

'The land, the people who work on it, horses, cattle, game, the best way to do things for everybody. Besides, ain't I interested in the children? The two girls' careers at Bedales? Young Ralph at Rugby and going up to Cambridge next year?'

'You know they're there, but how much interest you take, I couldn't say.'

'What is it you want me to do, my dear?'

'I think you might bestir yourself to get amongst better people. The girls will be leaving school soon and coming home. We know no one, no one at all in the neighbourhood.'

'No one at all! Jiminy! Why, we know everyone!'

'You spend all your time among horse-breeders and cattle-dealers, and people like Mounthead, and occasionally call on the Vicar, but who is there of any importance that we know?'

'Lord! What do you want? Do you want me to go and call at Crawshay Park, and ask Sir Septimus and Lady

Letter to come and make up a four at bridge?'

'Don't be absurd! You know quite well that the Letters are entirely inaccessible. He's not only an M.P. and owner of half the newspapers in the country, but a millionaire. They entertain house parties of ministers and dukes, and even royalty. They can afford to ignore even the county people themselves. But there are others. We don't even know the county.'

'Who, for instance?'

'Well, the Burnabys. You met St John Burnaby at the Constitutional Club two or three times and yet you have never attempted to follow it up. They're very nice people and neighbours. And they have three boys all in the twenties, and the girl Sheila—she's just a year younger than Ralph.'

'My word! Who's being material now?'

'It isn't material, it's just—thinking of the children.'

'Women are wonderful,' muttered Lewis Wonnicott into his white stock, without raising his head. Mrs Wonnicott swept to the door. Her thin lips were drawn in a firm straight line. Her refined hard little face appeared pinched and petulant. With her hand on the door-handle she said acidly:

'If you can spare half an hour from your grooms and pigs, I think you might at least do this to please me—call on Mr Burnaby to-day.'

And she went out of the room, shutting the door crisply.

'Oh, Jiminy-Piminy!' muttered Mr Wonnicott. 'Jiminy-Piminy!'

'He stood up and shook himself. Then with feline intentness he walked quickly to the French window, and opening it walked down the steps into the garden. All the way to the sunk rose-garden he kept repeating, 'Jiminy-Piminy!'

Once among the rose bushes he lighted his pipe. (His wife objected to smoking in the house). He blew clouds of tobacco smoke amongst imaginary greenfly.

Occasionally he would glance furtively out at the view across the downs. Half-buried amongst the elms near Basted Old Church he could just see the five red gables of the Burnabys' capacious mansion.

'I can't do it,' he thought, 'I can't do it, and I shall have to do it.'

It was perfectly true he had been introduced to St John Burnaby and had spoken to him once or twice. It was also true that Burnaby had never given any evidence of wishing to follow up the acquaintanceship. Bit of a swell, Burnaby, connected with all sorts of people, member of half a dozen clubs, didn't race but went in for golf, and had a shooting box in Scotland. Some said he had political ambitions, and meant to try for Parliament at the next election. He didn't racket round in a check suit and a white stock and mix with grooms and farm hands; he kept up the flair of the gentleman, the big man, acres of conservatory, and peacocks, and a son in the diplomatic service, a daughter married to a bishop. His wife, too, came of a poor but aristocratic family. Over at the 'Five Gables' they kept nine gardeners and twenty-odd servants. Everything was done tip-top.

Lewis Wonnicott turned and regarded his one old-man gardener, trying the new mower, which Mrs Mounthead had been so rude about to Dorothy. Poor Dorothy! She was touchy, that's what it was. Of course she did think of the children—no getting away from it. She was ambitious more for them than for herself or himself. She had given up being ambitious for him. He knew that she looked upon him as a slacker, a kind of cabbage. Well, perhaps he had been. He hadn't accomplished all he ought to. He had loved the land, the feel of horseflesh, the smell of wet earth when the morning dews were on it. He had been a failure...a failure. He was not up to county people. He was unworthy of his dear wife's ambitions. Jiminy-Piminy! It would be a squeeze to send Ralph up to Cambridge next year!

He looked across the valley at the five red gables among the elms, and sighed.

'Lucky devil!' he murmured. 'Damn it all! I suppose I must go.'

VII

'You don't seem to realise the importance of it,' said Gwendolen St John Burnaby as her husband leant forward on his seat on the terrace, and tickled the ear of Jinks, the Airedale. 'A career in the diplomatic service without influence is about as likely to be a success as a—as a performance on a violin behind a sound-proof curtain. There's Lal, wasting his—his talents and genius at that wretched little embassy at Oporto, and all you've got to do is to drive three miles to Crawshay Park and put the matter before Sir Septimus.'

'These things always seem so simple to women,' answered St John, a little peevishly.

'Well, isn't it true? Do you deny that he has the power?'

'Of course he has power, my dear, but you may not realise the kind of life a man like that lives. Every minute of the day is filled up, all kinds of important things crowding each other out. He's always been friendly enough to me, and yet every time I meet him I have an idea he has forgotten who I am. He deals in movements in which men are only pawns. If I told him about Lal he would say yes, he would do what he could—make a note of it, and forget about it directly I turned my back.'

Mrs St John Burnaby stamped her elegant Louis heels.

'Is nothing ever worth trying?'

'Don't be foolish, Gwen, haven't I tried? Haven't I ambition?'

'For yourself, yes. I am thinking of Lal.'

'Women always think of their sons before their husbands. He knows I've backed his party for all I'm worth. He knows

I'm standing for the constituency next time. When I get elected will be the moment. I shall then have a tiny atom of power. For a man without even a vote in Parliament do you think Letter is going to waste his time?'

'Obstinate!' muttered Mrs Burnaby with metallic clearness. The little lines round the eyes and mouth of a face that had once been beautiful became accentuated in the clear sunlight. The constant stress of ambitious desires had quickened her vitality, but in the process had aged her body before its time. She knew that her husband was ambitious, too, but there was always just that little something he lacked in the great moments, just that little special effort that might have landed him among the gods—or in the House of Lords. He had been successful enough in a way. He had made money—a hundred thousand or so—in brokerage and dealing indirectly in various manufactured commodities; but he had not even attained a knighthood or a seat in Parliament. His heavy dark face betokened power and courage, but not vision. He was indeed as she had said—obstinate. In minnow circles he might appear a triton, but living within the same county as Sir Septimus Letter—Bah!

About to leave him, her movement was arrested by the approach of a butler followed by a gentleman in a check suit and a white stock, looking self-conscious.

Mrs St John Burnaby raised her lorgnette. 'One of these local people,' she reflected.

On being announced the gentleman in the check suit exclaimed rapidly:

'Excuse the liberty I take—neighbours, don't you know. Remember me at the Constitutional Club, Mr Burnaby? Thought I would drop in and pay my respects.'

St John Burnaby nodded.

'Oh, yes, yes, quite. I remember, Mr—er—Mr—'

'Wonnicott.'

'Oh yes, of course. How do you do? My wife—Mr Wonnicott.'

The wife and the Wonnicott bowed to each other, and there was an uncomfortable pause. At last Mr Wonnicot managed to say:

'We live over at Wimpstone, just across the valley—my wife, the girls are at school, boy's up at Rugby.'

'Oh, yes—really?' This was Mrs Burnaby who was thinking to herself:

'The man looks like a dog fancier.'

'Very good school,' said St John Burnaby. 'Hot to-day, isn't it!'

'Yes, it's exceedingly warm.'

'Do you golf?'

'No, I don't golf. I ride a bit.'

'You must excuse me,' said Mrs St John Burnaby, I have got to get a trunk call to London.'

She fluttered away across the terrace, and into the house. Mr Wonnicott chatted away for several minutes, but St John Burnaby was preoccupied and monosyllabic. The visitor was relieved to rescue his hat at last and make his escape. Walking down the drive he thought:

'It's no good. He dislikes me.'

As a matter of fact St John Burnaby was not thinking about him at all. He was thinking of Sir Septimus Letter, the big man, the power he would have liked to have been. He ground his teeth and clenched his fists:

'Damn it!' he muttered, 'I will not appeal for young Lal. Let him fight his own battles.'

VIII

On a certain day that summer when the sun was at its highest in the heavens, Sir Septimus Letter stood by the bureau in his cool library and conversed with his private secretary.

Sir Septimus was wearing what appeared to be a ready-made navy serge suit and a low collar. His hands were thrust into his trouser pockets. The sallow face was heavily marked, the strangely restless eyes peered searchingly beneath dark brows which almost met in one continuous line. The chin was finely modelled, but not too strong. It was not indeed what is usually known as a strong face. It had power, but of the kind which has been mellowed by the friction of every human experience. It had alert intelligence, a penetrating absorption, above all things it indicated vision. The speech and the movements were incisive; the short wiry body a compact tissue of nervous energy. He listened with the watchful intensity of a dog at a rabbit-hole. Through the door at the end of the room could be heard the distant click of many typewriters.

The secretary was saying:

'The third reading of the Nationalization of Paper Industries Bill comes on at five-thirty, sir. Boneham will be up, and I do not think you will be called till seven. You will, of course, however, wish to hear what he has to say.'

'I know what he'll say. You can cut that out, Roberts. Get Libby to give me a précis at six forty-five.'

'Very good, sir. Then there will be time after the Associated News Service Board at four to see the minister with regard to this question of packing meetings in East Riding. Lord Lampreys said he would be pleased if I could fix an appointment. He has some information.'

'Right. What line are Jennins and Castwell taking over this?'

'They're trying to sidetrack the issue. They have every un-associated newspaper in the North against you.'

'H'm, h'm. Well, we've fought them before.'

'Yes, sir. The pressure is going to be greater this time, but everyone has confidence you will get them down.'

The little man's eyes sparkled. 'Roberts, get through on the private wire to—Lambe; no, get through to all of them, and make it quite clear. This is not to be a party question. They're to work the unctious rectitude stuff, you know—liberty of the subject and so on.'

'Very good, sir. The car comes at one-fifteen. You are

lunching with Cranmer at Shorn Towers, the Canadian paper interests will be strongly represented there. I will be at Whitehall Court at three with the despatches. It would be advisable, if possible, to get Loeb of the finance committee. Oh, by the way, sir, I had to advise you from Loeb. They have received a cabled report of the expert's opinion from Labrador. There are two distinct seams of coal on that land you bought in '07. A syndicate from Buffalo have made an offer. They offer a million-and-a-quarter dollars down.'

'What did we pay?'

'One hundred and twenty thousand.'

'Don't sell.'

'Very good, sir.'

'Have you seen my wife lately?'

'I have not seen Lady Letter for some days, sir. I believe she is at Harrogate.'

The little man sighed, and drew out a cigarette case, opened it and offered one to Roberts, who accepted it with an elegant gesture. Then he snapped it to, and replaced it in his pocket.

'Damn it, Roberts, Reeves says I mustn't smoke.'

'Oh, dear!—only a temporary disability I trust, sir.'

'Everything is temporary, Roberts.'

With his hands still in his pockets, he walked abstractedly out of the room. A little ormolu clock in the outer corridor indicated twenty minutes to one. The car was due at one-fifteen. Thirty-five minutes: oh, to escape for only that brief period! Through the glass doors he could see his sister talking to two men in golfing clothes, some of the house party. The house party was a perpetual condition at Crawshay. He turned sharply to the right, and went through a corridor leading out to the rear of the garage. He hurried along and escaped to a path between two tomato houses. In a few moments he was lost to sight. He passed through a shrubbery, and came to a clearing. Without slackening his pace, he walked across it, and got amongst some trees. The trees of Crawshay Park—his trees! ...He looked up at the towering oaks and elms. Were they his trees—because he had bought them? They were there years before he was born. They would be there years after his death. He was only passing through them—a fugitive. 'Everything is temporary, Roberts—' Yes, even life itself. Jennins and Castwell! Of course they wanted to get him down! Were they the only ones? Does one struggle to the top without hurting others to get there? Does one get to the top without making enemies? Does one get to the top without suffering, and bitterness, and remorse? The park sloped down to a low stone wall, with an opening where one could obtain a glorious view across the weald of Sussex. The white ribbon of a road stretched away into infinity.

As he stood there, he saw a dark swarthy figure clamber down a bank, and stand hesitating in the middle of the road. He was a tramp with a stubbly red beard nearly concealing his face, and a filthy black-green suit. In his hand he carried a red handkerchief containing his worldly belongings—a door-knob, a portion of a foot-rule, a tin mug stolen from a workhouse, some date stones, an onion, the shutter of a camera, and two empty match boxes.

Sir Septimus did not know this fact; he merely regarded the tramp as an abstraction. He observed him hesitate, exchange a word with a field labourer, look up at the sky, hunch his shoulders, and suddenly set out with long swinging strides down the white road. Whither? There stirred within the breast of the millionaire a curious wistful longing. Oh, to be free! To be free! To walk across those hills without a care, without a responsibility. The figure, with its easy gait, fascinated him. The dark form became smaller and smaller, swallowed up in the immensity of nature. With a groan, Sir Septimus Letter buried his face in his hands and murmured:

'Lucky devil! ...lucky devil! O God! If I could die...'

—*XIX*—

The Song of Praise

GEORGE ARTHUR always began the day with song. Almost directly he awoke he would sit bolt upright against the pillow, his small chest thrust out, his bright blue eyes fixed on the sky and the nodding branches of the elms visible from the night-nursery window, and he would sing.

It was a wonderful song. It had no recognisable air and no recognisable words. It was a volume of sound that rose and fell, rushed onward, sometimes repeated itself, sometimes hung poised, sometimes rumbled with a deep mock-manly note, sometimes lingered and sometimes scurried. But whatever its tempo, and whatever its rhythm, it always contained that quality which it shared with the birds on the branches below, the quality of triumph, the quality of praise.

It was as though, after the pause of darkness, when everything fell apart and became detached, one could not accept these golden gifts of the awakening and uniting god without due recognition. The story must be continued from where it left off when the sun departed.

To the sophisticated this interruption of darkness is accepted with the insolent assumption that in precisely so many hours and minutes it will again be light. But why? Why regard this astounding miracle with cynical indifference?

George Arthur and the birds had no cause to doubt the coming of the light, but it still remained a miracle. It still remained a subject upon which to pour out one's heart in praise. Through his open door he could see through the open door of Nan-Nan's room, and observe her bustling movements, but he never felt impelled to offer her any kind of greeting until the song had run its full course. And not even then in the general sense of the term greeting.

When, on this particular morning, she appeared some twenty minutes later, he immediately broke into a lively torrent of discourse concerning two rabbits, one of which the gardener's son had allowed to escape into Major Towle's kitchen garden, and how it had been chased and nearly killed by the red setter.

The unabated frenzy of the narrative lasted well into breakfast time. And breakfast was no inconsiderable trifle with George Arthur, consisting as it did of wheat flakes and cream, a boiled egg, toast, butter, jam and some stewed prunes, this solid nutriment being helped down by two cups of warm milk.

These matters being disposed of, George Arthur was aware that the serious business of the day was about to start. But not quite yet. For the first and most important business of the day was the visit to *Her*. And for some reason or other she did not like him to visit her until a certain time known only to Nan-Nan and herself.

So in a spasmodic way he continued his song, lying on his tummy on the nursery floor, and making a drawing of a steamer with clouds of smoke pouring out of the funnels, until she sent for him.

This was always a golden hour to George Arthur, the time when he had her entirely to himself, without fear of interruption. He was intimately aware of her astounding beauty, her gold-brown hair framed by the white pillow, her wonderful pink and white skin, those large, wistful, blue-grey eyes. There was a wonderful perfume about her body, which he could only recognise vaguely as the essence of their intimacy.

In bed she wore a wonderful pale blue thing trimmed with white fur. In fact, everything she wore was beautiful, far more beautiful than things worn by other women.

He had even heard people say so. And she moved more gracefully, and her voice was deeper, gentler, more musical than any other voice in the world. By the side of the bed was her breakfast-tray. Her breakfast never seemed to consist of anything but tea, toast and letters. And sometimes, while she was talking to him, she would pick up one of the letters and glance through it abstractedly.

He forgave these aberrations because, knowing that she was the most beautiful woman in the world, everyone wanted her. The house always seemed to be full of people wanting her. And they stayed to meals, played cards, or made her sing; and sometimes they took her away with them for long stretches of time, all night sometimes, and even several nights. But when, on these occasions, she returned, he always noticed an added pressure of her arms, a kind of breathless expression of her nearness.

Particularly did he notice this when 'Dadda' was away, and Dadda was away quite a lot. A curious person, Dadda, not a bit like her. There was nothing beautiful about him. He was rather bald with heavy black moustaches. Everything about him was rather heavy. He wore heavy dark clothes and watch-chains, and rings, and although he was always in a hurry he moved heavily. Sometimes he would come across George Arthur, and exclaim in his heavy voice:

'Well, my old cockalorum!' and he would pat him and admire his drawings, but very quickly he would seem to get tired of this and he would keep on looking at his watch, or else Mr Lanyard, his secretary, would come bustling along with a brown leather case, and would say:

'The car is here, sir.'

And then they would go off together, and nothing more would be seen of Dadda until the next morning, or until many next mornings. There was something unsatisfactory about this. Of course Dadda didn't matter in the way *she* mattered. He was not indispensable. But George Arthur always felt a kind of queer pity for him. He would have liked to know him better; but they were always both a little shy in each other's company.

It seemed to George Arthur that Dadda was always driven along by some hidden power to do the things he didn't want to do. He so often seemed worried and distracted, and sometimes when at home he would sit forward on his chair and look at *her*, with an odd, appealing look in his eyes, just like Jimmy, Major Towle's red setter, when his master had told him to 'Wait'. But George Arthur seldom saw them together. There were all these people always wanting her, and there was Dadda driven hither and thither by Mr Lanyard, and the brown leather case.

There were occasions, as on this morning, when Dadda had been away some time, that George Arthur would feel a sudden need for him, as though he felt there were something missing in the general scheme of things, and nestling in the crook of her white arm he said abruptly:

'When is Dadda coming back?'

There was a pause and she seemed to laugh a little uncomfortably.

'I don't quite know, darling. Not yet.'

'What is he doing?'

'Oh, he's busy. Business, you know.'

'What is business?'

'Being busy, darling. Selling things, making money—'

'Is it hard to make money?'

'To some people, not to others.'

'To Dadda?'

'I don't know. He—there, don't lean on me, darling. I must go and have my bath.'

On some mornings he accompanied her into the bathroom. He liked to watch her long white body glistening under the water. But this morning he refrained. He wanted to think something out.

For the last few weeks he had determined—and he had elaborated the idea minutely to Nan-Nan—that when he grew up he was going to be a policeman. Not, as he explained, an ordinary policeman, but an 'important' policeman, one who rode on a horse and wore white gloves and ordered the motorcars about. He had seen one on his last visit to London town, when they stayed at a large dark house in a square. He had seen this policeman in one of the busy streets near a park and he had been duly impressed. But now he was wondering whether it wouldn't be nicer to be a business man, to have a lot of cases and papers, and dash about in a motorcar, with everybody very deferential, and handing you bags of gold over counters.

The only great objection to this seemed to be that one had to be so much in London town, a place he did not like. When they went to stay at that dark house in the square he was always conscious of a feeling of depression. It seemed no place for games and make-believe, and sometimes he went into the garden of the square, and he noticed that the trees were dirty. The seats were dirty, and everything you touched made your hands black. And the other children and their nursemaids never seemed disposed to be friendly.

Which reminded him! In a leap he was off the bed and down the stairs. This was the morning that Joan and Nigel were coming in to play Red Indians. Joan was five and Nigel eight, and they belonged to Major Towle's, next door.

Of course they had not come, and Nan-Nan called out of the window that they would not be here yet, not till eleven o'clock. Oh, bother eleven o'clock! What a world of waiting this was! Nothing ever seemed to happen at once. It was always: soon, or presently, or by-and-by, or one day, or later on, or we-shall-see, or eleven o'clock. How he hated these expressions! When was eleven o'clock? It sounded a remote and sinister hour. Wasn't the whole essence of everything to do it immediately?

However, the sun was shining brilliantly, and he rushed

to the hutches behind the garage and engaged the rabbit in conversation. He pushed cabbage stalks through the wire and told 'Joey' he was an old silly. And the rabbit's nostrils worked up and down so rapidly it seemed just as though he were eagerly corroborating this criticism.

Then there was Beauchamp, the chauffeur, turning the hose on to the Daimler. He also had to be interviewed. There were, indeed, a great number of garden activities that required attention, and the time passed quickly. George Arthur had, in fact, forgotten all about his fellow Red Indians until a familiar war-whoop greeted him from the other side of the vegetable garden. Nigel was in full war paint with feathers and tomahawk complete, and Joan was wearing a headdress and a coloured shawl.

'Wait a minute!' was his greeting. 'I'm not ready.' He dashed indoors and yelled out to Nan-Nan for his Indian suit. There were times when her dilatoriness infuriated him. It was not that she was actually so slow in movement as that she did not always appreciate the importance of certain things.

There she was calmly ironing something out, and laughing and talking with Annie, the parlour-maid, while 'the tribe' were waiting for him below! However, by the employment of a certain amount of violence, both physical and vocal, he managed to persuade her to help him into his suit and feathers.

Down in the hall he ran into *her*. She was exquisitely gowned in some pale mauve colour with a small black hat. She was just going out to the car.

'Oh, darling, how splendid you look!' she exclaimed, drawing on her gloves. 'I shan't be long. I shall be home to tea in any case.'

In the ordinary way he would have protested at her going out for so long a time, but in an instant he sensed that she, too, like Nan-Nan, failed to judge the true importance of the situation. There was a shade of insincerity in her admiration. She was, he knew, anxious to get off 'without a fuss'. She had her interests and he had his, and there it was. Moreover, this was not the time of day for emotions and regrets.

He allowed her to kiss him on the cheek, and then with a quick: 'All right, then,' he dashed past her into the garden.

Beyond the vegetable garden, was a narrow strip of copse, and here the Indians pitched their tent. It was a glorious morning. There was much spying and creeping through the undergrowth, and waving of tomahawks. There were muttered whispers of 'Walla, walla, walla,' and similar sounds, alien tribes were defeated, victims scalped, bears and buffaloes tracked, and slain, and Joan rescued from the clutches of the enemy about to burn her. The morning seemed to go like a flash.

A smiling ayah glided into view almost simultaneously with Nan-Nan.

Oh, bother, bother, bother, bother, bother! What a tyranny were the interventions of these grown-ups. In the same way that nothing ever happened at once, neither did it ever happen continuously. There were always these absurd interruptions and intervals—just when one was getting into things.

'Now children, your rest before lunch.'

It was not even as though they could resume the game quite soon. After lunch Joan and Nigel had to go out, he knew. He, too, would probably have to go out for a walk with Nan-Nan. Mum didn't like him to play in the garden all day—then home to tea. Perhaps they could come after tea? But, no, Joan and Nigel, it seemed, had promised to go to tea with some other children, to play with them. To play with other children!

George Arthur felt a little stab of jealousy. He turned abruptly away and ran into the house. Lying on his bed, during his rest before lunch, he began again to think about Mum. Why did she always want to be going about seeing other people, leaving him to his own and Nan-Nan's devices? Had he treated her rather brusquely that morning, though? Oh, well, there were moments when he felt a queer desire to punish her in some fantastic way, or at least if not to punish her, to show his power over her. He hummed to himself, and turned to his drawing-book.

He found that Indian warfare had given him an appetite, and he did full justice to a meal consisting of roast chicken, vegetables, stewed damsons, custard and cream, and ending up with a nectarine.

It seems a significant comment upon the nature of the animal that immediately after this he could stand on his head in the corner of the room with his legs bent and balance the kitten on his knees, amidst shrieks of laughter from himself, mild protests from Nan-Nan, and dubious acquiescence from the kitten.

After the excitement of the morning the afternoon seemed a mild and rather uneventful experience. He went on to the common with Nan-Nan, and he took a kite, but owing to lack of wind this was not a success, neither was sailing a boat on a small muddy pond. These failures, however, were a little discounted by the sight of a large rat, which scuttled away from the reeds of the pond, and disappeared under a culvert. Then they sat down on a rug and Nan-Nan read to him. It was a lovely story about 'Winnie, the Pooh'. He had heard it before several times, but he did not like stories that were unfamiliar.

Nan-Nan had a pretty voice—Scotch. Sometimes he found it difficult to understand her, and he would stop her and ask her to repeat something. Sometimes he found himself just listening to the cadence of her voice, and not following the story. There was something very attractive about it when she read; much more attractive than when she just talked in the ordinary way.

He began to wonder how much he loved her. Her hair, pulled tightly back, was turning grey. Her cheeks were red and a little rough, but her eyes were deep and grey and understanding. She was very dear to him, sitting there bolt upright, with her back to a furze-bush and reading in her pretty Scotch voice. She was dear to him because she was so familiar, and reliable, and understanding. Of course it wasn't like Mum—there was nothing exciting about it. But he leant against her for a moment, and without stopping her reading, she put an arm round him, and pressed him to her.

Bees were droning in the yellow gorse. Little specks of white cloud drifted idly overhead. An aeroplane appeared from nowhere, the sound of its engine drowning the hum of the bees.

Tea-time was always the most important and exciting time of the day, especially when *she* was to be there. It seemed to mark the crisis of the day's adventures. The only danger lay in people. Mum had an unfortunate habit of bringing people home to tea. When they were strangers, or people he objected to, then the meal was spoilt. But sometimes people whom he liked came—you never knew.

There was Uncle Arthur, Dadda's elder brother. He was a big, clumsy man, too solemn in his manners. He and George Arthur had much in common. What he liked about Uncle Arthur was that he talked to him quite seriously, as between man and man. He never seemed to be laughing at him, or patronising. He knew the importance of things. And there was Aunt Mildred, and Betty Smallpiece, and Grandmamma, and, oh, quite a number of nice people.

From the edge of the common they could see that tea was set in the sunk rose garden. There was the gleam of white napery, and the glitter of silver and china. Two or three people were wandering around, admiring the roses. There was Mum, two people he could not recognise, and then to his profound disgust—'that man'! He always called him 'that man' to Nan-Nan, who reproved him mildly with:

'Oh, hush, Georgie! I'm sure Mr Sievewright is very nice.'

She, as any adult might, found it very difficult to explain George Arthur's bitterness against Oswald Sievewright. A more charming gentleman Nan-Nan had never met. Young, good-looking, boyish, gay, no one had made greater efforts to ingratiate himself with George Arthur; but it had all been in vain. The small boy would have nothing to do with him. He showed his dislike openly.

Whatever it was, George Arthur regarded him as his secret enemy, his pet aversion. And he had noticed of late that, when 'that man' was there, there was something subtly different about *her*. She spoke differently, moved differently, and what was most unpardonable, behaved slightly differently to George Arthur. She seemed worried by his inimical attitude, and was always trying to wheedle him into a more friendly one.

During tea he sat at his mother's elbow, and wouldn't speak. The two strangers, a man and a woman, seemed harmless. In any case, they didn't try to be familiar. But 'that man' seemed to monopolise everyone's attention, and his attempts to draw George Arthur out or be friendly with him were so persistent and abortive that Mum eventually said:

'Oh, leave him alone, Ossy. He's a funny boy.'

A few minutes later she was conscious of a disturbance at her elbow. She glanced round and saw that her small son was shaking, and tears were assembling on the brink of his eyes. Tea was in any case nearly finished, and she arose and said calmly:

'Excuse me, good people. Georgie and I are going for a little stroll.'

She tried to chatter to him dispassionately of other things, but when they were out of sight the storm burst. She picked him up, patted him, and tried to comfort him.

'What is it, Georgie? What's the matter? Tell Mum.'

But he would not speak. In the midst of his tears he uttered small groans of pain like one whose soul has been stricken. She knew him well enough to realise that it was no use to cross-examine too closely in an emotional crisis; moreover, she had a shrewd suspicion of the cause of the trouble. In a conflict between two personalities she had for an instant taken the side of the enemy. She said, in her effort to appease:

'There, there, darling, policemen don't cry.'

This statement had in any case the satisfactory effect of eliciting a reply, jerked vehemently through diminishing sobs:

'I'm not going to be a policeman. I'm going to be a business.'

'Oh, you're going to be a business, are you!'

She smiled weakly, wondering what this might portend.

A few minutes later something exciting happened.

Nan-Nan came out to say that the new 'fairy car' promised by Uncle Arthur had just arrived by the carrier. All troubles were instantly forgotten. The car was unpacked. It was painted scarlet and green. George Arthur mounted it and raced round the lawns, violently ringing the bell. The garden immediately became a playground, a paradise, a fairyland. He squealed with delight, and grinned with pride at the onlookers' praise of his skill.

The two strangers went, but 'that man' stayed on. In the corner of the rose garden he was sitting very close to Mum. They seemed absorbed in each other. He was whispering to her and smiling. Her eyes were lowered. They appeared to be concentrated on the ground, but now and then she would look up at him and sigh. Neither of them was any longer interested in the skill of the cyclist. The latter kept pausing and looking in their direction. Once or twice he felt deeply stirred to protest, but something prompted him to bide his time.

Nan-Nan had disappeared, but it was getting near the time when she would come for him for his bath. Sometimes when they were alone Mum would give him his bath, but not very frequently. Certainly no chance of it while 'that man' was there.

He rode down past the copse, and out of sight. There was no one about. He felt a little stab of melancholy. At the end of the copse was a little wooden gate and bridge that crossed a tiny stream, dividing the garden property from the common. He dismounted and stood staring about him. Then he heard Nan-Nan call.

Acting on a sudden impulse, he conducted his fairy car across the stream. Then he tipped it up on edge, and ran away into the common. He heard Nan-Nan calling, and he crept into the heart of a thick bush, where he was entirely hidden, but where he had a good view of what might take place near the bridge. Indians with a vengeance!

Her calls became louder, and at last she appeared at the bridge, and caught sight of the car. She hurried towards it, picked it up, gave a quick glance at the stream, and then peered all around her. She was obviously a little bewildered and frightened. She called on a higher note:

'Georgie! Georgie! Where are you?'

She seemed about to make a search of the common, then she crossed the bridge again and ran in the direction of the house. This was a lovely game! In a few minutes she returned, accompanied by Mum, and 'that man'. He heard the latter exclaim:

'I bet you he's only hiding.' And he began whistling and calling loudly, and then started a running trot across the common. He passed within two yards of Georgie, who crouched down, and held his breath. When his enemy passed he chuckled with glee. Mum was calling out in her deep musical voice:

'Geor-gie!'

There was a note of anxiety in it. She drifted uncertainly in his direction, continuing her call. He waited until she was within pouncing distance, then he sprang out with a triumphant yell. He saw her stagger for a moment, and put her hand across her eyes.

'Georgie,' she said quietly, 'you shouldn't do that.'

He had accomplished what he had set out to do! He had established the fact that his hold over her was greater than the hold over her of—any rival. He danced around her with savage delight. Her relief had its reaction. She was a little angry.

She said: 'You're a silly boy,' and she called out to 'that man'. But the latter had already heard, and came running back, laughing.

'Where was the young monkey?'

They all went back to the house. George Arthur didn't care very much if she was angry. He had won. He mounted his fairy car and rode vigorously around the lawns. He elected to be perverse. When Nan-Nan called him he rang his bell, laughed, and dodged her. The chase went on until it was late for his bath-time. Nan-Nan herself was getting winded and a little angry.

Mum showed her disapproval by leaving him and going into the drawing room with 'that man'. At last he dismounted and pushed the tricycle away. He crept into the drawing room after her. She and 'that man' were sitting on the Chesterfield. He went up and whispered in her ear:

'You give me my bath to-night.'

She whispered back: 'No, I can't tonight, darling. I—I've got something else to do. Run on upstairs, there's a darling. I'll come up and see you when you're in bed.'

It was all nonsense. She had nothing to do. She was just sitting there talking to 'that man'. He wheedled and coaxed, but she would not come. He had never known her so obstinate. He had his ultimate weapon—tears, but he was not going to use it in front of 'that man'. Besides—with a sulky wriggle he left her.

'Good-night, old man,' called out 'that man'.

He did not answer. George Arthur was not a well-behaved little boy. And tonight he was angry. Something was all wrong with the world. He didn't know exactly what it was, but he felt disasters and disappointments crowding upon him. He proceeded to take it out on Nan-Nan. He splashed her and threw the soap out of the bath, and also the three motor boats which usually afforded such absorbing entertainment while ablutions were being performed. Nan-Nan struggled bravely with her exasperations. She had had strict instructions from both parents that in no circumstances was she ever to slap or physically chastise the child. Neither had she any desire to do so, but there were moments—like the present—when she rather envied the people who had not so much conscience in these matters. But when she was drying him he seemed to change suddenly. He looked at her and said:

'Are you tired, Nan-Nan?'

'You make me tired sometimes, Georgie, when you are a naughty boy.'

Sitting up in his small bed, when she was out of the room, he felt a wave of pity for her sweep over him. Poor Nan-Nan! She, too—there was something all wrong with the world these days. She returned with his banana and biscuits, and as though to make atonement for his misdeeds he told her the full details of his adventures with Joan and Nigel, and he gave imitations of bears and tigers and the language of Indians.

He was interrupted in the performance by the entrance of Mum, who had come to say good-night. Nan-Nan went out of the room. As soon as he was alone with her he was aware of some unusual disturbance. Before she came he had entirely calmed down. He had become quite normal and himself. But now he felt not only that curious emotional thrill which her presence always gave to him, but the sense of something else, something more disturbing. She was looking pale, and seemed to be struggling to be matter-of-fact. Once or twice she looked at him, and then looked around the room curiously, as though she had never seen it before.

Her voice shook when she said: 'Was it a nice banana, darling?'

She kept touching things in an odd, jerky manner. And when she kissed him good-night she hurt him with a kind of savage hug. And though she looked into his face and there was the old familiar hungry look in her eyes, he noticed that she looked away almost immediately, and made some casual remark about the stuffed elephant on the chest of drawers.

She had gone before he had time to determine the shape of his own attitude towards her. He had felt aggrieved, and in need of comfort and loving assurance, and she had not given it to him. He felt an immediate desire to cry out, and yell for her return, but some stubborn impulse made him hold his peace. He had learnt that in dealing with grown-ups one had to invent one's own weapons. They didn't always fight fair. They had all the advantages, and their reserves were inexhaustible. There were, nevertheless, ways of defeating them. In this cumulating sense of a world against him Mum had somehow got involved. He struggled to think the matter out, but it eluded him. It began to get dark.

Nan-Nan came in and talked to him a little. He would have liked to tell her of his trouble, but he didn't know what his trouble was. It was indefinable. Neither was she somehow quite the person to tell, much as he loved her. She was neither in it, nor out of it. He didn't feel that she could help him. He was almost relieved at last when she went.

It was quite dark now, for he would never have a night-light. He lay there struggling with his load of trouble, trying not to cry. He thought of other things, flying impressions of the day, his new fairy car, Uncle Arthur and the rabbits, but the load remained.

He slept at last, still suffering as the dumb suffer. He did not know how long he slept, or what had happened in his dreams, but he knew that after what appeared a great lapse of time he awoke quite suddenly as though someone had touched him. He looked around.

It was daylight, but there was no one in the room. What hour was this? It was some unfamiliar time, much earlier than usual. He heard the birds outside, but there were no sounds of activity within the house. It was a forlorn, deserted hour. The recollections of yesterday had faded, but suddenly the burden of them came back to him in a concentrated form. He knew he could stand it no longer. He must cry. Not an ordinary whimper which one may do in bed, but an important cry. Something which would definitely relieve his depression.

He jumped out of bed and pattered across the room in his pyjamas. Nan-Nan's door was open, but he ignored it. He was in search of bigger game. He ran down the passage, opened Mum's door, and trotted in.

The fact that she was sitting on the edge of her bed partly dressed gave him no surprise, the fact that when she saw him she turned quite pale, and started like a person who had seen a ghost, seemed of small consequence. He flew at her, like an arrow to its mark, flung his arms around her and began to sob. His little bosom beat against hers, his tears ran down her neck. What could she do but hug him, and sway, beating time on his back with each rhythmic sob coming from his entire body?

'There, there, darling. It's all right. What is it? What is Georgie crying about?'

No answer; only the continual sob and the pat upon the afflicted back. She swung up her legs, and lay down on the bed still holding him close, and crooning softly. In that first fierce assault the defences of her own personal interest in the matter were carried, and she knew instinctively that she would never recover the ground lost. But her own tears were not far away.

'Oh, Georgie, why did you—how did you know?'

He heard her say this and he remembered it afterwards, but he did not answer. Know! know what? It was largely the fact of not knowing that had brought him to this condition. He was fighting with his own weapons, and he continued to sob.

Through his tears he caught a glimpse of her face. It still had that haunted scared expression, as though there was something she could not understand. She was desperately anxious to calm him.

'It's all right, darling, it's all right. Mum's not going. She's staying here with Georgie.' He was not going to acknowledge his goal, or gloat over the spoils of an uncertain victory. His business was to make sure. He clung to her the tighter, and for a long time neither spoke. But his sobs gradually diminished and he appeared to sleep. But her deep, troubled eyes were very wide-awake. They travelled from the chintz curtains of her beautiful room to a small hand-bag, partially packed, and then back to her son. They alighted upon a Limoges enamel box, brought back from her honeymoon, and from there to a note, addressed to Nan-Nan, propped up on the flap of the rosewood escritoire, and then back to her son. She knew that she was beaten. And amidst the anguish of defeat she was already conscious of the balm of relief which would eventually heal her wounds.

'Wait for me, darling. Mum must go and telephone to—someone. She won't be long.'

He saw her glide out of the room, closing the door behind her. He heard her go down to the little room off the hall, and there was that funny click of a bell which meant someone was asking for a number. Then followed a long interval. Then the click of that bell again, which meant the receiver had been put up. Another short interval, and she glided back into the room. She looked pale. She put her hand to her brow, and stared about vaguely. Then she seemed to shiver, and to emit a little sigh. She picked up the letter from the escritoire and tore it into a thousand pieces.

'I must go and have a bath, Georgie.' She said this almost petulantly, as though she were struggling to force herself into the normal observances of the working day.

He again watched her go without comment. He heard the bath water running, and the usual splashing which follows soon after. Other sounds of activity from the house and garden reached him. He knew that it would soon be *his* time to get up. Nan-Nan would be wondering where he was.

And then suddenly he remembered that it was time for his song. In a crystalline instant he realised that whatever happened in this world, the song must go on. And so, propped up against Mum's pillow, with his little chest thrust out, he began his morning song of praise and triumph.

With his bright blue eyes fixed on the blue of the sky there seemed to flood through him a praise of all living things, and a faith of man to surmount all obstacles. Tigers and Indians, elves and elephants, the menace of darkness, unseen and unknown powers ever conspiring to beat him down.

But the mission of man was to rise above all this. He must stand by his fellowman. Perhaps that was the true purport of George Arthur's song. Divided, he was at the mercy of the powers of darkness. The world was a battlefield where real blood and anguish flowed. United, it was the happy playground of a thousand dreams. And while he played and dreamed there would flow forever through his heart the golden melody of song—the song of praise, the song of triumph.

—XX—

The Persistent Mother

THE REFINEMENT OF THE BINDLOSS FAMILY was a by-word in Tibbelsford. Mr Bindloss himself was a retired printer. Now as everyone knows printing is the most respectable of professions, but retirement is the most refined profession of all. It suggests vested interests, getting up late in the morning, having a nap in the afternoon, and voting for keeping things stable. But Mr Bindloss was by no means an inactive man. He was a sidesman at St Mark's Church, tended his own garden, grew tomatoes, supervised the education of his two daughters, sat on the committee of the Tibbelsford Temperance League and the Domestic Pets Defence League. Mrs Bindloss was even more refined, for it was rumoured that she was distantly related to a lord. She certainly spoke in that thin precise manner which was easily associable with the aristocracy, a manner which her daughters imitated to perfection. The elder daughter Gwendoline, who was sixteen, was in her last term at Miss Langton Matravers' school; whilst the younger daughter Mildred was in her first term at that same institution. One might mention in passing that Miss Langton Matravers prided herself that she only catered for daughters of the gentry. The family lived in a neat semi-detached villa in the Quorn Road.

Now it came to pass in the fullness of time that Mr Bindloss realized that he was not so well off as he thought he was, or as he used to be. He discovered that the money that he had made by honest toil in the printing trade was now described as unearned increment, and taxed accordingly. Moreover, it did not go so far as it did in the good old days of his early retirement. In those days Mrs Bindloss was able to secure a nice pliable servant, who would work twelve hours a day, sleep in, and only ask for every other Sunday afternoon off, for fourteen pounds a year. Now, the only domestic help she could secure was a fugitive procession of strange women, who came daily and demanded a pound a week, all their evenings off as well as Sundays. Even then they did not appear eager for the work. They would turn up, take stock of the household, eat a few huge meals, smash a few plates, and vanish. It was very trying. Why couldn't things remain as they were?

One spring morning Mr Bindloss was in the garden thinning out some young cabbage plants, when his wife came out to him, holding a letter in her hand.

'I've had a letter from Agnes,' she said.

'Oh!' said Mr Bindloss.

'She says that the Northallertons have gone to live at Tollinghurst.'

'Really!' said Mr Bindloss.

'Yes. Do you know that young Archie Northallerton may one day be Lord Windlass?'

'Oh, that's nice!' said Mr Bindloss, who was apt to be a little preoccupied when gardening.

'Put that trowel down, Julian, and listen to me,' said his wife.

Mr Bindloss knew when he was spoken to, and he obeyed.

'Young Archie is just fourteen. Tollinghurst is only half-an-hour's journey by train. Does anything strike you?'

'Not forcibly,' replied Mr Bindloss scratching his head behind the left ear.

'No, I suppose it wouldn't,' snapped the refined Mrs Bindloss. 'Does it not occur to you that this boy is fourteen, that is to say that he is two years older than Mildred and two years younger than Gwen?'

The eyes of Mr Bindloss narrowed. His wife's implication became clear to him.

'What a thing it is to have a clever wife,' he said defensively, then added:

'It's a bit young though to think of—er—marriage.'

'It's not too young to *begin* to think about it.'

'No, no, that's true, that's very true. What do you propose to do, my dear?'

'Write to his mother, and suggest their bringing or sending the boy over for the day.'

'Excellent, you know her, of course?'

'I haven't actually met her, but she will know of me naturally. We are distantly related.'

'You say that boy *may be* Lord Cutlass. Let's see, what is the exact relationship? You did tell me but I have forgotten.'

'Windlass not Cutlass. It's like this—my sister married a Bream, who are cousins to the Northallertons. Henry Bolsover Northallerton, the father of this boy, is the younger brother of Lord Windlass, who is a middle-aged bachelor. If he leaves no heirs Archie will inherit the estates and the title.'

'I see, your's is not exactly a blood relationship, then. I mean to say there would be no obstacles—'

'No obstacles at all. The Northallertons in any case are a very good family and very wealthy.'

'Well, of course, my dear, I shan't stand in your way. Indeed, I'll do my best to make the young gentleman's visit enjoyable.' So Mr Bindloss returned to his cabbages and Mrs Bindloss to the library, where she wrote the following letter:

Dear Mrs Northallerton,

Forgive my writing you as I don't think we have ever actually met. My dear sister's husband, Samuel Bream, used to speak so affectionately about you all. Happening to hear that you have come to live in the neighbourhood I wonder whether you would give us the great pleasure of a visit. My dear husband, who has retired from business and my two daughters and myself, would be delighted to welcome you. We live in a modest way, but we have a very pleasant garden, as this is my husband's special hobby. I hear you have a small boy. We should be so pleased if you would bring him too, as we are all devoted to boys. Believe me, dear Mrs Northallerton,

Yours cordially,

CORA BINDLOSS.

This letter elicited no reply for five days. At length one morning came the following:

DEAR MRS BINDLOSS,

Thank you for your letter. Yes, I remember hearing my cousin speak of you. I'm afraid I cannot come over to see you just now, as I have several house-parties coming on, and Archie is attending school. Perhaps some time when you are in the neighbourhood you will give me a call.

Yours sincerely,

CONSTANCE NORTHALLERTON.

To some people this reply would have been accepted as rather in the nature of a snub, but not so to Mrs Bindloss.

'It gives me a loophole,' she explained to her husband. 'I shall wait a decent period, and then happen to be in the neighbourhood.'

As a matter of fact she waited fourteen days. It is possible that she might have called on Mrs Northallerton sooner, but this interlude had been devoted to the making of an ill-afforded new frock. At the end of that period she took the train to Tollinghurst, and walked sedately up to 'The Three Gables', only alas! to find Mrs Northallerton had gone up to town for a few days.

Whatever faults Mrs Bindloss may have had, a lack of tenacity of purpose was not one. Three times during the course of a fortnight she 'happened to be in the neighbourhood' of Tollinghurst. On the third occasion she ran her quarry to earth. Mrs Northallerton was just going out but she was graciously pleased to entertain Mrs Bindloss for a quarter of an hour. The latter, was at her very best. She flattered her hostess about her house, her clothes, her appearance, and her intelligence in accents so refined as to be almost painful. No one is entirely immune to flattery and Mrs Northallerton could not help but be polite and a little cordial. Towards the end of the interview Mrs Bindloss said:

'And how's that dear boy of yours? Archie, isn't his name?'

'Oh, he's very well. He's at school. He goes to Headingley, you know.'

'Really, *how* interesting!' exclaimed Mrs Bindloss. 'I hear it's such an excellent school. It is the great grief of my husband and myself that we never had a boy. My husband adores boys. It would be *so* delightful if you would let er—Archie come over and see us one day—perhaps during the holidays?'

'Why, of course, I expect he would like to come very much,' replied Mrs Northallerton, without any great show of enthusiasm. 'He's just got his school cap—maroon and black stripes. He's very pleased with himself.'

'How delightful! I *do* think maroon and black is a delightful combination. I expect he's a very clever boy, isn't he?'

'They seem to think so, Mrs Bindloss. He's very good at Latin and botany.'

'Really, how splendid, Mrs Northallerton. He would get on admirably with my husband. He doesn't know *much* Latin. He can't speak it you know; but he knows *all* about botany. You should see the tomatoes he grows.'

'Indeed! Well, it's very good of you to call, but I'm afraid I really must be going now.'

'Of course, oh dear! I'm afraid I'm an awful chatterbox, especially when I meet someone *really* interesting.'

When Mrs Bindloss returned home that evening she was able to announce that she had made a conquest, that Mrs Northallerton was charming, and that the boy was certainly coming over to visit the family during the holidays. She also said that her husband and both the girls were to study hard at Latin and botany.

Now this command led to a good deal of unpleasantness. The little Latin that Mr Bindloss had learnt at school he had almost entirely forgotten. It seemed rather much to expect, at his time of life, that at the end of a day's gardening when his natural inclinations were to sit down and read the newspaper, he should have to try and learn up passages from Virgil. The girls said they hated botany and had no books on it. This defect was rapidly put right by Mrs Bindloss, who went into the town and bought Green's *Life of the Plant* and Morgan's *Botany for Beginners*.

'You will study these books, Gwendoline and Mildred, or there will be no flower show and Church bazaar for you next month.'

Under this dire menace the two girls steeled themselves to grasp the first principles of plant life. And during the ensuing summer months Mrs Bindloss did her best to train their minds in some of the principles of human life. She did it quietly and insinuatingly. She pointed out how in a few years' time they would come to the stage when they would require to marry. She limned all the beauties and advantages of married life. She dwelt upon her own happy married life, only handicapped by the eternal lack of funds. Everything was so expensive now. Unless one was very, very rich one had to do one's own housework. (The two girls she knew hated housework.) Then she began gradually to talk about young Archie Northallerton. She had heard that he was a perfectly charming boy, very kind, clever, and gentlemanly. He would one day probably be Lord Windlass; in any case he would be very rich. A woman who married him would be a real lady, and would never have to do any housework at all. She did not think it advisable to go any further. The affair did not make much impression on Mildred. She was of the age which is more interested in meringues than marriage. But Gwendoline was sixteen, and was beginning to be absorbed in erotic literature. In reading of the doings of Ivanhoe and Lancelot it occurred to her sometimes that Tibbelsford was a drab little town. And she dreamed of a knight on a white charger, riding up to number 27, Quorn Road, and snatching her up—one evening perhaps when she was watering the syringa in the front garden—and carrying her off and whispering in her ear:

'Come, my beloved, I will make you a Lady. Come with me to my castle on the other side of the dark wood.'

She dwelt rather unduly on these visions.

As the summer advanced the family began to discuss the best way to entertain the future lord. It was to be assumed that it would be a fine day. Now Mr Bindloss took a great pride in his lawn, which he kept rolled and cut himself. He had never allowed tennis or any other game to be played on it, but discussing the matter in bed one night with his wife, they agreed that a game of some sort would have obvious advantages. It would bring the young people into more intimate relationship. But tennis? none of the family played tennis, and it was doubtful if the lawn was quite large enough. But what about croquet? Croquet was a nice quiet game that didn't require running about, and would not be likely to do damage to the flower beds. Yes, croquet they decided was just the thing.

The next day Mr Bindloss wrote up to town and had a croquet set sent down. When it arrived he and his wife poured over the rules. They seemed extremely complicated, and the girls were called in to give their help. The only solution seemed to be set up the hoops and experiment.

'We must be able to play a decent game when Archie comes,' said Gwendoline, who quickly showed herself the most proficient performer of the family. Nearly every afternoon for some weeks the Bindloss family practised croquet, much to the astonishment of their neighbours. Mr Bindloss had to explain to Mr Longman next door that the exercise was good for the girls. This was a good enough reason, but whatever physical benefits may have accrued, it cannot be said that the mental effect was satisfactory. There is perhaps no game at which people can so easily and persistently lose their tempers as croquet. There were furious arguments and disputes about the rules. Moreover, Mr Bindloss objected to being beaten, and the girls accused him of cheating. Mr Bindloss always played with the wrong ball, and swore it was the right one. Eventually the parents gave it up, and left the girls to play alone. Mildred hated the game, and was forced to play as though it were taking medicine. They also bought a box of draughts, and a box of Halma, in case it should be a wet day when Archie came. Early in July Mrs Bindloss again wrote to Mrs Northallerton, a chatty friendly little letter, ending up by hoping that at the end of the term Mrs Northallerton would remember her promise to bring Archie over for the day.

She received no reply to this, so she wrote again a week later, saying that she feared her letter must have miscarried and repeating her invitation. There was still no answer and it was near the end of July. The situation was desperate. She knew the school must have broken up. Some women would have given up in despair, but not so Mrs Bindloss. She wrote once more, and said that as the weather was so fine and Mr Bindloss's roses were now at their best, wouldn't Mrs Northallerton and Archie come over the following Wednesday to lunch and spend the afternoon? Her persistence reaped its reward. Two days later came a telegram from somewhere in Yorkshire:

> Many thanks am arranging to send Archie next Wednesday Train arrives 12-45 NORTHALLERTON.

Triumph! Mrs Bindloss glowed with it. And then what

a to-do there was. The girls' new taffeta frocks had been in preparation for some time and were quickly finished off. Mr Bindloss was bought a new alpaca coat and a Panama hat. A new loose cover was made for the best armchair in the drawing room. And a man was sent for to mend all kinds of household defects, attention to which was considerably overdue.

'And now we must consider the lunch and the tea,' said Mrs Bindloss.

It was decided that you could not give a potential lord anything less than chicken. The question was ought they to have soup and fish as well. After a deal of argument they decided to have soup only, for the reason that they were short of plates, and if Annie, the daily help, had to wash up plates between courses, she would probably lose her head. Of course there must be some nice sweets and pastry, but these could be prepared beforehand. And for the tea there must be a goodly assortment of cakes, jam and cream.

'A young gentleman like that is sure to appreciate such things,' said Mrs Bindloss, 'and if we do it well he will be more likely to come again.'

At length the great day dawned. Mrs Bindloss was up early. She peered out of her bedroom window anxiously. Yes, the day promised to be fine. She got up and dressed and roused the rest of the family. There would be plenty to do for everyone. Annie couldn't be relied on to cook such an elaborate meal by herself. Mrs Bindloss had had to scold her the day before for carelessness. Mrs Bindloss dressed feverishly. Annie of course was late. She *would* be on such an important occasion. Came half past seven and then eight and still no Annie. The girls were bustled out of bed and made to get breakfast. The family started the day with bad tempers.

'It's no good getting agitated,' said Mr Bindloss, coming into the dining room just as the breakfast was on the table.

'It's all very well for some people,' snapped Mrs Bindloss. 'Some people don't have all the work and worry of it.'

After a sketchy breakfast Mildred was sent into the town on her bicycle to beat up the lagging Annie. She returned in half an hour's time with a message from Miss Annie Woppins to the effect that that lady had no longer any intention of 'obliging Mrs B. after the saucy way she spoke to her yesterday.'

Consternation and fury in the Bindloss family.

'We must make the best of it,' said Mr Bindloss, lighting his pipe. 'We must meet the situation with Christian fortitude.'

'Yes, and perhaps you'll go and get some coals in,' said Mrs Bindloss. 'Mildred, get on your bicycle again and go and see if you can get Mrs Betts, or that other woman in Stone's passage—what's her name? the one with a moustache.'

'We can't have that awful apparition about for Archie to see,' exclaimed Gwen.

'You'd better get on with the housework,' said Mrs Bindloss, 'and be quick about it. And, Mildred, on the way back, call at Fleming's and order the dogcart to be here sharp at twelve to take some of us to the station. Julian, after you've got the coals in, you can clean the knives, and then roll the lawn and put up the croquet hoops.'

Mrs Bindloss's annoyance about the defection of Annie was mellowed by a certain cynical enjoyment at rubbing it in about the sordidness of domestic drudgery. It would be an object lesson to the girls. Having borne the burden of the fight so far, she meant to stand no nonsense from the family. For the next few hours the house was in a turmoil. Mildred returned to say that neither Mrs Betts nor the woman with a moustache was available. Mrs Bindloss proceeded with her preparations for lunch, whilst her husband and daughters were sent flying round at her commands. It was decided that the correct thing to do was for Mr and Mrs Bindloss to go to the station themselves in the dogcart to meet the future Lord Windlass, whilst the girls remained behind to change into the new taffeta frocks and at the same time to keep an eye on the fowl and the vegetables. It must be acknowledged that under the very trying circumstances Mrs Bindloss managed efficiently. All the preparations were carefully made, and when the dogcart arrived at twelve o'clock, she was ready in the hall pulling on her new white gloves.

They arrived at the station a good quarter of an hour before the train came in. Mrs Bindloss was one of those women who are always pecking at their husbands. That is to say she was always darting at him and pulling his waistcoat down, putting his tie straight, or picking little bits of cotton off his coat. This quarter of an hour was fully occupied in this way, amplified by various wishing-to-goodnesses he would do this, that, and the other in regard to his clothes.

At length the train came in. It was a slack hour, and a mere handful of people got out. In this company it was not difficult to discriminate which was the future Lord Windlass. The rest were ordinary market folk. Apart from being obviously what is known as 'upper class', he was wearing the maroon and black striped cap which his mother had spoken to Mrs Bindloss about. He came swinging along the platform, and he was carrying—curiously enough—two fishing-rods in canvas coverings and a brown paper parcel.

'Leave this to me,' whispered Mrs Bindloss. When the boy was within hailing distance she cried out in her most refined accent:

'So here you are, Archie! Welcome to Tibbelsford!'

She held out her hand, and he took it shyly. On close examination it could not be said that the future Lord Windlass was exactly of prepossessing appearance. For a boy of fourteen he was distinctly too fat. His round, fat face was flabby and, indeed, the lower part of his face even gave the appearance of having double chins. His expression was taciturn, with a shy reserve of maliciousness.

'You're just in time for lunch,' added Mrs Bindloss, who was avid to begin the lavish entertaining. 'I expect you're ready for your lunch after your journey.'

Archie mumbled something about being 'able to peck a bit,' and the three walked out of the station and got into the dogcart.

When they were seated, Mrs Bindloss broke out:

'Now, my dear Archie, I have a most dreadful confession to make. I don't know what you'll think, considering what you—er—are used to. But the whole of our domestic service has broken down. I don't know whatever kind of lunch we shall be able to provide. I do hope you won't mind taking pot luck. Our cook is ill in bed, and we're in *such* a muddle.'

They couldn't hear what the boy replied, owing to the rattle of the wheels and the noise of the town. Mrs Bindloss continued:

'And how is your dear mother?'

'She's all right.'

'Such a charming woman, *so* handsome, so intellectual!'

The rest of the conversation on the way to the house, consisted of a wild babble of effusive comment from Mrs Bindloss, a certain amount of forced hilarity from Mr Bindloss, checked by almost inaudible monosyllables from the boy.

'He's very shy,' Mrs Bindloss whispered to her husband as they descended from the dogcart. Gwendoline was on the lawn.

Mrs Bindloss called out:

'Ah here we are, dear! This is my eldest girl, Gwendoline. I hope you'll be great friends. Where is Mildred? Reading, I expect. Both my girls are great readers. Are you fond of reading, Archie?'

He was understood to say either 'yes' or 'no'.

It was then Mr Bindloss's turn to have something to say.

'Hullo, I see you've brought fishing-rods. I'm afraid we haven't any fishing here.'

'Haven't you?' said Archie quite distinctly.

They entered the hall, and he put down his rods, and his brown paper parcel, and took a stone bottle of ginger beer out of his pocket and laid it beside them.

'Oh, dear! boys will be *pueri*,' said Mr Bindloss, who was preparing for his Latin campaign. 'He's brought a bottle of ginger-beer, and I do believe—this parcel—'

'Really, Julian, Archie's parcel is no business of yours.'

'They're sandwiches,' said the visitor. This rather surprising statement was robbed of further comment by Mildred's entrance, rubbing her hands on her apron, which she had forgotten to remove. She had been dishing up the vegetables.

'Ah!' exclaimed Mrs Bindloss, 'here's our younger pride, Mildred. Mildred, dear, what are you wearing that apron for? Have you been working at your plants in the conservatory?'

'No mother I—er—' she held out her hand to Archie and said timidly: 'How are you?'

'Pretty dicky,' replied the boy.

'What!' exclaimed Mr Bindloss. 'Pretty dicky! but my dear boy, why didn't you tell me? What can we do? Is there anything you'd like? A little sal volatile, perhaps. How do you feel?'

'Oh, I don't know,' he answered.

'But this is most distressing. Do you feel like having any lunch?'

'I expect I could peck a bit.'

There is no denying that the future Lord Windlass had not made a very auspicious start. He was plain, surly; he arrived with fishing-rods, sandwiches and ginger beer—whatever kind of people did his mother think they were?—and on the top of this he announced that he felt 'dicky'.

'Come on, then, Julian, take Archie upstairs. Perhaps

he would like a wash. He may feel better after lunch.'

While he was upstairs the lunch was whipped on to the table. It must be acknowledged that for an invalid Archie 'pecked' remarkably well. He had two wings of chicken, a large slice of breast, the parson's nose, two sausages, a liberal helping of sprouts and potatoes, some coffee jelly, three mince pies, a banana, an apple and some nuts, and chocolates. Apart from eating his enthusiasms appeared dormant. They could get him to talk about nothing at all. Mrs Bindloss talked about the Royal family, the weather, politics, her two daughters' cleverness—she didn't mention that it was Mildred who had smitched the Brussels sprouts—the church, and the lower classes. Mr Bindloss talked about Headingley College, the decay of society, and the beauties of plant life. Gwendoline recounted a beautiful romance she had just been reading called *The Mother Superior*. Mildred stared at the future lord open-mouthed, too nervous and agitated to eat or speak. The young gentleman himself remained stubbornly monosyllabic. He only ventured two remarks during the meal. Once he cocked his head on one side and said:

'That picture's out of the straight.'

And towards the end of the meal he said to Mildred:

'Do you hunt?'

On receiving an answer in the negative, he relapsed into a settled gloom.

Once Mrs Bindloss said: 'After lunch we thought you dear children might have a nice game of croquet. Do you play croquet, Archie?'

'No,' he said, 'I hate croquet.'

This was distinctly discouraging in view of the time and expense that had been devoted in preparing this innocuous game. However, concessions have to be made to the eccentricities of a future lord. By an elaborate process Mr Bindloss led up to the value of doing things promptly, and came out proudly with:

'As you know, Archie, *corripe tempus quod adest, O juvenes, ne hori moriemini.*

Anyone who happened to know the trouble that Mr Bindloss had had to memorize this old tag would sympathize with him in his disappointment when he regarded the face of his guest. It expressed an uncomfortable disgust. Neither did he display any excitement over the girls' drawings of flowers and fauna.

After lunch, however, he appeared in a better humour. On his own responsibility he suggested a game with the girls which he called 'Yoics'. It had to be played in a room, so they repaired to the drawing room. The game was this. Each of the three players had to occupy a wall, touching it with their hands. Then the one facing the blank wall had to call out: 'Yoics! I'm going over.' Then he or she had to throw themselves on the ground and scramble on all fours to the opposite wall before the other two—also on all fours—met in the middle and touched hands. If he or she failed to get there, then they all changed walls and someone else tried.

It was not a game that Mrs Bindloss would have recommended because for one thing it meant rearranging the furniture, furthermore, it did no good to the girls' new taffeta frocks. Nevertheless, she and her husband looked on and gave the impression of being greatly amused. They kept the game up for about twenty minutes, until in an excess of anxiety to reach the opposite wall, Archie barged into the mahogany side table and knocked it over, smashing the vase which dear Aunt Emily had given as a wedding present, and spilling the flowers and water all over Gwendoline's frock. Gwendoline had to go and change, and Mr Bindloss suggested that as it was such a fine day they might play some game in the garden.

Archie was now getting more at home with the girls, and his greater intimacy was principally demonstrated by pushing them about. He had quite a pleasant wrestle with Mildred while Gwen was changing her frock. He guaranteed to throw her three times in five minutes, pinioning her head to the ground, and he did so quite successfully. He was less successful with Gwen, as he only threw her twice in ten minutes, and then at the expense of tearing her skirt.

'It's a pity you don't play croquet, Archie,' said Mrs Bindloss. 'It's a most interesting game.'

'No, I hate it. I'll tell you what we will do though. Let's play croquet polo. You know, you have a goal at each end of the lawn, and you try and score goals.'

This sounded a harmless enough game, and they played Archie and Mildred versus Mr Bindloss and Gwen. They started gently tapping the wooden ball across, but no goals being forthcoming, Archie began to hit harder, and suddenly there was a yell. Mr Bindloss had received a fierce blow on the ankle from Archie's drive. He limped off the field, and the girls protested that the game was too rough and dangerous.

'All right,' said Archie, 'but I bet I'll drive a croquet ball further than you two girls put together.'

Mr and Mrs Bindloss retired to the security of the drawing room.

'He's a very curious boy,' said Mr Bindloss, rubbing his ankle.

'I'm sure he's really very nice. I expect he improves on acquaintance,' replied his wife.

There was a sudden terrific crash and they rushed to the window. Archie had driven his ball right through the glass of the tomato house.

'Oh dear, oh dear!' Mr Bindloss called out feebly.

It required great tact to dissuade the young gentleman from continuing this game, without being definitely rude to him. It was not till he had trampled on a bed of lupins, broken a croquet mallet, and nearly knocked Mildred's eye out, that they were able to get him to turn his attention to something else.

The nerves of Mr Bindloss were getting on edge. He was accustomed to an afternoon nap, but of course such a thing was out of the question on a day like this. He was inclined to be querulous with his wife, an attitude which was hotly resented.

'You never think of the girls' interests,' she said.

'Interests!' exclaimed Mr Bindloss. 'A nice sort of son-in-law he'd make. I wish he'd go.'

'He's getting on very well,' said Mrs Bindloss, looking out of the window. 'I'm sure he's enjoying himself.' Then she added breathlessly, 'Julian, would you believe it! He's—kissing Gwen in the tomato house!'

'Kissing!'

'Yes, he's got his arm round her waist.'

'Well, I—really—I—what ought we to do?'

'Leave them alone. They are only children. Besides—'

She turned from the window and took up some knitting. There was silence from the garden for nearly twenty minutes. Then Mildred came running in.

'I say, mother, Archie says he feels sick,' she exclaimed excitedly.

'Sick!' exclaimed Mrs Bindloss.

'Sick!' echoed Mr Bindloss.

'Yes, he looks it too.'

'Oh dear, oh dear!' exclaimed both the parents. They hurried out into the garden. There was Archie sitting on the grass fanning himself. He certainly looked very queer.

'Oh, my dear Archie,' exclaimed Mrs Bindloss, 'I'm so sorry. Won't you come in? Let me get you something. Hadn't you better lie down?'

He said, 'Yes,' and they led him in. He looked so ill that they took him up to Mr Bindloss's bedroom and got him to lie down on the bed.

'Gwen,' said Mrs Bindloss, 'run down the road and see if Dr Burns is in. I'm sure Archie's mother would like us to have a doctor to him.'

They gave him a little soda water and left him.

Gwen went for the doctor. And while she was gone a most surprising thing happened. A telegram arrived addressed to 'BINDLOSS.' Mrs Bindloss naturally opened it, and having opened it, gave a gasp of astonishment. She handed the telegram to her husband. It ran as follows.

> Archie has mumps regret could not send him
> NORTHALLERTON.

Mr Bindloss repeated the word 'mumps' three times, and stared helplessly at his wife.

'What does it mean?' said Mrs Bindloss savagely, as though accusing her husband of some wicked treachery.

'How can they say they couldn't send him when he's upstairs all the time lying on my bed?' said Mr Bindloss, as though he had made a brilliant riposte.

'He must have escaped,' interjected Mildred. Mr Bindloss was feverishly biting his nails. Suddenly he waggled his first finger at his wife.

'Does anything strike you? Does anything strike you?' he said.

'What?'

'He's got mumps. That's what the matter is with him. When he arrived I thought he had double chins. But he's got mumps.'

Mrs Bindloss gasped.

'He's got mumps, and he's been kissing the girls, and now he's lying on my bed.'

'It's an outrage,' screamed Mrs Bindloss. 'What are we to do?'

'The only thing we can do is to wait for the doctor and then telegraph to Mrs Northallerton.'

Gwendoline happened to catch the doctor starting on his rounds. He came in and he and the two parents went up to the bedroom. The doctor examined the boy.

'Yes,' he said, 'he's got mumps all right. He must remain here and not be moved.'

'Oh, my dear Archie,' said Mrs Bindloss, 'what a pity you didn't tell us! But look here, my dear, here's a most curious letter from your mother, read it.'

Archie was sorry for himself and surly. He read the telegram and said:

'That's not from my mother.'

'How do you mean?'

'My mother's name is Bloggs.'

'What!' yelled Mr Bindloss.

'What!' screamed Mrs Bindloss.

'You never asked me my name. I was going out to do a bit of fishing and you asked me home to lunch. That's all.'

'But we called you Archie.'

'My name is Archie, Archie Bloggs.'

'But the maroon and black cap!'

'Yes, I know, I go to Headingley. I know young Northallerton, awful little ass. There was an epidemic of mumps just as the school broke up.'

'But who the devil!' exclaimed Mr Bindloss. 'I mean who is your father?'

'Don't you know? Blogg's Sausages.'

Mrs Bindloss was nearly in tears.

'Do you mean to say we've taken all this trouble and your father is only a sausage—'

Mr Bindloss saw red.

'It's an outrage!' he yelled. 'I shall prosecute you. You come here and get a good meal on false pretences. You smash up the drawing room. You smash the greenhouse and the croquet mallet. You nearly break my leg. And on the top of it you go kissing the girls with mumps on you, and all the time you're not—you're not who you're supposed to be. You're only the son of a sausage— By God! I'll have you locked up.'

The doctor intervened.

'You must excuse me, Mr and Mrs Bindloss, as I'm here in a professional capacity I must ask you to keep the patient quiet. And he should not be moved from this room.'

'We won't have him here.'

'Well, that's not my business. I've given you my advice.' And the doctor went.

There are many people in Tibbelsford who consider that Mr and Mrs Bindloss behaved heartlessly in this matter. It is a point of controversy to this day. The visit from an indignant Mr Samuel Bloggs, the father, did not help perhaps to pour oil on the troubled waters. There was certainly an acrimonious argument, and various cross threats of legal proceedings, but in the end the boy was sent home in an ambulance. The critics of the parents' behaviour did not of course know the inner history of their spiritual duress. People are apt to underestimate what parents will suffer for their children's interests, what indignities they will submit to. The girls fortunately did not get mumps, and two days later Mrs Bindloss wrote to Mrs Northallerton:

> DEAR MRS NORTHALLERTON,
>
> We were so grieved to hear about dear Archie. I do hope he is making a good recovery. We waited lunch nearly three quarters of an hour for him. I hope before the holidays are over he will be well enough to come over for the day, and that you will be able to accompany him. It was so sweet of you to have tried to arrange it, and to have sent us the telegram. My husband joins me in sending our very best greetings, and hopes for Archie's speedy recovery. Believe me, dear Mrs Northallerton,
>
> Yours very sincerely,
>
> CORA BINDLOSS.

That is the kind of woman Mrs Bindloss is. And that is the kind of spirit that has built cities, founded colonies and enlarged empires.

—XXI—

'Straight Griggs'

THERE WAS NO DOUBT but that the meeting of the parents had been a great success. During their seven years of married life Alec and Barbara Griggs often discussed the regrettable fatality that when his parents came over on a visit from America to stay with them, her parents always happened to be abroad. In a way it is not surprising, because although old Mr and Mrs John Griggs were pretty methodical and punctilious in their way of going on, and always gave plenty of notice of an intending visit, Barbara's father, Colonel Whetstone, was one of these restless old gentlemen with a passion for travel, and his wife shared this enthusiasm. In spite of his seventy-two years he was erect and agile, and if he once got the 'go fever', go he must, despite any arrangements that might have been made. But at last it had come off. Old Mr and Mrs Griggs had come from Florida to spend a couple of months, and Colonel and Mrs Whetstone were at home at their house across the valley. The month was August, and the visit coincided with that unusual English experience—a heat wave. The weather was indeed glorious. During the day Barbara was fairly occupied with her three children, and Alec motored in to Tellinghurst, where he managed the 'South Downs Agricultural Implements Ltd.' Consequently the parents were thrown very much together. At first Barbara was in a fever of apprehension. One never knew who was going to get on with whom, did one? But her mind was soon set at rest. Mrs Griggs and Mrs Whetstone, drawn together instinctively by the adoration of their children and grandchildren, were soon immersed in each other's company, whilst the two men struck up an immediate intimacy. Both had travelled and knocked about the world, and sitting side by side in the shade during the day, or on the verandah at night, these two, the Colonel, with his pipe, and John Griggs, with an endless procession of formidable-looking black cigars, would yarn and discuss world affairs all day, and half through the night (if they were allowed to by their womenfolk). Barbara was delighted. The whole thing was a great success. Alec's position at the Agricultural Implement Works was a good one and the firm was prospering, but neither he nor his wife made any pretence to their neighbours that it was his income which supported and sustained 'Guestling', one of the most beautiful houses in the whole of the Sussex weald. High up, but protected on the north and east by a thick belt of pine trees, it faced south, with a glorious view right down the Tellinghurst valley towards the sea. It had been a farmhouse in a very dilapidated condition when the Griggs bought it, but had been restored and enlarged by Lutyens. It showed that scholarly reverence for tradition, combined with the happy application of material, breadth, airiness, comfort and fine proportion which one associates with that eminent architect. It had a sunk rose garden, a Dutch garden, a bathing pool, and two tennis courts. Perhaps its most attractive feature, however, was the broad terrace in front of the dining room. On this was set a lime-wood pergola, over which trailed azaleas, clematis, and jasmine. The ground was flagged with broad rough stones, between which grew exquisite little crimson, white and blue rock flowers. It was, of course, Alec's father, John Griggs, who had paid for all this. He was known to be a very rich man and Alec was the only child. The Griggs were very popular on the countryside, and though many may have been envious, no one begrudged Alec 'an American millionaire' father, especially as the hospitality at 'Guestling' was notorious. Whether old John Griggs was actually a millionaire or not need not concern us. He was certainly a very rich man, but what the natives of Tellinghurst and district did not know—or only a few of them knew—was that although he was an American, he was only an American by naturalization. He was born and had spent the first twenty-three years of his life in England. Indeed, many Englishmen took him to task for thus forswearing the land of his birth, but his argument was that, although his heart was loyal enough to the motherland, you could not spend over forty years in a country, enjoy all its opportunities of advancement and make your fortune there, without ceding it whatever benefits your citizenship might afford. America had made him and he was, moreover, indebted to it for the most priceless asset of his career—his wife, the daughter of a professor of physics at Columbia University. No one seemed to know the details of John Griggs' chequered career. He had been most things. But it was at St Louis that he had laid the foundation of his fortune, first in connection with a bleaching business and then through a patent of his known as 'Griggs' Fertilizer'. It was in this city too that he acquired a soubriquet, which had stuck to him ever since: 'Straight Griggs'. No one was prouder of this title than Alec, his son. If his father had handed down to him one of the most honoured titles in the peerage, it would not have given him such a thrill of pride as this simple and well-earned description of his father's character. If his proprietorial conscience smote him a little when he looked around the beautiful house and grounds of 'Guestling', he consoled himself with the reflection that his possession of them was a source of infinite gratification to the man who had really bought and paid for that possession—'Straight Griggs'.

During the first fortnight, owing to the excessive heat, the Griggs hardly went outside the grounds, but the colonel and his wife, who were used to tropical climates, would come over in the afternoon, and very often in the early part of the evening the two elderly gentlemen would have a game of bowls, before settling down to their usual evening's 'pow-wow'. In the third week the colonel had to go up to London for four or five days to attend one or two committee meetings. John went with him in the car to the station and their parting had quite a note of melancholy regret. The colonel said he was afraid he would find the club he was staying at extremely boring after their delightful talks, while John said feelingly that he would be all the time looking forward to his friend's return.

Now if there was one feature about Griggs which had impressed the colonel more than another it was his innate buoyancy of disposition. It was a quality which conveyed itself to the listener. His eyes were the eyes of an incurable optimist. And when he spoke, in spite of his sixty-three years, the bulk of which had been spent struggling against adversity, his voice had almost a boyish ring. He was full of enthusiasms, sensitive to impressions, and eager to listen. It is advisable to keep these facts in mind in gauging the colonel's apprehensions on the night of his return. He had parted with 'Straight Griggs' in the manner described, and with these impressions of him indelibly graven on his mind. But on the Friday night when he returned he was conscious of a subtle change in his friend. It was not very marked, but it was there—quite definitely. He was just as affable, just as prepared to talk and to listen, but his manner was preoccupied. Some of his buoyancy had gone, some of his enthusiasm. He was not talking quite so well, or listening quite so well. Perhaps it was the heat. Sometimes during the evening his eyes would wander. When they were seated on the terrace he would let those terrible black cigars of his go out and then restlessly light another. When the colonel was talking to him he would suddenly turn and look down the valley, and the colonel knew that there was something on his mind. Moreover, it was something which had happened during his absence. He made occasion to take Barbara on one side, but she knew nothing. There had been no mail in from America during his absence. The Griggs had received no letters. How had they spent their time? Well, Mrs Griggs had hardly been out of the grounds, but Mr Griggs had taken the car out on two afternoons and gone for a run round the country, nowhere special, that she knew of. The colonel was perplexed. He returned to the terrace and found his friend still sitting alone in the dark. He determined to be as matter-of-fact as possible. Perhaps this mood would pass.

'Well, John,' he said breezily. 'I hear you have been for a run or two in my absence. Where did you get to?'

Without moving his cigar Griggs mumbled: 'Oh, one or two round trips—nowhere special. Except—' he paused and looked away down the valley. 'I got to the sea, and took a look at Ticehurst and Brynne—came back through Wantney and Glendisham—nowhere special—' There was an awkward little interval. The colonel wanted to hear more of the story of these wanderings, but he felt that any interruption might snap their flow. He merely murmured: 'Um—um', and refilled his pipe. Then John suddenly got up and appeared to stroll casually to the window that looked into the drawing room. The rest of the family had just settled down to what had become an evening ritual—a few casual rubbers of bridge. It was essentially a family game, in which the three ladies talked all the time about dressmaking and the bringing up of children, Alec behaved like a cheerful martyr, and no one seemed to know whose deal it was, or what were trumps, or what the score was. John's return to his seat had a more furtive character. He almost tiptoed. When he had lighted a fresh cigar he leaned forward confidentially towards the colonel, and the latter noticed that his eyes had an unusual brightness.

'Colonel,' he said quietly, 'as you pass through Glendisham, going east, there is a broad stretch of marshland on your left, but the road leads up through a pinewood to Worsleydale Common. But looking down through the trees you can just see the roofs of a long stretch of rambling buildings, built of granite and slate-coloured brick.'

He stopped, and looked at the colonel as though asking a question. The latter nodded his head and said almost under his breath:

'Yes, that's right. Deadmoor prison.'

John Griggs turned his head from left to right and back again, like a large benevolent-looking eagle. He seemed to be assuring himself thoroughly that he had heard aright. When he spoke again his voice had a husky quality. 'Deadmoor! Yes, I...I knew it was.'

The colonel felt himself on peculiarly delicate ground. His upbringing decreed that the poking of one's nose into another man's private affairs was a detestable form of ill-breeding. On the other hand here was a fellow creature—and one for whom he had developed an affection—obviously anxious to relieve himself of some oppressive mental load. After a decent interval he said as casually as he could:

'You—you knew of it then?'

There was an obvious sense of relief about the face of 'Straight Griggs'. He seemed to rejoice that the question had been put to him so squarely, that in fact the issue had become so defined. Leaning towards his friend he said in a deep clear voice:

'I escaped from there forty-one years ago last fall.' The two men looked at each other closely. It was the colonel who was the more disturbed. He gasped and repeated under his breath:

'Good God! Good God!'

Griggs, added calmly, as though meditating:

'I don't know how the law stands. Whether there's a time limit or what. But I suppose if they knew they would put me back.'

At this astounding revelation the colonel gave a quick apprehensive glance at the beautiful house silhouetted against the night sky. Through the open window came the sound of Alec's laughter, and his voice:

'Come on, Mother, you owe me one and threepence. Pay up!'

Griggs spoke more quickly, as though anxious to bridge the chasm that was suddenly yawning between them.

'You will first of all, of course, wonder what I was doing in prison. I will tell you in a few sentences. My father died just after I came down from Oxford—my mother had died when I was a small boy. He left me what seemed to be a pretty considerable fortune—about £32,000. I was young, high-spirited and I had no ties. I immediately proceeded to do all those things which dashing youth regards as "living". As you may imagine I had no lack of friends and acquaintances eager to help me in my anxiety to dissipate this fortune. Without, I hope, being vulgarly excessive, I did most of the usual things—travelled luxuriously, entertained and gambled. Incidentally, I'm afraid I gave a lot away to worthless people. Anyway at the end of eighteen months I was astonished to find that my capital of £32,000 had been reduced to rather less than £6,000! It was then that I began to make up my mind to pull myself together. This wouldn't do. I must settle down and find remunerative employment. And it was then, unfortunately, that I came in touch with Millingham. Millingham was one of the most ingratiating people I have ever met. He was tall, good-looking, and about twenty years older than I. We met, I remember, at a coffee stall about five o'clock one morning. I told him a good deal about my position, and afterwards went back with him to his flat in Golden Square. Millingham, it seemed, had a successful outside brokers business in the City. To cut it short he persuaded me to join him, and I put £4,000 into his business. I was to have a salary of £1,000 a year and a liberal percentage on the profits. The job suited me admirably. I could live comfortably on £1,000 a year. I was learning a business, and I was still my own master. I'm afraid dancing and other dissipations of youth still claimed a lot of my time, and my hours at the office were rather irregular. Nevertheless, I did a certain amount of work, and the whole thing seemed to be going swimmingly. It was two years later that the dreadful crash occurred. It was September, and I was going away with a friend to Norway fishing for a month. On the day of my departure I lunched with Millingham. We lunched lavishly, I remember—cocktails, champagne and liqueurs. His hospitality knew no bounds. About an hour before my train was due to depart he suddenly said: "Why, you never signed those Tilbury and Co. documents. I must have your signature before you go. If we take a taxi now you just have time to pop into the office and then have plenty of time for your train." I nearly said: "What are the Tilbury and Co. documents?" but I wasn't sufficiently interested. My mind was on fjords and fishing. We dashed into the office. I signed everything he put before me, about eight documents in all. His signature was already on them. I caught my train. I had a grand time in Norway. It was perhaps as well, for the day after I returned I was arrested.

'It seemed that I had put my signature to what was nothing more than an appalling kind of bucket-shop swindle. It came out at the trial that Millingham's real name was Malini. He had done this kind of thing once before in New York. He got seven years and I have never seen him since. As for me what could I say or do? As you know ignorance is no excuse in the eyes of the law. I did not even claim not to have read the documents I signed. I made no defence. Legally I had none. On account of my youth, and the fact that I was probably influenced by my senior partner, I was let off with two years.

'Gee! but I *was* young in those days. I was sent to Wandsworth first, and when I found myself in that forbidding prison I set my teeth, and determined to go through with it. I would make good somehow. I didn't *feel* a criminal, that was the great thing, and I was young and buoyant. At the end of four months I was transferred to Deadmoor. Deadmoor was a less depressing prison than Wandsworth, but Golly! how the time dragged! The dreadful monotony of that routine, and then the—how can I describe it?—kind of filthy undercurrent of confirmed vice running through the bulk of that unhappy crowd. I lie awake at night now sometimes and think of it. It's horrible. Living in it you gradually feel it gripping you. I don't pretend to know what can be done, but the system's wrong.'

Griggs licked his dry lips and frowned into the darkness.

'It was about six months later that the idea of escape occurred to me. There was a saying that no man had ever escaped from Deadmoor. I can quite believe it. I had very little real hope of escaping. But I felt that the mere effort of trying—however much I was punished for it afterwards—might sustain my momentary interest in life, and stimulate my self-respect. I began to take my bearings. At that time I was put to work making mailbags in a large building near the centre of the prison. I was passed daily from my cell to the exercise yard, and then to the mailbag building, and so back again to my cell, always, of course, under the eyes of warders. I could not see the slightest loophole of hope. The outer wall of the prison was a most formidable-looking structure, about 16 ft high and crowned with a close array of steel spikes. About the end of October, however, I was transferred for two days a week to the laundry sheds. Our "working party" consisted of about fifteen convicts, and in a long black shed near the south wall we did all the laundry work of the prison. On the second occasion of my visit there I began to take an alert interest in certain possibilities that this new situation offered. The windows of this shed faced north. The door was on the east side. But on the south side, where there were no windows, there was a space of less than twenty yards between the shed and the outside wall. In this space we used to hang out clothes to dry on clothes-lines. I noticed when I was out there that the position was not overlooked at all except by certain upper cells never occupied in daytime, and by the back windows of the sanatorium. But it was, I think, these attractive lengths of clothesline that put temptation into a young fellow's head.

'I came to the conclusion that this was one of those things that wanted doing without too much planning and forethought. It must be like an act of inspiration done at the exact psychological moment. It came a fortnight later. It was early November, late in the afternoon, and already getting dark. There was a slight mist about. I was sent out to collect some runner towels that had been out there all the afternoon. I found myself alone in this secluded space. Looking back on it after all these years I simply gasp at my own coolness and audacity. Without a moment's hesitation I untied about twenty feet of clothesline. In a few seconds I had made a noose at the end of it. I flung it up to the spikes. At my third attempt the noose caught over one of the spikes. I then tied one of the roller towels loosely round my neck—an inspiration this, as you shall see. It was again only a few seconds before I was at the top of that wall. But it was then that my more serious difficulties began. In the first place, although in the yard below I was not exposed, up here I seemed to be silhouetted against the skyline for the whole country to see. I was visible from the upper part of the deputy-governor's house, the doctor's house, the sanatorium, and various parts of the prison grounds. It seemed incredible that I was not immediately spotted. But I was too occupied to worry about this. My position was perilous. The slightest slip, and I should be impaled on those spikes. There was no space for a foothold, and it looked utterly impossible to leap clear of that wall, which appeared to slope outwards. It was then that my towel came in. I suppose it was again only seconds, but it seemed an eternity while I twisted it into a kind of pad. This I perched myself on gingerly on the top of the spikes. There was still no chance of jumping, so I simply let myself slither down the side of the wall. I fell with an unholy crash. When I reached the bottom the skin was torn off both my hands and arms, and my legs and body were badly cut and bruised, but I realised that no bones were actually broken. I staggered to my feet and ran.

'It is a curious fact when I look back on it, and I won't say whether I should take credit for it or not, that during the whole of that night's proceedings I never felt any fear. I reckoned the odds against me about ten thousand to one. I made up my mind to regard it as a kind of gallop and not to be broken-hearted when they caught me. Sportsmen aver that the fox enjoys the chase. I don't know anything about that, but I know that I got a curious kind of thrill out of it. I seemed to regard myself in a detached way, like a man looking down from a race stand on an outsider he has backed.

'Going direct south led, I knew, to the marsh, so I just ran till I was out of sight, then I made a wide detour and worked my way to the north side of the prison. As you know, about half a mile north is a pine wood, as the gradient of the hill begins to get steeper. As I say, it was getting dark, and I reckoned if I could make that wood before they caught me my chances would improve considerably. The trouble was I had to keep on stopping, hiding and dodging, because there were a few stray people about. But I must have had a good quarter of an hour's start before the gun went off. I knew what that meant, but the immediate danger was that it made the people I was likely to meet more alert. That confounded prison garb!

'But my luck held. I knew if I could make the wood, so far as men are concerned, I could give them a good run for their money, for that night anyway; but what I didn't like the thought of was *dogs*, which I knew they sometimes used on these occasions. Just before reaching the wood, I had to cross a road and an open field. A cart came blundering along the road, and I crouched down under a hedge. While hiding there a sound reached my ears which gave me a certain satisfaction—the sound of trickling water. It was true. After the cart had gone I found a narrow stream by the side of the field. I stepped into it, and waded over a hundred yards, until I came to the edge of the wood. I reckoned that might put the dogs off a bit, It was beastly cold and uncomfortable, but as I say I was young in those days. In the wood I had a good drink of water and a rest. Whether they used dogs or not, I cannot say. I heard no sound of them. In fact I heard nothing of my pursuers that night. I did not run any more, but walked quickly, keeping my eyes and ears on the alert. I walked for about another two hours and then had a rest on a fallen tree trunk. I felt it necessary to have a kind of committee meeting of one. The trouble was I didn't know the country at all, or where I was, or in what direction I was going. Not that this knowledge would have been very much use to me. The night was dark, but although one's eyes get used to it, it was impossible to see more than one's immediate surroundings. I could, however, just tell whether I was on a road or a common. After a time I decided to stick to a narrow road. A road in any case must lead in one direction, and I knew I was heading north. If I met anyone with a lantern or a lighted cart or trap I hid in the hedge, otherwise I did not hesitate to call out a cheery "good night" to passing travellers. The sound of my own voice gave me confidence. You must remember there were no motor cars in those days! I was beginning to get very hungry, and coming to a field I grubbed up a swede and ate it. It was better than nothing. I could see that my most urgent problem was going to be that of clothes. Unless I could get hold of other clothes the odds were going to remain 10,000 to 1 against me. I dare not go near a village or habitation.

It would mean hiding in the daytime and travelling at night, both at great risk; and where and to what end was I to travel? In the meantime, how was I to live? With a change of clothes I could take risks. It would be fatal to be merely seen. I don't know how long I plunged on through the darkness. Sometimes I tried to approach some sleeping farm, but I was invariably scared by the barking of dogs. But passing along my lane at some unholy hour of the night, I caught sight of a long bungalow-looking building almost hidden amidst trees. There appeared to be a few dim lights about the place. I determined to reconnoitre, and avoiding the carriage drive which led up to it, I got through the hedge, and approached it Indian fashion, moving noiselessly from cover to cover. When I got near enough I could see that it had the character of a hospital or sanatorium. Not a very suitable place to burgle, you may say, but still it held out the possibilities of my most vital need—clothes. When I got to the gravel path that ran all round the outside I took off my boots. I then went carefully across it and approached a window. To my surprise the window was open about two feet at the bottom, and the room was dimly lighted by a gas jet. My first glance told me that my surmise was correct—it was a hospital, apparently a small private hospital. In this room were three beds, only one of which was occupied, and that at the far end by a man who was asleep. I tried to take in the details of the room, and suddenly my heart gave a jump. On a chair at the end of the man's bed and neatly folded up, was a suit of clothes and a collar and shirt! Acting on my inspirational policy I was through that window like a knife. I shot silently across the room and gripped my treasure. As I lifted it I caught sight of a small pile of money on the mantelpiece. It is amazing how quickly one's mind acts in cases of this kind. During my stay in prison I had vowed to myself again and again that when I regained my freedom I would never do a thing that was not meticulously honest and straightforward, and here I was after a few hours' liberty committing a deliberate burglary! At the same time my instinct of self-preservation was telling me that in this lay my one chance in the 10,000, while my mind was registering a decision that these trifles could be easily replaced when I had made good. I had just gripped the money when I heard a brisk step in the passage outside. If I had darted into the room, my outward journey was even quicker. When I alighted on the flower bed outside the window I had to peep back to see what happened. A nurse entered and after glancing at the patient she went straight to the chair were the clothes had lain! Then she stopped, and looked puzzled. She looked on the floor, at the patient, and then around the room. She was obviously bewildered. Without waiting for her bewilderment to develop into suspicion of an outside burglary I crossed the gravel path, collected my boots, sprinted across the garden, got through the hedge and in a few minutes' time was among the furze bushes of an adjoining common. It was an unpleasantly cold night to change one's clothes in the open, but excitement kept me warm. I had no matches and I could not see how much the money amounted to. But this seemed of less importance than the clothes. They fitted me quite well, and I stuffed the convict garb as far up as I could into a rabbit hole. After walking on for another half hour there seemed to be no point in plunging about in the dark, so I leant against a tree and tried to get a little sleep. I must have slept an hour or two, for when I awoke there was a glimmer of light in the sky, which served the useful purpose of enabling me to locate the east. I was soon able to count my stolen money. There was a sovereign, a half-sovereign, and eight shillings in silver. A very useful accretion of capital upon which to start my new career!

'I was feeling stiff and very hungry, but when I looked at my new brown suit my spirits rose. I should now have to risk entering a town or village. I washed my face in a stream and did my hair as well as I could with my fingers.

I was bothered by having no hat. Not that I particularly wanted to wear one, but in those days "the hatless brigade" was almost unknown, and I feared that this little defect might make me conspicuous. I decided, however, that when I came to a town I would amble along the streets very slowly with my hands in my pockets, as though I had just strolled out of a house. I made for a road and after walking rather less than a mile I found myself coming to the outskirts of what appeared to be a fair-sized town. It turned out afterwards to be Brindlehampton. I passed a policeman, who I thought looked at me questioningly. I ambled by him, whistling, and to my relief found that he was not following me. The shops were shut, but a little further on I came to a sight which gladdened me—a cheap eating house for carters and market people. I strolled in and sat down, and a girl came up to serve me. I ordered two fried eggs some grilled ham, bread, butter, marmalade and a pot of coffee. Oh, that breakfast! During the whole course of my life I have never enjoyed such a meal. Afterwards I strolled out and bought cigarettes, and matches. I then came across a hosier's. There I invested in a three-and-ninepenny felt hat and a walking stick. The walking stick was a luxury but I felt it added conviction to my make-up. I looked at myself in the long mirror. In my brown suit, collar, tie, felt hat, with a cane hanging over my arm, a cigarette in the corner of my mouth, there was nothing about me to betoken the convict. Strolling up the town, my body sated with good food and hot coffee, the odds of 10,000 to 1 against me suddenly seemed to shift to a good level chance. Such is youth!'

'Straight Griggs' sighed. During the whole course of this narrative the colonel could not but be impressed by the extraordinary simplicity of the narrator. Having decided to tell the story he never hesitated. He seemed to be living through the exploits of that night all over again, and although he must have done so a thousand times, the recounting of them appeared to give him a certain boyish satisfaction. On account of 'youth' he had nothing to sigh about.

'I knew of course that the safest place in the wide world to hide in was London, and thither I made my way. I even had the audacity to ask a policeman the way to the station, and when he addressed me as "sir" I thrilled with delight. I really wonder I didn't travel up first class. In London I made for the inconspicuous neighbourhood of Camden Town, and took a furnished bedroom in a meagre street. I paid the landlady a week's rent in advance and told her my luggage was on its way from Scotland. It was impossible, of course, to make any definite plans. My immediate problem was to remain hidden until the keenness on my search had somewhat abated. Later on I might manage to get out of the country. In the meantime it would be necessary to get some kind of job—however menial—in order to keep body and soul together, and at the same time not to mix among a crowd of men, any one of whom might recognize me from my photograph, which had appeared in the newspapers. I must say I had managed to alter my appearance pretty considerably from the photograph. My luck was in. Two days later I heard from a man on a seat in the Park about a big rush order a large firm of stationers was dealing with for some continental government. They wanted men for all-night work. I called and applied and was taken on at once, without any question of reference or character. My job consisted mostly in folding circulars, putting them in envelopes and stacking them. I had to work on a nine-hour night shift, and I was paid twenty-five shillings a week. A hard job, you may say, but I realized that I was lucky. I saw no one but a lot of down-and-out scallywags like myself.

'Towards the end of the week I had a queer little experience. Every evening I used to go for a two hours' walk before going on duty. I walked about the streets, avoiding the more conspicuous and well-lighted thoroughfares, but

I enjoyed this plunge into adventure. One night I went as far as Oxford Street. I was walking briskly down Margaret Street when a man who was passing me stopped and exclaimed: "Good God!" My heart gave a violent jump as I looked up. It was Rusbridger. Rusbridger had been one of my pals in the old halcyon days. He was a good chap but a bit reckless, and unfortunately a bit of a drunkard. Many a wild night had we had out together. Almost instinctively he said: "Come and have a drink, old boy." I hesitated. Rusbridger made the situation a little more dangerous. At the same time I was in no position to flout a man who might be friendly towards me at that moment. A few minutes later we were in the corner of a saloon bar. Rusbridger knew that I had escaped from prison and of course he wanted me to tell him everything. I realized that he only meant well, but I also realized that he was a dangerous man to tell things to. He was obviously rather thrilled at the adventure of meeting an escaped convict, but I was certain that in his cups he would go and tell others all about me and they would tell others, and eventually the wrong person would get to know. I showed my delight at his friendly greeting, but was a bit evasive. At last he remembered he had an appointment. We went out and he hailed a hansom cab, and got in. Just as he was saying goodbye, he thrust his hand into my top waistcoat pocket and said: "Well, good luck, old boy!" When he had driven off I found two five-pound notes in my pocket.

'During the next few days I developed a new obsession. I kept on thinking of the man in the hospital whose suit I was wearing and whose twenty-eight shillings I had stolen. I felt an overwhelming desire to pay him back while I had the opportunity. With Rusbridger it was different. I could regard the £10 as a gift (he had meant it as such), or knowing his address, I could pay him back at any time. I decided to devote the weekend to this act of atonement. We did not have to work on Saturday night, but were supposed to begin again on Sunday night. On Saturday morning I took the train down to Brindlehampton. I wanted to be there in good time, for this reason. I should have to restore the stolen property after dark. I did not know the name of the hospital, and was not quite certain of its position. I wanted to take my bearings in daylight. I decided to stay at a cheap little commercial hotel, to buy a ready-made suit in the town, to change, make a parcel of the brown suit, put the money in an envelope inside, and then—if I had any luck—just drop it through the open window.

'There was one thing causing me considerable perturbation. For the last two days I had been feeling far from well, and when I reached Brindlehampton on the Saturday morning I was feeling much worse. This was the eleventh day after my escape from prison. I booked my room at the hotel, and then started out to try and rediscover the hospital. I thought I would leave buying the suit till I got back. I reached the outskirts of the town and then realized that it was not going to be any good. My head and back ached and I could hardly see which way I was going from giddiness. Somehow I managed to get back to the hotel, and when I got there I just had the wit to tell the proprietor that I was unwell and going to bed, and I thought I had better have a doctor. It was as well I did. I don't remember the doctor coming. I knew I had a very high temperature and was delirious. I think they gave me sleeping draughts. I seemed to be in a stage of unconsciousness for an interminable wretched time. At one time I knew they were carrying me in a stretcher. I got it into my head they were going to bury me, thinking I was dead. I cried out and struggled. There was a long interval of blackness after that…Then one night I seemed to emerge, and look around me. And do you know where I found myself?'

John Griggs shook his long index finger, as though lecturing a small boy.

'I found myself in the same room from which I had

stolen the clothes! There was the same man asleep in the corner bed, and I was occupying the bed next to his. Almost instinctively I looked round for some sign of the police. "They've got me all right," I thought. But there was no sign of police. After a time the same nurse entered the room. She came up and smiled. Close to, I could see she had a kind face. She gave me something to drink, and I whispered: "Where am I, nurse?" She wouldn't tell me at first, but after a time, I got it out of her. I was in a *smallpox isolation hospital!* To cut this part of the story short for your benefit, for twelve days I had been wearing the suit just removed from the smallpox patient in the bed next to me! On the night of my burglary when I had looked back through the window and saw the nurse enter she had just come to take all his things to the disinfecting chamber. Of course I did not learn this at the time. I pieced it all together afterwards.

'During my moments of consciousness during the next few days I tried to anticipate the result of my burglary of the smallpox hospital. Would it lead to my apprehension? There was nothing at present to suggest that I was under suspicion. I had given a false name at the hotel, of course, and was supposed to be a commercial traveller. I gathered from the nurse that there had been a mild epidemic of smallpox in the county recently, but it was now well in hand. In this hospital there were only my room companion and myself, but there were seven women cases in the other section. She told me that my case was considered a mild one, but that my companion was very bad. The doctor who visited me twice a day was kindness itself. But what about the suit? I kept on thinking. When I was brought in and undressed, did either the nurse or my fellow-patient recognize it? The latter I could almost dismiss without question. He was in no state to worry about a suit of clothes. As to the nurse, I guessed that she would have been too occupied at the time of the undressing, and if afterwards it struck her that there was something familiar about the suit, she would hardly suspect it could be the same one. This would be stretching the large arm of coincidence too far. Besides, there is not, as a rule, anything peculiarly striking about a man's clothes. She may not even have observed it very closely before. In this surmise I discovered afterwards that I was correct. But who would get the suit of clothes when we got well? It would, I presume, be brought to me. But then, of course, would come the danger. I could assume that by that time he would be much better and alert. He would assuredly recognize the suit. Then how could I explain? It is wonderful how, when one is ill, one's imagination seems to become so active over trifles. I lay there for hours during both the day and the night, tossing about and visualizing all kinds of compromising situations arising out of the brown suit. At the end of another ten days, however, I gave up worrying, and I noticed that my companion was beginning to show signs of some slight improvement. He had nodded and smiled at me on several occasions, and at last we began to have brief whispered conversations. I learnt that his name was Broome. He was only a few years older than I, and had followed several trades. Lately he had been quite successful, I gathered, as a dealer in brass furnishings, had saved a little money, and was talking of going out to Canada as soon as he was well enough.

'As the weeks went by it became more and more obvious that, in spite of the fact that I did not enter the hospital till twelve days after Broome, so far as condition was concerned, I had already overhauled him. His face was still a dreadful sight. I came through it with only these few little scars on my left chin, and many people now do not recognize them for what they are.'

'I certainly had not,' remarked the colonel.

'Broome, nevertheless, was quite hopeful. He had no idea how ill he was. When he found a difficulty in writing he got me to attend to his correspondence. There was always a certain amount of trouble over this. They did not mind us receiving letters, but everything we sent out had to be carefully disinfected and so on, and so they didn't encourage us.

'At the end of two months the doctor said that in ten days' time they would be able to let me go. My mind became active with plans for the future. What on earth was I to do? I realized that I was a fool to have escaped from prison. I had only had about another nine months to serve, and then I could have started out, to work out my own salvation in my own way. But as it was, I had contracted this filthy disease and was liable to arrest at any moment. If caught, all this period of liberty would be set against me, and I should get a further stretch as a punishment. It was, moreover, almost inevitable that I should eventually be caught. In any case, I could make no kind of honourable and successful career. My only hope lay in being able to get out of the country.

'When I told Broome they were going to let me go, he somehow or other got it into his head that he was to be released on the same date, and began to make his plans accordingly. He got me to write to a shipping company for him and book a passage to Quebec. This was for just three weeks hence. I also wrote and got hold of a passport which he already possessed. Broome became tremendously excited. He had, I gathered, saved quite a useful sum of money, and he had apparently no one dependent on him. He was full of the fortune he was going to make as a brass furnisher in Canada. He would talk far into the night, with corresponding rises of temperature. The doctors could not make out what was the matter with him. It went on for a week like this, and then the thing happened which was to affect my whole career. Broome died. A curious chap, and I can't profess to have felt any special interest in him, beyond the fact that he left in my possession a passport and a second-class single ticket from London to Quebec! Three days later I calmly donned the brown suit again and strolled out to the cab that was to take me to Brindlehampton Station. I had a few busy days in London. The first was devoted to getting an interview with Rusbridger. The good chap lent me £50. And so one morning I turned up with a cabin trunk and a valise for the boat train to Southampton. I felt full of confidence. It was three months since I had escaped from prison, and the search for me had probably relaxed, and the attack of smallpox had altered my appearance, to say nothing of the fact that I had grown a beard. In any case, I found myself ten days later a free man walking the streets of Quebec. I cannot describe to you the queer sense of thrill I experienced the first night I strolled about the streets of that quaint old town. I had a kind of inspired feeling. I was bursting with hope: determination, and good resolves. I seemed to detect the hand of Providence in all my later experiences. It was as though I had been duly punished and warned, but was now to be given another chance. The escape, the extraordinary coincidence of my burgling the smallpox hospital, resulting eventually in my free passage to Canada, the lucky meeting with Rusbridger. All these things seemed to stimulate my anxiety to make good. I don't propose, colonel, to bore you with an account of my life until I did make good. In no case was it very interesting, of course I had my ups and downs, but generally speaking I was lucky from the first. I worked hard, and discovered that I was no fool, but the thing I kept foremost in my mind was, even in the smallest dealings to play straight. I think you—you know that in later years I succeeded pretty well. Of course, a fellow doesn't forget, not entirely forget, not even after forty years. Do you think, colonel, do you think a thing like that can be entirely lived down…redeemed, as it were?'

The colonel hesitated. 'Yes, I do. I believe everything is redeemable. Your wife knows?'

Griggs nodded. 'I told her before we became engaged.'

His eyes glowed. 'I believe—I believe she has almost forgotten. It is so very long ago.'

The colonel nodded, and then in a low voice he whispered:

'And so you are Alec Stratford!'

The expression of utter amazement had hardly had time to fill the eyes of 'Straight Griggs' before he felt his forearm gripped in a friendly pressure, and the colonel was saying:

'I'm sorry. Forgive me, John. I did not mean to be so theatrical. The temptation was too great. Understand at once that not a word you have told me will ever pass my lips. Only it is rather strange. Do you know that at the time of your escape, I had just returned from the East and had accepted an appointment as deputy governor of Deadmoor Prison. I had not been there a month when one of the convicts—Alec Stratford—escaped. I got into trouble about it. In fact, they were so rude to me that I resigned. I did not mind much. I did not like the job. I remember the escape quite well. Our cook, an Irish girl, saw you on top of the wall from one of our upper windows. She did not tell us for two days, and when I taxed her with this neglect afterwards, she burst into tears. She said her first instinct was to call out, but when she saw how young and brave and sad you looked, instead of doing this she went down on her knees and prayed to the Holy Mother to spare you. You may care to cherish this vision of Kathleen. She has since died.'

Griggs leant forward, deep in thought. There came the sound of a piano from the drawing room. Barbara was playing a Schubert impromptu. A large white moth fluttered across the table between the two men. From below there arose the heavy perfume of freesia.

The colonel was continuing in his gentle voice:

'There is one point about which I may allay any fears you may have. You mentioned about being "sent back to Deadmoor". This shows that on your ride the other day you did not get very near the prison. If you had you would have observed one striking fact about it. It is dismantled.'

'Dismantled!'

'Yes. Some four or five years ago, owing to the general decrease in crime the Home Office decided to close four prisons. Deadmoor was one of them.'

'But what are they going to do with it?'

The colonel smiled.

'Oh, what does a government do in a case like that? Nothing at all for years and years. And then—oh, I don't know, something happens. The place gets pulled down and disappears. You could probably buy it yourself for an old song!'

Griggs looked up quickly. He waved his long forefinger in front of the colonel's face.

'There's an idea in that, colonel,' he said.

* * *

Should you at some time be motoring through Sussex and you pass through the valley of Tellinghurst, just beyond Glendisham, where the road turns northward, you will come to a plateau. On this plateau is a large stretch of intensively cultivated land, dominated by a low white building of elegant design in the Colonial style. Around the grounds are numerous glasshouses, potting sheds, and so on. At the entrance to the drive a white board with dark green lettering announces the fact that this is: 'The Anne Griggs Agricultural College for Women.'

For a month or so every summer you might observe at odd times a sprightly old couple walking amidst the flowers, talking to the superintendent or the students, helping, planning, scheming. No one seems to remember that in years gone by hardened convicts traipsed the dead monotony of the exercise yard, where now on that same spot fresh-complexioned girls move smilingly amidst the flowers, or stoop in loving solicitude above the soil. Perhaps sometimes the old man remembers it, but he gives no sign. The leaves fall, and the soil takes them to its bosom, against the coming of a new and distant birth. The cycle revolves, and in time everything is forgotten…

But the soil goes on, producing, producing. Indifferent to the frailties of man, reorganizing neither good nor evil, but eternally concentrated on the perpetuation of life. And the new birth comes, and the young buds thrust themselves forward, eager for whatever life may hold, regardless of the tribulations of the past.

—*XXII*—

Dark Red Roses

'TWIXT SLEEPING AND WAKING there came to him a moment of quiet exaltation. His consciousness was revelling in the surf of some far distant and yet familiar sea where the sirens whispered:

'You are well. You are happy. You are virile. You have achieved great things, and you will achieve more. You are enveloped in love and beauty and youth.'

The sun was creeping between the cracks of the dark blind. Spring! In a short while he would be out in it all. He would grasp it in his hand—love, and beauty and youth. He lay there vividly intent upon himself, his environment, his happiness.

Below the window the dew would be sparkling upon daffodils and jonquils, primula and violets. A starling up in the apple tree was chanting a eulogy of spring. In the next room—the white door slightly ajar—his wife was sleeping. He could almost see her, curled up in that way she had, like a little round ball, her glorious fair hair scattered over the pillow, her dark lashes, her beautiful fair skin, her small mouth firmly shut, just the tilt of that little wilful chin—how he loved her!

In two rooms at the end of the corridor, Mervyn, aged nine, and Diana, aged eleven, were sleeping as only youth can sleep...children of this cloudless love match. The fullness and the richness of their day was before them, and he possessed it as much as they.

Half-dozing, half-dreaming, he lay there an infinity of time absorbed in this sense of happiness...he was creating. He saw form, and the beauty of form, and the building of form. He was a sculptor...

And then his mind abruptly registered the probable reason of his exultant mood—the letter which had arrived by the last post the previous night, announcing that his model had been accepted by an important Corporation in the North. He had received this sought-after commission above all his fellows. The work would take him a year to accomplish, but what a year! His consciousness cleared. He began to work on the details of his undertaking. Technical problems were being faced, the frenzy of creation, with its pains, penalties and ecstasies. He would give to the world all that was best in him. Dear life! to be happily married, to have children, to be healthy and virile, and at the age of forty-seven to be recognized as one of the foremost sculptors in the world, was it not enough on this Spring morning to work him into a state of fevered anticipation and delight?

'I mustn't think too much of myself, about myself. I don't want it all for myself, it's for the others—the people I love, even the people I don't love. It's all too big, too overpowering to take to oneself. Oh, the glory and the beauty of the world.'

He restrained the temptation to get up and rush into the garden until he heard the familiar sound of domestic movements. Then he arose and went into the bathroom. The thrill of cold water down his spine urged him to song, deep-chested and passionate, even if a little out of tune. He rubbed himself down, his eyes glimpsing, not without pride, the fine proportions of his legs and torso. He completed his toilet with care and discretion, and then visited his wife. She was already drinking tea and reading an illustrated paper. He kissed her and exclaimed:

'Well, my darling, sleep well?'

'I always do. You've been making an awful noise in the bathroom.'

He laughed tempestuously, teased her a little, discussed the petty arrangements of their daily routine, and then went downstairs to the breakfast-room. He always regretted that Laura insisted on having her breakfast in bed. Breakfast was the most glorious meal in the day. The sun poured into the breakfast-room. The garden was ablaze with green and white and yellow and red. 'Rags', the old sheep dog, bounded to him, buried its nozzle between its master's knees, and peered at him, its sentimental eyes gleaming amidst the profusion of shaggy fur.

'Rags, Rags, dear old Rags, what is the day going to bring forth for us? I'm hungry, Rags, what about you?'

But Rags never seemed to be hungry. He seemed quite content to sit at the feet of his master and to feed on the glorious vision. A maid appeared with glittering silver dishes and a coffee urn. A gong sounded. He moved to the sidetable and picked up his letters and his newspapers. His interest quickened. The letters, mysteriously intriguing in their uncut state, linking him to friends, and the glamour of his career; the newspapers equally so with the whole cosmic creation. What had the world to tell him today? He stood there happily bemused, turning the letters over. And then suddenly what a to-do! The children and their governess. He was enveloped in a swirl of pulsating vital forces. Youth consumed with the prescience of a terrific day's programme. A terrific business having breakfast, making arrangements, anticipating, discussing. He was almost overlooked in the important trifles. Just pleased to have him there, happy at seeing father well and happy, but no time for endearments, no time for questions or solicitude. The rabbits had to be fed. George, the gardener, was reputed to have promised to bring along two guinea pigs. A cousin was coming to tea. Mervyn's cricket bat had got to be sent to the makers to be re-bound. Diana had to be reproved by the governess for calling Mrs Weak, the housekeeper, a 'silly sausage'. There was a picture postcard of Zermatt from Uncle Walter. All terrifically important...breathless. In the midst of it all he laughed loudly in sheer happiness. And the children laughed too, for no reason—just contagion, and Rags joined in the din.

Breakfast over at last, he lighted his pipe and went out into the sun. He sat on the bench below the tennis lawn, and looked at the spring flowers, entranced. At the end of the garden the black wooden studio partly concealed by foliage was calling him. He enjoyed the tumult of restraint. There was no hurry. Was he not fully conscious of his powers? Was he not even now, working, creating? A wood-pigeon was cooing in the coppice beyond the vegetable garden. His senses tingled with the thrill of the sweet, pure air, the perfume of wallflowers, the familiar comfort of good tobacco. His mind was working rapidly. Thus and thus would he do to improve upon that model. A curious sense of detachment crept over him, as though he were looking down on himself. Almost impatiently he arose, and wandered through the grounds, his grounds and—hers. He was consumed with a kind of contemplative lust of possession. He found himself in the white panelled drawing room. There indeed could he give his sense of possession full play. Was there ever such a beautiful room? A genuine Queen Anne room with French windows leading on to the lawn. There was the jolly walnut tallboy which they had bought on their honeymoon, from a dealer in Falmouth. He could almost see Laura now, leaning on his arm. He could hear the tone of her adorable voice:

'Oh, darling, wouldn't it be lovely to have it?'

It meant a lot in those days. They were very poor when they married. But somehow he managed to buy the tallboy because Laura wanted it so much. And there it stood to this day. And it had collected around it a company of worthy fellows, a William and Mary cabinet which he bought at a sale in Seven Oaks, a set of original seventeenth century walnut chairs which he got at Christie's at an appalling price…Things were different now. On the further wall was his choicest possession—an interior by Pieter de

Hoogh in an ebony and tortoiseshell frame. He sank back in an easy chair and regarded it lovingly. Everything in the room was beautiful from the Pieter de Hoogh to the daffodils in a cut glass vase on the bureau. Everything was symbolical of the unity of his married state. His taste and hers—what joy it had been to struggle, to select, to build. He thought of the old days when he had been a poor boy apprenticed to a builder at Nottingham, showing little aptitude or ambition. It was not till he was nearly thirty that he suddenly developed the passion to express in form the strange surgings of his soul. He had saved up money and been to Italy and studied Donatello...Thirty-five he was when he first met Laura. She seemed a slip of a girl, almost boyish. For a long while he had pondered over the problem of their mutual infatuation. He was twelve years older than she. Would it be right? Could he make her happy? 'When I am so-and-so, she will be so-and-so,' he envisaged every phase of the married state.

Well, well, he had nothing to regret. When they marry a man may be a little older than a woman. Especially if he keep himself fit, and sane, and temperate. A man has all the advantages. He was hardly conscious of the passing years, except as they added to his spiritual stature. He had mastered his art. He had wrested from the social conflict honour, and fame, and wealth. His love had developed into a finer, richer passion than it had been when he first met her. She was linked to him indissolubly by the ties of children, and the associations of passion and tenderness. O God! how happy, how happy...And they had built this beautiful nest in the Surrey hills. Step by step, piece by piece, their tastes ever in common, every little thing in the house was a symbol of their mutual understanding. And they were surrounded by friends. There was old Morrison, the painter, who lived at 'The Seven Gables' across the valley, a wealthy and entertaining old man who frequently came to dine. There were the Stapleys, and the Brontings, and Guy Lewisham, and there was that young violinist, Anton Falk, who had come to live with the Brontings, an engaging and romantic figure. Several evenings a week he would come, and play glorious passages from Bach and Paganini in this very room. And Laura would accompany him. He loved to lie back on the window seat and watch her bending over the keys, the pink glow from the lamp suffusing the beautiful room, the tense, pale face of the young fiddler frowning over his instrument. In music one finds the solution of all one's spiritual unrest.

He rose again impatiently, moved by an impulse to touch his possessions. He moved from piece to piece, smoking his pipe, and passing his hand affectionately over glossy surfaces. He buried his nose in flowers. There were flowers everywhere, flowers that *she* had gathered and arranged—spring flowers. Then once more he sat back in an easy chair and sighed contentedly.

The door opened abruptly, and the room appeared to receive the final note of its ultimate expression. Laura glided in, wearing a frock of thick white lace, and in her hand she carried a bunch of dark red roses, wrapped in that thin paper that florists use. She started slightly at sight of him and exclaimed:

'Hullo, dear, you're not working then—'

He laughed gaily at her momentary confusion, and at the exquisite vision of her supple movements.

'How clever of you,' he said, 'to come in at that moment. I was looking at the room. It just wanted that note—the girl in a white frock holding a bunch of dark red roses.'

'Aren't they lovely!' she exclaimed and bent over them. She removed the paper, scrumpled it up into a ball and threw it into the paper basket. Then she produced a glass bowl and a pair of scissors. With loving care she arranged the roses, humming to herself as she cut their stalks, and set them in the bowl on the centre table. His eyes caressed her every movement. When she had completed her task she went across to him and sat on the arm of his chair.

'Don't they look lovely!' she murmured.

'Yes,' he said. 'They are exquisite—almost exotic. It is early in the year for roses.'

She sighed as though a little impatient of his plaint.

'They must come from abroad,' he ruminated. 'Or perhaps bred under glass. We do not get such roses here till June.'

'They come from Stoole's, the florists,' she explained, fluttering towards the window like a little bird restless for flight.

'Davy,' she suddenly added, 'is it quite easy to take a cast of anyone's hands?'

'Yes, quite easy.'

'I thought it would be rather jolly to have a cast of Anton's hands. Have you ever noticed what beautiful hands he has?'

'Yes, they are beautiful hands.'

'There's something romantic about the hands of a musician, something one would like to preserve. He is coming this evening. Do you think you could spare time?'

'Why, of course. It would take less than an hour of my valuable time. You shall have a cast of your fiddler's hands, my dear.'

'Thanks so much, Davy.'

The little bird fluttered through the French window and down into the garden. But the man continued to sit there, intent on his happiness and the serene beauty of the room. The dark red roses produced in the artist in him a queer emotion. They were extraordinarily beautiful, and yet they left upon him a slight impression of disquiet. The room was no longer so serene or tranquil. They were a note of luxury and defiance. In the fullness of their blooming two petals had already dropped, and lay upon the dark table like little pools of blood. It was the season for daffodils and primroses, the virgin flowers which herald in the spring, but these spoke of warm summer nights or southern climes.

'It is early in the year for roses.'

Very slowly he rose, and walked towards them. The richness of their perfume assailed his nostrils. Much as he loved them they jarred his sensibilities, like a perversion or a wanton feast. He turned away, and went as though driven by some subconscious force to the waste-paper basket. With quiet deliberation he unfolded the paper they had been wrapped in. A piece of card had apparently escaped his wife's detection. He picked it up and read it. On it was scribbled in pencil, 'To my darling'. There was no signature. Guiltily he tore it up, and returned it and the paper to the basket.

And that morning he worked with the fury of creation. With long strides he reached his studio. His hands clutched and fashioned great masses of clay. Forms emerged from chaos, forms expressing beauty and humility. So engrossed was he with his new concepts that he did not return to the house for lunch. He sent his assistant over for a tray of food, which he devoured savagely, standing by his model all the while, like a mother fearful of some treacherous attack upon her child.

Sometimes the laughter of the children, playing in the garden, reached him, and once he heard his wife singing...The long day drew on. At six o'clock his assistant left. A little later there was a tap at the door, and it opened before he had time to say, 'Come in.'

Laura came gaily in, followed by the young man.

'Here's Anton, dear. Are you very, very busy?'

Her eyes were sparkling with the love of life. The young man was grave and deferential.

'Very, very busy. How are you, Anton?'

'What about those hands, David?'

'Ah, yes, I had forgotten. Those hands—let me see them, Anton.'

The young man held out his long delicate fingers.

'Yes, they are indeed beautiful hands, beautifully proportioned. The fingers long and tapering, the tips slightly flattened. Beautiful hands. I will take a cast of them. But you must excuse me for the moment. I have something to finish. Anton will stay to dinner. Afterwards we will have a little music perhaps? And then I will take a cast of Anton's hands.'

'You mustn't work too hard, Davy. You haven't left the studio since ten o'clock this morning. You'll be knocking yourself up.'

'Thank you for your solicitude. I'm feeling remarkably robust. Now run away and play, children.'

Any feeling of constraint which might have marred the dinner party that evening was dissipated by the arrival of Laura's mother, a dear old lady who was extremely garrulous and amusing. As a matter of fact the dinner was unusually merry. Laura was in the highest spirits, and David talkative and reminiscent. Only the young man seemed self-conscious and reserved, plainly anxious for the meal to end. But if his tongue was silent, he was sufficiently eloquent with his eyes.

The music that followed was not a success. Anton was obviously not in the mood, and Laura was apt to be frivolous. The old mother acknowledged frankly that classical music bored her.

David was restless and eager to consummate his preconceived purposes.

During a pause he arose abruptly and said:

'Come. I'm afraid we must terminate this concert if I am to take a cast of Anton's hands to-night.'

'Why, yes,' exclaimed Laura. 'I was forgetting all about it. Shall we all go over to the studio?'

'No.' David was emphatic. 'You stay here with your

mother. Anton and I will go over there alone.'

He almost relished the tinge of disappointment which flickered at the back of his wife's eyes. Out in the hall he said:

'Put on your hat and coat, Anton. These April evenings are treacherous.'

They walked the length of the dark garden and entered the studio. David switched on the light.

'I shall not detain you long,' he said. 'The process is quite simple. Here is a bowl of sweet oil. Will you please dip your hands in it, and get them thoroughly saturated.'

Anton did as he was bidden whilst the elder man prepared a mixture of plaster of Paris and water.

'Does it take long to set?' asked the violinist, advancing to the bench where David was at work. He was holding out his oily hands.

'Oh, no, two or three minutes at the outside. But it is very necessary to keep the hands quite still. Now, lay them face downwards on this plaster bed. So.'

He covered up the young man's hands with the cold wet plaster. Then he continued:

'I have been handling plaster all my life. It is treacherous stuff, shifting, unstable, unreliable—not unlike human nature. In a case like this we usually use irons to keep it from shifting. Allow me.'

He passed the iron bands over the pool of plaster and bolted it down into the bench.

'Does it feel cold?'

'It's not too bad, Mr Cardew. Will you explain the process to me?'

'With pleasure. We leave your hands there for a few moments till the plaster sets. Then we remove the irons, and you will be able to withdraw your hands quite easily. There remains then what we call a mould. This I fill with more plaster mixed with soap and oil. I leave this to set. I then chip away the outer mould and we arrive at the completed cast. Quite simple and painless, you see. Laura was most anxious to have a cast of your beautiful hands.'

He laughed a little recklessly as he uttered the last sentence in a cold incisive voice, and then he lighted his pipe. The seconds ticked by, and neither man spoke. At the end of two minutes Anton said:

'I think the plaster has set, Mr Cardew. It feels like it.'

David Cardew was perched on a high stool. He looked thoughtfully into the bowl of his pipe. In passionless accents he suddenly remarked:

'Dark red roses do not grow in April.'

The young man looked up at him quickly.

'Dark red roses?'

'Nature makes laws, and men make codes. It's all very much the same—the struggle for survival. Nature is cruel and relentless, man less so. He does not want to set up these codes. He is forced to do so. It is a blind subconscious force not so much for the protection of the individual as for the preservation of the type. We have our English saying, "It isn't done". It sounds inane and foolish and conventional, but in effect it is quite a sound dogma, founded on experience and tradition. It isn't done, Anton Falk.'

The young man gave him a quick glance and shifted his position.

'Why do you say all this to me, Mr Cardew?'

'Dark red roses in April—an exotic fancy! This is the time of year when the hedgerows are alive with little innocent buds, when the birds are mating, and youth and purity are at the helm. The flowers of darker passions are out of place. As a fellow artist you will appreciate this point of view, I'm sure.'

The young man gave a sudden scared look and made a violent movement with his wrists.

'If you had the strength of ten men you could not draw your hands from that mould, Mr Falk.'

The two men then looked full into each other's eyes, and both understood. Anton's face was the colour of the plaster which encased his hands.

'What are you saying, Mr Cardew?' he said breathlessly. 'What are you implying? It's all false, I swear. My God! what are you going to do?'

This latter query was caused by David Cardew's sudden action. He had reached out and taken down from the wall a Japanese sword in a carved ivory scabbard. Almost languidly he drew the sword and remarked:

'An interesting old sword this. It was given me by an American print collector, who brought it from Japan. It belonged to a famous Samurai. Wonderful people the Samurai, with a code of honour and morality that has never been surpassed. It is said that three people have already died by this sword—the wife, the lover, and then the man himself. Rather drastic you may say. In these days we should think it sufficient to kill the lover.'

The young man who was hanging limply by his hands suddenly uttered a cry of terror.

'My God! you're mad, Mr Cardew. Help! help!'

'They won't hear you in the house. The walls are thick, and the wind is stirring in the trees.'

'Don't talk like this. It's all false I tell you. I know what you think, but it isn't true. I'm not your wife's lover.'

The older man laughed cynically, and muttered:

'Dark red roses in the Spring.'

'I'm fond of your wife, very fond, but there's nothing else, I swear. I've never—Oh, for God's sake release my hands!'

'Very fond, very fond. Yes, yes, yes.'

Suddenly the tones of his voice changed. He went up to his captive and said savagely:

'I'm not going to kill you. It isn't done. Only listen

to me, killing is not the only thing that isn't done. Do you understand me? I told you to bring your hat and coat because the April nights are treacherous. The reason is that when I release you, you will take the path through the vegetable garden and drop down into Hood's Lane. You will go right away and never darken my doors again. Do you understand that? Do you promise that? or would you prefer to die?'

Hanging inert against the bench the young man whispered:

'Yes, I promise. But it's all false—it's all false—'

'I want no lies, no protestations.'

He sheathed the sword, and replaced it on the wall. He was trembling all over when he unbolted the iron bands. Controlling his passion he managed to say in a calm voice:

'Steady now, steady, Mr Falk. Withdraw your hands carefully. I must finish my work. Laura will be distressed if she does not have the cast of the beautiful hands of the young violinist. There! that's it, so. In the corner you will find a sink and some soap. You may wash your hands. I'm afraid they're badly soiled. Then I will see you into the lane.'

The young man was completely unnerved. He withdrew his hands and staggered towards the sink. He washed and wiped them on a towel, but he was careful never to turn his back on his late captor. He watched him furtively, prepared for flight. But David Cardew appeared already pre-occupied. His eyes were solemnly regarding the mould. There was nothing more to say on either side. When he had put on his hat and coat, both men went silently out. David led the way through the vegetable garden. At the end of it, he opened a gate that led into the lane.

'You know your way, I think,' was all he said, and the other replied, 'Yes.' They parted without salutation, and Cardew returned to the studio.

His emotions were in a state of riot. He could neither focus nor decide upon his next actions. Youth, and beauty, and love—shop-worn! Savagely he chipped away at the outer mould. One sardonic desire pressed itself upon him.

'She shall have the beautiful white hands of her lover.'

What was he going to do? How far was she involved? Could she possibly love this man?

'He won't come back anyway. I've frightened the life out of him. Spineless wretch!'

A few hours ago his happiness had been unbelievable. And now—could it all be destroyed so easily? Could all the associations of love, and passion, and tenderness be suddenly uprooted? No, no, no, a thousand times no. She *had* loved him. Of that there was not a shadow of doubt. This must be some mad spring infatuation. It would pass. He would go to her. There would be a little scene, and then she would weep on his breast, and he would forgive her. And oh, he would be so gentle, and forgiving, and loving, and she would fall asleep at last in his arms, like the little child she was. A kind of fierce pride surged through him when he thought how forgiving he would be. He completed the cast of the fiddler's hands. There they were, the beautiful long, tapering fingers with the slightly flat tips. He restrained the desire to hurl them to the ground. He had promised them to Laura. It would be a dramatic and potent way of starting their little scene. He would say:

'Look! Here are the white hands of your lover. Shake them. They have come to say Good-bye.'

And Laura would give a little scream, and throw herself on the bed. He hated the thought of hurting her, but the position had got to be faced. The nettle had got to be gripped before its stalk became too strong.

He wrapped the plaster hands in paper, shut up the studio, and went stealthily towards the house. A light was burning in the library. He hoped the mother had gone to bed. He would feign exhaustion and suggest that they went up at once. The bedroom was essentially the place for their little scene. He entered the hall noiselessly. To his disappointment he heard the voice of his wife's mother in the library. A sudden idea occurred to him. Perhaps Laura had already confessed; perhaps she was confessing even now. He tiptoed towards the door, which was ajar. He pushed it quietly open another two inches, and stood there listening, holding the plaster cast in his hand.

And this is what he heard—his wife's voice speaking cheerily:

'Oh, mother darling, I forgot all about thanking you for those lovely dark red roses you sent me from Stoole's.'

The mother's voice: 'Oh, my dear, my dear, don't be absurd. As though I should forget.'

His wife's voice again: 'Do you know, darling, isn't it a scream! but Davy *did* forget. He was so taken up with his silly old commission that he forgot all about my birthday! Isn't it too funny! Mother darling, don't remind him. He would be so upset, the poor dear!'

David Cardew fumbled his way through the door, but so agitated was he that he dropped the plaster cast on the parquet floor and it smashed to smithereens.

—XXIII—

The Accident of Crime

EVERY SEAMAN who makes the city of Bordeaux a port of call knows the Rue Lucien Faure. It is one of those irregular streets which one finds in the neighbourhood of docks in every city in the world. Cordwainers, ships' stores, cafés and strange foreign eating houses jostle each other indiscriminately. At the further end of the Rue Lucien Faure, and facing Bassin à Flot No. 2, is a little cul de sac known as Place Duquesne, an obscure honeycomb of high dingy houses. It had often been pointed out to the authorities that the Place Duquesne was a scandal to the neighbourhood; not that the houses themselves were either better or worse than those of adjoining streets, but that the inhabitants belonged almost entirely to the criminal classes. A murderer, an apache, a blackmailer, a coiner, hardly ever appeared in the Court of Justice without his habitation being traced to this unsavoury retreat.

And the authorities did nothing. Indeed Chief Inspector Tolozan, who had that neighbourhood under his special supervision, said that he preferred it as it was. He affirmed—not unreasonably—that it was better to have all one's birds in one nest rather than have them scattered all over the wood. Tolozan, although a practical man, was something of a visionary. He was of that speculative turn of mind which revels in theories. The contemplation of crime moved him in somewhat the same way that a sunset will affect a landscape painter. He indulged in broad generalities, and it always gave him a mild thrill of pleasure when the actions or behaviour of his protégés substantiated his theories.

In a detached way, he had quite an affection for his 'birds', as he called them. He knew their record, their characteristics, their tendencies, their present occupation, if any, their place of abode—which was generally the Place Duquesne. If old Carros, the forger, moved from the attic in NO. 17 to the basement in NO. 11, Monsieur Tolozan would sense the reason of this change. And he never interfered until the last minute. He allowed Carros to work three months on that very ingenious plant for counterfeiting one franc notes. He waited till the plates were quite complete before he stepped in with his quiet:

'Now, *mon brave*, it distresses me to interfere...'

He admired the plates enormously, and in the van on the way to the police court he sighed many times, and ruminated upon what he called 'the accident of crime'. One of his pet theories was that no man was entirely criminal. Somewhere at some time it had all been just touch and go. With better fortune the facile Carros might now be the director of an insurance company, or perhaps an eminent pianist. Another saying of his, which he was very fond of repeating, was this:

'The law does not sit in judgment on people. Laws are only made for the protection of the citizen.'

His colleagues were inclined to laugh at 'Papa Tolozan', as they called him, but they were bound to respect his thoroughness and conscientiousness, and they treated his passion for philosophic speculation as merely the harmless eccentricity of an urbane and charming character. Perhaps in this attitude towards crime there have always been two schools of thought, the one which regards it—like Tolozan—as 'the accident', the other, as represented by the forceful Muguet of the Council of Jurisprudence at Bayonne, who insists that crime is an ineradicable trait, an inheritance, a fate. In spite of their divergence of outlook these two were great friends, and many and long were the arguments they enjoyed over a glass of vermouth and seltzer at a quiet café they sometimes favoured in the

Cours du Pavé, when business brought them together. Muguet would invariably clinch the argument with a staccato:

'Well, come now, what about old Laissac?'

Then he would slap his leg and laugh. Here, indeed, was a hard case. Here, indeed, was an irreconcilable, an *intransigeant*, an ingrained criminal, and as this story principally concerns old Laissac it may be as well to describe him a little in detail at once. He was at that time fifty-seven years of age. Twenty-one years and ten months of that period had been passed in penitentiaries, prisons and convict establishments. He was already an old man, but a wiry, energetic old man, with a battered face seamed by years of vicious dissipations and passions.

At the age of seventeen he had killed a Chinaman. The affair was the outcome of a dockside *mêlée*, and many contended that Laissac was not altogether responsible. However, that may be, the examining magistrate at that time was of the opinion that there had been rather too much of that sort of thing of late, and that an example must be made of someone—even the Chink must be allowed some show of protection. Laissac was sent to a penitentiary for two years. He returned an avowed enemy of society. Since that day, he had been convicted of burglary, larceny, passing of counterfeit coins, assault and drunkenness. These were only the crimes of which he had actually been convicted, but everyone knew that they were only an infinitesimal fraction of the crimes of which he was guilty.

He was a cunning old man. He had bashed one of his pals and maimed him for life, and the man was afraid to give evidence against him. He had treated two women at least with almost unspeakable cruelty. There was no record of his ever having done a single action of kindliness or unselfishness. He had, moreover, been a perverter and betrayer of others. He bred crime with malicious enjoyment. He trained young men in the tricks of the trade. He dealt in stolen property. He was a centre, a focus, of criminal activity. One evening, Muguet remarked to Tolozan, as they sipped their coffee:

'The law is too childish. That man has been working steadily all his life to destroy and pervert society. He has a diseased mind. Why aren't we allowed to do away with him? If, as you say, the laws were made to protect citizens, there's only one way to protect ourselves against a villain like Laissac—the guillotine.'

Tolozan shook his head slowly. 'No, the law only allows capital punishment in the case of murder.'

'I know that, my old cabbage. What I say is—why should society bother to keep an old ruffian like that?'

Tolozan did not answer, and Muguet continued:

'Where is he now?'

'He lives in an attic in the Place Duquesne, NO. 33.'

'Are you watching him?'

'Oh, yes.'

'Been to call on him?'

'I was there yesterday.'

'What was he doing?'

'Playing with a dog.'

Muguet slapped his leg, and threw back his head. Playing with a dog! That was excellent! The greatest criminal in Bordeaux—playing with a dog! Muguet didn't know why it was so funny. Perhaps it was just the vision of his old friend, Tolozan, solemnly sitting there and announcing the fact that Laissac was playing with a dog, as though it were a matter of profound significance. Tolozan looked slightly annoyed and added:

'He's very fond of dogs.'

This seemed to Muguet funnier still, and it was some moments before he could steady his voice to say:

'Well, I'm glad he's fond of something. Was there nothing you could lay your hands on?'

'Nothing.'

It is certainly true that Muguet had a strong case in

old Laissac to confute his friend's theories. Where was 'the accident of crime' in such a confirmed criminal?

It is also true old Laissac was playing with a dog, and at that very moment. Whilst the representatives of law and order were discussing him in the Café Basque he was tickling the ribs of his beloved Sancho, and saying:

'Up, soldier. Courage, my old warrior.'

Sancho was a strange forlorn-looking beast, not entirely retriever, not wholly poodle, indeed not necessarily dog at all. He had large sentimental eyes, and he worshipped his master with unquestioning adoration. When his master was out, as he frequently was on strange nocturnal adventures, he would lie on the mat by the door, his nostrils snuggled between his paws, and watch the door. Directly his master entered the house, Sancho would be aware of it. He would utter one long whine of pleasure, and his skin would shake and tremble with excitement. The reason of his perturbations this morning was that part of the chimney had fallen down with a crash. The brickwork had given way, and a little way up old Laissac could see a narrow opening, revealing the leads on the adjoining roof. It was summer time and such a disaster did not appal him unduly.

'Courage,' he said, 'tomorrow that shall be set right. Today and tonight we have another omelette in the pan, old comrade. Tomorrow there will be ham bones for Sancho, and a nice bottle of fine champagne for the breadwinner, eh? Lie down, boy, that's only old Grognard!'

The dog went into his corner, and a most strange-looking old man entered the room. He had thin white hair, a narrow horse-like face with prominent eyes. His face appeared much too thin and small for the rest of his body, which had unexpected projections and convolutions. From his movements it was immediately apparent that his left side was paralyzed. On the left breast of his shabby green coat was a medal for saving lives. The medal recorded that, at the age of twenty-six, he had plunged into the Garonne, and saved the lives of two boys. He sat down and produced a sheet of dirty paper.

'Everything is in order,' he said dolefully.

'Good,' said Laissac. 'Show us the plan.'

'This is the garage and the room above where you enter. The chauffeur left with Madame Delannelle and her maid for Pau this morning. They will be away three weeks or more. Monsieur Delannelle sleeps in this room on the first floor; but, as you know, he is a drug fiend. From eleven o'clock till four in the morning he is in a coma. Lisette and the other maid sleep on the top floor. Lisette will see that this other woman gets a little of the white powder in her cider before she retires. There is no one else in the house. There is no dog.'

'It appears a modest enterprise.'

'It is as easy as opening a bottle of white oil. The door of the room above the garage, connecting with the first landing in the house, is locked and the key taken away, but it is a very old-fashioned lock. You could open it with a bone toothpick, master.'

'H'm. I suppose Lisette expects something out of this?'

The old man sniggered, and blew his nose on a red handkerchief.

'She's doing it for love.'

'You mean—young Léon Briteuil?'

'Yes, now this is the point, master. Are you going to crack this crib yourself, or would you like young Briteuil to go along? He's a promising lad, and he would be proud to be in a job with you.'

'What stuff is there, there?'

'In the second drawer on the left-hand side in a bureau in the salon is a cash box, where Monsieur keeps the money from his rents. He owns a lot of small property. There ought to be about ten thousand francs. Madame has taken most of her jewels, but there are a few trinkets in a jewel case in the bedroom. For the rest, there is a collection of old coins in a cabinet, some of them gold. That is in the library here see? And the usual silver plate and trinkets scattered about the house. Altogether a useful haul, too much for one man to carry.'

'Very well, I'll take the young —, tell him to be at the Place du Pont, the other side of the river, at twelve-thirty. If he fails or makes the slightest slip, I'll break his face. Tell him that. That's all.'

'Right you are, master.'

Young Briteuil was not quite the lion-hearted person he liked to pose as, and this message frightened him. Long before the fateful hour of the appointment, he was dreading the association of the infamous Laissac more than the hazardous adventure upon which he was committed. He would have rather made the attempt by himself. He was neat with his fingers and had been quite successful pilfering little articles from the big stores, but he had never yet experienced the thrill of housebreaking.

Moreover, he felt bitterly that the arrangement was unjust. It was he who had manœuvred the whole field of operations, he with his spurious lovemaking to the middle-aged coquettish Lisette. There was a small fortune to be picked up, but because he was pledged to the gang of which Laissac was the chief, his award would probably amount to a capful of sous. Laissac had the handling of the loot, and he would say that it realized anything he fancied. Grognard had to have his commission also. The whole thing was grossly unfair. He deeply regretted that he had not kept the courting of Lisette a secret. Visions of unholy orgies danced before his eyes. However, there it was and he had to make the best of it. He was politeness and humility itself when he met old Laissac at the corner of the Place du Pont punctually at the hour appointed. Laissac was in one of his sullen moods and they trudged in silence out to the northern suburb where the villa of Monsieur Delannelle was situated.

The night was reasonably dark and fine. As they got

nearer and nearer to their destination, and Laissac became more and more unresponsive, the younger man's nerves began to get on edge. He was becoming distinctly jumpy, and, as people will in such a condition, he carried things to the opposite extreme. He pretended to be extremely light-hearted, and to treat the affair as a most trivial exploit. He even assumed an air of flippancy, but in this attitude he was not encouraged by his companion, who on more than one occasion told him to keep his ugly mouth shut.

'You won't be so merry when you get inside,' he said.

'But there is no danger, no danger at all,' laughed the young man unconvincingly.

'There's always danger in our job,' growled Laissac. 'It's the things you don't expect that you've got to look out for. You can make every preparation, think of every eventuality, and then suddenly, presto! a bullet from some unknown quarter. The gendarmes may have had wind of it all the time. Monsieur Delannelle may not have indulged in his dope for once. He may be sitting up with a loaded gun. The girl Lisette may be an informer. The other girl may have heard and given the game away. Madame and the chauffeur may return at any moment. People have punctures sometimes. You can even get through the job and then be nabbed at the corner of the street, or the next morning, or the following week. There's a hundred things likely to give you away. Inspector Tolozan himself may be hiding in the garden with a half-dozen of his thick-necks. Don't you persuade yourself it's a soft thing, my white-livered cockerel.'

This speech did not raise Léon's spirits. When they reached the wall adjoining the garage, he was trembling like a leaf, and his teeth began to chatter.

'I could do with a nip of brandy,' he said sullenly in a changed voice.

The old criminal looked at him contemptuously, and produced a flask from some mysterious pocket. He took a swig, and then handed it to his companion. He allowed him a little gulp, and then snatched the flask away.

'Now, up you go,' he said. Léon knew then that escape was impossible. Old Laissac held out his hands for him to rest his heel upon. He did so, and found himself jerked to the top of the wall. The old man scrambled up after him somehow. They then dropped down quietly on to some sacking in the corner of the yard. The garage and the house were in complete darkness. The night was unnaturally still, the kind of night when every little sound becomes unduly magnified. Laissac regarded the dim structure of the garage with a professional eye. Léon was listening for sounds, and imagining eyes peering at them through the shutters...perhaps a pistol or two already covering them. His heart was beating rapidly. He had never imagined it was going to be such a nerve-racking business. Curse the old man! Why didn't he let him have his full whack at the brandy?

A sudden temptation crept over him. The old man was peering forward. He would hit him suddenly on the back of the head and then bolt. Yes, he would. He knew he would never have the courage to force his way into that sinister place of unknown terrors. He would rather die out here in the yard.

'Come on,' said Laissac, advancing cautiously towards the door of the garage.

Léon slunk behind him, watching for his opportunity. He had no weapon, nothing but his hands, and he knew that in a struggle with Laissac he would probably be worsted. The tidy concrete floor of the yard held out no hope of promiscuous weapons. Once he thought: 'I will strike him suddenly on the back of the head with all my might. As he falls I'll strike him again. When he's on the ground I'll kick his brains out...'

To such a desperate pass can fear drive a man! Laissac stood by the wood frame of the garage door looking up and judging the best way to make an entrance of the window above. While he was doing so Léon stared round, and his eye alighted on a short dark object near the wall. It was a piece of iron piping. He sidled towards it, and surreptitiously picked it up. At that exact instant Laissac glanced round at him abruptly and whispered:

'What are you doing?'

Now must this desperate venture be brought to a head. He stumbled towards Laissac, mumbling vaguely:

'I thought this might be useful.'

Léon was left-handed and he gripped the iron piping in that hand. Laissac was facing him, and he must be put off his guard. He mumbled:

'What's the orders, master?'

He doubtless hoped from this that Laissac would turn round and look up again. He made no allowance for that animal instinct of self-preservation which is most strongly marked in men of low mentality. Without a word old Laissac sprang at him. He wanted to scream with fear, but instead he struck wildly with the iron. He felt it hit something ineffectually. A blow on the face staggered him. In the agony of recovery he realized that his weapon had been wrenched from his hands! Now, indeed, he would scream, and rouse the neighbourhood to save him from this monster. If he could only get his voice! If he could only get his voice! Curse this old devil! Where is he? Spare me! Spare me! Oh, no, no...oh, God!

Old Laissac stuffed the body behind a bin where rubbish was put, in the corner of the yard. The struggle had been curiously silent and quick. The only sound had been the thud of the iron on his treacherous assistant's skull, a few low growls and blows. Fortunately, the young man had been too paralyzed with fear to call out. Laissac stood in the shadow of the wall and waited. Had the struggle attracted any attention? Would it be as well to abandon the enterprise? He thought it all out dispassionately. An owl, with a deep mellow note, sailed majestically away towards a neighbouring church. Perhaps it was rather foolish. If he were caught, and the body discovered—that would be the end of Papa Laissac! That would be a great misfortune. Everyone would miss him so, and he still had life and fun in him. He laughed bitterly. Yes, perhaps he had better steal quietly away. He moved over to the outer wall.

Then a strange revulsion came over him, perhaps a deep bitterness with life, or a gambler's lure. Perhaps it was only professional vanity. He had come here to burgle this villa, and he disliked being thwarted. Besides it was such a soft thing, all the dispositions so carefully laid. He had already thought out the way to mount to the bedroom above the door. In half an hour he might be richer by many thousand francs, and he had been getting rather hard up of late. That young fool would be one less to pay. He shrugged his broad shoulders, and crept back to the garage door.

In ten minutes' time he had not only entered the room above the garage but had forced the old-fashioned lock, and entered the passage connecting with the house. He was perfectly cool now, his senses keenly alert. He went down on his hands and knees and listened. He waited some time, focussing in his mind the exact disposition of the rooms as shown in the plan old Grognard had shown him. He crawled along the corridor like a large gorilla. At the second door on the left he heard the heavy, stentorian breathing of a man inside the room. Monsieur Delannelle, good! It sounded like the breathing of a man under the influence of drugs or drink.

After that, with greater confidence, he made his way downstairs to the salon. With unerring precision he located the drawer in the bureau where the cash box was kept. The box was smaller than he expected and he decided to take it away rather than to indulge in the rather noisy business of forcing the lock. He slipped it into a sack. Guided by his electric torch, he made a rapid round of the reception rooms. He took most of the collection of old coins from the cabinet in the library and a few more silver trinkets. Young Briteuil would certainly have been useful carrying all this bulkier stuff. Rather unfortunate, but still it served the young fool right. He, Laissac, was not going to encumber himself with plate...a few small and easily negotiable pieces were all he desired, sufficient to keep him in old brandy, and Sancho in succulent ham bones, for a few months to come. A modest and simple fellow, old Laissac.

The sack was soon sufficiently full. He paused by the table in the dining room and helped himself to another swig of brandy, then he blinked his eyes. What else was there? Oh, yes, Grognard had said that there were a few of Madame's jewels in the jewel case. But that was in the bedroom where Monsieur Delannelle was sleeping, that was a different matter, and yet after all, perhaps, a pity not to have the jewels!

H'm, Monsieur Delannelle was in one of his drug stupors. It must be about two o'clock. They said he never woke till five or six. Why not? Besides what was a drugged man? He couldn't give any trouble. If he tried to, Laissac could easily knock him over the head like he had young Briteuil—might just as well have those few extra jewels. His senses tingled rather more acutely as he once more crept upstairs. He pressed his ear to the keyhole of Monsieur Delannelle's bedroom. The master of the house was still sleeping.

He turned the handle quietly, listened, then stole into the room, closing the door after him. Now for it. He kept the play of his electric torch turned from the bed. The sleeper was breathing in an ugly irregular way. He swept the light along the wall, and located the dressing-table—satinwood and silver fittings. A new piece of furniture—curse it! The top right-hand drawer was locked. And that was the drawer which the woman said contained the jewel case. Dare he force the lock? Was it worth it?

He had done very well. Why not clear off now? Madame had probably taken everything of worth. He hesitated and looked in the direction of the sleeper. Rich guzzling old pig! Why should he have all these comforts and luxuries whilst Laissac had to work hard and at such risk for his living? Be damned to him. He put down his sack and took a small steel tool out of his breast pocket. It was necessary to make a certain amount of noise, but after all the man in the bed wasn't much better than a corpse. Laissac went down on his knees and applied himself to his task.

The minutes passed. Confound it! It was a very obstinate lock. He was becoming quite immersed in its intricacy when something abruptly jarred his sensibilities. It was a question of silence. The sleeper was no longer snoring or breathing violently. In fact he was making no noise at all. Laissac was aware of a queer tremor creeping down his spine for the first time that evening. He was a fool not to have cleared out after taking the cash box. He had overdone it. The man in bed was awake and watching him! What was the best thing to do? Perhaps the fool had a revolver! If there was any trouble he must fight. He couldn't allow himself to be taken, with that body down below stuffed behind the dust-bin. Why didn't the tormentor call out or challenge him? Laissac crept lower and twisted his body into a crouching position.

By this action he saved his life, for there was a sudden blinding flash, and a bullet struck the dressing-table just at the place where his head had been. This snapping of the tension was almost a relief. It was a joy to revert to the primitive instincts of self-preservation. At the foot of the bed an eiderdown had fallen. Instinct drove him to snatch this up. He scrumpled it up into the rough form of a body and thrust it with his right hand over the end of the bed. Another bullet went through it and struck the dressing-table again. But as this happened, Laissac, who had crept to the left side of the bed sprang across it and gripped the sleeper's throat. The struggle was of momentary duration. The revolver dropped to the floor. The man addicted to drugs gasped, spluttered, then his frame shook violently and he crumpled into an inert mass upon the bed. A blind fury was upon Laissac. He struck the still cold thing again and again, then a revulsion of terror came over him. He crouched in the darkness, sweating with fear.

'They'll get me this time,' he thought. 'Those shots must have been heard. Lisette, the other maid, the neighbours, the gendarmes...two of these disgusting bodies to account for. I'd better leave the swag and clear.' He drained the rest of the brandy and staggered uncertainly towards the door. The house was very still. He turned the handle and went into the passage. Then one of those voices which were always directing his life said:

'Courage, old man, why leave the sack behind? You've worked for it. Besides, one might as well be hanged for a sheep as a lamb!'

He went quietly back and picked up the sack. But his hands were shaking violently. As he was returning, the sack with its metallic contents struck the end of the brass bed. This little accident affected him fantastically. He was all fingers and thumbs tonight. What was the matter? Was he losing his nerve? Getting old? Of course, the time must come when—God! What was that? He stood dead still by the jamb of the door. There was the sound of the stealthy tread on the stairs, the distinct creak of a board. How often in his life had he not imagined that! But there was no question about it tonight. He was completely unstrung.

'If there's another fight I won't be able to face it. I'm done.'

An interminable interval of time passed, and then—that quiet creaking of another board, the person whoever it was, was getting nearer. He struggled desperately to hold himself together, to be prepared for one more struggle, even if it should be his last. Suddenly a whisper came down the stairs:

'Léon!'

Léon! What did they mean? Eh? Oh, yes—Léon Briteuil! Of course that fool of a woman, the informer Lisette. She thought it was Léon. Léon, her lover. He breathed more easily. Women have their uses and purposes after all. But he must be very circumspect. There must be no screaming. She repeated:

'Léon, is that you?'

With a great effort he controlled his voice.

'It's all right. I'm Léon's friend. He's outside.'

The woman gave a little gasp of astonishment.

'Oh! I did not know—'

'Very quietly, mademoiselle. Compose yourself. I must now rejoin him. Everything is going well.'

'But I would see him. I wish to see him to-night. He promised—'

Laissac hurried noiselessly down the stairs, thankful for the darkness. He waited till he had reached the landing below. Then he called up in a husky voice:

'Wait till ten minutes after I have left the house, mademoiselle, then come down. You will find your Léon waiting for you behind the dust-bin in the yard.'

And fortunately for Lisette's momentary peace of mind, she could not see the inhuman grin which accompanied this remark.

From the moment of his uttering it till four hours later, when his mangled body was discovered by a gendarme on the pavement just below the window of the house in which he lived in the Place Duquesne, there is no definite record of old Laissac's movements or whereabouts.

It exists only in those realms of conjecture in which Monsieur Tolozan is so noted an explorer.

Old Laissac had a genius for passing unnoticed. He could walk through the streets of Bordeaux in broad daylight with stolen clocks under each arm and it never occurred to anyone to suspect him, but when it came to travelling in the dark he was unique. At the inquest, which was held five days later, not a single witness could come forward and say that they had seen anything of him either that evening or night.

That highly eminent advocate, Maxim Colbert, president of the court, passed from the cool mortuary into the stuffy courthouse with a bored, preoccupied air. Dead bodies did not greatly interest him, and he had had too much experience of them to be nauseated by them—besides, an old criminal! It appeared to him a tedious and unnecessary waste of time. The old gentleman had something much more interesting occupying his mind. He was expecting his daughter-in-law to present his son with a child. The affair might happen now, any moment, indeed, it might already have happened. Any moment a message might come with the good tidings. A son! Of course it must be a son! The line of Colbert tracing their genealogy back to the reign of Louis XIV—must be perpetuated. A distinguished family of advocates, generals, rulers of men. A son! It annoyed him a little in that he suspected that his own son was anxious to have a daughter. Bah! Selfishness.

Let us see what is this case all about? Oh, yes, an old criminal named Théodore Laissac, aged fifty-seven, wanted by the police in connection with a mysterious crime at the villa of Monsieur and Madame Delannelle. The body found by a printer's devil, named Adolp Roger, at 4.15 o'clock on the morning of the ninth, on the pavement of the Place Duquesne. Witness informed police. Sub-inspector Floquette attested to the finding of body as indicated by witness. The position of body directly under attic window, five stories high, occupied by deceased, suggesting that he had fallen or thrown himself therefrom. Good! Quite clear. A life of crime, result—suicide. Will it be a boy or a girl? Let us have the deceased's record…

A tall square-bearded inspector stood up in the body

of the court, and in a sepulchral voice read out the criminal life record of Théodore Laissac. It was not pretty reading. It began at the age of seventeen with the murder of the Chinaman, Cheng Loo, and from thence onward it revealed a deplorable story of villainy and depravity. The record of evildoings and the award of penalties became monotonous. The mind of Maxim Colbert wandered back to his son, and to his son's son. He had already seen the case in a nutshell and dismissed it. It would give him a pleasant opportunity a little later on. A homily on the wages of sin...a man whose life was devoted to evildoing, in the end driven into a corner by the forces of justice, smitten by the demons of conscience, dies the coward's death. A homily on cowardice, quoting a passage from Thomas à Kempis, excellent!...Would they send him a telegram? Or would the news come by hand? What was that the Counsel for the Right of the Poor was saying? Chief Inspector Tolozan wished to give evidence. Ah, yes, why not? A worthy fellow, Inspector Tolozan. He had known him for many years, worked with him on many cases, an admirable, energetic officer, a little given to theorizing—an interesting fellow, though. He would cross-examine him himself.

Inspector Tolozan took his place in the witness box, and bowed to the president. His steady grey eyes regarded the court thoughtfully as he tugged at his thin grey imperial.

'Now, Inspector Tolozan, I understand that you have this district, in which this—unfortunate affair took place, under your own special supervision?'

'Yes, *monsieur le président*.'

'You have heard the evidence of the witnesses Roger and Floquette with regard to the finding of the body?'

'Yes, monsieur.'

'Afterwards, I understand, you made an inspection of the premises occupied by the deceased?'

'Yes, monsieur.'

'At what time was that?'

'At six-fifteen, monsieur.'

'Did you arrive at any conclusions with regard to the cause or motive of the—er accident?'

'Yes, *monsieur le président.*'

'What conclusions did you come to?'

'I came to the conclusion that the deceased, Théodore Laissac, met his death trying to save the life of a dog.'

'A dog! Trying to save the life of a dog!'

'Yes, monsieur.'

The president looked at the court, the court looked at the president and shuffled with papers, glancing apprehensively at the witness between times. There was no doubt that old Tolozan was becoming cranky, very cranky indeed. The president cleared his throat—was he to be robbed of his homily on the wages of sin?

'Indeed, Monsieur Tolozan, you came to the conclusion that the deceased met his death trying to save the life of a dog! Will you please explain to the court how you came to these conclusions?'

'Yes, *monsieur le président;* the deceased had a dog to which he was very devoted.'

'Wait one moment, Inspector Tolozan, how do you know that he was devoted to this dog?'

'I have seen him with it. Moreover, during the years he has been under my supervision he has always had a dog to which he was devoted. I could call some of his criminal associates to prove that although he was frequently cruel to men, women and even children, he would never strike or be unkind to a dog. He would never burgle a house guarded by a dog in case he had to use violence.'

'Proceed.'

'During that day or evening there had apparently been a slight subsidence in the chimney of the attic occupied by Laissac. Some brickwork had collapsed, leaving a narrow aperture, just room enough for a dog to squeeze its body through and get out on the sloping leads of the house next door. The widow, Forbin, who occupies the adjoining attic, complains that she was kept awake for three hours that night by the whining of a dog on the leads above. This whining ceased about three-thirty, which must have been the time that the deceased met his death. There was only one way for a man to get from his attic to these leads and that was a rain-water pipe, sloping from below the window at an angle of forty-five degrees to the roof next door. He could stand on this water pipe, but there was nothing to cling to except small projections of brick till he could scramble hold of the gutter above. He never reached the gutter.'

'All of this is pure conjecture, of course, Inspector Tolozan.'

'Not entirely, *monsieur le président*. My theory is that after Laissac's departure, the dog became disconsolate and restless, as they often will, knowing by some mysterious instinct that its master was in danger. He tried to get out of the room and eventually succeeded in forcing his way through the narrow aperture in the fireplace. His struggle getting through brought down some more brickwork and closed up the opening. This fact I have verified. Out on the sloping roof the dog naturally became terrified. There was no visible means of escape; the roof was sloping, and the night cold. Moreover, he seemed more cut off from his master than ever. As the widow, Forbin, asserts, he whined pitiably. Laissac returned some time after three o'clock. He reached the attic. The first thing he missed was the dog. He ran to the window and heard it whining on the roof above. Probably he hesitated for some time as the best thing to do. The dog leaned over and saw him. He called to it to be quiet, but so agitated did it appear, hanging over the edge of that perilous slope, that Laissac thought every moment that it would jump. *Monsieur le président*, nearly every crime has been lain at the door of the deceased, but he has never been accused of lack of physical courage. Moreover, he was accustomed to climbing about buildings. He dropped through that window and started to climb up.'

'How do you know this?'

'I examined the water pipe carefully. The night was dry and there had not been rain for three days. Laissac had removed his boots. He knew that it would naturally be easier to walk along a pipe in his socks. There are the distinct marks of stockinged feet on the dusty pipes for nearly two metres of the journey. The body was bootless and the boots were found in the attic. But he was an old man for his age, and probably he had had an exhausting evening. He never quite reached the gutter.'

'Are the marks on the pipes still there?'

'No, but I drew the attention of three of my subordinates to the fact, and they are prepared to support my view. It rained the next day. The body of the dog was found by the side of its master.'

'Indeed! Do you suggest that the dog—committed suicide as it were?'

Tolozan shrugged his shoulders and bowed. It was not his business to understand the psychology of dogs. He was merely giving evidence in support of his theories concerning the character of criminals—'birds'—and the accident of crime.

Maxim Colbert was delighted. The whole case had been salvaged from the limbo of dull routine. He even forgave Tolozan for causing him to jettison those platitudes upon the wages of sin. He had made it interesting. Besides, he felt in a good humour—it would surely be a boy! The procedure of the court bored him, but he was noticeably cheerful, almost gay. He thanked the inspector profusely for his evidence. Once he glanced at the clock casually, and said in an impressive voice:

'Perhaps we may say of the deceased—he lived a vicious life, but he died not ingloriously.'

The court broke up and he passed down into a

quadrangle at the back where a pale sun filtered. Lawyers, ushers, court functionaries and police officials were scattering or talking in little groups. Standing outside a group he saw the spare figure of Inspector Tolozan. He touched his arm and smiled.

'Well, my friend, you established an interesting case. I feel that the verdict was just, and yet I cannot see that it in any way corroborates your theory of the accident of crime.'

Tolozan paused and blinked up at the sun.

'It did not corroborate, perhaps, but it did nothing to—'

'Well? This old man was an inveterate criminal. The fact that he loved a dog—it's not a very great commendation. Many criminals do.'

'But they would not give their lives, monsieur. A man who would do that is capable of—I mean to say it was probably an accident that he was not a better man.'

'Possibly, possibly! But the record, my dear Tolozan!'

'One may only conjecture.'

'What is your conjecture?'

Tolozan gazed dreamily up at the Gothic tracery of the adjoining chapel. Then he turned to Monsieur Colbert and said very earnestly:

'You must remember that there was nothing against Laissac until the age of seventeen. He had been a boy of good character. His father was an honest wheelwright. At the age of seventeen the boy was to go to sea on the sailing ship *La Turenne*. Owing to some trouble with the customs authorities the sailing of the ship was delayed twenty-four hours. The boy was given shore leave. He hung about the docks. There was nothing to do. He had no money to spend on entertainment. My conjecture is this. Let us suppose it was a day like this, calm and sunny with a certain quiet exhilaration in the air. Eh? The boy wanders around the quays and stares in the shops.

Suddenly at the corner of the Rue Bayard he peeps down into a narrow alley and beholds a sight which drives the blood wildly through his veins.'

'What sight, Monsieur Tolozan?'

'The chinaman, Cheng Loo, being cruel to a dog.'

'Ah! I see your implication.'

'The boy sees red. There is the usual brawl and scuffle. He possibly does not realize his own strength. Follow the lawcourt and the penitentiary. Can you not understand how such an eventuality would embitter him against society? To him in the hereafter the dog would stand as the symbol of patient suffering, humanity as the tyrant. He would be at war for ever, an outcast, a derelict. He was raw, immature, uneducated. He was at the most receptive stage. His sense of justice was outraged. The penitentiary made him a criminal.'

'Then from this you mean—'

'I mean that if the good ship *La Turenne* had sailed to time, or if he had not been given those few hours' leave, he might by this time have been a master mariner, or in any case a man who could look the world in the face. That is what I mean by the accident—'

'Excuse me.'

A messenger had handed Monsieur Colbert a telegram. He tore it open feverishly and glanced at the contents. An expression of annoyance crept over his features. He tore the form up in little pieces and threw it petulantly upon the ground. He glanced up at Tolozan absently as though he had seen him for the first time. Then he muttered vaguely:

'The accident, eh? Oh, yes, yes. Quite so, quite so.'

But he did not tell Inspector Tolozan what the telegram contained.

—*XXIV*—

One Thing Leads to Another

I

'THAT'S ALL VERY WELL,' said Mr William Egger. And after a pause he repeated: 'That's all very well.'

In his shirt sleeves, carpet slippers, and embroidered skullcap, he shuffled restlessly from the breakfast-table to the window in the sitting room above his general shop. His wife began to clear away, with the obvious suggestion that it was her place to make herself scarce. This was a father's duty. The boy stood sheepishly staring out of the window. The day was going to be scorching.

Of course it was his duty. It was always a father's duty. He must be firm, admonishing, a little forensic. And all these things came a little difficult to William. He was no orator. It was too early in the morning. He had breakfasted well, and at the back of his mind lurked the old hint of palliation: 'Boys will be boys.' He cleared his throat and rumbled:

'You say pinching apples isn't stealing. You're wrong. Anything you do becomes a habit. This is the second time Farmer James has written to complain. That doesn't mean that it's only twice you've stolen his apples. It means it's only twice you've been found out.'

'I swear it's only twice,' said Tom, sulkily.

'That'll do. Don't answer me back. You acknowledge you stole them. Well, what does it mean? You took what didn't belong to yer. It's sinful. You steal apples, and it becomes a habit. Perhaps tomorrow you steal pears, then peaches, then grapes—'

'I've never stolen no grapes!'

'Be quiet, will yer! It's just a question of—one thing leading to another. The downward path, the slippery slope, the—er—Gadarene swine, and so on. If you take these things p'r'aps one day you'll pinch a little money out of the till—my till!—p'r'aps someone else's penknife, umbreller, or whatnot. That's not the end. You're slipping down. Stealing leads to other things—weakness, giving way all the time. In the end, drinking, forgery, goin' to the pictures, all the deadly sins—'

Mrs Egger had re-entered the room with a brush and crumb-tray and she exclaimed:

'Tom's a very bad boy, William. But you needn't drag in all the deadly sins. One doesn't need to go to hell for pinchin' a few apples.'

William showed annoyance. Just like Agnes—to put him on to the job and then interfere.

'I tell yer—one thing leads to another,' he barked.

'Yes, but—'

'There's no "but" about it. Sin is sin, and once on the slippery path, down yer go.'

'It's not so bad as all that,' replied Mrs Egger, quickly. 'What I ses is—it's not nice it getting about, us with the shop and that—'

'Oh! ... agh!'

The whole matter might have petered out at that point, but for the fact that, in the disturbance caused by Farmer James's letter, Mrs Egger had left the bacon-dish on the sideboard. On the bacon-dish were several rinds from their breakfast. Ambling between the window and the sideboard, Mr Egger's attention had been divided between this dish and a company of fowls in the yard below. The situation was a little too embarrassing to glance at his son. When his wife stood up in defence of the young man he pretended to be annoyed, but he was really relieved. He had landed into this tirade of abuse and admonition, and didn't see quite how to end gracefully. In a moment of distraction he picked up one of the bacon-rinds and flung it out to the fowls.

For the purposes of this story it is necessary to drop the curtain on this domestic scene for the moment and follow the adventures of the bacon-rind.

The fowls were white leghorns, and from their appearance they fared sumptuously. Doubtless a small general shop is a liberal ground for scraps, apart from the supply of grain which their kind demands. But there is something about a bacon-rind that is irresistible to nearly all living creatures. Dogs will fight to the death for it, cats desert their kittens, birds and poultry perform prodigious acts in the way of running, doubling, and ducking. The bacon-rind is never safe until safely ensconced in the maw of some hungry champion.

On this occasion three hens rushed at the bacon-rind, and one, a little longer in the legs than the others, got possession. She scampered towards the hedge, followed by seven others, clucking and screaming. Before the hedge was reached the rind had changed hands—beaks, rather—three times. The original bird had regained possession and was about to force her way through a gap when the cock flew from a savoury refuse heap and savagely pecked her neck. Scandalous that a female should be allowed to enjoy this essentially masculine luxury! There was a rough-and-tumble in the hedge, and the cock got possession. But do not think that he was allowed to enjoy his triumph in peace. The fight was by no means over. So great is the appeal of bacon-rind that the weak will attack the strong, wives will turn on their husbands, the desperate will perform feats of valour which no other incentive could stir them to.

The cock half-flew, half-ran, across the angle of the adjoining field, followed by five of his screaming females. He knew a thing or two, and doubled under an alder-bush and entered a narrow coppice that ran alongside the road. But when he arrived there three of the hens were still on his track.

Now it is one thing to capture a piece of bacon-rind, but quite another thing to swallow it. The latter operation requires several uninterrupted seconds, with the head thrown back. Even at the last moment a rival may seize the end projecting and a fierce tug-of-war take place. And that happened in this case. He ran and ran and ran. He had no recollection afterwards how far he had run, but at last he seemed to have outdistanced his pursuers. There was a moment's respite somewhere by the side of someone's kitchen garden. He threw back his head, closed his eyes, and began to gulp the succulent morsel inch by inch. Oh, the ecstasy of that oleaginous orgy! Was there ever such a rind?

And then, of course, the thing happened! Someone had seized the end just as it was disappearing, and was tugging it back energetically. Curse! He opened his eyes and blinked. If it was one of his own hens, he would—well, give her a very bad time. Perhaps kill her, perhaps only neglect her. But, no! As he looked into his rival's eyes he realized that he was up against a large brown cock, one of the Rhode Island wretches that belonged to Mr Waite, the wheelwright. Venom and hatred stirred in his blood. When this little matter of the rind was determined he would settle with this Rhode Island upstart. He was somewhat exhausted and nearly two inches of the rind had been reclaimed by his rival. Backwards and forwards they swung, their feathers sticking out with sinister promise of the real fight that was to follow. The white cock had regained a quarter of an inch when the rind snapped. He gulped his remaining portion, and drew back ready for the fray. Both beaks were lowered, when suddenly the white cock beheld an approaching terror, a large, savage mongrel dog rushing towards them. With a scream he turned, flapped his wings, dashed through the bushes, and left the brown cock to his fate.

II

'Jim! Quick! Quick!' exclaimed Mrs Waite, running out of the cottage. Jim Waite appeared at the door of his shed, a hammer in his hand:

'What is it? What's the matter, Ida?' he called out, running towards her.

'That dog! That savage mongrel dog of the Beans has killed one of our fowls! O Lordy, it's the cock, too! It's killed the cock!'

'Where is it?'

'Look! Running across the road.'

Jim Waite was angry. This was not the first time that mongrel dog of the Beans had raised his ire. It always growled savagely at him and at his wife and children. On one other occasion he had found a fowl murdered, and he had had his suspicions.

He ran into the road in pursuit. The dog, scared at first by the shouts of Mrs Waite, had left its victim and darted under a culvert the other side of the road. Jim bent down, picked up a stone, flung it into the opening of the culvert and, as chance would have it, hit the dog on its flank. The dog became angry. It saw red, and likewise Mr Waite. It ran out and round him in a circle, growling, and then made a sudden rush. Jim was a powerfully built man, and he brought the hammer down plomp on the mongrel's skull. It would kill no more fowls.

The matter might have ended there had not Mr Bean, the retired corn-chandler, at that moment turned the corner in his dogcart and beheld Jim with the hammer in his hand, standing above the corpse of his pet dog. Now Mr Bean was a thin, wiry man of rather bucolic and eccentric temper. Moreover, he had a great affection for this most unpopular dog of indeterminate breed. Long before he reached the group he roared out:

'What the devil have you done?'

Equally angry Mr Waite roared back:

'I've ridded the neighbourhood of this vile beast that's just murdered my cock!'

'Your cock! What the devil does it matter about your cock!'

The dogcart pulled up, and Mr Bean jumped out.

Before either of the men could say another word, Mrs Waite pointed to the other side of the hedge and screamed:

'Look! Our only cock! Your blamed dog's killed it. It's always trying to bite everyone.'

Mr Bean followed the direction where she was pointing.

His side-whiskers shaking, he exploded:

'Well, then, it was in my ground. If your cock comes into my ground, my dog is justified in killing it.'

'There was another cock there—'

'Be damned to that!'

Mr Waite appeared, a formidable figure towering in the road, with the hammer in his hand, as he said, savagely:

'You shall pay for my cock!'

Nevertheless Mr Bean replied with spirit:

'You shall pay for my dog!'

'Dog, you call it? Bah!'

III

The attitude of both men appeared threatening, particularly as Mr Waite handed the hammer to his wife and began to take off his coat. What would have been the immediate outcome is difficult to say. But the uproar and disturbance upset the rather highly strung young horse, which began to trot off up the road. Mr Bean did not notice this till it had gone about twenty yards. Then he called after it, but the horse took no notice. So Mr Bean began to run. He would probably have caught it, but a little farther on a farmhand, late for his breakfast, came swinging down a narrow lane into the road on a solid-tyre bicycle. He did not expect to find a horse and trap there, and he just ducked under the horse's nose and his back tyre struck the left shaft, and he was thrown. So far as the horse was concerned, that put the lid on things. He put back his ears and bolted, with Mr Bean a kind of forlorn 'also ran'.

The farmhand picked up his bicycle and swore. Jim Waite picked up the dead dog, and flung it into Mr Bean's strip of land. Mrs Waite picked up the dead cock, and muttering to Mr Waite: 'Well, we'd meant to kill this week, anyway,' she took it inside and plucked it while it was warm.

Mr Bean was a good runner, and he tore down the road, yelling: 'Stop him! Stop him!'

He had lost his dog, and the prospect of losing his horse also spurred him on. But a young horse, even encumbered by a dogcart, can run faster than the fastest man. The distance between them widened. He could see the dogcart swaying and swerving, but the horse stuck to the road. Mr Bean ran over half a mile. It was a deserted part of the country, and nothing passed him. The horse and cart were out of sight. He rested for a few moments, and then ran on. When he had travelled about another four hundred yards he beheld a group of dark objects at the angle of two narrow roads. For some moments he could not distinguish what they were, but his instinct told him that something had happened. On approaching nearer, he beheld a large car, apparently jammed into the embankment by the side of the road; his dogcart appeared to be hugging its mudguards. Two or three figures were moving about, but there was no sign of the horse. He rushed up, panting. When within hailing distance, he called out: 'What's up? What's happened? Where's my horse?'

IV

Three busy men turned and regarded him. One was a young chauffeur. The other two were a curious contrast: a tall, white-moustached man of the Indian Army type, and a thin, aesthetic young man in the early twenties.

Now Mr Bean was in the mood when the great thing he needed in life was sympathy. He was having a bad morning. It was therefore an unpleasant shock to have the white-moustached gentleman turn on him in a blaze of anger and exclaim:

'Who the devil are you? What the devil do you mean, letting your damned horse and trap rush about the country? My God! you've buckled both our front wheels, and I've a most important appointment in forty minutes in Hornborough.'

'Where's my horse?' wailed Mr Bean. 'I got out of the trap for a moment, and he bolted.'

'What the devil did you get out of the trap for?' roared the stentorian individual. The younger man grinned and said, casually:

'Your horse is all right, old boy. He's trotting about in the meadow yonder, eating lotus-leaves.'

Mr Bean climbed up the embankment and looked over; and, sure enough, there was the horse, two hundred yards down the meadow, nibbling grass in the intervals of staring nervously around. He did not appear damaged at all, but the left shaft of the dogcart was snapped at the base and the wheel badly twisted. Mr Bean, however, was not allowed to devote too much attention to his own troubles. The elder man, whom he heard the other address as 'General', ordered him down in such a commanding way that he had not the power to disobey.

'Now, my man, listen to me,' roared the parade-ground voice. 'How far is it to Hornborough?'

'Nine miles,' replied Mr Bean, almost involuntarily adding 'sir'.

'God!' said the General. 'And where is the nearest place we can get a car?'

'There isn't a garage nearer than Hornborough that I know of.'

'Isn't there anyone in this God-forsaken part of the country who has got a car?'

'Only Sir Samuel Lemby, and I know he's motored up to town today.'

'God!' repeated the General, and turning to the younger man, he said:

'What the devil are we going to do, my lord?'

It occurred to Mr Bean that the younger man, addressed as 'my lord', was vaguely amused. He scratched his chin and said:

'It looks like a wash-out, unless we walk, General.'

'Walk! Nine miles in forty minutes.'

'Perhaps we could hire bicycles.'

'Bicycles.'

The General's face was a study in stupefied outrage. He turned to Mr Bean and exclaimed: 'Are there no traps about here?'

'Plenty, sir,' answered Mr Bean, who by this time had completely succumbed to the overwhelming atmosphere of a general and a lord. 'But no trap could do nine miles in forty minutes.'

'But what the devil are we to do? The Minister can't wait. The train won't wait. The House sits at two.'

Mr Bean was enormously impressed. He felt personally responsible for some mysterious national disaster. He said, weakly: 'I don't know, sir. It's very awkward.'

Then a bright inspiration occurred to him. 'A racehorse could do it. Sir Samuel Lemby has race-horses, but he's away, and it's not likely the head-groom would lend any out for such a purpose.'

The eyes of the General started out of his head.

'He wouldn't, wouldn't he? How far is it to this Lemby's?'

'There's the house, just up there, sir. Five minutes' walk.'

V

The General appeared to be calculating savagely. At last he turned to the younger man and said:

'Gevenah, it's our only chance. You could do this. You rode in the Grand National. What you don't know about horses isn't worth knowing. For God's sake run up the hill. Cajole, bribe, steal—do anything to get the horse. Five minutes, say another five minutes arguing—half an hour to do nine miles. Perhaps you can get across country, save a bit, eh? There's just a chance. The train goes at twelve thirty-two. Oxted is bound to catch it.'

The young man's face lighted up. A queer smile twisted his mouth.

'All right,' he said. 'I'll have a shot. Give me the report.'

'Here it is. I'll follow you up the hill as fast as I can move, in case they want more persuading.'

Mr Bean was left alone with the useless car and the broken dogcart. He saw the younger man sprinting up the hill like a professional runner, and the elder chasing after him like some valetudinarian crank trying to keep his fat down.

As luck would have it, the younger man came slap on the head-groom and a subordinate leading two silk-coated mares out of the paddock for a canter. He approached the head-groom and smiled.

'My friend,' he said, 'I'm going to ask you to break all the Ten Commandments in one fell swoop. I am Lord Gevenah, a lover of horseflesh and metaphysics. The gentleman you observe coming up the hill is not training for the Marathon. He is General Boyd-Boyd, of the War Office Intelligence Staff. You may suggest that War Office and intelligence are a contradiction in terms, but we have not time to argue the matter. The point is, Sir Samuel is a very old friend of the General's and we are convinced that he would come to our rescue in the circumstances.'

The head-groom leant forward and said: 'Excuse me, sir, but would you mind telling me what you're talking about?'

'A very reasonable request. Farther down the hill, at the crossroads, you may also observe a car jammed against the embankment. Both the front wheels are buckled. It is essential that we deliver a report—this report, my friend—to Sir Alfred Oxted, the Minister. He is catching the twelve thirty-two train at Hornborough for London. The report affects the whole aspect of the argument affecting a Bill that is being discussed in the House this afternoon.'

'What is it you want me to do, sir?'

'I want the loan of that beautiful roan mare which for the moment your figure so gracefully adorns, for the purpose of riding to Hornborough.'

'What! Lend you one of Sir Samuel's racers!'

'Precisely, my friend.'

'Not on your dear life! Lend you Iconoclast to go monkeying about the high roads on! Why, it's more than my place is worth.'

'Is your place worth more than the interests of the people—the vital necessities of the nation?'

'I know nothing about it. I work for Sir Samuel Lemby. If you get his permission—'

'We have his permission—morally. He is one of the General's oldest friends.'

'I've only got your word for it. Sir Samuel paid four thousand seven hundred and fifty for this mare. It can't be done.'

'Come! this is quibbling; time is precious. The General said we should waste five minutes arguing. But if you will kindly dismount, I shall still have half an hour to get to Hornborough. I promise to bring the mare back safely.'

'It can't be done, my son. For all I know the whole thing may be a cock-and-bull story.'

'Ah! here comes the General. General, I'm afraid our friend demands security.'

'Well, for God's sake give it to him. What the devil does he think we are?'

'Produce everything you've got, General. Pocketbook, money, despatches. I will do the same.'

The head-groom beheld wallets of notes being produced, and he became frankly interested. In the end he accepted a bribe of two hundred and twenty-five pounds in cash for the loan of Iconoclast for one hour.

'It's an awful risk,' he said, dismally, as he dismounted.

'If you do not take risks you will never arrive,' replied the young man, leaping into the saddle. 'Without taking risks great battles would not have been won, colonies founded, discoveries made. Iconoclast! an excellent name! Come, old friend! Iconoclast, breaker of idols, shatterer of illusions, trusted enemy to false prophets! Come!'

He pressed the mare's flanks gently with his knees, and she responded.

'Only twenty-nine minutes!' roared the General.

The young man turned a laughing face and waved his hand. His progress was visible to the anxious General's eye for nearly half a mile. The narrow road flanked a sixty-acre field and led into a bridle path through a chain of little coppices. By taking this bridle-path, the head-groom had explained that he would save a mile or two, as well as the horse's feet. The last they saw of him, he appeared to be leaning over, whispering in the mare's ear. Iconoclast was travelling like the wind.

It was certainly a very beautiful ride. The bridle path, which once had been a Roman road, ran for nearly six miles in almost a dead straight line. The ground was gently undulating. Woods flashed by, and open spaces, commons with sparse trees, sandy cuttings with gorse and furze projecting at tantalizing angles, stretches of blue distance with cattle grazing, sleepy rivers. On, on, raced this famous offspring of Babylon and Happy Days (you shall read of her in Borwell's *History of the Turf*).

The young man's face was alight with pleasure. Occasionally he slackened the mare's speed to glance at his wristwatch. When the road was reached there were three miles to go, and twelve minutes to accomplish it. Iconoclast had justified her good name.

'Steady, now, old girl, steady! We're reaching the stormy outposts of Christian gentlemen.'

A signpost pointed eastward to Hornborough. Fortunately the road was still what is known as a secondary road. A few cars flashed by, their drivers a little nervous of this bolting apparition of man and beast. Hay-carts lumbering leisurely out of fields were the serious source of danger, men on bicycles, market carts, all the slow-moving things.

Twelve minutes, eleven minutes, ten—the road sloping upwards violently to the headland that looks down on the Horn valley.

Nine minutes, eight and a half, eight—the summit reached. Down below, the sleepy valley, almost impervious to the thrusts of time. Thus it must have looked in Boadicea's time. A few more hamlets, a few more cultivated fields.

'Whoa up, old girl!'

The signboard said one-and-a-quarter miles to Hornborough Station. One mile and a quarter, and eight minutes to go! His faith! a worthy beast, this Iconoclast! One mile and a quarter, and all the way a gentle slope downward. If ever there was a pleasant sporting prospect, here was one. To travel at the rate so far maintained would bring the horse and rider to their destination with some minutes to spare. Away on the horizon appeared tiny white balls of smoke, like little lumps of cotton wool being shot out of a toy gun. It was the train. He again consulted his wristwatch and estimated the distance. 'It's four minutes late!' he exclaimed, a shade of disappointment in his voice. It would appear, in any case, not an occasion to tarry. One mile and a quarter, and twelve minutes to go. But, curiously enough, the young man seemed in no hurry. He tethered the mare to a gate, on the top bar of which he perched himself, and lit a cigarette.

'A glorious ride, Iconoclast, old friend!' he said, stroking the mare's nozzle. He appeared to be making a careful calculation, his eyes wandering from the little blobs of cotton wool to his watch. After some minutes he flung his cigarette away, and again took to the saddle. The last mile-and-a-quarter was done at express speed, but certainly not at the greatest speed of which the mare was capable. The rider seemed a little agitated by some meticulous calculation. Some of the road was covered in whirlwind fashion, but there were unaccountable slackenings and halts.

When the little market town of Hornborough was reached, the blobs of cotton wool arrived simultaneously. There was a furious ride along the broad High Street, terrifying the owners of booths and stalls. Shopkeepers ran to their doors, women clutched their children, and dogs barked. But horse and rider swung round the corner into Church Street, dashed across Ponder's Green, up the slope into the station-yard, and arrived *just as the train went out!* The whole town must have observed that dramatic ride and commented on it. A young man, on one of Sir Samuel's racehorses—some said it was Iconoclast herself—racing to the station to catch the London train—why?

VI

He flung the reins to an outside porter, and dashed into the station and on to the platform.

'The train has just gone, sir,' exclaimed the ticket collector, grinning. It may be observed, at this juncture, that there is a type of individual who loves to impart information of this kind. He loves to tell you you have just missed your train, or that you are in the wrong train, or that there isn't another one for four hours. His supreme idea of joy is to be able to tell you that you have just missed your last train. It isn't nice.

On this occasion our hero—for so he surely must be—merely muttered the formal exclamations of disappointment, and then went back and remounted his steed, after flinging the improvised groom a purse of gold. (No, if we remember rightly, it was a shilling.) Anyway, he galloped back through the town for all the world to see.

Instead, however, of returning the way he had come, he bore off to the west and, after ten minutes' ride, cantered up the chestnut avenue that led to a Georgian house. In the circular drive in front of the entrance-hall he espied a butler taking a parrot in a cage out for an airing. He called out:

'Hi, Fareweather, can you hold my mare for five minutes? I can't stop. Is Miss Alice in?'

'Yes, my lord. With pleasure, my lord. She's in the Dutch garden, watering the gentians.'

The girl looked up at him with that dreamy, does-anything-else-exist-but-thou-and-I expression, and he crushed her in his arms. These preliminaries being concluded, she said:

'Well?'

And appropriately enough he answered:

'There's a destiny which shapes our ends, rough-hew them how we will!'

'You look as though you had just invented a new religion.'

'And so I have, but I haven't had time to patent it. This afternoon the Government will fall, and it will be my work. Religion and opportunity are old bedfellows.'

'Tell me.'

'You know the storm that has raged round the Subsidies Bill. It has been working to a crisis. The Government have staked their all on squashing the amendment which our people are putting this afternoon. A delicate subject like this is largely a question of figures. Figures can be impressive, but a clever man can use them either way. That is what they've been doing. They have the control end of statistics, and statistics can be wangled. Over the weekend I was at Clive Hall. I was supposed to be there for polo, but I found myself in a mare's nest of conspirators and wanglers. Brigadiers and carpet-salesmen, they've been all over the country, drawing up a report.'

'Is it a false report, Mervyn?'

'Yes, and no. A report can be false not so much by what it says as by what it leaves out. See? This was a devilish, wanglish, naughty, spiteful report, and they were going to spring it on the House this afternoon, to crush our people's amendment. I didn't show my hand. I'm only a polo player. I was full of sympathy. A chutney-biting brigadier named Boyd-Boyd fixed an appointment on the 'phone with Oxted, at Hornborough Station, for the twelve thirty-two. He was to deliver the goods. I offered to accompany him, making the excuse that I had to go to town. Cyril lent us his car. We had got as far as some God-forsaken spot in the Weynesham Valley. I was desperate. I couldn't make up my mind whether to dot the old chap over the head and bolt or whether to pinch the report and let it blow away, when fate supervened.'

'What happened?'

'A horse in a dogcart bolted. The fool of a man had

got out, for some reason or other. In trying to avoid it, our chauffeur ran into a bank, and buckled both the front wheels. We had nine miles to go, and there wasn't such a thing as a car in the neighbourhood. The old Purple Patch nearly went off his nut. Then some magician produced a race-horse.'

'A race-horse?'

'Wasn't it sweet? I jumped at the idea. I knew that it would be up to me to do the flying handicap stuff, and with the report once in my possession all would be well. I rode hell-for-leather, and missed the train gracefully by a minute.'

'But what will you do with the report?'

'Give it back. It doesn't matter. It will be too late. Figures like that are only useful when used at the right moment. To-morrow the Government will be down, and no one will care a rap about their blinking old report.'

'Oh, dear! I'm glad I don't have anything to do with politics.'

'You do. You are politics. You are what we fight for, and lie for, and wangle for. You are religion. You are beauty. Haven't you heard the saying: *Homo solus aut deus aut demon*? You are the rose in the heart of the world. You—'

'Talking about roses, Mervyn, how do you like my gentians?'

'There you go! You always spoil my best periods. Darling, one kiss and I must away.'

'Whither, O Lord?'

'To take the mare back, and face the fury of my bonny brigadier.'

'He *will* be angry!'

'What does it matter? Did you ever know a brigadier who mattered? When the big story is told, you'll find he's about as important as a—as a—piece of bacon-rind!'

EPILOGUE

'You didn't ought to have talked to the boy like that,' said Mrs Egger, as she poured out Mr Egger's glass of stout at suppertime. 'It's set the boy on thinking; and when a boy like Tom starts thinking it's—it's—bad for his health.'

'I like that,' replied William, blowing the froth off the stout. 'Why, it was you put me up to it. Didn't you say—?'

'I told yer to give him a good scolding. It would have been better if you'd boxed his ears. Instead of all this talk.'

'What talk?'

'Saying one thing leads to another, and so on.'

'Well, isn't it true?'

'In a kind of way it's true. In a kind of way it's silly. Anyway, it sets him on thinking. I saw him in the shop this afternoon staring at them cooking-pears. I know he was thinking about what you said. Now if he took apples today, he might take pears tomorrow. It put the notion there, like. He'd never have thought of it. And this evenin' he comes up to me and says, "Mum, dad said one thing leads to another," and I says, "Yes, Tom?" and he says, "Mum, what was the first thing from which the other things come?" Did you ever hear such notions? Pass the pickles, dear.'

—XXV—

'Face'

IT WILL NOT, OF COURSE, SURPRISE YOU to know that it was at the Cravenford National School that he was first known as 'Face'. The people of Essex are well-known for their candour and lucidity of expression. He was an exceptionally—well, plain boy. There was nothing abnormal, or actually malformed about him, it was only that his features had that perambulatory character which is the antithesis of classic. It was what the Americans call a 'homely' face. The proportions were all just wrong, the ears actually protruding, the jaw too lantern, the eyes actually too wide apart. Moreover, his figure was clumsy in the extreme. He seemed all hands, and feet, and knees, and chin. It was impossible for him to pass any object without kicking it. Neither was his personality enhanced by his manner, which was taciturn and sullen, gauche in the extreme. The games and amusements of other boys held no attractions for him. He made no friends, exchanged no confidences, distinguished himself at nothing. Yet those of the impatient world who found time to devote a second glance to this uncouth exterior were bound to be impressed by the appeal of those deep brown expectant eyes.

They were not essentially intelligent eyes, but they had a kind of breadth of sympathy, a profound watchfulness, like the eyes of some caged animal to whom the full functions of its being had not so far been revealed.

It was the universality of this nickname, 'Face', which preserved it, for the boys of Cravenford National School knew that Caleb Fryatt resented it, and individually they feared him. That very clumsiness and imperviousness of his was apt to be overwhelming when adapted to militant purposes. Not that he was easy to rouse, but it was difficult to know when he was roused—he gave no outward manifestation of it—but when he was, it was difficult to get him to stop. He was a grim and merciless fighter, who could take punishment with a kind of morbid relish. It only inspired him to a more terrible onslaught. The boys preferred to attack him in company, and then usually vocally, by peeping over the churchyard wall and calling out:

'Face! Face! Oh, my! There's a face!'

The tragic setting of his home life explained much. He had had a brother and two elder sisters, all of whom had died in infancy. He lived with his father and mother in a meagre dilapidated cottage a mile beyond the church. His father worked at a stud farm, at such moments as the mood for work was upon him. He was a man of morose and vicious temper, quickened by spasmodic outbreaks of alcoholic indulgence. Of poor physique, he was nevertheless a dangerous engine of destruction in these moods, particularly in respect to the frailer sex. Caleb had been brought up in a code which recognised unquestioningly the right of might, which accepted tears and blows as a natural concomitant to its reckoning. He had stood powerless and affrighted at the vision of his little mother beaten unreasonably almost to insensibility, and he had never heard her complain. His own body was scarred by the thousand attentions of sticks and belts. He, too, had not complained. In some dumb way he suffered more from the blows his mother received than he did from those he received himself.

But he was growing up now—ugly, clumsy old 'Face'. When at the age of fourteen he passed through the first standard and out of the school, he was already as tall as his father, and somewhat thicker in girth, more agile, tougher in fibre. The significance of this development did not occur to him at the time. He was sent to work at

Sam Hurds', the blacksmith, a dour, intelligent, religious giant, who instructed him in the intricacies of his craft with relentless thoroughness, but without much sympathy. The boy liked the work, although he showed no great aptitude at it. He had a way of plodding on, appearing to understand, serving long hours, and then in a period of abstraction forgetting all that he had been told. He loved the blazing forge, the clang of metal upon metal, the sheen upon the carters' horses that came in to be shod, the sunlight making patterns on the road outside...

He was two years with Sam Hurds. At seventeen his muscles were like a man's. His overgrown, hulking body like a fully developed farm labourer's. His appearance had not improved. Even the smith adopted the village nickname and called him 'Face'. At first it was 'Young Face', then 'Face', then as their sombre familiarity developed, and the smith realised the boy's sound qualities and the something far too old for his years, it became 'Old Face'. He knew that his assistant had no powers of adaptability, little invention, not a very real grasp of the essentials, but at the same time he knew he could trust him. He would do precisely as he was told. He would stick to it. He could be relied upon like a sheepdog. Nothing could shift him from his post of duty.

The smith was right, but he had not allowed for those outward thrusts of fate which upset the soberest plans.

One night Caleb arrived home and found his mother crying. He had never seen her cry before. He regarded her spellbound.

'What is it mother?'

'Nothing, lad, nothing. Come, your tea's keeping warm upon the hob. There's a pasty—'

'Nay, you wouldn't cry for nowt, mother. Lift up your head.'

She lifted up her head and dashed the tears away, but as she moved toward the kitchen he noticed that she was trying to conceal a limp. He caught her up.

'He has been striking you again.'

'It's nothing, lad.'

'Show me.'

He pulled her down to him and she wept again. Lifting the hem of her skirt, she revealed her leg above the ankle, bound up in linen.

'He kicked me, dear, but it is nothing. It will pass.'

Caleb ate his tea in silence. His table manners were never of the finest, and on this occasion he masticated his food, and swilled his tea, like an animal preoccupied with some disturbance of its normal life. Afterward he sat apart and thought, his mother busy with household matters. Later she popped across the road to a neighbouring cottage to borrow some ointment.

While she was out his father returned. It was getting dark, and a fine rain was beginning to fall. His father came stumbling up the cottage garden singing. Caleb blocked his passage in the little entrance hall, and said deliberately:

'You didn't ought to have kicked mother.'

His father, emerging from the shock of surprise, scowled at him.

'What's that?'

'You didn't ought to have kicked mother.'

For a moment Stephen Fryatt was speechless, then he lurched forward and pushed his son away.

'What the devil's it to do with you, whipper-snapper?'

Caleb thrust his father back against the wall and repeated:

'You didn't ought to have kicked her.'

Then Stephen saw red. He struck at his son with his clenched hand, and the blow split the boy's ear. Caleb took his father by the throat and shook him. The latter tried to bring his knee into play. At this foul method of attack Caleb, too, became angry. Those long powerful fingers gripped tighter. He closed up, and flung his father's body against the lintel of the door. He did not realise his own newly developed strength. When his mother returned a little later she found her man lying in the passage with the back of his head in a pool of blood, her son hovering ghost-like in the background. She gave a cry:

'What's this ye've done, Caleb?'

A hollow voice came out of the darkness:

'He didn't ought to have kicked ye, mother.'

She screamed and, kneeling upon the floor, she supported the battered head upon her knee. It appeared an unrecognisable thing, the hair so much blacker in the ivory-hued face, the eyes staring stupidly.

Followed then a shifting phantasmagoria, scenes and emotions incomprehensible to the defender. Neighbours, and doctors and policemen, talking and arguing, whispering together, pointing at him. He was led away. In all that early turmoil, and in the more bewildering proceedings which followed, the one thing which impressed him deeply was the attitude of his mother. She had changed towards him entirely. She accused him, reviled him, even cursed him. He would ponder upon this in his dark cell at night. He had never imagined that his mother could have loved his father—not in that way, not to that extent. His brown ox-like eyes tried to penetrate the darkness for some solution. He had no fear as to what they would do with him, but everything was inexplicable...unsatisfying. The days and weeks which followed—he lost all sense of time—added to the sense of mystification. He appeared to be passed from one judge to another, beginning with a gentleman in a tweed suit and knickerbockers, and ending with a very old man in a white wig and gold-rimmed glasses, of whom only the head and the thin pale fingers seemed visible. Yes, yes, why did they keep on torturing him like this? He had answered all the questions again and again, always giving the same replies, always ending up with the solemn asseveration:

'He didn't ought to have kicked her.'

At the same time he had never meant to kill his father.

He had underestimated his strength. He had become very strong in the forge. His father had attacked him first. It was unfortunate that the back of Mr Fryatt's head had struck the sharp corner of the lintel post. He was in any case crazy with drink. The boy was only seventeen. He believed he was defending his mother. Of course, these pleas were not his. This version of the case had not occurred to him, but to his surprise a learned-looking gentleman, who had visited him in his cell, had stood up in Court and made them vehemently. And hearing the case put like that, Caleb nodded his head. He hadn't thought of it in that light, but it was quite true. Oh, but the arguments which ensued! The long words and phrases, the delays, and pomp and uncertainty. Never once did the question seem to come up as to whether his father 'ought to have done it', or not. According to his mother, his father appeared to have been almost a paragon of a father.

It was all settled at last; and he was sent away to a 'Home' for two years.

Home! The ironic travesty of the word penetrated his thick skull immediately he had passed what looked like a prison gate. There were two hundred boys in this home. It seemed strange to live in a home ruled over by a governor in uniform, policed by gaolers and superintendents. Strange to have a home one could not leave at will, where iron discipline turned one out at dawn, drove one like a slave to long hours of hard and uncongenial work. Strange that home should breathe bitterness and distrust, that it should be under a code which seemed to repeat eternally:

'Don't forget you are a criminal. Young as yet, but the taint is in you!'

It was true there were momentary relaxations, football and other games which he detested, bleak and interminable services in a chapel, organ recitals and concerts. The other boys disgusted him with their endless obscenities and suggestions, their universal conviction that the great thing was to 'get through it', so as to be able to resume those criminal practices inherent in them, practices which the home did nothing to eradicate or relieve.

If 'Old Face' had not been of the toughest fibre, dull witted, impervious, and in a sense unawakened, those two years would have broken him. As it was they dulled his sensibilities; even more, they embittered him. Those brown eyes had almost lost that straining glance of expectancy, as though the home had taught him that there was nothing for him in any case to expect. He was a criminal, hallmarked for eternity. When he had been there six months they sent for him to go and visit the chaplain. That good man looked very impressive, and announced that the governor had received information that Caleb's mother was dead, and that it was his solemn duty to break the news to him. He appeared relieved that the boy did not at once burst into tears. He then delivered a little homily on life and death, and pointed out that it was Caleb's evil and vicious actions which had hastened his mother's death. He advised him to pour out his heart in penitence to God, who was always our Rock and Saviour in times of tribulation. He quoted passages from Leviticus, and Caleb stared at him dully, thinking the while:

'I'll never see my mother again, never, never.'

He did not give way to grief. The news only bewildered him the more. He went about his duties in the home stolidly. He was quite an exemplary inmate, hardly up to the average standard of quickness and intelligence, but quiet, obedient, and well behaved. At the end of his term of service he was sent up before the governor and other officials. The clumsy scrawl of his signature was demanded upon innumerable forms. He believed he was once more to be a free man. And so he was in a qualified sense. But he was not to escape without the seal of the institution being indelibly stamped upon him. In roundabout phrases the governor explained that he was to leave the home, but he was not to imagine that he was a free agent to go about the world murdering whomever he liked. He was still a criminal, requiring supervision and watching. Out of their Christian charity the governors had found employment for him at a timber merchant's at Bristol. Thither he would go, but he must remember that he was still under their protection. Every few weeks he must report to the police. Any act of disobedience on his part would be treated—well, by a sterner authority. On the next occasion he would not be sent to a nice comfortable establishment like the home, where they played football and had concerts, but to Wormwood Scrubbs or Dartmoor. Did he understand? Oh, yes, Caleb understood—at least, partly. He was to be free, free in a queer way.

The arrangement did not exactly tally with his sense of freedom, any more than this building tallied with his idea of home, but he was only nineteen and his body was strong and his spirit not completely broken. Any ideas he may have entertained that the new life was going to spell freedom in any sense were quickly shattered. The timber merchant at Bristol was a man named Barnet, a tyrant of the worst description. He knew the kind of material he was handling. Most of his employees were ex-convicts, ticket-of-leave-men, Lascars, or social derelicts. He acted accordingly. Caleb slept in a shed with nine other men, four of whom were coloured. They worked ten hours a day loading timber on barges. They were given greasy cocoa and bread at six o'clock in the morning, a meal of potatoes and little square lumps of hard meat at twelve, then tea and bread at four o'clock in the afternoon. In addition to this he was paid twelve shillings a week. The slightest act of insubordination or slackness was met with the threat:

'Here, you! Any more of that and you go back to where you came from!'

Before he had been there a month he felt that the home was indeed a home in comparison. It was one of the coloured men who rescued him from his thraldom, a pleasant-voiced man with only one eye. He appeared to take a fancy to Caleb. One night he came to him and whispered:

'Say, boss, would you like to beat it?'

It took some time for the boy from Cravenford to understand the coloured man's phraseology and plan, but when he did, he fell in with it with alacrity. The following Saturday they visited a little public-house down by the docks and were there introduced to a grizzled mate. Hands were wanted on a merchantman sailing for Buenos Aires the following week. The coloured man was a free agent and he signed on, and Caleb signed on in the name of J. Bullock.

Two nights before sailing, he hid in a barge and joined his ship the following morning. All day long he experienced the tremors of dread for the first time in his life. The primitive instinct of escape and the call of the sea was upon him. He could have danced with joy when he heard the rattling of the chains and the hoarse cries of the deck hands as the big ship got under way at dusk.

The voyage to Buenos Aires was uneventful. The work was hard and the discipline severe, but he was conscious all the time of sensing the first draught of freedom that he had experienced since he left his village. This feeling was accentuated at port when he realised that after being paid off, he was free to leave the ship. But the rigid magnificence of Buenos Aires depressed him. He learnt that after unloading they were to refit and convey cattle to Durban in South Africa, so he signed on again for the next voyage. This proved to be a formidable experience. A week out they ran into very heavy seas. He was detailed to attend the cattle. The cattle superintendent was a drunken bully. The stench among the cattle pens, added to the violent heaving of the ship, brought on sickness, but he was not allowed any respite. The cattle themselves were seasick, and many of them died and had to be thrown overboard. The voyage lasted three weeks, and when he arrived at Durban he determined to try his luck once more as a landsman. At that time there was plenty of demand for unskilled labour for men of Caleb's physique in South Africa, but it was poorly paid. He drifted about the country doing odd jobs. He visited Cape Town, Kimberley and Pietermaritzburg. The fever of wanderlust was upon him. He never remained in one situation for more than a few months. He was the man who desired to see over the ridge. Perhaps further, just a little further, would be—he knew not what, some answer to the inexpressible yearning within him, deep calling unto deep. At the age of twenty-two he was working on the railroad near Nyanza. They came and told him about the great war, which had just started in Europe. A keen-faced little man, one of the gangers, tapped him on the shoulder, and said:

'It's lucky for you lad you're out here. Otherwise they'd be telling you that "Your king and country need you".'

The phrase disturbed him. Night after night he lay awake dreaming of England. Memories of the home and of the timber-merchant at Bristol vanished. He thought only of Cravenford, the grey ivy-coloured church, the rambling high street, the pond by Mr Larry's farm, the cross-roads where he and another boy named Stoddard had fought one April afternoon, his mother's cottage, now, alas! deserted, but always sacred, old Sam Hurds banging away in the smithy, the rooks circling above the great elms in the park—all, all these things were perhaps in danger whilst he lay sulking in a foreign land. They had called him 'Face'. Well, why not? He knew he was not particularly prepossessing. The fellow workmen had always been at great pains to point this out to him. But still—stolidly and indifferently he went about his work, and then one day in the old manner he vanished…

We will not attempt to record Caleb's experiences of the war. He had no difficulty in joining a volunteer unit in Cape Town, which was drafted to England. There he asked to be transferred to one of his own county regiments. The request was overlooked in the clamour of those days.

He found himself with a cockney infantry regiment, and he remained with it through the whole course of the war. His life was identical to that of his many million comrades. In some respects he seemed to enjoy lapses of greater freedom than he had experienced for a long time. He was better fed, better clothed, better looked after. He had money in his pocket which he knew not what to do with. He made a good soldier, doing unquestioningly what he was told, sticking grimly to his post, being completely indifferent to danger.

Save for a few months on the Italian front, he served the whole time in France. He was slightly wounded three times, and in 1917 was awarded a military cross for an astounding feat of bravery in bombing a German dug-out and killing five of the enemy single-handed in the dark. Those queer spiritual strivings so deep down in his nature derived no satisfaction from the war. It was all quite meaningless and incomprehensible. When he left South Africa he had an idea that the fighting would be in England. He visualised grim battles in the fields beyond Cravenford, and he and the other boys from the school defending their village. He had never conceived that a war could be like this. Sometimes he would lie awake at night and ruminate vaguely upon the queer perversity of fate which suddenly made murder popular. He had been turned out of England because he had quite inadvertently killed his father for kicking his mother across the shins, and now he was praised for killing five men within a few minutes. He didn't know, of course, but perhaps some of those men—particularly that elderly plump man who coughed absurdly as he ran on to Caleb's bayonet—perhaps they were better men than his father, although foreigners, although enemy. It was very perplexing…

After a grey eternity of time, the thing came to an end. He found himself back in England. During the war much had been forgotten and forgiven. No one asked him for his credentials. The police never interfered with him.

With his three wound stripes, his military cross, and his papers all in order, he was for a time a *persona grata*.

He had a bonus beyond the pay which he had saved, and he had never been so wealthy in his life. He stayed in London, and tried to adapt himself to a life of luxury and freedom, but he was not happy. In restaurants he was self-conscious, in theatres bored, in the streets bewildered. And so one day he set out and returned to his native village. Strangely, little had it altered! There was the church, the smithy, and the old street all just the same. He called on the smith, who was startled at the sight of him, but on perceiving his strips and ribbons, reasonably polite. He ransacked the village for old friends. Alas! How many of his school associates had gone, never to return. He called on Mr Green, the miller, Mrs Allport, at the general shop, Bob Canning, the carrier. Oh, dear me! yes, they all remembered him, were quite courteous, glad he had done well at the war, got through safely. Well, well! And soon the story got round. 'Old Face has returned. Old Face! The boy who murdered his father!'

The novelty of his re-appearance and return soon wore off, and he knew that he was held in distrust in the village. He wandered far afield, and eventually obtained employment at a brick-works at Keeble, four miles down the valley toward Blaizing-Killstoke. Here the rumours concerning him gradually percolated, but they carried little weight or significance. He was a good workman, and time subdues all things.

Then the strangest miracle happened to Caleb Fryatt. He was nearly thirty, hard-bitten, battered, ill-mannered, with a scar from a bullet on his left cheek, little money, no prospects and no ambition—an unattractive chunk of a man. But what should we all do if love itself were not the greatest miracle of all? Anne Tillie was by no means a beauty herself, but she was not without attraction. She had a round, bright red ingenuous face, a heavily built figure with rather high shoulders and long arms. She was a year older than Caleb and inclined to be deaf, but there was a transparent honesty and simplicity about her. One could see that she would be honest, loyal, and true to all her purposes. She was the daughter of the postman at Blaizing-Killstoke. She and Caleb used to meet in the evenings and wander the lanes together. They did not appear to converse very much, but they would occasionally laugh, and give each other a hearty push. To her father's disgust, these attentions led to marriage the following year. They went to live in a tiny cottage on the outskirts of Keeble, ten minutes' bicycle ride from the works. Anne made an excellent wife. She seemed to understand and adapt herself to her husband's idiosyncrasies. She kept the cottage spotlessly clean, tended his clothes, and kept him in clean linen, cooked well, and studied all his little wants and peculiarities. She found time to attend to the garden, grow her own vegetables, and even see after a dozen fowls.

Caleb had never enjoyed such material comfort. In the evening they would sit either side of the fire, he with his pipe and she with her sewing. They were an unusually silent couple. Apart from her deafness, they never seemed prompted to exchange more than cursory remarks about the weather, their food, or some matter of local gossip. In the summer they sat in the garden, and watching the blue smoke from his pipe curl away into the amber light of the setting sun, Caleb felt that he had reached a haven after a restless storm. He worked remorselessly hard at the brickworks, and in two years' time was made a kiln foreman, receiving good wages. Malevolent people still whispered the story concerning the boy who murdered his father, and pointed an accusing finger at the back of his bulky form, but no one dared to remind Anne of that tragic happening. She knew the full details of it quite well, and woe to any unfortunate individual who dared to suggest that her man was in the wrong! In course of time he built a barn, and a toolshed, and they bought an adjoining orchard. They kept pigs, and then a pony and trap, and on Thursdays Anne would drive to market, and sell eggs, and chickens and apples. Oh, yes, they were becoming a prosperous pair. Caleb had surely outlived the ugly vicissitudes of his face. Was he happy? Was he completely satisfied? Who shall say? The promptings from the soul come from some deep root no one has fathomed. He was conscious of a greater peace than he had ever known. He sometimes hummed quite unrecognisable tunes as he went about his work. The mornings enchanted him with gossamer webs gleaming with dew, swinging between the flowers. But the eyes still sometimes appeared to be seeking—one knows not what.

They had been married five years and seven months when the child was born. It came as a great surprise to Caleb. He had hardly dared to visualise such an eventuality. What a to-do there was in the cottage! Another room to be prepared, strange garments suddenly appearing upon the line in the kitchen, a visiting nurse somewhat important and discursive.

'A boy! Ho!' thought Caleb, as he trundled along on his bicycle the following morning. A boy who would grow up and perhaps become like himself. Well, that was very strange, very remarkable. Most remarkable that such a possibility had never occurred to him. All day long, and for nights and weeks after he thought about the boy who was going one day to be a man like himself. The thought at first worried and perplexed him. Was he—had he been—the kind of man the world would want perpetuated? He felt the fierce censure and distrust mankind had always lavished upon himself beginning to focus upon the boy, and gradually the protective sense developed in him to a desperate degree. The boy should have better chances than he ever had, the boy should be protected, cared for, shown the way of things...Caleb ruminated. His wife became very dear to him. He was a man on the threshold of revelation. But before his eyes had fully opened to the complete realisation of all that this meant to him, a wayward gust of fever shattered the spectrum. The little fellow died when barely four months old. For a time Caleb was most deeply concerned for the health of his wife, who was a victim of the same scourge, but, as she gradually recovered, a feeling of unendurable melancholy crept over him. He began to observe the grey perspective of his life, its past and future. When Anne was once more normal, their intercourse became more taciturn than ever. There fell between them long, empty silences. There were times when he regarded her with boredom, almost with aversion. The years would roll on...wander-spirit would assail him. He would be tempted to pick up his cap and go forth and seek some port, where a ship under ballast might be preparing to essay the vast insecurity of heaving waters. But something told him that that would be cruel. His wife's love for him was the most moving experience of his life, far greater than his love for her. She was middle-aged now, and her deafness was more pronounced than ever.

Once she went away to stay with her father for a few days. The morning after she left, a wall in the brickyard collapsed and crushed his right foot. He was carried home in excruciating pain. A neighbour came in and attended him and they fetched the doctor. They wanted to send for his wife but he told them not to bother her. All night he was delirious, and for the next two days and nights he went through a period of torment. As the fever abated a deep feeling of depression crept over him. He began to yearn for his wife profoundly. The neighbour, an elderly woman, wife of the local corn-chandler, was kindness itself. But everything she did was just wrong. How could she know the way Caleb liked things, and he lying there silent and uncomplaining?

On the third evening Anne arrived. She had heard the news. She came bustling into the cottage, dropped her bag, pressed her lips to his.

'Silly Billy, why didn't you send for me?'

Silly Billy! That was her favourite term of raillery when he had behaved foolishly.

He choked back a desire to cry with relief.

'It's nothing, nothing to bother about.'

But a feeling of deep contentment crept over him. His eyes regarded her thick plump figure moving busily but quietly about the room. There would be nothing now to disturb or annoy him. Everything would be done just—just as he liked it. She deftly re-arranged the positions of tables, and cups, and curtains. As the evening wore on she hovered above him, watching his every little movement, like a tigress watching over its cub. She eased the pillow, stroked his hair, and by some adroit manœuvre relieved the pressure on his throbbing leg. A deep sense of tranquillity permeated him. For the first time for three days he felt the desire to sleep, the cottage seemed so inordinately quiet, secure. Once when she was stooping near the chair by the bed, he seized her rough, strong forearm and pulled her to him. He believed he slept at last with her cheek pressed against his own…

They treated him very well at the brick-works, and his wages were paid every week during his absence. It was nearly two months before he could get about again, and the doctors said he must expect to have a permanent limp. Summer vanished in the October mists, and a long winter dragged through its course. Spring again. Its pulse a little feebler than in the old days? Well, well, what could a man expect? Some of the old desires raised their heads and tugged at his heart-strings. He was very happy—off and on a little soiled, perhaps, by the stress of bitter years, a little more ordinary, a little more sociable. He sometimes visited 'The Green Man' and would drink beer with Mr White, the corn-chandler, and old Tom Smethwick. And after a glass or two he would be quite a social acquisition, and would be inclined to boast a little of his deeds in the Great War, and of his adventures in foreign lands. No harm in it. Not such a bad sort, Old Face, the boy who murdered his father.

Heigho! But how the years ravage us! 'Twas but a while when things were so and so, and now...He was forty-four when two disturbing factors came into his life, threatening to wreck its calm tenor, and they occurred almost simultaneously. There was a girl at the brickworks who came from London. She was the manager's secretary and she worked in his office. Oh, but she was a smart piece of goods, and the men never tired of discussing her. In the early twenties, distinctly pretty, with a mass of chestnut hair, pert manners and a wrist watch. Passing through the yards, she would sometimes chat with the men at the kilns, and in their dinner hour she would laugh and joke with them. Their estimate of her was not always expressed in very refined or flattering language. Old Ingleton, the time-keeper, swore she had given him the 'glad eye', but as one of his own eyes was glass, his confession did not carry great weight. She had never singled Caleb out for any particular attention although she was always friendly with him. The cataclysm came upon him quite suddenly one day in late September. He was digging a trench by a mound covered with nettles and a few sunflowers. He rested on his spade and was enjoying the pleasant tranquillity of the scene, when the girl came round the corner and looked at him. She smiled and exclaimed:

'A lovely day, Mr Fryatt!'

He instinctively touched his hat and said 'Ay.'

And that was the end of the conversation. But Caleb watched her walking up the narrow path toward the manager's shanty, and some restless fever stirred within him. She was unique. He had seen such women from a distance, smartly apparelled, walking about the streets of London and Cape Town, but he had always looked upon them as creatures of a different world from his own, and hardly given them a thought. But here was one smiling at him, speaking to him. After all, she was not so remote. She was a girl, indeed a working girl, quite accessible and friendly. And what a lithesome, dainty figure! What an appealing pretty face! Those lips! Ah! A large worm wriggled free from the side of the little trench, and quite unreasonably he cut it in half with his spade.

From that moment forward Caleb began to think of Agnes Fareham. Alas! He began to dream about her also. She was a note of bright and vivid colour in the drab monotony of his life. He began to lie in wait for her, to force his clumsy attentions upon her and she did not seem to resent it unduly. The affair became an obsession. His faculty for reasoning had never been considerable. In some dim way he felt that here was the solution of all those buried yearnings and thwarted desires which had accompanied him through life. Here was an explanation. He was content to be held by the experience, without formulating any plan or definite resolution. Whether the girl would ultimately succumb to his solicitations, whether she would go away with him, and if so how he was to manage to keep her; moreover, how he was to face the appalling cruelty of his own attitude toward Anne—all these questions he put behind him. For the moment they appeared immaterial to the blinding obsession. One day while still in this indeterminate mood he went home as usual to his midday dinner. As he dismounted his bicycle and leant it against the garden fence, Anne came out of the cottage and said:

'Caleb, there's a gentleman to see you.'

He went inside and beheld a small keen-faced elderly man, who nodded to him and said:

'Mr Caleb Fyatt?'

'Ay.'

The little man examined him closely.

'I will come straight to the business I have in hand. I am the head clerk of Rogers, Mason and Freeman, solicitors of Blaizing-Killstoke. You, I believe, are the only child of Stephen and Mary Fryatt, late of Cravenford?'

'Ay.'

'You may be aware that your father had a brother, named Leonard, in Nova Scotia?'

'I've heard tell on 'ee.'

'Your uncle died last year. He left a little property and no will. My principals are of opinion that you are the lawful legatee. They would be obliged if you would pay them a visit so that the matter may be fully determined. Here is my card.'

Caleb stared dully at the piece of pasteboard but Anne, who had entered the cottage just previously, asked to have the business explained to her. Caleb shouted in her ear. Then she turned to the lawyer and said:

'And how much money did his Uncle Leonard leave? Do you know, sir?'

'Quite without prejudice, and entirely between ourselves, I believe it is a matter of approximately four thousand pounds.'

It took the whole of the afternoon for this news thoroughly to penetrate the skull of the fortunate legatee. Indeed, it was not till he had had a pint of beer at 'The Green Man' on the way home that the full significance came home to him. It is to be regretted that after his supper he returned to 'The Green Man', and for the first time in his life Mr Caleb Fryatt got drunk. He stood drinks lavishly and indiscriminately. He told everyone his news. The amount became a little distorted. It may have been due to the lawyer's use of the word 'approximately'. This orgy acted upon him disastrously. As he reeled up the village street, only one vision became clear to him. Agnes! He could take her away, buy her a mansion and smart frocks. He could take her to hotels and theatres in London. At the same time, he could settle money on Anne. He was a millionaire. The world belonged to him.

With a tremendous effort he controlled his feet and voice when he reached the cottage, but he went to bed at once. In the morning he had a headache and Anne bound his head in damp linen handkerchiefs and brought him tea.

By Monday everyone on the countryside from Cravenford to Billows Weir knew that 'Old Face', the ugly man, known as the boy who murdered his father, had come in for a huge fortune left by an uncle in Canada. The first person he met in the brick-works on Monday was Agnes, who came up to him and held out her hand:

'I believe we are to congratulate you, Mr Fryatt.'

He smiled at her foolishly and held her hand an unnecessarily long time. There was no doubt she had taken to him. She liked him. Could he stir her deeper emotion?

The weeks went by in a dream. He visited the lawyers. Everything was in order. They even offered to advance him money. He could not visualise the full dimensions of his fortune; neither had he the power to act upon it. He still went on at the brick-works and the cottage, listening to Anne's sensible admonitions to invest the money in small amounts so as to have a nest egg for their old age. But he could not detach this miracle of wealth from the figure of Agnes. They had come together. They belonged to each other, fantastic phenomena jerking him violently out of the deep rut of his existence. One day he went into the town and bought a gold locket, set with blue stones. He gave four pounds ten for it. He waited for Agnes that evening and gave it to her. He had been in an agony as to whether she would accept it, but to his delight she received it with gratitude and thanked him bewitchingly. This seemed to bind her to him indissolubly. A few evenings later he met her in the lane. There was no one about. Without a word he took her in his arms and pressed his lips to hers. She gasped and spluttered:

'Oh, Mr Fryatt, please…no.'

But she wasn't angry. Oh, no, not really angry—just provocative, more alluring than ever ... They met frequently after that, in secret disused corners of the brickfield, in the lanes at night. He bought her more presents, and one Saturday they went secretly to a fair at Molesham and only returned by the last train. The men naturally began to get wind of this illicit courtship, but as far as he knew no rumour had penetrated the deafness of Anne. He was drifting desperately beyond care in either respect. Two months of this intensive worship and the madness was upon him. He said:

'You must come with me. We will run away.'

'Where, Caleb?'

'We'll go to London.'

'Where should we stay?'

'At swell hotels. We will have a carriage. I will buy frocks and jewels.'

The girl's eyes narrowed.

'What about your wife?'

'I'll make it all right. I'll settle some money on her.'

But Agnes was not so easily won. Oh dear, no! There were tears and emotion. You see, she was only a young and innocent girl. Suppose he deserted her? What assurance had she? This scheming and plotting went on for weeks. At length they came to an agreement. Agnes would go to London with him if he would first settle a thousand pounds upon her. It was very cheap at the price, and a fair and reasonable bargain. One Saturday they journeyed together to his lawyers at Blaizing-Killstoke. The deed was drawn up, and they both signed various papers. The elopement was fixed for the following Saturday. All the week Caleb walked like a man unconscious of his surroundings. The purposes of his life were to be fulfilled. True, he had odd moments of misgivings. He dared not think about Anne. Also at times he had gloomy forebodings concerning London hotels, how to behave, whether the people would laugh at him, what clothes to wear, whether Agnes would quickly sicken of him. But still he had pledged himself. He jingled the money in his pocket... His destiny.

Friday was a disastrous day. It was cold and damp, and to his disgust he awoke with a severe twinge of rheumatism in his left shoulder. It made him irritable and nervous all day. Agnes was very preoccupied. He had advanced her some money to buy frocks, and she went backward and forward to her lodgings with large cardboard boxes. He had selected the morrow, because Anne was going away to spend a few days with her father. In the afternoon his rheumatism became worse, and he became aware of the symptoms of a feverish chill. He left off work at his usual time and cycled home. The cottage was all in darkness. He lighted the lamp. Anne had left his supper ready for him on the tray. The little room looked neat and tidy. She had also left a note for him. He picked it up carelessly and held it under the lamp. This is what he read:

> CALEB DEAR,
>
> I hear that you have made some money over to Agnes Fareham and that you are wishful to go away with her. My dear! I do not want to interfere with your happiness. I thowt I had been a good wife to you but you know best. I am goin to my father and I shall not come back. Please God you may be happy.
>
> Your broking hearted wife,
>
> ANNE.
>
> Bless you dear for all you have been to me
> and the happiness you have give me.

And Caleb buried his face in his hands. Without touching his supper he carried the lamp into the bedroom and went to bed. Curse it! How his teeth were chattering! He would have liked a little brandy, but there was none in the cottage, and there was no one to go and fetch it. He wrapped himself up and rolled over, the interminable night began. What a weak fool he was! All the experiences and temptations of his life crowded upon him and tortured him. Idle dreams! Idle dreams! His shoulder ached insufferably. If Anne were here, she would rub it with that yellow oil. He could not rub his own shoulder and back. Then she would wrap it up in a thick shawl and say:

'Silly Billy, you must be careful of the damp.'

He could visualise her moving about the room, arranging the curtain so that there was no draught, stirring something in a cup, giving those little dexterous pokes to the bedclothes which meant so much, sitting placidly by the window, his coarse woollen socks in her hand. She loved darning his socks...doing things for him, even all the unpleasant, ugly things of domestic life.

He ought to have some soup or gruel or something, but he could not be bothered to make it. He turned out the lamp. And all night long Caleb turned and fretted, and strangely enough he gave little thought to Agnes. She was now becoming the unreality, the vain fancy! a feather drifting on the ocean. She was nothing to him. She had no part in that deep consciousness, amongst whose folds he had sought so desperately to find inner relief. What was it? Where was it? Toward dawn he slept fitfully, struggling to keep awake on account of the disturbing dreams that crowded upon him. When things at last became visible the first thing he was aware of was an old shawl of his wife's on a nail by the door, and the cap which she wore to do the housework in. The things became to him an emblem of the love she bore him, and truth came to him with the rising of the sun. Love—the deep secret her hand had sought; the love that struggles to endure through any conditions, the love that as far as human nature is concerned is permanent and indestructible. He observed its action upon his own career. His mother's love for his father, a love which he had so tragically misinterpreted.

Later his love for his country, which had crept upon him across the years and whispered to him across the endless waste of waters. And lastly the love that existed between his wife and himself, a love that was so near and familiar to him that he could not always see it. He sighed and the dreams no longer worried him. It must have been some hours later that he awoke and made himself some tea. He was still shaky, and his shoulder hurt, so he went back to bed.

In the middle of the morning he heard the latch of the front door click, and his heart beat rapidly.

'She has come back,' he thought. He heard some one moving in the passage, his door opened, and on the threshold of the room stood—Agnes! It was queer that on observing her his first thought was with regard to his teeth. During the war he had lost three front teeth. A loving government had presented him with a plate and three false teeth which he always wore in daytime, but which at night, on Anne's advice, he always kept in a glass of water by the side of the bed. He stretched out his hand for the teeth, and then he felt that he would be ridiculous putting the plate in, so he left the matter alone. She advanced into the room, and neither of them spoke. It is difficult to know precisely what attitude Agnes had resolved to take, but the appearance and atmosphere of that room may have altered or modified it. She merely grinned rather uncomfortably at Caleb. He could not have been an attractive sight. He had slept badly, and he had not washed or shaved. He was wearing a coarse woollen nightgown, and his three front teeth were missing. Perhaps it occurred to her abruptly that in the round of life one has to take the unshorn early morning with the gaily bedecked evening, and she was already wondering whether the combination was worth while. In any case she merely said:

'Well?'

And Caleb replied, 'Hullo!'

They both looked a little ashamed then, and Agnes glanced out of the window as though dreading someone's approach. As he did not speak further, she turned and said:

'You're not coming then?'

He turned his face to the wall and answered 'No.'

There was a definite expression of relief on the girl's face. She was very smartly dressed in a tailor-made coat and skirt. She edged toward the door. Then she said in a mildly querulous voice:

'I knew you'd back out of it.'

Caleb sat up and exclaimed feelingly:

'I'm sorry, Agnes.'

This seemed to quite appease her, and she said:

'Anything you want, Caleb, before I go?'

The man stared thoughtfully at the ceiling before replying:

'Yes; wait a minute, Agnes.'

He took a pencil and a sheet of paper, and wrote out a telegram addressed to his wife:

'Come back, dear, I want you.'

The girl took up the telegram and read it through thoughtfully. Then she once more edged toward the door. She fumbled with the latch. Suddenly she turned and said:

'That'll be elevenpence.'

'Eh?'

'That'll be elevenpence—for the telegram.'

He fumbled with his trousers on the chair by the side of the bed and produced a shilling.

'There, lass, I haven't any change. Don't bother about the penny.'

She took the shilling and went back to the door.

'Good-bye, Caleb.'

'Good-bye.'

When she had gone he thought it was rather queer of her to ask for the shilling. He had already given her a thousand pounds, and many frocks and presents. She might in any case have offered to give him the penny change. However, he soon forgot her in the fever of anxiety he was in as to the return of his wife. All day long no one came near the cottage. The day was wet, and a thick white mist drifted with the rain. He could not trouble to light the fire. He ate some bread and cheese at midday, and vainly tried to rub his shoulder with the oil. Soon after five it began to be dark again. He was in a terror of remorse and fear. Had he destroyed the lamp of his happiness? He buried his face in the pillow and groaned: 'I didn't understand! I didn't understand!'

He began to feel so weak; he was losing sense of time. He awakened once with a start. The room seemed suddenly filled with an enveloping comfort. He held out his arms. He felt those wet cheeks pressed close to his. That voice so dear and familiar to him was whispering in his ear:

'Silly Billy, I knew ye would send for me.'

—XXVI—

Freddie Finds Himself

TALENT IS an elusive quantity. It never does to despair concerning the lack of it. Some people will dig, and dig, and dig, and find nothing, and then suddenly—perhaps when they are reaching middle-age—they will discover that they can do something as well as, if not better than, anyone else.

It cannot be said that up to the age of twenty-six Freddie Oppincott had shown any particular ability. Indeed, he was the butt of his family, as he had been of his school. He had tried seven different professions and had foresworn them all, or perhaps it would be truer to say that the professions had foresworn him. In spite of all this, Freddie was an incurable optimist. There was no holding him. He lived with his father, his elder brother John, who ragged him mercilessly, and his two sisters, Emma and Jane, who mellowed their ragging with a genuine streak of affection. Fortunately for Freddie, his father was a fairly well-to-do coal merchant. The family lived at Highgate. Mr Oppincott had long since given up all hope of Freddie accomplishing anything, except perhaps marrying a rich girl. He was by way of being good-looking, and he could talk. Talking was certainly his one talent. But the trouble is that to exploit talking profitably you must be able to talk well. And that could not be said of Freddie Oppincott.

At the time when this story commences he had been in a state of unemployment for two months. And then one morning he sprang the latest bombshell on the family. He announced that he was going to be a private detective!

Even Mr Oppincott was forced to laugh. And Emma and Jane said:

'Don't be so utterly absurd, Freddie.'

But the matter was already a partial *fait accompli.* He had taken a little room, described as an office, in Bloomsbury.

And in the morning paper was an advertisement worded as follows:

> Must hubby really stay at the office till midnight? Is it really mother that wifey spends the weekends with? What is your partner always going to Paris for? If in doubt on all these problems, consult Pimpleton's Detective Agency, 9, Eurydice Street, Bloomsbury.
>
> Pimpleton never fails.

Freddie announced that he was Pimpleton. He was quite impervious to the shafts of derision hurled at him by the other members of the family. Having had a good deal of time on his hands during the last two months, he had been reading detective stories. His mind had become obsessed with visions of himself in a cloth cap (with ear flaps) tracking down murderers, discovering the duchess's stolen tiara, bringing the faithless to justice.

'Don't you make any mistake,' he said. 'I'm not such a fool as I look.'

'No; but even then there's a wide margin to fill up,' replied John. And Emma said sternly, in that delightfully candid manner that characterizes family life:

'Freddie, you have got every quality which a detective should not have, and you've not got a single quality that he should have. You've no perception, no logic, no reasoning power, and, moreover, you talk too much. You give yourself away every time you open your mouth. Don't be a complete ass.'

And Jane said:

'Why don't you *write* detective stories? It's much easier, and far less dangerous.'

And Papa Oppincott said:

'I must be off. Where are my boots? Don't smoke too many cigarettes, Freddie, sitting in your chamber waiting for the Countess to call.'

And they all departed to their various vocations.

It would be painful to record the sarcasm, gibes, and derision to which Freddie was subjected during the ensuing ten days. It reached a degree of cruelty that could only happen amongst people who are really fond of each other.

Freddie went out and bought a cloth cap (with ear flaps). Then he hired a roll-top desk, and littered it with papers, ink, and pens. And then—a really bright inspiration—several cardboard files which he labelled conspicuously, 'The Lord Harridge Case', 'Mr Jocelyn Mountjoy and others', 'The Weir Case', and so on.

He purchased many tins of cigarettes, and he sat at his desk all day long, waiting for answers to his advertisement, which appeared regularly in several daily papers. He smoked cigarettes and read detective stories. He always had a drawer open so that if anyone called he could slip the book away. He had a shrewd suspicion that real detectives didn't read detective stories.

It was on the tenth day that the astonishing thing happened. He had gone out to lunch and was feeling a trifle discouraged concerning his enterprise. On returning to his 'office' he found a dark, foreign-looking gentleman reading his notice printed on the door: 'Out at lunch, back in twenty minutes.' The foreign gentleman started at sight of him and exclaimed:

'Mr Pimpleton?'

'That's me,' said Freddie.

'I wish to see you urgently.'

'Come inside, Mr—er—'

They went inside, and Freddie smuggled away *Jim Slooth's Last Case* just in time. They both sat down and Freddie said:

'Well, now, what can I do for you?'

The mysterious visitor looked furtively around. Then he said confidentially:

'You, I believe, handled ze case concerning ze stolen bonds for Count Tisza?'

'No.'

'What! But my sister understood from the Baron himself on the telephone this morning that you—'

'Oh, well, perhaps I did,' said Freddie, realizing he had made a bloomer. 'I have so many cases, you see, I'm apt to forget.' And he glanced significantly at his labelled files.

The foreigner glanced at the files, too, and seemed satisfied. Then he leant forward and tapped Freddie's knee.

'It does not concern that, anyway. It was only a recommendation. My sister, the Countess Sforza, is in great trouble. Listen!'

Fame at last! Freddie listened.

'Doubtless you know of her by reputation? Hein? Well, she has the beautiful place at Steeplehurst, in Sussex. This week she entertains a small house-party—seven guns. The guests arrived on Saturday last. On Sunday evening she goes to dress for dinner. Her pearl necklace, worth thousands of pounds, is missing. A search is made, but ze guests are not informed. Zey have all announce to stop one veek. All ze servants has been searched, and zeir boxes and properties. A detective arrive from Scotland Yard on ze Monday afternoon. He passes as a guest—a Mr Battesley. Zis is Wednesday afternoon. So far no clue, nozing discovered.'

'Perhaps it was a burglar,' said Freddie, brightly.

'Zere is no sign of burglary. No one has entered ze house unknown, or left it. Ze guests still remain. My sister—she is in despair. She rings up Count Tisza, an old friend. "Go to Pimpleton," he says; "he'll solve ze mystery for you." My sister bade me come to town at once to try to persuade you to return mit me. Zere is a train at five-ten vich gets us down in comfortable time for dinner.'

'All right, Mr—er—Forcer?'

'My name is Baron Hunyadi Sergius Szychylimski.'

'Oh, really! I see. Well, I'll just have to go home first.'

'Home!'

'Yes. I must go to Highgate and tell Dad and the others, and then pack up. I suppose you wear evening-dress for dinner down there, don't you?'

The baron seemed a little mystified. Perhaps he had misunderstood the English of this famous detective. He said:

'I will meet you on ze train, zen, Mr Pimpleton. And—one vord!—my sister suggest zat you come as a private gentleman, not a sportsman. Zat would give you ze excuse to hang about ven ze others are out. She suggest you come as a professor or scientist, or explorer. If zere is any special branch of science you have exceeded at or—doubtless you have travelled a lot. Vat do you suggest? Vat is your special genius?'

Freddie considered for some moments, then he said:

'Well, I'm not bad at snooker-pool.'

'Snookerpool!' The Baron turned the word over in his brain. Snookerpool sounded distinctly erudite. He was too polite to make enquiries. 'Goot, zen! We vill say ze eminent authority on Snookerpool. What name shall we announce?'

'My name's Oppincott. I mean—why not call me Mr Oppincott?'

'Mr Oppincott, se Snookerpoolist. Goot!'

Luckily for Freddie, when he got home neither his father nor John had returned from business. The two girls were there, and he announced with magnificent calm that he was called away on a case to recover the Countess Forcer's pearl necklace. The girls for a long time thought he was fooling. It was not until he had commandeered John's evening dress, shoes, collar, tie, and splutter brush and packed these things that they began to take him seriously.

He caught the train by the skin of his teeth. He would, indeed, have missed it, but for the fact that the Baron was waiting for him feverishly by the booking office, with two first-class tickets already taken. They scrambled into the train.

The journey down was uneventful. Freddie talked all the time, but it was difficult to know how far the Baron was impressed. He wanted to talk about the case, but he got little opportunity. He only managed to impress one thing on Freddie. He was not to make himself known to the other detective—Mr Battesley. The Countess was disappointed that Mr Battesley had so far not even got a clue. Pimpleton was to work on his own lines, and of course he was to have free run of the house.

When they arrived at Steeplehurst Towers, they found two tired colonels drinking cocktails in the lounge hall. The rest of the party were dressing for dinner. The Baron introduced Freddie to the two colonels as 'Mr Oppincott, ze eminent authority on Snoddlepole.' It was fortunate that he had forgotten the word snooker-pool, because if the matter had been put to the test either of the tired colonels could have given Freddie fifty per cent on any game played on the green baize. They regarded him languidly, either too polite or too bored to inquire what Snoddlepole was.

The Countess was very anxious to see Mr Pimpleton, and he was ushered up to her boudoir at once. He felt a little dubious about removing his cloth cap (with ear flaps). No detective looks the real thing without such. It was only the questioning and rather challenging glances of the two colonels in the hall which prompted him eventually to leave it behind.

The Countess was small and dark and agitated. The loss of her pearl necklace seemed to have driven her to a frenzy of lapidary display. She appeared to be wearing the remainder of her jewellery, in case that too was stolen. Her knowledge of English was far more limited than that of her brother. She began by saying:

'I spik English bad. My brozzer tell you of the lost pearl. Zis man, Battesley, he find nozing. It ees to you I look now. Zese guests depart Saturday. Zis is Vednesday. Ze house is disposed to you. Inquire, look, search as you vill. One vord also. Ze Baron and I, ve know of zis. No von else. Not even my daughter.'

'Righto,' said Freddie.

She came up to him and said, tensely:

'Listen. In ze short vile ze bell gongs to dinner. You gom to dinner? Or no? You stay here, perhaps, search ze guests' effects vile we hold zem at dinner? Perhaps you have dinner after by yourself. Hein?'

By the base of the hall staircase Freddie's nostrils had been assailed by an aroma that might have been roast pheasant, or it might have been roast quail. He was hungry. He replied:

'No, I think I'll start making my depositions after dinner, Countess. Work like mine can't be done on an empty stomach.'

He did not quite know what 'depositions' meant, but it was a word he had frequently come across in *Jim Slooth's Last Case*. It apparently impressed the Baron too, for he repeated, 'he makes depositions', and he translated it into the rummy lingo they spoke between them. The Countess appeared satisfied, and he was allowed to retire to his room and to put on John's evening clothes.

When he found himself seated at the dining table, after having been introduced to the company as Mr

Toddingpot, the eminent authority on Snoddlepole, he rejoiced that he had made this decision. In the first place, the dinner was unbelievably good. He had never imagined such foods and wines existed. In the second place, he found himself sitting next to the daughter of the house. She was an extremely pretty girl, with dark, mischievous eyes, and she spoke English like a native. (He found out afterwards that she had been educated at Girton.) He found her an enchanting listener. There were nearly twenty guests seated round the table, and the noise of conversation was so loud that he almost had to shout into her ear. They were eating red mullet, when she suddenly said:

'I'm most thrilled that you are an authority on Snoddlepole, Mr Toddingpot.'

'Oppincott is my name,' said Freddie, in order to gain time.

'Of course. I'm so sorry. By the way, do you consider the Einstein theory is going to affect the practice of Snoddlepole?'

It was obvious that this was a dangerous woman. He was not going to enjoy himself so much as he had hoped. The only way to treat this onslaught was to counter it by asking questions of his own. He said, 'No' rapidly, and almost in the same breath:

'Are you Oxford or Cambridge?'

'Cambridge.'

'Good! I'm so glad. So am I. Can you float?'

'What? Companies?'

'You're pulling my leg, Miss Forcer.'

'You're asking for it, Mr Hottentot.'

There was a lot of fun in this girl. If she would only talk sensibly, about lawn tennis, for instance, or music-halls, or tobacco, he could have a good time with her.

He found himself eating pheasant when he suddenly remembered that he was a detective. He had to discover which of these guests had stolen the pearl necklace. He glanced round the table. A more unthieving-looking crowd had surely never foregathered. They all looked well off, well fed, and slightly vacant, entirely innocent of anything except the knowledge of what is done or what is not done. Stealing pearl necklaces is not done. No, there was only one saturnine-looking individual present at all. He was seated in the far corner.

'Who is that chap over there?' Freddie asked his neighbour.

'That's Mr Battesley.'

The real detective! That was no go, then. But still, you never could tell. A sleek exterior sometimes concealed an itching palm. That wasn't right. He was mixing things a bit, especially wines. He would have to keep a clear head for the great work in front of him. Depositions, eh?

When the dinner was over and the ladies had retired, Freddie realized that this was a good opportunity for him to commence his work. He went stealthily out of the dining room. He had reached the foot of the stairs when he heard a quiet voice behind say:

'Mr Oppincott!'

He turned. It was Battesley, the detective. An uncomfortable feeling crept over him. He had been told not to have anything to do with his rival. But there was a sense of power about this man a little difficult to ignore. The detective said:

'May I have a word with you in the billiard room?'

Freddie hesitated.

'Well, I don't mind playing you fifty up, but I've got some work to do.'

'Yes, yes, of course,' said Battesley, and led the way in. Having shut the door, he turned to Freddie and said:

'I have received information that you are a private detective that has been sent for at the Countess's direction. Here is my card. You know my mission here. The Countess is a very highly strung woman, a little impetuous. I think it will be to the advantage of all parties concerned, and most likely to be conducive of results, if we work together.'

'Oh, I don't know,' said Freddie, weakly.

'I am quite prepared to place at your disposal all the information I have so far acquired,' continued the detective, ignoring Freddie's protest. 'The Countess was wearing the necklace on the evening of the twelfth. On retiring to bed she locked the necklace up in her jewel cabinet. On the following evening, when she went to put it on, she found it to be missing.'

'Well, I never!' said Freddie.

'The key of the cabinet she kept in her chatelaine, which she carried about with her all day. No one could have entered her bedroom during the night. The doors were locked. The key must have been taken from her chatelaine during the day and replaced. The Countess says that, so far as she can remember, the chatelaine was never out of her sight. Of course, she put it down many times, on the piano for instance, and on the luncheon-table, but she never observed anyone touch it. It must have been done very deftly by someone who was near to her and very intimate.'

'Fancy!'

'I have made a careful inquiry into the character and record of everyone of the servants, and also of the guests. One of the under-gardeners has a bad record, but he was never seen to approach the house all day. There is no one else upon whom one would dare to cast the slightest suspicion. But in order not to run any risks I have, unbeknown to them, searched all their rooms, luggage, and effects. It seems probable that, if one of the guests had taken it, he would have made some excuse to get away as quickly as possible. But no one has intimated any desire to leave before next Saturday.'

'It's extraordinary, isn't it?' said Freddie. 'Perhaps she dropped it somewhere. Did you look under the bed?'

'Now you are a young man,' the detective continued. 'And I observed that you were not altogether repulsed in your attentions to the daughter of the house, Miss Olga

Szychylimski. It is there that I think we may stumble on some solution.'

'The daughter! You don't mean to say that you think she pinched it?'

'You may have observed that the Countess and her daughter are hardly on speaking terms. There has been a row. The daughter wishes to marry a profligate young man named Julius Stinnie. The mother won't hear of it. She has not even informed her daughter about the necklace. This young man has been forbidden the house, but he haunts the neighbourhood. The daughter meets him clandestinely.'

'Well, you do surprise me!' exclaimed Freddie. 'I thought she seemed a top-hole girl—a bit too clever, perhaps.'

'I am, of course, working entirely on a supposition. The young man has no money and is a *roué*. Nevertheless, he is well-connected. He would probably be able to dispose of a pearl necklace among some of his associates. Whether he has been able to persuade the daughter to connive at the theft remains to be seen. Whether it was she who actually removed the necklace and passed it on to him remains to be proved, but no one has more intimate knowledge of the Countess's movements and habits, or an easier access to her person. I have tried to make friends with her, but she repulses me. That is where I think you might succeed. She has obviously taken to you. You could keep her under observation. Take her out on the river, pump her, make love to her if you like.'

Oh, if only John could hear all this! He, the despised Freddie, being appealed to by a real detective, and urged to make love to the daughter of a countess! A glow of manliness crept over him. He wanted to say:

'Yes, we professionals must stick together. I will sacrifice myself. The girl shall be made love to.'

And yet he did not like Battesley. There was something hard, cruel, and forbidding about the man. It seemed shabby to make love to a girl in order to worm secrets out of her. It seemed shabbier to get someone else to do it for you. The manliness wavered.

'I will think over what you say, Mr Battesley,' and he bowed in quite a dignified manner and left the room.

In the morning he wondered whether the other detective had told him the story to put him off the scent. If he went punting about the river with Olga he would be out of the way, and the coast would be clear for Battesley to do as he liked. Ha, ha! No, he was not going to be taken in like that. He went down to breakfast determined to act on his own. But how? He hadn't the faintest idea how to begin. Thank goodness, Battesley had searched all these people's private rooms and effects. It would save him from a most distasteful task.

After breakfast the Countess sent for him.

'Vell?' she said. 'You make some discover? Yes?'

'Not yet,' replied Freddie. 'I am making my depositions. I have several people under close observation.'

'No clue yet?'

'Not yet.'

'Vell, the house is disposed to you. It is urgent. I trust you.'

'I'm sure, Countess, you'll have no cause to ultimately regret it,' said Freddie, splitting his infinitive with a magnificent gesture.

In the garden he found Olga among the phlox and campion. She looked wickedly attractive.

'Good-morning, Mr Oddinglot,' she said. 'Come for a little punt up the reach, will you?'

Now this was just what he had decided not to do. It was what Battesley wanted him to do—to get rid of him. His duty was to hang about the house and search for the pearl necklace. Great bumblebees hung heavily on the phlox. The air was filled with their droning, and with the song of birds, and the distant lowing of cattle.

'I should love to,' he said.

In half-an-hour's time they were gliding up a backwater.

Fortunately he could punt—not very well, but sufficiently well to get the boat along. He slowed up among the reeds and rested.

'Now I want you to tell me all about Snoddlepole,' she said.

Freddie lit a cigarette.

'As a matter of fact,' he replied, after a lengthy pause, 'I'd rather not talk about Snoddlepole. When I'm on a holiday I like to get away from it.'

'Are you on a holiday?' she said. Olga was one of those ingenuous girls who exude omniscience, or if there is something they do not know, *you* are not going to find out. Her dark eyes mocked him.

'I'm having a very nice holiday, thank you,' he said, simply.

She laughed. 'Tell me all about yourself. You amuse me.'

This was the kind of invitation Freddie liked. Without any preamble he told her all about Dad and John and Emma and Jane, about his own chequered career right up to the time when he became a detective.

'And what are you doing now?' she asked.

'I'm resting on my punt pole,' he answered.

Oh, very clever, Master Freddie! He was feeling extremely happy and pleased with himself.

'This is all very interesting,' the girl said. 'Only, considering what a lot of things you've crowded into your brilliant career, I don't see how you could have found time to become an authority of Snoddlepole.'

'Look here,' answered Freddie, 'that's all nonsense—it's a mistake. I don't even know what Snoddlepole is.'

The punt shook with the girl's laughter.

'What I want to know is—what are you doing here? Mother doesn't know you. Uncle doesn't know you. None of the guests knows anything about you. Uncle went up and fetched you from town, and now you don't even know what Snoddlepole is!'

She was too clever for him. She was manœuvring to defend her lover, of course, the man who had stolen the necklace.

'Do you want me to go away?' he said, not without bitterness.

'Oh, no. I like you. It's jolly to have someone really young and innocent about the place.'

Little devil! 'I think we'll push on a bit.'

They did not get back till lunchtime: the girl, mischievous and provocative; the boy, bewildered and fascinated.

'I'll play you at tennis this afternoon,' she said.

'She doesn't mean to leave me alone,' he thought. 'Oh, well—'

After lunch the Countess sent for him.

'Vell, have you any clue yet?'

'Not yet, Countess, but I have every hope.'

'Is there anyone you suspect?'

'I'd rather not say for the moment.'

'Bien!'

Battesley nodded at him approvingly as he entered the luncheon-room. Most of the elder men were out shooting and would not be back until the evening. During the course of lunch Freddie decided that Battesley was right. It was this girl's lover who had stolen the necklace. Her whole manner indicated it. She suspected him of being there as a spy and she was going to look after him. Instead of him spying upon her, she was going to spy upon him. She had him in her clutches. Well, he wouldn't play tennis with her. He would refuse. He would begin to make his own researches. But—? It seemed much more difficult to be a detective than the storybooks had led one to suspect. This man Battesley apparently worked on a system. He would go up to his own room after lunch and think the whole thing out.

When the rest arose from the table he avoided Olga's glance, slid out of the room, and dashed upstairs and locked his door. He then remembered that he had never sent a postcard home, as promised. So he wrote, saying that he had arrived, that he had not yet traced the Countess's necklace, but that he was getting together some important information and hoped to trace the thief by Saturday, when he returned. (He afterwards put this postcard on the hall table with some other letters for the post.)

He had just written his postcard when there was a knock at the door. He opened it. It was Olga. She said demurely:

'Oh, Mr Loppinott, I'm so sorry to disturb you, but a young couple have just arrived and want to play tennis. I do wish you would come and make up a four. There is no one else.'

What was he to do? He played tennis till teatime. The young couple departed, and then Olga said:

'Now, wouldn't you like to take me on the river again?'

No. A thousand times, no! She touched him ever so gently on the forearm.

'You had better put on your sweater. It sometimes gets suddenly chilly in the evening.'

A starling was making an awful to-do up in the apple tree.

'Right. Oh, thanks awfully. Of course I would.'

When he found himself once more among the reeds up that backwater, and Olga was playfully letting the stream trickle through her white fingers, he knew that the reason he wanted to avoid her was that if it were true that her lover had stolen the necklace, he didn't want to be the one instrumental in discovering the fact. He didn't want to be associated with anything that would give her pain. Indeed, he wanted to bring her joy and happiness. He wanted to take her in his arms and say:

'I love you. I love you. I love you.' Or words to that effect.

Her face caught the reflected glitter from the water. She was wearing most exquisite openwork silk stockings.

'I'm not cut out for a detective,' he thought to himself.

'Well, my pensive friend?' she said, after he had been gazing at her abstractedly for at least five minutes.

'Life's a rummy go,' he said, dolefully.

'It is, indeed,' agreed she, eagerly. 'Your perspicacity leaves me breathless.'

As though accepting that as a challenge, Freddie stumbled across the punt and sat in the seat facing her. Her eyes were watching him questioningly. He took his courage in both hands and both her hands. He said:

'I shan't want to go back on Saturday.'

She made no attempt to withdraw hers. She looked at him quizzically.

'Won't you? But your mission will be accomplished.'

'What mission?'

'Oh, I forgot you're just here on a holiday, Mr Polyglot.'

'Be serious with me for five minutes. This fellow you're engaged to—'

'What's that?'

She withdrew her hands. Her eyes narrowed.

'I know all about it. You're going to marry that chap Julius Stinnie.'

'Who told you that?'

'It wouldn't be fair to say.'

The expression of her face suddenly changed. She spoke rather bitterly.

'Since it seems to interest you, I'll tell you the truth. I'm not going to. It's off. I found out things that—well, anyway, it's off.'

Freddie's mentality received various shocks. Firstly, a shock of exultation. If Julius Stinnie was off, why should not Freddie be on? Secondly, but a much milder shock, a shock to his professional vanity as a detective. He was on the wrong track. He was doing just what Battesley wanted him to do—wasting two days making love to the daughter of the house, and it was all on a false scent. He registered a mental vow of revenge against Battesley. He must give this girl up and return to the fray.

He certainly did return, but it was nearly dark when the punt glided into the boathouse. The lawn was damp with evening dew, and the girl's hair was all awry.

The position, he now realized, would soon be getting desperate. After dinner another bright idea. He asked the Baron if he might see him and the Countess alone. Naturally. They received him in the boudoir.

'Please show me the key of the jewel-case at once, will you?'

The Countess produced it. He turned it over, held it up to the light, and repeated, 'Ah!' three times. The Countess was very impressed.

'Vell?'

'I can say nothing more tonight. Tomorrow I hope to spring a surprise—'

'Vat ees dat?'

'He springs a surprise to-morrow,' explained the Baron.

Freddie appeared to be thinking profoundly. He said 'Ah!' once more, and left the room without another word.

'This will be difficult to follow up,' he thought, as he went downstairs, not having the faintest idea what his various 'Ahs!' implied.

He found Olga in the drawing room with the rest of the party. She was in a high-spirited, ragging mood. He could not detach her from the rest. Her mocking laughter jarred him. He did not understand her. She was never serious for a moment. It was the first time he had met a girl of this kind. He was bewitched by her, and at the same time she made him feel wretched. Before the others she went out of her way to make him look a fool. And yet on the river—

He retired early and lay in bed trying to evolve 'depositions'. If only the Countess didn't keep on demanding clues! In the stories he had read they were usually footprints, or hairpins, or tobacco pouches. In any case, something solid. On the morrow he simply *must* find a clue. It would be his last chance. He slept at last, dreaming of the perfume of dark hair and of some very expensive and mysterious scent.

The next day was finer than ever. A thin mist hung over everything, presaging heat to come. After breakfast the Countess sent for him as usual. He experienced the familiar sensation of the schoolboy being hauled up before the headmaster for not learning his prep.

'Vell?'

How sick he was of it!

'To-day I expect to find a clue,' he said.

'He expects to find a clue,' echoed the Baron.

The Countess was looking annoyed and a little suspicious.

'Tomorrow they go,' she snapped.

'You may rely upon me, Countess,' wheedled Mr Freddie, his mind concentrated on a last day on the river.

But Olga didn't want to go on the river. She took him for a walk over a common. He was deliciously happy. Away from the others she was quite amenable and rather more than friendly. She did not object to his squeezing her hand, putting his arm round her waist, and on two occasions kissing her. Beyond that there seemed to be a kind of blank wall. He could not think of the right thing to say. She never attempted to talk to him seriously. She was amusing herself with him.

It took Freddie the whole morning to realize this, and when he did he felt desperate. He was madly in love with her, and she was as intangible as a myth.

Lunch was a dismal meal. He almost made up his mind to confess to the Countess and to return to town forthwith. But the lunch was a very excellent lunch, and afterwards he felt fortified. He strolled out into the rose-garden, sat on a bench in the sun, and smoked. It seemed a shame to have to leave all this. That wretched Countess with her clues! He simply must find something.

Suddenly he saw her coming in his direction through the pergola. He looked desperately around. The only solid thing that caught his eye was a small garden trowel. He stooped and picked it up. As she approached him, he went up to her and handed her the trowel.

'Look, Countess,' he said. 'I have found a clue.'

And without giving her time to ask questions, he hurried away in the direction of the house. He found Olga near the boathouse.

'Come,' he said, 'for the last time. Down the river. You must.'

She was carried away by his decisiveness, and in a short while they were gliding away down the river. And they had a very pleasant afternoon. Pleasant, in that youth is pleasant, and a sunny day. And dalliance is pleasant under a willow tree with the water musically lapping the sides of a punt. And it is pleasant to hold hands and to imagine that one is in love—if only for an hour. It is pleasant to believe that life is perpetuated in a gesture. To the girl it was a pleasant pastime. To the young man a desperate spiritual adventure. He knew that nothing would come out of it, and he didn't care. He saw himself clear and whole for the first time. During the most intriguing moments of this new ecstasy he was registering a vow to improve himself, to work, to learn, to study. He would go back and begin life anew.

'I love you so much that I am going to give you up,' he said.

'Before you talk of giving up, you must first postulate possession,' she answered.

He didn't know the meaning of the word 'postulate', so he kissed her lips, presumably in order to close them.

He decided to catch the six-fifteen back to town, and so, in spite of her protests, he manfully guided the punt back to Steeplehurst boathouse in time for tea. On arriving at the house, one of the servants told him that the Baron wished to see him in the rose-garden.

'My doom!' he thought. However, he went eagerly enough thither, anxious to get the whole thing over. He saw the Baron in conversation with an old man with white hair. As he entered the garden the Baron exclaimed:

'Oh, Mr Oppincott, Count Tisza himself has come over to see us.' The old Count came forward and then started at sight of Freddie.

'But this is not Ponderton!' he said.

'Ponderton?' said the Baron. 'Ponderton? Did you not say Pimpleton on ze 'phone?'

'Pimpleton! No, Ponderton. Ponderton, the great detective. Who is this fellow?'

It was an embarrassing position, but it was relieved in a most astonishing manner. The Countess came hurrying down the grass path. Within earshot she cried out:

'Oh, Mr Pimpleton! Mr Pimpleton!'

The three men turned. The Countess came up. In her right hand she held out a pearl necklace.

'Oh, Mr Pimpleton! how can I zank you?'

'But zis is not Pimpleton,' cried the Baron. 'I mean it is Pimpleton. It is not Ponderton.'

'Who vas Ponderton?'

'It should be Ponderton, but it is Pimpleton.'

'I know nozing. But I know it is he who find ze necklace. Listen, you all. I know not how Mr Pimpleton or Mr Ponderton work, on vat lines, no. But he zink, and zink, and zink, for two days. He not poke about like zis Battesley. He keep quiet and hide. And then, lo! presto! he find ze clue quick.'

'How do you mean?' exclaimed the Baron.

'Listen. Zis afternoon I find him here zinking in zis garden. I goes to him. He gives me a little—vat you call—trowel! He says, "Look here, ze clue!" Zen he go away. I hold ze trowel in my hand and I zink also. And suddenly it all come back to me. It was here in zis garden on ze Saturday ven ze pearls was stolen. I had put my chatelaine down on ze zeat here, so! Zey call to me to go to ze telephone. Ven I gom back I zee zat man, Ben Burnett, ze unter-gartener. He vas vorking quite near in ze beds. I zink he give me one funny look, but I take no notice. Ze chatelaine vas as it is! So! I zink no more about zis until just so soon. Ven I see ze trowel it all gom back. I suspicion him with certainty. I go right down quick to his cottage. I go in. He is there vis his wife, I accuse him. I say, "Vere is ze necklace you vas taken?" He says, no, but his wife burst vif tears. Zen I know. He too quite vite he goes. He bends ze knee. He tells me all. He vas vat you say, a tickets-of-leave man. He vas a bad man. But he lives straight, vasn't it? He implores forgiveness. His wife cries. She will ruin herself if he is taken. I give vay. I am veak. I restore me the necklace. I fogive him. I am so happy. Oh, Mr Pondleton, how can I zank you?'

'I only did my duty,' said Freddie, quickly.

'You will stay mit us over ze week-end, shust as a guest? Yes?'

'Alas, no,' answered Freddie. 'I must catch the six-fifteen. I have another urgent case.'

'Vell, vell!' cried the Baron. 'I must congratulate you, Mr Pinderton. Perhaps I was fortunate after all to make zis mistake on ze telephone, eh, Count?'

The Count was annoyed, but he shrugged his shoulders and bowed politely to Freddie.

He did not see Olga again. Close by the box-hedge near the summerhouse he heard her laughter, and her merry voice calling out, 'Fifteen-forty!'

She was playing a single with the curate.

'It's a rum, funny life,' he thought, as he sat back in the

corner of a first-class carriage going back to London. In his breast pocket was a cheque for one hundred pounds.

* * *

All this happened three years ago. It seems strange that after his brilliant start in the career of a private detective he no longer follows that calling. Indeed, he never received another commission.

He is now running a little shop where he sells foreign postage stamps, and is doing fairly well. He is married to a little girl, the daughter of an ironmonger. She is not clever, nor even pretty, but she has redeeming qualities. One is that she adores Freddie. She thinks he is handsome, loyal, and clever. She is enormously proud of him, and she believes in his story about the recovery of the Countess's pearls. Perhaps that is because he told her the truth about it. He also told the truth about it to John and Emma and Jane, but so embellished was it with romantic tissues that the Father of Lies himself might almost have claimed it as his own. What would you? A man must defend himself.

—XXVII—

'Page 189'

THERE IS ONE THEME over which the philosopher never tires of wagging his finger at us. It is that of the illusory character of riches. And there is, perhaps, no field in which his propaganda has been less fruitful of results. One does not argue with him, of course. No one argues with a philosopher; one treats him like a child. One may say that philosophy is and always has been one of the least potent factors in shaping human actions. Passion, greed, prejudice, heredity, love—even the daily press—have all done more.

And so again and again the philosopher and his father and his grandfather, right back to the days of Diogenes, have enlarged upon the fact that wealth cannot buy any of the things that matter; that riches do not make for happiness; that high thinking and low living is the better programme; that the rich man cannot pass through the eye of a needle. And we say: 'Yes, father. You're quite right.' And directly his back is turned, we immediately begin to think how best to collect the filthy impedimenta to true happiness. We are willing to take our chance about the needle. Perhaps we shall be the one in ten thousand who gets through. Anyway, it will be a pleasant journey. We are in good company. Smith, Jones, and Pierpont Morgan are all on the same road. If they negotiate the eye, why shouldn't we?

It is an undoubted fact that a vast percentage of the inhabitants of this earth, living in poverty, are in a condition of constant anxiety; are held together, are sustained through years and years of drab existences, by the vague hope that somehow, somewhere, by some means of which they see no tangible evidence, they will acquire—wealth. It is their constant dream; their obsession. If they knew for certain that there was no possibility of their ever becoming rich, they could not go on.

Old Tobias Tollery was not one of these unfortunate creatures. He was enormously wealthy and he despised wealth. Possibly because he had made his money himself, and for fifty years of his life had been a comparatively poor man. Now a wealthy man who despises wealth is, in the opinion of all right-minded people—a crank. And there is no gainsaying the fact that Old Tollery was a crank in every way. He looked like a crank. He dressed like a crank. He talked like a crank. He was a crank.

At the age of seventy-three he lived alone in a large house in the Cromwell Road, attended by two old servants. He spent most of his time in a laboratory which he had built on the top floor. He wore—anything comfortable which happened to be lying about. Flannel trousers and a tweed coat and a scarf; never a collar or a tie. He shuffled along at a great pace in his felt slippers, as though his body was trying to catch up with his large, bald head, which was always occupied with some urgent matter connected with test-tubes, and cylinders, and microscopes. He had innumerable relatives, who had discovered him in his old age, and who were always calling upon him, and to whom he was extremely rude. The sycophantic manner in which they accepted his rebuffs may have been one of the causes of his somewhat cynical regard for wealth. An old bachelor, seventy-three years of age, rather asthmatic, no particular ties or responsibilities—to whom was he going to leave all his money?

He had, however, one and—from the relatives' point of view—dangerous friend, old Simon Occleve. Simon Occleve was his lawyer: a man of similar age and disposition to Tobias himself. He was, indeed, his only friend: the only person in whose society Tobias expressed any pleasure. They dined together twice a week; sometimes lunched together at an imposing club in St James's Street, and on occasions Tobias would go down to Simon's house at Haslemere and spend a few days. Tobias would assuredly leave Simon part of his fortune unless, happily, the lawyer should die first.

It may be advisable at this point to enumerate the old gentleman's relatives. They consisted, roughly speaking, of two families—the Tollerys and the Bowers. All his immediate family were dead; but he had a married niece, Laura, married to a stationer in West Kensington, whose name was Valentine Bower, and they had living with them two middle-aged, unmarried daughters, Ethel and Clara Bower.

He also had a married nephew, the Reverend Guy Tollery, whose living was at Highgate, and whose wife—a keen-featured, domineering person—rejoiced in the name of Lettice. They, in their turn, had a profligate son, Harold, who had married a barmaid named Annie, a pretty, common, warm-hearted little thing, of whom he was quite unworthy. Harold and Annie Tollery had a small boy of five, named Richard.

These were the sum total of the old gentleman's relatives.

The financial status of the two families was somewhat similar. They had enough, but not sufficient. They suffered from a kind of financial unrest, owing to the unexpected propinquity of this rich uncle. Otherwise, they seemed to have plenty of money to pay their rent, buy good food and clothes, take reasonably long holidays, and get postage stamps (the postage stamps being principally required for the purpose of sending tactful appeals to Uncle Tobias). These appeals were always wrapped up in most plausible covers—church funds, extension of shop premises, education, etc. The old man always said: 'Rubbish and nonsense! Fiddlesticks!' But he invariably paid.

The only one he had ceased to help was Harold, who

was a notorious gambler, and had been caught out on two occasions telling Uncle Tobias a lie. But before dismissing him, he had delivered himself of a little homily. He had said:

'It's no good your coming to me again. I shan't help you. Go and educate yourself. You are not trying. My whole life has been spent on educating myself, and I'm still doing it. I ran away to sea at fifteen—the best education in the world. I settled in South Africa and observed. That is what education is—applied observation. I studied mining and chemistry. I went to South America, Mexico, and then the States. It was in the States I made my money—eventually, and quite unexpectedly. You know—the Tollery Tripod, an electric portable cooker. A ridiculous invention. I take no pride in it. It was just an accident during the course of my education. Go away and observe, and perhaps you'll learn not to be a fool.'

One night Tobias and Simon Occleve were dining alone in the large house in Cromwell Road. Their dinner consisted of a lemon sole, a cutlet, and a very ancient cheese. Tobias drank barley water, and Simon had a little weak whisky-and-water. When the meal was finished, Tobias lighted a long, thin cigar. He never offered them to his friend, because he knew he preferred a pipe. He waited till the old woman had cleared the things away, then, making himself thoroughly comfortable in the easy chair by the fire and observing that Simon was in a similar happy position opposite, he picked up the black cat from the rug and put it on his knee. He stroked the cat gravely with his long, knobbly fingers, until the purr of contentment attuned itself to the gentle harmony of the hour. Then he said:

'Simon, I am anxious to put myself under a further obligation to you.'

'Come, come,' smiled Simon; 'I don't realize any past obligations, Tobias. I am a professional man—a lawyer—one of these "thieving lawyers", you know. I always charge you for whatever I may have the good fortune to be able to do for you.'

Tobias pursed up his lips.

'Rubbish and nonsense! Your charges to me, I know, are nominal. But the obligations I am under do not principally concern professional matters.'

'Well, what can I do?'

'I want you to find me an acid test.'

'A chemical experiment?'

'Almost. Let us call it a psycho-physiological experiment.'

'You excite me profoundly, Tobias.'

'These people!' Tobias left off stroking the cat and waved his arm impatiently in the direction of the door. 'I am tired of it. Something has got to happen. Those two women, Laura, you know (Mrs Bower) and that clergyman's wife (Lettice)—they were here again this afternoon. It is "Uncle Tobs!" and "dear Uncle Tobs, won't you come to our Christmas party?" I'm not a hard man, Simon, although I've led a hard life. Even at my age I am loath to shut out all affection. I realize that my blood relations have a certain call on me. Only the holding of wealth makes one suspicious. I suspect everyone, and yet how do I know? Some of them may have a real affection for me. Since my return I have disbursed among my relatives some four thousand pounds; Harold alone relieved me of five hundred before I had been in the country a year. But my suspicions, founded upon close observation, are that the matter which interests them most deeply is the question of my demise. As you know, Simon, I have made no will. In the event of my death, the money will be divided by your meticulous care between all these people.'

'I have always wanted you to make a will, Tobias.'

'I know. I know. And I have always put it off. I am now coming to the opinion that I can put it off no longer.'

'I think you're right, Tobias. Have you formed any general or individual feelings with regard to your relatives?'

Old Tollery put the cat down and looked meditatively at the fire.

'I cannot abide that clergyman; but Lettice, although objectionable in many ways, I feel to be an honest woman. It is deplorable to have a profligate son. At the same time, I am sorry for Harold's wife—one of the pleasantest and least offensive of them all—and the boy might be a nice boy, if he had the chance of proper education. As for the Bowers, Valentine is a greedy nonentity, Laura is kind in a way, but embittered by a long life with a feeble partner. I sometimes think Ethel is a nice woman. I'm not sure that she has not a real affection for me, or if not, it is most cleverly simulated. I find her more companionable than the gloomy Clara, though Clara, curiously enough, is the only one who has never deliberately begged from me. I am wondering about Clara. I'm not quite certain...'

Simon took a spill and re-lighted his pipe.

'It is not for me to influence you in any way...Of course, there are institutions, hospitals. You have a pretty considerable fortune, Tobias.'

'Yes. I think I shall leave the bulk of my savings to Scientific Research, but I will reserve a sum—say twenty thousand pounds—for my relatives.'

Then he leant forward and added:

'Of course, old friend, if *you* would be happier with—'

But Simon immediately patted the other's knee vigorously.

'I appreciate what you are going to suggest thoroughly. But no, no, no. I am an old man, Tobias. It is very doubtful whether I shall survive you. In any case, I have more than enough for my needs to the end of my days. I should be happier if you willed the money elsewhere. Nevertheless, it is very kind, very kind and thoughtful.'

'Well, it must be like that then.'

'But this is all quite simple. What do you mean by the acid test, Tobias?'

'What I want to ask you to do is to find some way by which I can test the affection and friendship of my relatives. Give them all an equal chance. The one who proves him or herself the loyalest to me shall inherit—nay, shall have at once—the sum of twenty thousand pounds.'

Simon looked down into the bowl of his pipe; then he smiled and answered:

'Well, I am your lawyer. I must obey instructions. But you must give me time.'

'There is no hurry. In any case I do not mean to die for some months—not till I have completed a little experiment I am making concerning the extraction of nitrogen from the air.'

Simon spent three weeks thinking out his scheme, then he came to Tobias and said:

'I think, old friend, it would be better for me to reveal my plan to you by installments. In the first place, it will be necessary for me to relieve you of all your money.'

'I expected that.'

'Naturally. The most obvious plan, but a good groundwork.'

'Is it necessary to actually do so?'

'Not at all. They will accept my word.'

That same week every member of the Bowers and the Tollerys received an identical letter.

DEAR SIR OR MADAM,

Owing to the sudden liquidation of a large company in which he held important interests and the financial crisis arising therefrom, I am instructed by my client, Mr Tobias Tollery, to warn you that he will require the return of the sum of —— advanced to you as a loan by him on ——. My client will be glad if you will return the same without interest, or in lieu, as great a part of it as you are capable, by Saturday week next, the 4th prox.

Yours faithfully,

SIMON OCCLEVE.

The effect of this letter was electrical. At ten o'clock the next morning the old gentleman was disturbed at his breakfast by the appearance of Lettice Tollery and Harold.

'What does this mean, Uncle?' screamed Lettice. 'It doesn't mean you're losing your money, does it? It isn't serious, is it?'

'You see what my lawyer says. I leave everything to him.'

'Is he to be trusted?'

'Yes, he is!'

'But all your money is surely not in this company.'

'Practically.'

'It's madness! I can't believe it. Let us call in another lawyer.'

'Why add the expense?'

'What's the name of the company, Uncle?' asked Harold.

Before the old man had had time to formulate an answer, the door flew open and Mrs Bower and Ethel burst into the room. Ethel threw her arms round his neck.

'Oh, Uncle Tobs, tell us it isn't true!' she exclaimed.

'What does it amount to, dear?' breathlessly asked Mrs Bower.

'It's no good your all pestering me,' snapped the old man. 'I can tell you nothing. What Simon Occleve says—stands.'

'But I haven't got five hundred and sixty pounds to return,' said Mrs Bower.

'And I haven't got two hundred to my name,' said Mrs Tollery.

'And I haven't got a bean in the world,' said Harold, and he picked up his hat and walked out.

The storm raged for ten days. It was very trying for Tobias. It interfered with his experiment.

They swept backwards and forwards between the

Cromwell Road and Simon Occleve's office in the Temple. The old lawyer was terse and uncommunicative. No, Mr Tollery was not ruined. But he was badly hit. It all depended upon certain delicate financial operations during the next few weeks. In the meantime all available capital was necessary. The difficulty might right itself if Mr Tollery's debtors would fulfil their obligations. He could tell them nothing more.

The dreaded Saturday, the 4th prox., arrived. The two old gentlemen dined alone at the end of the day.

'I am quite surprised that our request has met with the response it has,' said Tobias, when they had reached the nicotine stage. 'Clara has surprised me most. She has sent forty pounds and a formal note of regret that it is not more. Lettice has sent fifteen pounds and a letter of vituperative aggression. No one else has sent money. The Reverend Guy has written a long letter forgiving me my past sins and hoping I may yet find grace in the eyes of God. He promises to send something later on. Valentine, a long whine of excuses. Ethel, gush and regrets. Mrs Bower, more excuses, and a kind of veiled threat. Harold, nothing at all. His wife, nothing at all. Now, what is the next move, Mr Lawyer?'

'We must be thorough. We must clean you of every penny.'

'The furniture?'

'My "bailiffs" will arrive next week to take possession!'

'I don't like doing this, Simon. It seems mean.'

'I am giving you the acid test.'

'Very well.'

The 'bailiffs' arrived on the same day that every member of the family received a letter, this time from Tobias:

DEAR —,

I have very serious news for us all. I regret to say that Mr Simon Occleve, whom I have always trusted and looked upon as my greatest friend, has absconded.

I am completely bankrupt. Another firm of lawyers is winding up my accounts.

Yours, etc.

T. T.

Within the hour Mrs Bower appeared with her husband, Valentine, and Ethel, and they were quickly joined by Lettice, who came alone. Tobias was busy in his laboratory, and thither they all pushed their way, and there was a great scene. It reached its climax when they learned that the two gentlemen in the hall were bailiffs. Even the furniture was lost. There was nothing to sell at all.

'And you sit here,' shouted Lettice, 'messing about with those stinking chemicals!'

'You've treated us disgracefully,' echoed Mrs Bower.

'What are you going to do, Uncle?' asked Ethel. 'You'll have to go to a workhouse.'

'I told you all the time that that lawyer was a common thief. You could see it in his face.' This was Lettice.

'You should never trust lawyers,' piped Valentine.

'I could see he was dishonest. Are the police on his track? We shall demand to know all the details.' The thin face of Mrs Bower was thrust forward, and she shook her curls at him threateningly.

'You'll mind your own business,' snapped Tobias, who was beginning to feel uncomfortable and angry. But the mask was off. There was no need for any further politeness.

'I shan't trouble to tell you what I think of you, you old fraud!' added Mrs Bower.

'If you had been a little more informing and friendly to your relations you wouldn't have got into all this mess. You might, for instance, have consulted the Reverend Guy. He's not an adventurer, and he's not wealthy, but he has sound practical sense. He would have looked after your affairs with pleasure.'

The old man surveyed Lettice through his thick glasses and remarked:

'Yes, I expect he would. Harold too, perhaps?'

'Harold has never robbed anybody.'

Just as they were all going, Tobias had a surprise. Valentine shuffled uncomfortably on the fringe of the crowd. The party had reached the door, when the little stationer returned and furtively thrust out his hand.

'Well, I'm damned sorry,' he said in his reedy voice, twirling his thin grey moustache with the other hand. 'It's damned hard lines.' Then he slunk away to the protection of his wife's skirts.

Simon wished to be thorough, but, like a good organizer, he always had an eye to economy. The next day several men appeared. The halls and staircase were gutted of furniture and carpets, which were placed carefully inside various rooms. Then the doors were locked and the shutters were put up. When the family next called, Tobias was apparently living in the laboratory, where an iron bedstead had been put in. He was to remain in possession of the house till quarter day, when he was going to Fulham Workhouse. He was also to be allowed to retain his laboratory equipment to that date. The old woman who waited on him had kindly consented to remain also. The house appeared to be empty and utterly desolate. The metamorphosis was complete. Tobias had everything he wanted in the laboratory, but it cannot be said that he was happy. The thing assumed larger dimensions than he had bargained for. It disturbed horrid emotions. 'Damn Simon,' he thought. 'It's positively cruel.'

He experienced sudden waves of pity for these unfortunate relatives which interfered with his work. The more contemptible and pitiable they were, the more sorry he was for them. What a terrible thing is this money-lust! They were not really in need. They could all, indeed—possibly with the exception of Harold—have paid him back. But they were mad to get his wealth. And in each one it produced an individual eruption. It made them give themselves away. It made him ashamed to enjoy the secret vision of so many naked souls. It was like eavesdropping, uncannily unfair. But he had placed himself in the hands of Simon, and he could not go back. During the weeks that followed he learnt all there was to learn about his blood relations.

Mrs Bower and Mrs Tollery called every day for a week, as though they could not credit the disaster. Mrs Bower continued her abuse and threats to the end of that time; then she vanished, and he never saw her again. Lettice called twice more, and was almost as vindictive, but in the end she said:

'Oh, well, if you want anything you must let us know. I don't say we'll do it, but you can let us know.'

Ethel did not come at all, but one day Clara appeared. She was surly and diffident. She neither criticized nor pitied him, but as she went, she put down another five pounds and said:

'I know I owe you more. That's the best I can do.'

Valentine did not call, but he wrote a letter marked '*private*', and said again that he was damned sorry and that it was a damned shame. Of Harold, of course, there was no sign; but one day his wife called with the little boy, Richard, who was five years old.

The mother looked worn and worried. She was losing her good looks and her quick little birdlike movements. Her eyes were ringed with dark circles. The boy, however, was a fresh-complexioned, jolly little fellow. He put out his arms and kissed 'Uncle Tobs' soundly and moistily on the cheek. And Tobias thrilled surprisingly. It was many years since he had been kissed by a child. A pleasant boy...If only he could be educated—escape from the demoralizing influence of his father. Tobias moved uneasily in his chair. He was under a compact with Simon. He must be entirely impartial with all the relatives. They must all have an equal chance. Above all, he must be reserved, abrupt, and rather taciturn.

'Are you reely ruined, Uncle Tobs?' said Annie Tollery. 'It's an awful thing. I know Harold treated you bad. What can we do? I hoped he might get another chance. It's the horses, you know, and the cards. He can't let it alone. He's not reely bad, Uncle, not vicious like, except sometimes when they make him drink. It's terrible for us, Uncle.'

She pleaded as though she, too, could not credit the disaster. Things must right themselves. Tobias said nothing, but once he patted the little boy on the head. Then he turned away to his bottles and powders.

'I must be getting on with my work,' he grunted.

Annie sniffed and blew her nose. As she was going out she put a paper bag down on the table and said:

'Here's just a little something. I made it myself.'

When they had gone he opened the parcel and found it contained a pork pie! And Uncle Tabs turned it over and stared at it. His lips trembled a little, and he replaced it on the table.

'It's very queer,' he mumbled.

That evening he dined again with Simon, and their dinner consisted of turbot, pork pie and salad. He did not tell Simon where the pork pie came from, but the lawyer gave it as his opinion that it was excellent. Over the fire he said:

'It is rather fortunate that just at this time I have opened a new office in Brick Court. Quite an inaccessible spot to the uninitiated. Of course, my old offices are still going, and it is also a little fortunate that the style of my firm is still "Messrs Mulberry & Platt", for, as you may imagine, we have had many visitors. It has been necessary to let my head clerk, Peters, into the secret. He reports that practically all your relatives have called. Peters is very mysterious and secretive. He is enjoying himself. "Yes," he says, "our Mr Occleve is away just now. I can't tell you more. Have you any demand or complaint against him?" And, of course, they haven't. It's no business of theirs. Peters is quite masterful. He tells them nothing, but gives an appearance of nervous agitation. He asks them endless questions. He is very sympathetic. When they go away they realize that they have done all the talking. They have learnt nothing but their feelings have been soothed by a kind of vague insinuation that "our Mr Occleve really must have absconded. It will all come out in due course. In the meantime, if you have any definite charges to make, etc."'

'I am beginning to wish the whole thing was over.'

'My dear Tobias, of course you are; and I am willing to end it at any time. But I should be glad of, at any rate, one more week of general discomfort. I want to disillusion you of the idea that people are wholly good or wholly bad. It is very unlikely that in the end you will feel that any one of your relatives stands out from the rest. You may want to divide the money equally, or shall we say equitably, according to the various ways they have treated you.'

'I am certainly learning a lot.'

During that last week Lawyer Occleve put three more tests to these good people, and they were all a repetition. They consisted of a letter from Tobias to each member of the family. He said he was unwell and obliged to keep his bed. He specified three nights, Tuesday, Thursday or Saturday. He had not the means to invite them to dinner, but would they come in afterwards and read a scientific book to him for a couple of hours? It was November and the nights were cold, and dark, and wet.

In reply to this the Reverend Guy sent him a tract called, *Am I Walking in My Master's Footsteps?* Valentine wrote and said he would have come, but he was no reader; at the same time, he thought it was a damned shame.

No one else answered. On the Tuesday, much to his surprise, Lettice appeared. She was in a very bad temper, and she had lost her umbrella on the bus coming along. She bullied him, but read a few chapters of a book on *Crystals*. She read so badly that Tobias was rude to her at the end of half an hour. She rounded on him for having dragged her all that way for nothing. She said she had had a headache and must go. Tobias was relieved when she went. He noted that she had read as far as page sixty-three. On Thursday no one came at all, but Ethel sent a postcard to say she had meant to come on Tuesday, but was prevented at the last minute. She couldn't possibly manage either of the other two nights. She hoped he was going on all right, and that things might right themselves. On the last night of the tests the two old gentlemen dined together again. It was considered so remote a possibility that anyone would come that they decided to sit upstairs in the laboratory. Tobias would wear his dressing gown, and if anyone should come, he would slip into bed, whilst Simon would hide behind the curtain which concealed the sink and lavatory at the end of the room.

The night was very dark and the wind was moaning round the skylight, but the two old friends were in good spirits. Tobias lighted his cigar and Simon his pipe, and they discussed cheerfully the better times to come.

'I am very grateful to you, Simon,' said Tobias. 'I certainly know how I stand, but I am very relieved that it is all over.'

'Yes, yes. Well, we will make plans. We'll soon get you straight again. And while the change is being effected you must come down to Haslemere with me. But come, you were just going to tell me of this new idea of yours with regard to the fourth dimension.'

Tobias's eye lighted up. He peered above the ash of his cigar and cleared his throat.

'The idea came to me on reflecting over this discovery

of Professor Einstein with regard to the curvature of light. One presupposes that the stellar system—damn!'

'What's the matter, Tobias?'

'Didn't you hear? It was the bell.'

'Oh!'

Simon walked stealthily to the door and opened it. The wind seemed to have found its way into the great corridors and passages. He heard the heavy laborious tread of old Mrs Turner coming slowly up the stone staircase from the basement. She carried a lantern, for the house was in complete darkness, the electric light being presumably cut off. Tobias switched off the light in the laboratory and lighted a paraffin lamp.

'Thank God!' he murmured. 'This is the last test. If it's Lettice, I shall simply be rude again.'

'No, no, you must be fair,' said Simon. 'Remember she got as far as page sixty-three.'

Tobias got into bed, but Simon hovered by the door. He heard the old woman go wheezing across the hall and slip back the chain on the front door. He listened intently and then drew back into the room.

'It's a man,' he said. 'I couldn't see whom.'

He walked quietly across the room and took up his position behind the curtain. Tobias again muttered 'Damn!' and settled down to the posture of the invalid. He was in a very bad mood. He had been robbed of a cigar in its most intriguing phase, and of the development of an interesting theory at its very birth. They could follow the slow progress of Mrs Turner, in the van of her late visitor, from floor to floor. Her steps resounded on the bare boards, but the man they could not hear at all. On the landings she stopped to get her breath, and her pulmonary disturbances carried above the wind. The journey seemed interminable. At last she fumbled against the latch of the door.

'A gentleman to see you, sir.'

Simon peered through the crack of the curtain and Tobias turned his weary head in her direction.

In the doorway stood—Harold!

'He's shaved off his moustache,' was the first thought which flashed through the mind of Tobias.

There was something phantom-like, unconvincing about the figure of Harold. He appeared almost to hesitate whether to advance or to bolt from the room again. He looked sideways at Mrs Turner and did not speak until she had closed the door. Then he walked gingerly up to the bed and said: 'Hallo, Uncle.'

The visit was so unexpected, and the appearance so surprising, that the old gentleman had no difficulty in simulating the dazed outlook of the invalid. He put out his hand without speaking.

Harold took it and laughed nervously.

'I've come, you see,' he stuttered at length, and glanced from the invalid to the dim recesses of the laboratory. He seemed to be listening to the retreating footsteps of Mrs Turner.

'Sit down,' said Tobias, and he pointed to a chair by the lamp.

'Bit lonely here, ain't you, Uncle? All alone in the house, eh? Except for the old—' he jerked his thumb in the direction of the door.

'What's his game?' thought Tobias, and he began to idly speculate upon the young man's motives and character. His thin, rather clever, dissolute face appeared in blotches of irregular colour. His eyes were unnaturally bright. He was red round the temples, but his lips and chin were white. He appeared to be shivering, although the room was warm.

On the table, by the lamp, was an old and heavy volume on *Crystals*. Tobias pointed a long finger at it and remarked:

'There's the book.'

Harold appeared startled, as though he did not understand. He muttered:

'Eh? ... the book?'

'Yes, you have come to read to me, haven't you?'

He stared at the book as though mesmerized by its ancient pattern. He touched it with his fingers and turned it over. Then he sniggered again.

'Eh? Oh, yes, of course.'

'Sit down then and begin at page one.'

Harold obeyed. He thrust the book as near under the lamp as possible and found the place. Then he coughed and looked round at Tobias.

'Go on. Begin at the first paragraph.'

He stared at the page for a long time, as though he was not seeing it. Then hesitatingly he began to read. Curiously enough, after the first few paragraphs, he read quite well. His voice was thin and without resonance, but he spoke distinctly and as though the words had meaning. Now and then he would stop and glance furtively round the room. He did not look at Tobias. The wind was still moaning against the skylight; otherwise the room seemed unnaturally silent and remote. At the end of a chapter he sat feverishly rubbing his chin and temple, like an animal heated in the chase. Then he plunged into the book again as though it held some secret charm against a sinister menace. Tobias made no comment; he lay there listening and watching. The night grew late and still Harold read on. Doubtless by this time the old woman would have gone to her bed in the basement. She was rather deaf...very feeble. A long way off could occasionally be heard the hoot of a motor-horn. The room was getting cold. Harold stumbled on, beginning to read huskily. Suddenly he turned over a page and gave a cry...

He started up and stared hard at Tobias. The old man was observing him intently.

'What is this? What is the meaning of this, Uncle?'

In his hand he held a thin, half-sheet of notepaper on which was written the word 'Stop'. Beneath this sheet of paper was a Bank of England note for one thousand pounds. Across his face there swept a mingled expression of amazement, fear, greed, and a kind of desperate resolve. What his immediate action would have been is open to conjecture, for he was subjected to a further startling shock. He seemed to hear a movement behind him and turning, he beheld the trim figure of Lawyer Occleve, standing by the curtain and idly toying with a long, steel straight-edge.

'Perhaps you will allow me to explain on behalf of my client.'

The acid tones of the lawyer's voice seemed to bite the air. He pointed at the chair and continued:

'You may sit down. There is nothing to be alarmed about. The money is yours. My client, as you know, is what is known as a crank. In one of his eccentric moods he set his relatives this little test. When he is old, penniless, and ill, of no use to any of them, whoever has sufficient charity of heart to turn out on a cold night and come and read an uninteresting book to him so far as page 189 shall have a thousand pounds. This is only one of many little tests which, in his fanciful way, he has conceived.'

Harold stood up.

'But I don't get the thousand pounds? Not for that? Not just for doing that!'

'Yes, the money is yours.'

And suddenly the young man behaved in a most peculiar way. He flung the note from him, and burying his face in his hands, he burst into sobs.

'No, no, no . . . I can't. You don't know. I'm bad, but—my God! no!'

'My client is not so poverty-stricken as circumstances may appear.'

'I know all that.'

He looked at Tobias and fell on his knees by the bed.

'Do you know why I came to-night?' he said hoarsely.

'Why?'

'I came to rob you.'

He spoke rapidly, as though the relief of confession might be thwarted by some further development. 'I've signed on for an oil ship leaving Tilbury at eight in the morning for South America. I was desperate. Do you remember, Uncle, telling me about education? Applied observation, you called it. Well, I've done a bit of applied observation over this game. I knew there was something on. I've been watching. I followed one of these "bailiffs" to an office in Brick Court, and I watched that, and one day I saw Mr Occleve come out and get into a car, in which was Mr Peters. I was outside here one morning at six o'clock. I saw the men gutting the halls and staircases, but I never saw no furniture vans come to take the things away. So I reasoned they were still here, and the house was full of valuables, and there was some game on. I didn't know what it was. But it looked like some plan to let the whole family in. Whatever happened, I knew I stood to get nothing. If there was a will I shouldn't be in it. My only chance was to find a will and destroy it; then I should be in the share-out. I came tonight to—see if I could find a will. If I couldn't, I was going to take anything I could find and clear out. I was going to take it, mind you. I wasn't going to be scrupulous how. There was only the old woman...I never saw you come in, Mr Occleve.'

'No? Well, since you are making an honest confession, I will tell you that I have an entry from the mews at the back through the basement. And might I ask what you were prepared to do if any of the other relatives called?'

'Yes. I got Annie to write to them all to say that she was coming. And, as a matter of fact, she was. She wanted to come. Then at the last minute I sent her a telegram to say that her mother was sick at Hendon. I knew that would fetch her off.'

'Then your wife didn't know you were coming here?'

'No.'

'Does she know you're going away?'

'No.'

'Well, how will she manage?'

'She'll be glad. She'll manage somehow like the others. I've never been no use to her.'

Suddenly he turned to Tobias and said eagerly:

'Uncle, if you can spare it—send her this thousand quid. I don't want it. I've always been a gambler, and ready to take my chance. Perhaps, in a way, it would make up a bit for the way I've mucked things. She's been a good girl and little Dick…'

Tobias coughed and spoke for the first time.

'Very well. Give me an address. I can write to you.'

'My name's Thomas Carter. I suppose "*Poste restante*, Buenos Aires" would find me. You're not going to give me in charge, then, Uncle?'

'No. I've nothing to charge you with except—stupidity. When you get to South America, try and apply your observation to more worthy ends. Your wife shall be provided for. Good night!'

And the little old man got out of bed and lighted a cigar.

Harold stumbled forward and held out his hand.

'Good-bye, Uncle, and God bless—'

Tobias gave the hand a little jerky pressure and muttered:

'All right, all right. If you are in difficulties, call on my agent in the Plaza Gonzalo in Buenos Aires. He may have word from me. Switch on the electric light in the hall as you go out, and pull the door to. Goodbye.'

The two old gentlemen sat facing each other. They heard the footsteps of Harold hurrying down the stairs, the click of the electric light switch, and the bang of the front door. Then Tobias stood up and walked slowly across the room.

'It is late, Simon; but I think a little night-cap, eh?'

'I am of opinion that it would be appropriate, and well-deserved.'

They each compounded their own mixture. Tobias took three short sips; then he said:

'With regard to the theory of the curvature of light, my opinion is…'

* * *

If you had access to the secret archives locked in one of Lawyer Occleve's safes, you might come across a very remarkable document. It is the will of Mr Tobias Tollery. It would astound you with its lucidity. You would be in a quandary to know whether to praise more highly the fine craftsmanship of its construction or the broad-minded liberality of its intention. Various institutions working for the betterment of mankind are not only generously endowed, but are given an invaluable lead in the wide interpretation of their activities. Towards the end, under the head of 'Family Bequests', the phraseology appears to belong to another mood, as though a lawyer had worded the earlier portions, but had left this purely domestic section to the will-maker himself. It runs as follows:

> To my relatives I bequeath such sums as appear to be merited by their behaviour to me when I endured a period of great distress. To those of them who returned me a portion of the money I lent them, I bequeath it a hundredfold. That is to say, to Clara Bower, who returned me forty-five pounds, I bequeath four thousand five hundred. To Lettice, Mrs Guy Tollery, who returned fifteen pounds, I bequeath fifteen hundred pounds. To

Valentine Bower, because he said he was 'damned sorry', I leave five hundred pounds. To the Reverend Guy Tollery I leave a dressing-case and a new set of false teeth, as a memento of me. To Mrs Valentine Bower and her daughter Ethel, I leave two hundred pounds each, for no reason other than that I am a fool. To Annie, wife of Harold Bower, because she one day brought me a pork pie when she thought I was hungry, and who would have read to me quite disinterestedly only that her husband prevented her, I leave the residue of my estate to be held in trust for her son Richard, for whom I have formed a real affection.

This represented the family bequests of Tobias Tollery, no mention being made of what he had done for them in life, or of a Quixotic act of generosity he afterwards performed for a man who would have murdered him.

Whether all these liberal benefices will ever be distributed as ordained is still an open question, for old Tobias is still alive, and he hasn't yet completed his experiment with regard to the question of extracting nitrogen from the air.

—*XXVIII*—

The Brown Wallet

GILES MEIKLEJOHN was a beaten man. Huddled in the corner of a third-class railway carriage on the journey from Epsom to London, he sullenly reviewed the unfortunate series of episodes which had brought him into the position he found himself. Dogged by bad luck! … Thirty-seven years of age; married; a daughter ten years old; nothing attained; his debts exceeding his assets; and now—out of work!

He had tried, too. A little pampered in his upbringing, when the crisis came he had faced it manfully. When, during his very first year at Oxford, the news came of his father's bankruptcy and sudden death from heart failure, he immediately went up to town and sought a situation in any capacity. His mother had died many years previously, and his only sister was married to a missionary in Burma. His accomplishments at that time? Well, he could play cricket and squash rackets; he knew a smattering of Latin and a smudge of French; he remembered a few dates in history, and he could add up and subtract (a little unreliably). He was good-looking, genial, and of excellent physique. He had no illusions about the difficulties which faced him.

His father had always been a kind of practical visionary. Connected with big insurance interests, he was a man of large horizons, profound knowledge, and great ideals. Around his sudden failure and death there had always clung an atmosphere of mystery. That he had never expected to fail, and was unprepared for death a week before it happened is certain. He had had plans for Giles which up to that time he had had no opportunity of putting into operation. The end must have been cyclonic.

Through the intervention of friends, Giles obtained a situation as clerk in an insurance office, his wages amounting to fifteen shillings a week, a sum he had managed to live on. In the evening he attended classes, and studied shorthand and typewriting. At first the freshness of this experience, aided by youth and good health, stimulated him. But as time went on he began to realize that he had chosen work for which he was utterly unsuited. He worked hard but made no progress. He had not a mathematical mind; he was slow in the up-take. The chances of promotion were remote. The men around him seemed so quick and clever. At the end of two years he decided to resign and try something else. If only he had been taught a profession! After leaving the insurance office he went through various experiences: working at a seedsman's nursery, going round with a circus, attempting to get on the stage and failing, working his passage out to South Africa, more clerking, nearly dying from enteric through drinking polluted water, working on an ostrich farm, returning to England as a male nurse to a young man who was mentally deficient.

It was not till he met Minting that he achieved any success at all. They started a press-cutting agency in two rooms in Bloomsbury. Minting was clever, and Giles borrowed fifty pounds (from whom we will explain later). Strangely enough the press-cutting agency was a success. After the first six months they began to do well.

It was at that time that he met Eleanor. She was secretary to Sir Herbert Woolley, the well-known actor-manager, and she happened to call one day concerning the matter of press cuttings for her employer. From the very first moment there was never any question on either side but that both he and she had met their fate. Neither had there been an instant's regret on either side ever since. They were completely devoted. With the business promising well, he married her within three months. It is probable that if the business had not existed he would have done the same. They went to live in a tiny flat in Maida Vale, and a child was born the following year.

A period of unclouded happiness followed. There was no fortune to be made out of press cuttings, but a sufficient competence to keep Eleanor and the child in reasonable comfort. Everything progressed satisfactorily for three years. And then one July morning the blow fell. At that time he and Minting were keeping a junior clerk. Giles and Eleanor had been away to the sea for a fortnight's holiday. Minting was to go on the day of their return. When Giles arrived at the office he found the clerk alone. To his surprise he heard that Minting had not been there himself for a fortnight. He did not have long to wait to find the solution of the mystery. The first hint came in the discovery of a bank counterfoil. Minting had withdrawn every penny of their small capital and vanished!

Giles did not tell his wife. He made a desperate effort to pull the concern together, but in vain. There were a great number of outstanding debts, and he had just nine shillings when he returned from his holiday. He rushed round and managed to borrow a pound or two here and there, sufficient to buy food and pay off the clerk, but he quickly foresaw that the crash was inevitable. He had not the business acumen of Minting, and no one seemed prepared to invest money in a bankrupt press cutting agency. In the midst of his troubles the original source of the fifty pounds, upon which he started the business, wrote peremptorily demanding the money back. He went there and begged and pleaded, but it was obvious that the 'original source' looked upon him as a waster and ne'er-do-well.

He went bankrupt, and Eleanor had to be told. She took it in just the way he knew she would take it. She said:

'Never mind, darling. We'll soon get on our feet again.'

She had been a competent secretary, with knowledge of French, bookkeeping, shorthand and typewriting. She set to work and obtained a situation herself as secretary to the manager of a firm of wallpaper manufacturers, housing the child during the day with a friendly neighbour.

Giles was idle the whole of August. They gave up the flat and went into lodgings. In September he got work as a clerk to a stationer. His salary was thirty shillings a week, a pound less than his wife was getting. He felt the situation bitterly. Poor Eleanor! How he had let her down. When he spoke about it though she only laughed and said:

'If our troubles are never anything worse than financial ones, darling, I shan't mind.'

They continued to be only financial ones till the following year when Eleanor became very ill. She gave birth to a child that died. In a desperate state Giles again approached the 'original source'. After suffering considerable recrimination and bullying he managed to extract another ten pounds, which quickly vanished. It was three months before Eleanor was well enough to resume work, and during that time they lived in a state of penury. Giles lived almost entirely on tea and bread, and became very run down and thin. He pretended to Eleanor that he had had an increase, and that he had a good lunch every day, so that all the money he earned could be spent on her and the baby. In the meantime he dissected desperately that grimmest of all social propositions—the unskilled labour market. If only he had been taught to be a boot maker, a plumber, or a house painter he would have been better off. Manners may make men, but they don't make money, and one has to make money to live. He became envious of his fellow clerks and shop assistants who had never tasted the luxurious diet of a public-school training. That he had brains he was fully aware, but they had never been trained in any special direction. They were, moreover, the kind of brains that do not adapt themselves to commercial ends.

He had always had a great affection for his father, but he began to nurture a resentment against his memory. His father had treated him badly, bringing him up to a life of ease and assurance, and then deserting him.

It would be idle and not very interesting to trace the record of his experiences during the next years up to the time when we find him in the train on the way back from Epsom. It is a dreary story, the record of a series of dull underpaid jobs, a few bright gleams of hope, even days and nights of complete happiness, then dull reactions, strain, worry, hunger, nervous fears, blunted ambitions, and thwarted desires. Through it all the only thing that remained unalterably bright and inspiring was his wife's face. Not once did she flinch, not once did she lose hope. Her constant slogan: 'Never mind, old darling, we'll soon be on our feet again,' was ever in his ears, buoying him up through the darkest hours.

And again he was out of work, again Eleanor was not well, and again he had been to the 'original source'.

The 'original source' was his uncle, his father's brother. He was a thin, acid old gentleman, known in commercial circles as a money-maniac. Living alone in a large house at Epsom, with all kinds of telephonic connections with the city, he thought and dreamed of nothing at all but his mistress—money. Between him and Giles's father had always existed a venomous hatred, far more pronounced on the side of his uncle than of his father. It had dated back many years. When his father died and Giles appealed to his uncle, the old gentleman appeared thoroughly to enjoy giving him five pounds as an excuse for a lecture, and a subtly conveyed sneer at his father's character.

He was a very wealthy man, and he could easily have launched Giles into the world by putting him through the training for one of the professions, but he preferred to dole out niggardly little bits of charity and advice, and to boast that he himself was a self-made man, who had had no special training.

'No,' thought Giles, 'but you have an instinct for making money. I haven't. You don't have to train a duck to swim.'

Naturally, they very quickly quarrelled, and his uncle seemed to rejoice in his failures. It was only in his most desperate positions that he appealed to him again.

Lying back in the dimly lighted railway carriage he kept on visualizing his uncle's keen malevolent eyes, the thrust of the pointed chin. The acid tones of his voice echoed through his brain:

'It's quite time, my lad, you pulled yourself together. You ought to have made your fortune by now. Don't imagine I'm always going to help you.'

Giles had humbled his pride for his wife and child's sake. He had spent the night at his uncle's, and by exercising his utmost powers of cajolery, had managed to extort three pounds. Three pounds! and the rent overdue, bills pressing, his wife unwell and he out of work. What was he going to do?

The train rumbled into Waterloo Station without any satisfactory answer being arrived at. He pulled his bag out from under the seat, and stepped slowly out of the carriage.

Walking along the platform it suddenly occurred to him that he was feeling weak and exhausted. 'I hope to God I'm not going to be ill,' he thought.

The bag, which only contained his night things and a change of clothes, seemed unbearably heavy. A slight feeling of faintness came over him as he passed the ticket collector.

'I believe I shall have to have a cab,' flashed through him.

Two important-looking men got out of a taxi which had just driven up. Giles engaged it, and having given his address he stepped in and sank back exhausted on to the seat. It was very dark in the cab, and he lay huddled in the corner—a beaten man. Everything appeared distant and dim, and unimportant. He had hardly eaten any lunch, and his uncle seemed to have arranged that he should leave his house just before dinner. It was late, and he was hungry and overwrought.

The cab turned a corner sharply, and Giles lurched and thrust his hand on to the other end of the seat to prevent himself falling. As he did so his knuckles brushed against an object. Quite apathetically he felt to see what it was. He picked it up and held it near the window. It was a brown leather wallet, with a circular brass lock. He regarded it dubiously, and for an instant hesitated whether he should tell the driver to go back to the station, the wallet presumably belonging to one of those two important-looking men who had got out. But would it be possible to find them? By that time they would probably have gone off by train. No, the right thing to do was to give it up to the police, of course.

It was a fat wallet, and he sat there with it in his hand ruminating. He wondered what it contained. Quite easy just to have a squint anyway. He tried to slip the catch but it wouldn't open. It was locked. It is difficult to determine the extent to which this knowledge affected him. If it had not been locked Giles Meiklejohn's immediate actions, and indeed his future career, might have been entirely different. It irritated him that the wallet was locked…tantalized him. If it was locked it meant that it contained something…pretty useful. All round the park he lay back in the cab hugging the wallet like one in a trance.

A desperate, beaten man, holding a fat wallet in his hand. Contrary forces were struggling within his tired mind. Going up Park Lane one of these forces seemed to succumb to the other. Almost in a dream he leant out of the cab, and said quietly to the driver:

'Drive to the Trocadero. I think I'll get a bit of supper first.'

Arriving there, he paid the cabman, concealed the

wallet in his overcoat and went in. He entered a lavatory and locked himself in. With unruffled deliberation he took out a penknife and began to saw away at the leather around the lock.

'I just want to have a squint,' he kept on mentally repeating.

It took him nearly a quarter of an hour to get the wallet open, and when he did his heart was beating like a sledgehammer.

The wallet contained eight thick packets of one-pound treasury notes! He feverishly computed the number which each packet contained, and decided that it must be two hundred and fifty. In other words, he had two thousand pounds worth of ready cash in his possession!

A desperate, beaten man, with a wife and child, hungry…out of work…two thousand pounds!…

There seemed no question about it all then. One side of the scale was too heavily weighted. He took seventeen of the one-pound notes and put them in his pocket book, the rest he divided into the pockets of his overcoat, where he also concealed the wallet. He went up into the bar and ordered a double brandy and soda. He drank it in two gulps and went out and hailed another taxi. On the way home he stopped at a caterer's, and bought a cold fowl, some pressed beef, new rolls, cheese, a box of chocolates, and a bottle of wine. Then he drove homewards.

Up to this point his actions seemed to have been controlled by some subconscious force. So far as his normal self was concerned, he had hardly thought at all. But as he began to approach his own neighbourhood—his own wife—the realization of what he had done—what he was doing—came home to him…

'It is practically stealing. It *is* stealing, you know.' Yes, but what would anyone else have done in that position? He couldn't let his wife and child starve. There was only one thing he was afraid of—his wife's eyes. She must never know. He would have to be cunning, circumspect.

He must get rid of the wallet, conceal the notes from his wife—eke them out in driblets, pretend he was making money somehow. But the wallet? He couldn't leave it in the cab. It would be found and the cabman would give evidence. He mustn't drive home at all. He must get out again, think again. Between Paddington and Maida Vale runs a canal. Happy thought! a canal! He stopped at the bridge and dismissed the man again, tipping him lavishly. The banks of the canal were railed off. It was only possible to get near enough to throw anything in from the bridge. Thither he walked at a rapid stride. The feeling of exhaustion had passed. He was tingling with excitement. He looked eagerly about for a stone, and cursed these modern arrangements of wooden pavements. There were no stones near the canal. Never mind, the thing would probably sink. If it didn't, who could trace its discovery to his action? The point was to get rid of it unseen.

He reached the bridge. A few stray people were passing backwards and forward—must wait till everyone was out of sight. He hung about, gripping his portmanteau in one hand, and the wallet in his right-hand overcoat pocket. He crossed the bridge once, but still seeing dark figures about he had to return. Why not throw it now? No, there was someone watching in the road opposite—might be a policeman! The police! never had cause to feel frightened of the police before. There would be a splash...Someone might come out of the darkness, a deep voice:

'What was that you threw in the canal?'

No, no, couldn't do it. The bridge was too exposed, too much of a fairway. He hurried off walking rapidly down side streets in the direction of his home. At last an opportunity presented itself. Shabby, deserted little street, a low stone wall enclosing a meagre garden. Not a soul in sight. Like a flash he slipped the wallet over the wall and dropped it. Instantaneously he looked up at the house connected with the garden. A man was looking out of the first floor window, watching him!

He turned and walked quickly back. He thought he heard a call. At the first turning he ran, the portmanteau banging against his leg and impeding his progress. He only ceased running because people stopped and looked at him suspiciously.

'It's all right! It's all right!' he kept saying to himself. 'I've got rid of it.'

Yes, he was rid of that danger, but there loomed before him the more insidious difficulty of concealing the notes. His pockets bulged with them. When he arrived home, Eleanor would run out into the landing and throw her arms round him. He could almost hear the tones of her gentle voice saying:

'Whatever have you got in your pockets, darling?'

If he put them in the portmanteau she would be almost certain to open it, or she would be in the room when he went to unpack. Very difficult to conceal anything from Eleanor; she knew all about him; every little thing about him interested her. Nothing in their rooms was locked up. Moreover, she was very observant, methodical and practical. Someone had called her psychic, but this was only because she thought more quickly than most people, and had unerring intuitions.

Giles would have to be very cunning. His mental energies were so concerned with the necessity for deceiving Eleanor that the moral aspect of his position was temporarily blurred. He plunged on through the darkness, his mind working rapidly. At the corner of their meagre street he was tempted to stuff the notes in a pillar-box and hurry home.

'Don't be a fool,' said the other voice. 'Here is comfort and luxury interminably—not only for yourself, for the others.'

He went boldly up to the house and let himself in. He heard other lodgers talking in the front ground-floor room. He hurried by and reached his own landing. To his relief Eleanor's voice came from the room above:

'Is that you, darling?'

He dumped the bag down and in a flash had removed his overcoat and hung it on a peg in a dark corner. Then he called out:

'Hullo, old girl. Everything all right?'

Within a minute his wife's arms were around him, and he exclaimed with forced triumph:

'I touched the old boy for twenty pounds! I've brought home a chicken and things.'

'Oh! how splendid! A chicken! Rather extrav. isn't it, darling?'

'One must live, dear angel.'

Her confidence and trust in him, her almost childish glee over the gay feast, her solicitude in his welfare, her anxiety that little Anna should have some chicken, but keep the sweets till the morrow, her voice later crooning over the child—all these things mocked his conscience. But he couldn't afford to have a conscience. He couldn't afford to say:

'I stole all this and more.'

He was eager for the attainment of that last instance—crooning over the child. Whilst she was putting the little girl to bed, he crept out into the passage and extracted the packets of notes from his overcoat pocket. He took them into the sitting room and wrapped them up in brown paper. He wrote on the outside, 'stationery'. Then he stuffed the parcel at the back of a cupboard where they kept all kinds of odds and ends.

'That'll have to do for to-night,' he thought. 'I'm too tired to think of anything better.'

When she came down he enlarged the claims of his exhaustion. He had a bit of a head he explained, just as well to turn in early. In the darkness he clung to her fearfully, like a child in terror of separation.

It was not till she was sleeping peacefully that the enormity of his offence came home to him.

If he were found out! It would kill her.

He remembered her expression:

'If our troubles are never anything worse than financial ones, darling, I shan't mind.'

Good God! What had he done? He could call it what he liked, but crudely speaking it was just stealing. He had stolen. He was a criminal, a felon. If found out, it meant arrest, trial, imprisonment—all these horrors he had only vaguely envisaged as concerning a different type of person to himself. In the rough and tumble of his life he had never before done anything criminal, never anything even remotely dishonest. And she, Eleanor, what would she think of him? It would destroy her love, destroy her life, ruin the child.

He must get up, go into the other room and—what? What could he do with the notes? Burn them? Eleanor had that mother's curious faculty for profound, but at the same time, watchful sleep. If he got out of bed she would be aware of it. If he went into the next room and began burning things, she would be instantly alert.

'What's that burning, darling?'

An ever-loving wife may be an embarrassment when one is not quite playing the game. By destroying the wallet he had burnt his boats. If he returned the money he would have to explain what the wallet was doing in a neighbour's garden with the brass lock cut away.

'Besides, you've already spent some,' interjected that other voice. 'You're horribly in debt. Here's succour. The money probably belongs to some rich corporation. It's not like taking it from the poor. Don't be a fool. Go to sleep.'

For hours he tossed feverishly, the pendulum of his resolutions swinging backwards and forwards. If he was to keep the money, he would have to invent some imaginary source of income, a fictitious job, perhaps, and that would be very difficult because Eleanor was so solicitous, such a glutton for details concerning himself. He might have made out that his uncle had given him a much larger sum of money, but in that case there was the danger that in her impetuous manner Eleanor might have written to the old man, and the old man would smell a rat. Doubtless the affair of the lost wallet would be in the papers the next day, and wouldn't the old man be delighted to bring it home to Giles!

There was nothing to be done but to trust to fate. The milk carts were clattering in the road before he slept.

It was hours later that he heard Anna's merry little laugh, and his wife's voice saying:

'Hush, darling, daddy's asleep. He's very tired.'

He got up and faced the ordeals of the day. The place at the back of the lumber cupboard seemed the most exposed in the world. He racked his brains for a more suitable spot. But whichever place he thought of danger seemed to lurk. One never quite knew what Eleanor might do. She was so keen on tidying up and clearing things out. He decided that a crisp walk might clear his mind. He made up the excuse that he was going to the public library to look through the advertisements and went out. He meant to smuggle the parcel of notes out with him, but Eleanor was too much on the spot. She helped him on with his overcoat and said:

'It'll soon be all right again, darling.'

Poor Eleanor! What a capacity she had for living! She ought to have married a rich, successful and clever man. She ought to have everything a beautiful woman desires. Well? . . . He walked quickly to the nearest newsagent and bought a paper. There was nothing in the morning paper about the loss of the wallet. He felt annoyed about this, until he realized that, of course, there wouldn't have been time. It would come out later. And indeed whilst standing on the curb anxiously scrutinizing his morning paper, boys came along the street selling the *Star* and the *Evening News*.

A paragraph in the *Star*, headed '£2,000 LEFT IN A TAXI', supplied him with the information he needed. It announced that Sir James Cusping, K.B.E., a director of a well-known bank, and a chief cashier, left a wallet containing two thousand pounds in treasury notes in a taxi at Waterloo Station. The money was the result of a cash transaction concerning certain bank investments. Anyone giving information likely to lead to recovery would be suitably rewarded. It also announced that Scotland Yard had the matter in hand.

So far the information was satisfactory. Sir James Cusping was a notoriously wealthy man, and the chief cashier was hardly likely to be held seriously responsible for a loss for which such an important person was jointly responsible. The bank mentioned was a bank that advertised that its available assets exceeded four hundred million pounds. Two thousand pounds meant less to it than twopence would mean to Giles. No one was hurt by the transfer of this useful sum to his own pocket. The sun was shining. Why be down in the mouth about it? What he had done he had done, and he must see it through.

How could anybody trace the theft to him? The two cabmen? They would be hardly likely to remember his face, and neither of them had driven him home. There was no danger from anyone except Eleanor. A sudden fever of dread came over him. She would assuredly turn out that cupboard today, find the packet of 'stationery'. Then—what?

He hurried back home. Approaching the house other fears assailed him. He had visions of policemen waiting for him on the other side of the hall door.

Damn it! His nerves were going to pot. He opened the door with exaggerated nonchalance. There was no one there. No one up in his rooms except his wife and child. Eleanor was singing. The kettle was on the gas-ring, ready for tea.

'What a cad I am to her,' he thought.

The condition of frenzied agitation continued till the following afternoon when it reached a crisis. He was feeling all unstrung. Seated alone in their little sitting room he was struggling with the resolution to confess everything to Eleanor, when she entered the room. He glanced at her and nearly screamed. *She was holding up the parcel in her hand!*

In her cheerful voice she said:

'What is this parcel marked stationery, darling? I was turning out the cupboard.'

Like an animal driven to bay he jumped up and almost snatched it from her. The inspiration of despair prompted him to exclaim:

'Oh!...that! Yes, yes, I wanted that. It's something a chap wanted me to get for him...It doesn't belong to me.'

A chap! What chap? Giles didn't usually refer to chaps. They had no secrets apart. She looked surprised.

'I was just going to open it. As a matter of fact we have run out of stationery.'

'Eh? No, no, not that. I must send that back. I'll get some more stationery.'

He tucked the packet under his arm and went out into the hall.

'You're not going out at once?' said Eleanor, following.

'Yes, yes, I must post it at once. I'd quite forgotten.' He slipped on his coat and went out without his customary embrace.

Beads of perspiration were on his brow.

'That's done it!' he muttered in the street. 'I must never take it back.'

An extravagant plan formed in his mind. He went to the library and looked at the advertisements in a local paper. He took down some addresses in St John's Wood. In half an hour's time he was calling on a landlady in a mean street.

'You have a furnished room to let?' he said when she appeared.

'Yes, sir.'

'Well, it's like this. I am an author. I want a quiet room to work in during the daytime.'

'I've got a nice room as would suit you.'

'Come on, then, let me see it, please.'

He booked the room, a shabby little overcrowded apartment.

'I'll be coming in to-day,' he said.

'Very good, sir. What name might it be?'

'Er—name? Oh, yes, name—er—John Parsons.'

He fled down the street and sought a furnishing establishment.

'I want an oak desk which I can lock up—a good strong lock.'

He paid seven pounds ten for the desk, and got it taken round at once on a barrow. He then bought scribbling papers, paper and ink. He established himself in his room, stuffed the packet of notes in the desk and locked it. Then he went out into the street again. The fresh air fanned his temples. He almost chuckled.

'By God! Why didn't I think of this at first?' he reflected. 'After the life I've led one forgets the power of money.'

He felt singularly calm and confident. It was dark when he got home. He kissed Eleanor and made up an elaborate story about a fellow clerk named Lyel Bristowe, who used to work in the same office, and whom he had met in the street recently. He had wanted this particular stationery most particularly. He had been to see him, and Bristowe was giving him an introduction to a man who might be able to offer him a good situation. The story went down reasonably well, but he thought he detected a pucker of suspicion about his wife's brow.

He was too involved now to turn back. The following day he visited his furnished room. He anxiously unlocked the desk, took out the notes, examined them, put them back, took them out again, stuffed them in his pocket…Very dangerous after all leaving them there, a flimsy lock…there might be a burglary. He had told the landlady that he was an author, and it is true that he spent a great portion of the day inventing fiction…lies to tell Eleanor. He eventually locked the notes up again and went home.

He assumed a somewhat forced air of triumph. He had been successful. Through the influence of Bristowe, he had secured a position as chief cashier to a firm of surgical instrument makers in Camden Town. His salary was to be five pounds a week to commence. Eleanor clapped her hands.

'Oh, but how lovely, darling! I suppose you can do it? You're such an old silly at figures!'

He explained that the work was quite simple, and added ironically that the great thing Messrs Binns and Binns wanted was a man they could trust.

Then the narrow life of lies proceeded apace. Every day he went to his room, fingered the notes, took some when he needed them, deliberately invented the names and characters of his fellow workers at Messrs Binns and Binns, even made up little incidents and stories concerning his daily experiences. The whole affair was so inordinately successful. No further reference was made in the newspapers to the missing wallet, and though Scotland Yard were supposed to have the matter in hand, what could they do? Even if by chance suspicion fell on him, there was nothing incriminating to be found in his lodgings. His wife and child were living comfortably. He was gradually paying off his debts.

But if the purely material side of his adventure was successful, the same cannot be said of the spiritual. He was tortured beyond endurance. Lies bred lies. The moral lapse bred other moral lapses. He was conscious of his own moral degeneration. He was ashamed to look his wife in the face. In the evening when he intended to be gay and cheerful, he sat morosely in the corner, wishing that the night would come—and go. In the daytime he would sit in his room, fretful and desolate. In a mood of despair he began to set down his experiences in terms of fiction, ascribing his feelings to an imaginary person. Sometimes when the position became unbearable he would go out and drink. Often he would go up to the West End and lunch extravagantly at some obscure restaurant. He came into touch with unsavoury people of the underworld.

The marks of his deterioration quickly became apparent to his wife. One morning she said:

'Darling, you're working too hard at that place. You look rotten. Last night when you came home you smelt of brandy.'

Then she wept a little, a thing she had never done in their days of adversity. He promised not to do such a thing again. He swore that the work was not hard; the firm was very pleased with him and was going to give him a rise.

The weeks and months went by and he struggled to keep straight. But little by little he felt himself slipping back. He managed to write a few things which he sent off to publishers, but for the most part he avoided his room for any length of time, and sat about in obscure cafés in Soho, drinking and playing cards.

Between himself and his wife the great chasm seemed to be yawning. She was to him the dearest treasure in the world, and he was thrusting her away. In that one weak moment he had destroyed all chance of happiness—hers and his. Too late! Too late! In six months' time he found that he had spent nearly five hundred pounds! At this rate in another eighteen months it would all be gone, and then—what? His moral character destroyed, his wife broken in health, the child without protection or prospects.

One morning he observed his wife glancing in the mirror as she did her hair. It came home to him abruptly that she had aged, aged many years in the last six months. Soon she would be turning grey, middle-aged, old-aged.

And he? His hair was thin on top, his face flabby, his organs becoming inefficient and weak, his nerves eternally on edge. Sometimes he was rude and snappy to her. And he buried his face in the pillow and thought:

'Oh, my darling, what have I done? What have I done?'

That day he concentrated on a great resolve. This thing would have to stop. He would rather be a starving clerk again, rather a bricklayer's navvy, a crossing-sweeper, anything. He wandered the streets, hugging his determination. He avoided his old haunts. There must be no compromise. The thing should be cut clean out. He would confess. They would send back the remainder of the money anonymously, and start all over again. It was hard, but anything was better than this torture.

He returned home early in the afternoon, his face pale and tense. His wife was on the landing. She said:

'Oh, I was just going to send a telegram on to you. It's from your uncle. He says come at once.'

A queer little stab of the old instinct of conspiracy went through him. If she had sent the telegram on, it would have come back: 'No such firm known at this address.'

What did his uncle want? Come at once? Should he go, or should he make his confession first?

'I think you ought to go, darling. It sounds important.'

Very well, then. The confession should be postponed till his return.

He caught a train at a quarter to four, and arrived at his uncle's house in daylight. An old housekeeper let him in and said:

'Ah! Your uncle's been asking for you. The doctor's here.'

'Is he ill?'

'They say he hasn't long to live. The poor man is in great agony.'

He was kept waiting ten minutes. A doctor came out to him, looking very solemn.

'I've just given him an injection of strychnine. He wishes to see you alone.'

His uncle was propped up against the pillows. His face unrecognizable except for the eyes, which were unnaturally bright. Giles went close up to him, and took his hand. The old man's voice was only just audible. He whispered:

'Quickly! quickly! I shall be going—'

'What is it, uncle?'

'It mustn't come out, see? Mustn't get into the newspapers, nothing, the disgrace, see? That's why…no cheques must pass; all cash transaction, see?'

'What do you want me to do?'

'On that bureau…a brown paper parcel…it's yours, all in bonds and cash, see? Twenty-eight thousand pounds… it really belongs to your father…I can't explain…I'm going. He—I swindled him…he thought he was…it's all through me he…bankrupt, death, see?'

'Do you mean my father…killed himself?'

'Not exactly, see? Hastened his end…thought he would get into trouble. Take it, Giles, for God sake! Let me die in peace.'

'Why did you? Why did you?'

'I loved your mother…Take it, Giles, for God's sake. Oh, this pain!…it's coming…God help me!'

It was very late when Giles arrived home. His wife was asleep in bed. All the way home he had been repeating to himself in a dazed way:

'Twenty-eight thousand pounds. No, twenty-six thousand. Two thousand to be sent back anonymously to the bank. No need for confession. Twenty-six thousand pounds. Eleanor, Anna. Oh, my dears!'

On the table in the sitting room was a letter from a firm of publishers, addressed to Mr John Parsons. It stated that the firm considered the short novel submitted to be a work of striking promise, and the manager would be glad if Mr Parsons would call on them.

'Perhaps I've found out what I can do,' Giles meditated.

Eleanor came into the room in her dressing gown and embraced him.

'All right, darling?'

'Very much. Uncle has given me twenty-eight—I mean twenty-six thousand pounds. He said he cheated my father out of it.'

'Darling!'

No, there was no need for confession. The sudden wild change in their fortunes got into his blood. He gripped her round the waist and lifted her up.

'Think of it, old girl, money to live on for ever. A place in the country, eh? You know, your dream: a bit of land and an old house, flowers, chickens, dogs, books, a pony perhaps. What about it?'

'Oh, Giles, I can't realize it. But how splendid, too, about the publishers' letter. Why didn't you tell me you were writing? Why do you call yourself John Parsons?'

No need for confession, no, no, let's go to bed. But oh! to get back to the old intimacy…

And so in the silent night he told her everything.

And the tears she shed upon his burning cheeks gave him the only balm of peace he had enjoyed since the hour he had destroyed the wallet.

It was Eleanor's hand which printed in Roman lettering on the outside of a parcel the address of Sir James Cusping, K.B.E. Inside were two thousand pounds in treasury notes, and on a slip of paper in the same handwriting: 'CONSCIENCE MONEY. FOUND IN A TAXI.'

—XXIX—

A Good Action

It is undoubtedly true that the majority of us perform the majority of our actions through what are commonly known as mixed motives.

It would certainly have been quite impossible for Mr Edwin Pothecary to analyse the concrete impulse which eventually prompted him to perform his good action. It may have been a natural revolt from the somewhat petty and cramped punctilio of his daily life: his drab home life, the bickering, wearing, grasping routine of the existence of fish-and-chips dispenser. A man who earns his livelihood by buying fish and potatoes in the cheapest market, and selling them in the Waterloo Road, cannot afford to indulge his altruistic fancies to any lavish extent. It is true that the business of Mr Edwin Pothecary was a tolerably successful one—he employed three assistants and a boy named Scales, who was not so much an assistant as an encumbrance and wholesale plate-smasher. Mr Pothecary engaged him because he thought his name seemed appropriate to the fish trade. In a weak moment he pandered to this sentimental whim, another ingredient in the strange composition which influences us to do this, that, and the other. But it was not by pandering to whims of this nature that Mr Pothecary had built up this progressive and odoriferous business with its gay shopfront of blue and brown tiles. It was merely a minor lapse. In the fish-and-chip trade one has to be keen, pushful, self-reliant, ambidexterous, a student of human nature, forbearing, far-seeing, imaginative, courageous, something of a controversialist with a streak of fatalism as pronounced as that of a high priest in a Brahmin temple.

It is better, moreover, to have an imperfect nasal organ and to be religious.

Edwin had all these qualities. Every day he went from Quince Villa at Buffington to London—forty minutes in the train—and back at night. On Sunday he took the wife and three children to the Methodist Chapel at the corner of the street to both morning and evening services. But even this religious observance does not give us a complete solution for the sudden prompting of an idea to do a good action. Edwin had attended chapel for fifty-two years and such an impulse had never occurred to him before. He may possibly have been influenced by some remark of the preacher, or was it that twinge of gout which set him thinking of the unwritten future? Had it anything to do with the Boy-Scout movement? Someone at some time had told him of an underlying idea—that every day in one's life one should do one pure, good and unselfish action.

Perhaps after all it was all due to the gaiety of a spring morning. Certain it is that as he swung out of the garden gate on that morning in April something stirred in him. His round puffy face blinked heavenwards. Almond blossoms fluttered in the breeze above the hedgerows. Larks were singing... Suddenly his eye alighted upon the roof of the Peels' hen-house opposite and Mr Edwin Pothecary scowled. Lord! How he hated those people! The Peels were Pothecary's *bêtes-noires*. Snobs! Pirates! Rotters!

The Peels' villa was at least three times as big as the Pothecarys'. It was, in fact, not a villa at all. It was a 'court'—whatever that was! It was quite detached, with about fourteen rooms in all, a coach-house, a large garden, and two black sheds containing forty-five fowls, leading an intensive existence. The Pothecarys had five fowls which sometimes did and sometimes didn't supply them with two or three eggs a day, but it was known that the Peels sent at least two hundred and fifty eggs to market every week, besides supplying their own table. Mr Peel was a successful dealer in quills and bristles. His wife was the daughter of a post-office official and they had three stuck-up daughters who would have no truck at all with the Pothecarys. You may appreciate then the twinge of venom which marked the face of Edwin as he passed through his front gate and observed the distant roof of the Peels' fowl house. And still the almond blossoms nodded at him above the hedge. The larks sang...After all, was it fair to hate anyone because they were better off than oneself? Strange how these moods obsess one. The soft air caressed Edwin's cheek. Little flecks of cloud scudded gaily into the suburban panorama. Small green shoots were appearing everywhere. One ought not to hate anyone at all—of course. It is absurd. So bad for oneself, apart from the others. One ought rather to be kind, forgiving, loving all mankind. Was that a lark or a thrush? He knew little about birds. Fish now!...A not entirely unsatisfactory business really, the fried fish trade—when things went well. When customers were numerous and not too cantankerous. Quite easy to run, profitable. A boy came singing down the road. The villas clustered together more socially. There was a movement of spring life...

As Edwin turned the corner of the Station Road the impulse crystallized. One good action. Today he would perform one good, kind, unselfish, unadvertised action. No one should ever know of it. Just one today. Then perhaps one tomorrow. And so on. In time it might become a habit. That is how one progressed. He took his seat in the crowded third-class smoker and pretended to read his newspaper, but his mind was too actively engaged with the problems of his new resolution. How? When? Where? How does one do a definitely good action? What is the best way to go to work? One could, of course, just quietly slip some money into a poor-box if one could be found. But would this be very good and self-sacrificing? Who gets money put in a poor-box? Surely his own family were poor enough, as far as that went. But he couldn't go back home and give his wife a sovereign. It would be advertising his charity, and he would look silly doing it. His business? He might turn up and say to his assistants: 'Boys, you shall all have a day's holiday. We'll shut up, and here's your pay for the day.' Advertising again; besides, what about the hundreds of poor workers in the neighbourhood who relied for their midday sustenance on 'Pothecary's Pride-of-the-Ocean Popular Plaice to Eat'? It would be cruel, cruel and—bad for business in the future. The public would lose confidence in that splendid gold-lettered tablet in the window which said 'Cod, brill, halibut, plaice, pilchards always on hand. Eat them or take them away.'

The latter sentence did not imply that if you took them away you did *not* eat them: it simply meant that you could either stand at the counter and eat them from a plate with the aid of a fork and your fingers (or at one of the wooden benches if you could find room—an unlikely contingency); alternatively you could wrap them up in a piece of newspaper and devour them without a fork at the corner of the street.

No, it would not be a good action in any way to close the Popular Plaice to Eat. Edwin came to the conclusion that to perform this act satisfactorily it were better to divorce the proceeding entirely from any connection with home or business. The two things didn't harmonize. A good action must be a special and separate effort in an entirely different setting. He would take the day off himself and do it thoroughly.

Mr Pothecary was known in the neighbourhood of the Waterloo Road as 'The Stinker', a title easily earned by the peculiar qualities of his business and the obvious additional fact that a Pothecary was a chemist. He was a very small man, bald-headed with yellowy-white side whiskers, a blue chin, a perambulating nostril with a large wart on the port side. He wore a square bowler hat which seemed to thrust out the protruding flaps of his large ears. His greeny-black clothes were always too large for him and ended in a kind of thick spiral above his square-toed boots. He always wore a flat white collar—more or less clean—and no tie. This minor defect was easily atoned for by a heavy silver chain on his waistcoat from which hung gold seals and ribbons connecting with watches, knives, and all kinds of ingenious appliances in his waistcoat pockets.

The noble intention of his day was a little chilled on his arrival at the shop. In the first place, although customers were then arriving for breakfast, the boy Scales was slopping water over the front step. Having severely castigated the miscreant youth and prophesied that his chances of happiness in the life to come were about as remote as those of a dead dogfish in the upper reaches of the Thames, he made his way through the customers to the room at the back, and there he met Dolling.

Dolling was Edwin's manager, and he cannot be overlooked. In the first place, he was remarkably like a fish himself. He had the same dull expressionless eyes and the drooping mouth and drooping moustache. Everything about him drooped and dripped. He was always wet. He wore a grey flannel shirt and no collar or tie. His braces, trousers, and hair all seemed the same colour. He hovered in the background with a knife, and did the cutting up and dressing. He had, moreover, all the taciturnity of a fish, and its peculiar ability for getting out of a difficulty. He never spoke. He simply looked lugubrious, and pointed at things with his knife. And yet Edwin knew that he was an excellent manager. For it must be observed that, in spite of the gold-lettered board outside with its fanfare of cod, brill, halibut, plaice and pilchards, whatever the customer asked for, by the time it had passed through Dolling's hand, it was just *fish*. No nonsense about it at all. Just plain fish levelled with a uniform brown crust. If you asked for cod you got *fish*. If you asked for halibut you also got *fish*. Dolling was something of an artist.

On this particular morning, as Edward entered the back room, Dolling was scratching the side of his head with the knife he used to cut up the fish, a sure sign that he was perplexed about something. It was not customary to exchange greetings in this business, and when he observed 'the guv'nor' enter he just withdrew the knife from his hair and pointed it at a packing case on the side table. Edwin knew what this meant. He went up and pressed his flat nose against the chest of what looked like an over-worked amphibian that had been turned down by its own Trades Union. Edwin sneezed before he had had time to withdraw his nose.

'Yes, that's a dud lot,' he said. And then suddenly an inspirational moment nearly overwhelmed him. Here was a chance. He would turn to Dolling and say:

'Dolling, this fish is slightly tainted. We must throw it away. We bought it at our risk. Yesterday morning when it arrived it was just all right, but keeping it in that hot room downstairs where you and your wife sleep has probably finished it. We mustn't give it to our customers. It might poison them—ptomaine poison, you know…eh, Dolling?' It would be a good action, a self-sacrificing action, eh? But when he glanced at the face of Dolling he knew that such an explosion would be unthinkable. It would be like telling a duck it mustn't swim, or an artist that he mustn't paint, or a boy on a beach that he mustn't throw stones in the sea. It was the kind of job that Dolling enjoyed. In the course of a few hours he knew quite well that whatever he said, the mysterious and evil-smelling monster would be served out in dainty parcels of halibut, cod, brill, plaice, etc.

Business was no place for a good action. Too many others depended on it, were involved in it. Edwin went up to Dolling and shouted in his ear—he was rather deaf:

'I'm going out. I may not be back today.'

Dolling stared at the wall. He appeared about as

interested in the statement as a cod might be that had just been informed that a Chinese coolie had won the Calcutta sweepstake. Edwin crept out of the shop abashed. He felt horribly uncomfortable. He heard some one mutter: 'Where's The Stinker off to?' and he realized how impossible it would be to explain to anyone there present that he was off to do a good action.

'I will go to some outlying suburb,' he thought.

Once outside in the sunshine he tried to get back into the benign mood. He travelled right across London and made for Golders Green and Hendon, a part of the world foreign to him. By the time he had boarded the Golders Green bus he had quite recovered himself. It was still a brilliant day. 'The better the day the better the deed,' he thought aptly. He hummed inaudibly; that is to say, he made curious crooning noises somewhere behind his silver chain and signets; the sound was happily suppressed by the noise of the bus.

It seemed a very long journey. It was just as they were going through a rather squalid district near Cricklewood that the golden chance occurred to him. The fares had somewhat thinned. There were scarcely a dozen people in the bus. Next to him, barely a yard away, he observed a poor woman with a baby in her arms. She had a thin, angular, wasted face, and her clothes were threadbare but neat. A poor, thoroughly honest and deserving creature, making a bitter fight of it against the buffets of a cruel world. Edwin's heart was touched. Here was his chance. He noticed that from her wrist was suspended a shabby black bag, and the bag was open. He would slip up near her and drop in a half-crown. What joy and rapture when she arrived home and found the unexpected treasure! An unknown benefactor! Edwin chuckled and wormed his way surreptitiously along the seat. Stealthily he fingered his half-crown and hugged it in the palm of his left hand. His heart beat with the excitement of his exploit. He looked out of the window opposite and fumbled his hand towards the opening in the bag. He touched it. Suddenly a sharp voice rang out:

'That man's picking your pocket!'

An excited individual opposite was pointing at him. The woman uttered an exclamation and snatched at her bag. The baby cried. The conductor rang the bell. Everyone seemed to be closing in on Edwin. Instinctively he snatched his hand away and thrust it in his pocket (the most foolish thing he could have done). Everyone was talking. A calm muscular-looking gentleman who had not spoken seized Edwin by the wrist and said calmly:

'Look in your bag, Madam, and see whether he has taken anything.'

The bus came to a halt. Edwin muttered:

'I assure you—nothing of the sort—'

How could he possibly explain that he was doing just the opposite? Would a single person believe a word of his yarn about the half-crown? The woman whimpered:

'No, 'e ain't taken nothin', bad luck to 'im. There was only four pennies and a 'alfpenny anyway. Dirty thief!'

'Are you goin' to give 'im in charge?' asked the conductor.

'Yer can't if 'e ain't actually taken nothin', can yer? The dirty thievin' swine tryin' to rob a 'ard workin', 'onest woman!'

'I wasn't! I wasn't!' feebly spluttered Edwin, blushing a ripe beetroot colour.

'Shame! Shame! Chuck 'im off the bus! Dirty sneak! Call a copper!' were some of the remarks being hurled about.

The conductor was losing time and patience. He beckoned vigorously to Edwin and said:

'Come on, off you go!'

There was no appeal. He got up and slunk out. Popular opinion was too strong against him. As he stepped off the back board, the conductor gave him a parting kick which sent him flying on to the pavement. It was an operation received with shrieks of laughter and a round of applause from the occupants of the vehicle, taken up by a small band of other people who had been attracted by the disturbance. He darted down a back street to the accompaniment of boos and jeers.

It says something for Edwin Pothecary that this unfortunate rebuff to his first attempt to do a good action did not send him helter-skelter back to the fried-fish shop in the Waterloo Road. He felt crumpled, bruised, mortified, disappointed, discouraged; but is not the path of all martyrs and reformers strewn with similar débris? Are not all really disinterested actions liable to misconstruction? He went into a dairy and partook of a glass of milk and a bun. Then he started out again. He would see more rural, less sophisticated people. In the country there must be simple, kindly people, needing his help. He walked for several hours with but a vague sense of direction. At last he came to a public park. A group of dirty boys were seated on the grass. They were apparently having a banquet. They did not seem to require him. He passed on, and came to an enclosure. Suddenly between some rhododendron bushes he looked into a small dell. On a seat by himself was an elderly man in a shabby suit. He looked the picture of misery and distress. His hands were resting on his knees, and his eyes were fixed in a melancholy scrutiny on the ground. It was obvious that some great trouble obsessed him. He was as still as a shadow. It was the figure of a man lost in the past or—contemplating suicide? Edwin's breath came quickly. He made his way to him. In order to do this it was necessary to climb a railing. There was probably another way round, but was there time? At any minute there might be a sudden movement, the crack of a revolver. Edwin tore his trousers and scratched his forearm, but he managed to enter the dell unobserved. He approached the seat. The man never looked up. Then Edwin said with sympathetic tears in his voice:

'My poor fellow, may I be of any assistance—?'

There was a disconcerting jar. The melancholy individual started and turned on him angrily:

'Blast you! I'd nearly got it! What the devil are you doing here?'

And without waiting for an answer he darted away among the trees. At the same time a voice called over the park railings:

'Ho! you there, what are you doing over there? You come back the way you came. I saw yer.'

The burly figure of a park-keeper with gaiters and stout stick beckoned him. Edwin got up and clambered back again, scratching his arm.

'Now then,' said the keeper. 'Name, address, age, and occupation, *if* you please.'

'I was only—' began Edwin. But what *was* he only doing? Could he explain to a park-keeper that he was only about to do a kind action to a poor man? He spluttered and gave his name, address, age, and occupation.

'Oh,' exclaimed the keeper. 'Fried fish, eh? And what were you trying to do? Get orders? Or were you begging from his lordship?'

'His lordship!'

'That man you was speaking to was Lord Budleigh-Salterton, the great scientist. He's thinkin' out 'is great invention, otherwise I'd go and ask 'im if 'e wanted to prosecute yer for being in 'is park on felonious intent or what.'

'I assure you—' stammered Mr Pothecary.

The park-keeper saw him well off the premises, and gave him much gratuitous advice about his future behaviour, darkened with melancholy prophecies regarding the would-be felon's strength of character to live up to it.

Leaving the park he struck out towards the more rural neighbourhood. He calculated that he must be somewhere in the neighbourhood of Hendon. At the end of lane he met a sallow-faced young man walking rapidly. His eyes were bloodshot and restless. He glanced at Edwin and stopped.

'Excuse me, sir,' he said.

Edwin drew himself to attention. The young man looked up and down nervously. He was obviously in a great state of distress.

'What can I do for you?'

'I—I—h-hardly like to ask you, sir, I—' He stammered shockingly. Edwin turned on his most sympathetic manner.

'You are suffering. What is it?'

'Sh-sh-shell-shock, shir.'

'Ah!'

At last! Some heroic reflex of the war darted through Edwin's mind. Here was his real chance at last. A poor fellow broken by the war and in need, neglected by an ungrateful country. Almost hidden by his outer coat he observed one of those little strips of coloured ribbon, which implied more than one campaign.

'Where did you—meet your trouble?' he asked.

'P-P-P-Palestine, sir, capturing a T-T-Turkish redoubt. I was through G-G-Gallipoli, too, sir, but I won't d-d-distress you. I am in a—in a—hospital at St Albans, came to see my g-g-g-girl, but she's g-g-g-gone—v-v-vanished...'

'You don't say so!'

'T-t-trouble is I l-l-l-lost my p-pass back. N-not quite enough m-mon—'

'Dear me! How much short are you?'

'S-s-s-six shill—s-s-s-six—'

'Six shillings? Well, I'm very sorry. Look here, my good fellow, here's seven-and-sixpence and God bless you!'

'T-t-thank you very much, sir. W-will you give me your n-name and—'

'No, no, no, that's quite all right. I'm very pleased to be of assistance. Please forget all about it.'

He pressed the soldier's hand and hurried on. It was done! He had performed a kind, unselfish action and no one should ever hear of it. Mr Pothecary's eyes glowed with satisfaction. Poor fellow! even if the story were slightly exaggerated, what did it matter? He was obviously a discharged soldier, ill, and in need. The seven-and-sixpence would make an enormous difference. He would always cherish the memory of his kind, unknown benefactor. It was a glorious sensation! Why had he never thought before of doing a kindly act? It was inspiring, illuminating, almost intoxicating! He recalled with zest the delirious feeling which ran through him when he had said, 'No, no, no!' He would *not* give his name. He was the good Samaritan, a ship passing in the night. And now he would be able to go home, or go back to his business. He swung down the lane, singing to himself. As he turned the corner he came to a low bungalow-building. It was in a rather deserted spot. It had a board outside which announced 'Tea, cocoa, light refreshments. Cyclists catered for.'

It was past mid-day, and although tea and cocoa had never made any great appeal to the gastronomic fancies of Edwin Pothecary, he felt in his present spiritually elevated mood that here was a suitable spot for a well-merited rest and lunch.

He entered a deserted room, filled with light oak chairs, and tables with green-tiled tops on which were placed tin vases containing dried ferns. A few bluebottles darted away from the tortuous remains of what had once apparently been a ham, lurking behind tall bottles of sweets on the counter. The room smelt of soda and pickles. Edwin rapped on the table for some time, but no one came. At last a woman entered from the front door leading to the garden. She was fat and out of breath.

Edwin coughed and said:

'Good-mornin', madam. May I have a bite of somethin'?'

The woman looked at him and continued panting. When her pulmonary contortions had somewhat subsided, she said:

'I s'pose you 'aven't seen a pale young man up the lane?'

It was difficult to know what made him do it, but Edwin lied. He said:

'No.'

'Oh!' she replied. 'I don't know where 'e's got to. 'E's not s'posed to go out of the garden. 'E's been ill, you know.'

'Really!'

''E's my nefyer, but I can't always keep an eye on 'im. 'E's a bright one, 'e is. I shall 'ave 'im sent back to the 'ome.'

'Ah, poor fellow! I suppose he was—injured in the war?'

'War!' The plump lady snorted. She became almost aggressive and confidential. She came close up to Edwin and shook her finger backwards and forwards in front of his eyes.

'I'll tell yer 'ow much war 'e done. When they talked about conscription, 'e got that frightened, 'e went out every day and tried to drink himself from a A1 man into a C3 man, and by God! 'e succeeded.'

'You don't say so!'

'I do say so. And more. When 'is turn came, 'e was in the 'orspital with Delirious Trimmings.'

'My God!'

''E's only just come out. 'E's all right as long as 'e don't get 'old of a little money.'

'What do you mean?'

'If 'e can get 'old of the price of a few whiskies, 'e'll 'ave another attack come on! What are yer goin' ter 'ave—tea or cocoa?'

'I must go! I must go!' exclaimed the only customer Mrs Boggins had had for two days, and gripping his umbrella, he dashed out of the shop.

'Good Lord! there's another one got 'em!' ejaculated the good landlady. 'I wonder whether 'e pinched anything while I was out? 'Ere! Come back, you dirty little bow-legged swipe!'

But Mr Pothecary was racing down the lane, muttering to himself:

'Yes, that was a good action! A very good action indeed!'

A mile farther on he came to a straggling village, a forlorn unkempt spot, only relieved by a gaudy inn called 'The Two Tumblers'. Edwin staggered into the private bar and drank two pints of Government ale and a double gin as the liquid accompaniment to a hunk of bread and cheese.

It was not till he had lighted his pipe after the negotiation of these delicacies that he could again focus his philosophical outlook. Then he thought to himself: 'It's a rum thing 'ow difficult it is to do a good action. You'd think it'd be dead easy, but everythin' seems against yer. One must be able to do it *somewhere*. P'raps one ought to go abroad, among foreigners and black men. That's it! That's why all these 'ere Bible Society people go out among black people, Chinese and so on. They find there's nothin' doin' over 'ere.'

Had it not been for the beer and gin it is highly probable that Edwin would have given up the project, and have returned to fish and chips. But lying back in a comfortable seat in 'The Two Tumblers' his thoughts mellowed. He felt broad-minded, comfortable, tolerant...one had to make allowances. There must be all sorts of ways. Money wasn't the only thing. Besides, he was spending too much. He couldn't afford to go on throwing away seven-and-sixpences. One must be able to help people—by helping them. Doing things for them which didn't cost money. He thought of Sir Walter Raleigh throwing down his cloak for Queen Elizabeth to walk over. Romantic but—extravagant and silly, really a shrewd political move, no doubt; not a good action at all. If he met an ill-clad tramp he could take off his coat and wrap it round his shoulders and then—? Walk home to Quince Villa in his braces? What would Mrs Pothecary have to say? Phew! One could save people from drowning, but he didn't know how to swim. Fire! Perhaps there would be a fire. He could swarm up a ladder and save a woman from the top bedroom window. Heroic, but hardly inconspicuous; not exactly what he had meant. Besides, the firemen would never let him; they always kept these showy stunts for themselves. There *must* be something...

He walked out of 'The Two Tumblers'.

Crossing the road, he took a turning off the High Street. He saw a heavily-built woman carrying a basket of washing. He hurried after her, and raising his hat, said:

'Excuse me, madam, may I carry your basket for you?'

She turned on him suspiciously and glared:

'No, thanks, Mr Bottle-nose. I've 'ad some of that before. You 'op it! Mrs Jaggs 'ad 'ers pinched last week that way.'

'Of course,' he thought to himself as he hurried away. 'The trouble is I'm not dressed for the part. A bloomin' swell can go about doin' good actions all day and not arouse suspicions. If I try and 'elp a girl off a tram-car I get my face slapped.'

Mr Pothecary was learning. He was becoming a complete philosopher, but it was not till late in the afternoon, that he suddenly realized that patience and industry are always rewarded. He was appealed to by a maiden in distress.

It came about in this way. He found the atmosphere of Northern London entirely unsympathetic to good deeds. All his actions appeared suspect. He began to feel at last like a criminal. He was convinced that he was being watched and followed. Once he patted a little girl's head in a paternal manner. Immediately a woman appeared at a doorway and bawled out:

''Ere, Lizzie, you come inside!'

At length in disgust he boarded a south-bound bus. He decided to experiment nearer home. He went to the terminus and took a train to the station just before his own. It was a small town called Uplingham. This should be the last dance of the moral philanderer. If there was no one in Uplingham upon whom he could perform a good action, he would just walk home—barely two miles—and go to bed and forget all about it. Tomorrow he would return to fish-and-chips, and the normal behaviour of the normal citizen.

Uplingham was a dismal little town, consisting mostly of churches, chapels and pubs, and apparently quite deserted. As Edwin wandered through it there crept over him a sneaking feeling of relief. If he met no one—well, there it was, he had done his best; he could go home with a clear conscience. After all, it was the spirit that counted in these things...

'O-o-oh!'

He was passing a small stone church, standing back on a little frequented lane. The maiden was seated alone in the porch and she was crying. Edwin bustled through the gate, and as he approached her he had time to observe that she was young, quietly dressed, and distinctly pretty.

'You are in trouble,' he said in his most feeling manner.

She looked up at him quickly, and dabbed her eyes.

'I've lost my baby! I've lost my baby!' she cried.

'Dear, dear, that's very unfortunate! How did it happen?'

She pointed at an empty perambulator in the porch.

'I waited an hour here for my friends and husband and the clergyman. My baby was to be christened.' She gasped incoherently. 'No one turned up. I went across to the Vicarage. The Vicar was away. I believe I ought to have gone to St Bride's. This is St Paul's. They didn't know anything about it. They say people often make that mistake. When I got back the baby was gone. O-o-o-oh!'

'There, there, don't cry,' said Mr Pothecary. 'Now I'll go over to St Bride's and find out about it.'

'Oh, sir, do you mind waiting here with the perambulator

while I go? I want my baby. I want my baby.'

'Why, yes, of course, of course.'

She dashed up the lane and left Mr Pothecary in charge of an empty perambulator. In fifteen minutes' time a thick-set young man came hurrying up to the porch. He looked at Edwin, and pointing to the perambulator, said:

'Is this Mrs Frank's? or Mrs Fred's?'

'I don't know,' said Edwin, rather testily.

'You don't know! But you're old Binns, aren't you?'

'No, I'm not.'

The young man looked at him searchingly and then disappeared. Ten minutes elapsed and then a small boy rode up on a bicycle. He was also out of breath.

'Has Mrs George been 'ere?' he asked.

'I don't know,' replied Edwin.

'Mr Henderson says he's awfully sorry but he won't be able to get away. You are to kiss the baby for 'im.'

'I don't know anything about it.'

'This is St Bride's, isn't it?'

'No, this is St Paul's.'

'Oh!' The boy leapt on to the bicycle and also vanished.

'This is absurd,' thought Edwin. 'Of course, the whole thing is as plain as daylight. The poor girl has come to the wrong church. The whole party is at St Bride's, somebody must have taken the baby on there. I might as well take the perambulator along. They'll be pleased. Now I wonder which is the way.'

He wheeled the perambulator into the lane. There was no one about to ask. He progressed nearly two hundred yards till he came to a field with a pond in it. This was apparently the wrong direction. He was staring about when he suddenly became aware of a hue and cry. A party of people came racing down the lane headed by the thick-set man, who was exclaiming:

'There he is! There he is!'

Edwin felt his heart beating. This was going to be a little embarrassing. They closed on him. The thick-set man seized his wrists and at the same time remarked:

'See he hasn't any firearms on him, Frank.'

The large man alluded to as Frank gripped him from behind.

'What have you done with my baby?' he demanded fiercely.

'I 'aven't seen no baby,' yelped Mr Pothecary.

'Oh! 'aven't yer! What are yer doin' with my perambulator then?'

'I'm takin' it to St Bride's Church.'

'Goin' in the opposite direction.'

'I didn't know the way.'

'Where's the baby?'

'I 'aven't seen it, I tell yer. The mother said she'd lost it.'

'What the hell! Do you know the mother's in bed sick? You're a liar, my man, and we're goin' to take you in charge. If you've done anything to my baby I'll kill you with my hands.'

'That's it Frank. Let 'im 'ave it. Throw 'im in the pond!'

'I tell yer I don't know anythin' about it at all, with yer Franks Freds and Georges! Go to the devil, all of yer!'

In spite of his protestations, some one produced a rope and they handcuffed him and tied him to the gate of the field. A small crowd had collected and began to boo and jeer. A man from a cottage hard by produced a drag, and between them they dragged the pond, as the general belief was that Edwin had tied a stone to the baby and thrown it in and was then just about to make off.

The uproar continued for some time, mud and stones being thrown about rather carelessly.

The crowd became impatient that no baby was found in the pond. At length another man turned up on a bicycle and called out:

'What are you doing, Frank? You've missed the christening!'

'What!'

'Old Binns turned up with the nipper all right. He'd come round the wrong way.'

The crowd was obviously disappointed at the release of Edwin, and the father's only solatium was:

'Well, it's lucky for you, old bird!'

He and his friends trundled the perambulator away rapidly across the fields. Edwin had hardly time to give a sigh of relief before he found himself the centre of a fresh disturbance. He was approaching the church when another crowd assailed him, headed by the forlorn maiden. She was still in a state of distress, but she was hugging a baby to her.

'Ah! You've found the baby!' exclaimed Edwin, trying to be amiable.

'Where is the perambulator?' she demanded.

'Your 'usband 'as taken it away, madam. He seemed to think I—'

A tall frigid young man stepped forward and said:

'Excuse me, I am the lady's husband. Will you please explain yourself?'

Then Edwin lost his temper.

'Well, damn it, I don't know who you all are!'

'The case is quite clear. You volunteered to take charge of the perambulator while my wife was absent. On her return you announce that it is spirited away. I shall hold you responsible for the entire cost—nearly ten pounds.'

'Make it a thousand,' roared Edwin. 'I'm 'aving a nice cheap day.'

'I don't wish for any more of your insolence either. My wife has had a very trying experience. The baby has been christened Fred.'

'Well, what's the matter with that?'

'Nothing,' screamed the mother. '*Only that it is a girl!* It's a girl and it has been duly christened Fred in a Christian church. Oh! there's been an awful muddle.'

'It's not this old fool's fault,' interpolated an elderly woman quietly. 'You see, Mrs Frank and Mrs Fred Smith were both going to have their babies christened today. Only Mrs Frank was took sick, and sent me along with the child. I went to the wrong church and thinkin' there was some mistake went back home. Mrs Frank's baby's never been christened at all. In the meantime, the ceremony was ready to start at St Paul's and Frank 'isself was there. No baby. They sends old Binns to scout around at other churches. People do make mistakes—finds this good lady's child all primed up for christening in the church door, and no one near, carries it off. In the meantime, the father had gone on the ramp. It's him that probably went off with the perambulator and trounced you up a bit, old sport. It'll learn you not to interfere so much in future perhaps.'

'And the baby's christened Fred!' wailed the mother. 'My baby! My Gwendoline!' And she looked at Edwin with bitter recrimination in her eyes.

There was still a small crowd following and boys were jeering and a fox-terrier, getting very excited, jumped up and bit Mr Pothecary through the seat of his trousers. He struck at it with his stick and hit a small boy, whose mother happened to be present. The good lady immediately entered the lists.

'Baby-killer...Hun!' were the last words he heard as he was chased up the street and across the fields in the direction of his own village.

When he arrived it was nearly dark. Mr Pothecary was tired, dirty, battered, torn, outraged, bruised, and hatless. And his spirit hardened. The forces of reaction surged through him. He was done with good actions. He felt vindictive, spiteful, wicked. Slowly he took the last turning and his eye once more alighted on—the Peels' fowl-house.

And there came to him a vague desire to end his day by performing some action the contrary to good, something spiteful, petty, malign. His soul demanded some recompense for its abortive energies. And then he remembered that the Peels were away. They were returning late that evening. The two intensive fowl-houses were at the end of the kitchen garden, where all the young spring cabbages and peas had just been planted. They could be approached through a slit in the narrow black fence adjacent to a turnip field. Rather a long way round. A simple and rather futile plan sprang into his mind, but he was too tired to think of anything more criminal or diabolic.

He would creep round to the back, get through the fence, force his way into the fowl-house. Then he would kick out all those expensive Rhode Island pampered hens and lock them out. Inside he would upset everything and smash the place to pieces. The fowls would get all over the place. They would eat the young vegetables. Some of them would get lost, stolen by gypsies, killed by rats. What did he care? The Peels would probably not discover the outrage till the morrow, and they would never know who did it. Edwin chuckled inwardly, and rolled his eyes like the smooth villain of a fit-up melodrama. He glanced up and down to see that no one was looking, then he got across a gate and entered the turnip field.

In five minutes' time he was forcing the door of the fowl-house with a spade. The fowls were already settling down for the night, and they clucked rather alarmingly, but Edwin's blood was up. He chased them all out, forty-five of them, and made savage lunges at them with his feet. Then he upset all the corn he could find, and poured water on it and jumped on it. He smashed the complicated invention suspended from the ceiling, whereby the fowls had to reach up and get one grain of corn at a time. To his joy he found a pot of green paint, which he flung promiscuously over the walls and floor (and incidentally his clothes).

Then he crept out and bolted both of the doors.

The sleepy creatures were standing about outside, some feebly pecking about on the ground. He chased them through into the vegetable garden; then he rubbed some of the dirt and paint from his clothes and returned to the road.

When he arrived home he said to his wife:

'I fell off a tram on Waterloo Bridge. Lost my hat.'

He was cold and wet and his teeth were chattering. His wife bustled him off to bed and gave him a little hot grog.

Between the sheets he recovered contentment. He gurgled exultantly at this last and only satisfying exploit of the day. He dreamed lazily of the blind rage of the Peels…

It must have been half-past ten when his wife came up to bring him some hot gruel. He had been asleep. She put the cup by the bedside and rearranged his pillow.

'Feeling better?' she asked.

'Yes. I'm all right,' he murmured.

She sat on a chair by the side of the bed, and after a few minutes remarked:

'You've missed an excitement while you've been asleep.'

'Oh?'

'Yes. A fire!'

'A fire?'

'The Peels came home about an hour and a half ago and found the place on fire at the back.'

'Oh?'

'Their cook Lizzie has been over. She said some straw near the wash-house must have started it. It's burnt out the wash-house and both the fowl-houses. She says Mr Peel says he don't care very much because he was heavily insured for the lot. But the funny thing is, the fowls wasn't insured and they've found the whole lot down the field on the rabbit-hutches. Somebody must have got in and let the whole lot out. It was a fine thing to do, or else the poor things would have been burnt up. What's the matter, Ned? Is the gruel too hot?'

—AN ESSAY—

The Thrill of Being Ill

IT'S NO GOOD getting a cold in the head, or any kind of absurd bilious attack. This doesn't help you at all. Your friends regard you as a bore. The people who have an affection for you display only an impatient interest.

You must do the thing properly. There must be in the first place a sudden shifting of all physical and mental values. You must glide away into a curious twilight where the division of time seems a little uncertain. And then you notice an unfamiliar figure, all in white, gliding hither and thither, performing rites that contribute to your general comfort. And a man in a grey suit, with an air of forced geniality, takes arbitrary possession of your body. And he says 'Ha!' and 'H'm!' in a discreetly non-committal way. And he vanishes and comes again, and vanishes and comes, and other people come and vanish, and your vanity forbids you asking too many questions, as though you think you are so important!

And then, you become subtly aware of a change of attitude in the manner of certain people. They are anxious. At this realization the ego-maniac in you rises and swells. You have come into your kingdom. You have become dramatically a centre of interest. No miserable cold in the head for you, but something with a name that has the power to frighten and disturb. Its direct bearing on you is purely objective. It seems of no great consequence, except as it affects these social relationships. Indolently you think of various friends who will say, 'Poor old chap! He's got it!' and you visualize them discussing the matter with others.

There is a latent thrill about all this. You have bought the luxury at the price of many pains and penalties, and you rightly demand your pound of flesh. You become somnolently autocratic. You accept the attention and service of those who hover around you as the toll due to a person of special privilege. If you were commanding a ship at sea, or sitting in judgment on your fellow-man, you could not feel more secretly elated. The fact that your physical powers are dissipated, that even the actions of your own body are controlled by others, seems to add to rather than diminish this sense of personal exultation. Of course it's all wrong. But illness itself is all wrong. It is attributable in nine cases out of ten to some unnatural pressure of which this very exultation is one. In the ordinary course of social life we set up and demand a certain standard of exultation. If we fall below it we are unhappy. That is why we smoke thirty cigarettes a day and—do all the other things we do. We are constantly keying ourselves up to our own arbitrary standard of exultation. And then one day comes a crash, and the first thing the Medicine Men say, after having picked up the pieces, is: 'Ah! too much exultation!'

And then we are sent away to where such a thing is apparently inaccessible. Ninety-nine per cent of the exultation is cut off. We slowly emerge. And as we emerge we realize how wise and yet how unseeing the Medicine Men are. For though their precepts are good, they have overlooked the fact that if you knock 99 per cent off a thing the remaining unit is still divisible by a hundred. The thrill shifts its ground, but it is still there.

We discover in the first place that whereas in the old days our time was divided between night and day—that is to say a time when it was light and a time when it was dark—we now enjoy a cycle of twenty-four complete hours. We make friends with hours that are strangers to us. I met such a one last week. It was between two and three in the morning, and an owl went slowly by, hooting around the eaves of the house.

I have an idea he must have been a young owl—one, perhaps, just starting up in business for himself—for although his cry was plaintive and very beautiful, it had not that deep velvety note of the older owl, surely the most beautiful sound in Nature.

Exultation! You cannot escape it, whatever the scale of your activities. In the early morning you hear a rustling in the corridor outside. You know that in twenty minutes' time someone will be bringing you tea. Tea! You await the thrill of the early morning tea with the same avidity that in former days you have awaited the rising of the curtain on a first night. After the tea the day proceeds on a carefully modulated progression of thrills. The post comes. That is in itself as exciting an experience as man could desire. One's whole destiny may be affected by a post. One reads the letters through very attentively twice, and even circulars about sales of jam and women's *coiffure* arrest one's attention. Whilst the pathetic offer from the gentleman who is anxious to lend you £20,000 on note of hand, without security, sends one off into vivid dreams of southern seas or Persian palaces.

In due course follow the newspapers. In the bad old days one glanced at the cricket and skimmed the general news. One now reads the newspaper from cover to cover. Not an over is missed in county cricket. Even letters to the editor, weather forecasts, and political speeches have an arresting significance. And so as the day proceeds one is reminded of the poem about the little fleas and the lesser fleas. The unit functions within its restricted area with complete success. The proportion remains undisturbed. I am writing this seated among pine-trees in Berkshire. I cannot see very far because the view is cut off by the pines. A Russian lady was here the other day. She said the view made her feel homesick. 'But think,' she added, 'in Russia we have this'—and she waved her arms towards the pines—'the same thing, stretching away for thousands of miles.'

Well, dear lady, we none of us can see more than we can see. So far as my happiness is concerned there are just as many pine-trees in Berkshire as there are in Russia. It is quite likely that the lesser fleas get just as big a thrill biting the little fleas as the little fleas do biting the big fleas. It is all a question of scale.

For the editor and publishers, the compilation of this volume of Stacy Aumonier stories has been a labour of love. The more we probed into this writer's life and background, the better we liked him—he emerges as attractive a human being as he was an artist.

We wish to express our profound thanks to all those who helped us in finding out more about Stacy the man, including his family members with whom it was such a pleasure corresponding: Richard Aumonier, sculptor and grandson of Stacy; and Ann McGill, grandniece of Stacy and author of the invaluable *The Aumoniers, Craftsmen and Artists*. Both were generous with their time and resources. Richard provided the arresting photograph of Stacy used in the frontispiece, and Ann gave us the benefit of her extensive research, in the course of which she had located (in the Beinecke Rare Book and Manuscript Library at Yale University, which we also thank) the very moving letters written by Stacy to Rebecca West shortly before he died.

We also thank sincerely: Mike Payne, retired history master of Stacy's alma mater, Cranleigh School, Surrey, and Old Cranleighan Liaison Officer, who provided us with much useful information from the records of *The Cranleighan*, including an Obituary and a copy of a 1901 cover designed by Stacy (reproduced below); the *New York Times* for Stacy's article 'Britain Also Has Her Babbitts' (8th November 1925) and 'Will Sing On Honeymoon' (8th February 1907); Sandra Darra MBE Honorary British Consul, Montreux; Yaël Bruigom of Clinique La Prairie, Clarens, Switzerland; Trinity College Library, Dublin; and the U.K. National Archives, London, for war service, census and personal records.

Also from Phaeton Publishing (and set in 1927):

The Secret of Jules and Josephine
—An Art Deco Fairy Tale
by Artemesia D'Ecca.

'... impressive and imaginative ...'—INIS
CHILDREN'S BOOKS IRELAND MAGAZINE

'One of the best books I've ever read ... Irish fairies flying all over Opéra Paris—magic, suspense and humour ...'
—KATE LONGMORE, BRENTANO'S-PARIS

ISBN: 978-0-9553756-2-0

'An orange juice, Mr Fitzgerald?' the barman asked in surprise.

'I have work to finish tonight,' the American said. 'Yes, an orange juice.'

'Cornelia, this is a huge piece of luck,' Tansy whispered to her eagerly. 'Do you know who that is? It's Scott Fitzgerald, the writer.'

...once again, Cornelia's parents could only stare at this scene, flabbergasted. The truth is that, no matter how many times one has seen a dog jump up and sink its long yellow teeth into its owner's bottom and keep them there, the spectacle never ceases to be very surprising.

'You are due to be murdered by a gang of apaches in the Place de l'Opéra on May 21st, the night Lindbergh arrives in Paris. You must stop that happening.'

'Well, I'll do my best,' he said, and surprised them by laughing. 'But who's this Lindbergh? Is he an associate of Omera?'

PHAETON PUBLISHING LIMITED
28 LEESON PARK, DUBLIN 6 · TEL: 353-1-498 1893 · FAX: 353-1-496 4410 · EMAIL: PHAETON@IOL.IE